A LONG WAY
FROM HEAVEN

Like a death knell the station bell signalled the train's departure and a great keening arose from those left behind. The train jerked into motion, its tall funnel belching smoke, weeping men and women clinging to its brass rails. They pressed their faces to the carriages, attempting to catch a last glimpse of their kin. Gathering speed, the train shook them off like a dog ridding itself of fleas. Some of them fell under the clattering wheels and were crushed. Wretched white faces peered from its carriages, watching their homeland fall further and further behind them. Those on the station watched the train grow smaller until it was a mere dot on the horizon.

Then all went home to certain death.

AUTHOR'S NOTE

Though Britannia Yard was a real place — my own great-grandfather was born there — the similarly named yard in this novel is fictional, a composite of Walmgate's courtyards. I have also taken the liberty of adding a slaughterhouse which many of the yards did have but Britannia Yard did not. All the streets and public houses which I name exist or did exist in that period. Dunworthe Hall alone is fictional, as are all the characters, with the exception of James Hack Tuke. Though the episode in which he briefly appears is purely imaginary, the fact that he and the Society of Friends were instrumental in saving hundreds of immigrants is not.

A LONG WAY FROM HEAVEN

Sheelagh Kelly

ARROW BOOKS

For David, Gayle and Vanessa

Arrow Books Limited
62-65 Chandos Place, London WC2N 4NW

An imprint of Century Hutchinson Limited

London Melbourne Sydney Auckland
Johannesburg and agencies throughout
the world

First published by Century 1985
Arrow edition 1986
Reprinted 1986 (twice)

Printed and bound in Great Britain by
Anchor Brendon Limited, Tiptree, Essex

ISBN 0 09 946090 4

PROLOGUE

July 1846

THE SUN STRUGGLED to break free of the early-morning mist, bathing the land with a lazy, golden tranquillity. Out of the swirling haze a chequered blanket of colour unfolded: wild thickets of gorse, though they had shed their saffron gowns no less resplendent in their dew-kissed tiaras; whispering, blood-sprinkled oatfields; lush pastures, no larger than a pocket handkerchief; a winding stream whose banks glistened with wild angelica and blue forget-me-not. Even the granite mountain which provided a backcloth to this beautiful setting seemed less forbidding in the gentle light of morning; its harsh summit lost among the clouds, its foot melting into the vast expanses of pink and purple heather.

Slowly the inhabitants of this small corner of Ireland began to come alive. A hare ventured a tentative whisker from his hollow secreted amid a tangle of briar and gorse. His wide brown eyes cast nervous glances over his shoulder, long ears twitched, alert for the sound of predators. Emboldened, now that the air held no alien scent, he succumbed to the urgent desire to stretch his cramped limbs, bounding with great, joyous leaps over the springy turf, pausing occasionally to nibble at a sweet, young shoot.

Some unseen hand conjured up a breeze, dispersing the last of the wispy clouds that had erstwhile draped the sun, teasing them into fragile cobwebs to leave the sky clear and blue. With the unveiling of the sun the hare suddenly realised he was no longer alone; a dark, aeronautical shadow hovered ominously beside his own. He made a frantic dash for cover, the muscles in his powerful hindquarters rippling under the tawny fur. His heart beat wildly as he slipped into the undergrowth to await the hawk's departure.

His action had been instinctive but unwarranted; the hawk had already eaten when the sun had been but a glimmer of orange on the horizon. The bird was merely re-enacting the hare's impulse to stretch his limbs, slicing the firmament with an easy, gliding arrogance; flying simply for the joy of it. Idly he tipped his handsome wings and veered abruptly away from the hare's hiding place, leaving the relieved animal to settle back into its hollow and relax.

In the crystal clear stream that wound its route between aromatic ferns and secret rockpools two otters frolicked, intertwining to let the stream carry them on its laughing course. Sleek bodies rolled and cavorted. Each sank playful teeth into the other, chattering and squeaking until the sound of barking sent them darting away, leaving only an eddying cloud in the water to tell of their passing.

The dogs, pink tongues lolling, plunged headlong into the stream, drawing howls of good-humoured protest from the two men they accompanied. At first glance one would not have imagined the men to be father and son. The grizzled head of the older man barely reached the other's shoulder, and whilst Richard Feeney was wiry, his son, Patrick, was powerfully built with wide chest and long, muscular limbs.

Richard smiled up at his son and wondered how on earth he had sired such a giant, and such a handsome one at that. He was by far the most good-looking man for miles around, as his bevy of admirers would bear witness. Ah yes, there had been many a fight over Pat, but much good would it do them now, thought Richard. Today Patrick would wed Mary McCarthy and put an end to the speculation of whom he would finally choose, no doubt breaking countless hearts.

He was Richard's only child. Patrick's mother had died shortly after the birth of her second – stillborn – baby, leaving Richard to bring up the boy alone. When his grief had abated he had toyed with the idea of remarrying, but had soon cast this notion aside. While his wife's eyes shone out of Patrick's face he would never be able to forget her.

Ah, *muirnin, muirnin!* cried his heart. 'Tis a tragic shame you could not live to see what a fine man our son has become. He raised his eyes to the sky, trying to picture her sweet face smiling down at him. God be good to her.

Patrick saw the moisture in his father's eye and wondered

what thought had provoked it – but then it took little to set Richard weeping; he was such an emotional man. They would be treated to many such displays of emotion today, thought Patrick, turning his glance to the harp which his father carried. It was somehow as if the strings were connected to his tear ducts, for the moment the first chord was struck the tears would invariably flow.

As well as producing such a wondrous sound, the harp was an object of great beauty in its own right. Its bowed forepillar was carved, in meticulous detail, with scrolls and vines, flowers, birds and fishes, all sleeping within the wood – sleeping, until someone caught at the strings, when each of the carvings would spring to life! Its graceful neck swept with an inward curve to meet the body, inlaid with a marquetry so fine as to defy description. But, to Richard, none of these things meant so much as that the harp to him was Ireland herself. When he played, he could feel the love and hate of centuries vibrate within the harp's form. He had promised faithfully that there would be no rebel songs today, knowing even as he said it that the promise was as hollow as the inside of Crazy Declan's head. Once the poteen was flowing through everyone's veins, they would be dancing on the tables and roaring the old, fighting songs with the usual gusto.

These thoughts were interrupted by the appearance of the village: a small cluster of white dwellings, flung by some careless gesture over the green landscape. Outside the priest's house the wedding guests were assembled. Patrick's eyes searched for his bride. It was no hard task to single her out, a tiny fragile creature who looked as if a puff of wind would blow her over. At sixteen she was the youngest of five surviving children and, with her alabaster skin, glossy black mane and eyes the colour of Lough Conn, she was also the prettiest.

Mary stood with her hands clasped in front of her, making a church steeple with her forefingers which she nibbled anxiously as she waited for a sign of her man. It was nothing short of miraculous, she thought, that he had chosen her when he had had the whole of the village to select from. She knew that her two unmarried sisters would have made sparks to the altar had he asked either of them – as she herself had expected him to. Why hadn't he, she asked herself again.

Why had he picked *her* when the others were so much prettier? She did not know and she had never asked him, but when he strode over the brow of the hill her heart soared at the sight of him . . . How beautiful he was, with his crisp black hair and strong jaw, the tip-tilted nose that belied his twenty-six years – but it had been his eyes that had first fired the attraction. Their irises were of the lightest blue ringed with grey and had a piercing effect as if they could see into her very soul. She now drank deeply of those eyes as he stood before her, feeling the blush rise from her throat under that bold appraisal. Then the throng of delighted guests encircled the couple and bore them into the priest's house to be joined in the sight of God.

Later, when the ceremony was over, they spilled into the sun-drenched morning; how much later not one of them could tell, for who among them possessed a timepiece? In this ageless land of theirs the time to rise was when the rooster filled his lungs and shrieked a noisy reveille, the time to sleep was when the sun had passed behind the granite mountain, and the time now, their grumbling stomachs informed them, was to eat and make merry. Headed by the fluter the gay procession made its way back to the bride's house for the wedding feast which would continue for as long as the poteen held out. With the strawboys dancing behind them, wearing their long, pointed hats and white shirts decorated with coloured ribbons, the happy participants began their celebrations.

Many hours later, when the cerulean day had given way to deep purple shadows and the mountain bore a halo of burnished gold, the creatures of the night began their rituals. The owl paused in its meticulous preening to watch the passage of a lone vixen. It blinked its great, inscrutable eyes as the russet shadow threw back her head and emitted a blood-curdling scream. The eerie sound was transported over the hillside by a gentle breeze to where two lovers sought out a clump of ferns for their marital bed. The sound did not alarm them; they knew it for what it was – a call of love.

Mary Feeney lay in the strong, protective arms of her husband, staring at the twinkling constellations that scattered the black velvet above them. If there were truly a Heaven up

4

there how could it better the one which enveloped her at this moment? The thought was blasphemous, she knew, but she could not help the thinking of it. A similar thought ran through Patrick's mind: what man could ask for more? He had a beautiful wife to bear his sons, a warm roof over his head and a plot of land for his livelihood. Below him he could see the nodding heads of the potato flowers reflected in the pale light. Fields full of the tiny, silvery beacons bursting white and healthy from the kind earth. He filled his lungs with the scent of peat and bracken, of wild honeysuckle and meadowsweet. If God had created man in His own image then surely He must have adopted a similar criterion for the land, for if ever a place were akin to Heaven then this was it.

He turned to look at his wife and all thoughts were suddenly lost in desire. He bent his dark head over willing lips, oblivious to all else. He was deaf to the vixen, the owl and the muted strains of merriment from the wedding guests, blind to the beauty around him – for the loveliness of his bride outshone all other things.

But deep in some crevasse of Fate, lurking in the rich, black soil between the ranks of bobbing potato flowers another creature waited. His name was Death.

PART ONE

CHAPTER ONE

August 1846

MARY OPENED HER eyes and stared up into the rafters where the hens roosted, red and speckled puffballs of feathers. Stretching, she placed an exploratory palm on her flat abdomen and her lips parted in a secret smile as she recalled Pat's rapturous expression when she had told him. She hoped that it would be a son, for her husband had made it clear that this was what he expected of her; many sons to help him with the land. Perhaps later it might be nice to have a daughter who would assist her mother – *mother!* 'Mammy' – how great it sounded. Perhaps . . . ah no, she chided herself, there's no time for idle dreaming today – or any day come to that, for it was a strenuous life they led, working the soil. Giving the child in her stomach a last tender pat she threw back the blanket and leapt to her feet. She drew on the red flannel petticoat, musing over the absence of any nausea – she knew that this was the secondary indication of pregnancy but as yet had no experience of it. She just felt wonderful and happy and alive.

A grunt assailed her from the bed of rushes that she had vacated as Patrick missed her warmth. Devoting a moment to gaze down at him, she marvelled how she could ever have felt nervous of marrying a man so much older than herself. How like a child he looked in sleep, with his long dark lashes and parted lips. Feeling her scrutiny, his eyes slowly opened. He did not return her smile at once, for he was still in that state of limbo between sleep and consciousness.

She gave him a light prod with her bare foot, and when she spoke it was in her native tongue, the only language spoken in this wild corner of Connaught. '*Hóra! a dhuine!* Is

9

it the life of a gentleman ye'd be after or are ye thinking of getting up to do some work?'

Patrick yawned and stretched his great frame, then his hand shot out to grasp her ankle. 'Sure, isn't that a fine way to illustrate the splendour of wedded bliss, kicking a sleeping man.'

She laughed and extricated her ankle. 'Ah, come on now ye lazy good for nothing. Ye'll not be leavin' the work to me in my condition – you too, Dad!' she added to the lump in the blanket beside Patrick. Receiving no response she nodded meaningfully to her husband who jumped up and whipped the blanket from his father's complaining carcase, wishing him a vociferous good morning.

'Ach, not so loud, son,' groaned Richard. 'Ye're enough to wake the Devil himself.' He tried to retrieve the cover but his son flicked it out of reach.

'Away up, ye lazy old rogue or I'll set the wife on ye, bruiser that she is.'

Mary grinned up at him from the hearth where the fire glowed beneath the ovenpot; the fire that was never allowed to go out or bad luck would befall them.

Richard raised a gnarled hand to his temple and glared at his son, his eyes shot with scarlet – a testament to the previous night's revelry at Murphy's shebeen. Reluctantly, he hauled his bony, work-abused body from the bed and pulled on his breeches, at the same time putting out a coated tongue to show his distaste of the morning.

'Sure, you're not going to put that filthy thing back in your mouth?' asked his son. 'The mere sight is enough to make the hens stop layin'.'

'In the name o' God what's that smell?' Richard wrinkled his nose in distaste.

'An' how would I be knowing? Sure, your nose is too near your arse.'

'Patrick!' Mary almost flung two bowls on the table by the window. 'I'll not have such talk in my house.'

Patrick, laughing, seated himself on a stool. 'Her house, says she. Throwing her weight around already an' hardly married above a month. Ye'll need to grow a bit before ye're big enough to give this one orders.'

'I don't need brawn to deal with the likes o' you, Pat

Feeney.' A stack of potato bread was placed alongside his bowl. 'Doesn't everyone know I can twist ye round me little finger.'

He knew that what she said was true but strenuously denied it. 'God forbid that a woman could get the better of a Feeney. What do you say, Dad?'

'I say, if the pair o' yese go ranting on much longer me head's going to drop off,' muttered Richard grumpily.

'Ah, y'old misery,' voiced his son loudly. 'Ye were talkative enough last night.' Big hands broke the bread which a grinning mouth consumed.

Mary agreed. 'Aye, kept us awake half the night with his tales, the scoundrel.'

'Enough! Enough, the both o' yese.' Richard covered his ears.

'See, Mary, he doesn't care for the taste of his own medicine,' laughed Patrick. 'Come on, Dad, give us an old rebel song just to start the day right.'

His father pushed away an untouched bowl. 'I'll remember your kindness the next time Father Brendan asks me why ye haven't been to Confession.' He screwed up his face. 'An' I can still smell whatever it is. 'Tis as if something crept in here an' died.'

Mary lifted her own finely-chiselled nose and sniffed audibly. ' 'Tis right he is. I can smell it too.'

Patrick scraped his bowl clean. 'Sure, is there any wonder when you're standing right next to Brian?'

Brian hoisted his pink snout and grunted his disapproval over the bales of straw that imprisoned him in the corner.

'Ah, now don't go blaming the poor pig,' cried Mary, scratching the animal's rough skin and stooping to speak to it. 'He cannot help it if he stinks, can ye, Bri? Will I let y'out in the fresh air, then?'

'Aye, sling the filthy poltroon out,' Richard answered for the pig. 'An' those crazy hens too, they're doing nothing for the headache.'

'Will ye have a little respect when you're addressing the creatures that pay the rent,' said Mary. 'Which is more than could be said of you. Just look at ye – fit for nothing!'

'Why, the damned cheek o' the woman!' retorted the elderly man. 'Whose cottage is this anyway, I'm askin'?' Instead of

Patrick moving out when he married it had been decided he would stay here and the two would work the land in one chunk. It had seemed stupid to split it into even smaller portions. Being a good-natured sort the girl had voiced no objection, but Patrick wondered regularly if his wits hadn't been addled on the night of that decision; his father was not the most affable of bedfellows after a skinful the night before.

The big man sprang up as Mary began to lug away the bales. 'Away now, I'll be doing that.' He gave her a knowing look, the corners of his mouth twitching, then delivered a slap to the pig's rump and steered it to the door.

At the pig's exit a green mist swirled into the cottage, curling and licking round Pat's legs as he opened his mouth in astonishment. 'Will ye ever look at this.' He turned to his father as the swine disappeared into the haze. 'Sure, I've never seen a mist that shade in all me born days.'

Richard raised his head slowly and stared through the doorway. No, 'twas the drink playing tricks; there was never a mist that colour. The smell was even stronger now, overpowering. The old man suddenly felt sicker than ever as a terrible thought came to his fuzzed brain. His legs trembled as he rose from the stool and shuffled towards the door. Ignoring the questions from his son and Mary he stepped outside into the hideous fog. The others exchanged glances, then followed him into the garden where all were to discover the source of the malodorous wave of putrefaction – the field which last night had burst with ripe potato plants was dead.

They stared about them in disbelief and growing horror at the clouds of foul-smelling steam that rose from the stricken field. Patrick was the first to break the stunned silence. 'Jesus, Mary an' Joseph . . . what in the name o' God is it?'

Richard wiped a hand over his mouth and took a few steps away from his son, his back towards him. 'D'ye remember that travelling man who came by last year an' told us of the strange blight that'd ruined a lot o' the crop?'

Patrick frowned. 'I do. If I recall rightly he said it looked as if the field had been . . . burnt. Ah sure, but it couldn't happen that fast, could it? 'Twas only yesterday we were saying what a fine crop we had this year. I can't believe it could happen overnight.' With an abrupt turn he strode back to the house, his father calling to ask where he was going. 'To fetch a spade!'

Richard shook his head at the other's return. 'I've this feeling on me that ye've had a wasted journey.'

Patrick thrust his spade into the soil. 'Sure, there's bound to be something among this that we can use.' But a curse escaped his lips as the implement yielded only a foul black pulp. 'Holy Mother, 'tis like digging into a latrine.' A disgusted poke from the toe of his boot.

Mary covered her mouth to fend off the rush of nausea, spoke through her fingers. 'Will they all be like that?'

Richard glanced at her and nodded, his eyes closed, a man in defeat.

But Patrick disputed this, ramming his spade back into the earth. 'There must be something we can salvage – God Almighty there's got to be.'

He unearthed another cluster of the slimy tubers then, as if there was no time to lose, began to dig and dig with increasing agitation. Sweat ran down his face and with it rose the panic as each spadeful produced the same agonizing sight.

'Don't waste your strength, son,' Richard advised gravely. 'Ye'll find nothing worth the effort.'

'But why, *why*?' demanded Patrick harshly, then flung down the spade in frustration.

' 'Tis as the tinkerman said,' was Richard's reply. 'One day ye've a fine, healthy crop, the next . . . well, ye can see for yourself.'

'But dammit where does it come from?'

Richard shrugged. 'Who knows? I did catch the whisper that all was not well with Dermot Laughlin's crop, but I thought 'twas just the leaf-rot or something – an' our crop was fine, there was no reason to worry.'

'No reason to worry?' barked Patrick. 'The slightest hint o' disease would seem to me a good enough reason to worry. Why the divil didn't ye tell me about Dermot's praties? We could've dug ours up early an' avoided all this. Ye'll see reason enough to worry when ye've nothing to fill your belly with.' He glared angrily at his father. Mary placed a pacifying hand on his arm.

Richard stormed back, 'Oh, is it blaming me y'are for all this, then? D'ye imagine I'd be eejit enough to let it happen if

13

there was some way to avoid it?' His son waved a conciliatory hand, sorry that he had spoken so hastily, but Richard went on, 'Well, I'll tell ye this: there're better men than Patrick Feeney who've tried to beat the blight at its own game by sneaking their praties in early, thinking that once they're out o' the ground they're safe. Didn't that tinker tell us that last year the market was flooded with seemingly good praties that'd been dug up early? People were buying 'em up right left and centre, only to find when they got 'em home that what they had was a bagful o' mush. 'Tis a sad fact that this blight cannot discriminate between a pratie in the soil and one in a sack . . .' With these words came a horrible dawning.

The others had experienced it too. Each looked at the other as they remembered the remaining potatoes from last year's crop which they had recently taken from the pit to make room for the new harvest and had stored in a sack. Stumbling and tripping over each other all three raced towards the cottage. Patrick, whose long legs assured his first arrival, was the one to make the discovery. Even before he felt the pulpy remains squelch through his clutching fingers the same putrid stench rushed from the opened sack. He brandished soiled fingers at his father and knew that Richard's thoughts were similar to his own: God in Heaven, what were they to do? Their whole lives revolved around this humble vegetable. It was the mainstay of their diet – Patrick himself could easily consume thirteen pounds in one day – and without it they would be destitute. And with what would they drown their sorrows when there were no potatoes to make their poteen?

Patrick barely saw his father sink to his knees and begin to wail, barely saw the white, questioning face of his young wife as she thought of the child inside her. All he could see was the whole year's work lying dead before his eyes, the sack of invaluable potatoes which had already begun to suppurate, the evil-smelling slime which oozed through the cloth to form black puddles of death at his feet.

In despair he turned his face to the valley and, as he did, small patches of the same green mist began to appear and multiply until every one of his neighbours' fields was clothed with a mantle of corruption.

CHAPTER TWO

AFTER GIVING UP hope of saving any healthy potatoes Richard, Patrick and his wife called upon Mary's parents to investigate the extent of their losses. Patrick glanced around him as he strode down the hillside. The land was changed. Like a beautiful woman whose face had been blemished by some dread disease, so the country was dominoed with the scars of the blight. Burnt patches marred the landscape, denoting the cancerous path of the virus and at every step of the way there were people prostrate with shock, draped in utter hopelessness over the fences that hedged their plagued gardens.

When they arrived at the McCarthy dwelling they found Liam, Mary's father, squatting alone on a boulder, his head cradled in his arms and the familiar stench of death all around him. He raised lack-lustre eyes at their approach. 'No need to waste good breath for I know what you're going to say. Couldn't I see that filthy mist hanging over your own field?'

Mary bobbed down and took hold of one of his hands as Richard replied wearily: ' 'Tis not just ours that's blighted, Liam. I've yet to hear of anyone who's escaped.'

Liam appeared not to have heard. 'How could it happen so fast?' he whispered in disbelief. 'What have I done to deserve this? All gone, every last one. 'Tis as if . . . as if the Devil has spit upon the land.'

'Don't take on so, Dad,' begged Mary, squeezing his hand.

Liam noticed her for the first time, reared. ' "Don't take on so," says she. Would ye expect me to be organising a *ceilidh* with our livelihood in jeopardy?'

'I didn't mean . . .'

'Is it stupid y'are?' raged Liam. 'Can ye not see we're all in danger o' starving to death? An' the only constructive thing you've got to offer is "don't take on so".'

Patrick saw the tears begin to form in Mary's eyes and intervened. 'Sure there's no need for us to go falling out over it, Liam. I'm certain we can work something out.' He craned his neck, trying to see into the cottage. 'Where's the mother, is she taking it hard?'

Liam grimaced. 'Hard is not the word. The wailing got so bad I was expecting any moment to see the banshee. It sounds as though they've plugged it now. Will we go in?'

Inside the cottage Carmel McCarthy sat glassy-eyed, not bothering to acknowledge their presence as the three men and Mary entered. The room was without its usual mouth-watering smell of baking, the atmosphere one of dejection. Mary's three sisters observed her with round, doleful eyes, fidgeting, picking at nonexistent specks on dresses, biting hangnails. She seated herself on a rush mat beside her mother and stared back at them, unable to think of anything to lighten their despair.

Sean, her only brother, stood and addressed Patrick. 'I've been trying to tell them 'tis no use sitting here waiting for a miracle. I say you an' me oughta take the cart an' see if we can buy ourselves some seed.'

'I'm in agreement with ye, Sean,' answered Patrick. 'The thing is,' he ran his fingers through his black hair and frowned, 'I can't for the life of me think where we'll get any. Everyone hereabouts seems to have been hit.'

'Sure, it can't have affected the whole county,' argued the other.

'Can it not?' put in Richard grimly. 'This is a different blight to any we've known before. Faith, 'tis so powerful. Ye've seen what it can do in the space of a few hours. What's to stop it repeating that process over the county – over the entire country, come to that. Didn't that tinker tell us . . .'

'Gob, ye're as bad as this lot!' Sean jabbed a thumb at his family. 'I've seen livelier faces at a wake – an' that was the corpse's. It'll do no good talking like that, else we might as well all shoot ourselves now. There's bound to be someone can sell us some seed.'

Patrick was infected by Sean's optimism. 'An' if ye recall the tinker's words so well,' he told his father, 'Then ye'll remember he said the country was like a checkerboard; some fields black, some untouched.'

'Oh, an' d'ye think if anyone's escaped they're likely to be parting with any o' their precious praties?' scoffed his father.

'Ach, away with us, Pat,' said Sean exasperatedly. 'It'll do no good arguing with the ould fella.'

Patrick turned to follow him but Richard grabbed hold of his son's arm.

' 'Tis not my place to stop ye if you're intent on wasting your time, but heed this: last night I heard the sound of your mother's grave calling to me an' her voice was joined by a million others. 'Tis dead we'll all be before the year is out.'

'Oh, Jazers!' Patrick shook off his father's hand in disgust. 'Let me out while I'm still sane.'

'Sure, 'tis right he is,' agreed Carmel miserably. 'The fate is on us.'

Patrick was at the door now. 'Mary, I'd away home if I were you. They'll not be happy till they've made ye as wretched as they are.' He joined Sean who had hitched up the Connemara pony. With a slap of the reins and a last backward wave the cart went bumping and jarring on its journey.

Mary had followed them to the door and now watched the cart disappear into the distance, her eyes troubled and bright. When it had finally vanished she crossed the room to sit beside her mother again.

Carmel wrung the hem of her petticoat and sobbed. 'Lord save us! We're all going to perish.'

Mary stroked her hair. 'Oh no, Mam, everything's going to be fine. You'll see – Pat an' Sean they'll find some praties, they'll not let us down.'

Carmel dried her eyes and patted Mary's hand. 'Ah, 'tis a good girl y'are, trying to cheer me up, an' me not caring to ask me daughter how her new husband is treating her.'

Mary's face lost its worried look and took on a secretive warmth. 'Oh, very well, Mam ye could say, very well indeed. I'm . . .' she paused, wondering if this was the right moment to break the news.

Red-eyed, Carmel waited for her daughter to complete the sentence, then from long experience in these matters guessed the reason for the healthy bloom on the girl's cheeks. 'Oh, ye're not, child,' she cried. 'Tell me I'm wrong.'

The smile faded. 'I thought ye'd be pleased for me.'

Carmel looked at her youngest child and her heart wept. She was so small, so fragile. Carmel was hardpressed to decide to which Mary would fall victim first; the hunger or the strain of bearing the child of a giant. She sighed and affected a weak smile. 'Pleased, pet? Well, I suppose I would be at any other time – but, oh, what a time to choose.'

'Now what sort of a greeting is that to be giving the news of another grandchild?' asked Liam, attempting to repair the earlier hurt he had inflicted on his sensitive daughter. 'Don't be worrying your head, *Iníon*. Tonight when Sean an' Pat come home with the praties we'll celebrate your news.'

Carmel knew that Liam did not believe his own words for one minute but was only trying to reassure his daughter – as she should have been. She tried to instill some confidence into her tone. 'Sure, 'tis right your father is. I'm just a silly old woman who should know better than to put the fear o' God into me own baby daughter. I'm only worried for ye, Mary. He's such a big fella, that Pat. It'll be a brute of a baby an' no mistake. He oughta be ashamed of himself.'

Mary's red lips parted in laughter. 'Oh, Mam! What on earth is marriage for if not for having babies? Pat's a big fine fella 'tis true, but it doesn't necessarily mean our babies are going to be giants.'

Siobhan, the eldest, who had come to tell the family that her own land had been hit, chipped in. 'Look at it this way, Mam. There's Pat about six feet two an' our Mary, well I guess she'd be about five feet nuthin', so things oughta even themselves out in the baby, don't ye think?'

Carmel nodded thoughtfully at this sagacity, until Bernadette remarked, 'By my reckoning that'll make the baby about five feet seven.'

For the moment the tragedy was forgotten as everyone rocked with laughter at the thought of such a baby. Bernadette, pleased with herself for dispelling the gloom, sprang up and smoothed her skirts. '*Dia linn*! I'm forgetting me duties,' she sang at the sight of the hens who scratched around the floor in the hope of finding a crumb. 'Look at the poor creatures, they must be starving.'

There was facial collapse as her words brought the laughter

to an abrupt halt. 'Oh, come on now!' she cried. 'Don't be such a load o' whipped curs. Pat an' Sean'll be back before ever ye know it, an' long faces won't bring them back any sooner. Kathleen!' She shooed the hens out into the mist. 'Fetch that bowl an' come help me feed the hens.'

Kathleen, at seventeen twelve months her junior, grumblingly obliged. She scattered the food amongst the foolish, clucking livestock while the rest of the family watched through the open doorway, the incongruity of such an act lost upon them.

'I didn't hear y'offer your congratulations to Mary,' murmured Bernadette slyly, knowing full well the reason behind her sister's lack of enthusiasm at the news. While Bernadette had accepted Patrick's choice philosophically – after all, weren't there plenty of other men around? – Kathleen had made it patently obvious that she had hoped to be Mrs Patrick Feeney and ever since had nurtured an unsisterly bitterness.

But then, hadn't it always been the same? thought Kathleen, always Mary, the youngest, as the centre of attention. The memory of being told that she was no longer her mother's little angel, that Mammy had a new baby to take care of, still rankled and she recalled the fights to gain admittance to her mother's embrace, the sharp slaps when she had tried to push her new sister out of her rightful place – 'Ye naughty child! don't go hurting the baby like that. You're a big girl now, Mammy can't be nursing ye any more.' All through her growing years it had been Mary who was singled out for the compliments – 'Ah, she's the bonniest of the bunch!' and 'Don't ye wish ye had pretty hair like your sister, Kathleen?' That was the thing that hurt most, being compared to Mary all the time . . . And it was just not fair, for she *did* have pretty hair, only hers was a dark brown colour while her sister's was as black and gleaming as a rook's wing – or the Devil's heart, thought Kathleen uncharitably. But there was no stopping folk's thoughtless comments when they set eyes on Mary and Kathleen had just had to learn to live with it. That was not to say she had grown used to it though, and she took every opportunity to take a dig at her sister.

'I don't see anything to put the flags out for,' she answered sourly, tossing the grain at the hens. 'Sure, 'tis not as if it'll be the first grandchild or anything.' Siobhan, at twenty, had been the first to marry and the first to bring forth a new generation.

'Ah, sour grapes,' goaded Bernadette persistently. 'Ye'd be excited enough if it were you who were carrying his child.'

'I can't for the life of me see why it isn't,' replied Kathleen. 'I mean, if you were a man wouldn't ye rather have somebody built like a woman instead of a bag o' skin an' bones? Our Mary's bonny enough in a skinny sorta way, I suppose, but she's so green, isn't she? Sure, I could've shown Pat a thing or two if he'd married me.'

Bernadette laughed, an infectious, bubbling giggle and the onlookers smiled, unable to hear the joke, wondering what it might be. 'That's precisely why he didn't choose you – he's probably got to hear about the thing or two ye've shown half the village.'

'Huh, I like that,' spat Kathleen venomously. 'You're not so bloody innocent yourself. Don't think I haven't noticed y'almost undress Pat with your eyes every time ye see him.'

Undaunted, Bernadette's blue eyes twinkled roguishly. 'Now, now, your whiskers are showing. Ah, I've been looking sure enough – what girl wouldn't look at a pair o' well-filled breeches like his? Haven't I seen yourself peeping an' all, trying to guess if 'tis all him.'

Kathleen was unable to resist the barb. 'That's where you're wrong.' Her face was smug. 'I don't have to play no guessing games when I know well enough what's in Pat's breeches.'

Bernadette gasped and put a hand to her mouth, staring past her sister's mocking face in dismay. Mary, who had hoped to join in her sisters' fun, stood momentarily nonplussed, the smile frozen on her face. She opened her mouth but no words came out. Her hands dropped involuntarily to her stomach as she stared at Kathleen who returned her gaze triumphantly – At last! At last I've been able to pierce that saint-like exterior, thought Kathleen. Unlike previous occasions when nasty remarks had failed to make Mary angry or believe that her sister harboured anything other than love for her, the reference to Patrick was like an arrow piercing her heart. The large eyes welled tears then, with a little sob, she spun away and ran down the hillside like a frightened rabbit.

'Well! Ye've really gone and done it now,' breathed Bernadette, watching the fleeing figure disappear.

'Sure an' it wasn't my fault,' snapped Kathleen. ' 'Twas you who got me mad. Anyway, she shouldn't've been listening; eavesdroppers never hear anything good about themselves.'

'Ye don't need to be an eavesdropper to hear a few home-truths,' responded Bernadette darkly. 'An' if ye don't go find her an' apologise ye'll be sure to catch a few yourself. Go tell her ye were only joking now.'

'An' what makes ye think I was?' asked Kathleen, her crafty smile returning. 'He's not a saint, ye know. Somebody had to ease him while Miss Pious kept him waiting all these months.'

Bernadette's anger spread in a red flush over her cheeks. 'Ye'd better be joking,' came the warning, 'or not just me but everyone will know ye for the harlot y'are.'

Without further utterance she left a somewhat deflated Kathleen to ponder on her words. Did Bernadette really think that of her? Did Pat? Was that the reason he had not asked her to marry him as she had hoped he would? A sudden emptiness engulfed her. What if Mary were to tell him what she had boasted? How would she ever be able to face him again? She tried to justify her treatment of Mary: it had been her turn to wed – well, that was not strictly correct, there was Bernadette before her, but even so it should never have been Mary's turn – not the youngest, it wasn't fair! If only Pat knew how she felt about him, didn't he know from the way she looked at him? Ah, but no, he was blind to everyone save the little saint.

Oh, if only he knew how much she wanted him. If only her name were Mary and not Kathleen. If only. If only.

CHAPTER THREE

MARY LAY ON her stomach listening to the gurgling of the stream, watching the moonlight play over the silvery waters. She had been here for hours; couldn't go home. Her mind ached, her heart ached. Oh, 'twas foolish to have expected him to be as pure as herself – men were not made the same way – but did it have to be with her sister? Did anyone else know? How silly, of course they would. They would all be laughing at her; at her innocence. This morning her world had brimmed with happiness. Now that world had exploded into hurt and shame, for added to Kathleen's cruel words had come the discovery that there was not, after all, to be a baby. What was she going to say to everyone? How could she ever face Pat again?

A trout suddenly leapt through the moon's watery reflection, invading her misery with a noisy splash – Why, you fool. You eejit! She sat bolt upright to gaze at the rippling shadow beneath the surface. Here you are making out that you're the one to blame when all the time you should be thinking of what you're going to say to him when he gets in. He'll come swaggering into that cottage, all proud of himself for bringing home the praties, when pride is the last thing he should be feeling after the shame he's brought on you. Go on home and give him a piece of your mind.

'I will!' she cried aloud. 'Damn me if I don't have your hide for boot leather, Patrick Feeney.'

Springing from the mossy bank she began to walk purposefully towards home. He must surely be back soon and then, by God, she'd show him.

The McCarthys had been reluctant to go to bed until Sean and Pat returned but it was growing very dark. Richard had decided that his son would not be back until morning now and had himself gone home to his bed. Those who remained began to strip off their clothes. Carmel arranged the rushes on which they would sleep. Each took their place, lying side by side in sequence of age under the communal blanket.

'Did herself go home?' asked Carmel, referring to Mary. 'I don't recall her saying goodbye.'

Bernadette gave Kathleen a nip before answering. 'Aye, Mam, she went home to wait for Pat. I think she was a bit upset, that's why she never said anything.'

Kathleen turned to her sister in alarm: was she going to inform! Was Kathleen to face the wrath of the priest? But – don't worry, you bitch, said Bernadette's face – I'll not be the one to admit what a slut of a sister I have. She deliberately turned her back on Kathleen and closed her eyes.

They had not been abed long before the sound of the cartwheels brought them springing to life. 'They're back!' Kathleen was the first up and began to pull on her petticoat, much to Bernadette's amusement.

'Sure, I can't think why you're bothering,' she mocked under her breath. 'Has he not seen it all before?'

Kathleen replied by sticking out her tongue, 'Come on. Let's go help with the praties, Mam,' and ran out into the moonlight.

'I don't see the rush,' said Liam doggedly. 'There'll be none.' But with an elbowing from his wife pulled on his own clothes and went to assemble with the others.

Patrick and Sean made no attempt to get down from the cart. They sat dumbly, looking from one face to the next, not knowing how to tell them.

'Didn't I tell ye?' Liam had no need to look into the empty cart to know. He now collapsed against the cottage wall.

The girls were gripping the sides of the cart, staring at the empty space. 'Perhaps ye didn't look far enough?' said Bernadette hopefully. 'Ye could try again tomorrow.'

It was Patrick who answered. ' 'Tis futile, colleen. The countryside is dead from here to Sligo – and beyond for all I know. We saw sights ye'd never believe. There were people there living like animals. God knows the last time they saw a healthy crop.' He climbed wearily from his perch. 'I'd best be away home anyhow an' break the news to Mary. She'll be getting worried.'

Kathleen and her sister exchanged guilt-ridden glances. The last thing on Mary's mind would be praties. Pat would have something less wholesome on his plate when he got home.

He tried to apologise to the older ones but Carmel set up such a wailing, 'Oh, Jesus help us, we're all going to starve!' that Liam bade him go.

They allowed him to leave with no word of goodnight. As he reached the brow of the hill he looked back over his shoulder and saw them as he had left them, a mute circle of standing stones against the heavy sky.

They reached the cottage simultaneously. Breathless with anger Mary waited to hear what he had to say before discharging her tirade. It was not to come.

'I'm sorry, Mary,' he said softly. 'I've let ye down. We searched everywhere we could think of, there's no praties to be had. 'Tis like trying to find fairy gold.' He dropped his chin to his chest and sighed. 'I feel so useless. You were all relying on me an' I failed ye.'

In more ways than one, thought Mary, but her anger had died at his admission. So sure had she been that he would succeed in his quest that it had never entered her mind what she would say if he came home defeated. A moment ago she had almost hated him, but now the sight of his wounded pride rekindled her warm and forgiving nature. She took hold of one of his big, rough hands and whispered falteringly, 'You're not the only one to have failed, Pat, I'm afraid.' At his look of expectancy she went on, 'I'm sorry, I made a mistake . . . there's not to be a baby.'

He nodded wearily. 'Ah well, perhaps 'tis for the best. The sights I've witnessed today I'd not inflict on a child o' mine.' He pulled her into the cottage where Richard snored peacefully and the pig twitched silently in his dreams. A soft chuckle. 'Will ye look at the old fella? Sure he sounds more like the pig than the pig himself.' Then he was serious and hugged his young wife protectively. 'God, I don't know what we're going to do if we cannot find any seed.'

'We'll find a way out, you'll see,' answered Mary optimistically. ' 'Tis not the end o' the world though it might seem like it at the moment. With the hens an' Brian we can hold out till help comes.'

' 'Twon't be help coming but the landlord – had ye thought o' that?'

'Well, tomorrow I'll go see Father Brendan – we'll both go. An' I'll say a special prayer to the Holy Mother. She'll not let us starve.'

Patrick agreed without conviction. 'You do that, darlin'. We're going to need all the prayers we can muster.'

The priest delivered grave news when they gathered for Mass with the rest of the community. On one of his infrequent visits to Westport he had obtained a newspaper and had discovered to his horror that what was happening in his home county was a mirror image of the whole country.

'Is there nowhere we can buy praties, Father?' enquired Patrick anxiously. 'I'm prepared to visit the other side o' the county if needs be.'

The clergyman could hardly bear to look at him, to see that hope doused. 'Pat . . . there *are* no potatoes. The entire crop has failed. They tell me every single potato in Ireland has been lost.'

'In one week?' Patrick's face showed disbelief.

A grim nod. 'Unbelievable, I know. Apparently we've been extremely fortunate here till now. This is the second failure for many.'

'Like the people I saw in Sligo?' He remembered a woman, naked save for a rag tied around her loins, the filthy, scab-ridden baby at her empty breast.

'Aye, an' some not so far from home,' replied the priest. 'Just the other side o' the mountain. I knew nothing . . . Strange, how a catastrophe like this can pass unnoticed till it affects your own.'

'So what's to be done? I mean, what have the others been living on?' Not simply concern for those already starving; he had to learn for his own family's sake.

'Well, the Government's been shipping in this Indian corn . . .' Patrick interrupted to ask where he could get some. 'A lot further afield than our own district, I'm afraid,' Father

Brendan divulged. 'The Relief Commission doesn't extend to such remote corners as this.'

Patrick laughed bitterly. 'Do they think we don't eat, then? Do we pluck our nourishment from the air?' He rammed his fists into his pockets. 'With the famine growing is there any likelihood that they'll extend the Commission's boundaries?'

Father Brendan looked doubtful. 'I'd love, for all the world, to tell ye there was, but I fear there's a possibility that not even those who're receiving it now will see any more corn.' He produced an envelope, taking out some pieces of paper. 'A colleague of mine in England sent me these. This is what the English people are being fed with.' They were newspaper clippings, cartoons depicting the Irishman as a slovenly pug-nosed brute with a begging bowl in one hand and a rifle secreted behind his back, illustrating that this shriek of 'Famine!' was just a ploy to get more money for weapons.

Patrick showed his disgust by scattering the clippings on the priest's desk. As a child he had learnt English at the priest's knee and though some of the longer words eluded him their implication was all too clear.

While he tried to control his anger the Father added, 'I suppose 'tis understandable that they get this impression, what with the trouble over the Corn Law going on. Some o' these young Repealers are a bit wild.' A sigh. 'They don't seem to realise that their violence is condemning fellow countrymen to death.'

'Is there nothing positive ye can offer us, Father?' begged Patrick.

'Well . . . this here Relief Commission has instigated a lot of road-building; 'twould provide ye with the money to buy food I suppose.'

'That's it then,' declared Patrick with a glance for his fellows. ' 'Tis on the roads I'll be for I'd sooner not sell Brian yet.'

'Brian?' The priest was somewhat perplexed, and seemed relieved when Patrick informed him that Brian was only the pig. 'Oh . . . right, Pat, I'll find out for ye where the nearest roadworks are an' let ye know.' He addressed the congregation. 'I suppose there'll be more who want the work?' The whole male population raised their hands. 'Right, as soon as I find out the details I'll inform ye.'

The priest kept his word, though he had to escort them miles to do it. There was a brief skirmish, for thousands were applying for this type of work and were prepared to use their spades as weapons to achieve the post, but after soothing words from Father Brendan all was settled and though it was a strange way of making a living, thought Patrick, he was glad of the wage it brought.

Alas, their triumph was tainted. The wage of ten pence per day, though it kept the three Feeneys, proved to be pitifully inadequate for those with six or seven in the family. As August neared its end food was becoming so scarce that people were travelling miles in the hope of securing a meal. The 'gombeen men', the meal-dealers and moneylenders, had been buying grain in enormous quantities and the price had soared beyond the pockets of the poor and the relief committees. Orders for more Indian corn had been sent, but it was too late, since supplies would not reach Ireland now until 1847.

Autumn passed into winter. The wild fruit and nettles which had meant the difference between life and death had gone. Not an edible root nor rotten cabbage leaf could be found. And if Mary had been mistaken before, then she was well and truly pregnant now. Would that the rest of the countryside were as fruitful as her belly, she sighed.

Patrick, exhausted by his daily exertions, had only the strength to slump to the cabin floor when he got home. The coins jingled in his pocket but there was nothing on which to spend them. The chickens had long since stopped laying and had met with the same fate as the rest of the livestock in the village. The dogs were still here, but not for long if Patrick could judge the way folk eyed them. Everyone was now totally dependent on the soup kitchens that the parish priests and the Quakers had set up. Each time Patrick closed his eyes he saw lurid pictures of dying children, some unable to speak, puffy-eyed, others with no hair on their heads but a wierd, downy growth on their faces, making them look like little monkeys. Was his child to look like this, or would they all be dead before the child saw light? And how long would it be before he was among the band that pressed their faces to the poorhouse window, savouring every mouthful that their more fortunate fellows ate. Oh, how could he have inflicted a child on Mary, on top of everything else? Yet it was the only comfort they had.

The pain suddenly gripped his vacant belly and he drew up his knees to his chest, waiting for the spasm to pass. When it did he put his arms around his sleeping wife and held her close, waiting for his own, merciful release.

All night long the freezing gales howled and whistled through the rafters, making the people inside the cottage shiver and huddle together in their fretful dreams. The fire glowed red in the hearth as the wind roared down the chimney. Soon there would be no peat left to keep it burning, and the ground was now so hard that it was impossible to cut any more.

In the morning when Mary woke and went to open the door she was met by a wall of whiteness. It seemed now as if even the weather was against them. The years in which they had seen snow were few and far between. Now, when their suffering was at its height, came the severest winter in living memory.

CHAPTER FOUR

PATRICK WOULD HAVE thought it a miracle that they had
survived the winter, had he still believed in such happenings.
His visits to Mass became less frequent, finally stopping
altogether. Father Brendan was greatly concerned, not simply
for Patrick's welfare but for his soul. Did the man not know
that he risked eternal damnation, not only for himself but for
his unborn child by turning his back on the true faith? His
harassment of the Feeney household became a source of
intense irration to Patrick and today's encounter was sufficient
to unleash his accumulated frustration.

'If you're going to tell me once more to put my trust in
God I'll . . . I'll . . .'' So incensed was he, speaking through
gritted teeth and holding both clenched fists to his head, that
what he wanted to say refused to come. He was unable to
think clearly any more. The lack of food had affected his
brain as well as his body. He was dizzy and sick, sick to death
of hearing that Our Lord would help them. If God was so
merciful how could He allow this devastation? ' 'Tis all very
well for you to talk, who don't rely on the potato for your
livelihood,' he raged. 'How ye've got the gall to churn out
all this rubbish about the will o' God while there's children
crying with the pain o' their swollen guts. What sorta God is
He, for Christ's sake?'

Silence ensued while the priest mulled over these bitter
words. On any other occasion this reversal of roles – Patrick's
chastisement of the priest when normally it was the other
way around – would have brought a swift rebuke, but today
the outburst was accepted dumbly.

'God forgive me I have no call to go on at you like that.'

The fire in Patrick, given a free rein, had burnt itself out. It took energy to be angry and he was lately lacking in this commodity. 'I know how hard ye've been working to feed people. I understand your feelings . . . I don't know where we'd all have been without your soup kitchen.'

The priest raised one eyebrow. 'I'd prefer that folk need me for my spiritual guidance rather than for a free meal ticket.'

Patrick barely heard, so obsessed was he by his own private suffering.

' 'Tis just that I feel so helpless watching me wife get thinner and thinner, hearing stories of how they're shipping boatloads o' grain to England while our own people die. 'Tis bloody marvellous, is it not, that those of us whose land is rich enough to grow wheat an' corn cannot even afford to eat it ourselves?'

'There's talk of more help from the English,' ventured the priest.

'I'll believe that when I've got the evidence in me belly,' said Patrick. 'Sure, what help have the English ever given us – except to help themselves to our land.'

'Now that's not strictly true in your case,' the priest reminded him for Patrick's landlord was Irish.

'Aye, well I reckon there's not a deal o' difference when we're owing them money. Boyne's due again any time now. This'll be his second visit an' still we've not enough for him.'

The futility of his expression brought an all too familiar feeling of helplessness to the priest. These people looked to him, as their leader, for help – and all that he was able to give them was advice to have faith and put their trust in God. But he could see by the doubt on countless faces that this was not enough. Words, however rich in meaning, held no nourishment. Trying to inject some enthusiasm into his voice he said, 'Ye know, a lot of folk have gone to America. They say 'tis a fine country. Ye could make a fresh start there if ye could get hold o' the fare.'

'Haven't I heard the tales?' replied Patrick grimly. 'They're packed in their hundreds into the holds like slaves, existing for weeks in their own filth. Those left alive – which I'm doubting are very many – are cast ashore with not a penny left between them.'

'Have ye ever considered England, then? Surely the ferry from Dublin cannot be as bad as that?'

Patrick's reaction was swift. 'England ye say? God Almighty, they're the last people on earth I'd choose to live with.'

Father Brendan sighed. 'Ah, Pat, is there no helping ye? I've suggested all I can think of.'

'The only way ye can help is to magic up a few seed potatoes an' I doubt that even you could do that. No, when God set the blight on my land He really made a fine job of it, didn't He?'

The priest was about to tear a strip off him, then resigned himself to the fact that Patrick would believe what he wanted to and no amount of cajolery would make him think otherwise. 'You're a devilish stubborn man, Patrick Feeney,' he sighed. 'D'ye not think Our Lord has enough on his doorstep without you turning against Him an' all?' He moved to the door, still speaking. 'An' you're wrong, ye know. This isn't the work o' God.'

'I don't want to hear it,' Patrick interrupted tersely. 'All I want is some seed, an' I'm not likely to get that am I?'

'There's hope yet. Maybe the Government might send us some.'

'If might was bread we'd all be very fat.' Patrick opened the door for him. In doing so he caught sight of his wife fighting her way through the snowdrifts, hugging a thread-bare shawl to her meagre bosom. 'I was beginning to worry!' he shouted. 'Where've ye been?'

'There and back,' evaded Mary as she reached the two men. 'Hello, Father, sorry I was out. Will ye not stop for . . .' she paused. What was there left to offer the man?

Father Brendan noted her humiliation. 'Thank ye no, Mary. I'll tarry no longer with this ass of a husband o' yours. Try to talk some sense into him, will ye. God be with ye.' He turned to Patrick. 'Both of ye. Even though ye choose not to believe it, Pat, He is with ye.' He marched off towards the village.

Once inside Mary revealed the prize she had been hiding under her shawl – a turnip. 'Isn't it wonderful? I found it under a hedge-bottom sticking out of the snow. It must've fallen off a cart ages ago. I'm surprised no one else found it.' She held up the frozen turnip, turning it this way

31

and that as though it were a prize exhibit at a show.

' 'Tis a clever wife I have indeed.' Patrick bent to pick up a stool that he had kicked over in his anger at the priest. 'Sit ye down, Mary, there's something I'm wanting to ask ye.' He squatted on his heels in front of her, carefully weighing the words before asking, 'How would ye feel if we had to leave here?'

'What's that you're saying?' His father came in from the cold, adjusting his breeches with skeletal fingers.

'Ah, ye've decided to surface at last, have ye?' scoffed Patrick. 'Leaving me to face the priest alone. Ye must've been crouching out there for ages. 'Tis a wonder ye didn't leave the skin o' your buttocks behind.'

A frown creased Richard's forehead. 'A pox to the priest. What was that I heard ye say about leaving?'

'If ye'd honoured us with your presence ye wouldn't need to ask.'

'Well, 'tis asking I am. An' where is it ye'd be thinking of going?'

Patrick told him of the priest's suggestion.

'What!' roared the old man, veins standing out on his temples.

'Now don't go giving yourself a seizure.' Patrick tried to calm him. 'We haven't the fare so 'tis out of the question. But whether we go to England or no, we'll still have to leave here one way or the other.'

'England, huh! The man's mad. I'd sooner take my sup from the Devil's navel. The only way I'm leaving this cottage is in a wooden box – an' that's not unlikely the way things are going.' Richard turned angrily to his daughter-in-law. 'You'll not be wanting to go surely, Mary?'

Mary looked at Patrick. 'Wherever my husband goes then I go too.'

'Saints preserve us,' howled Richard. 'Is it mad y'are too? An' you in your condition. D'ye not know the English roast babies alive?'

Mary's blue eyes widened in fear and she cradled her swollen abdomen protectively.

'Ye daft old eejit,' stormed Patrick. 'Don't be goin' filling her head with all that nonsense. Ye'll be having us believe they eat the blessed things next.'

'And so they do!' insisted Richard loudly. 'Didn't my own grand-daddy tell me about King Billy's soldiers.'

'Ah, don't go listening to the old woman, Mary. He'd tell ye pigs lay eggs just to frighten ye.' He went to comfort his wife but Mary pulled away from him.

'What sorta land is this where you're taking me, Pat?' she whispered fearfully. 'I'd rather stay here an' face things than risk the baby being harmed.'

' 'Tis a load o' nonsense I'm telling ye,' Patrick reiterated, glaring at his father. 'If we stay here we'll die for certain. Have ye not seen enough over the past six months to realise that? An' would I be taking ye anywhere ye'd be in danger? Would I, Mary?'

She searched his honest face. 'If you're sure 'twill be safe . . .'

'I'm sure,' he responded firmly, daring his father to say more.

Richard sat on the floor. What was the use in telling them? Nobody believed an old man.

Mary wandered to the window, casting her eyes over the dormant land. The naked trees pointed their fingers at a snow-laden sky – I'll never see the spring again, she thought sadly. Never smell the peat bogs, never see the newly-born fern curl its way through the brown crackling remnants of last year's growth, never watch my child race up and down that green hillside like a mad March hare filled with the joy of being alive.

She could no longer bear to look and turned her gaze back to the room. The men bowed their heads as if sharing her unspoken thoughts.

'If staying here means the child will never see the light of day, then I'm thinking we must go where we have a chance of survival. Though God knows where we'll get the money for it.' Having said this Mary closed her mind on the matter. 'Will ye go break the ice on the rain barrel, Pat? I'll cook this turnip.' She was acting as if everything was normal; it was ridiculous. She wondered as she sliced the vegetable how she was going to coax the heat to cook it from that pathetic little fire.

– Oh, you're so ungrateful, she charged herself. There were those who fared much, much worse. She had seen them travelling in droves to the coast, their matchstick legs barely able to support their emaciated, sore-covered bodies. Children with heads too large for their shrunken shoulders to carry who collapsed at the roadside to die. Occasionally a cart would arrive to collect the corpses, pack them into coffins and trundle them to a communal grave. The coffins had false bottoms so that the bodies were slipped discreetly into the ground, leaving the boxes to be used again. Now, they had even dispensed with the coffins altogether.

She shuddered as the bone-chilling air followed Patrick and the man now with him back into the cottage. Seamus Boyne removed his hat and loosened his scarf, blowing on his hands to restore the circulation although he was wearing gloves. His well-clothed, well-fed frame seemed out of place here. He was a peacock amongst broiling fowl, a pig among skeletons. Boyne was the agent for the Irish lord's estate and as such, was responsible for collecting the rents. Although his lordship was anxious to rid himself of his non-paying tenants, he did not hold with the methods employed by other landlords and being unsure of the best direction to take, had prudently left it to Boyne to sort out the matter, thereby divesting himself of blame should there be repercussions.

The man came straight to the point. 'I have some news which may not please you, Feeney.'

Patrick had no need to ask the nature of this news, was only surprised to be given prior warning of the inevitable. He had heard of the evictions in other parts of the county, how the people had been compelled to watch the soldiers stack their pitiful belongings in the dead gardens and demolish the flimsy mud dwellings that had been their homes, leaving them no place to turn but the small dank caves amid the bracken. To be fair, some of the soldiers took no pleasure in their orders, sometimes dipping into their own pockets to compensate the cottiers for the harsh manner in which they were treated. But this did not detract in any way from the landlords' callousness.

'You're a brave man to come without the lobsters, Boyne,' he spat bitterly. 'Are ye thinkin' to evict us all on your own? 'Cause 'tis a fight ye'll have on your hands an' no mistake.'

'Don't be classin' me with them English,' replied Boyne, affronted. 'Oh, I'll be turning y'out sure enough,' he nodded to Patrick's scornful smile. 'His lordship needs the land to turn to more profitable use. He's been having a thin time of it lately.' Here Patrick laughed, a loud, derisive echo off the mud walls. 'Ah, ye can laugh,' said Boyne. 'But 'tis true. How d'ye expect him to maintain his standard of living when you idlebacks aren't paying your quarter?'

'Idlebacks!' roared Patrick, stepping towards Boyne. 'Why ye miserable poltroon, I'll push your teeth to the other side o' your head.'

Mary struggled to restrain her husband while a terrified Boyne fumbled inside his jacket. Finally reaching the object of his search he pulled out a purse and waved it as a means of defence. 'Here, Feeney, take this,' he stammered. 'I meant no harm, truly.'

'What is it?' asked the other suspiciously.

'Call it what ye will,' said Boyne, relieved that the purse had had the desired effect. 'Compensation if ye like. There's enough in this purse to pay your way to England.'

'An' what makes ye think I'd want to go there?' But Patrick still eyed the purse.

'Ye'd be a fool not to, there's nothing left for ye here.' As he spoke Richard made sounds of derision. Boyne ignored him. 'Come on, man! Is it not better than having your home pulled down around your ears?'

Patrick was silent for a moment. He looked at his wife, who evaded his unspoken question; it must be his decision. Slowly, and to the sound of condemnation from his father, he reached out and clutched the purse. 'Maybe I misjudged ye, Boyne. I took ye to be just like the rest. We're grateful.'

Boyne lost some of his bluster and looked embarrassed. He had omitted to mention the confrontation he had had with the priest on his way up here. Father Brendan had really laid into him as he straddled his well-nourished pony. He had never seen the man so angry, raving on about helping one's fellow man, rebuking him for the food he had so obviously stuffed down his pony's throat instead of into the mouths of crying babes, breathing hellfire and damnation down his collar until he had thought the man might attack him physically, too. Boyne would have promised anything to get away. As it was he had escaped rather lightly. With the offer of this small sum the land would be retrieved peaceably. Yes, his lordship should be well pleased with his solution.

After Boyne had left Patrick waved the purse in the air and said, 'Now isn't that a real turn of events?'

'Charity,' spat his father. 'An' ye needn't think I'm going.'

' 'Tis not charity! Damn me if I'd take that, 'tis compensation like Boyne said – an' what d'ye mean you're not going?'

'Is it soft in the head y'are? Ye don't seem to understand: I was born here – not just in this county or this village but on this very land.' The old man stabbed a finger at the floor to strengthen his point. 'So, don't be telling me that rubbish about ending up in the poorhouse – I *know* that's where I'll be!'

' 'Tis lucky ye'll be, then,' said Patrick sarcastically. 'The poorhouse is burstin' its walls already.'

'Then I'll die,' came Richard's zealous retort. ' 'Tis as simple as that. Anything is preferable to moving in with me enemies.'

Mary listened to his words with alarm. 'But we cannot go without you.'

'Ah, ye know ye'll be a lot happier without a cantankerous old devil like me,' joked Richard. 'Many's the time ye'd've liked to throw me out, I'll be bound.' Mary strenuously denied it and was upset that he should even think so. ' 'Tis true all the same,' replied Richard. 'Ye'll be a lot better off without me round your necks. Ye must go, 'tis the only chance my grandchild will have – even if it will mean he'll be born a foreigner.'

Her large eyes shone with tears. 'No, never that. We'll make sure he knows where his heart lies.'

'I'm sure you'll keep Ireland alive inside o' ye, Mary,' sighed Richard. 'But who can say what the little fella will feel, brought up amongst heathens?'

Rising creakily he moved to where the harp still reclined in the corner of the almost empty room. His refusal to part with it had brought many violent outpourings from his son, who could not understand his reasoning that he would rather starve than surrender his heritage. It had been handed down for generations, and to sell it would be like severing a limb. Braving the icy blast he limped outside and, sitting with the harp between his legs, began to lure a haunting melody from the instrument. The sound of its lament filled the air and wafted over the valley, pervading each cottage as it flowed, and filling each heart with a heaviness that was unbearable in its pain.

CHAPTER FIVE

AND SO, WITH Boyne's help, they had found a means of escape from the blight. The pity of it was that the same compassion had not been extended to the McCarthys. With the months of famine, Mary had seen the size of her family drastically reduced; not so much from the hunger, for Father Brendan's soup kitchen had blunted the effects of starvation, but from the deadly famine fever which raged through the country. Boyne had been shrewd enough to see that here was one place where he would not have to dig into his pocket. The McCarthy cottage would soon be vacated by natural processes.

Surprisingly, Sean had been the first to fall victim to the fever; healthy, robust Sean with his ready laugh and good nature. His death was closely followed by Liam's, then Siobhan's husband – it was odd how the menfolk perished first – and finally Siobhan's baby, since when she had left her lonely cott and joined the remaining members of her family. There had been no deaths since little Rory's three days ago, but as Mary entered now she knew that the rest of her kin would soon follow. Carmel's head lolled against her chest. The lack of sleep and the strain of constant nursing had finally caught up with her. She and Siobhan had, up until now, escaped the fever, but were just as likely to drop dead from the fatigue of the last few weeks.

Bernadette and Kathleen lay on the rush-covered floor, both near to death. Mary had experienced increasing guilt that she would soon be on her way to a new life while they were left to rot. That was why today, as every day, she had come to tend her dying siblings in the hope that it might cleanse her conscience. Trying not to wake her mother she stepped over the prostrate form and knelt beside Siobhan, balking at the harsh, racking cough that exploded from Kathleen's lips.

'I thought ye promised me ye wouldn't come again,' said Siobhan apathetically.

'I know. I'm sorry, but 'twould be wrong to stand by an' do nothing while my family needs me.' She put a hand towards Kathleen's greasy brow.

'Don't touch her!' Siobhan snatched her wrist fiercely. 'Have I not told ye time and again? If ye must come here at least try to touch them as little as possible.' Her voice softened at Mary's hurt expression. 'Look, I'm sayin' this for your own good. Ye can't help, Mary. Ye'll only succeed in taking the fever home to Pat – an' ye've the child to think of too.'

'I have to come, Siobhan,' answered her sister desperately.

'Sure, an' d'ye think I don't know why?' exclaimed Siobhan. ' 'Tis 'cause ye feel guilty over Boyne giving ye the money an' not sparing any for us, am I right?' Mary hesitated, then nodded. 'Didn't I know it,' said her sister. 'Well, I'll tell ye there's no call for you to feel guilty. Boyne is quite capable of answering his own sins, may the devil take his ugly hide. D'ye think our mam'd want ye to stay behind an' risk death just because we have to?' She answered her own question. 'No, ye must go an' start a new life for yourself, Mary. You, Pat an' your lovely baby when he comes. We don't think ill of ye for going. We're glad one of us is left to carry on.'

Mary accepted absolution gratefully. It had demanded all her courage to come here every day, risking her own life and defying her husband who had forbidden her to come. Now that some of her guilt was assuaged she felt free to go to England.

Kathleen coughed again. Her eyelids fluttered and her mouth moved in an attempt at speech. Mary looked down upon the sister who had wronged her and felt nothing but sorrow. When she had first heard Kathleen's words she had thought her world shattered forever, but she had come to realise that it was Kathleen, not herself, who deserved the pity. She had Pat, what did poor Kathleen have? She ignored Siobhan's warning and took hold of her dying sister's hand.

'Hush, Kathleen,' she whispered to the girl, who was still trying to speak. 'Don't tire yourself, just rest an' get well again.'

Kathleen strained to lift her head from the floor, becoming more and more frustrated with herself because the words she wanted to say emerged as incoherent croaks. Mary felt the tears prick her eyes. She knew that Kathleen was trying to ask her forgiveness. 'It's all right! I understand you love him too, an' I forgive ye, Kathleen, truly I do. Don't fret yourself.'

Rage and impotence mottled Kathleen's face – I didn't do it, you fool! her mind screamed. Can't ye understand? It was all talk. God knows I offered it, but would he have me? Hah, he would not. An' for the life of me I still can't see why he preferred a mealy-mouthed little saint like you. Why isn't it you who're lying here instead of me? She sank back, panting.

'What was all that about?' asked Siobhan.

'I thought ye'd know,' replied Mary. 'I thought everybody'd know. Ah well, no matter, 'tis all past.'

Siobhan did not press her further and they sat in silence for some minutes before Mary asked, 'Has anyone sent for the priest?'

– Is it dying I am, then? thought Kathleen with a jolt, an' me with all these wicked things in my head.

'Nobody's sent for him,' replied Siobhan, 'but like as not he'll be payin' us a visit. He never seems to be away from the place nowadays. Sure, I'm sick o' the sight of him.'

'Ye shouldn't oughta talk like that about the Father,' Mary rebuked her elder sister. 'You're as bad as that husband o' mine. Sure I keep telling Pat the man only comes to help.'

'We're past helpin',' sighed the other. 'An' anyway, what help can his preaching possibly be?'

'May God forgive ye for your wicked talk,' cried Mary.

'Aw, Mary you're such an innocent. Don't tell me ye still believe in all that rubbish he gives ye?'

'Stop it!' The girl covered her ears so that she would not be party to her sister's blasphemy. 'I won't listen. How can ye talk that way when . . .'

'When I'm in danger o' going next?' Siobhan finished for her. 'Ye think I'm putting my soul at risk? Well, Mary I never did go for all that talk, an' I believe it even less after watching my family snuffed out like candles. If there is a God how come He allowed all this to happen? Ah, forget it,' she patted Mary's hand. 'I can see I'm upsetting ye an' I'd hate to poison such short time we have together.'

Mary placed a damp rag on Kathleen's brow. 'I hope Father Brendan does come. 'Twould be a terrible thing if . . .' she bit her lip. Suddenly she rose to lift the wooden crucifix from the wall. Stooping beside Kathleen again she folded the clammy hands round it.

– My God! Kathleen's mind cried, I am going to die. I don't want to. Oh, please I don't want to. Just because I can't find the strength to speak doesn't mean I cannot hear what you're saying! She clawed Mary's hand desperately, hanging on to life – I'm sorry, Mary, I didn't mean it, 'twas just talk.

Her body was seized with one, great convulsive fit of coughing and the vomit belched noisily from her throat. Mary tried to pull her hands away as the revolting bile ran over them but Kathleen held on, would not let her escape. After what seemed like hours the coughing subsided to an ominous gurgle and Kathleen's fingers went limp. Mary snatched the opportunity to free herself and stared down at the slime-coated fingers in horror. Why had she come here? How would she evade the fever now with the filth clinging to her skin?

Siobhan's voice cut through her terror. 'Go down to the stream,' she ordered, suddenly finding the energy to stand and take control. 'Scrub that mess off ye straight away, an' when ye've done that go home to your husband and never come here again. D'ye hear?' Mary nodded woefully and made for the door. 'And, Mary,' Siobhan picked up the wooden cross from the floor. 'Ye may as well take this with ye. I hope it does ye more good than it's done for us.'

'Oh, Siobhan, please don't talk like that,' pleaded Mary. 'What if Mam should ask after it?'

Siobhan looked to where Carmel lay in an exhausted heap. All the commotion had failed to wake her. 'If she asks I'll be sure to tell her I gave it to you. She won't mind you taking it, Mary.' The other took the crucifix and leaned to kiss her. 'Go!' commanded Siobhan taking a step backwards, then relenting, she grabbed the girl and kissed her before roughly shoving her through the doorway and barring the door behind her.

Mary ran from the cottage and did not stop until she reached the stream. She stepped into the chilly, babbling waters, sucking in her breath at the extreme coldness of it.

When she had scrubbed her body thoroughly all over she bent her head into the water. Her long, ebony tresses mingled with the water's course; like dark strands of seaweed it spread out into the crystal stream, rippling serpent-like over the pebbled bed.

When it came to putting her clothes back on she found it too sickening, with the contents of her sister's stomach clinging to them. There was nothing for it but to wash them too. This she did, sloshing them violently in the water then laying them on the bank to pound at them with a large flat stone. Once done, she draped the sopping garments on a tree to dry, though much hope of that there was in this climate. Her teeth chattered and her thin body began to quake. She folded her arms in front of her chest, rubbing her hands up and down her goose-pimpled flesh. She would have to go back to the cottage and collect her clothes later, though what Patrick would have to say . . .

'In the name o' God, what is it you're at?'

She turned, startled, trying to cover herself with her hands, then saw that it was her husband. Patrick hurriedly stripped off his shirt and held it out to her. 'Is it trying to catch your death y'are?' he demanded angrily. 'Here, put this on at once.'

As she lifted the shirt over her damp head he winced at the sight of her starveling body. True, she had never been plump, but now the skin hung loosely over her fleshless form, the bones jutting out at right angles. Only the swollen belly bore evidence to the fact that this was a woman. Strange, he had always thought of her as a girl before – as chronologically speaking she was – but all the months of suffering had driven away any vestige of immaturity; to call her a girl now would be an injustice. She had been every inch a woman to her family.

She tugged the shirt to her knees and looked back at him beseechingly, still shivering violently.

'Now, would ye care to tell me what ye were doing?' he demanded. 'Did a pebble trip you into the stream?'

She shook her head, then told him what had happened.

'Aw, Mary,' he breathed noisily. 'Ye promised me ye wouldn't go any more.'

'I'm sorry to disobey ye, Pat, but 'tis my family we're talking about, not some strangers. I couldn't stand idly by without offering comfort.'

'I'm your family Mary,' he reminded her sternly. 'Did ye not give a thought that ye might bring the fever home to me while ye were playing the righteous nursemaid? Do I not count?'

'Patrick, that's not fair!'

'Ah, I know, I'm sorry, I'm sorry.' He pulled her to him and buried his face in her wet hair. 'Ye know I'm not really bothered about meself. 'Tis you an' the child I worry about. Here's me trying to keep ye alive while we can get to England an' you intent on killing yourself.'

'Well, ye need worry no more,' she said sadly. 'Siobhan's told me not to go again. Oh, Pat, I fear for her, she said the most terrible things; about not believing in God and the like. I cannot believe 'twas her who was saying it.'

'Can ye not?' he asked, holding her at arms' length to study her face. 'Can ye honestly expect her to keep faith with a God who kills off all her family?'

'Please, please I know what you say, but ye don't really feel that way, do ye, Pat? I know ye don't go to Mass an' I know you're rude to the Father, but surely, surely there must be something still there? How can I make ye both see what you're doing? What can I say . . .'

'Say nothing, darlin',' he told her. 'You hang on to your faith if it brings ye comfort, but don't ask me to do the same 'cause I'm out an' finished with all that. We've been through it an' I'll say it no more. Finished. Now, come away home, we've more pressing issues to discuss.' He turned towards home, steering her with him. She asked what he meant.

'We've hung around long enough,' he answered grimly. 'Tomorrow we go.'

The two men stood facing each other; down one man's face the tears coursed unashamedly, his shoulders racked with sobs. On the features of the other a different emotion was mixed with the grief – that of anger, anger that he had been forced to come to this, to leave his land, his father.

'Oh, Pat I'll miss ye, son,' wept Richard, flinging his arms around his son, feeling their bones grate at the contact.

'Will ye not change your mind, Dad?' begged Patrick, the anger fading as he witnessed his father's distress. ' 'Tis not too late, ye know.'

' 'Tis too late for me, son,' sighed Richard, wiping a filthy claw under each eye. 'Besides, this is where I belong.' He limped across the room and picked up his harp, holding it out to the other man. 'Here, take this to remember me by.'

'I don't need nothing to remember ye by, ye great soft lump o' soda bread,' answered Patrick thickly. He tried to push the harp back into his father's hands. ' 'Tis the only thing ye have left, for God's sake!'

Richard insisted. 'Take it! That's the only piece of Ireland ye can take with ye.'

'No, not the only one, Dad.' Mary showed him the small parcel in her hand, unfolding the piece of rag to reveal the square of turf she had hacked from the frozen ground that morning.

Richard stared down at it for a moment, then folded her fingers back over the tiny package and patted her hand warmly. 'Keep it safe, Mary,' he told her gruffly. Then silently to himself – I'm thinking 'tis the last ye'll see of Ireland . . .

Patrick fingered his father's gift. 'Before I leave, will ye tell me the tale one more time? Just to carry with me.'

'About the harp?' Richard sank to the floor. 'Sure, are ye never sick o' hearing it?' He rubbed a finger around his painful, spongy gums, swearing as another tooth came away. ' 'Tis just as well there's nothing to eat for I've nothing left to eat it with.'

'Come on, y'old rogue, give me something to cheer me,' urged Patrick, and Richard launched into the tale of how the magnificent instrument had come to be in his possession.

While this was in progress Mary quietly excused herself and slipped away. She could not leave without first discovering the fate of her family. The snow was packed hard and her feet kept slipping out from under her. On the brow of the hill she paused to look down upon her family's cottage, almost invisible in the whiteness. There was something odd about the scene, something not as it should be. Suddenly she realised what it was: there was no smoke coming from the chimney. Walking as fast as her weakened limbs would allow she made her way down the hill and stood for a few seconds outside the door. She tried to peer through the window but a thick layer of frost on the inside obscured her view. The door was stuck in its jamb. She put her shoulder to it and pushed with all her might. It gave with a groan and she stumbled into the cottage. Something scuttled over her feet. With a scream she lifted the hem of her tattered garment – then her eyes fell on the bodies.

Kathleen, Bernadette and Carmel lay beside each other on the floor. It was as though someone had laid out sticks in a neat line; their lifeless shells were frozen, making hardly a swell under the torn blanket. Next to them lay Siobhan. Hers was not a neat and tidy death. She had obviously collapsed whilst tending her mother, beside whom she was slumped, a rag still clutched in her hand.

But it was her face that transfixed Mary with horror – or the lack of it. She did not understand what had happened at first, until she noticed the inquisitive, beady eyes studying her from a shadowy corner, waiting for her to leave so that the creatures could resume their meal. With a moan of disgust and rage she looked around for a broom – anything – with which to beat them. There was nothing, all had been pawned long ago to buy food. Her hands flailed about in uncontrollable fury, but the wretches merely scurried to another corner of the room and twitched their filthy whiskers at her.

It was too much. She ran sobbing from the cabin, tripping in the ice, the tears freezing on her face to make sore, red patches. At the top of the hill she fell to the ground to regain her breath. She must pull herself together before encountering Patrick. He would be so mad if he knew where she had been. The act of digging her fingers into the snow helped to calm her, which was just as well for at that moment the door of the cottage opened and Patrick stepped out to seek her.

'God, have ye hurt yourself?' He hurried forward to help her to her feet.

She wiped a hand across her face, attempted a smile. 'No, I'm fine. No damage done. 'Tis time to go, then?'

Patrick looked at his father as he spoke. 'Alas, it is.'

Richard started to weep again and clung to his son, prolonging the agony of parting. Why was it, when they had but a few seconds left together that he could think of a million things to tell his son? He sank to his knees as Patrick wrenched himself free and, hooking his wife's arm, strode away down the hill without a backward glance.

The wailing had stopped now. A quiet madness came upon him. Leadenly he went back inside the house.

'Stop pushing!' blared the angry porter, while he himself tried to force the emigrants onto the train.

Mary, standing back with her husband, looked beyond him to a group of noisy departees who clung to their relatives, the free-flowing tears carving channels on their ravaged faces. Women prostrated themselves on the railway track, weeping and wailing their misery. Mary clasped her little bundle of possessions to her chest. Through the cloth she felt the outline of the crucifix that Siobhan had given her, saw again the rats that had eaten her sister's pretty face.

After they had left Richard, she and Patrick had called at the priest's house in the hope of receiving a meal before they embarked on their journey. He had given them soup and wished them God speed. Patrick had offered no rudeness this time, indeed, Mary doubted he had even heard Father Brendan's last attempt at retrieving his soul. He had been very subdued.

Apart from the sermon and the soup the priest had also made the suggestion that they take the train to Dublin instead of walking the breadth of the country. After all, had not Boyne given them enough to cover the fare? Neither Patrick nor Mary had ever seen a train before and the idea of speeding along on one of the fire-breathing monsters filled them with apprehension. But then Patrick had seen the wisdom of Father Brendan's words; Mary was in no condition to tramp hundreds of miles unnecessarily.

Even after being pointed in the right direction they had had to walk a considerable distance before finding the railway and were now exhausted, too much so to be afraid of the strange contraption that was going to spare them further exertion.

'Right, move!' The shout went up, making people cling more wildly than ever to their departing relatives. The impatient porters were upon them, roughly grasping Patrick's arms and thrusting him onto the train. Mary soon followed, sobbing pitifully as she thought of the corpses of her loved ones, left to the mercy of the rats. Others, too, were wrenched from their families and hurled crying and complaining onto the waiting train.

Like a death knell the station bell signalled the train's departure and a great keening arose from those left behind. The train jerked into motion, its tall funnel belching smoke, weeping men and women clinging to its brass rails. They pressed their faces to the carriages, attempting to catch a last glimpse of their kin. Gathering speed, the train shook them off like a dog ridding itself of fleas. Some of them fell under the clattering wheels and were crushed. Wretched white faces peered from its carriages, watching their homeland fall further and further behind them. Those on the station watched the train grow smaller until it was a mere dot on the horizon.

Then all went home to certain death.

Some days after this, when Seamus Boyne rode up the hill to supervise the tumbling of the vacated cottage, he spied a figure who sat, his back supported by a frost-covered tree stump, smiling at the vast panorama below him. Puzzled as to who might be mad enough to be sitting outside on a freezing day like this, he went closer to investigate.

Boyne recoiled in shock at the discovery. What he had at first imagined to be the man's smile was, in reality, a gaping wound that ran from ear to ear. Richard Feeney, the knife still in his lifeless hand, sat frozen solid. His last view, before the red mist had shrouded his sight forever, had been that of his beloved land.

CHAPTER SIX

LIVERPOOL DOCKS SWARMED with life of varying forms and the stench of fish greeted their nostrils as the ferry spewed forth its luckless cargo. The voyage had been a nightmare. The entire crossing had been plagued by squalls which had buffeted the steamer relentlessly, rendering even the most resilient of passengers green-faced and bilious. The pain of trying to vomit on an empty stomach had left Patrick wishing he was dead.

But now, as they stepped giddily onto the quayside, Patrick resolved to make the most of this new life. The question was – where did one start? He looked down at his fragile wife who was trying to suppress the discordant music that gurgled around her intestines. Heading the list of priorities must be food. He examined his pocket. There was little left of the money Boyne had given them but enough, perhaps, for a meal and a place to stay until he could find employment. He wished he had possessed more foresight and not bought that frugal meal in Dublin. It had been a foolish decision in more ways than one, for after relying on soup for so many weeks their stomachs had revolted at the solid food. He could have wept at the waste of it for the moment that the ferry began its rocking and swaying the food on which he had spent precious coins had refused to stay down.

Dragging Mary behind him, he elbowed a passage through the crowd, weaving his way between coils of rope and discarded fish crates; past the fishermen who sat mending their nets, deftly threading the giant shuttles in and out of the torn mesh; past the blind beggar who held out his cup as they stepped over his legs and who spat contemptuously when his ears failed to catch that welcoming chink; past the organ grinder who bellowed at a gaggle of urchins who tormented his monkey. The seething crush of sweaty, unwashed bodies made Patrick dizzy. It was claustrophobic and alien after the green fields of his homeland. He had never thought to be surprised again after encountering the busy streets of Dublin, but this colourful glimpse of Liverpool society made the capital of Ireland appear genteel in comparison. He quickly averted his face – then looked again – as gaudily-dressed females with painted faces lifted their skirts almost to the calf in advertisement of their profession. The provocative sway of their hips held his startled eyes, which he only tore away at the foul-mouthed retorts as a prospective client informed the girl her fee was too high.

'Gerrout the bloody way!' Patrick jumped hastily aside as a netload of crates was lowered from a hoist and deposited on the wharf.

The stevedore swung his hook into the ropes that bound the crates and moved them towards the landing stage. Patrick and Mary stood watching dumbly as he carried out his work.

'Pat, d'ye think y'oughta ask the fella where we might find something to eat?' whispered Mary, clinging to his arm. She was as much – if not more – in awe of her surroundings as her husband.

Patrick was uncertain – the man looked a surly character. Still, he told Mary he could but try. Anglicizing his request he said, 'Excuse me.'

'What is it?' snapped the man, pushing Patrick to one side with a curse as the person who was controlling the hoist miscalculated and sent a large container hurtling to the ground. 'Have a care, Chalky for Christ's sake!' He examined the contents of the smashed crate. 'Look at that,' he told Patrick disgustedly, pointing at the pile of broken crockery, then hollered aloft: 'If yer gonna drop one yer could at least pick one that's got somethin' useful in it!' He started to clear up the mess, then realised Patrick was still at his shoulder. 'Are you still 'ere? What the 'ell are yer hangin' about for like a bad smell? Can't yer see yer in the road?'

Patrick apologised. 'I was just wonderin' if ye could be after telling us where we might find work or at least somewhere to lay our heads?'

The stevedore laughed, baring a set of stubby brown teeth. 'I doubt if yer'll find either work or shelter 'ere, mate. No room at the inn, sorta thing,' he joked, pointing to Mary's condition, then seeing Patrick was unamused, cleared his throat. 'Please yerself – but I can tell yer that Liverpool's teemin' with your lot. Thousands there's been arriving every week. There's talk of 'em not letting any more in. In fact,' he tapped Patrick's chest with a nicotine-stained finger, 'I've heard they might be sendin' some of 'em back, so if I were you I'd move on, sharpish-like.'

Patrick stiffened at the man's words. Had they undergone all that discomfort just to be sent back? He muttered thanks for the information then ushered Mary away.

'Oy!'

Patrick started at the stevedore's afterthought.

'There's one o' them soup kitchens round the corner,' the man shouted, making signals with his thumb. 'Yer missus looks as if she ain't seen a square meal in months. It won't cost yer nuthin'.'

Patrick raised a hand in acknowledgement and, following the man's hand-jabs, soon found the soup kitchen.

He groaned as he saw the mass of people waiting for the handouts, standing in queues that stretched beyond the capabilities of his vision. There must be five – no, ten thousand paupers here, most of them children. Nevertheless the couple took their place in the line and sat down patiently to wait their turn.

Pending nourishment Patrick turned to a young man at his side. 'Have ye managed to find any work?'

The youth nodded. 'Maybe, but not here. I normally come over every year for the chicory-picking at York. Sure, I'm a little early for it this time but what with the situation being what it is at home, well, I thought there might be a couple o' thousand more after the job so I'm seeing I get my name down early.'

'Might there be work for me there?' asked Patrick eagerly.

'There might, but not till the summer I doubt.'

'God, that's no good, I need the money now.' He told the young man of the money given to him by Boyne. 'It didn't last very long, I fear. So, what're you going to do while you're waiting on the chicory?'

'Oh, I dare say there'll be something I can turn me hand to.'

'Are ye going to this York place straight away?' Patrick made a sound of acknowledgement at the young man's affirmation. 'Aye, I'm thinking we should be going too, Mary.' The stevedore's words still worried him. He began to rise.

'Faith, you're not thinking to go right now, are ye?' asked the young man. 'D'ye not know how far it is? A hundred miles, give or take. At least have the sense to get a good meal down ye first.'

Patrick remained seated but was still on edge. 'I'm fearing they might send us back if we clutter up their roads for long. An' by the time we're served I coulda walked there an' back. I think they must be breeding down the other end o' this queue.'

'Look,' said the youth. 'I'll be settin' off meself tomorrow nice n'early. If ye'll just have patience I'll take ye there. If we get separated in this place meet me back here in the morning. There's about thirty of us joined together; 'tis safer to travel in numbers.'

Five hours later their long wait was rewarded by a bread ticket and a bowl of gooey substance which tasted surprisingly good. His belly warmed and comforted, Patrick realised that he hadn't thought to ask the young man where he would be staying the night. There was no hope of finding him again in this tangle of famine-flesh but perhaps one of those women attendants could give him an address.

'Could ye be after helping us with a problem, ma'am?' he asked politely, with careful formation of his little-used vocabulary of English.

The woman continued to scour out the giant soup container, glancing at him only briefly as if she had not understood his words. With this supposition he repeated his question more distinctly.

'The Lord helps those that help themselves,' replied the woman without looking up this time.

Patrick's friendly smile vanished and after a second's pause his fist crashed heavily onto the table, sending the clean pans crashing to the floor. 'Help ourselves?' he raged bitterly. 'D'ye think we'd be here relying on your bloody charity like paupers if we were able to help ourselves? D'ye think we let our children die deliberately? Don't you talk to me about the Lord, I've finished with Him. He's been no bloody help whatsoever – an' neither have you damned English . . .'

'Welsh, actually,' the woman interposed, not the least bit afraid of this wild-eyed man. 'And if you hate the English as much as your tone implies why do you come here?'

'I'm beginning to ask meself that question,' yelled Patrick, interspersing his angry speech with Irish words which tripped more easily from a raging tongue, but fell on uncomprehending ears. He took hold of himself, forming the protest into English. 'I was led to believe I'd find help here but so far I've received none – an' 'tis not just the English who're an uncharitable lot.'

'Now look, you! Don't you be accusing me of uncharitableness. I've been here for seven days solid with hardly a moment's rest. You seem to think the world owes you a living and here I am flogging myself to death, for what? To have some big oaf of an Irishman undoing all my work.' She clashed the pans together. 'I'm sick of the ingratitude of you people.'

'Who said anything about being ungrateful?'

'Why, you did, you clown.'

'Only 'cause I was pushed to it by a sharp-tongued old biddy like yourself. If ye'd have had the courtesy to listen to my original request ye'd have found all I wanted was directions to a lodging house.'

The woman opened her mouth to speak, then closed it again as a great-eyed spectre appeared at the Irishman's elbow. The girl could be no more than sixteen but looked thirty, the responsibility for the unborn child resting heavily upon her. Yet despite the filth and lice the woman could tell that the girl had once been beautiful – Oh, you're getting hard, Bronwen Evans, she told herself. In the beginning the sight of so much suffering had overwhelmed her, so that she had had to turn off her mind to avoid becoming emotionally involved with these people. But this child was the same age as her own daughter . . .

She flopped down onto a bench, squeezing her nose between thumb and forefinger. 'I'm sorry. I must have sounded callous and indifferent to your plight . . .'

'So ye did.' Patrick was still annoyed. 'An' now I'll bid ye good-day.' He turned on his heel and made for the exit. Mary gave the woman one last imploring look then hurried after him.

'Wait!' cried Bronwen, anxious to redeem herself. 'Where are you going?'

'Sure, ye said to help ourselves, didn't ye?' shouted Patrick. 'Well, that's what I intend to do. Perhaps we'll be treated with more sympathy in York.'

Bronwen marched down the hall, hands on hips, and demanded into his face, 'Don't you know it can make you bow-legged?' He frowned. 'Riding high-horses,' she enlightened. 'For Heaven's sake vent your spleen on me if you must – I dare say I deserve it – but don't go taking it out on that poor girl. Dragging her across the countryside just to spite me . . .'

Mary asked what the woman was saying and Patrick translated for her.

'Tell her not to worry about me,' she told her husband then. 'I'm well enough to make this journey.'

Patrick interpreted. 'Well, of course she'd say that!' Bronwen almost screamed at his insensitivity. 'She'd follow you to the ends of the earth if you asked her. Can't you see she worships the ground you walk on? No, of course you can't, with all those clouds of self-importance round your head . . . God, what is it about you that gets people's backs up? I've no desire to start another argument. Let me tell you where there's a lodging house then get you out of my sight.' She gave directions. Patrick asked how much this would cost him. 'Fourpence per night,' she replied and, satisfied, he made to depart once more. 'Don't you go letting that oaf drag you all over the place neither!' she warned Mary who did not understand but inclined her head as her husband had seemed to have been accommodated.

'Silly old crow,' muttered Patrick when they were outside. 'Making out I don't know how to look after me own wife.'

'I'm sure she was only tryin' to be kind, Pat,' soothed Mary.

'Ah, y'always think the best of everybody, don't ye, Mary?' He put his arm around her and pondered over the crowd of unfortunate fellows still waiting to be fed. 'Ah well, let's be finding this lodging place of ours.'

When they did find the accommodation, however, the conditions were such as to make the sleep they so desperately craved virtually impossible. They were packed into a room with forty or fifty strangers, lying side by side like matches in a box. Whenever one person turned over the rest were disturbed – often to ignition point – and by next morning poor Mary did not feel as if she had had a wink of sleep at all.

But the cheery good morning offered by their young travelling companion when they met at the arranged place helped to make her troubles seem less. When the rest of their fellows arrived it was with renewed spirit that the party set off on the long road to York.

CHAPTER SEVEN

OVER THE NEXT few days they came to know and like their companion, Denny O'Halloran. He hailed, he informed them, from County Clare. His mother and sisters had perished in the famine. With his father already dead some years before, that left Denny and his brother to seek their fortunes in England. At Dublin, however, his brother had met with a young lady and having a liking for the city life had decided to risk things in his mother country. A personable chap, Denny was always finding ways to cheer the Feeneys when they had begun to doubt that their suffering would ever end, entertaining them with tales of Irish folklore to wind away the cold nights spent shivering under the hedgerows.

Whenever they came across a farm it was always Denny who would knock at the door and beg for a crust of bread, always Denny who ran the risk of being savaged by the farmers' dogs. Being a regular visitor to these shores he had picked up the language. When Patrick argued that he too spoke English and that he should take his turn at the farm door, Denny replied that it would not do for his friend to take an unnecessary gamble when he had Mary to think about. No, if there was any courting with death to be done Denny would be the one to do it – for who would miss him if the worst happened? The other travellers, even though some of them were familiar with the language, supported his claim – much to Patrick's disgust.

Mary grew very fond of Denny. He reminded her of her brother, Sean – he had the same easy-going outlook on life. She liked the way he protected her, on brief occasions feeling that she had more in common with this young boy than with

54

her husband . . . a thought for which she immediately felt guilty.

On they tramped, mile after mile. Although greatly fatigued their hearts grew lighter as each sign they came upon spoke a lower mileage. Between the grimy cities and inhospitable towns – in which they stopped only long enough to seek food and rest – the stretches of countryside were pretty much like their own land. The sun sparked grand proposals: maybe, once they'd found work a scrap of this countryside would be theirs some day. If so, it would not be dissimilar to the life they had been forced to leave. All at once the future took on a rosy hue.

'Ye know, Denny,' said Patrick as they ambled along the track, 'I'll miss your company when we get there. Ye've a mouth on ye for the tales.'

'Oh, that's nice. I escort yese all the way to York an' the minute I'm no longer of any use to ye I'm ditched.' It was said jokingly.

'Sorry, I'd be pleased enough to keep in touch but I thought ye'd maybe want to make a life for yourself.'

'Now don't be giving me that, you're sick o' the sight o' me I can tell. Ah, no,' Denny smiled. 'I just got to thinking, wouldn't it be nice if the three of us stuck together? I could be of use to ye, Pat. I know me way round the town, all the dodges. I wouldn't be a nuisance, honest.' It had begun to sound as if he was pleading. 'Truth to tell, I don't really get on with any of the others – not like I do with you an' Mary – you're the only friends I have.'

'Well, thank ye for the compliment, Denny an' I agree, it'd be nice to have kinfolk in this land full o' foreigners. I'll be glad of any help ye can give me, an' who knows?' he smiled widely. 'With our wages pooled we may just be able to afford a piece o' land by next year, once we get our bearings. I'll tell Mary, she'll be pleased.' He looked back. His wife had fallen some way behind due to having to relieve herself behind a bush.

Denny stopped. 'Your lady wife looks as if she could do with a rest.'

Patrick shook his head despairingly. 'I know . . . sure why does she never say anything? I go marching off an' forget all about her she's so quiet.' He took the harp from his shoulder, laid it on the grass and retraced his steps. 'God, I wish ye wouldn't keep playing the martyr, ye make me feel a right louse.'

'I don't want to hold you up,' she said breathlessly.

'Sure, 'tis me who'll be doing the holding up when I grasp ye by the hair and clout some sense into ye. Away an' sit down. Look, they're all taking a rest.' He brought her to where Denny was seated at the roadside amid a pathetic pile of belongings, telling her what he and the young man had decided between them.

She took no insult when he had told her rather than asked, and smiled at Denny though her face was weary. 'I'm glad, Denny. We'll be like a family again.' With a sigh she lay back against a milestone. 'God, I'm hungry. What I'd give for a drop o' buttermilk even.'

Denny felt her discomfort. Her fragile beauty never failed to move him. Sometimes he felt angry at his friend for his apparently indifferent treatment of his young wife. If Mary had been married to him he would . . . but she wasn't, she was married to his friend, and he must dispell all such notions if he was to share their home. 'You just sit yourself there, Mary,' he told her. 'Denny will go an' charm the farmer's wife for a drop o' something.'

'He's a lovely young fella.' Mary smiled at her husband. 'I'm so glad ye said he could stay with us.'

'Hearing that I'm beginning to wonder if it was the right thing,' said Patrick teasingly. 'Sure, ye never call me a lovely young fella.'

'That's 'cause you're a lovely old fella.' Mary watched the boy's jaunty walk along the path of the nearby farm. She could still see him as he knocked at the door.

'Ah, good day to ye, ma'am!' Denny doffed his hat at the sour-faced woman who answered his knock, taking care not to soil the whitened step. ' 'Tis a kind day we'll be having.'

'State your business,' snapped the woman, eyeing him up and down disdainfully.

'I was wondering, could ye find it in your heart to spare a drop o' buttermilk for a poor woman who's expecting a child any day?' He pointed down the path to the group of ragged travellers who observed his polite overtures with growing unease. This one was not going to be so easily swayed by his charm.

The woman's mouth dropped open as she followed his finger. 'Didicois!' she screeched. 'Joshua, them bloody Didies are back. Get the dogs out.'

'Ah, no, ma'am,' begged Denny. 'You're making a terrible mistake. Sure, we're only a band of starving immigrants. We'll do ye no harm. I can see ye've got a kind face, lady, we'll work for our sup . . .'

'Joshua!' screamed the woman again, grabbing hold of a broom and brandishing it threateningly at Denny who was now backing away. 'Joshua, where're them dogs?'

The sound of furious yelping made Denny turn tail and retreat down the path. 'I'm sorry, forget I ever asked ye!'

'You'll be even sorrier when my lads get hold of you,' bellowed the woman, braver now that he was in retreat. 'As if it weren't bad enough you lot pinchin' my eggs last week you have the cheek to come back here begging for milk. Ah, Josh!' A heavy-jowled man had appeared flanked by two burly youths and a pack of snarling collies. 'It's them gyppos back again, trying it on.'

'Oh, so you're the ones, are yer?' roared Joshua, advancing on poor Denny. 'Well, I'll bloody well teach you a lesson yer won't forget in a hurry.'

Denny increased his step. At the end of the path Patrick and the others had leapt to their feet and now watched as the men pursued him towards his friends. Suddenly one of the collies caught hold of Denny's heel, bringing him down and knocking the breath from his body. As he fell the men started to lay into him, beating him about the body with the farm tools they carried, swearing and cursing as the dogs got in the way.

'Pat!' screamed Mary. 'Ye have to help him, 'tis my fault, he went to fetch the milk for me.'

Patrick set off, thinking his partners would follow, yet they did not. Realising they were not with him he spun back angrily. 'Do I have to help him all on me own?'

'I'm not sure me poor bones can stand up to a beating,' moaned one member of the party. 'An' anyhow 'twas his choice to go.'

'Why, ye miserable coward! That boy's been providing ye

57

with food every day, risked his skin a hundred times to save your worthless hide from a beating. Tut, Mother o' God we've three times as many men as they have, we'll soon have them beaten. Now come on will yese, before they knock the brown stuff out o' him.'

A handful grudgingly followed, though not feeling at all confident with no weapon in their hands. The lack of food had made once proud men weak and lethargic, caring only for their own welfare.

The dogs were the first to hear their approach and raced towards them. One or two Irishmen lost their nerve and made a rapid detour through the hawthorn hedge, howling as the sharp branches cut their exposed skin. The dogs' natural instincts were to follow those who were running away, thereby leaving Patrick and his companions to press a counter-attack.

The farmer saw that he and his sons were outnumbered. 'Away, lads, he's had enough. Let's gerrin t'ouse, sharp.' His offspring saw the Irishmen charging at them and, dropping their weapons, made for the farmhouse. 'Ey!' shouted their father, pointing to the tools. 'Don't be leavin' them there for that lot to use on us.' But his sons ignored him. Indeed, he had only just managed to slam the door behind him and drop the bar into place when the Irishmen reached the house to rain heavy blows upon the woodwork.

'The devil take ye!' shouted Patrick, while his companions tried to break down the door.

Inside, the farmer, trying to sound braver than he felt, shouted, 'I've got friends coming in a minute! A constable, one is. You'd best clear off before you get what the other one got.'

Patrick, breathless with the assault on the door, looked back down the path at the limp figure of his friend. 'Come on, we'd best tend Denny.'

Denny opened his eyes as Patrick lifted his head from the stony path. 'D'ye think I said something to upset them?' he asked with a bloody grin.

'Quiet now, Denny,' commanded Patrick, attempting to hoist the boy. 'We'd best be taking ye back to the others before those rogues have another go at ye.'

'I'll not be going anywhere,' winced Denny, obviously in great pain.

'Sure, ye will. 'Tis only a couple o' knocks ye've taken. We'll soon have ye . . .' He faltered as a trickle of red seeped from Denny's mouth. Laying his young friend down again he opened his jacket to look for any sign of injury. There was nothing. It was then that he felt the stickiness on the hand that supported Denny's back. Very gently he eased the youth onto his side. The ground beneath was red. Between Denny's shoulderblades were two puncture marks. One of the prongs of the pitchfork had been deflected away from the heart by a rib and, though clearly inflicting great discomfort, the wound it had gouged could be mended. But the other, judging from the blood which coloured Denny's agonized snarl as Patrick moved him, had punctured a lung.

Patrick's face darkened with rage. 'Why, the bastards,' he breathed. 'The cowardly stinking hounds!'

He sprang to his feet and pushed through the crowd of stunned Irishmen to where the discarded weapons lay. He picked up the pitchfork and glowered. It had blood on it; Denny's blood. With a roar he hurled it at the farmhouse door where it embedded itself with a thud, its shaft trembling with the impetus of his savage thrust.

The farmer emitted a terrified shriek as the prongs appeared two inches above his right shoulder. He shelved any thought of using his body to wedge the door and scuttled to hide with the rest of the family behind the upturned pine table.

Outside, the immigrants returned to their fearful spouses and children, bearing Denny's battered carcase between them. They laid him on the grassy verge at Mary's feet. His eyelids fluttered open as Mary knelt down beside him and touched her cold fingers to his pallid brow. 'Ah, Mary I'm sorry, I never did manage to get ye that milk.' Then he lost consciousness.

For the last stage of their journey they took it in turns to carry their injured compatriot. Mary walked beside the makeshift bier that they had cut from a blackthorn hedge, dabbing at the pink frothy bubbles on Denny's lips. Mercifully, he was insensible most of the time, but when he was jerked awake by his stumbling bearers Patrick had to keep up a steady conversation to take the boy's mind off his pain.

When they made Denny comfortable for the night Patrick

said, 'The lad'll have to see a doctor soon else he's going to die.'

Mary sank to the grass at Denny's side and wiped his face. 'Sure, it can't be far now. How many miles on the last stone?'

'God, don't mention miles.' Patrick grimaced. ' 'Tis a good job my feet don't have ears; they couldn't walk another inch.'

Mary unfastened her little bundle of possessions and brought out her rosary. She bowed her head over Denny's prostrate form and began to thread the beads through her fingers. Patrick lay on his back, hands clasped behind head, listening to her pious whisperings with mixed feelings, hoping her prayers would work, but fearing they would not. Long before Mary replaced her beads and curled up beside him, he was asleep.

When they awoke the next morning it was to a clear sky and a mist-free horizon. Patrick crawled from the musty hedgebottom and stretched himself. Mary followed suit, rubbing her knuckles over her sleepy eyes and coming to stand beside him. She linked her arm with his and laid her chin against him. On a morning like this they could almost be back home. He smiled down at her, thinking the same thing: this land was nearly as beautiful as his own.

They were both suddenly aware that their companions were not listlessly searching the hedgerows for berries or pulling burrs and lice from their hair, as usually went on in a morning, but gesticulating animatedly and buzzing like an upturned hive.

'See there!' cried a man when Patrick approached him, and pointed into the distance. Patrick looked, but saw nothing, save a great saucer-like valley spreading out for miles. ' 'Tis the Vale o' York! Can ye not see that great building over there?'

Patrick shaded his eyes and after a moment said yes, he could just make out the gleaming monument.

'That's York, son,' the man laughed. 'We're there.'

Patrick spun triumphantly to inform Mary and found her at his shoulder. 'Did ye hear that, darlin'? We're there, we're there!' He picked her up and swung her round, making her laugh as she had not done for months. 'Let's go tell Denny.'

Hand in hand they ran back to the hedgerow and gently

coaxed Denny awake. The boy responded by breaking into a fit of coughing and spraying the pair of them with his blood.

Mary took out a rag and wiped his pallid face. 'Oh, Denny we're nearly there. We'll soon have ye to a doctor now.'

Denny smiled bloodily. 'Soon be there, soon be there, fifty miles to County Clare, what will ye buy me when we get there?'

Mary threw an anxious look at Patrick, who summoned three of his fellows.

'The sooner we get there the better,' he said grimly.

'Well, don't expect us to break into a trot,' said the man. 'Sure, it might look near but 'tis miles we have to go yet.'

The raggle-taggle band set upon the final stage of their journey, limping and shuffling, their rags blowing in the breeze. Denny remained conscious, crying out in torment as his bearers heaved his pain-racked body awkwardly between them.

'Mam!' he sobbed deliriously. 'Mam, I can't see ye. Jimmy, I can't find Mam an' here's Winthrop for the rent. Will I make him a cup o' tea? No, tea's for special visitors, not for scum like him. Ah, Mam I can see ye now. Were've ye been hiding?'

And so he rambled on as his perspiring bearers grumbled about his weight and Patrick chastised them for their callousness.

The sun had reached its pinnacle and was well into its westwards descent when they finally reached the ancient fortress of York. The medieval walls glistened welcomingly in its light. At this sighting the travellers somehow found the energy to increase their pace, their tired and hungry faces smoothing out in relief as they reached their journey's end.

'Denny, we're there!' Mary hobbled at the side of the injured youth's stretcher and took hold of Denny's shoulder, shaking him gently. There was no response. Her eyes flooded with alarm. 'Pat . . . I think he's gone.'

Patrick stopped the men who were helping to carry the stretcher and bade them put it down. He caught his breath and bent over the young man.

'Aw, Denny, could ye not hold on for a wee bit longer? We'd've had ye there.'

'God!' uttered an indignant stretcher bearer. 'Is it a corpse we've been breaking our backs with? 'Tis a pity that farmer didn't do for him right an' save us all a lot o' trouble.'

'Patrick!' shrieked Mary, making a dive for him as he lunged towards the complainant. 'Stop! That won't do Denny any good now, will it?'

Patrick shook her off and stood glaring at the man. 'Just say that again,' he challenged, 'if ye've an urge to be carried into that city the same way as poor Denny.'

The man backed off, unwilling to pick up the thrown gauntlet, and made to walk on.

'Hey, ye lousy bastard,' spat Patrick. 'Aren't ye even going to help me carry him the last few steps to the city so's we can give him a proper burial?'

'We could've dropped him off at that place back there,' muttered the man to one of the others. They had just passed a cemetery.

But after much grumbling he, two others and Patrick picked up the stretcher and made their way to the city gates. Those in the group who had been to York before had lodged in the Walmgate area. It was because of this familiarity that they had steered towards this Bar, having crossed the river at an earlier stage in order to bring them into the city at this point.

Mary linked her arm through her husband's to lean against him, then remembered that he had enough to support and straightened her back. She knew that she should have felt sorrow at Denny's death – which indeed she did – but her main emotion was one of relief; relief that their long, hard struggle was finally coming to an end.

Had she but known it, the struggle was just about to begin.

CHAPTER EIGHT

'THA'LL NOT LET any more o' them buggers in 'ere, Mr Tuke, an' that's final!' The effort of so much arguing had brought a crimson flush to the man's face, creating a startling contrast to his ginger hair. Morosely he eyed the group of Irish immigrants who sat in hopeless disarray outside the city walls.

Edwin Raper, a man of porcine appearance who hardly ever smiled – if he did it was usually at someone else's expense – had been appointed spokesman for a group consisting of some fifty citizens, gathered to prevent the newcomers from entering. Someone had spotted their arrival from the city walls and had run to inform Raper who had then gathered reinforcements to check the invasion. Over the past months he had watched a seemingly endless influx of destitute Irish, bringing with them strange customs and deadly diseases, and now he and others were determined to end that flow.

There were, however, one or two stalwarts ready to plead the immigrants' case. James Hack Tuke, the man whom Raper addressed, was a member of the Society of Friends. Living quite nearby he had come to learn of this disturbance and had come to offer support. Tuke had not long returned from Ireland where he had been appalled at the suffering he had witnessed. He and his friends had championed the cause of the evicted cottiers many times during their stay in Ireland so he was not easily deterred by the belligerence which he now faced.

'Friend,' he began.

'I'm not your bloody friend,' muttered Raper, no diplomat.

'Mr Raper! I am certain that if you had witnessed such

sights that I have then you would not be so ready to turn these wretched people away. I can assure you that their suffering is far too acute for me to begin to describe it. These poor souls have travelled on foot across the country to find work and shelter. They tell me that some of their fellows have dropped dead on their journey. Please reconsider. If they are not given food and medicine for their ills then they will surely die.'

If he had hoped to prick the man's conscience then he was to be sadly disappointed. Raper's face remained immobile. He tried again. 'If their diseases are contained under the one roof the safer it will be for all.'

' 'E'll be tryin' to tell us hoss tods are figs next,' murmured one wag, sending a ripple of amusement through the crowd.

Tuke experienced an uncharacteristic surge of anger, then promptly quelled it – anger would only serve to antagonise the mob further and he must gain their pity. 'For the love of God, their children are dying by the thousand. Think how you would feel if they were your children. Do exercise a little Christian charity, I beg you.'

'Christian charity!' spluttered Raper, sending a spray of spittle onto the other man's frock-coat. 'What d'they know about Christian charity? They're bloody papists.'

Tuke closed his eyes in exasperation at this illogical state-ment and opened his mouth to reply.

'Hold on!' his opponent interjected. 'I haven't finished yet. Look, you can't say as 'ow we 'aven't taken our quota. There's already thousands of 'em in t'city spreadin' their muck an' lice. Take Hungate an' Bedern, ghettoes, they are, bloody ghettoes.' A buzz of agreement came from the crowd as he continued. 'An' violent? What? Decent people daren't walk down Walmgate without fear for their lives. You let any more in an' in a few months we'll be overrun by rats an' God knows what diseases. I know that for a fact, 'cause I 'ave to live among the filthy ingrates.' Raper was a butcher whose slaughterhouse was situated in the very heart of the immigrant community. 'They'll be pinchin' me meat an' God knows what – I can't leave a blasted pig outside but that it disappears up somebody's sleeve.' He shook his head firmly and gave a mirthless laugh. 'No, Christian charity my arse, beggin' yer pardon, sir but our folk come before that lot.' He clasped his hands behind his back and raised himself up and down on the balls of his feet, signifying that the argument was at an end as far as he was concerned.

Among the band of hollow-eyed, lice-ridden Irish, Patrick sat and listened to all the familiar words with growing contempt. He should have been used to the insults by now – Heaven knew he had heard them in every town and city since arriving on English soil – yet the anger never failed to simmer resentfully inside him at the lack of compassion and rejection they had had to endure. He smouldered at Raper's smug pink face and had a sudden urge to smash it; but as Mary would say, that would get them nowhere. Instead he examined his sore and bleeding feet, wincing as he probed the abscesses which had cracked open with the severe conditions under which they had been forced to travel. His attention was suddenly drawn back to the speakers: Tuke was by no means finished yet.

'Well, all I can say, *gentlemen*,' – he laid scornful emphasis on the word, deriving some satisfaction from having made one or two of his opponents look extremely uncomfortable – 'is that I hope not one among you should ever have to undergo the same fate as these people. I wonder how many of you would fare if the food on which you relied suddenly vanished overnight, which is what has happened in Ireland. How many of you would be able to survive on nettles or grass?' He looked around at the mixed expressions. 'Eh? Not many, I'll stake my life on it – especially some of our more portly friends.' He fixed his eyes on Raper's waistcoat, the buttons straining over his rotund frontage, the vertical stripes wrinkling into crooked waves. 'You would not take very kindly to being denied your roast beef and glass of porter, would you, friend? Well, these folk do not ask for such rich fare; all they ask is to be allowed to come into the city to earn a living. For pity's sake do not turn them away when they have come to this noble city of ours for help.'

Raper glared at his companions who seemed about to give way to Tuke's relentless persuasion. 'Don't let 'im make fools o' yer!' he shouted at them. 'Tryin' to play on yer conscience, he is. Well, it isn't 'im who has to live with 'em, is it? Look!' He jabbed a finger to where Denny's body lay between Patrick and Mary, his face even redder. 'If yer need any more evidence that they're riddled with disease well there yer 'ave it. They're droppin' like flies – an' so will we be if we let the buggers in.' He snorted triumphantly as the crowd were behind him once more and said, 'There y'are, Mr Tuke.' – The clever devil, all high an' mighty, looking down on them as likes a drink. – 'I'm sure we're all very sorry for 'em, but like I said, our folk 'ave to come first.'

Patrick looked at Tuke and knew by the man's eyes that he was about to give in. Well, Tuke might be but he wasn't. Tired as he was he rose to his feet and strode over to place himself between Tuke and Raper. The butcher took a step backwards as he looked up into the Irishman's livid face.

'Keep away!'

'Afraid I'll infest ye with the fever, are ye?' asked Patrick, taking a step towards him and causing Raper to take another step back. 'Well, ye needn't worry on that score, but I'm thinkin' ye should be pretty wary of these.' He presented two huge, clenched fists and nodded grimly as Raper tried to back away again but was hampered by the press of bodies at his rear.

'What did I tell yer?' yelled Raper. 'Ravin' lunatics, the lot of 'em. Look at the madness in them eyes. He can't wait to get hold o' me, look at 'im!'

'Friend, I think you had better . . .' Tuke began.

'Ah, don't worry, sir,' Patrick growled. 'I'd not be soiling me hands with the varmint. I'd just like to set the record straight on poor Denny there. 'Twas not the fever that did for him, you fat old Pharisee, 'twas an Englishman. Cut down in the flower of his youth by a man not unlike yourself, Raper. Indeed he was so similar as to be your brother. A nice fella he was, kind-hearted, generous, aye very much like yourself.' He finished with a sudden swipe at Raper's nose, making the man jump and snort his alarm, then with an expression of disgust he walked back to his friends.

Tuke sighed. There seemed no point in further argument now. Had it not been for Raper he was sure he could have won them over, but the big Irishman had just extracted any chance of that. Perhaps once the immigrants were loused and cured of the fever they so obviously carried the people of York might relent.

'My friends, it appears you are not to be allowed entry to

66

the city. However, if you can summon up the energy to walk a few miles further I can promise you a place where you will not be turned away.'

Hardly daring to entertain much hope – their hopes having been dashed too many times for that – the immigrants listlessly picked up their belongings and doubled back from whence they had come to follow the Quaker. Leaving behind the medieval walls that sparkled in malevolent defence of the city, walls which an hour ago had appeared ready to embrace them in the bosom of that city and now served only to hold them at bay, the paupers limped, shuffled and dragged themselves along the Heslington road until Tuke finally came to stop at the gates of a field.

'I am sorely afraid I can offer you no shelter as yet. The Board of Guardians does propose to erect a fever hospital here as soon as is humanly possible, but until that time we shall have to make do with what we can lay our hands to. I shall procure as many blankets as I am able and bring them to you immediately. If you could segregate those amongst you who are in need of medical attention it would be most helpful.'

He watched them file into the field then, after a brief and successful tangling with the farmer who rented the remainder of the field for his cows, went to seek the aid of a physician.

Every day the Tuke family visited the Irish. They helped to feed and nurse the fever victims, running the risk of becoming infected by the deadly typhus which was now rife in the camp, along with dysentery and other types of fever. The shed which was to serve as a fever hospital was near completion, which was as well for now added to the camp were those members of York's immigrant community who had hitherto been left to fend for themselves and with its swelling numbers was like a boil ready to burst. Makeshift tents had been imported to supply temporary accommodation. It was in one of these that Patrick and his wife were living, still unable to gain access to the city.

The Irishman, having regained some of his former strength with the regular diet, helped with the construction of the fever hospital. The fact that he gave his services for mere coppers induced the goodwill of the carpenters and before they departed one of them whispered to Patrick that he knew of employment if the man was interested.

'Am I interested?' Patrick laughed. 'I've been doing nothing but trying to find a job since I set foot here. I'd hoped to work in the chicory fields but Mr Tuke tells me there's near riots going on over who gets the jobs an' apparently the harvest isn't till autumn.'

'Well, I'm sorry I can't offer you owt like that,' replied the man. 'What I had in mind was a bricklayer's labourer.'

'Sure, I'm a farmer,' protested Patrick. 'What do I know about building?'

'You don't need to know about building, just do what you've been doing for us – passing tools an' that. Anyway, think about it – but not too long or it might be gone. It's for a builder name o' Baxter.'

'I don't need to think about it,' answered Patrick. 'An' 'tis very good o' ye to offer me first chance.' He had been told by Tuke that people were often reluctant to employ the immigrants, seeing them as workshy.

'Aye well, he's not a bad bloke isn't Baxter. I think you'll get it if you nip in quick.'

Patrick cheered. 'All I need now is a place to live.'

'Oh, God aye.' The man scratched his head. 'Eh, wait there a minute – I might be able to help you there an' all.' He approached one of the other carpenters and engaged in a short conversation. When he returned he told Patrick that his partner knew of a landlord with vacant accommodation in Britannia Yard. 'Don't expect much though, but it's better than nowt.'

Patrick asked him if he would scribble down the address of the house and its landlord, also that of the builder. The man showed surprise. 'You can read an' write an' you're wasting your time with labouring jobs?'

The other grinned. 'Ah no, I'm not pretending to be a scholar but I learnt enough in Ireland to get me by.' He thanked the man and, taking the piece of paper that bore his future, went to share it with his wife.

Mary was thrilled. 'Oh, but we'll have to go see Mr Tuke before we go, he's been so good to us.'

Patrick agreed and they did just that. Tuke, after congratulating them, asked Patrick if he had any money. The Irishman became uncomfortable. He divulged that he had earned a small amount from helping the carpenters but it was not enough to last the week. Tuke then presented him with a sum from the Board of Guardians, for which he received another effusive bout of thanks.

'The good Lord knows there is no call to thank me.' The austere face softened. 'I have done little. Indeed, the efforts of your good wife this past week have put me to shame.'

Patrick's frown showed incomprehension and Tuke explained that Mary had done a splendid job of nursing the sick. The Irishman pressed his lips together so as not to swear before the gentleman but he threw his wife a look of rebuke which – as she hadn't followed the interchange – she failed to understand.

'So that's what ye were doing while me back was turned.' It was delivered in Irish and with a smile for Tuke's benefit but she felt his annoyance and knew that Mr Tuke must have disclosed her little secret – and after she had been so careful that Pat shouldn't find out, always being there in the tent when he came back from helping with the shed. However, she saved her excuses for later, thanking God Mr Tuke was present to save her from her husband's displeasure, at least for the moment.

Tuke smiled his goodbyes, watched as they picked up their meagre possessions and walked to the gate. Their shoulders, previously bowed, were now held straight in a token of renewed optimism. After hearing where Patrick was proposing to live, he hoped that spirit would last.

CHAPTER NINE

THEY DRIFTED ALONG Walmgate, a thoroughfare composed of centuries of building styles, medieval to modern. There were dingy stuccoed dwellings with crumbling gables and tiny shuttered windows, the more sedate Georgian facades with gold lettering above the fanlight windows and row upon row of shops, punctuated by the buildings that seemed to make the most frequent appearance of all – public houses. There were scores of them, enough to cater for the whole of Dublin, thought Mary uneasily. She had often said how splendid it must be to be a city-dweller, but this place did nothing to verify that opinion. Yet it was certainly grand to gaze into all these shops, for never had she seen such variety. The people around here must have pots of money.

'Oh, Pat!' She pressed her nose to the window of a pawn-shop. 'Look at that lovely gown.'

'Ah, wouldn't you be the dangerous sight dressed in that,' remarked her husband, then wiped the smudge of dirt from her nose. 'But, no second-hand clothes for you, my love. Now, I've chance of a job I'll buy ye the finest gown in all the city – when you're not looking like a pouter pigeon that is.' He laughed as she punched him lightly in the ribs. It was remarkable what a little hope could do, he thought, recalling her sad face of yesterday. He gave another glance at the paper in his hand. He had found the landlord's address all right and had paid the advanced rent but his own accommodation wasn't so easy to pinpoint. 'Well, I'm jiggered if I can find this place, Mary.' They had almost reached the end of Walmgate. 'Ah dear, looks like we'll have to go all the way back down the other side – but won't we feel better from the exercise?' He grinned.

In fact they were almost within reach of Walmgate Bar again before Patrick spotted a defaced sign. 'Jaze, no wonder I couldn't see it. Still, I suppose we couldn't expect a brass plaque.' He stopped to consider the passageway, trying to get a glimpse of what lay at the other end.

'Surely there aren't any houses down there,' put forward Mary, following him down the narrow, litter-strewn alley which opened onto a courtyard.

They emerged from the passage and stopped dead. The first thing that hit them was the smell; the all-pervading stench of excrement, both animal and human, joined forces with the smell of fear to invade their already battered senses and send them reeling. There were houses, sure enough. At the doorway of each small dwelling was an ashpit and midden, all overflowing. The gutters that were channelled into the unpaved yard ran with blood and filth, flowing in a steady stream from a slaughterhouse, from which also erupted bellows of fear and pain.

Amid all this revulsion scores of people, grey-skinned and unkempt, lounged or squatted, puffing unconcernedly at their pipes, their passionless eyes sparing nary a glance for the newcomers. Tousle-haired infants with dirt-ringed mouths – some not yet walking – played amongst the piles of raw sewage. The only hint of colour was provided by the glossy-backed bluebottles which flitted happily from dungheap to child's face, where they were absent-mindedly brushed away, only to land again a few seconds later.

'We must've come to the wrong place,' ventured Mary hopefully, looking to her husband for reassurance; but all she received was a rather scathing expression.

– God, but she is innocent, thought Patrick, but *me*, I should've know better – should've known that we'd be sent somewhere like this. 'God damn them!' he raged. 'How can we be expected to live like this?' With a dolorous sigh he smoothed out the paper which he had crumpled tightly in his anger. 'Well, we've paid a week's rent now. I've not enough cash left to be choosy. Looks like that one's ours.' He pointed to where the framework of a door had partially fallen away. Such a desirable residence.

They climbed over the débris and filth, disturbing the bluebottles which rose in a buzzing cloud as the dismayed couple entered the house. Inside was no improvement. Someone had obviously been using the place as a latrine. Mary opened the window to admit a little more light; the ageing paintwork flaked away like dead skin as she touched it. Decomposed flies scattered the sill. Damp patches punctuated the chipped and scarred walls. Patrick set a foot on the rickety staircase and gingerly ascended it to examine the solitary bedroom.

He rubbed a peephole in the clouded window and peered out, trying to close his mind to the squalor below. So this was what it was like to live in the city. What a contrast to the lush, open spaces of home. He tried in vain to catch a glimpse of greenery over the dingy houses. There was nothing to be seen but black, grey and brown – not the warm and friendly brown of the earth but a brown of decay, of old age, of hope extinguished. It terrified him.

Then the feeling of panic subsided. There were voices below. He dashed the beads of perspiration from his brow. His shirt was saturated at the armpits and down his spine. Taking one more deep breath he went back downstairs.

'Pat, this is Mrs Flaherty.' Mary gestured at the angular figure in the doorway.

Patrick managed to control his voice. 'Ah, good day to ye, Mrs Flaherty. Won't you come in? I'm sorry we've nowhere for ye to sit nor anything to offer ye at the moment.'

'Ah, don't you fret, son.' Molly Flaherty brushed aside his apology and swept into the room, sending a swirling cloud of dust around the hem of her skirt. 'We don't stand on ceremony here. I just thought I'd come an' make your acquaintance an' see if there's anything I can do.' She spoke in her native tongue, eyes like black slits above the finely-sculptured cheekbones lingering fleetingly on a point below Patrick's belt. She took in the broad – if somewhat bony – shoulders, the large capable hands, then her eyes encountered his amused, startlingly-blue ones and she hastily looked away. He was a fine figure of a man, she thought, comparing him to the balding and portly father of her children – though Jimmy's robustness was caused not by over-indulgence of food but from the large quantities of ale he drank in order to forget his poverty.

'It looks as if ye'll be needin' some help shortly.' She nodded towards Mary's distended figure.

Mary agreed and hopelessly indicated the house with a sweep of her skinny arm. 'An' with this lot, too.'

'Ah, sure we'll soon have that in order,' cried Molly, rolling up her sleeves to reveal strong, sinewy arms. 'Ye're very fortunate to be having this place to yourselves.'

Patrick laughed disbelievingly. 'Oh aye, 'tis a privilege to pay two shillings for it. A veritable palace.'

'What I meant was, won't ye be taking any lodgers? Sure I take in a couple meself. It helps with the rent.'

'An' how many would I be taking in a mousehole like this?' he demanded.

Molly laughed. 'Ye think this is cramped. Sure there's twenty in the house next door.

Mary scratched viciously at her head. 'Before I consider new lodgers I'll have to get rid o' the old ones. These dratted lice are driving me insane.'

Molly found this hilarious, also Patrick's suggestion that he must take a bath, but said that if they were intent on wasting good money on soap she would show Mary where to buy it.

Patrick thrust his hand in his pocket and gave her the remainder of his money. 'Ye'd best get some food in too, love. It looks like this is going to be our new home.'

As Mrs Flaherty took Mary's arm and piloted her through the dust and rubbish he let out a noisy sigh and, brushing a handful of tiny corpses from the windowsill, he began the thankless task of bringing the house into some semblance of respectability.

When Mary and Mrs Flaherty returned, they set to work cleaning and scrubbing. Molly enlisted the help of her eldest daughter, while Patrick went to ask if anyone could lend him a hammer and nails with which to repair the doorpost. Whilst in the process of this he received a second taste of what life in Britannia Yard was going to be like. He turned sharply as a medley of howls and bellows interrupted his conversation and his heart sank as he recognised the person at the centre of the row.

'Get tha booit up its arse!' Edwin Raper bawled at a crimson-faced assistant who was trying to persuade a terrified steer to enter the hell-hole.

The youth's shoulder was rammed against its rear when

suddenly the frightened beast evacuated its bowels over his straining back. He stood there, arms outstretched, incapable of removing the steaming green cape.

Raper doubled over with coarse laughter. 'Well, wouldn't thee shit thissen if tha' were gonna get topped?' He wiped the tears from his piggy eyes and asked himself what in Heaven's name had possessed him to employ a daft lummox like Leach. In exchange for half an hour's pleasure from the idiot's attractive mother when her husband was at his work he was now well and truly saddled with the dolt.

Jos Leach danced about in circles, trying to pull off his jacket. Raper snorted and, filling a bucket with none-too-clean water, marched up to the youth and emptied the contents over him. At the same instant that he lifted the bucket his eyes fell on Patrick's disdainful face.

'Well, by 'ell,' he breathed, slinging down the pail with a crash. 'Tha's managed to come creepin' in after all, has tha?'

'Would ye care to throw me out?' asked Patrick casually.

Raper eyed the Irishman, wondering whether to take him on, but thought better of it. He spun away with a sharp expletive and slapped Jos Leach on the back of the head. 'Stop bawlin', useless bugger an' let's gerron wi' summat.' Grabbing the rope that was attached to the steer he hauled it after him into the abattoir.

Jos Leach flicked back the wet hair from his forehead and, picking up a stick, poked and prodded the animal's rear until he too disappeared into the slaughterhouse and fastened the blood-spattered doors behind him.

Patrick turned to the man to whom he had been speaking and made a sound of disgust. Then, after thanking him for the hammer, returned to his own dwelling, promising himself that as soon as he was able to he would be out of this place.

'Ah no, pet!' Molly was shouting as Mary started to brush the floor, sending the dust flying in choking clouds. 'Ye'll have to damp it down first, else we'll all be smothercated.' She sent her daughter, Norah, to fetch some water from the yard.

Mary then noticed the swelling under the woman's coarse dress. 'Why, Molly, you're having one too.'

'What? Oh, the bairn, ye mean. Sure, I get that used to having a child in me that a flat belly would be abnormal.

Eight children, I've had – they've not all survived, mind. One died when we moved in here – of the fever, ye gather; another was born dead. Then, there's no wonder, living in this filth.'

Mary's face paled as the woman's words struck a chord of fear.

Molly was quick to note this. 'Ah, don't go fratching yourself. Ye'll've felt the little fella move lately, have ye not?'

Mary grew even more alarmed. She suddenly realised that she had not felt so much as a flutter for days. Clasping her hands to her belly she stared down at it.

Patrick came in to catch her anxiety. 'Now what's wrong with ye?'

'Sure, she's a bit worried about the child, 'tis all,' provided Molly, completing her task of scrubbing the floor and rising to her feet. 'It'll be all right, pet. 'Tis probably such a big baby that it hasn't much room to move in there, that's why ye haven't felt it lately. My last one was built like the tower o' the gasworks. Oh, the pain.'

Patrick could see that if he did not get rid of Molly his wife was going to start labour there and then. 'Well, thank ye very much, Mrs Flaherty for your help,' he said, firmly leading her to the door. 'We'd best let ye see to your own family now. Perhaps ye'd like to call with your husband tonight for a jaw?'

Bemused at finding herself so quickly sent packing Molly answered faintly, 'I would, thank ye – an' ye must call me Molly.'

'Molly, it is then,' said Patrick, backing through the door and beginning to close it.

'Now mind what I said,' shouted Molly through the gap.

'I will.' Patrick virtually pushed her back outside and fastened the latch. 'Soft eejit. Take no heed of her, Mary. Everything's going to be just fine.'

Mary gave a weak smile and went to unwrap the purchases she had made. Putting the two battered pewter plates on the floor, as there was nowhere else, she picked up some potatoes and turned to the fireplace, then realised there was no fire on which to cook them.

'Isn't there enough rubbish in that yard to keep a fire going for a year,' declared Patrick. 'You prepare the praties an' I'll have one fixed in no time at all.'

'There's no oven-pot either,' answered Mary dully.

He gripped her shoulders. 'Mary, I know 'tis a bitter blow to find ourselves come to this, but we have to make the best of it. If we've no oven-pot then ye must stick them in the fire an' be satisfied. Ye cannot expect to have everything ye want straight away.' He went to collect rubbish for a fire.

Later, they sat in front of the fire, each with a plate of potatoes on their knees. Even their eating styles were altered; at home they would take their potatoes from a communal basket. Mary had been very quiet since his admonishment. Patrick stole a glance at her now and saw that she was crying.

'Aw, Mary.' He flung his half-eaten potato back onto the plate and put his arms around her. 'I'm sorry I snapped at ye.'

She sniffled into his shoulder. 'Oh, Pat, 'tis not you. 'Tis just silly I am – but oh, I never thought it'd be like this.' She indicated the dark depressing room. 'An' ye should've seen the going-on we had at the shop. The man didn't know what I was talking about . . .'

'I'll bet he understood the colour of your money, though,' cut in Patrick.

She continued as if he had not spoken. 'An' Molly, she was no use at all. She cannot speak a word of English either. 'Tis funny, what with all the Irish voices ye get to feeling like you're at home. Only when ye open your eyes . . .'

'Don't I know?' replied Patrick and squeezed her. 'But it'll not be like this always. Once I've had a few weeks' wages we'll be able to buy ourselves out o' this filth. An' like it or not ye've got to agree 'tis better than starvin'.'

She conceded. 'I'm just being soft. If we'd stayed in Ireland we'd probably be in our graves now.'

'Ah, you're homesick, *muirnin*,' he hugged her. 'An' so am I, Mary, so am I.' His eyes misted over as he thought of his father; was he still alive? 'One day,' he promised, 'we're going home. When all this is over. I promise, we'll go home.'

'Oh, Pat ye're so good to me.' She kissed him. 'I feel so safe with you.' They hugged each other for a long time, touching and stroking and sighing until their forgotten meal grew cold on the hearth.

Eventually Patrick pulled away. 'I know one thing though.'

Mary indicated the cold potatoes. 'Come on, don't waste

them, they cost me the earth. What d'ye know?'

'Someone will have to get things organised around here. No wonder the English think of us as shirkers and dirtmongers with all that trash out there. I'm going to call a meeting, an' tell these lazy so-and-so's to pull theirselves together – an' I'm gonna give English lessons too. How the hell do they expect to get themselves out o' this mess if they won't even bother to learn the language?'

Mary was gathering enthusiasm. 'An' we could invite some of them round for a song an' a tale or two,' she chattered excitedly. 'It'll be even more like home then.'

Having made his proposal Patrick reminded his wife that she was in need of an English lesson or two herself.

'Oh, teach me now, Pat!'

'What, right this minute? I have to go down to that building site shortly.'

'Oh, go on,' she begged. 'Just a few words . . .'

'Sure, I'm not claiming to know any more meself.'

'. . . the really important ones that I should be knowin'.'

So he patiently repeated over and over the words Father Brendan had taught him, the ones she would need for everyday conversation. 'How much? . . . how much? Too dear . . . too dear,' and so on. Mary was quick to learn and within half an hour had a sufficient vocabulary to make her shopping trips less confusing. After making certain that his wife was happier Patrick went off to look for the builder's yard.

CHAPTER TEN

MR BAXTER EXPLAINED to Patrick that he would be on a month's trial – any trouble and he would be out on his ear! The wage was twelve shillings per week and if he didn't like it or he wasn't prepared to work he could go now. Patrick hurriedly accepted the offer and was taken off to meet his five workmates – three bricklayers and two labourers.

'Another Mick, eh?' said the first man, who had been introduced as John Thompson.

Patrick's wary smile hardened into a straight line. Was it to be like this always? He withdrew his hand before it made contact with Thompson's.

'Eh, I'm only kidding!' exclaimed the other. 'Touchy, aren't yer!'

'How was I to know your mood when that's the way I've been treated since I arrived in this wretched land?'

'Oh, poor soul, proper 'ard done by, aren't yer?' replied John lightly. 'Away then, Mick an' meet the rest o' the lads.'

'The name is Patrick – or Feeney if ye prefer.'

'All right, keep yer hair on. Ey, lads watch what yer say to this'n, he'll 'ammer yer as soon as look at yer.'

'I just treat like with like, 'tis all,' said Patrick. 'You be civil to me an' I'll cause ye no bother.'

'I'm very glad to 'ear it,' answered the other, examining him amusedly. He introduced Patrick to the others, two of whom, it transpired, were also Irish. '. . . and Jimmy Riley, ah! an' if ever you're needin' a fiddler for yer sing-songs this is your lad: Ghostie Connors, the best Jeremy Diddler in York.'

'That's yourself ye'd be describin',' muttered Ghostie and

78

nodded at Patrick. The chalk-white face had eyes that held a faraway look; wherever Ghostie was, it was not here.

John nudged the new man. 'See, if we get laid off we do a bit o' grave-robbin' on the side. If yer look close enough yer'll see t'maggots comin' out of his ears.'

The man in question snorted and shambled away. John shouted, 'Right, lads, back to work!' and turned to Patrick. 'Are you 'ere to do some work then, Mick or just to cause trouble?' He marched off.

'He's a bit of a clever so an' so, is he not?' grumbled Patrick to Riley.

The man picked up his spade. 'Ah, sure he means no harm. He's like that with everybody. Once ye get to know him he's a generous body.'

'Away, Mick!' shouted John, flourishing a trowel. 'Don't stand there like a soft pillock else somebody'll think yer a permanent fixture an' pour cement in yer boots. Shove some bricks into that 'od, yer can be my man this aft.'

'I'm nobody's man but me own,' returned Patrick.

'All right, clever bugger, there's plenty more'll snap t'job up.'

Patrick smouldered, but knew that what Thomspon said was true. He could ill-afford to throw this job away – but just let that one overstep the mark. Filling his hod he tramped over the rubble and placed the bricks in a pile next to John.

'Now, yer can go mix some mortar,' said the man without looking up.

This induced more anger but Patrick laid down the hod – deliberately gently, and did as he was told. One of the other labourers gave him instructions on how to make the mortar, telling him the ratio of lime and horsehair and helping to shovel it into a barrow which was then wheeled over to Thomspon.

John turned at his arrival. 'Right, now yer can . . . Christ!' he stared down at Patrick's feet.

'What's the matter now?' enquired Patrick irritatedly.

John blinked. 'I've just noticed . . . you 'aven't got no bloody boots.'

'An' how d'ye expect me to afford boots when I haven't yet had a wage?'

'Shit, man, yer can't work in bare feet! They'll be torn to

ribbons before t'day's out.' John's eyes rose from Patrick's feet to his angry face, then fell to his feet again.

'No, they won't,' argued Patrick. 'I haven't worn proper boots in months, my feet've become hard as nails. Feel.' He rammed a foot at John's groin but the man avoided it.

'Get!' Nevertheless he felt sorry for the new man and resolved to ask Baxter if Patrick could have an advance so as to get something to protect his feet; hard or no, they would break the same as anyone else's should a brick fall on them.

Towards the middle of the afternoon all work stopped for tea. Patrick sat beside the others, wiping the dirty sweat from his brow and wishing that he had had the foresight to bring some refreshment.

' 'Ere y'are.' John held out a napkin which displayed thick wedges of bread and butter. Patrick ran his tongue over his lips but declined the offer. 'For Christ's sake what's the matter wi' you?' cried John. 'Are yer too good to eat wi' the likes of us or summat?'

'I'm not,' replied Patrick hastily. He took one of the sandwiches. 'Thank ye kindly.' The man was a paradox, he thought as he ate. All afternoon he had been dishing out orders as though Patrick was his personal slave, insulting him, calling him all sorts of unsavoury names, and now he was offering to share his food with him. Would he ever understand these English?

John's grimy face creased into a grin, exhibiting a wide gap between his front teeth. 'I can 'ear yer mind whirring away like clockwork. Yer thinkin' what a funny bugger I am, aren't yer?' He laughed as Patrick's face told him he was right. 'Aye, I thought so. Yer'll not be first, but I dare say yer'll get used to me. I'm a nice lad really, aren't I?' he asked the others who made derisory noises. 'See, they love me. Eh, Ronnie, are y'off t' shop?' he shouted to one of the bricklayers who replied that he was. John dug into his pocket. ' 'Ere, get Mick – sorry – Patrick,' he grinned at his neighbour, 'get Patrick a twist o' tea from Mrs Mouncey's, will yer?' He spun a penny into the air which the other deftly snatched.

'Hey, no,' objected Patrick, digging into his own pocket. 'I'm not that hard up.'

'Oh, sit down, yer proud bugger. Yer can buy mine tomorrow. Hurry up, Ron, else water'll boil dry.'

Patrick threw a penny onto John's lap and leaned back to continue eating.

The man picked up the coin and turned it over thoughtfully as he spoke. 'Is my money not good enough for yer, then?'

Patrick looked askance. 'I meant no offence. I just like to pay me own way as does any man.'

'If I offer to buy Ronnie a drink in the bar he doesn't say no, does he? If he offers to buy me one I don't say, I'll buy me own, do I? Pride's all well an' good in its place, but seems to me yer can't afford it at the moment.' He looked pointedly at the other man's feet. 'An' if yer continue to throw people's good intentions back in their faces they'll be wary of offerin' owt again. Tek my advice: if anyone's willin' to do thee a favour, tek it, whether yer need it or not. We all help each other round here – or most on us – an' if you're gonna live among us then yer'll have to get used to it.'

'I really am sorry,' said Patrick sincerely. 'No offence was meant.'

'None taken.' John flicked the coin back at him with a thumb.

The conversation progressed in desultory fashion until Ronnie returned with the tea and Patrick borrowed a jug in which to make it. John asked where he lived.

'Britannia Yard.' Patrick used a pencil to stir the brew.

'Oh, s'truth, ol' Raper's residence, eh?'

'Ye know the man?' Patrick frowned as he sipped from the jug.

'Who doesn't? Edwin Raper, master butcher, Irish-hater, sheep-shagger, scourge of our womenfolk. Are yer married? Well, yer'd best keep yer missus locked up while he's around, dirty old get.'

Patrick was all for going right home but the other clapped him on the shoulder. 'Nay, it's only a jape, kidder. I think yer wife's safe enough – lest she's got a fleecy coat an' goes *baa*. He's that used to shovin' sheep's legs down 'is boots he's probably forgotten where it is on a woman.'

Patrick joined in the laughter, but nevertheless made a note to warn Mary to keep well clear of the butcher.

As the weeks progressed the house became more habitable – which was more than could be said for the exterior. Patrick had done his best to keep the piles of refuse away from his door – unlike some of his neighbours who seemed unconcerned at the sort of conditions in which they lived, creating more filth as quickly as he disposed of it. Soil was piled high in the midden privies until it overflowed and spilled out onto the yard. No one made any attempt to move it. Small wonder that disease flourished here.

At the first official gathering of the residents Patrick had told them that they would be expected to contribute to the upkeep of the yard. There had been cries of derision. What was the point, some asked – it would not make the houses any better.

'No! But perhaps it might help to keep your children alive a bit longer,' he had goaded. 'I'll wage not one of you here can say he's not lost a child.'

There had been mumbled acceptance of what he said, but some still grumbled. 'Ye'd think the corporation'd do more to help. Why should the responsibility fall on us?'

'Because it *is* your responsibility,' answered Patrick. ' 'Tis you who subscribe to the state o' the privies an' you who must see they're kept clean.'

'Sure, I'm not shovelling shit for two hundred people,' exclaimed another.

'I'm not suggesting ye should. We must all take our turn at emptying the closets so that they stay in reasonable condition.'

'An' what do we do with the stuff we empty?'

'Look, ye're grumblin' about the corporation not doing anything to help,' said Patrick. 'If we pile it into the street then they'll have to have it shifted unless they want to be knee-deep in the stuff. An' another thing: d'ye not think 'tis time ye learnt to speak the lingo?'

'Sure an' how come you know their miserable tongue?' demanded Molly, 'when ye've only just arrived?' Patrick told her of his lessons from the parish priest. 'Well, that's all clever stuff,' she sniffed, 'but we've no need of it.'

Patrick smiled condescendingly. 'Had ye no need for it the other day when ye were charged twice the normal amount for your provisions?'

'*What! Where?* I don't believe ye.'

' 'Tis right, I tell ye. The old skinflint tried it on me, thought I couldn't read the prices on his merchandise.' An angry rumble rocked the hovel as the poor Irish realised how they were being swindled. ' 'Tis your own silly faults an' no one else's,' Patrick continued. 'But now I'm here to change all that.'

'Gob, will y'ever listen to him,' said Molly. 'The Second Messiah. All right, Pat Feeney, you're so clever ye can teach me the English – an' while ye're at it ye can turn this here tea into poteen.' She cackled, baring long, horse-like teeth and setting the others off laughing.

So the meeting had turned out equably. There was, however, no solution at all to the effluence from the abattoir. The stench crept into their very skin, causing people to give them a wide berth when passing them on the street. The horrible cries and foul language – the latter coming from the drovers who had a difficult task in getting the condemned beasts through the narrow passageway – demanded great stoicism. Patrick often remonstrated with the butcher, but each admonishment served only to alienate the man even further.

Patrick felt the man's hate now as he unlatched his door and momentarily turned to counter the butcher's stare. Raper dropped his eyes and went back to paring his nails, allowing Patrick to step inside.

'Mary, for the love o' God will ye put that table down!' He slung down his pack and went to assist her.

'I was just rearranging the furniture,' panted Mary, referring to the broken-legged table and two well-used stools. 'I can't seem to sit still.'

'Where d'ye want it?' asked her husband, then dragged the table to the specified point. 'God, woman, I'll have the hide off ye if I come home again an' find ye moving heavy things like that. What's got into ye?'

'I think I'm getting near my time.' Mary rubbed the small of her back. 'I feel as though I've loads to do – they tell me 'tis that way, like the birds with their nest-building.'

'I'll give ye nest-building,' answered Patrick. 'An' what might ye be giving me for me tea – worms?'

Mary chuckled and drew the cooking-pot away from the fire. 'Be quiet an' sit down else ye'll get nothing.'

'Hah, it'll be no less than I've been getting lately. I'll be glad when that child comes. I'm beginning to know what a priest feels like.'

Mary blushed. She was still not accustomed to his forward speech. 'Stop that at once, Patrick or ye'll get this pot over your head.' She waved a spoon at him as they sat down to their meal.

Later they sat side by side watching the flames lick at the fireback, thinking, as they usually did at this time of day, of their homeland. Mary tried to position herself more comfortably on the stool, keeping her hands busy by sewing a tiny garment. Molly had very kindly given her a cast-off dress belonging to the girls to cut up for baby clothes. She was proving to be a good friend, despite her sometimes thoughtless remarks and her liking for the ale, and Mary would be glad of her help when the time came. As her needle flashed in and out of the material she urged the child to make quick his arrival and hoped her prayers would be answered with a live healthy baby.

As if by some telepathic message the child had heeded her words, he began to make his entry into the world the very next day. Patrick was roused from his sleep that fine morning by small animal utterances from the woman at his side.

'It's started,' gasped Mary as he peered anxiously into her face. Actually it had started during the night but she hadn't wanted to wake him.

'I'll get Molly.' He leapt up trying, unsuccessfully, to get his legs into his breeches.

'There's no call for panic.' Mary relaxed as the pain subsided and giggled at her husband who was shoving both limbs down one trouser leg for the second time. Despite the light laughter she felt a pang of fear at the thought of what was going to happen to her body and held out her hand to him. 'Don't go, Pat.'

He turned an encouraging face at the door. 'I'll be but five minutes. Now don't go away.' He held up his hand. 'I'll be back before ever ye know I'm gone.'

Molly answered his pounding at her door, bewilderment on her sleepy face. 'Oh, 'tis you, Pat.' She yawned and hooked a finger into each eye, ridding them of sleep. 'An' why would you be in such a state – as if I didn't know. Ye're all alike, you men. Jimmy! Jimmy, ye'll have to get yourself off to work, I have to see to Mary.'

A young girl squinted blearily round the bedroom door to

see what the commotion was about. 'Ah, Norah, kick your father's backside an' give the mob their breakfast, will ye?' Molly instructed her eldest daughter, then followed fast-disappearing Patrick.

Mary groaned as the contraction gripped her, clutching with steely fingers, trying to force the new life from her.

'How is it, love?' Molly planted herself at the foot of the mattress and bent to examine the girl.

'I've never felt anything like this,' hissed Mary through clenched teeth, then breathed out as the spasm receded.

'Don't I know it, pet.' Molly laughed ruefully. 'The men get all the pleasure an' we get all the pain. Ye'll find it gets easier, though.'

'Holy Mother o' God never again,' swore Mary, another pain rippling through her tortured body. She gnawed at the twisted and torn sheet that she clutched in her fists.

'Ah, they all say that but sure ye'll soon forget about the pain.' Molly turned to the anxious husband. 'Ye'd better be off to work; there's nothin'll happen here for a while yet.'

Patrick refused. 'I'm stayin' right here.' He moved to Mary's side and took hold of her hand.

'Is it that ye'd not be trustin' me?' asked the woman airily. 'For if ye want to play the midwife yourself ye're welcome.'

'No!' cried Patrick. 'I meant nothin' o' the sort an' well you know it, Molly – but this is my first child an' I'm bound to be worried, aren't I?'

'Huh, *his* child says he,' sniffed Molly. 'Sure, an' what's this poor girl screamin' an' cryin' for if you're the one that's havin' it?'

'Molly are ye going to help or aren't yese?' cried the desperate father.

'Ah, ye won't be needin' me for a while yet,' replied Molly. 'There's nothing I can do for a moment. I might as well go see if me own are coping.' She made for the door.

'You're not leavin'? For God's sake, Molly, how will I know what to do?'

'Didn't I tell ye?' replied Molly patiently. 'There's nothin' to be done for ages yet. If ye want to throw away a day's wage ye can make yourself useful an' hold her hand.' With that she was gone.

'Pat, you go,' grunted Mary between pains. 'We can't afford for ye to be off work.'

'But . . .'

'Ye can't help an' I'd rather not have ye watching my pain. Go . . . oh, for God's sake go!' Her face contorted.

He still attempted to stay but she grew so agitated at the loss of wages that in the end he did as she asked, promising to get away early if one of the lads would cover for him.

All day the young girl rolled frantically over the palliasse, trying to escape the red-hot pincers that tore at her innards until it seemed that she could bear no more. 'Mam!' she cried out in her anguish, but no one could help her.

'Not much longer now,' said Molly who had kept popping in and out all through the day. 'Come on, keep pushing.' She held Mary's straining legs apart, offering words of encouragement. 'Good, keep goin', I can see its head. It's got a load o' black hair. Come on, push, push!'

To Mary it seemed that she might split in half at any minute. Suddenly something gave, a gush of hot moisture shot up her back and the head of the child emerged, heralding its birth with a lusty scream of rage at the indignities perpetrated upon it.

'Lord above!' Molly helped the infant to make its exit from its mother. ' 'Tis cryin' before it's all the way out.' She dangled it upside down.

Mary craned her neck to get a view of the child. 'Is he all right?'

'Not he, love – *she*; 'tis a fine colleen ye'd be having an' a right lusty one at that.' Molly wiped the blood-speckled infant and, wrapping her in a clean sheet, passed her to her mother.

Mary cradled the child and gazed wearily into the disdainful face. The child seemed to be accusing her for the pain it had suffered.

Patrick, now home from work, had been pacing the floor in the room below. The high-pitched wail brought him to a halt. Silence followed and he thought he must have imagined it, until Molly appeared at the top of the rickety stairs and shouted: 'Does this child have a father or not?'

He bounded up the stairs three at a time and stopped at the bedroom door, overcome by emotion at the sight that met his eyes. Mary, her damp hair spread over the straw-filled palliasse, beckoned and he moved closer. She looked different – what was it? Her face appeared the same with its translucent skin and piquant features, the mouth was parted in the usual kindly smile – then what had changed? Ah, now he knew – it was her eyes. She had always had wide beautiful blue eyes but now there was an added beauty; they glowed in sapphire-like brilliance, brimming with love and newly-discovered motherhood. It was an effort to tear his eyes away but somehow he directed them at the tiny bundle in her arms.

'I didn't expect a girl,' he told her foolishly at her announcement.

'Neither did I – ye don't mind, d'ye?'

'How could I mind? Just look at her and anyway there'll be plenty of time for those sons.' He missed Mary's wince and laid a rough finger in the sleeping baby's palm; the tiny hand curled around it involuntarily. 'Will ye look at that grip? I expected her to be . . . well, a bit weedy-like, what with the famine an' all, but there's nothing wrong with this one, is there?'

Her face shone. 'There's not, thank God. Ye know, I felt so sure he was going to die, Pat – ah, will ye listen to me, calling her "he". It takes some getting used to after all these months. I don't know what we'll call her.' It was usually the custom to name a first boychild after the paternal grandfather and a girl after the grandmother, but Patrick never spoke of his mother – had never really known her.

He thought for a while then his face lit up and he spoke quietly. 'I have just the very name that'll serve to remind her of her heritage.'

And as he told her, Erin Feeney opened her navy-blue eyes and, with an all-knowing gaze, erased the horrors of the past, bringing a new joy and meaning to their empty lives.

CHAPTER ELEVEN

LIKE A ROSEBUD unfurling its petals with each new day, so the child grew and flourished, adding to their little dwelling an atmosphere of contentment. True, their environment had not altered noticeably, but when the door was shut fast against the filth and squalor outside, their humble abode was a warm haven of security.

Now that Mary was back on her feet again she had secured a post in the chicory fields, working with the child slung on her back. Patrick was greatly displeased at his wife going out to work, but he had to admit that the money brought its benefits. Over the previous months they had added various items of cheap furniture to the house and had also purchased more clothes for themselves. They had made their place as much a little Ireland as was possible. Each night the residents of the yard would gather around the fireplace of one of its families, singing, sharing a pot of tobacco, telling tales; it was only when the dawn showed up the grassless yard and the twin towers of the gasworks instead of the granite mountain, that they had to live with the fact that this was not home.

For Patrick work helped, the physical effort it entailed alleviating the stress of his cramped living conditions. His workmates, too, he had come to understand better, even going so far as to form a precarious friendship with the man Thompson. The insulting nicknames, he had discovered, were not intended as a personal affront. John employed this tack with everyone, it was just his way. All in all, life was a little easier than it had been.

With Mary things were somewhat different. Although reasonably happy, it was of great concern to her that they had not sought guidance from the church since leaving Ireland. Her faith was still important to her – more so, now she had the child – and it hurt that she must enact it in private. Several times she had tried to discuss it with her husband but he would cut her dead; Patrick could be so hard. She feared what this rejection must do to his soul. There came a time, however, when she could stand it no longer, and it was as they sat by the fireside that night, watching the babe drum her heels on the rug that Mary had created from strips of rag that she spoke.

'Pat, you're not going to like this – no, I beg you, listen this time.' He had guessed what the subject was to be and his mouth had opened to stall her. 'I know how ye feel about the church, but . . .' here she took a deep breath, 'leaving aside my desperate need to go to Confession, that child's got to be baptiscd. 'Tis terribly wrong o' ye to risk her soul because o' your bitterness. I want – I demand – to see Father Kelly.' The priest had attempted time and again to breach the Feeney stronghold but had always been repulsed. Pat wouldn't even allow the fellow to see his wife.

'Sure, ye've had your answer, Mary.'

There were the stirrings of anger. 'Patrick, 'tis not often I disobey you but by God I'm going to see that child baptised if I have to beat ye senseless. Look,' she became coaxing, 'I could've taken her any time while you were out o' the house, could I not? Had her baptised, gone to Confession an' you'd've known nothing about it; but I didn't. When I go to church I want to do it properly – with my husband.'

'Then ye'll need to find another fool.'

'Patrick, damn you for a selfish hound! I've never known the like o' ye, turning a priest away from our own door – 'tis unheard of.' Whilst she had been preparing to follow her husband to work yesterday Father Kelly had been sharing a joke with Jimmy Flaherty in the yard. Patrick had gone right up to him, no less, and interrupted rudely, 'Ye needn't waste your time knocking on my door while I'm away.' Father Kelly could be as rude as he: 'Sure, haven't I better things to be doing than bruising me knuckles on a heathen door? I'll thank ye not to interrupt my conversation with the faithful.' And had turned his back on Pat. Mary could have died with shame – had not dared set off for the fields till he had gone.

Patrick took stock of his wife's indignation. He knew from experience that on the rare occasions she employed this tone she could not be shifted. He heaved a sigh. 'If I give my approval of your going to church will ye cease hounding me?'

Eagerness. 'An' have the baby baptised?'

'No. That'd mean I had to be present.'

'Very well,' she answered stiffly. 'If that's the limit of your generosity I'll stop hounding ye, Patrick Feeney – in fact I'll never utter so much as one word till you see sense.'

'Mary . . .'

But she bent her head over her darning and pressed her lips together and not another word did he get from her for the rest of the evening. The morning found her no more approachable. His breakfast was delivered with no whisper of regret. God, she could be a stubborn little minx when she chose. He raced down the meal, eager to be out of here. Church, church, church, that was all he ever seemed to get.

His premature departure had singled him out for some more. As he made his exit from the yard a stentorian voice assailed him from the far end of the passage. The priest blocked his way, though Patrick could easily have pushed him aside had he wanted. Liam Kelly was a wiry man. His originally dark brown hair was now peppered with grey, the product, Liam supposed, of listening to so many strange confessions over the years. He had often wondered if they made them up just to see his face when he left the confessional afterwards; the face that gave the first impression of cherubic mildness – which the eyes then belied; when provoked they could burn like two fiery emeralds and set the biggest brute of a sinner to instant repentance.

'I was hoping to catch ye, Patrick Feeney.'

'Were ye indeed?'

'I was. I've been doing some serious thinking about you.' Merely a raised eyebrow from Patrick. 'Could we have a chat?'

'I'm not very talkative at this time of a mornin'.' Patrick sought a way round the priest.

'Sure, you're not very communicative at any time o' the day,' said Liam, then suddenly: 'Ye think you're getting at God through me, don't ye?'

'An' why would I put meself out to do that?' Patrick

marvelled at why he was still standing here. Yet the voice did have some restraining quality to it.

'Ah, haven't I seen it all before? Hundereds of Patrick Feeneys, blaming Our Lord for all their problems.'

'How long've ye been in this place?' enquired Patrick, to which Liam replied several years. 'Then what would ye be knowing o' the problems I had at home, sat in your big English house with its full larder . . .'

'Hah, full larder is it? Remind me to tell that to my housekeeper when she's serving me faggots for the sixth time in a week.'

Patrick tried to end this. 'Look, all I'm askin' is to be left alone to look after my family.'

'An' is this how ye look after them, Patrick Feeney, by keeping them from the church? 'Tis a wicked thing you're doing here.'

Patrick gave an exclamation to the air, then made to move away. 'Ah, don't be giving me that, you're all the same.'

'The same as what? Just what am I, if ye'll spare a second to enlighten me.'

The question was just puzzling enough to put a brake on Patrick's feet. 'Sure, you're a priest, what else?'

Liam tugged at his garb. 'As ever was – but under all this, what am I then? I'll tell ye, I'm a human being like yourself. This outfit doesn't somehow make me invincible to doubt an' pain; those feelings are not the prerogative of the layman.' His green eyes were penetrating. 'D'ye not think I sometimes ask *why*? Why, if Our Lord is so loving and merciful He permits these terrible things to happen?'

'An' how does He answer ye?' asked Patrick sarcastically, trying to match the piercing stare but, unable to dismiss the years of Catholicism try as he might, finally looking away. They had always been taught to respect the priest; he was the head man, the one with all the answers.

'Is it a kicked arse you're looking for, Mr Feeney?' warned Liam angrily, then tempered the flow at the other's look of shock. 'All right,' he presented his palms, 'all right. Ye want to know what He says? I'll tell ye. He says to me that all these bad happenings, these trials, are for a purpose – to sort out the grain from the chaff. I want no chaff in my parish, Mr Feeney. 'Tis a very tight ship I run an'

I'm thinkin' we may have to consider the yardarm for you.'

'Threats, is it?'

'D'ye not think I could carry them out?'

Patrick eyed the much smaller man. 'I've used bigger than you to dip into my egg.'

'An' did they taste good? Would ye care to sample me? 'Cause I'm thinking my foot should slip quite easily into that big hole in your face.' He threw up his hands. 'Ah, will ye listen to me. There's no call for any o' this badness is there? Look, 'tis no arm-lock I'm trying to fit on ye. I'd like to see ye in church but only if ye want to be there. I'll not be yelling for the coals o' Hell to swallow ye up if ye truly feel unable to come.'

'Then you're like no other priest I met.'

'I'll never make Pope, 'tis true.' A wry smile, which Patrick was forced to match; against his feelings for the cloth he was warming to the man inside it. 'Look, I must admit that my prime concern is for your soul. I wouldn't be in the job otherwise – but I also care for your earthly body . . .' There was a pause, then, 'Ye got no help from your priest in Ireland?'

'His soup kept us from dying, aye, but 'twas always served up with a sermon: Our Lord will hear your prayers; He won't let ye down; God will provide.'   '

'An' it was true, was it not?' demanded Liam to much scepticism. 'Just wipe away your bigotry for a spell an' think rationally. Ye could've died of starvation but ye didn't. Who d'ye think brought ye through it? I don't really have to supply the answer do I, Pat? I may call ye Pat, mayn't I? An' He brought ye through for a reason. Who's to say what that reason is? Perhaps 'tis for some important cause – such as buying your parish priest a measure down at the King Willie, seven o'clock tonight,' the flicker of a grin, 'or maybe 'twas simply to allow ye to perpetuate your kind – that's a very important reason in itself, creating children. I couldn't help but notice, though I never got into that nice little kitchen o' yours, that ye've not long been a father.'

'That's right – may God take me for a fool.'

'Oh, ye do still call upon Him from time to time?'

Impatience. 'All right, look, if ye want to go see Mary I've told her she can let ye in.'

'Such gallantry. Can I anticipate a warmer welcome from the wife o' this stubborn block o' granite?'

'Ah, she'll no doubt feed ye the dinner that was meant for me. Isn't seein' the priest more important than her own husband? Ye'll no doubt be hearin' her plea about the child's baptising too.'

' 'Tis not baptised yet?' A frown, then his face relaxed. 'No matter, we can soon remedy that.'

'Ye could if I wanted ye to.' For these last few seconds Patrick continued to oppose him. Then all interest seemed to vanish. 'Ah, do what ye like, the pair o' yese. I'm away to me work.'

'No, no that won't do.' Liam caught at his sleeve. 'Ye've got to want this yourself.'

'An what does it matter to you?'

'Sure, it matters a great deal. I care about you.'

Patrick had to accept that there was obvious sincerity in the green eyes, but still resisted. 'Why should you care?' All these fellows were interested in was collecting souls like medals.

'Why shouldn't I?' asked Liam perversely.

'We could bounce that one back and forth all day.'

'And so we could. Listen, I tell ye what, Pat, I can see you're raring to be at your labours an' I've no wish to force your wife into depriving a workin' lad of his dinner. Fetch them both to evening Mass an' we'll see about getting this child baptised.'

'Ah, I'm not sure.' To like the man was one thing, to go into his church another.

'I'll not leap on ye the minute you're through the door an' string ye to a pew. Ye'll be free not to listen to my ramblings if ye so choose – sure, ye'll be no different from your neighbours; don't they tell me my sermons are a great cure for insomnia? We'll baptise the babe then see if we can do something about that black soul o' yours.'

'Father . . .'

'Father is it? That's an improvement, anyway.'

'I lost faith once. Even if I agree to come to your church an' make all the responses an' drown meself in holy water, who's to say I'll ever get that feeling back or, even if I do, that I won't lose it again in hard times?'

'Faith's not a jacket ye put on and take off when ye feel like it, Patrick. God has His rights too. It shouldn't be a one-sided commitment. I'm thinking ye've been expecting too much of Him, letting Him be the one to do the giving when you're not prepared to give of yourself. Ah, my poor friend,' Liam gripped him fiercely, 'I know, I know how ye've suffered – but you're not the only one. Do please take this step.'

Patrick forced a smile. 'Ye know, Father Kelly, ye've a tongue on ye like a yard o' velvet.'

'Aren't I regularly asked to supply the ladies' gowns? Now will ye come?'

'Oh, I don't know.'

'Isn't that what attracted me to ye, Pat Feeney? You're such a decisive soul. Remind me to send for you when my house is on fire. Ye wouldn't know whether to turn to the pump or pull down your breeches.'

'If I come an' sit there an' not believin' in any of it 'tis a hypocrite I'd be.'

'Hypocrite or no, I sense the faith's still in you, Patrick an' I'll do my damndest to fetch it out. An' if not . . . well, I can surely still be your friend?'

'I never had a priest for a friend.'

'Now isn't that a thing? I never had a bricklayer's labourer for a friend neither. Such blether. I like to think I'm everbody's friend. So, we've got that settled. We'll see ye at Mass tonight an' wet the baby's head directly afterwards.'

'The things some people do to get a free drink,' said Patrick, then chuckled as he went on his way, leaving the priest still uninformed on whether he would be there or not.

After much heart-searching, Patrick took his wife and child to Mass. They were accompanied by the Flahertys and their six children. It was a mild, summery evening and the dying sun cast long shadows over the pavements. They strolled along Walmgate, viewed idly by the ancient Irish grandmothers who sat at the roadside peering through the clouds of smoke that rose from the clay pipes clenched between toothless gums.

Mary felt a surge of freedom and gladness. She was going to church. She was really going at last. The guilt she had felt at her enforced exile from Catholicism was now to be put to rights. While his wife was experiencing this joy Patrick was asking himself what had persuaded him to be led by the priest's charm – for that was what had swung the matter, the man, not the power of his religion.

They passed from Walmgate into Fossgate and from there to Whip-ma-whop-ma-gate and Colliergate, street names which seemed to increase the foreignness of the place, thought Patrick. At their arrival at the chapel in Little Blake Street he followed the others inside, emulating their automatic gestures of obeisance by dipping his fingers into the vessel of holy water and applying it to his forehead and breast. He did not even realise he had done it, so naturally did it come. He shuffled into the pew alongside his wife, taking the baby from her so that she might pray in comfort. He bounced Erin on his knee as she started to turn crotchety, inwardly recoiling at Mary's look of sublime happiness as she raised her face to the altar. How could she find the stomach for it?

Mary turned to him and held out her arms for the baby so that her husband could do as she had done, but he shook his head resolutely and held onto the child.

The priest toured a brief eye over his congregation as he mounted the altar, offering a prayer of gratitude as he spotted Patrick sitting head and shoulders above the rest. He launched into Mass, the Latin incantations flowing easily from his tongue, but whenever he snatched a look he was dismayed to see that the dark head was not bowed as were the others, but looking fixedly in front, an expression of stubborn defiance on his tanned features.

Later, when Mass was completed and most of the worshippers had departed, Father Kelly approached the small group which remained. 'Good to see ye here, Patrick.'

' 'Tis only through the wife I'm here,' replied the other, somewhat peeved at the slight man's power over him. He introduced the shy girl at his side.

'An' who might this fine personage be?' Liam tapped the baby's cheek, making her gaze in awe at her new admirer.

'This is our daughter Erin, Father.' Mary, her voice filled with evident pride, kissed the baby's cheek.

'Ah, a little bit o' the old country, is it?' observed Liam. 'An' a real Irish temper to go with it,' he added as the child let out a wail.

'Could ye find it in your heart to baptise her, Father?' whispered Mary as if expecting a rebuff for her absence from the church.

'Now how could I refuse such a charmingly-delivered request?' said Liam. 'I take it ye've discussed this, the pair o' ye?' A nod from Patrick. Ascertaining that Molly and Jimmy were to act as sponsors Liam proceeded to give the child her name. At the end of which he found that the babe was not the only one to receive a wetting. 'Will ye look at that?' He flapped his wet sleeve. 'Don't they always do it to me.'

Mary apologised and offered to wash the vestments but Liam turned down her offer, saying that his housekeeper would see to it. 'Well, would ye honour us with your presence at supper, Father?' she asked, a little to her husband's annoyance.

'The offer of food I have never refused, my dear,' smiled Liam. 'I should be delighted – that's if I won't be taking it out of your own mouths?'

'We're not in the habit of chewing food before we feed it to our guests,' said Patrick.

'Oh, a joker is it?' And wasn't Liam encouraged by this fact.

So ended the evening, with Liam taking sup from the Feeney's meagre larder. Patrick still felt uncomfortable at the way the priest seemed intent on making a friend of him. He could not understand it and the feeling showed in his treatment of the guest. When Mary slipped upstairs to tend to the child he blurted out his incomprehension.

'Why're ye doing this, Father?'

'I was invited, was I not?'

'I don't refer to your taking sup with us. What d'ye see in me that makes ye bent on trying to save me? 'Cause I know that's what's behind all this.'

'Is it the simple answer you'd be wanting or the complicated one? Either way they're both the same: I just don't know. Just say 'tis 'cause I like ye – an' don't ask me why that either for you're as unworthy a Teague of saving as ever I met.' A smile. 'Ah, who can say why one person takes to another. Can you define the quality?'

A shake of head from Patrick; he who was unable to explain the reason for his friendship with the wily John Thompson.

'I sense a terrible amount o' pain in you, Pat Feeney. I'd like to take a little off your shoulders if ye'll let me.'

There was still that obstacle of the man's vocation. 'I've no inclination to return to the church. I know I brought Mary tonight but I felt nothing.'

'An' who mentioned anything about church?' Liam suddenly reached in his pocket and brought out a flask. 'Some of my parishioners are a darned sight more generous than you, thank the Lord. Instead o' going to the alehouse why don't we take our dram here?'

Patrick grinned and sought out receptacles for the whiskey. When his wife came down some time later the men were onto their third. The whiskey serving to ease some of the guilt he felt, he found himself overlooking the priestly attire and actually regarding Liam as a friend.

'Sure, d'ye not realise what ye were doing?' asked Mary on closing the door after the priest. 'Using the man's proper name an' no hint of a title.'

'Isn't that what friends do? Call each other by their first names?' The whiskey had made him happy.

'He's not our friend, he's our priest.'

'Then you can call him Father an' I'll call him Liam,' stated Patrick. 'Sure, I've quite got to likin' the fella.'

CHAPTER TWELVE

OVER TWO YEARS had passed since they had left County Mayo, but for Mary time could not erase the memory of the green and golden fields, the purple mountain that dwelt in a corner of her mind. On certain days, when the mood was upon her, she would take out the little piece of Ireland that had accompanied her all those miles. Lifting the child on her lap she would show Erin the piece of dried turf and speak to her of her own childhood, telling tales of leprechauns and banshees, while the child looked up enthralled.

Erin had just celebrated her second birthday and had grown into a beautiful child, inheriting the long black hair of her mother, which already hung past her shoulders in thick waves. She lifted her wide blue eyes to meet her mother's, the sooty lashes fluttering precociously.

'Show harp, Mam.' Her stubby fingers pointed to the instrument in the corner of the room. Mary reverently took up the harp. It was odd how the child had taken a liking to the thing – no, more than a liking, an obsession; she seemed to want to play with nothing else, which was strange for a child. She would finger the intricate carving, talking to the birds and animals within the wood and even making crude attempts to play the instrument. 'You tell me story?' asked Erin, clutching the harp, and Mary repeated the much loved story of their lives in Ireland, trying to convey the love that she felt for her homeland.

When her husband came home for his midday meal she commented upon the girl's attachment to the harp. 'We'll have to get someone to teach her when she's a wee bit older, Pat. She seems to have inherited your daddy's gift.'

Patrick smiled sadly as he thought of his father. 'Aye, he'd be real proud o' that . . . but 'tis no use lookin' to me to teach her: I never mastered the thing. We'll have to ask round.'

'Ah well, there's a few years yet,' replied Mary. 'Perhaps by that time we'll be back home.' She put the dinner on the table, a meal consisting of bacon and a bowl of potatoes which Patrick proceeded to dip thoughtfully into the plate of salt.

'Ye aren't eating, Mary?' He examined his wife's face for signs of illness as she bustled about the room.

'I'm not hungry. Just lately I've been feeling like I've a bellyful o' worms.' She lifted eyes that held a secret and told him shyly, 'Pat, I think I could be havin' another.'

'Oh, that's great.' Patrick mopped his plate with a piece of bread and leaned back in his chair to give her a cheeky grin. 'I was beginning to think I was putting it in the wrong place.'

'Patrick Feeney!' Mary snatched the plate from under his nose. 'What have I told you about sayin' things like that in front o' the child?'

'Oh, woman, let yourself go.' He sprang up to grab her around the waist.

'I'll let something go in a minute if you don't get out o' this house an' back to work.'

'Did ye hear that, Erin?' Patrick asked the child as he pulled on his jacket. 'The woman's a tyrant.' He kissed them both then left for work, whistling merrily.

As soon as he had left the room Mary's smile evaporated. She put her hand to her aching head and decided to postpone the washing-up. Instead, she took Erin's hand and went to lie down upstairs. It had not been as bad as this the last time.

In the evening when Mary undressed in front of the fire she suddenly doubled over and cried out. Patrick shrugged off his shirt, left it inside out and went quickly to her side. 'What is it, *muirnin*?'

' 'Tis nothing.' She tried to make light of it. 'Just a touch o' belly-ache.'

'Will I get the doctor?' It looked like more than a touch of belly-ache to Patrick; her face was contorted with discomfort.

'No!' Her sharp tone implied that this was the last thing they could afford. 'I'll be fine tomorrow.'

'But it might be the baby.'

'No, Patrick,' she said firmly. 'Ye'll bring no doctor. 'Tis only the body's way o' telling me to cut out all these cherries your friend John keeps plying me with.' The bricklayer often brought them presents for which Mary – thinking he had paid for them – scolded him. She straightened and took a deep breath. 'Look, I'm fit now.'

'Sure, ye don't look fit to me,' replied Patrick dubiously.

'Oh, an' isn't that a compliment to aid recovery.'

'I think I will fetch the doctor.' He started to dress.

'Patrick, I've said no and I mean no. Now get undressed and come to bed.'

He saw it was no use arguing with her; once Mary had set her mind on something she would not budge. Anyway, she probably knew best how she felt. He snuffed out the candle and followed her upstairs.

It wasn't a surfeit of cherries; Patrick could see that as, over the next few days, his wife's condition worsened. She was still refusing to see a doctor, arguing strenuously that they could not afford it. At first he gave in to her, making do with Molly's nursing skills, but as others of his acquaintance began to go down with a similar ailment he knew that it was something serious. Finally she became too weak to protest and he sent a friend to bring the doctor.

As he waited he looked down helplessly at the frail creature on the palliasse. The illness had weakened her so much that now, to her shame, she had not the strength to reach the privy. The dry, cracked lips emitted a rasping cough and a cold sweat had broken out on her forehead. Patrick, damning himself for listening to her argument so long, wrung out a cloth in the bowl of water that Molly held and laid it over his wife's brow.

'She's not getting any better, Molly. Sometimes it's as if she doesn't even know me.'

The girl mumbed something about Erin.

'Ah, don't worry yourself, pet, she'll be fine enough.' Molly put down the bowl and stroked Mary's hair. 'Sure, isn't her Aunt Molly takin' care o' her?' Still, she was concerned.

The two were still with Mary when the doctor arrived. After a perfunctory examination he snapped his bag shut. Patrick asked what ailed his wife.

'Cholera,' replied the man. 'And you've left it a little late to inform me, haven't you?'

Patrick was stunned. 'God . . . I didn't know . . . she said it was just a belly-ache . . .'

The doctor mentally condemned these people's ignorance. Were they too stupid to realise it was their own filth provided a haven for the disease?

'She'll have to be taken to the fever hospital.' He had taken out a handkerchief, through which he now spoke. 'Though God knows when I can arrange it, the damn place is full up.'

Patrick asserted himself. 'Then they'll just have to find room!'

'I'll try . . . but really, man you shouldn't have allowed it to get as bad as this. You must have known what it was – the city's crawling with the disease!'

Patrick looked shamedly at Molly. The doctor, telling the Irishman he would return when he was able, left to arrange a hospital bed.

At his revelation Molly had backed away from the bed. Fever! and she had been nursing the girl. Giving her excuse as wanting to see the children, she left.

Patrick barely noticed the pounding of Molly's retreating feet. He slumped beside the writhing girl to await her removal to hospital. The disease being rampant in the city this was not arranged until the next day, by which time Mary's condition had deteriorated even further. Patrick did not go to work but played sentinel whilst she moaned deliriously of events long past, shouting out the names of her dead brother and sisters. There were moments of lucidity, though few. In one of these she asked him to bring her the little piece of Ireland so that it might give her comfort. At this time she also asked why he was not at work. His lightly delivered explanation did not convince her: she knew how things were.

'Pat,' she said croakily. 'Will ye fetch Father Kelly?'

He took the rag from her brow, dipped it into water and replaced it. 'Sure, what would ye be wanting with Liam right this minute? Didn't he promise to come an' see ye again the other day?'

'Pat, ye know well enough what I'm wanting him for.'

'No!' He laid a finger over her dry lips. 'Don't talk like that, Mary. Ye're going to get better.'

'Please, Pat I must have the priest,' she begged. 'Don't leave it too late. Don't let me die a sinner.'

'Mary, you are not going to die! I won't let ye.' Where the hell was that doctor?

'For the love of God, Patrick!'

'No!' He refused to believe that she was going to die, despite the evidence before him; to fetch the priest would be admitting defeat. A slight softening: 'All right, I'll send word for Liam to come a little sooner than he'd intended – but sure, 'tis only to keep you from nagging me. There'll be none o' this Extreme Unction rubbish. Once you're in that hospital you'll be leppin' about like a spring lamb.'

Her eyes lost their pleading as the pain overtook her again and once more she slipped into her twilight memories, flinging her head restlessly from side to side as he stared down at her. The pitiful object on the bed bore no resemblance to the girl he had married. Even in the months of famine she had never looked so bad. A stronger stench from the bed indicated that the sheets would need changing again. The last ones that Molly had washed for him were not dry. What could he do? He clutched the damp sheet in his fists and rent it viciously, the threadbare material making hardly a sound of complaint. He flung down the two halves of the sheet and paced the room, gripping handfuls of hair, hurting himself for the shabby way he had treated her. He knew that what he should be doing was kneeling and praying, but he couldn't; he just couldn't. The sleepless nights when he had washed and cared for her had taken their toll. He dashed his head against the wall in futility and guilt.

A croak from the bed brought him rushing to her side again and he sat beside her, bowed his head and eventually closed his eyes.

He must have slept, for when he opened them the room was dark and the girl on the bed was silent. 'Mary?' He picked up the cold, half-clenched fist, searching for life. '*A Dhia na bhfeart!*' he whispered, as the fragile hand fell open to reveal the piece of dried turf, which crumbled through her fingers and turned to dust . . . as would his wife.

He could not cry. Guilt forbade it, guilt, that he had not sent for the priest and now she was dead. Dead. The stairs creaked and Molly slowly appeared at the bedroom door.

'There's a cart here to take Mary to hospital, Pat.' Her black slitty eyes narrowed even further as she stood on tiptoe to see over his hunched shoulder.

'Tell him he's too bloody late,' came the choked reply.

She crept closer then, seeing Mary's glazed eyes, took an involuntary step backwards and crossed herself. Recouping her courage she moved alongside the mattress and kneeling down took hold of the edge of the sheet, making to draw it over the dead girl's face.

'Leave it.'

Molly looked up at him quizzically but did not release the sheet.

'I said leave it!'

The eyes that bore into her were full of such anger, such hatred that Molly dropped the cover and rose slowly to her feet, looking down at him. 'D'ye want me to do anything for ye? I'll send for Father Kelly . . .'

'Just go.'

'Pat, she'll have to be prepared an' . . .'

'Go!' he yelled. 'Get out, will ye? For Christ's sake leave me be.'

Molly was about to do this but as she turned she encountered the tiny figure in the doorway. 'Erin, darlin' come back to Aunt Molly's house an' have a cup o' tea, ye shouldn't've followed me.' She tried to shield the child's view of the bed but the tiny hand pushed her out of the way.

'Mammy?' Erin sensed the tragedy, evaded Molly's grab and ran to the makeshift bed, flinging herself at her dead mother. 'Mammy, wake up!'

She felt herself being grasped roughly and lifted from the mattress. Her father gripped her by the shoulders and glared into her face. He was trembling, she could feel the vibrations running from his body into hers where his hands joined her arms. His eyes looked funny. He was hurting her. Daddy had never hurt her before.

Molly found it hard to believe this was the same man. His handsome face was disfigured by a mask of bitterness. Overcome with sorrow for him, Molly went over and firmly disentangled the child's arms, gently pushing her away from the bed.

'Get that child out o' my sight!'

'Oh, Pat . . .'

'Get her out, Molly, now!'

'Daddy!'

'Come on now, Erin,' said Molly gently. 'Daddy wants to be on his own for a while. Ye can come back later.'

'No.' Patrick was less vociferous now, but just as militant. 'You take her, Molly. Take her an' don't bring her back. Sure, I can't stand the sight of her.'

– You callous bastard, thought Molly as she saw Erin's face screw up in pain. You lousy, pig-headed bastard.

– How can she know, thought Patrick, who guessed what was going through her mind – how can she know how I'd feel, looking at that child every day and seeing her mother? I could not bear it. Tentatively he reached out and passed a hand over Mary's eyes. Then he took hold of the sheet and slowly pulled it up over her face. She was gone.

It was then that the most distressing factor of all hit him. In all those months of famine, in their two, nearly three years of marriage, even in the throes of love, he had never told her – he had never told her he loved her.

CHAPTER THIRTEEN

FOR A LONG time after Mary's death Patrick endured his existence with bad grace. The cholera epidemic was on the wane but his escape from the disease was of no consequence. He was barely able to drag himself from his bed in a morning. Despair flooded over him, carving deep furrows on his brow and around his mouth. Any offers of sympathy from friends were quickly withdrawn on meeting the hostile madness in his eyes. His moods varied from apathy to anguish to hatred – hatred, mainly of himself. His workmates steered well clear of him when he was wielding his pick and not even John's humour could pierce the sullen barricade he had erected.

Erin, bewildered and forsaken, was cared for by the Flahertys, spending her days collapsed listlessly against her old harp and her nights snuggled up between Norah and Peggy on the lumpy, flea-ridden mattress. Often she would sneak into her father's house and gaze down at him where he lay on the floor in a drunken stupor. She could not understand what she had done to make him hate her so.

Day after day Molly Flaherty watched the bereaved child rock to and fro, staring sightlessly out of the cracked window. She had tried every method she knew to make Patrick aware of the harm he was doing the child, but it was all utterly useless. Her entreaties were met with vitriolic retorts, sometimes nearing physical violence.

Liam Kelly had also racked his brains for some way to shake Patrick from his self-pity. The man no longer washed and his clothes were filthy. Jaunty arrogance had collapsed into morose languor – and what he was doing to that child was criminal. Liam himself enjoyed a drink but Patrick had taken this pleasure to extremes, no longer visiting the pubs for companionship and a friendly chat but to find a quiet corner where he could drink himself into oblivion, in a vain attempt to eradicate his sorrow. The priest had more sense than to tell Patrick that it was God's will that his wife had been taken. He knew any interference would only be misunderstood. He realised from the drunken, incoherent ramblings that had greeted him when he had spoken to Patrick after the funeral that this time the man blamed not God but himself, was steeped in guilt at not sending for the priest when his wife had begged him to. He shunned all who tried to help him; had never shed so much as one tear; was merely escaping further and further inside himself.

Father Kelly knew that he desperately needed to be brought out of that self, to face his suffering. Just how he would go about helping Patrick escaped the priest for the moment. Perhaps Patrick was the kind who needed someone to provoke him. If so, then Liam must be the one to do it. Liam, who would not retaliate, would take whatever Pat needed to fling.

– Let's hope 'tis not hammers, thought Liam grimly as he hung up his cassock and put on his street clothes. Opening the solid oak door he went forward to battle.

'A firkin o' your finest ale, landlord,' slurred Patrick, already beginning to sway though the night was still young.

'A firkin?'

'Aye – a firkin big potful,' roared Patrick, thumping the bar and laughing at his own joke.

'All right, clever bugger – out!' The landlord lifted the hatch on the bar and made to escort Patrick from the house. 'You've had enough.'

On feeling himself grasped firmly by the collar, the Irishman gave vent to all the pent-up emotions that the priest had hoped to take upon his own shoulders. Instead, the landlord was to feel their violent effect. With a bellow Patrick threw up his arms, causing the landlord to fall against a customer, who in turn stumbled into his neighbour, who pushed him back, giving the signal for a general free-for-all. Patrick's long-forsaken workmates, eager to renew their friendship with him, leapt over the tables to join the affray, kicking over glasses and tankards and bringing forth further violence from their beer-drenched victims.

Patrick, spurred into further action by the rumpus he had initiated, was having a whale of a time. Picking up the landlord by the lapels he drew back his great fist and aimed it at the man's jaw. Unfortunately, where Patrick thought the man's jaw to be and where it actually was were two different places. The blow was neatly dodged, allowing the landlord to implant one of his own. His was more accurate; it sent Patrick crashing to the floor, upturning spittoons, splintering chairs and tables in his downfall.

The battle was in full swing now, with bottles and pots hitting the walls, emptying their contents over the paintwork and leaving brown stains. Blood and teeth flew from all quarters and chairs were smashed over unsuspecting heads.

It was at this point that Father Kelly came upon the scene. After investigating several public houses in search of Patrick he had been instructed by one of the walking wounded who had escaped the fracas that he would find the man in The Angel. Of all places, thought Liam, then ducked as a hurtling projectile – earlier identifiable as a meat pie – struck the woodwork behind him with a splat. Wearing an expression of determination he rolled up his sleeves and strode into the mêlée, forging a path through the struggling combatants in an attempt to reach the main culprit. The latter was drawing back his fist yet again when, feeling a hand grasp his shoulder, he ducked and spun round, delivering to the intruder the only accurate punch he'd thrown all night.

As though a bell had sounded the end of the bout a sudden hush came over the room. Clenched fists were dropped as the men gathered silently to stare down at the unconscious priest who lay like a sleeping babe among the broken glass. Somebody chuckled nervously. The noise was joined by another, then another, until the sound grew into a crescendo of inebriated merriment.

John Thompson's face split into a grin, blood edging each tooth. 'By, yer won't half be in for a bollockin' when he comes round.' He slapped Patrick on the back and reached for a magically intact tankard of ale.

Patrick, who had been staring, dumbstruck, at the trickle of blood at the priest's mouth, turned slowly and looked around the room at his laughing friends, then back at the priest. His mouth slowly curled up into a half smile, which gave way to laughter, filling the room with its intensity. He laughed and brayed, bending over with side-splitting mirth. Oh, what a joke! Honking uncontrollably now he woke the priest from his slumber and Liam staggered to his feet, hauling himself up by the belt at Patrick's waist. Patrick was still roaring with amusement. What a tale to tell Mary . . .

The priest's hand moved like the head of a snake to land with a resounding slap on the man's cheek, killing the hysteria. The big Irishman's reflexes demanded that he pull back his fist and retaliate. The eyes that stared back at the priest were wild and full of madness. Then, dispiritedly, his arm was lowered to his side, the anger in his eyes was doused by the sudden welling of tears which spilled over his lashes and trickled down his bruised cheeks. The room was deathly quiet now. The men hung their heads in embarrassed silence, not wanting to see those brawny shoulders shake with misery as he sobbed and sobbed.

'Is there anyone other than the landlord paying rent?' demanded Liam. 'Then get you to your own houses!' A rapid evacuation followed, leaving only the two men and a disgruntled landlord.

Father Kelly patted the weeping man's shoulder. 'Let it go, boyo, let it go.'

And Patrick let the hot tears run their course to wash away all the pain and misery of the past and herald a new beginning.

Part Two

CHAPTER FOURTEEN

THOMASIN FENTON YAWNED and gazed through the bakery window at the bustle of activity outside. Idly she scratched her head. The early morning sun revealed particles of dust as they floated airily about her, captured on a thermal. Her attention suddenly focused on a group of workmen who were busily attacking the facade of the shop opposite the bakery. One man in particular caught her eye. The great hammer that he wielded bit into the ancient brickwork, sending up a cloud of reddish dust. Despite his unkempt appearance he was by far the most handsome man she had ever seen. A rampant imagination entertained her for the next few minutes in which she watched the powerful shoulders and forearms. She could almost feel them around her. The thought made her shiver.

'More bread, Thomasin!' The shout from the bakehouse brought her reluctantly from the window, her thoughts clinging stubbornly to the man outside as she drifted in.

'What the hell's up with you this mornin'?' asked the baker. 'I had to shout three times.' His hands busily pressed the pastry around a mould, creating a shell. Thomasin watched as he filled the pie-case with minced pork then put on the lid – His fingers are like hairy sausages, she thought, watching them crimp the edges of the pie; couldn't fancy 'em touching me.

She always judged a man by his hands and had long since put the baker into the category of 'completely useless'. Oh, he was a nice enough chap to work with, it was just that Thomasin tended to put every man into one of three categories: there was the 'very useful but not fanciable' category, which meant that the man was wealthy but had to be kept at arms' length for as long as his patience would permit; then there was 'fanciable but useless' which indicated that the man might have breathtakingly good looks but was also penniless; 'completely useless' meant just that. Thomasin had yet to find a man who fell into the pigeonhole of 'fanciable and extremely useful'.

'There, that's that lot done.' The baker made a space on the tray, putting the pie and its companions into the oven. 'Well, get crackin', lass!'

The shop bell proclaimed another customer. Thomasin carried the tray of freshly-baked bread through to the shop, where the man who had made the bell jangle greeted her.

'Good morning, Thomasin, my dear.' He laid his hat and gloves on the counter to grin at her.

If Roland Cummings had sported a forked tail and horns he could not have appeared more demonic. His hooded black eyes were canopied by brows that sprang from the bridge of his nose and swept outwards like the wings of some bird of prey. The wide nose curved, beak-like, to meet thick lips which were, at this moment, attempting to give the impression of a smile. His thick, bull-like neck sprang from enormous shoulders, the latter threatening to break free of the fine frock-coat he wore at any moment.

'Oh, we are formal this mornin',' said Thomasin, conversant that the horrific exterior concealed a kind and generous nature; the power in those shoulders was put to no greater use than spreading his butter on his morning toast. If Roland had any faults they would not incline towards violence – as his appearance might imply – but weakness, both in character and in his associations with the gentler sex. The latter he adored.

Which was how it had all begun between Thomasin and himself. She had been sitting in the tea shop, cradling a cup of steaming tea in her frozen hands and had looked up to answer the question directed at her.

'Is anyone sitting here?'

Thomasin examined the chair with exaggerated scrutiny. 'Not unless they're suffering from chronic malnutrition.'

The man laughed – it emerged as a leer – and said, 'May I?'

She nodded and, after putting him into the category of 'completely useless' took no further notice.

Although all the other seats were occupied it was no act of Providence that had brought Roland to her table. He had been standing outside for an age, shivering, while the tea shop filled up, silently urging everyone who entered to take any seat but the one next to the pretty girl's, for that was where he wanted to be. Indeed, he had watched this attractive young woman for weeks, had followed her with his eyes as she made her journey to and from her work and in doing so passing the chambers where he pursued his career. Fascinated, he had watched her make her daily perambulation, stopping frequently to chatter and flirt with acquaintances – of whom there were many – and drawing admiring glances from both labourer and gentleman alike.

One could hardly describe her as beautiful – her nose was too large for beauty – but her smile was as brilliant as the auburn hair that snaked in coils around the well-shaped head and her eyes held an undoubtable sensuality. Excitement invariably caught at his belly as he watched the swaying hips that provided entertainment for her male audience. That midday as he had seen her leaving the cake shop he had rashly ignored the business luncheon with a client and at a discreet distance had followed her.

'Seen enough?' objected Thomasin, glaring at her ugly table-mate over her teacup.

'I do humbly beg your pardon,' replied Roland, though showing no discomfiture at having been caught blatantly ogling her body. 'You must forgive me. If I stare it is only because I have never in all my life seen such beauty as yours.'

Thomasin was unimpressed; she had met his sort before – poets and actors who mouthed love-struck rhetoric and had not two halfpennies to rub together.

Roland looked downcast. 'I can see that you do not believe me.'

She shrugged. 'Does it matter?'

'Oh, my dear of course it matters!' Roland leaned earnestly towards her, in so doing upsetting his own cup of tea over her dress.

She leapt up and twisted her mouth bad-temperedly as the hot tea soaked through to her skin.

'I'm so dreadfully sorry.' Roland pulled out his handkerchief as he stood. 'Here, let me help you.' He tried to mop at the tea stain on her dress but she brushed his hand away.

'Eh, mind what yer doin'!' she spluttered as the handker-chief stroked her thigh. Snatching it from him she dabbed at the mark. 'Look what yer've done. It'll not come out, yer know.'

'I really cannot apologise enough,' said Roland, waiting while she sat down again then joining her. 'You must allow me to replace the gown or make some other recompense.'

'Yer know what I think?' said Thomasin. 'I think yer did that on purpose.'

'Oh, no,' cried Roland. 'It was truly an unfortunate accident. Please, you must believe me.'

She pulled down the corner of one eye and stuck her face into his. 'See any green?'

Roland appeared mortified. 'But why should I do a thing like that?'

' 'Cause I wasn't takin' no notice of yer, that's why. I'm not as daft as I look.'

He grimaced and gave up the charade. 'Am I as transparent as all that?'

For the first time since he had sat beside her Thomasin smiled. 'Not really. It's just that I'm pretty good at seein' through people, even if I do say it missen.' She was studying him now with a speculative gleam in her grey eyes. At first glance his scruffiness had dismissed him from any designs she may have had, but now she saw that his clothes, despite their ill-fit, were quite well-tailored; it was only the body underneath that made them hang badly. He must be a tailor's nightmare, she thought. 'All right then, come clean.'

'I beg your pardon?'

'What is it yer after?' she prodded.

'I'm afraid I do not . . .'

'Oh, come on! Stop actin' soft beggars. Any road, yer never gerrowt if yer don't ask.'

He was somewhat taken aback by her broad accent, staring at her speechlessly until she grew tired of his reticence and suddenly rose from the table. 'Right, I might as well be off then.'

'No, wait!' He grabbed her arm and she sat down again.

'Well, out with it, I haven't got all day.'

'Very well.' He sat ramrod straight in his chair. If she

wanted bluntness she could have it. 'I want you for my mistress.'

The woman at the next table gave a snort into her cup. She brought out her handkerchief to mop up the spilt tea and nudged her companion, inclining her head at the couple who provided the sport.

Unmoved, Thomasin looked him up and down, then cupped her chin in her palms and tried to categorise him. How old was he, thirty-six, thirty-seven? He was certainly no oil-painting; she had never seen anybody quite so ugly. But, having reversed her former evaluation, she decided that he was obviously a man of high status, judging by the expensive clothes and confident manner – he was fully expecting her to say yes. She stared into the smouldering eyes; there would be no holding this one at arms' length, and strangely she found that a point towards acceptance. It had been a long time since there had been anything resembling excitement in her mundane life.

'All right.'

He could scarcely believe her rapid decision. 'You mean . . .?'

'Why not?' Why not indeed? It was not as if she was an innocent young maid. In the village where she had been born and had lived for twenty years before coming to live in York, there had been few more interesting pastimes than a tumble in a hayloft or cornfield, no feeling of shame over such a natural act as there might be in the city. One had to be extremely careful, though, when playing these dangerous games; but luck had always seemed to be with her on these occasions – well, part luck, part careful planning; she had never had the misfortune to be saddled with a misbegot. Now, at the age of twenty-five, she was the only one of five sisters to remain unmarried, and it sometimes felt as though the years were passing more quickly than ever. Why not grab a little excitement?

'I must inform yer though I've got expensive tastes.' She stood once more.

'Anything you want will be yours,' Roland promised rashly, rising too.

'Yer can meet me after work tonight if yer like. Seven o'clock at Dawson's Cakery. It's round by . . .'

'I know where it is,' he forestalled her.

She raised an eyebrow and continued on her way then, as if suddenly remembering something, returned to where he stood. 'I don't even know yer blasted name.' He told her. 'Mine's Thomasin Fenton,' she said in a businesslike manner, then swept from the tea shop looking to neither right nor left.

Roland picked up his gloves, gave an amused glance to the woman at the next table then followed her out, pausing outside to feast his eyes on her retreating figure. 'Thomasin.' He tested the name on his tongue, rolling it around and savouring the taste of it. 'Thomasin – yes, I like it.' And congratulating himself on his conquest, marched briskly back to his work with a spring in his step.

Later that day Roland made his excuses to a client, all but pushing the man from his office in his eagerness to be off. He snatched a quick glance at his pocket watch, a procedure that had been repeated throughout the afternoon. Grabbing his coat he left his clerk to lock up.

Outside, the frost had begun to twinkle under the gaslight and his breath rose in clouds on the cool evening air. He walked hurriedly away from the slummy end of Piccadilly – that so illustrious a man as he should be forced to have his chambers here!—but it was near the Castle where he performed his art. Soon he reached the little bakery. It was closed; the door was locked and the shutters were down. He leaned his head against the cold window in disappointment.

'Right one, you are, tellin' a girl yer'll walk her 'ome an' leavin' 'er to get frozen to death!'

He spun round quickly, the relief evident on his face. 'I'm so sorry, my dear, I was unavoidably delayed.'

'Yer'll 'ave to do better than that if we're gonna be friends. I can't abide folk who're late all time.'

He apologised again, then laughed. 'I seem to be spending the whole time apologising. Here, take my gloves.' He held them out then stepped into the road and hailed the cab that was unloading a few doors away.

Thomasin slipped on the gloves, admiring their suppleness, then looked up at the arriving hansom. 'God's truth, I can't go 'ome in one o' them.'

Roland would not accept her argument. 'You must. I

myself have no intention of walking. Get in.' He helped her up then climbed in himself and closed the half-doors in front of them. Having received instructions the driver whipped up his horse.

Thomasin studied the devilish profile. 'What'll yer wife say if yer late home?'

'Your perceptiveness amazes me.' Roland turned his face to hers, although he could barely make out her features in the darkness of the cab. 'How did you know I was married?'

'Same way as you could tell I was a good sport,' she grinned. 'Experience.'

Roland warmed to her pithiness. 'I can see we're going to make a good team. As to my wife, I doubt that she will even notice my absence. Besides, my home is in this direction also, so I shall not be late.'

'I'll bet yer live in next street an' I've never noticed yer before.' A jest.

'Well . . . perhaps not in the next street – but my house is not such a great distance from yours.'

'I daresay it's a damned sight grander though,' said Thomasin.

He searched for a trace of bitterness in her tone but found none. 'Perhaps just a little.' To her next question as to his employment he answered that he was a barrister.

She thought for a moment, then said, 'Mr Cummings – Roland – yer sure y'aren't mekkin' a mistake? I mean, won't yer be embarrassed bein' seen wi' me? I talk like this all time, yer know, an' I'll not change for no bugger. See! There y'are – common as muck. I ask yer, what lady would talk like that?'

'Believe me, Thomasin, I am sincerely glad you are not a lady – oh, dear me, I didn't mean . . . oh well, you did say it yourself. It makes a refreshing change to feel at ease with a woman. You see, my wife considers me to be less than a gentleman so perhaps we have more in common than you imagine. No, my dear, I do not consider myself to be making a mistake. I think you and I are admirably suited. I can make you very happy. The only sad fact is that I cannot offer to marry you. I could not leave my daughter to the mercy of that woman for anyone.'

'Who's askin'?' replied Thomasin. 'How old's yer daughter then?'

'Seven years old.'

'Is that all?'

'Do I judge by your tone that you think I am rather too old to be the father of such a young child?'

'Did I say so?' she held out her hands.

'Well, you may be correct,' continued Roland. 'I married rather late and would possibly not have done so at all had it not been for the child.'

'Ah,' said Thomasin.

'Quite,' he answered wearily. 'On the only occasion I have had too much to drink I happened upon the most ravishing creature – or so I believed – and lost my usual, er, control. Being hopelessly besotted by this heavenly girl I did not find it too distasteful at being blackmailed into marrying her by her father. It was only after several months of matrimony that I began to be disillusioned. After the birth of the child Helena showed her true colours by rejecting our newborn daughter and on regaining her strength took a never-ending stream of lovers.'

'But, isn't that what you're doin'?' she asked. 'Seems to me yer've got double standards.'

'Ah, no you mistake my point, Thomasin. It is not so much the fact that she takes lovers – I can quite understand that element of her behaviour, after all I was not a very good catch for her, was I? No, it is the heartless manner in which she treats the child which distresses me most. She has disowned her completely, abhors the sight of her.'

'Couldn't yer leave her an' tek the bairn wi' yer if it's that bad?'

'For someone who is seemingly a woman of the world you are very innocent, my dear,' he replied sadly. 'The fact is that my dastardly father-in-law has me in a tight corner. If I divorce her I risk losing everything. He has promised to ruin my career if there is any breath of scandal.'

'Clever bloke in your position should be able to deal wi' that.'

'I dare not risk it.'

'So, he doesn't mind yer both havin' a string o' lovers?'

'He would mind very much if he knew about it, but he doesn't; we are both very discreet, so discreet, in fact, that each of us pretends not to know about the other's misdemeanours.'

'Sounds a rum goin'-on to me,' declared Thomasin. 'Don't you two ever . . . yer know?'

'Oh, most certainly not.' Roland feigned horror. 'Helena would never dream of allowing my slippers to come within ten feet of her bedroom door – even without my feet inside them.' He mentally compared the two women. When it came to looks Helena could win hands down; with hair of spun gold and eyes of cornflower blue she was the epitome of every man's image of an angel. But there the similarity ended. Under the handsome, voluptuous casing lay a heart of neat vitriol.

The dialogue was growing too serious for Thomasin's liking. 'Enough of yer wife.' She slapped his knee. 'Let's talk about our little partnership.'

He snuggled up to her. 'Ah, most agreeable.'

'I 'ope yer still say that when I tell yer what I want,' she replied. 'First, I'd like a nice little house o' me own – none o' this slap n'tickle stuff then back to Mam's. Second, I expect to be wined an' dined in all the best places, an' third, I don't want no scenes when we come to the partin' o' the ways. I like the break to be nice an' clean.' Although his face was barely visible she could feel his smile. 'Think I'm kiddin' d'yer?'

'Oh, Thomasin it is simply your manner which makes me smile. You certainly do not mince words, do you? Still, I have to admire a woman who knows her own mind. Some of the silly little creatures I've . . . well, never mind, suffice to say that I respect your businesslike attitude. My only fear is that it will extend to the bedchamber.'

'Yer'll 'ave to wait an' see, won't yer?' she replied lightly.

He folded his arms, leaned back into the musty upholstery and grinned to himself. 'You are the most open person I have met. Here we are, discussing our intended affair as if it is a business venture.'

'Well, that's what it is, isn't it?' said Thomasin. 'A business deal. You gimme a good time an' I gi' you one.'

'Quite so, but you seem not to show the faintest sign of discountenance in speaking of it.'

'Why should I? I'm not one of yer hypocritical townies, one o' them women who puts drawers on their piano legs and don't wear any themsels.'

He burst out laughing. She was a real tonic.

'Things're different in t'country, Roly – more open. People in cities are so two-faced about it; pretendin' they're so virtuous when they're in company, when everybody knows they're as bad as everybody else really.'

He took hold of her hand and squeezed it, suddenly hoping that this would last a long time. They sat in silence as the carriage rolled on, the only sound being that of the horse's hooves. Roland peered over the doors, noting the poor district they had entered. 'We're almost there.'

'Aye, ye'd best tell 'im to stop 'ere. I'll walk rest o' way.'

Roland banged on the roof and the horse clip-clopped to a halt on the cobblestones. 'Before you go,' he said, 'would you agree to meet me tomorrow? I should like to show you around your new home.'

Thomasin made a noise. 'By, you were tekkin' things for granted, weren't yer? What would yer've done if I'd said no to your proposal?'

'I can assure you I would not take you for granted, Thomasin. I acquired the property some years ago.'

'Mm, that sounds ominous. What 'appened to all the other ladies who've been through yer hands? Did they get chucked out on their ear when yer got tired of 'em?'

'Actually, they're buried in the back garden but don't let that concern you.'

'I won't. As for tomorrow, your luck is in, it's me afternoon off. You can collect me at one o'clock at shop.' She picked up her skirts and stepped down from the cab then, as he pulled the doors shut, said, 'Will yer do me a favour?'

'Anything.'

She tiptoed up and kissed his cheek. 'For God's sake stop callin' me Thomasin, will yer? I allus thought it were too grand a name for the likes o' me, but there y'are, that's me mother all over; all us lasses've got daft names.'

'Then what do I call you?' asked Roland as she stepped back onto the pavement.

'Tommy!' she shouted and picking up her skirts once more ran full pelt down the streets and disappeared into the shadows.

*

All that had taken place six months before, since when Roland Cummings had provided Thomasin with the house on Hull Road, an extensive wardrobe, tons of trinkets and many nights of pleasure – the latter being reciprocal. Only one thing had changed. Roland, philanderer though he was, had fallen hopelessly in love with her. Alas, to Thomasin everything was as it had been – purely a business relationship. To her he was still good old Roly who gave her anything she asked. He doubted she even knew how he felt.

'You're dreaming, Tommy!' Roland waved a hand in front of her face, abruptly ending her recollections.

'Sorry, I was just thinkin' on how we met – it seems ages ago.' She put down the tray of bread and wiped her floury hands on a cloth, not caring to soil the pristine apron that she had donned that morning. 'What're you 'iding?' She eyed the large box that he was trying, unsuccessfully, to conceal.

'I thought we should do something special tonight,' he told her, handing over the package. 'There's a good play on at the Theatre Royal – would you care to go?'

'Oo, don't yer think that's temptin' Providence a bit? I mean, we were on the town every night last week and we're bound to get caught out one o' these days. We might just bump into somebody who knows yer wife an' they'd tell her.'

'Bugger being caught,' declared Roland. 'Anyway, I told you my wife and I have an agreement.'

Thomasin laughed in surprise at hearing him swear. 'No cussin' in front o' ladies, if yer don't mind.' She lifted the lid from the box and let out a cry of delight. 'Oh, Roly it's lovely! Oh, I can't wait to see it on.'

'Personally I can't wait to see it off.'

'Eh, control yerself, Lothario.' The green satin was cool to her touch as she held the dress against her. Though he had bought her many gifts this was quite the nicest. In a fit of girlish enthusiasm she began to waltz around the shop. The frilled sleeves floated about her as she spun, sending a pile of neatly-stacked cake boxes flying in all directions. Round and round she twirled, the dance becoming more frenzied by the second. Spinning, whirling, the unimaginable yardage of the dress billowing out, speckled with flour in the confined space of the shop. Her abandoned laughter obscured the sound of the shop bell.

Suddenly she stopped: a man stood in the doorway – a man she had seen before but not at such close quarters – and now as she looked, breathless and admiring, she saw that he was even more handsome than she had imagined. From his crisp black hair and bright blue, quizzical eyes, to his long, lean body and muscular thighs.

Roland turned, smiling, to discover what had caused the cessation of movement. The smile froze when he saw the way the man returned her discerning stare – and he knew that he had lost her.

The night that he had intended to be so enjoyable proved to be a disaster. Roland sat uncomfortably beside her in the dimly-lit theatre, growing more and more annoyed at the slurping of oranges, coughing and fidgeting from the audience who waited for the play to commence. Every time he instigated a conversation she would answer in the briefest possible manner as though it was an intrusion into her thoughts and making him feel like some insignificant adornment. At last he could bear it no more.

'It's that man, isn't it?'

'What yer talkin' about?' she said absently, nibbling the edges of her fan.

He gripped her arm, making her painfully aware of his presence. 'Ow! Roly, that 'urt.' She rubbed the spot in discomfort. 'What did yer do that for?'

'Because when I spend a lot of well-earned money on a woman I expect her to listen when I have something to say,' snarled Roland, black eyes blazing. 'I said it's that man that so preoccupies you, is it not?'

'Who? What're yer talkin' about? Let go.'

'That . . . that peasant in the shop this morning! The one who looked as though he'd like to rip off his clothes and take you there and then before my eyes.'

'Oh, don't talk rubbish,' said Thomasin. 'I don't even know 'im.'

'You'd like to though, wouldn't you? Deny it if you can.'

'I don't 'ave to deny anything, Roland. You don't own me yet!' She lowered her voice as people started to stare, spoke kindly. 'Look, would I choose somebody like that when I've got you? Yer think that after all t'good times we've 'ad together?' She tapped him lightly on the shoulder with her fan. 'I do believe yer jealous.'

'You're damned right, I am!'

'Well, there's no need. I've told yer, I don't even know the fella so stop worryin'. Now, be quiet like a good boy, the play's gonna start.'

'Ssh!' said the woman in front as the curtain rose.

'Shush yerself,' retorted Thomasin and gave a reassuring smile to Roland who found it not the least reassuring.

She could deny it all she liked, but he had seen her face as she looked at the man and he knew. He smouldered in his seat, eyes on the ornate ceiling, and gave a deep sigh of regret. It was as he was lowering his gaze back to the stage that it alighted on a familiar face in the box opposite his. Helena had seen them the moment they had entered the box and now gave a satirical inclination of her golden head. She turned to her chinless companion and mouthed something behind her ostrich feather fan, then let out a tinkling laugh, eyes still on her husband.

Roland fumed – I am glad at least someone is amused, he thought acidly.

But despite the laughter Helena Cummings was not amused; she was very, very angry. It was an odd quirk in Helena's make-up that, although she did not want him for herself, she would be damned if anyone else was going to make Roland happy.

There was, however, some small satisfaction to be gained from the fact that, at this moment, Roland looked anything but happy.

CHAPTER FIFTEEN

IT WAS ALL too ridiculous, Patrick told his reflection in the triangular piece of reflective glass. He raised a hand to feel his cleanshaven jaw. As if she would look at you, a lovely lady like herself. He grinned and turned away from the mirror. It was worth a try though. From the moment he had felt the lurch in his stomach – the one that had hit him like a pole-axe as he opened the bakery door and saw her smiling back at him – then he knew that the memory of his dead wife was finally laid to rest. His mornings began earlier. He made a special effort to look presentable, drawing raucous comments from his workmates.

Pulling the tunic-shaped shirt into position he fastened a belt around his waist. The close-fitting breeches of brown worsted clung to his legs like a second skin. Brown woollen stockings began at the calf where the breeches ended and a tasselled cap of green tweed completed his outfit, lending him a rakish appearance – too rakish, perhaps? He studied his reflection, then decided it was. He would take it back to the pawnshop on his way to work.

His inspection was interrupted by the arrival of his daughter. 'Daddy, Aunt Molly says ye'll be late for work if ye don't hurry.' She hung back in the doorway, wondering what her reception would be this morning.

Patrick felt a rush of guilt at the little face which glowed in admiration for his new stylishness. How could he have treated her like he had? Swiftly he bent down and scooped her up in his arms.

'D'ye think Daddy looks nice?' he asked softly, brushing her tousled hair from her eyes.

'Oh, ye look lovely, Daddy. Ye'll have to be careful ye don't get your nice clothes dirty at work.' She put a tiny hand on his cheek and rubbed it. 'Ye're not all scratchy today.'

His breath caught at the soft sweetness of her. 'Oh, Erin.' He hugged her tightly making her squeal in discomfort. 'I'm sorry if I hurt ye – not just now but all the times. I've not been meself since your mammy died. An' I couldn't bear to look at ye; not because I didn't love ye – I do – but 'twas 'cause ye reminded me so much of her. D'ye see?'

The child nodded solemnly. 'But ye're better now?'

He kissed her and swung her up in the air. 'I am. I'm much better now. An' I'm gonna make it up to ye, I promise.' He dropped her gently back to the ground.

Erin, delighted at the change in him, scampered off to tell Aunt Molly he was on his way. Her skinny legs carried her into the Flaherty house, where Molly grinned at her breathless arrival, guessing that Pat had made it up with his daughter at last. It had taken a long time, and who knew what scars it had left, but the child was happy again and that was enough for the present. With a bit of luck, now that he had more or less returned to his old self, Patrick might find himself another wife and the child could return to her own home. Not that Molly minded looking after her – Pat paid for her keep and what difference did one more make – but all said and done the child's place was with her own family.

Patrick's head appeared round the door. 'I've not time for a cup o' tea, Molly, I'd best be straight off to work.'

'Ah, sure you're that busy preenin' yourself these days ye don't leave any time for eatin'. Ye'll have to be more careful or ye'll be fainting on her.'

'Who?'

'Ah, stop codding! 'Tis a woman ye've got hidden away somewhere. Joseph!' she shouted to a half-naked youngster. 'Stop swingin' that knife about else somebody'll be walkin' about with no legs.'

'Woman?' said Patrick. 'Sure, what woman in her right mind would take me?'

'There's one here,' answered Molly saucily.

'Sure, I'm not man enough for you, Molly.' His eyes twinkled. 'Anyway, I haven't the time, I'll be late for work.'

'Ye're just trying to wriggle out of it,' shouted Molly as

he disappeared, then, 'Here, wait a moment!' She hurried after him with an oblong package, shoving it roughly into his bag. 'That's for to eat with your break.'

He smiled down at her, looking healthier than he had for a long time, she thought. His eyes were shining, black hair neatly brushed. 'I want to thank ye, Molly,' he blurted out suddenly.

' 'Tis only a bit o' bread an' butter for God's sake.'

'That's not what I'm talking about as well you're aware. I don't know where I'd've been without you an' Jimmy – all of yese. These past years have been hell. I sometimes thought I was going mad.'

'Didn't I get to thinking the same?' replied Molly, her arms crossed over her bulging abdomen.

'Will ye not take me seriously? I'm tryin' to thank ye.'

'Ah, away with ye, ye'll be late for work,' said Molly gruffly. 'I don't want your thanks. I'd do it for anybody, so I would.'

'I know that, Molly,' he persisted. 'I just want ye to know if there's anything I can do to repay ye . . .'

She shoved him towards the alley. 'Yes, there is. Ye can find yourself a good Catholic girl who'll be willing to take this child o' yours off me hands; 'tis beginning to look like a baby farm here.' She gave a wink at Erin who smiled. She was used to Molly's rough talk and knew it was not to be taken seriously.

Patrick waved cheerfully as he vanished into the alley, feeling rejuvenated and full of excitement. His late arrival at work was greeted by catcalls and whistles.

'S'truth, look at Beau Brummel 'ere,' shouted John. 'Thinks he's gonna impress that fancy piece at cake shop.' He took hold of Patrick's shirt with a dainty thumb and forefinger. 'Yer'll not get anywhere with her, Demick; she don't look at any fella unless he's wearin' gold-lined clouts.'

'Can't a fella look smart without y'all thinking he's after some woman?' Patrick took his pick from the lock-up.

'Yer must think we're dummies,' laughed John. 'Don't think I 'aven't noticed yer creepin' off to cake shop every five minutes. Yer've eaten enough o' them pies to feed a bloody army this past week. They're puttin' a right kite on yer.'

'You're only jealous 'cause she'd not have any truck with

a jackeen like you.' Patrick swung his pick viciously at the ground.

John leaned on a spade. 'So, it is her yer after then?' Patrick gave no answer. 'She'll not 'ave yer. I had a go at her meself t'other day; she told me where to go.'

'An' ye're surprised?' grunted Patrick, hacking away at the ground. 'Anyway, I'll thank ye to keep away from my woman.'

John hooted. 'Hah, listen to it! His woman, he says.' Still laughing he went off to his bricklaying.

The morning wore on amid a strenuous bashing and digging, swearing and laughing as the men persistently tormented Patrick. The sun peeped over the rows of grimy buildings, bringing a fresh layer of moisture to his brow and making him hot and bad-tempered. He threw down the pick and straightened his back, feeling the dampness of his new shirt. He was a fool to have kept it on; it would smell; that would impress no one. Time for a breather anyway. Without addressing his companions he wiped his hands on a rag and made his way over the road to the cake shop.

John shook his head as he watched the Irishman cross the road, dodging the horse-drawn traffic with a spring in his step.

'Don't be pinchin' t'cherries off her buns!'

His jocular shout reached Patrick who raised a middle finger in a gesture of insolence. The bricklayer gave a dirty laugh and went to speak with the others.

Once inside the cake shop. Patrick approached the counter, trying to look confident. 'Could I be after havin' one o them pies, please?'

Thomasin felt herself blushing – an unusual occurrence as she was normally in command of a situation. She felt his eyes boring into her as she selected the biggest pie and wrapped it. Every day for the past week they had enacted the same roles; he asked for the pie, she handed it over with a 'thank you very much, sir'. It seemed the question she wanted to hear would never come.

Patrick stared at her adoringly. She was so . . . so full of colour – vibrant, effervescent. He could almost feel the aliveness of her. Just as it had on previous encounters his courage failed him. How could he ever have thought to ask her? What had he to offer? Taking the pie he dropped his eyes from her face and, putting his money on the counter, was about to leave. This was costing a fortune.

'Look, this is gettin' a bit ridiculous, don't yer think?'

He turned at Thomasin's words. 'I'm sorry?'

'Well, are yer gonna ask me or aren't yer? Yer've been comin' in 'ere every day; we both know what for – an' it's not meat pies.'

'Now wait a minute.'

'Well, I 'ad to say summat, didn't I? If I'd left it to you we'd've got nowhere.'

'Who says I want to get anywhere?' asked Patrick coldly.

'The Irish aren't always so shy. I know yer fancy me.'

Patrick showed amazement. The forward madam! 'Listen, if I've anything to say to ye I'll say it – all right? But I haven't.'

Thomasin was undeterred. 'Oh, no? Yer just like to undress people wi' yer eyes, d'yer?'

Patrick's heart sank; she was not living up to her image. He became annoyed. 'Now listen, ye may be right when ye said I was interested in ye, but that was before I was better informed as to your character. The reason I haven't said anything was because I thought ye were a lady an' wouldn't be interested in the likes o' me. I can see now I was wrong – you're no lady.'

'Why, you ignorant bloody spud-basher!' She picked up the nearest thing to hand and hurled it at his retreating back. The trifle decorated his checked shirt with cream and jelly, much to the amusement of his friends who cheered and clapped the spectacle in noisy appreciation.

'Oh, the joys of love are sweet,' trilled John, mincing along with his hand on his hip as Patrick attempted to scrape off the offending mess.

The Irishman growled and stormed off to find a quiet corner.

John cupped his ear. 'What was that – rollocks? Yer can't use language like that in front o' these innocent young lads.' He turned to his mates. 'Right, hand it over.'

His companions made wry faces and dug into their pockets, handing over their threepences into John's grimy hand. 'Wharrabout you, Ghostie?' asked John. 'Away, cough up.'

'Could I give it ye on payday?' pleaded Ghostie, who today

was looking sicker than ever at having lost the wager. ' 'Tis a bit short I am.'

'Yer always short – especially in the arms.' John tutted. 'Oh, go on, I suppose it'll do on Sat'day.' He put the rest of the coins in his pocket. 'I told yer, didn't I? I said she'd 'ave nowt to do wi' him, but would yer listen?' He shook his head. 'I feel sorta guilty about tekkin' yer money.'

'Not guilty enough to give us it back, though,' replied one of them.

'Well, I reckon yer've learned a valuable lesson today, Ronnie. Yer know what they say about a fool an' his money.' He looked over to where Patrick bit savagely into his meat pie. 'An' yer can tek comfort in t'fact that yer not the only fools around 'ere. Look at yon. Fancy workin' yerself up into a state like that over a woman. He's biggest fool o' lotta yer.'

– Just who does she think she is? Patrick was thinking. The cheek of the woman. My God, ye nearly made a terrible mistake there, Pat me boy. Ye're well out of it. A hoyden, that's what she is. She'd've made your life a misery given half the chance – an' who wants her anyway? She's nuthin' special when ye get close. He bit into the pie and munched it as though it was her he was chewing up. Then he examined it half-heartedly and, with a curse, flung it as far as he could, watching it bounce off a rooftop and shatter in a cloud of crumbs. Oh, shit. Ye've really gone and messed things up, haven't ye? He sprang up and resumed his work, bringing down his pick in a strenuous arc and taking his anger out on the earth. For he knew that however she had behaved, whatever he had said about her, he could never give up.

The sun had gone down. Thomasin closed the shop door behind her and set off for home, a sense of emptiness inside her. What a fool she had been, ruining her chances with her bluntness. She should seriously consider having her tongue amputated. It was too late now; he knew what she was. His angry face came to mind – the tanned features creased into an unflattering frown, the blue eyes sparkling with vexation. Why, oh why when she felt as she had never done before about anyone, did she have to open her big gob? Before she had gone very far she felt a hand on her arm. 'What d'you want?' she muttered crossly, then cursed herself – Look, there you go again!

Patrick swallowed the angry retort that sprang to his lips and walked alongside her. 'I wanted to apologise. I had no call to say those things about ye. Ye were right, I did fancy ye – an' I would've asked ye if I could call on ye, like, given time.'

'How much time, though?' asked Thomasin, trying to keep pace with him, then grinned to show she didn't mean it as it sounded.

He smiled. 'I suppose I must seem a bit backward to you.'

'Makes a change. Wish the same could be said for that mate o' yours.'

'Ye mean John?'

'Long on cheek, brown hair, gappy teeth an' dirty laugh?'

'That sounds like John all right,' chuckled Patrick.

'By, he's a fly devil, that'n. D'yer know, yesterday he asked me for these cakes what I 'ad to go through t'back for. When I came back, he pays me and it's only when he goes out I notice there's half a dozen almond tarts missin'.'

'Sure, I thought 'twas unusually generous o' John to be treating us all!'

He threw back his head in laughter. She linked her arm familiarly with his and smiled up at him. 'Look at us, walkin' along an' laughin' as if we've known each other years.'

'You're very forward if I might voice an opinion without gettin' covered in jelly.'

Thomasin threw up her eyes. 'Eh, I can be a right scold. 'Ave yer gorrit off yer shirt yet? Let's 'ave a look.' She made him turn round. 'Tut, I've made a right mess of it. I'm ever so sorry. Tell yer what, you come 'ome wi' me an' I'll try to clean it for yer.'

'There's no need,' answered Patrick, then berated himself for his loose tongue. Wasn't that what he wanted, to go home with her?

Luckily for him she insisted. 'It was my fault I lost me temper. I'm allus doin' it.'

'Aye, made me look a right clown, didn't ye? Well, I dare say I deserved it.' He told her his name.

'Mine's Thomasin Fenton, how d'yer do?' She looked along the street, wondering whether Roland would put in an appearance tonight, then decided it was worth the risk. 'Away then, let's get 'ome an' get that shirt off.' Patrick was pleased to see she had the grace to blush. She wasn't such a hoyden then. He took her arm. The heat of her skin escaped the thin material of her sleeve – it burnt like the very Devil himself.

Roland Cummings, heading back from the castle, turned into Piccadilly with the intention of waylaying Thomasin before she left the shop. The sight of them brought him to a standstill and a wave of nausea rose to his throat. The couple sauntered arm in arm into St George's Terrace, the woman lifting her face adoringly to her companion who slid an arm possessively round her, pulling her to him. Both were blind to everyone and everything except each other – as is usually the way of people in love.

Chapter Sixteen

'Come in,' invited Thomasin as he stood outside rubbing his hands nervously.

He followed her inside, wiping his dusty boots on the mat and making a quick appraisal of the room. Doubt touched him fleetingly again – God, will ye look at this place, he told himself. Perhaps she was too good for him, was used to a better life than he could offer. But no, there was no mistaking the warmth in those eyes.

She offered him some tea which he gratefully accepted. In the kitchen she could barely keep the cups from rattling in their saucers and fought to calm her nerves. Huh, that was a good'n; Thomasin Fenton nervous of a fella! But even as she said it she knew that this one was different – special. Though God knew what it was she found so attractive; he obviously didn't have a penny to his name – I'll have to find a new category, she thought – though I don't know what I'll call it. He's one on his own is this'n. Those eyes.

Patrick thanked her for the tea, glad to note that most of it was in the saucer. Glad, because minutes earlier he had felt oafish and callow next to her and now he knew that she was as nervous as himself. It was crazy, the two of them behaving like children.

'Where d'yer come from, Patrick?' asked Thomasin politely whilst sipping her tea.

'Ireland.'

'Well, I know that, yer daft . . . sorry, I meant what part?'

He told her, adding, 'I mean to go back there some day.'

She saw the wistful expression in his eyes. 'What did yer come 'ere for in t'first place, if yer don't mind me askin'?'

'We were starvin',' he replied simply.

'We?'

'Me an' the wife, everybody, nearly everybody I knew. Don't ask me to describe it. I couldn't in a million years. 'Twas . . . devastating is the word that springs to mind, but even that isn't strong enough.' He sighed.

Her face had dropped when she heard the word 'wife'. 'Yer married then?'

Her forlorn mien prompted him to hasty explanation. 'Ah no, I've been a widower these last couple o' years.'

'Sorry. Did she . . . was it because of the famine?'

'No, she died in the cholera epidemic of forty-nine.' He saw that her face was without its usual smile. 'Cheer up, I didn't mean for to make ye miserable. 'Twas a long time ago, it doesn't hurt me to talk about her now.' It was with some surprise that he realised this was true.

She reached for the teapot. 'More tea, Patrick?' He thanked her and held out his cup. 'Tell me what life is like in Ireland.'

'Sure, 'twouldn't be as interesting as your own.'

'Let me be the judge o' that,' said Thomasin firmly. 'An' as for workin' in a bakery bein' interestin' that beats all, that does. Come on, tell us.'

Patrick did not know where to begin, but soon found himself telling her about the cottage where he had been born, the work he had done, the people amongst whom he had lived.

'An' what sorta things did yer do for pleasure?' she asked.

'Well, in the summer we'd be workin' the fields all day, there wasn't much time for pleasure as you'd know it. In the winter it was lazier, 'cause there were no praties to be tended. We'd pile the fire high with turf an' invite our neighbours in for a sing-song an' a tale, an' hope the poteen would see us through the end o' winter.'

'Yer'll find it a bit different round 'ere, then?'

'I do,' he sighed. 'Of all the things I miss 'tis the greenness most of all. The city is full of ugliness.'

'By, lad, yer must walk around wi' yer eyes shut! York's a grand ol' place.'

'Well, you're bound to say that, ye live here.'

'I weren't born 'ere though. I come from t'country, same as thee, but I can still find beauty in a city.'

Patrick laughed at her vehement defence of the place. 'Well, can ye show it to me for I've yet to come across it.'

'Right, I will,' vouched Thomasin. 'I'll tek yer on a tour o' York. When can yer come?'

Patrick said that Sunday was his only day of freedom, then had an idea. 'Thomasin, d'ye think 'twould be all right to bring me daughter along for part of the time? She doesn't get much enjoyment an' well – I've been awful hard on her since her mammy died. I'd like to make things up if I can.'

Though wanting him to herself Thomasin smiled warmly and said of course it would be all right. ' 'Ow old is she?' He told her five. 'I expect she misses her mam.'

A nod. 'One o' my friends looks after her for me, she's very good to her but 'tis not the same, is it?'

Thomasin played with the buttons on her dress. ' 'Ave yer never thought of marryin' again?'

'I have . . . but never seriously till now.' – God, what's wrong with you, Feeney, saying things like that? She's not the sort o' female a clean Irish boy weds.

– My God, thought Thomasin, what am I getting myself into? Look at him, poor as a church mouse. What sort of life could he offer? However attractive he might be, whatever her feelings for him she had not intended that it should come to this. Then just what did you expect? she asked herself. Lord, I don't know, but if I don't steer this conversation away from marriage, if he keeps looking at me with those eyes of his, it would be anyone's guess where it would all end. 'Er, more tea, Mr Feeney?' she stammered.

' 'Twas Patrick a moment ago. Have I said something wrong?' He declined the tea.

She put down the pot and answered lightly, 'No, 'course not – oh, I nearly forgot! I said I'd get that mark off yer shirt, didn't I? Best take it off an' I'll see what I can do.'

'I'm not sure that would be decent.' His eyes had darkened, his lips slightly apart. 'Besides, I've a feelin' on me that I won't be able to stop at the shirt.'

'Now who's bein' forward?' she joked, but her voice quavered.

They stared at each other for what seemed like an eternity, then Patrick began to unbutton the shirt and pulled it over his head. She found that she could not take her eyes off him.

Her breath came in rapid, heart-fluttering sighs. Never had she wanted anyone as she wanted him, wanted him so much that it was agony just standing there looking. It was this look that encouraged him to make his move. As she reached out for the shirt his hand shot out and manacled her wrist, pulling her close. The heat from his body wrapped itself around her, drawing her into him.

'Ye don't seem to have much to say for yourself now,' he said thickly. 'Are ye sorry y'asked me to take it off?'

She shook her head slowly as his mouth came down on hers. The actual effect far surpassed those vivid imaginings that had preceded it. She now knew what it felt like to drown. Each muscle and nerve of her body seemed to liquefy, to melt into a sensuous whirlpool of pleasure. Her tongue darted tentatively between his lips, shocking him. Never had he done such things – but he did them now – You're mad, you're bloody mad, she scolded herself but continued all the same.

Patrick was dying. The line between pain and pleasure became so fine that he no longer knew which side of it he trod. He could only pull her closer, moulding his body to hers, touching her, screaming out for her. They fell to the carpet, assisting each other in the shedding of clothes, their lips never parting as though bonded together. Thomasin pressed her palms against his chest, pushing him downwards, her breasts tumbling like lush fruits. She bent over Patrick's beautiful strong face, gracing it with light, loving kisses. His eyelashes brushed her lips as she touched them. Nose, lips, cheeks, throat – none escaped; she wanted to taste every part of him. A pause in her movements as she gazed down into his face brought his eyes open and the love there mirrored her own. So this was what it was like, love. God, what she had been missing. What did all the other things matter? All the jewellery, the clothes, the money, all were irrelevant now. This was the only thing that mattered; this moment. Such were the things one dreamed on when one grew old.

Patrick felt about to explode. He started gently to push her over, to assert his dominance.

'Please, not yet,' she begged. 'I want this to last.' She resisted the pressure and continued to lay her lips upon his body, shivering as she anticipated the feel of him inside her. His breath came in urgent gasps, belly contracting as her tongue slithered over him. He groaned her name. Ecstatically she brushed her lips against the silken hardness of him, making his tumescence too agonizing to bear. With a convulsive shudder he ejaculated high over his taut stomach, forcing a groan of pleasure and apology from his lips.

'Ah, Christ I'm so sorry.' He swallowed and pulled her up beside him, holding her small face in one great hand. 'It's been so long, an' I wanted ye too much. 'Twas like bein' a wee boy let loose in a sweety shop. God, woman ye're enough to drive a fella crazy doin' things like that.' It was never that way with Mary. Mary had never done things to him – he had never even known that women enjoyed it till now.

'Ssh.' Thomasin placed a finger to his lips. 'It doesn't matter, honest. It was my fault, any road. I just couldn't stop. I wanted it to go on an' on.'

He kissed her. 'It doesn't have to stop, does it? After all we've the rest of our lives for making it last.' He noticed the flicker in her grey eyes and propped himself on one elbow, looking down on her. 'I can't help noticing that every time I'm steeling meself to broach the subject o' matrimony ye go all defensive. Is it that you're married already?'

She pointed to her finger and asked softly, 'See any ring?'

'But you're living with a man at least.'

She started. 'What makes yer say that?'

'Sure, I'm not blind,' he answered with a kiss. 'There's plenty o' signs about the house. That robe over there, 'twould swamp you – an' I doubt if ye've taken to wearing trousers, although I'd not put anything past ye.' God, he still trembled with disbelief.

She followed his eyes and saw Roland's checked trousers hanging neatly over the back of a chair. It had never occurred to her just how much of him was here: a lone cigar on the mantelshelf, the gold cravat pin so carelessly mislaid under one of the armchairs.

'D'ye do things like this with him?'

'What if I do? What if I am livin' wi' someone? It's not really any o' your business, is it?'

'Ye can lie there an' say that?' he expostulated fiercely, winding his fingers into her hair. 'After what ye've just done with me? And yes, I reckon it is my business – leastwise I'm making it so.'

She felt his hardness pressing into her but resisted the urge to yield to it. 'Why? Why, is it?'

' 'Cause ye know the way I feel about ye, brazen though y'are, an' if I'm not mistaken ye feel the same about me. Is it the fella I saw ye with in the shop?'

She closed her eyes in affirmation and pulled his head to her breast but he struggled free pettishly. 'Y'ought to have told me before.'

'Yer never asked. Anyway, I'm not actually livin' with him, he just set me up in this 'ouse so he can come an' see me from time to time.'

Patrick felt the jealousy gnaw at brain and body, at the same time asking what sort of woman had he got himself mixed up with. 'Will he be likely to come tonight?'

She felt herself go hot at the thought of Roland coming in and catching them like this. After a look at the clock she sighed in relief. 'I don't think he'll come now, it's too late. To tell yer the truth I never even gave 'im a thought – isn't that awful?'

Patrick found it hard to summon any sympathy for his rival. He tightened his hold on her hair. 'Ye must tell him 'tis over when next ye see him.'

'But that means I'll 'ave to give up this 'ouse. We'll 'ave nowhere to be together.'

'We'll manage somehow. I don't relish the thought o' makin' love to you under another man's roof.'

'Have I any choice?'

'No. And there's something else: when ye see him ye'll not make love to him.' It was an order rather than a request. 'You're mine now, Thomasin; mine an' nobody else will have ye. If he does, I'll kill him.' He thrust himself inside her, using his body almost as a weapon, plunging for her very core, clamping his lips over hers and drowning her mews of passion, finally erupting in one last desperate thrust and filling her body with his burning seed.

The moon crept stealthily through the bedroom window to where they had retired, clothing their satiated bodies in its ethereal glow. Thomasin lay in the crook of his arm, tracing a delicate finger over his torso and making him shiver. He tugged the bedclothes over them, slinging a leg over her as he did so and taking her earlobe gently between his teeth.

'Ah, I shouldn't get too comfortable.' He peered at the clock on the bedside table. ' 'Tis sinful late.'

Prising herself loose she reached over, opened the window that encased the dial and, instead of, as he thought, merely putting the hands back, twisted them almost into knots. 'That's what I do to spoilsports.'

He laughed and rolled with her. 'D'ye know you're a bloody crazy woman?'

'Stay with me,' she answered.

He sighed into her ear, sending mind and body into turmoil. 'Ah, I wish I could, but Erin'll be worried enough as it is.'

She took his hand away from her breast and laid it firmly over her waist. 'Then don't set me off again else yer'll be lucky if I let yer out of 'ere next week, never mind tonight.'

He grinned into her neck. 'I've never met the like of ye. Insatiable ye are.'

'It's you I can't get enough of.' Her smiling face turned to his. 'Funny, it's as if I've known yer all me life. I can't believe we only spoke to each other properly for the first time today.'

'Don't I know what ye mean? There was I yesterday, minding me own business, when this woman grabs hold o' me, covers me in trifle an' ravishes me chaste little body till it feels like it's been through a mincing machine – an' all I ever did to her was ask for one of her meat pies. Ah well, I suppose I'd better go while I'm still able to walk.' He planted a smacking kiss on her cheek and rolled out of bed.

She lay back against the headboard and watched him dress, letting his glorious body imprint itself on her mind before he covered it. He took a brush from the dressing table and brought his springy hair under control, then stopped to gaze at her in the mirror. 'You're beautiful.' His eyes were alight with love.

'So are you.'

'Men aren't beautiful – dashing, yes.' He grinned and warning her to wash the brickdust from the brush before using it on her own hair, returned to sit on the bed. He placed his hands on either side of her and bringing his eyes level with hers said: 'Now, don't shy away this time.' She made no answer, but neither did she lower her eyes as she had done when he had approached the question before. 'I've no right to ask ye, I've not a penny to me name – just the few shillings I've managed to save – an' if ye say no then I'll go an' never trouble ye again – no, I'm lying; 'tis a desperate nuisance I'll make o' meself if ye don't say yes. Will ye marry me, Thomasin?'

In her mind she watched all the clothes, the money, the nights at the theatre fly out of the open window, and did not even put out a hand to stop them. Then, with a small cry, she flung herself into his arms, almost strangling him in her eagerness to reply. 'Yes, oh yes.'

'Ye will?' Patrick beamed delightedly. 'My . . . Holy Mother, I can't believe it. She'll have me! Ah, Thomasin,' a great hug, 'I'll try to make ye so happy. I'll work like a legion to buy ye a nice house like this. It'll be a long time coming but I won't stop workin' till I buy ye everything your heart desires.'

'Oh, Pat, those things don't matter. They did once, but not any more. There's only two things I want out of life now – you an' yer children.'

The fresh breeze caught at her hair and tossed it in gleaming strands to cover her smiling face. Thomasin withdrew her head from the open window, caught her wayward locks and secured them with a pin. Everything was lovely on this spring morning. Daffodils nodded a welcome as she looked out into the small garden below, blackbirds scuttled and pecked amongst the hyacinths, new life burgeoned within the naked trees.

Pinning a silver brooch to the blue woollen dress she wore she felt the pangs of guilt return. Her fingers touched Roland's gift. He had given her the brooch after their first night together; now it would have to be returned. She lingered undecidedly for a moment, then unpinned the brooch and returned it to the trinket box. She fumbled with the ribbons on her bonnet, her anxious fingers refusing to obey the command from her brain. He must be faced so, taking a fortifying breath, she stepped out to meet his disapproval.

The first person she encountered on emerging from St George's Terrace was Roland. In fact he appeared to have been waiting for her. They stood facing one another, uncertain of what to say. He knows! thought Thomasin aghast. She touched her face unconsciously in an effort to discover the signs of guilt that had told him.

'Good morning, Thomasin.' He doffed his top hat and took her arm. 'May I walk you to your place of work?'

She laid her fingers on his forearm and walked beside him. 'Yer never came last night.'

'Ah, no,' he replied carefully. 'I thought perhaps my presence would be unwelcome.'

She bit her lip. 'Yer know, don't yer?'

A nod. 'I saw you together last evening.' His voice was dull. 'I knew this would happen.'

'Yer knew more than I did then.'

'Don't be flippant, my dear, this is not the time.'

'No, yer right – oh, I'm sorry if I've hurt yer, Roly.'

He remained silent for a brief span, then said, 'Of course, if you were to tell me that it was only an unfortunate lapse, I would . . .'

She stopped him. 'I'm sorry, Roland, if I told yer that I'd be lyin'.'

He nodded resignedly. 'I guessed as much. Anyone could see that the man is infatuated with you.'

'An' me with him,' said Thomasin. 'He's asked me to marry him.'

'Oh, Tommy, Tommy,' he cried exasperatedly. 'Do not do it, I beg you. What has he to offer? A one-roomed hovel, a child every year, so that by the time you are thirty you will look fifty? I can give you so much more. Please, let us go on as we were, you cannot deny that we enjoy each other's company.'

'No, I'll not deny it,' she answered. 'But just what can yer give me, Roly? Oh aye, I know what a fine collection o' dresses an' things yer've bought me, an' I can't pretend yer didn't gimme any pleasure either, yer as fine a lover as I've ever had.' This was the highest compliment that she could think of. 'But, Roland love, that's not enough. I've found that out now. I love this man. I know that sounds daft comin' from a graspin' bugger like me, but I don't care that he hasn't a sou to his name, it's him I want, not his money. No, Roly, yer could never 'ope to gimme what he does.' She held out her hand. 'Goodbye, Roly. I'm sorry if I've let yer down, but I did make it clear at the beginnin', didn't I?'

Roland stared at the proffered hand, then slowly clasped it between his. 'Yes, a good clean break, that was what you said. There will be no tantrums from me, Tommy. But I suppose you do realise that I love you too?'

With a jolt she realised that he actually meant it. How blind she had been not to notice until now. But she tried, in a clumsy fashion, to lighten his loss. 'No, you only think you do, Roly. You watch, soon as I'm round the corner yer'll be feelin' randy as ever an' lookin' out for a new playmate.'

'Perhaps,' he answered dubiously. 'Nevertheless I shall miss you, and for all your fine sentiments I still say you are making a terrible error.'

'Oh, Roly, don't let's part on this note. Say yer'll forgive me an' that we can still be friends.'

He patted her hand kindly then released it. 'There is nothing to forgive, my dear. I realise that you must care deeply for this man, otherwise you would not be taking such a drastic step. I wish you every joy in your new life, Thomasin. Goodbye.' He seemed about to kiss her, then thought better of it and strode away with his cane tucked firmly under his arm, as if for support.

Thomasin gave a sad little smile, then turned her back on him and his way of life forever.

Chapter Seventeen

Patrick found the sight of John's slack-jawed disbelief highly amusing. 'I can see it's come as a great shock to ye, John,' he laughed. 'Would ye care to sit down for a few minutes over it?'

'Yer sure this isn't one o' your jokes?' asked his friend, declining Patrick's invitation. 'Yer really gerrin' married?'

Patrick grinned widely. 'I am.'

'Well, I'll go to 'ell,' breathed John, then laughed. 'By, yer crafty devil, 'ow long's this been goin' on an' who's t'lucky woman?'

'Sure, I thought ye'd know, since ye reckoned to know so much about her.'

'Yer don't mean . . .?' John pointed to the cake shop and Patrick nodded delightedly. 'Yer can't do! It was only yesterday she covered you in trifle. Yer were callin' her from a pig to a dog.'

'Ah, well I realised, ye see, 'twas all my fault, not being very educated in the idiosyncrasies of the female. So, I went to apologise an' it sort o' grew from there.'

John laughed. 'By, yer dirty little tomcat, grew from there. Yer a fast worker – an' she must be summat good if yer want to tie yerself down again.'

'She is something very good, John,' replied Patrick as he packed his haversack, ready for home. 'Very good indeed. She's the best thing that's happened to me in a long, long time.'

'Very accommodatin' too, judgin' by the way yer goin' on about her,' ventured his friend slyly.

'Hey, watch your tongue,' ordered Patrick sharply. 'I'll not have that sorta talk about me future wife.'

'I meant wi' the free cakes,' said John innocently, then clapped him on the back. 'May I offer me humblest congratulations – eh, an' I 'ope I'm invited to the weddin'?'

'If ye behave yerself,' replied the other, slinging his haversack over his shoulder. 'But don't mention it to anyone else; I've not told Erin yet. Hey, she's gonna be really excited when I tell her she's to have a new mammy. Right, John, I'm off. Goodnight, lads!' He strode off towards home imagining the pleasure on his daughter's face when he told her.

He was therefore taken completely by surprise at the reception that greeted his news. The five year old wore an expression of accusation. How could he have forgotten so soon? She hadn't. It seemed like only yesterday that her mother's lovely face had lain against hers, telling her stories and drying her tears. 'Don't want a new mammy!' her bottom lip came out in defiance. 'I've got you an' Aunt Molly, I don't need no one else.'

'Well, there's a fine howdyedo,' cried her father. 'An' here's me thinkin' ye'd be pleased.' He bent his knees and peered into her obstinate face. 'Don't ye want to come back home to live with me?'

' 'Course I do!' She flung her arms round his neck. 'But ye don't have to bring her to live with us, d'ye?'

'Sure, I can't be expected to look after ye all on me own, can I?' He ruffled her hair and walked to the window, peering out. 'I'm out at work all day, who'd take care o' your needs?'

'Aunt Molly can bring my meals in,' suggested Erin.

'Aye, she'd like that, I'm sure, running two households. D'ye not think she's enough to cope with?'

'I could cook me own meals then,' argued his daughter.

'Ah, you're too young, darlin'. Anyway, I'm afraid 'tis all settled now.' Patrick's eyes lit up as he thought of Thomasin. 'Ye'll like her when ye meet her, ye know. She's real nice an' she's dyin' to meet you. As a matter o' fact . . .' He looked over his shoulder to discover that he had been speaking to himself for the last thirty seconds. 'Why, the little she-cat. Erin! Erin, come back here.' He marched out into the yard in time to see her disappear into Molly's and, setting his mouth in a firm line, stormed after her.

'What's got into ye, child?' Molly had just finished saying. 'Ye look as though the divil himself were after ye.'

'An' well he might be,' donated Patrick coming into the room and shaking Erin's shoulders. 'Don't ye know 'tis rude to walk when someone's speakin' to ye?'

Erin broke into racking sobs and clung to Molly's grubby skirt.

'God in Heaven, Patrick, what've ye been sayin' to the child?' Molly dabbed the girl's face with a rag.

'Sure, all I said was she'll soon be havin' a new mammy.'

'Oh, Pat!' Molly's dirt-seamed face cracked in pleasure. 'I never thought I'd see the day. Well, isn't that a thing to treat the ears? When's the weddin' goin' to be? What's her name? Is she from these parts? Aw but, Pat,' she reproved him and cuddled the child closer, 'ye coulda put it a bit gentler to the lass. She misses her mammy somethin' terrible, ye know.' She stroked Erin's hair. 'Well, are ye goin' to keep it a secret or do we get to know her name?'

'Ye will if ye'll let me get a word in edgeways,' smiled Patrick, glad that someone was interested. 'Her name is Thomasin Fenton an' she's a real bonny lady, Molly. Ye'll like her.'

'Is she a good Catholic?' enquired Molly, wiping the bubbles from Erin's nose and sitting the child on her lap.

Patrick frowned. 'I never thought to ask – but sure, what does that matter to me? I've nothing to do with the church now.'

'Ye go, don't ye? Haven't I seen ye there meself?'

'Only to take Erin,' he explained. 'I feel I owe it to Mary to keep the child's faith going.'

'Ah, well ye see,' Molly pointed out, 'that's why I asked if your Intended was a good Catholic. She might not be as true to Mary's memory.'

'No,' he said defiantly. 'Tommy's not like that.'

Molly cocked her head and thought. 'Fenton, ye say? Fenton, Fenton – I don't seem to know that name. What part o' the old country is she from?'

'Ah no, Molly ye have it wrong, 'tis not Ireland she comes from; she's English.'

There was a shocked hiatus, then Molly threw up her bony arms in dismay. 'Oh, Mother o' Christ, a foreigner! How could ye ever bring yourself to do it, Pat? Oh, if poor dear Mary could see ye now she'd turn in her grave. Why, no wonder the child is upset if you're bringin' a foreigner into our midst.'

'Ye daft clot,' ridiculed Patrick. 'How can she be a foreigner? 'Tis England we're in – we're the foreigners.' He cringed as he said it. After all he had spouted about the damned English here he was marrying one of them. But then he didn't think of Thomasin as English, she was . . . well . . . she was just Thomasin.

Molly flapped her arms in slight agreement. 'Ah well, I take your meanin', Pat, but 'tis the mixin' of the blood I'm against, see. I can't bear the thought o' your pure Irish blood being tainted, like.'

'Rubbish!' shouted Patrick, his patience beginning to fray. 'There's nothing wrong with Thomasin's blood, 'tis as pure as your own.'

'I dare say it is,' replied Molly, then added wisely, 'but 'tis English blood.'

'Well, English or no, ye're goin' to have to get used to it, the pair o' yese, 'cause I'm off to marry her an' there's an end to it.' He glared at Erin who sucked her thumb and curled a lock of her hair around her finger, keeping close to her ally.

'Ye'll be bringin' her here, then?' Molly's lips pursed into an unforgiving button.

'Hah!' Patrick took a swipe at the wall, sending a shower of flaking distemper to the floor. 'I will not. It'll be something better than this for Thomasin.'

' 'Twas good enough for Mary,' objected Molly. 'An' I'll thank ye to stop knockin' me house to bits.'

'An' I'll thank you not to keep bringing Mary into this,' he countered angrily. 'Mary's dead.' He brushed the flakes from his knuckles.

'Have ye no thought for the child, ye great galoot?' cried Molly, pointing at Erin's shaking shoulders. 'D'ye have to be so brutal?'

'Oh, God I'm sorry.' He bent to pick Erin up but she shied away. 'Look, Molly, all I meant was that Thomasin isn't Mary. If ye could see the house she's livin' in at the moment ye'd not ask why I'm reluctant to bring her here.'

'Too good for the likes of us, is she?' sneered Molly.

'She's not like that at all,' he insisted. 'I'll tell ye the same as I told milady there,' he bobbed his head at Erin, 'ye're sure to like her when ye meet her.'

'Oh, we are goin' to meet her, then?' it was delivered sarcastically. 'I was beginning to think ye were ashamed of us.'

'Don't talk crazy. As a matter o' fact she's promised to come walking with me an' Erin on Sunday – tomorrow. I'll bring her to meet ye.'

Molly sniffed. 'Suit yourself.'

'I'm not going,' declared Erin.

'You'll do as you're damn-well told.' Patrick pointed a finger at his daughter. Damn them, damn them all. Why did they have to spoil his happiness? His mind wandered to Thomasin; what would she be doing now? One thing was certain, she would not be enduring the same hostility as himself.

A sharp knock at the door caused Hannah Fenton to ask of her husband, 'Who can that be at this hour?'

William slapped his newspaper onto his knee. 'In case thee hadn't noticed, me eyes are stuck on 'ere,' he indicated his face, 'not on t'other side o' bloody door.'

'William, language please.' It was Hannah's constant bewailment that he could neither praise nor damn without an expletive.

'Well, tha's not likely to find out lest y'answer t'blasted thing.' William reached for his pipe to produce clouds of tobacco smoke, at which his wife swiped with a dishclout before answering the door.

When the visitor was not spontaneously admitted William craned his neck. 'Well, who is it, woman?'

Hannah glanced at him vaguely. 'It's your daughter.' Thomasin had always been 'your daughter' having inherited William's lax morals and earthy language.

'Well, esta started chargin' admission fees? Away in, lass!' he bawled to Thomasin and, when she warily edged her way past her mother, 'Fancy knockin' on thy own door, soft bugger.'

She took off her shawl as her straight-faced mother closed the door. 'I wasn't sure I'd be welcome.' There had been uproar from her mother when she had announced she was going to live with Roland.

'What, just 'cause tha's been livin' over t'brush? Soft 'aporth, this is still thy 'ome. Hannah, get kettle on. Away an' sit down, Tommy.'

Hannah, a prim woman in lace cap and sombre clothing, made no move to comply. 'I see you've brought your bags with you. He's tired of you, then?'

Thomasin made no answer as she took a seat by the fire. It was a cosy room for all her mother's aloofness.

'Questions later, Mother,' said William firmly. 'An' didst not 'ear? I said we'd have kettle on. Now then, lass,' he pulled his chair closer to hers, 'Howsta been?'

Though being some man's mistress was hardly what William would have chosen for his favourite daughter he had never condemned, further than to tell her she was a soft bugger for doing it. If she was frightened of being left on the shelf she was going the wrong way about remedying it – no one was partial to another man's leavings. Essentially a man of the Dales, bluntness came naturally to him – uncouthness, that's what his wife termed it. Not that she didn't have affection for him nor he for her, but they were just totally different. It was for Hannah he had consented to move to the city and earn his living at the cocoa factory instead of at the loom. Hannah with mannerisms and ambitions far above her class had decreed that she wanted something better for her daughters than farmhands and labourers – and so she had, for all except this one; the other four had made excellent marriages.

'Oh, not so bad,' answered Thomasin noncommittally, feet rubbing the hearth.

'That usually means not so good. Yon's chucked y'out, am I reet?'

'As a matter of fact, clever-clogs it's t'other way round.'

'Fancy.' William raised his brow as his wife carried in a tray of cups.

'Aye, fancy,' grinned his daughter then, with a sly peep at her mother, said, 'I'm gettin' wed.'

'Wed?' William clapped a hand to his balding head. 'Eh, I'll go to . . . well.'

'Aren't yer gonna offer congratulations, then?' Thomasin

watched her mother's face.

It was her father who spoke. 'Eh, lass 'course I am.' The hand slid down his face to his whiskered chin. 'I'm just that tekken aback, like. By, tha could knock me over wi' a corpse's breath. Hannah, didst hear what lass said?'

Thomasin's mother showed reserve. 'When is the wedding going to be? If I am permitted to ask of course, only being your mother.'

'As soon as possible.' Thomasin experienced his arms around her.

'You're not?' breathed Hannah.

'Don't be daft, Mother,' replied Thomasin calmly. 'There's no bairn on t'way. We just want to be together, that's all.'

'Well, that's a relief,' muttered Hannah as William contributed to the exchange again.

'Eh, lass!' It was not merely emotion that boosted his tone, William's voice was always extremely loud. 'I'm reet glad tha's found somebody. By, it's quick though, in't it? Where'd tha meet him? What's lad's name?'

'Patrick, Patrick Feeney.' She was so pleased he had taken to her announcement.

The teapot lid crashed to the floor. 'An Irishman?' Her mother was horrified. 'Oh no, don't do this to us, Thomasin. This is terrible.' She ignored the broken china at her feet, growing paler by the second.

'D'yer know, yer can be such an obstroculous bugger sometimes, Mother,' sighed Thomasin. 'There you were, dead set against me livin' in sin, as yer so delicately phrased it, I thought yer'd be pleased now I'm gettin' the proper documents.'

'Pleased?' Hannah was amazed. 'Am I supposed to be pleased when my daughter is marrying a ditchdigger? At least this Roland fellow was well-to-do.'

'Don't be such a bloody snob,' William chastised, at the same time thinking – bloody hell, a Paddy for a son-in-law, I hadn't bargained for that!

'It's too bad of you springing it on us like this, Thomasin,' sobbed Hannah. 'It is customary for a gentleman to pay court to a girl and then ask her father if he will consent to the marriage.'

Her husband and daughter's response to this was to break into hoots of laughter. 'It's a bit academic now,' snorted William. ' 'Ave I got right word there? I mean, she's hardly a virginal young maid. She's been livin' over t'brush for t'past six months. It's a bit late for 'er to start behavin' like a lady.'

'How can you sit there and laugh about it beats me,' said Hannah between sobs. 'Any father worth his salt would have put his foot down years ago, but not you, you're as bad as she is, not one moral between the pair of you.'

Thomasin and William exchanged pitying looks, then the former said, 'Er, I'm not sure I liked your insinuation, Father, too late to be a lady indeed.'

William grinned and slapped her knee. 'Nay, I meant nowt. Now then, away, less o' this palaver, when are we gonna meet this fella?'

'Well,' replied his daughter. 'I've asked 'im to come for tea actually.'

Her mother paused in her lamentations to prick her ears. 'When?'

'Tomorrow.'

'Oh, Thomasin!' Hannah sprang into action, pushing William out of his chair to plump up the cushion and flick her apron over the pot dogs. 'What on earth will I give him to eat?'

'Well, yer could try pickled armpits or . . .'

'Don't be so revolting!' admonished her mother.

'Well, what d'yer think he eats? They're not cannibals across the Irish Sea, yer know. He'll have same as us an' like it. Any road, yer don't 'ave to make a start on it right now, d'yer?'

'I have to get the place looking respectable,' puffed Hannah, darting from pot dog to aspidistra. 'I can't have the man thinking we're all as common as you. Look at the condition of this place! It's like a rubbish dump.'

'Tell him he can come if he brings his own shovel.' William gave his daughter a knowing smile. It was typical of Hannah that one minute she classed the Irish as vermin and the next one would think it was the Prince himself who was coming to tea. 'An' are we gettin' this tea or not? That kettle's boilin' its arse off.'

Thomasin held her hands to the fire's warmth, the glowing

coals emphasising the happiness on her face as she thought of her lover. 'He'll be bringin' his daughter round an' all,' she informed them, matter-of-factly.

Another piece of china hit the floor. 'Daughter!' shrieked Hannah and put a hand to her brow. 'Oh, I've come over all faint. Help me to a chair, somebody.'

'Go get that whatsit out o' cupboard, Tommy,' urged William, wafting his wife's face with a newspaper.

Thomasin reached into the cupboard for the smelling salts and shoved them under her mother's nose while William still flapped his newspaper.

'Oh dear, I don't know what the world is coming to,' whined Hannah, then smacked viciously at William's efforts. 'Get out!'

'No need to take it out on me,' he said airily and resumed his seat.

'He's a widower, Mother, that's all,' explained Thomasin. 'People's wives an' husbands do die, yer know.'

'Wi' a bit of luck,' murmured William.

Hannah groaned. 'Think what you'll be saddling yourself with, girl. You've seen the way these people live, there are plenty of them around here to illustrate. They're so . . . unhygienic – and if his child is anything like the ones I've seen . . . well . . .' She shuddered at what the neighbours would say when they saw the Irishman and his daughter entering her spic and span home. 'Could you not bring them for supper instead?'

'Don't think I don't know what's goin' through your mind,' Thomasin told her sternly. 'Yer think I should bring 'em when it's dark so no one'll see 'em.'

'Nothing of the sort.' But Hannah blushed. Her daughter's shrewdness could be disconcerting sometimes. 'I just thought it might be more convenient that's all.'

Thomasin, though annoyed at her mother's attitude, decided to employ a rare diplomacy. 'All right, I'll bring 'em for supper then – but I 'ope you aren't gonna behave like this when they're 'ere?'

Hannah straightened her spine. 'Unlike some people I do know the meaning of good manners,' she said coolly. 'I hope I can expect the same of your Intended. For instance, where is he going to take you to live after you are wed?'

Her mother's question took Thomasin by surprise. Everything had happened so swiftly. 'I suppose he'll be takin' me to where he lives now; I hadn't really given it much thought.'

'Typical,' snorted Hannah. 'You rush into these things headfirst without a thought of what you may be getting yourself into. Ah well, I suppose it is too late now to change your mind?' She gave her daughter a hopeful glance, which Thomasin chose to ignore.

'Eh, look at me,' she yawned. 'Tired out, I am. D'yer mind if I get up to bed? I've had a 'ard day what with 'aving' to clean t'ouse from top to bottom. Well, I thought it were only right, I couldn't leave place in a tip, could I?' She thought of Roland's gifts to her which she had parcelled up and left in the drawing room with a note of explanation. She had not deemed it right to flaunt these trophies in Patrick's face. The only concession to this honourable line of thought had been the green satin gown that she had worn to the theatre that last night spent with Roland; it was so pretty that she could not bear to parcel it up with the others and had brought it to her parents' house, where it would stay. When she went to Patrick it would be with only the things she had bought from her own money. She stood and yawned again.

'You'll have to make up your own bed,' snapped her mother. 'We weren't expecting you.'

William winked and smiled fondly. 'Goodnight, lass, sleep tight, mind t'bugs don't bite.'

Chapter Eighteen

He looked a great deal smarter when next she saw him. In his top hat, frock coat and tight, striped trousers she thought it was a stranger who waved to her as she tripped along Goodramgate – their arranged trysting place – until she was close enough to see those twinkling eyes. The clothes had been a necessary purchase; what numskull would go to call on his prospective in-laws in his workaday togs? Even second-hand they had effectively scrambled his savings. He would have to return them to the pawnshop after they had served their purpose.

Thomasin was well-decked out for the occasion too. The straw bonnet she wore had deep pink ribbons that hung to her waist, breaking the monotony of her white blouse. A similarly coloured ribbon sashed her waist, from where fell a wide, flounced skirt of sage green.

She showed him the city then, revealing its finer points. Love making him see it through her eyes, it became not such a bad place after all. Truth to tell, he hardly saw anything but his partner, following her dutifully around the narrow streets, missing the minute detail that flavoured its character: the brightly-coloured cigar store Indians with their head-dresses of tobacco leaves, giant boots and brushes that advertised the commodity to be found within each quaint establishment. Then the bigger things: the city's defences, the Bars where the heads of traitors had been impaled, and the Minster.

'Now tell me York's an ugly place if yer dare,' she challenged as they stood in the shadow of the great cathedral.

He shook his head as if seeing it for the first time. 'I can't ever visualize anyone actually building it, can you?' Surely it had forced its way out of the earth; its gleaming towers raked the sky, making him feel dwarfish, a nonentity. He turned to study her face. 'Ye really love this place, don't ye? I can feel it.'

'Aye, I do – but not as much as I love thee.' It was the first time she had said it. How banal those three words could sound when not backed by physical enactment. She squeezed his arm. 'Eh, look at us, behaving like an old married couple.'

'Sure, I wish we were,' he returned the squeeze. ' 'Tis hard work being pure – not that you'd know.'

'Ey,' she straightened his cravat. 'That's no way to get yourself an invitation to supper.'

'Ye've done that before,' he said as her fingers patted the adjusted cravat.

'An' no more o' that neither,' she scolded, seeing the jealous tinge in his eye. 'All that's over with, yer not to keep fetching it up. I told yer I'd move back in wi' me parents an' so I 'ave.'

'I beg milady's pardon – an' what was that about supper?'

'Me mother's invited us.' Only a white lie. 'An' I thought yer were gonna take me to see where you live an' to collect yer daughter?'

'So I am.' He gave a tight smile. 'Though I doubt it'll be as edifyin' as this.'

Nothing could have prepared her for what lay at the end of that dingy passageway. She stood there, unable to stop the involuntary urge to cover her nose; the smell was atrocious.

'Diabolical, isn't it?' said Patrick sympathetically. 'Though I think I ought to warn ye it might not be as bad as the stink my friends kick up when they meet ye; see, they're not keen on me marrying an Englishwoman.'

'What a time to tell me,' she sighed, then lifted her skirts and followed him, attempting unsuccessfully to avoid stepping in something unsavoury. She scraped her boot along the step as Patrick opened the door to Molly's home.

'Hello to ye, Molly,' he shouted. 'Have ye got the water on to boil? 'Tis a nice cup o' tea I'm beggin'.' He pushed Thomasin forward into the circle of hostile faces. 'Tommy, I'd like ye to meet my friends. This is Molly Flaherty.' Thomasin held out her hand to the angular woman with wonderfully high cheekbones which were spoilt by deeply-set eyes.

Molly grunted at Thomasin then turned her back and busied herself with making the tea. Patrick tried to curb his annoyance and introduced her next to Jimmy Flaherty who grudgingly shook her hand and would have smiled at the good-looking woman had his wife not ordered him to assist her.

Patrick then pointed to an ancient crone who peered myopically through milky eyes. 'This is Bridie O'Hara, another of our neighbours. Bridie, this is my wife-to-be.'

The wizened old lady puffed energetically at the pipe that was clamped between toothless gums, then held out a claw-like hand despite Molly's reproachful glare. Thomasin took the hand, grateful that one person at least did not have to be won over. 'Hello, Mrs O'Hara.'

'Good day to ye, child.' The voice was surprisingly youthful and seemed wrong for this wrinkled ageing shell. 'Don't take no notice o' her.' She nodded at Molly. 'We're not all agen the English, ye know.'

'I'm glad to hear it,' replied Thomasin. 'I was beginnin' to wonder.'

'Ah no, we're not all like that,' repeated Bridie. ' 'Tis glad I am that someone's come to make this wee boy happy; life's not dealt him the hand he deserved.'

Thomasin smiled at Bridie's description of Patrick as a 'wee boy'. 'Well, I 'ope things'll change now, Mrs O'Hara. I'll do me best to make 'im 'appy, an' I'd like to think that Pat's friends can be mine.'

'So they can, darlin',' answered Bridie giving Molly a meaningful look. 'If some o' them put their narrow minds to it.' Molly sniffed haughtily.

Patrick ignored this and introduced the Flaherty children one by one until he came to a young girl with enormous blue eyes – eyes like saucers, thought Thomasin – and long black hair that was tousled and tangled into a bouffant nest.

Thomasin stared back into those brilliant orbs, so beautiful yet so full of hate and defiance. There was a black, sticky ring around Erin's mouth which was clamped together obstinately, and she could actually see tiny creatures creeping about in the infant's hair. How could she take her home to see Mother? That would be the final humiliation. Hastily unclipping her reticule she lifted out the doll which she had hoped might aid the introduction and held it out to Erin, trying desperately to think of something nice to say. 'I'm very pleased to meet you, Erin. Yer daddy's told me a lot about yer. I hope we can be friends.' Silence. 'Here, I've brought yer a little present.'

Erin refused to be charmed. Her pride and loyalty to her dead mother refused to allow her to accept the gift that Thomasin still tendered. The Flaherty children sidled round in awe and one of them even had the temerity to touch the doll's face until Molly chased them all into the yard and slammed the cracked mugs onto the table. Before Patrick could stop her Erin had slipped out also, leaving Thomasin looking disconsolately at the doll.

'She'll get used to the idea in time,' comforted Patrick.' 'Twas very thoughtful of ye to bring it for her.' She nodded and replaced the doll in her bag. 'Forget about that ungrateful spalpeen for the time being. Sit down an' drink your tea.'

Thomasin examined the grubby, cracked mugs that held the tea then noticed Molly's defiant expression. She took a sip, much as it disgusted her. 'That's the best cup o' tea I've tasted in a long while, Mrs Flaherty.' Who knew? – maybe flattery might help.

Molly inclined her head, then held out a plateful of stale-looking bread and butter which Thomasin declined politely. This was going to be much harder than she had thought.

'We'll be going to see our new home when we've finished here,' ventured Patrick.

Molly turned to Bridie conversationally. 'Ye know, people aren't what they used to be. Everyone used to stick together an' not bother with outsiders but now there are some that're more English than the English. They start movin' away to fine houses an' their old friends aren't good enough for them any more.'

Patrick shot to his feet. 'That's not the case an' you know it! Sure, 'tis only a few yards away I'm movin', an' if you're not good enough for me than what am I doin' sitting here?'

'Did I mention any names?' asked Molly, feigning innocence. 'Did I, Bridie? Did I mention . . .'

'I know an' you know what ye meant! An' I'm not stoppin' here to be insulted. Come on, Thomasin let's go an' sit for a while in my house where the company's more polite.'

Thomasin pursued him into the yard leaving Molly and Jimmy to hang in the doorway.

'She wasn't so bad,' muttered the latter, receiving a slap from his wife.

A fat man with piggy eyes approached Patrick. 'Oy, I want a word wi' you lot.'

'Not now, Raper,' growled the Irishman, trying to move round him.

'I want to make a complaint,' Raper persisted, barring Patrick's escape and addressing Molly and her husband also. 'It's about time you dirty buggers sorted yerselves out. I can't 'ave all this 'ere filth clutterin' up yard, there's no room for my stock.'

'Huh, I like that!' Molly stepped forward, her eyes narrowing even further. ' 'Tis you who contributes to the mess more'n any of us. Ye don't seem to be too concerned about our children gettin' sick from all the stuff that comes out o' your slaughterin' house.'

'I'm not,' announced Raper. 'Not concerned in the bloody least. I couldn't give the bloody Pope's balls if you lot all dropped dead, the more the better, I say. Vermin should be exterminated.'

'Why, did ye hear that?'ejaculated Molly. 'Jimmy, are ye goin' to stand there an' let him insult ye? Go give him a pastin'.'

Thomasin had spotted that Patrick's jaw had set into a dangerous angle and stepped between him and the butcher. 'Look, can't yer sort this out without all this bawlin'?'

'Oh, got yer bloody dollymop to fight yer battle, 'ave yer?' scoffed Raper, crossing his arms, a rather foolish action as it left him quite defenceless.

'I'll give yer bloody dollymop!' roared Thomasin and swung the bag at him. With the added ballast of the doll the bag provided a formidable weapon, taking Raper completely off balance and making him stagger backwards to land slap-bang in the middle of a dung heap.

Thomasin turned furiously to Patrick . . . then her face relaxed. He was shaking with merriment, throwing back his head and booming with laughter. To her astonishment he was not the only one. She peered round him at Molly whose grimy face was wreathed in amusement, the slitty eyes had almost disappeared, the bony hands clasped to splitting sides. Jimmy, too, was enjoying Raper's discomfiture; he chuckled bronchially, then nudged his wife and winked at Thomasin.

Molly wiped her eyes and nose on her sleeve and came to stand beside the red-haired woman, still laughing as Raper vanished into his abattoir with: 'I'll 'ave you buggers one o' these days.'

'How could I ever o' thought ye were English?' she asked a bemused Thomasin. 'Sure, the way ye sorted that varmint there's got to be a drop of Irish blood in ye somewhere.'

Thomasin grinned, assuming this to be a compliment. 'I don't think so, Mrs Flaherty, though it's kind o' yer to say so.'

'Ah, less o' the Mrs Flaherty.' Molly laced a dirty mitt through her new friend's arm. ' 'Tis Molly to me friends, an' anybody that can get the better of old Porkface is a friend o' mine. Would ye like to come back in for another cup o' tea an' some bread an' butter?' She saw the other's mouth twitch. 'Ah sure, I'll give ye fresh this time. I only put the stale out for I thought ye were all stuck up 'cause o' the way ye're dressed.'

Thomasin looked down at her outfit. It had been a mistake to wear it, but she had little guessed she would be stepping into such poverty. Small wonder Molly had been hostile. She declined the offer, explaining, 'We'd best not, we're meant to be going to visit me parents – but I'd like to come for a cup o' tea another day if that's all right?'

'Any time, pet, any time,' sang Molly. 'Oh, an' when ye find yourself wantin' a midwife, Molly's the one to send for.'

Thomasin laughed and looked at Patrick. 'Well, I don't think I'll be needin' one this week, but thanks for the offer.'

Molly returned to her house and Thomasin looked uncomfortably at Patrick. 'Pat, I don't really know how to put this – whatever I say it'll sound as if I'm pickin' fault – but here goes: d'yer think I could give Erin a bath before we take 'er to meet me parents?'

'A bath?' Patrick looked to where his daughter played ring o' roses amongst the dung heaps and saw her as Thomasin must see her: a dirty ragamuffin with lice abounding in the haystack of hair. 'Jazers, Tommy I see what ye mean, she's not exactly fit to meet anyone, is she?' He summoned the child over and chucked her under the chin.

'Come in the house, Erin.' He took his daughter's hand. 'Let's get ye tidied up before we go for our walk.'

Thomasin trailed after them. 'Where's yer bath?' She unfastened her bonnet and looked around for a clean surface on which to lay it, then instead hung it on a hook that protruded from the back of the door.

Patrick pointed to a tin bath which Thomasin dragged before the fire.

'Get me some pans an' we'll heat water. Ee, wait on, let me just 'ave a look in me bag t'see if that doll's still in one piece.' She opened the bag. 'Ah, yes no damage done – only to Raper's head.' She laughed and held out the doll again to Erin, who swung her shoulders round in mute antagonism. 'Ah well, maybe yer might change yer mind later,' sighed Thomasin, then began to roll up her sleeves.

Erin's apprehension grew as the water was tipped into the tin bath and Thomasin advanced on her. The child clamped her arms round her father's long legs.

'I'm not gonna bite yer,' soothed Thomasin. 'But we can't bath yer wi' yer clothes on.'

'Daddy!' shrieked Erin and ran up and down on the spot in a panic.

Thomasin sighed. 'All right, if yer don't want me to do it yer daddy'll 'ave to 'cause yer needn't think yer comin' out with us lookin' like a bag o' rags.'

'I don't want to come with you,' cried Erin. 'I don't like ye.'

'Erin!' Patrick gripped her shoulders and shook her. 'Say ye're sorry to Thomasin.'

'I'm not sorry. I don't like her,' Erin sobbed.

Patrick was about to reprove her once more than Thomasin stepped in.

'Don't, Pat,' she mouthed. 'It's only natural. I'm a stranger to 'er, she don't want me seein' 'er wi' no clothes on, d'yer, love?' She put out a sympathetic hand to Erin who ignored it. 'You get 'er ready an' put 'er in t'bath. I'll just nip out for some soap, there's bound to be a shop open somewhere.'

An hour later Erin looked like a different child, and the bathwater had an inch of silt at the bottom. Those lumps of hair which had been so matted that they had defied the comb had been trimmed away and the hair now hung, damply obedient, over Erin's shoulders. Her face was as clean as a newborn piglet's and her nails no longer capable of growing potatoes. It was a pity that the child did not have another set of clothes to change into, for the drab little pinafore she had worn before was soiled and creased.

Thomasin stood back to inspect the finished result. 'There, don't yer feel much better for bein' clean?' she asked brightly.

Erin scowled.

'Mm, yer just need somethin' to brighten yer dress up.' Thomasin chewed on a fingernail. 'I know!' She undid the sash from her own waist. 'If I cut a bit off 'ere it'll make a lovely ribbon for yer hair.'

'But ye'll spoil it,' objected Patrick.

'Nay, nowt's too good for our Erin, is it, love? Pass us them scissors will yer, Pat?'

'There,' said Thomasin, clipping off a length of the sash and fastening the remainder around Erin's hair. 'That looks lovely, don't it, Daddy?'

'He's not your Daddy!' Erin ripped off the ribbon and flung it to the floor where she danced upon it.

'Mm, what are you gonna be if yer grow up, love?' muttered Thomasin to herself, then to Patrick, who had raised his hand to strike the girl, 'No, don't! It don't matter, honest, she didn't mean it.'

Patrick and Erin glared at each other, both knowing that this was far from the truth.

'Any road, come on,' said Thomasin in an attempt to pacify. 'I thought we were off to see this new house of ours?'

'So we are.' Patrick, with a defiant glare for his daughter, caught the child's hand.

Although situated in another of Walmgate's many court-yards this place could hardly be grouped with Patrick's present address. The yard, though unpaved, was relatively clean and instead of ashpits and middens outside each door these were restricted to one corner of the yard. Two closets served the area, both amazingly clean, and the absence of an abattoir meant that access to one's entrance was not moated by blood. The house itself was bigger, having two rooms up and two down. The previous occupants had apparently taken great pride in their dwelling as there was not a speck of dust and the walls lacked the damp patches that plagued so many of these houses.

None of these agreeable points suited Erin who moaned constantly that she would be away from Aunt Molly and Granny and refused to say anything in its favour. 'I want to go home now,' she said decisively when they exited.

'Thomasin's kindly invited us to supper,' her father informed her.

'I don't want to go.'

He stopped and whispered. 'Erin Feeney, 'tis lookin' for a striped backside y'are,' then beamed at Thomasin. 'I'm sure we're both going to enjoy it greatly.'

The dazzlingly-white cloth floated down to cover the table and Hannah smoothed out the creases. Out came the best china, the only marring feature being the lidless teapot. It had grown quite dark outside, much to Hannah's relief. She made nervous, last-minute inspections of the table and room, then started as the door to the street was opened.

'Oh, William, that will be them!' She began to pace this way and that.

'I don't know what tha's gerrin' thissen all wound up for,' said William calmly. 'He's only a peasant like us, not one o' thy plumgobbed in-laws.'

'Typical,' hissed Hannah. 'Typical.' She spun round as the parlour door opened. 'Oh, our Thomasin what a surprise.'

Thomasin caught her father's eye, smiled then introduced Patrick to Hannah who perused the tall, handsome man before her and found him more expensively dressed than she had anticipated.

'How do you do, Mr Feeney?'

'Charmed, Mrs Fenton, charmed.' Patrick bowed low over Hannah's outstretched fingers. 'Your daughter has told me so much about ye, but she omitted to mention your beauty.'

Hannah laughed simperingly. 'Oh, Mr Feeney, you flatter me, I think.' The man was obviously a much better prospect than she had supposed and his manners were faultless. 'Thomasin has told us so much about you too,' she added as an afterthought.

Patrick smiled at his Intended. 'All good, I hope?'

'Of course.' Hannah took his hat, then peered around him as if looking for something. 'Thomasin, I understood Mr Feeney was bringing his daughter?'

'Oh, Patrick please,' insisted the Irishman. 'After all, with your kind permission I am to be part of the family.' He looked for his daughter who had lingered at the outside door. 'Erin, come in, child.'

If Hannah's hopes about Patrick's prosperity had been escalated at their meeting the appearance of his daughter dashed them to smithereens. She looked aghast from the smartly-dressed man to the ragged child, her disapproval evident. The girl was positively destitute; just look at that moth-eaten dress. Thomasin's heart sank as she watched her mother's face and realised that all her efforts had been wasted.

'Come on in, love an' 'ave summat to eat,' she softly instructed the child.

All Hannah's politeness vanished. 'You may as well sit down,' she said abruptly. There was little point in wasting niceties on these two.

'I find it somewhat remiss of you, Mr Feeney,' she said coldly, 'that you did not see fit to attire your daughter to the same standards as yourself for our meeting.'

'I'm sorry, Mrs Fenton,' replied her guest. 'I would have done so had she owned another set of clothes.'

Hannah was astounded. 'You can sit there in your finery and tell me that your daughter has only the rags she stands up in?'

Patrick looked uncomfortably at William who had not yet spoken. 'I know it sounds a poor excuse but had I known she'd be in such illustrious company I should've purchased more suitable clothes for her.' He tugged at his own suit. 'I know how it must appear – that I put myself before my child – but believe me it was only because I couldn't possibly have visited you in my everyday working clothes. It grieves me to admit it but after the wedding these will have to be returned to the pawnshop.'

'So, you sought to impress us with your finery,' condemned Hannah. 'Leading us to believe that you were a gentleman.'

'Mother!' objected Thomasin, wishing she had warned

Patrick that one was not allowed to be open and honest in this house.

Patrick held up his hand to stay the interruption. 'No, Mrs Fenton I did not wish to mislead anyone into thinking I was other than what I am. I'm not ashamed of my background. My intentions were merely founded on good manners, which I had hoped might be returned.' He looked past her to her husband who now approached the table. 'I believe we've yet to be introduced, sir?'

William leaned across his blushing wife and shook hands with Patrick who had risen. 'Nay, don't mind me, lad. I come last in this 'ouse. She usually keeps me locked up when we 'ave visitors in case I show 'er up.' Without ceremony he seated himself at the table and turned to his wife. 'Well, are we gonna sit 'ere an' look at it all neet – or are we gonna eat it?'

Patrick, sitting also, attempted more flattery. 'I must say, Mrs Fenton that pie looks particularly edible.'

Hannah gave Patrick a withering stare, making him feel more uncomfortable than ever, and passed him a plate laden with minute sandwiches. He had begun to sweat. His collar was chafing and the trousers were proving much too tight for comfort now that he was sitting. He thanked Hannah politely and took a sandwich. What a dragon.

Thomasin relieved her mother of the plate and offered it to Erin who shook her head and stared down at the table, though the sight of all this food provoked terrible hunger. At least the ginger-haired woman had seemed to like her, but this other one openly detested her; that was plain from the disdainful glances Hannah kept shooting at her.

Thomasin placed a piece of cake on Erin's plate without giving her the chance to refuse. 'Get that down yer. No wonder yer so skinny.'

Erin nibbled sullenly and though she found it absolutely delicious she would not have dreamed of informing the hoity-toity one who had probably made it.

Patrick, his own taste buds a-tingle, was about to place the whole sandwich in his mouth, then caught Hannah's look of repugnance and delicately nipped off one of the corners.

Thomasin narrowed her eyes at her mother and issued a mental warning – *be nice to him, or else.* Hannah pursed her lips and began to pour the tea. She supposed that she should show some form of politeness. 'Have you set a wedding date yet, Mr Feeney?' She flatly refused to use his Christian name.

Patrick maintained his well-spoken English. 'As yet, no. Perhaps when I've consulted Father Kelly . . .'

'Oh!' Hannah had knocked over her tea cup, staining the spotless cloth and now stared glassily at her guest.

'I'm sorry, have I said something wrong?' Patrick looked bewilderedly across at William who shook his head.

'Nay, lad it's just that I think t'wife's a bit concerned tha'll be wantin' our Tommy to convert.' He put down his cup with a clatter. 'Stop it, tha soft bugger,' he berated Hannah who had started to weep. His wife gave a squeak and rushed from the room.

'Eh, I don't know,' sighed William. 'Tommy, go get a whatsit to clean this tea up, lass.'

Thomasin went to the scullery to fetch a cloth. Whilst William was talking to her father Erin sneaked another piece of cake and crammed it into her mouth.

'Tha'll 'ave to excuse lass's mother,' the man told Patrick. 'She meant nowt by it, she's allus bealin' an' carryin' on about summat. She's just thinkin' to do best for her lass as she sees it.'

'An' yourself, Mr Fenton,' returned Patrick. 'How d'you stand on this marriage?'

'Will it make any difference to thy plans what I think?'

'No . . . I'm sorry,' admitted Patrick.

'Just as well tha said that,' nodded William satisfiedly. An unusual man, it was not that his other daughters' husbands weren't good enough but that they were too good; William detested his other sons-in-law and was delighted that this one did not – as they did – make him feel like muck. 'Well, lad, thee asked for my opinion so I'll tell thee: tha seems a nice enough bloke to me. It's way tha treats my lass, not which foot tha leads with as concerns me. It's not way a fella preaches but how far apart his eyes are that I use as yardstick; never trusted a bloke whose eyes are too close-set.'

'Should I get my tapemeasure out?' offered his daughter.

'Soft bugger – an' stop shovin' that pie down yer neck; gerrit passed round.'

Patrick then explained to William that Mrs Fenton was

worrying needlessly as he did not practise his religion any more. 'I only mentioned Father Kelly 'cause he's a personal friend. I didn't mean he'd be officiatin' at our weddin'; that'll have to be in a register office. About the nuptials, I've very little saved . . .'

William forestalled him, speaking through a section of pie. 'Nay, that's our worry, lad. We're used to forkin' out what with five lasses. Thee leave it to us. Pass us one o' them whatdyercallits, Tommy, then go sherrack tha mother. Tell her if she sits blubberin' up in that bedchamber all neet we'll have to consider who gets fishin' rights.'

'Does anyone else want owt to eat before I go?' asked Thomasin. 'Erin love, 'ave another piece o' cake.' She placed it on the child's plate. 'Right, I'll go persuade 'er to show her face, then.'

'Aye, well don't try too hard,' muttered William. 'This hot pastry's given me wind an' I shan't be able to let go if she's 'ere.'

Fifteen minutes later, during which time William and Patrick had come to know each other better, Hannah put in a reluctant appearance. Her husband hoisted his cup. 'Oh, back to the land of the livin' esta?'

Patrick smiled. The man had a comfortable roughness about him. He stood and went towards Hannah. 'Before we have to leave, Mrs Fenton I'd like to thank ye for the supper, also to explain my remark about the priest, if ye'll let me.' He had abandoned his refined speech, deciding that she must take him as he was.

'There's no need for explanations,' replied Hannah, still aloof. 'Thomasin has told me that you no longer practise your faith and though it is a relief to me that my daughter will not have to undergo a conversion I cannot help feeling that one who dismisses his faith so lightly is not to be depended upon. Will you abandon her in the same manner when you have grown tired of her, Mr Feeney?'

'Mrs Fenton, if you'd seen thousands o' your fellow countrymen and women – not to mention children – reduced to living skeletons and prepared to kill for a cupful of grain then I doubt that even one so pious as yourself could continue to believe in God. 'Tis a wonder that child there was ever born with the conditions that her poor mother had to suffer, so don't be givin' me any o' your holier-than-thou stuff, ye know nothing about it, any of it.'

Hannah stood erect. 'Well, I'm sure I beg your pardon, Mr Feeney. I did not fully appreciate your reasons for dismissing your faith. I suppose I must apologise.'

'Ah sure, 'tis me that should apologise,' he answered ashamed at his outburst. 'I was very rude – an' after that lovely supper; 'twas unforgivable. You weren't to know my circumstances. Well, I must be off an' get this child to bed. Thank ye once more for your splendid hospitality.'

Hannah summoned a weak smile.

'Ah, Thomasin!' exclaimed Patrick. ' 'Tis your mother ye've inherited your pretty smile from. Why, to put the two o' yese together one'd think ye were sisters.'

Thomasin giggled as she showed him and Erin out into the street. 'By, yer a charmin' devil. Tryin' to butter me mam up. I bet yer like that wi' all t'women, aren't yer? One look at them twinkly eyes an' they'll be fallin' all over yer.' She could feel his laughter though he made not a sound.

'Aye, I seem to have quite a way with the ladies; could have any woman I fancy – hold on, if that's true then what am I doing cavorting with the like o' you?'

Thomasin joined his laughter. 'By, wait till I get you married, yer won't half suffer.' She bobbed suddenly and attempted to kiss Erin. ' 'Night, Erin, see yer soon.'

Patrick answered for the child. 'Aye, very soon, *muirnin*.'

'Moowhat?'

'*Muirnin* – darlin',' answered Patrick softly, and kissed her.

CHAPTER NINETEEN

THOMASIN FOUGHT TO escape the nebulous confines of sleep. She opened her eyes, then quickly closed them again as the brilliant darts of morning sought to drive her blind. Turning her head away from the light's source she attempted once more to open them, experiencing the sharp thrill of surprise which had accompanied each waking second during that first week of married life. It took a great deal of getting used to, seeing another head on the pillow after sleeping for so long alone. She wormed her body into the hollow that his sleeping form offered, sliding a mischievous hand over his belly.

What a fiasco the wedding had been. There had been a fight – an actual full scale battle between her side and his, with people throwing food as well as punches and her poor mother ending up in floods of tears due to 'that dreadful Mrs Flaherty' who had started it all. And after all was over, the hall wrecked, food ruined, Molly had the audacity to say, 'Sure 'twas a lovely wedding, pet, just marvellous. If I have one little criticism to make 'twould be on the manners of your relatives – sure, they're so uncivilised.'

The insistent pressure of her hand brought him slowly awake to blink sleepily at her, then smile as he remembered where he was. Their bodies, relaxed and saturated with sleep, came together, an automatic fusing of magnets. Slow and easy, lazily engaging, their early morning love bore little similarity to the frantic throes of evening. Each sank inside the other, into a cavernous eternity of pleasure, of needing and belonging, until the burning core of passion was finally extinguished.

Thomasin's flushed face lay against the damp heat of his

shoulder, breathing in the sensuous musk of love. 'If I shut my eyes now,' she murmured dreamily, 'I could almost imagine I'd died an' gone to Heaven.'

Patrick ran tender fingertips over her breast as his eyes travelled around the stark room. 'Ah, 'tis a long way from Heaven, Tommy,' he sighed regretfully, then twisted his body so that he was looking down into her face once again. 'God, when I look at all this I still can't believe ye consented to marry me. You look outta place here, 'tis no fit life for a lady. Ye deserve more, an' I'm going to give it ye.'

'Oh, Pat, you are funny,' she stroked the sweep of his shoulder, 'calling me a lady. How many times do I 'ave to tell yer? I've got all I want here. Have I ever said it weren't good enough for me?'

He pulled free a scarlet tendril of hair that had clung to her mouth. 'I know ye'd never dream of asking me for anything, Tommy,' he replied softly. 'But I want to give ye nice things; I need to give ye them for me own self-respect. I can't expect ye to live like this for the rest o' your life; I'd be less than a man if I did. No, now that the fine weather has arrived there should be plenty of overtime and spare jobs that need doing, an' I'll be the first in the queue. We'll soon be able to add a couple o' nice bits o' furniture to the place to make it look nice until I've saved enough for another place.'

'Patrick, I don't want yer workin' all hours God sends just because yer've somehow got it into yer head that this isn't good enough for me,' she protested. 'An' neither do I want yer comin' home too tired to make love to me.'

'Sure, I'll never be too tired for that,' he reassured her, then rolled onto his back and stretched noisily as the knocker-up tapped on the window with his pole. 'Jazers, is that the time already? I'll be late for work.' He swung his legs over the side of the bed and began to pull on his clothes, then paused to ask over his shoulder, 'D'ye know what day it is today?'

'I do believe Friday comes after Thursday.'

' 'Tis me birthday.'

She sprang into a kneeling position and hooked her hands over his shoulders. 'Aw, why didn't yer tell me? I would've bought yer summat.'

'I thought I'd just had me present,' he joked.

She laughed and pulled him back onto the bed. 'Would yer like another one?'

'God forbid!' He escaped her and resumed dressing. 'I'll be worn out before ever I get to work.'

'Yer must be past it,' she scoffed. 'How old are yer?'

'Let me see,' he pondered whilst buttoning his breeches. 'I think I'd be thirty-two.'

'Why, yer poor old devil, no wonder yer not up to it.' She leapt out of bed and pulled on her clothes before taking his arm. 'Would yer like an' 'elpin' 'and down the stairs, me old soldier?'

He cuffed her lightly. 'I'll give ye helping hand. Ye can go butter some bread for me to take with me. I haven't time for breakfast what with all your wicked goings-on.'

Thomasin slipped past him and ran downstairs to the kitchen where she quickly prepared the bread and tucked it into his haversack. Patrick splashed some water onto his face, gave it a cursory wipe, then kissed his wife and left for work, seconds before Erin stumbled sleepily into the room looking for something to eat.

Thomasin had adapted remarkably well to her domestic role. Patrick had made it perfectly clear that there would be only one breadwinner in the house so she had given up her job at the bakery. Much as she valued her independence, she was loathe to start an argument over what Patrick obviously considered a paltry matter and, as he pointed out, who would look after Erin if Thomasin were at work all day? So for the first time in her life she had backed down; then had instantly regretted it for she soon found out that Patrick's wage was nowhere sufficient to run a household. But then, she kept reminding herself, had she not known what it would be like when she had married him? And, all in all, they were very happy.

The one thing that marred their contentment was Erin's animosity, which had not waned by one degree. Thomasin had tried incredibly hard – too hard perhaps – to win her over, but the child simply ignored her. The verbal enmity that she had offered at the beginning had reduced itself to a stony barrier of monosyllables – Sometimes, thought Thomasin, it's as if I'm not here.

Erin munched at her breakfast, closing her ears to anything

which her stepmother might have to say, and thought about her new friend Bridie O'Hara. Of course, Bridie had always been a friend, but not close like she was now. It had all come about when they were loading the handcart to move house. Bridie had spotted the harp strapped securely on top of the pile of furniture and had asked to whom it belonged.

' 'Twas my father's,' Patrick had replied. 'But it belongs to Erin now, or it will do as soon as we can find someone to teach her how to play it, for I've never been the musical sort meself.'

'Ye can stop looking,' Bridie had answered. 'Sure, I know everything there is to know about harp playing, I'll gladly teach her for ye.'

'Are ye sure ye don't mind?' said Patrick. 'She can be a bit of a handful at times.'

'I'll be glad o' the company,' Bridie had told him, and from thence had sprung the mutual bond often encountered between the very old and the very young.

Thomasin was speaking. 'I said do yer want to go see Granny today?'

Erin nodded and took her empty bowl to the sink.

'All right,' replied Thomasin. 'I'll just do these pots then we'll go. Shall we take your harp wi' us so's yer can 'ave another lesson?'

Erin nodded again.

Half an hour later the child was playing happily in Bridie's home while Thomasin sat gossiping to Molly.

'Have ye not brought Erin?' enquired Molly, placing a cup of tea in front of her guest.

'She's in Bridie's takin' her lesson,' explained Thomasin. 'To tell yer the truth I'm glad o' the rest. It's hard work tryin' to 'ave a conversation wi' somebody that hates the sight o' yer.'

'Aw, 'tis not just you,' Molly told her. 'She'd hate anyone who tried to take her mother's place; they were very close.'

'But that's what I keep tellin' 'er,' stormed Thomasin. 'I'm not tryin' to take anyone's place. It's like talkin' to a brick wall. I ask 'er all sorts o' questions about 'er mam, tryin' to show an interest like, but she just clams up. I don't know which is worst, havin' to deal with a load o' cheek or a wall o' silence.'

'Ah, she'll grow out of it,' said Molly, dropping a lump of fat into a pan which already had a liberal coating of grease. 'D'ye mind if I cook this here egg for Jimmy? Poor darlin', he's ill in bed so I thought I'd give him a little treat.'

'Aye, I'm thinkin' o' givin' Pat a treat, it's his birthday today.'

'Oh, sure ye'll be having a party then?' issued Molly hopefully.

'I most certainly will not,' replied Thomasin, putting her cup to her lips, 'I've had enough o' parties for the time being.' Once again she pictured the disastrous wedding.

The egg sizzled and spat over the fire and a wayward draught wafted the smell under Thomasin's nose.

'Are ye feeling all right, love?' asked Molly, looking at the sickly pallor on her companion's face.

'I will be in a minute.' Thomasin took in deep breaths, trying to fight down the wave of nausea. 'I don't know what's wrong wi' me this week, I can't seem to stand the smell o' fryin'.'

Molly laughed and gave her a knowing wink. 'When's it due?'

The meaning of her words escaped Thomasin at first, then suddenly the full impact of them smote her. There were quick calculations. No, it couldn't be! She had hardly known Patrick five minutes, it couldn't happen that fast – could it? A nagging doubt crept into her head: my God, it could be Roly's. She tried frantically to recall the last time he had made love to her, then fought to reassure herself. No, all those months with Roland had produced nothing, they had been too careful. It was only when she had met Patrick that all her meticulous planning had gone to pot. It must be Patrick's – had to be.

Molly misread the distraught expression. 'Don't give yourself kittens.' She patted her friend's hand. 'I fell with my first the very second I was wed. Ye'll get used to the idea.' She added congratulations.

'Don't tell Pat,' pleaded Thomasin. 'I haven't told him yet. S'truth, I didn't even know meself.'

'Sure, won't it be a nice surprise for him?' answered Molly.

'I hope so,' muttered Thomasin.

Despite Erin's protests, Bridie sent her out into the yard to play with the other children. It was not good for a child, she said, to be with an old lady all the time, she must go and seek younger company and leave Granny to have a nap.

So Erin slouched sulkily into the yard where Peggy and Norah Flaherty were playing kiss catchings with Jos Leach. Her peevishness was soon washed away by the girls' shrieking laughter as Jos tried to catch hold of them, and before long she was begging to join their fun. She ran screaming as the simple-minded youth lumbered merrily after her, leaping over the piles of dirt and trying to hide behind Peggy's skirts.

'Ah've got yers!' Jos's huge hand clamped her shoulder as he bent over and took his reward, his slobbering mouth soaking the side of her face.

'Ugh!' She wiped a hand over the wet patch, then smiled up at Jos to show there was no ill-feeling and took hold of his hand. She liked Jos, he was not like the other grown-ups, he always had time to play with her. 'Let's have another game,' she decided suddenly, and Jos willingly agreed.

He danced about the yard in his clumsy, childlike fashion, emitting guttural cries of glee in his attempts to ensnare Erin, forgetting about the other girls completely as she was his favourite.

'What the bloody hell's going on 'ere?' Edwin Raper came out into the daylight, his killing over for the time being. He wiped his gory hands on the filthy apron at his waist and advanced on the gumptionless apprentice. 'Oy! I don't pay thee to run about like a bloody looney all day, yer big daft kid. In't it time yer grew up? Look at yer, eighteen years old an' still playin' bairns' games. Get yer arse back inside an' clear up that pile o' guts.'

With a hangdog expression Jos Leach loped off towards the abattoir. Raper then turned his indignation on the three young girls. 'An' I'll thank you lot not to be takin' my assistant away from his work. Bugger off, the lot o' yer.'

The girls were adhered to the spot, especially Erin, who was absolutely terrified of the butcher. She thought him the ugliest man she had ever seen; he had hairy arms and smelly breath, and whatever he did behind those blood-spattered doors it was certainly something horrid. The thought made her shiver. Unlike the other children in the yard she was a sensitive child. She had watched sheep and cows enter the building, heard their cries. Ugh, nasty, nasty man.

'Well, what yer still stood gawpin' for?' cried Raper, then crouched down, made his hands into claws, opened his mouth wide in a snarl and stuck out his tongue. 'Blaaaargh!'

The girls screamed and fled as the butcher gave a blood-curdling laugh and returned to his work. They burst into Molly's kitchen and startled the life out of the poor woman.

'God in Heaven!' she cried, clutching her swollen stomach. 'D'ye want me to give birth to a monster? What's the matter with yese?'

'That nasty Mr Raper chased us,' panted Erin, flopping onto the floor to play with baby Martin.

'Oh, we'll soon sort him out,' announced Thomasin. 'Shall I go an' thump him for yer?'

Erin wrinkled her nose, then shook her head.

'Then we'll go to shop for some sweeties,' Thomasin decided and went towards the door. 'I'll mebbe see yer tomorra, Moll – an' keep mum about you-know-what.'

CHAPTER TWENTY

THAT EVENING THOMASIN made a small but significant mistake that worsened matters between Erin and herself. After the platefuls of Yorkshire Pudding – a delicacy new to the Feeneys – she served up a joint of mutton which she had purchased with her personal savings as a birthday treat. When Erin's plate remained untouched she was compelled to ask, 'Is there summat wrong, love?'

Erin gave Patrick a forceful stare then looked at the meat on her own plate. 'I can't eat it.'

Patrick rammed another forkful into his mouth. 'What d'ye mean ye cannot eat it? 'Tis wonderful stuff.'

' 'Tis Friday.'

His fork faltered. 'Gob, the child's right, an' here I am forgetting – still, 'tis no concern to me now an' surely you can forget about the rules for once, colleen. Thomasin's gone to a great deal of expense to buy this.'

Thomasin was still puzzled. 'D'ye not know that good Catholics never eat meat on a Friday?' asked Erin, coldly polite.

'Aw , . . aw dear.' Thomasin squashed her cheeks between her palms. 'Aren't I just the one? I'd clean forgotten. Eh, I'm that sorry, Erin.'

'Sure, you can't be expected to cater especially for her,' said Patrick. 'Erin, ye'll not waste a good meal. It won't matter just this once.'

' 'Tis a sin.'

'Since when has anybody who gives a Flaherty baby rabbit droppings to eat as currants ever bothered about sinful? When I say eat it you eat it.'

173

'I'll be sick,' protested Erin.

'So was Brendan Flaherty – eat it!'

'Here.' Thomasin snatched up the child's plate and scraped the meat onto Patrick's. 'That's that sorted out. There'll be no more arguin' now.'

Patrick flung down his cutlery, temper flaring. 'Thomasin, I have told that child to eat it and eat it she will.'

'Oh, stop makin' such a song an' dance about it! I don't know, here I am thinkin' I'm doin' yer all a favour an' we end up fightin'. Listen, it was your idea to bring that bairn up a Catholic, yer can't be choppin' an' changin' to suit yerself, yer'll only confuse 'er. If yer gonna do it, do it right.'

Patrick calmed down and picked up his knife and fork again. 'Aye, you're right o' course. 'Twas only you I was considering though. All that trouble . . .'

' 'Tisn't trouble if one o' yer's enjoyed it,' said his wife.

'I have, indeed. 'Tis just as well you're a good cook else I mightn't've married ye.'

'Is that all I'm good for then?' A seductive glance as she left the table.

His meal finished, he leaned back in his chair rubbing his belly. 'Well, as they say, the proof of the pudding is in the eating. Maybe I'll sample a little piece later on.' The suggestiveness of his tone provoked a grin.

Erin, tired of being either chastised or ignored, pushed away her plate and without a word left the room. It seemed to her that all of her father's love was directed at Thomasin, leaving none for her. He was punishing her for rejecting the interloper as her mother. She trudged sadly up the stairs and into her own room. Even though it was nice to have somewhere private, she missed the warmth of the Flaherty girls at night, sleeping alone on the small, lumpy mattress. Closing the door, she listened for any movement on the stairs, then, satisfied that she would not be disturbed, she pried up the loose floorboard and reached inside. Her fingers touched the cool face and she lifted the doll from its hiding place. She wondered if Thomasin had noticed it missing from the cupboard downstairs. The temptation had been too strong.

'Come and sit here, Mary, and I'll tell ye a story.' She shook the creases out of the doll's blue gown, smoothing the skirts into position and propped it against the wall. 'Now, if you're a good girl I might let ye listen to me harp,' she informed the doll, which stared back with sightless eyes. 'But if you're naughty,' she wagged a grubby finger, 'the gombeen men will come an' get ye.' She had no idea what a gombeen man was, but it must be pretty awful, for hadn't her mother threatened her with the same fate?

'Right, Mary, pay attention. This is a song about a great king of Ireland, that's where we come from, his name was Brian Boru.'

The light, airy chords sprang forth, lifting some of the loneliness from her heart. Whenever it was close to her, she felt her mother's presence.

Downstairs Patrick cocked his ear at the sound of her music. 'She's really taken to that thing hasn't she?'

Thomasin sighed. 'Aye, I wish I could say the same for me.'

' 'Tis still as bad with the two of ye?'

She nodded. 'I've tried my damndest to fetch her out of herself but she just won't take to me.'

'Does it upset ye?'

'Well, course it does,' she cried. 'What do yer think I'm made of?' She brushed off his apology. 'It's all right, I think it bothers me more for her sake than for mine. It can't be doin' her any good, an' I think what's upsettin' her most is that she thinks I've taken yer away from her. You're sometimes very hard on her yer know. Like just now. An' it allus seems to be me what's in the middle o' things. I know yer 'aven't 'ad much time lately, but I think yer should try to make time, after all she is yer daughter. Go tell her a story or summat while I get cleared up.'

Patrick wrapped strong arms about her. 'D'ye really think that's what's going through her mind?'

'I know it is.'

'I didn't realise 'twas as bad as that – so ye think I oughta go an' spend some time with her, d'ye?'

'Patrick Feeney, are them two baps yer've got stuck on t'side o' yer head? I just said so, didn't I? Now tear yerself away from me an' get upstairs.'

'I will.' He saluted and went towards the staircase. 'But I'm also goin' to have a serious talk with her. It can't go on like this. I'll not have you upset.'

'Not too serious though, eh?' she begged. 'Yer might make things worse.'

Patrick's foot caught at a loose stair and immediately the music stopped.

'Don't let me interrupt ye, darlin',' he told Erin, poking his face around her door. 'I like to listen to ye play. Sure, you're going to be a fine musician one o' these days.'

Erin bit her lip. 'I don't feel like playin' any more.'

He sat beside her, back against wall. 'Why's that, my pet?'

She hesitated for a moment, then asked in a tiny, quivering voice, 'Why don't ye love me any more, Daddy?'

If she had physically struck him it would not have compared with the pain he now experienced. 'Aw, Erin! Erin, darlin' I do love ye, I do.' He gathered her up into a tight embrace, fighting to keep the tears at bay. 'Ah, God, Erin, what makes ye say such a thing? Have I ever said I didn't love ye?' He stroked her hair roughly as she wept into his chest. 'Ye think that Thomasin has taken your place in me heart?'

'She's taken Mammy's place,' sniffed Erin.

'Nobody can take your mammy's place, Erin,' he said firmly. 'Not even Thomasin – even if she wanted to. Ye know that, don't ye?' His calloused hand smoothed the black curls from her brow. 'You loved her an' I loved her, but she's gone now, nothing's going to bring her back, and she wouldn't like it if she could see the way you're carryin' on – an' she can, ye know, she's up there with the angels watchin' over ye an' she knows that ye still love her. But she also knows that ye need a new mammy to take care o' ye. Ah, I know,' he nodded, silencing her interjection, 'you're going to tell me ye've got Granny an' Aunt Molly – but they don't belong to me, Erin. A man needs a wife – ye won't understand that now but ye will when ye get older – not somebody who cooks his meals then goes back home to her own family. I need someone who's there all the time; someone to love me.'

'But I love ye, Daddy.' The plaintive voice was a knife thrust. How could you explain to a five year old child that her love was not enough?

'I know ye do, darlin',' he whispered, kissing her soft cheek. 'An' I love you too. But so does Thomasin, can ye understand that? She isn't trying to take me away from ye, she wants to love the both of us.'

Erin was torn in half. On the one hand she was desperately in need of female affection, for even though she had Bridie and Molly, theirs was not the same as a mother's love. On the other hand she still felt that it would be disloyal to her mother's memory, whatever her father might say to the contrary. If she could only reach a compromise.

She finally decided. 'All right, I'll try an' like her, Daddy, but just for your sake, do you understand?'

'Aye, I understand,' replied Patrick quietly.

Her hand reached out and pulled the doll from under the mattress where she had hastily shoved it on his entry to her room. Patrick made no comment as she hugged it to her chest.

'Come on,' he whispered softly. 'Let's get ye ready for bed, then Daddy'll tell ye a nice, long story.'

Later, with the pots washed and replaced in the cupboard, Thomasin sat on the rug, leaning against Patrick's legs. Her long, auburn hair flowed over his lap as she pillowed her head there. The wide mouth curved in a secretive smile as she awaited the right moment to break her news. He stroked her hair and stared pensively into the fire.

'Pat?'

'Mmm?'

'I've got another birthday present for yer.' She did not look at him.

'Another? Sure I'm a lucky fella today. Is it as good as the one I got this mornin'?'

'Better,' she smiled.

'Then it must be something special.' He looked around the room. 'Where is it then?'

Only now she lifted her face to meet his, touching her stomach as she spoke. 'In here.'

His hand stopped its stroking. 'Ye mean . . .?'

She nodded, anxiously awaiting his approval.

And there it was. His eyes sparkled in the darkened room, outshining the candlelight. The smiling mouth opened to speak but paused, unsure of what to say. What words were adequate at a time like this? He had thought never to encounter such joy again when he had learned of the conception of his firstborn, assuming it to be a once in a lifetime experience, the thrill of finding oneself a parent for the first time. Yet here was that same feeling rising in his breast, the mixture of love and achievement. Tenderly he cupped her small face in his rough hands.

'God, I do love ye, ye red-haired demon.'

The light kisses that he gave her became more insistent and she returned them with equal fervour. Her fingers began to struggle with the buttons on his shirt. The feel of his smooth, warm skin made her shiver in anticipation and a feeling of urgency surged over her as she directed his hand inside her bodice.

'Let's go to bed,' murmured Patrick through the web of her hair, sending ripples of pleasure down her spine.

But she refused, saying, 'No, let's do it in front of the fire tonight. It's a celebration, let's go mad.'

He shrugged off his shirt as Thomasin rapidly undressed and leaned towards him. His belt buckle proved more difficult than the shirt buttons and she had to sit back impatiently while he did it himself. Soon, his hard body made contact with hers. Together they sank to the floor in a clumsy embrace, caressing and kissing as they lay down. The flame of the candle fluttered, casting dancing shadows on the stark walls. Raindrops began to tap at the window, but the sound was lost to them as their bodies united. Faster, faster fell the rain as though attempting to keep pace with their increasing rhythm, rising to a wild reverberation and culminating in a tremendous roar of thunder, drowning the cry that escaped her lips, seconds before his own climax.

The dying fire hissed its annoyance at the drops of water that invaded its territory. Rain cascaded relentlessly outside, but they were oblivious to its presence. Their bodies were still joined in love, his head cushioned on the white breast. She took a deep breath, arching her body and forcing him to support himself on his elbows, looking down at her rosy face. He bent and kissed her nose. Not satisfied, his mouth made frequent contact with her cheeks and lips, as if to devour her. She offered halfhearted objections, feeling him harden and pulsate within her.

'Haven't you had enough?'

'That's rich coming from you.' His laughing reply infected her and she pulled his face down to her breast, making a crescent of her body to join every part of it with his. The dance of passion began again.

So wrapped up were they in each other that the draught from the open door failed to alert them. The little intruder stared, fascinated and unnoticed, watching their bodies seek satisfaction, her eyes becoming even wider as he began his violent thrusting.

Erin observed for a few, quiet seconds, then closed the door gently behind her and went back to bed. The rain that had awoken her had subsided. She wondered what Thomasin had done to so incur her father's wrath. He must have been really angry to punish her so hard. A half-smile of satisfaction crept into her face. Perhaps he did not love Thomasin as much as her after all, because he never punished her like that. Funny though, she thought sleepily as she snuggled up under the blankets, funny that he had to take all his clothes off to do it.

CHAPTER TWENTY-ONE

THE MONTHS CRAWLED, frustrating Thomasin's impatient longing for motherhood. She wondered if her mother would feel any differently towards the child when it was born, for she had shown little interest up till now apart from saying that she would be present to assist at the birth. When Patrick had suggested that Molly act as midwife Mother had gone up in the air. Thomasin often despaired of the relationship between her mother and Patrick. Hannah would not even try to like him, belittling all his efforts to improve life for them. Had she known the source of some of their home comforts there would have been more reproof. By, he was a lad was that John, thought Thomasin, always rolling up with joints of meat, odds and ends for the house. The Lord – or the Devil – knew where they came from. Patrick, poor innocent soul that he was, seemed to attach nothing sinister to these gifts. Well, Thomasin wasn't going to be the one to put him right, although she did sometimes give John a ticking off if the 'gift' he brought was too extravagant. She wished that his powers would extend to magicking this baby into being. Oh, if only this dratted bulge would turn into a child.

Not until Christmas did she begin to visualise an end to her waiting. Why then, she could not say. It was just the way she felt when she awoke that morning. Her eyes opened tentatively, blinking in bewilderment as she studied the window. There were lace curtains where there had been none the night before. It was some seconds before she realised that the delicate filigree of fern and feather was composed not of lace but of frost. Her breath shone white upon the air as she studied the cracked ceiling, gathering up the strength to lift her weighty body from the bed.

Her husband turned to ask if she wanted assistance and when she nodded pathetically he leapt up and grabbed hold of her hands. 'Holy Mother o' God, we'll be wanting a winch if ye get any bigger.'

She gave him a look of pure loathing. 'What's up wi' you any road? Yer normally need gunpowder to shift yer from bed, an' 'ere y'are up at crack o' dawn.'

'Ah well, I have to look after me little wife, have I not – or me big wife, should I say. I can't be havin' ye stuck in bed all day when I'm wantin' me breakfast. Anyways, I couldn't sleep, I kept dreaming this elephant was squashin' the life out o' me.'

'You're lookin' for a clipped ear'ole.'

The cold December air sent a tremor through her naked body as, hastily, she wobbled over the room to get her clothes. Pulling aside a curtain she selected a drab woollen creation that had been altered to fit her increasing girth. Cursing at her ill-fitting underclothes she finally succeeded in pulling them on and over them the drab frock. Fastening her buttons she turned to address her husband who was hastily dragging on his own garments.

'Merry Christmas, Pat.' She moved heavily towards him, delivering a kiss to the bristly cheek.

'A merry Christmas, Tommy.' He returned the kiss. 'Our first together. I'm sorry 'twon't be all that festive.' He reached for his jacket which was slung over the end of the bed and thrust a hand into its pocket, searching for something. His fingers closed around the small package and withdrawing it he held it out to her.

'For me?'

'Don't sound as though ye weren't expecting anything.'

'Aye, you'd've been for it if yer'd bought me nowt.' Her face lit up as she took the gift then, before opening it, ducked behind the curtain once more, emerging with a gift of her own. 'Here y'are, open yours first.'

Patrick tore off the paper and lifted out a pair of grey woollen stockings. 'Elegant stuff, just what I need,' he told her. 'Thank ye kindly. Can I put them on now?'

She nodded and he bent to pull off his old, darned ones,

replacing them with the new while she unwrapped his gift to her. He looked up at her cry of wonder.

'Oh, Pat, it's beautiful.' She took the tiny silver locket from its box, feeling the cold metal on the palm of her hand. The tears sprang to her eyes. 'But yer shouldn't go spendin' all yer money on me. Yer must've saved up ages for that and yer know yer can't really afford it. Why d'yer do it?'

' 'Twouldn't matter if I spent every penny I had,' he replied. 'It still wouldn't be as much as ye deserve, putting up with the likes o' me. Anyway, 'twas worth every penny just to see your face.'

'God, yer've made me feel so guilty now, only givin' yer a pair o' stockings.'

A finger to her lips stopped her self-recriminations. 'They're the best present ye could've given me,' he said softly. 'I never had a pair o' stockings made with so much love – d'ye think I don't know how much ye hate knitting, haven't ye told me often enough? Yet ye spent all that time making these for me.'

She hugged him in gratitude and turned to the door as Erin burst in, face aglow with excitement.

'Look what I do be gettin'!' she bubbled, showing them the apple, orange and small packet of lovehearts that they had placed at the foot of her bed. 'Can I eat them now?'

Patrick laughed and ruffled her already tousled curls. 'Ye'd best ask the gaffer.' He gestured at Thomasin who refused at first, saying they would spoil the girl's breakfast then, seeing the resentment creep into the girl's face, she relented.

'Oh . . . go on then.' She laughed as Erin bit into the orange without taking off the peel. 'Here, let me do it,' but Erin had fled to her own room. Thomasin sighed. Would she ever truly find a place in Erin's heart?

Downstairs, Patrick raked out the ashes, a task usually undertaken by Thomasin who now found the job impossible. He then laid a fire. His wife buttered some bread and took some bacon from the cupboard, throwing it into the pan while she waited for the fire to establish itself. Apart from the gifts it would be hard to distinguish Christmas from any other day of the year. No smell of roast beef – the traditional dinner of the North – would invade their kitchen to set mouths watering. The recent bad weather had called a halt to building work and Patrick had found the effect on his wages had put paid to any lavish festivities. Thomasin's savings had run out long ago and she would not demean Patrick by asking her parents for financial help. But they had each other, and their friends.

Liam called whilst they were breakfasting, presenting Erin with her first rosary and demanding to know what Patrick was doing here eating when he should be saving that till after church. The Irishman was still no closer to the faith, but that did not seem to matter to Liam and he sat there talking with them for quite a while.

Shortly after the priest's departure John called. 'Top o' the mornin', Patrick,' he shouted through the crack of door, giving a poor imitation of an Irish brogue.

'My, we're certainly popular today.' Patrick ushered his pal into the kitchen. 'Come on, come on, let's be keepin' the cold where it belongs.' He eyed the parcel under John's arm. 'What's that ye've got there?'

John placed the object on the table and stood back smugly. Giving the impersonation of a conjurer he went through his paces. Indicating nothing up his sleeves he held his arms wide, telling his audience, 'Observe.' With pronounced movements he took hold of a corner of the newspaper and proceeded to reveal the parcel's contents. Leaving the last layer intact he held them in suspense until, with the flick of a wrist, he whipped it away. 'Da–da!'

'Bugger me with a blunt stick,' murmured Patrick, staring at the table on which lay a chicken, nude and trussed. 'Where in Heaven's name did ye get that?'

'What d'yer mean, where did I get it? It's me Christmas present to you. I saved up all me pennies to buy yer that.'

'Guess who's coming to dine with us – Prince Albert.' Thomasin gave a snort of derision. 'You never 'ave any spare pennies, they're all spent down at The Ham and Firkin.'

John made a pretence of taking the bird away. 'Ungrateful wretch. If yer don't want it . . .'

'I don't remember sayin' that.' Thomasin made a grab for the bird that John held above his head out of her reach. 'Aw, come on, John, let's 'ave it, she begged, dancing round him.

'Not until yer apologise for the insinuation that I pinched it,' he told her sternly. 'The cheek o' the woman,' he said amazedly to Patrick. 'She's callin' me a thief as well as a liar.'

'Aye well, I know you better than most,' said Thomasin, a twinkle of laughter in her grey eye, then, 'Oh, all right I'm sorry – now will yer give it us?'

John lowered his arms and she seized the fowl. 'I still say yer didn't buy it,' she laughed from a safe distance and stuck out her tongue.

John sat down. 'Tsk, I don't know. What sort o' friends 'ave I got that don't believe a word I say? Yer try an' do 'em a favour an' this is how they treat yer.'

'I've said I'm sorry,' replied Thomasin. 'Here, cleanse your tongue.' She handed him a cup of coffee.

John leaned over the table and stared down into the brown liquid, reliving the events that had provided him with the chicken.

He had been strolling along past Raper's shop, minding his own business, when pandemonium erupted. Raper and his brother had received that morning a consignment of chickens and geese to slaughter for Christmas fayre. Assisted by Jos Leach, they unloaded the crates of fowl from the cart and began to transfer them to the abattoir in Britannia Yard. Unfortunately – or fortunately, depending upon one's viewpoint – the witless Leach knocked one of the crates to the floor. The sound of splintering wood reached Raper's ears and he lumbered out into the street to investigate.

'Jesus Christ!' he roared. 'Yer fuckin' great useless pillockin' idiot.'

Leach threw himself at the escaping hens as the captive geese honked their appreciation, hoping he would let them out, too.

'George!' bellowed Raper. 'George, come an' give us a hand!' Even as he yelled he knew that it was hopeless; brother George was as deaf as a post and was busy in the slaughter-house.

A brown hen cocked its head and studied the stealthily approaching figure with a beady eye. Raper lunged at the bird which flew six feet into the air, a strangled squawk amid a flurry of feathers. The butcher hurled another string of abuse at the apprentice's feeble attempts to recapture the birds.

Meanwhile, John looked on in alert amusement, awaiting an opening. Suddenly it came in the form of an urchin who had somehow managed to stalk and capture two chickens and now raced off with a bird under each arm.

'Stop, thief!' cried Raper, trying to lift his portly body from the road, where he had fallen in another vain attempt at capture.

'I'll catch him, Mr Raper,' shouted John and gave chase, swiftly following the boy along Walmgate and into Paver Lane.

'Follow him, Jos,' ordered Raper, finally managing to stand upright. 'I don't trust that bugger.'

Leach turned a vacant stare at the butcher and indicated the birds. Raper clapped a hand to his forehead and looked at the sky. 'What 'ave I done to deserve 'im?' he asked, almost in tears. 'All right, yer stupid get, go-get-my-brother.' He mouthed the words exaggeratedly. 'Happen he'll be able to catch these little swines.' He sat down at the roadside and glared at the escapees who now roosted in various buildings along the street.

The urchin used numerous tactics to evade capture, all to no end. Unable to gather sufficient speed with the chickens under his arms he soon felt John's hot breath down his collar.

'Come 'ere, yer thievin' little devil.' John made a grab for the boy as he darted between some tinker caravans. He caught him, puffing triumphantly as he swung the culprit around to face him. 'Nah then, if yer gimme them chickens back, mebbe I'll think twice about callin' t'Law.'

The boy was unimpressed by this show of generosity and shot the man a look of defiance. 'I know your game, ye'll not take 'em back to that fella, ye'll eat 'em yerself!'

John tried the gentle approach. 'Look, son,' he put his hands on the boy's shoulders and looked him in the eyes. 'I'll overlook that remark, seein' as 'ow yer only a lad an' don't realise the seriousness of yer offence. Yer could be transported for this yer know.' A faraway look came into his eye. 'Just think, yer might never see yer mam an' dad again.'

The boy stuck out his jaw. 'D'ye think I'm bothered about that?'

This called for sterner measures and John sneaked a look down the lane, anxious that Raper should not arrive yet. He grabbed a fistful of the boy's ragged shirt and hauled him close to his face. 'Now look, yer little shit if yer don't gimme them birds I'll 'ave to alter yer appearance somewhat.'

The menace in his voice finally sapped the boy's courage and he thrust the hens at John who grasped them firmly by the legs and swung them upside down. The helpless creatures hung in silent mesmerisation, dizzy from the sudden rush of blood to their heads.

'There's a good lad, didn't hurt too much, did it?' John grinned and retreated.

'Bastard!' shrieked the urchin, dancing around like a demented frog. 'I do be tellin' me daddy, he'll be using your guts for bootlaces.' He ran off to complain to his father as John strode briskly away, the wings of his captives flapping uselessly against his legs.

Ducking through a snicket to avoid Raper he made his way home. Making sure that he was unobserved he swiftly despatched the hens and flung them onto the kitchen table, startling his wife and sending up a cloud of flour. Then she picked them up and tossed them aside as though he brought home chickens every day of the week; nothing he did could surprise her after ten years of marriage.

Returning by the route along which he had come, John strolled back into Walmgate. By this time Raper and his brother had succeeded in recapturing the birds and were dealing with the rest of the crates. Leach watched them unconcerned that they no longer trusted him to assist. Idly raking a finger around his wide nostril he wiped the outcome onto his jacket.

'Ah, Jos.' John strode up, hands in pockets. 'Can yer give Mr Raper a message, if it's not too much to ask?' The question was met by a gormless nod.

'What message would that be?' The butcher appeared from the alleyway.

'Oh, Mr Raper.' John threw up his hands in mock despair. 'That lad gave me the slip. I searched all down Paver Lane but I reckon he must've slipped into one o' them tinkers' caravans. Thievin' devils them tinkers, yer know. Sorry I couldn't help.' He touched his cap and departed.

Raper frowned and snorted, then delivered a hefty slap to Leach's head.

'I'm not payin' you to sit on yer arse all day, go get some bloody work done!'

John returned to the present as Thomasin tapped his shoulder. 'Are yer gonna sit there watchin' that coffee all day? I've got work to do yer know.'

He grinned. 'Right, I'll be off. Will I see yer tonight for a jar?' This to Patrick who looked at his wife.

'Oh, go on,' she told him. 'Seein' as how it's Christmas an' I'm feelin' charitable – but don't you be keepin' him out all night, Thomo.'

Patrick let his friend out. 'Where shall we meet?'

'The Bay Horse first,' John shouted from across the yard. 'Tara.'

'You're sure ye'll be all right on your own?' asked Patrick, kissing the back of her head. 'I'll only have the one or two.'

'Or three, or ten,' she scoffed, then, 'If I said I wouldn't be all right would that make any difference?' She removed his hands from her waist in order to prepare the vegetables for dinner. 'Aye, I'll be reet – as long as it is only one or two. I get a bit worried if yer late.'

Small flakes drifted gracefully to earth as Patrick shouted his goodbyes and closed the door. Earlier he had fulfilled the promise he had made to Father Kelly to take Erin to Mass, now he was going to keep his other appointment. By the time he had crossed the yard the snow was beginning to lay, clothing the grime with a virginal freshness. He entered The Bay Horse, shaking the glistening snow from his hair and looking round for his friend.

'Over 'ere, Pat!' shouted John, and Patrick passed between the drinkers to join him.

Ale flowing freely, the pall of smoke that was suspended above their heads in a grey blanket, the buzz of festive spirit, all subscribed to the steady intoxication of John and Patrick. Two drinks became three, three became five, until their empty glasses on the bar merged with those of the other drinkers and became innumerable.

'Shall we have a change o' scenery an' visit The Mass Glakers' Arms?' slurred Patrick, wondering why John cackled drunkenly at his words.

They lurched from the bar, steered an unsteady course

to the door and went outside. It had stopped snowing. In Walmgate the gaslight caught the silvery whiteness to set it sparkling with diamonds. The men pulled up their collars against the cold that sliced through their thin clothes and made their winding way to The Glassmakers Arms. Difficult though it was to gain entry to the busy inn, what with drunken revellers blocking the doorway, Pat and John elbowed their way to the bar.

In all innocence they had entered a lions' den. As they leaned against the bar, raising their glasses yet again, they were closely observed by a keen pair of eyes. Hugh Fallon knew instantly that one of these men was the one he had seen fleeing with the chickens as his son had dragged him from the caravan. Unable to catch up with his son's tormentor the Irish tinker had bided his time. The world in which they lived was small and there was a more than even chance that their paths would cross at some point. That point was here. He raised his glass, eyes never leaving the laughing face at the bar and watched, waited.

Patrick was refusing John's entreaties to have another drink. 'John, I loves ye like me own sweet darlin', but I's already had three more than I should've – or was it four?' He banged the glass down on the counter. 'Me dear little wife'll be thinkin' I've left her. She'll be sat there with murder in her heart an' a shillelagh in her gentle hand, ready to give me six heads.' He wavered unsteadily then, placing one foot in front of the other in drunken deliberation, he made for the door. John unwillingly gazed at his empty tankard, then followed his friend, swaying and weaving through the crush.

The sharp eyes noted their departure. As the door swung shut behind them Fallon lifted his glass, draining it in one gulp. He tapped his drinking companion on the forearm and inclined his head towards the door. In their purposeful stroll to the exit the two men halted at a group of drinkers and indulged in brief conversation. Then, accompanied by four more men, they slipped out into the night.

'Me an' Fin'll go this way.' Fallon indicated Fishergate Bar, his voice cutting the darkness with its harsh, grating quality. 'Two o' yese can circle round by Long Close Lane, the others can take Lead Mill Lane. We'll cut off their escape.'

They went their separate ways. Fallon and Maguire moved

through the ancient stone arch, their senses honed despite the drink in them. Fallon lifted his head. The breeze had carried sounds of inebriated singing to his alert ears. The hunters exchanged satisfied glances and followed the sound to Margaret Street where two men swayed and reeled from one side of the road to the other. Their loud chanting echoed between the rows of neat houses, bringing an angry complaint from one irate resident.

Maguire and Fallon pressed their bodies close to the cold brickwork while the man leaned out of the window and hurled abuse at John and Patrick. Then the window slammed shut, allowing the hunters to resume their stealthy pursuit.

Blithely unaware of the impending danger John and Patrick danced on. 'Merry Christmas!' shouted the former at two men who loomed up before him. The greeting was met by an unfriendly silence. The friends tried to focus on the blurred images that blocked their path, sensing that something was not quite right.

'An' did ye think ye'd get away wid it, Englishman?' The rasping voice made them rotate slowly to find two more men behind them.

'I don't take, pal.' John stared in puzzlement at the big man who had spoken.

'What the divil is this about?' asked Patrick.

Fallon picked up the lilt in his voice. ' 'Tis no argument I'll be wantin' wid another Irishman, there's just the business o' two chickens to be sorted out wid dis English fella here.'

The pieces of the puzzle came together and the awful truth dawned. John felt the adrenalin stir up inside him and an abrupt state of sobriety ensued. 'Ah . . . it were your lad, I suppose?' he ventured weakly.

'It was. An' ye see, Hugh Fallon is not a man to stand by an' see his son manhandled.'

'I'm sure we can come to some arrangement, Mr Fallon.' John stared at the large men who surrounded him.

'Oh, I'm sure we can,' Fallon agreed. 'If ye'll just be lettin' me have me property back I might even consider lettin' yese go.'

Patrick, though still befuddled with drink, began to grasp the situation.

'Would it be the chicken I had for me dinner he's talkin' about?'

John nudged him. 'Ssh! Don't get him any madder, yer silly bugger, 'ave yer seen size of him?'

'Sure I knew! I bloody-well knew ye hadn't bought it. 'Tis a hidin' ye'll get off Tommy when she sees ye.'

Fallon intercepted. 'An 'tis a hidin' he'll be gettin' off us if I don't get me birds back soon.'

'I'd give 'em to yer if I could,' pleaded John. 'But we've eaten 'em.'

'Sure, there's nothing left to discuss then, is there?' Fallon looked at his comrades.

'Four against one, that's not very fair, is it?' asked John.

'Your friend looks like he can handle himself,' was Fallon's reply.

'Now wait a minute.' Patrick presented his palms. ' 'Twas none o' my doin'.'

'Pat, yer me mate, yer not gonna let 'em gimme a bazzackin', are yer?'

'Sure, I'll give ye one meself when I get ye home,' replied Patrick strongly, and at the same time jerked his elbow back to catch one of the tinkers in the stomach. Grabbing his friend from under the nose of the surprised Fallon he raced off towards a nearby alley.

John laughed in nervous relief as he was dragged behind Patrick. 'By God, that were bloody close.'

'Shut up an' keep runnin',' gasped Patrick, stumbling into the alley. 'If we stick to these passages we'll lose them.'

But the tinkers knew these passages too. At the other end of the alley stood another two shadowy figures. The runners' boots skidded on the stone floor as they tried to retrace their steps . . . but there would be no escape. There stood Fallon and his cronies, blocking the exit.

John swore under his breath and watched the men's swaggering approach, twisted smiles of arrogance on their swarthy faces. The look that Patrick threw him needed no words of interpretation, he understood the Irishman's anger.

'Christ, I'm sorry to get yer mixed up in this, Pat,' he said, waiting for the first blow to fall.

' 'Tis a bit bloody late for that,' answered the other. 'Right now I'm concerned with gettin' out o' here in one piece. I think we should try an' charge them. When I shout the watchword get your thick skull down and point it at them – 'tis the only thing dense enough to make an impression.' He filled his lungs with deep, calming breaths then, as the tinkers drew closer, he gave his signal and both men charged headlong towards the end of the alley, crashing into the oncoming tinkers in their flight.

It was a splendid effort but totally ineffective against six ruffians. They fell to the floor, enveloped by musty, tinker flesh. Patrick writhed in agony as a vicious knee sank into his groin. A curious buzzing sound filled his ears, bringing the bitter taste of beer to his throat. Kicks and blows rained down upon the fallen men, forcing from them weird animal noises of pain. Rolling up like hedgehogs they tried to protect vital organs but to little effect. Another excruciating pain seared through Patrick's body, dealt by a rock-hard boot that crashed into his ribs. Then mercifully he felt himself float lightly away from the pain as a black miasma of unconsciousness descended.

John was not so fortunate.

It had begun to snow again. Soft white feathers drifted to earth, dissolving when they made contact with the warm hand that protruded from the alley. The steady trickle of melted snow on his fingers reached the sensory cells of Patrick's brain and a groan slipped wearily from his lips. An attempt to force his eyes open was met by abrupt and agonising pain. Its source was indiscernible, seeming to occupy every nerve in his body. The effort of trying to raise his head made him cry out and he lay still for a moment, turning his head to watch the white, hypnotic descent. Gathering what little energy he had left he raised his punished body onto his elbows. His head felt as though it was inhabited by a hundred sledgehammers that pounded his brain every time he moved it.

No longer was it night; the grey sky of morning hung oppressively over him. With great caution he tested his aching limbs. Remarkably they appeared to be in working order, albeit somewhat unsteady. A sharp, violent thrust as he tried to straighten bore evidence of more than one broken rib, bringing tears to his eyes. When his vision cleared the sight of so much blood set his belly a-shake. It was everywhere: the walls, the floor, some had even sprayed out of the alley, still faintly visible under the new layer of snow, staining the whiteness in scarlet assault – but the majority of the dark, congealing liquid formed an ominous pool around the head of his friend.

Unnecessary though it was to make a closer inspection to derive the fact that John was seriously hurt – if not dead, Patrick rolled onto his knees beside the man. No sound passed the blue swollen lips. His breathing was barely discernible as Patrick touched his chest. Only by putting his cheek close to John's slightly open mouth did he feel the barest whisper.

Horror and revulsion brought the bile to his throat as he moved John's head a fraction. The side of his face that had previously been concealed was a grotesque parody of its former self. Glistening splinters of bone jutted from the broken face, laid bare by the cleaved flesh. Even more appalling was the eye that dangled against the broken cheek like a cherry swinging daintily from its stem.

Patrick lurched away and threw up. Steaming, beer-scented vomit shot from his retching throat and he shuddered violently. Conflicting emotions raged inside him as the events of the previous evening returned with painful vengeance. He had felt angry and let down by his friend for involving him in all this, but now the anger was directed solely at the tinker, Fallon. It was understandable that the man had wanted revenge, but did he have to reduce a man to this, for two chickens? Trying to decide what course to take, Patrick wavered for a moment, then stumbled out of the alleyway towards the nearest house. His feet were encased in mortared boots, his body and mind numb. All he wanted was to be home, anywhere but here where he would have to gaze upon that terrible sight. His relentless pounding brought a bleary face to the bedroom window. A woman lifted the sash window and leaned over the sill.

'What time of morning is this to come banging on my . . .' The question remained unanswered. The man below had collapsed in an untidy heap on her doorstep.

CHAPTER TWENTY-TWO

THE DYING COALS noisily shifted their position, bringing
Thomasin awake with a start. She blinked rapidly, attempting to shake the sleep from her head. Over on the table the
glob of wax that had been a candle suddenly reached its end
and snuffed itself out, filling the room with an unmis-
takable odour. The chair in which she had spent the night
now held her like a vice, refusing to abandon its hold as she
heaved her burdened body up. It had not been much of a rest
either; this nagging backache had kept her awake half the
night.

She raised a hand as the realisation dawned. It was morning
and still Patrick was not home. Had he, seeing her sleeping
and unwilling to disturb her, crept past and up the stairs? She
moved as quickly as her bulk allowed up the tread and
opened the bedroom door. The bed was unoccupied, its fine
counterpane – a wedding gift from one of her sisters – still
lay as smooth and unruffled as it had yesterday. Before she
descended she peeped in on Erin who was sleeping soundly.
It must be very early, she thought, for there was no sound
from their neighbours or from outside. How maddening not
to possess a single timepiece – though the time was hardly
relevant; that it was morning and Patrick had not returned
was cause enough for alarm. She rubbed her aching back,
then listened, suddenly alert. Someone was lifting the sneck
on the outside door. The absence of a balustrade necessitated
resting her hands on the cool wall to steady herself as she
negotiated the stairs. The figure had his back to her, attempting to close the door quietly. She reached the last stair as he
turned into the room.

'Oh, my God!' her cry startled him, revealing more of his injured face.

Gone were the merry, twinkling eyes, hidden somewhere amongst black and swollen flesh. He tried to form a smile but the attempt made the cut on his mouth crack open and a thread of scarlet ran down his chin. Someone had tended his wounds, washing away most of the dirt from his sore face, but still the effect was painful to behold and the tears sprang readily to her eyes. Running to him she threw her arms round his waist, bringing forth a harsh complaint.

'Oh, I'm sorry! I'm sorry, love.' She released him quickly.

' 'Tis all right,' he forgave her as she fussed about him and helped him to a chair. 'Ye weren't to know.'

'What happened, for God's sake?' Her worried face searched his.

Patrick related the facts as he remembered them while Thomasin dabbed tenderly at his bloody mouth. 'I might've known!' she expostulated angrily. 'Where is the little swine? Let me get me hands on him, I'll give him what-for, gettin' you mixed up in his dirty dealin's.' She rubbed her back again.

'Oh no, Tommy,' he replied bitterly. 'Ye'd not say that if ye could see what the bastards did to him. Oh, the doctors say he'll survive, but I'm doubting he'll be the same man again.'

'Doctors? He's in hospital then?'

'Aye.' Patrick's eyes were bright with suppressed rage. 'I don't know how he got there though. I remember knocking on somebody's door for help an' then I musta fainted, 'cause when I woke up I was at the hospital an' all, getting these ribs strapped up.'

Thomasin asked about John's injuries and he told her, sparing her none of the grisly details.

His wife was contrite for her hasty condemnation of John. 'Oh, the poor little bugger.' She laid a hand on his arm. 'Eh, does his family know?'

Patrick moved his head in affirmation. When he had been sent home from hospital his first action had been to call at John's home, every step of the way trying to think of a way to phrase the bad news. How could you tell a woman that, apart from losing half of his face, her man might never work again? As it transpired, he did not have to. The police had been there before him having been called to the scene of the fight by the woman on whose door Patrick had chosen to knock for help. They had also wanted to know a few facts about the attack from Patrick, who told them he could not remember anything, for that would mean having to explain about the stolen chickens. Besides, a district such as this had its own law. He would settle the score himself.

John's wife had been beside herself with grief, though surprisingly her concern was more for the loss of John's wages than for the man himself.

'I'll help ye all I can,' Patrick had told her, though not a little upset by her apparent lack of concern for her husband's state of health.

The look which she had shot him had been a mixture of disbelief and contempt. 'Yer'll not be in a position to 'elp anybody,' she flung bitterly. Then taking some of the harshness out of her words had added, 'But I thank yer for yer concern. Good day.' She had then turned her back, a gesture of dismissal, and Patrick had let himself out.

Her words had nagged at him on his way home. She was right, how could he hope to help her? Lifting a pick was going to be well nigh impossible for some time. Damn and blast! Fate had dealt another of her cruel blows.

Thomasin's sudden cry of pain and surprise brought him out of his bitter wanderings. His wife stood clutching her belly, eyes wide open in shock. Leaping up he stifled his own yelp of anguish and went to her side.

'Is it the baby?'

'I don't know . . . oh, God it must be.' Erin, awoken by the noise, came to investigate.

'Erin, get dressed an' go fetch Aunt Molly,' commanded Patrick abruptly.

'What if she's in bed?' asked the child fearfully.

'Drag her out of it – now go!' The frightened girl dashed upstairs, dressed quickly and ran from the house.

'Surely it can't be the baby, 'tis too early.' Patrick held his wife, feeling useless.

A sudden gush of hot fluid burst from her, soaking her dress. 'Early or not it's on its bloody way,' she gasped, realising now what the backache had been trying to tell her.

She tried to remember how long she had had the ache but failed.

Patrick helped her up the stairs, the pain jarring his side with each step. He tried to make her laugh. 'God, we're like a couple o' bloody cripples.'

She stopped him as he was about to lay her on the bed. 'Take all these good sheets off, yer'll find an' old one in cupboard.' She arched her back again as he rushed downstairs. 'Ee, God, I didn't reckon on this.'

With the moment of solitude returned the nagging doubt of who had fathered the child, but as the crippling discomfort returned all she wanted was for it to be over, whoever's it was. 'Pat, for God's sake hurry!'

Patrick clattered up the stairs with the sheet which had been turned and restitched many times. Through her pain she noticed his sore, grazed knuckles as his hands clumsily gathered up the best sheets, replaced them with the old, then began to fumble with her dress. With difficulty he finally managed to strip off her wet garments and gently helped her onto the bed where she groaned and turned her head into the pillow, digging her teeth into fusty material. 'Oh, God, why did I ever get meself into this?'

A noisy chattering told of Molly's arrival and heavy footfalls brought her up into the bedroom. She took one look at the haggard face and rolled up her sleeves. 'My, ye're well on the way.' Turning to Patrick she said: ' 'Tis bad to be so quick for the first. I'll go get a little something to help her. You go boil some water – an' what the divil have ye been up to? Ye look as if ye've been in a shindy with ten navvies.'

'Something like that, ye could say.' Patrick rushed off to boil a kettle, followed by Molly.

'Don't leave me!' Thomasin raised her frightened face from the bed.

'Just goin' to wash me hands, Tommy, don't fret,' called Molly.

'I'll bet that's the first time that's ever been known,' muttered Thomasin. 'God, me mother'll go mad when she knows she missed it. Oooh!'

Molly returned to administer a potion that was supposed to make the woman feel better but didn't. In a way it made things worse as it took effect. She no longer seemed to inhabit her own body. It was as if she were a spectator, suspended above the heaving creature on the bed, watching and listening as the curses ripped from the grimacing lips, unable to stop them, not even caring to. Quick, had Molly said? It lasted for centuries.

'Jesus Christ!' she screamed, her tortured body thrashing wildly.

'Sure, He'll not be helpin' ye, love,' Molly shouted merrily. 'He's a fella like all the rest. Come on now, let's be after takin' a look at ye. Ah well, I know 'tis bad but it'll be over soon. Put your hands on your belly an' feel that – tight as a drum.'

'I don't 'ave to put me hands there I can already feel it!' shouted Thomasin. 'Aw, Molly, 'elp me, anybody 'elp me.'

'I'm helpin' ye all I can,' replied Molly. 'But 'tis only you can do it. Come on now, there's work to be done.'   .

'Oh, bugger off yer silly old cow,' screeched Thomasin ungratefully.

'Ye can call the Pope a randy dog if it'll help ye,' said Molly, unconcerned at the abuse. ' 'Tis a good job I left Erin at my place what with all the fuss you're creatin'.'

Thomasin was about to swear again when something like a belch caught her breath. The pain had altered, instead of ripping her apart it now felt that the very kernel of her being was trying to force its way out of the pain-racked shell.

'Oh, good,' said Molly at the obvious change. 'Ye can start pushin'.'

If Thomasin had thought this indicated an end to her suffering then she was wrong. How long she arched and writhed on the sweat-soaked bed she could not gauge. It just seemed to go on and on and on. All she wanted to do was sleep but the child who struggled for life would give her no peace. The hours seemed to bring no release, just an overwhelming monotony of pushing and straining. Somewhere, through the endless labyrinth of suffering, she heard Molly's voice urging her to make one more push. She wanted to tell her to go away, leave her alone, but instead of these words came a sharp squeal as the head of the child burst its way from her.

Patrick hung in the doorway. Unable to stay downstairs listening to his wife's torment any longer he had crept up, disobeying Molly's orders. Rapt fascination overtook him as he watched the tiny blue face squeeze itself free of the birth canal amid a fluid gurgling and snuffling. Molly manoeuvred its shoulder under the pubic bone, letting the rest of its body follow in a slithery, bloody rush.

Blue became angry lobster-red as the child drew his first breath and let out a squawk, making his mother peer anxiously between her thighs to ask: 'Is it all right?'

'Aye, 'tis a peacock of a boy ye have,' said Molly, cutting the cord and tying it off with great dexterity, advertising the fact that she had done this many times before. 'Which is more than can be said for him.' She gave Patrick a withering glance over her shoulder. 'Could ye not keep your nose out, eh? Well, now ye know what we women go through to pay for your pleasure. While you're here ye can make yourself useful; hand me that blanket.'

Patrick, still dazed by what he had witnessed, handed her the blanket which she wrapped around the baby.

'Here, hold this.' Without warning she thrust the bundle into his arms, telling Thomasin to have patience while she cleaned the mess up, then she would be able to hold the child.

Curbing the rush of apprehension that he had experienced when Molly had burdened him, he gazed down in wonderment at his son, hardly feeling the hot tears that coursed down his cheeks to sting his open wounds. Gently he opened the blanket and began to examine the tiny fingers and toes, then laughed as a tiny fountain spurted over his hand. He was wonderful, wonderful!

'Oh, peacock did I say – didn't I ask for it?' Molly, finishing with Thomasin went for another blanket. After changing the wrapping she transferred the child to Thomasin's arms. 'There y'are, what d'ye think to him? Is he not the image of his father?'

Thomasin was suddenly afraid to look. What if it were Roland who stared back at her? What if he did not look like either man, then how would she tell? It had to be faced. She turned her eyes slowly down to discover the truth . . . and a smile of relief and love flooded her tired face.

They named him Richard William; the first for Patrick's dead father, the second after hers. Despite his premature entrance, the baby was extremely lively, if somewhat small, holding onto life with a tenacity that amazed his parents as even full-term babies were lucky to survive such an environment.

'Look at the little guzzler,' laughed Thomasin as Richard, feeling the breast against his cheek, opened his mouth and searched for the nipple. Adoration gleamed in Patrick's eyes as he watched. No artist could capture such a vision on canvas as was before him now. The serene, beautiful mother looked down at the suckling infant, whose greedy pulling brought a sympathetic flow of milk from the other breast. Thomasin picked a strand of her hair from Richard's face and threw it back over her shoulder in a russet flourish, then smiled up at her husband.

'What're you thinking?' she asked, quietly happy.

Patrick came out of his trance and returned her smile. 'I'm thinking how beautiful y'are,' he answered softly. 'An' how lucky I am to be part of this. Sure, I could sit here all day an' watch the pair o' ye.'

For Patrick, Richard's arrival could not have been more timely; it helped to heal a little of the pain and gave him more to think about than his friend's tragedy. Though not all aspects of the situation were so enjoyable. His mother-in-law's presence in the house had interfered with his involvement with the newborn child.

'Oh, he's just like his mother,' she had exclaimed when she and William had first set eyes on their grandson. 'Look, William, is he not like Thomasin?'

'Eh, be right, Mother,' Thomasin had objected, pulling a brush through her tangled hair. 'He's nowt like me, he's image of his father.'

'Oh no, dear,' Hannah had insisted firmly. 'He's just like you were when you were a baby – apart from the hair of course. I suppose that could come from your husband.'

'Well, I think he's like Pat.' Thomasin had remained loyal. 'What d'you think, Dad?'

William had been unhelpful. 'Nay, they all look same to me – little goblins. I like 'em best when they're bigger an' yer can play games wi' 'em.'

Hannah had seen that she was to get no support from this quarter and shortly after this had sent William packing with instructions to return for her in the evening. 'It will be more convenient if I return to my own home at the end of the day instead of sleeping here,' she had told her daughter. 'After all I do not wish to impose.'

Thomasin had offered thanks for her mother's concern, guessing that the real motive for not wanting to sleep here was not out of consideration but because she feared an attack by bed bugs.

Now, Hannah's voice made Patrick spring up from his comfortable position. 'God save us she's here again!' He lifted the sleeping baby from his wife's arms and placed him gently into the box that had to serve as Richard's bed. 'I'd best be off to work before I get a tongue-lashing.'

Thomasin laughed. 'I do believe yer afraid of her.'

'I am.' Patrick leant over the bed to kiss her goodbye as Hannah came into the bedroom.

'You'll be late for work, Mr Feeney,' she warned sternly, her hands clasped in front of her, ready once more to take charge.

'Mother,' sighed Thomasin, 'don't yer think yer could at least try an' call Pat by his first name? Yer can't go on callin' him Mr Feeney for the rest o' yer life.'

Hannah bowed her head. 'Very well, dear, as you like. Before you go . . . Patrick,' the name tasted like vile medicine '. . . I should be obliged if you would put some coal on that fire. My grandson is in danger of being frozen to death.'

Patrick set his mouth and picked up the poker with which he could have quite happily taken Hannah's neck measurement. He rammed it forcefully into the fire, stirring up red sparks and swearing silently to himself, then placed half a dozen pieces of coal onto the flames.

'Thanks, love,' said Thomasin. 'Don't work too hard.'

'I doubt there's little danger of that,' muttered Hannah as Patrick left, then went to the crib to check on the baby.

Erin too was checking on him, though not for the same reasons as Hannah. It was her greatest hope that one day when she looked into the crib she would find it empty, that the tinkers had stolen this horrible red-faced creature who had replaced Erin in her father's affections. As if he had perceived her resentment the baby opened his mouth and let out a yell, making her step back in alarm lest she be accused of hurting him. The possibility had not eluded Hannah who now pushed Erin aside and lifted the baby from his bed, examining him for scratches.

'This child is wet,' she proclaimed and began to strip off the damp clothes, cooing and fussing over her grandson in a manner which completely sickened Erin. That was the reason they lavished so much attention on him, thought the child sullenly as the baby kicked his naked legs in the air, that . . . that thing there. How she would love to take a pair of scissors and cut it off, the thing that made him a boy and her, with the lack of it, only a girl. It was not fair. Nobody took any notice of her now that he had come – and what was so clever about being a boy anyway, she wanted to know?

She listened to Thomasin and Hannah discussing the child's attributes and felt desperately lonely – I shall go to Granny's, she decided suddenly. She still loves me. An announcement: 'I'm off to Granny's.'

Thomasin was tickling the baby's toes and looked up absently. 'All right, love.' Then her attention returned to her son.

She doesn't even notice I'm gone, thought Erin, stamping down the stairs. It was all that baby's fault. Well, shit. She liked the sound of the word and experimented with it, beating time on the tread: shit, shit, shit. She wasn't bothered about them either, she would run away, then see how they liked that. Lugging the harp which was almost as tall as herself from its place in the corner, she stormed out to Bridie's. Granny would give her a home.

Granny didn't go so far as to give her a home but she did succeed in making things a little better, telling Erin she must pretend to love her new brother, then everyone would say what a good girl she was and pretty soon it would cease being a pretence and become reality.

After spending an hour with the old woman and secure in the knowledge that not everyone in the world was against her, Erin left in search of younger company. Outside a watery sun made a weak attempt to melt the snow in the yard. As with most children the cold did not seem to bother Erin, which was fortunate for the thin dress she wore ill-afforded a sensitive body. Two of the Flaherty girls answered her knock and they stood in the doorway chatting loquaciously until their conversation was interrupted by an insolent-looking boy of about ten years old.

'What d'they call you then?' His question was directed at Erin, who turned her big blue eyes to the scabby face and gave her attractive smile.

'Erin Feeney.'

'Huh, another Irish, eh?' The mean little face sneered, curbing Erin's smile. She looked to Norah for support as the boy, without provocation, nipped her cruelly on the arm. 'As if we 'aven't got enough wi' all this lot.' He gestured at Norah and Peggy. 'Me Dad says we oughta send y'all back where yer belong.'

'Ye can shut your mouth, Ned Raper,' commanded Norah. 'An' leave her alone. We've as much right to be here as yourself – you don't even live in this yard.'

'Me uncle owns all this,' boasted Ned, sweeping his arm wide. 'I can throw y'out whenever I want – in fact I think I'll throw this mucky pig out now.' He made a grab for Erin who dodged behind Norah.

'Mucky, is it?' shouted Norah. 'At least she doesn't stink like a landlord's boot.' She gave a 'that'll show him' nod to Erin who laughed gleefully at the boy's morose face and decided to chance a rejoinder of her own.

'Stinky Raper! Stinky Raper!'

Ned was not brave enough to take on Norah – she was a good head and shoulders above him, even if she was a girl – and had to content himself by snarling at Erin, 'Just you wait, Feeney. Yer brave now but wait till I get yer on yer own.' He lashed out with his boot at a stone, kicking it at her legs with painful accuracy, then moved off towards his uncle's abattoir.

Erin could not understand why the boy should want to be so unfriendly.

'Take no notice, he's just like the rest o' them Rapers,' said Norah knowledgeably. 'A nasty piece o' work.' She opened the door to admit Erin who was examining her leg. 'Come on, let's go play mothers an' fathers.'

The door closed behind them, watched by a weasel-like face through a crack in the abattoir door – I'll get that clever bitch, Ned Raper promised himself.

CHAPTER TWENTY-THREE

THAT FIRST VISIT to the hospital had been dreadful. Patrick had toured the rows of beds in search of his friend. Twice he had gone back along the ward to see if he had somehow bypassed John, and in doing so had found him. Out of a bandage-swathed face the solitary eye observed him. A weak hand raised in recognition. 'I shouted yer once.'

'Sorry, I didn't hear ye.' Patrick moved briskly to John's bedside, trying not to betray the pity he felt. 'Now y'old bugger what're ye doing lyin' here? Sure, I thought ye'd be running a book on which patient snuffed it first.'

John closed his eye and swallowed. 'I doubt I'd be around to collect with my odds.' A groan.

'Don't think ye have to make conversation if 'tis painful.' Patrick gripped his hand. 'Sure, I'll just sit here an' look pretty.'

'I'd be lying if I said it wasn't,' answered the other with difficulty. 'It hurts like hell.'

'Is there anything ye're wanting?'

'Aye, there is . . . but you can't do it for me.' Tears of fury welled up in the eye. 'It'll have to wait till I'm out of 'ere. Christ, I'll 'ave that bastard, Pat, for what 'e's done to me. No matter 'ow long I 'ave to wait I swear . . .'

'Leave it, John.' The man's head had elevated from the pillow in his determination. Patrick now pushed him back. ' 'Tis mad he is. He'll likely kill ye next time.'

'He had a bloody good try last time an' all, but I'll 'ave him, you see.'

Patrick attempted to divert John's mind from the tinker, speaking of his new son and what was going on at work, but though John made the appearance of listening, the seed of revenge was taking root and spreading like an all-consuming cancer, the only reason for his being.

'Am I boring ye?' asked Patrick suddenly.

'No . . . no – I allus have this hole through me skull.' John attempted a grin. 'Ah well, I am a bit tired, kidder if yer don't mind.' Even as he spoke he knew it to be untrue; sleep would remain elusive until the plan of retaliation formed itself.

'I'll go then,' said his friend lamely.

'Aye – an' don't come empty-handed next time, tight bugger. I don't know, all that stuff I provide for him an' he never brings so much as an orange.'

'I'll bring ye a bagful, so I will,' promised the Irishman.

'Aye, an' I bet you'll've sucked the buggers first.'

'Erin, put that bairn in his crib an' come get yer tea,' called Thomasin from the kitchen. 'Never mind if he cries, he's gettin' too big for his boots, thinks everybody should be at his beck an' call.' It was no longer surprising to see Erin tending her brother; she seemed to have taken to him now. Probably just Mother's presence that had retarded the relationship, thought Thomasin, for as soon as Hannah had gone Erin seemed to experience a change of heart. Didn't Mother have that effect on everyone?

Erin ignored the screams of rage that rose from the box and arrived in the kitchen at the same time as her father.

'Hello, me darlings, who's for a beatin' first.' He ruffled her hair and flung his sack in a corner.

'Snowed off again?' asked his wife.

'We are, we are, an' I can't say I give a tinker's cuss.' The word brought a vision of Fallon. ' 'Tis nithered to the bone I am. Anyway, while I get the chance I thought I'd go see John.'

'Can I go with ye, Daddy?' asked Erin.

'Best not,' he replied kindly. ' 'Tis a long trail through the snow. Besides, the hospital's not a very pretty sight for young eyes. Ye'll see Uncle John soon enough.'

How glad he was later that he had taken this decision, for though John was vastly improved the face, divest of its bandages, was obscene and would likely have scared the child to death. The right cheek was seared by a long, raw-looking scar which transformed his whole visage, continuing over his lips and twisting the mouth down into an ugly grimace. The normally wide gap in his teeth had been expanded even further where the tinker's boot had smashed out three teeth. Mercifully for any onlooker his worst injury had been concealed behind a black eyepatch, which he occasionally touched as they spoke as if hoping that his eye had somehow reappeared.

Patrick arrived on the ward to find John learning to walk again with the aid of crutches. The leg, badly broken, had been the doctors' main concern and they had been greatly pleased when their fears had not been realised and John had felt the life return to it. Only he knew that it was the thoughts that raged within him, the single-minded yearning for reprisal, that had been channelled into healing the limb. He led Patrick over to his bed, stumbling awkwardly with the unaccustomed crutches. The Irishman put out a helping hand which was brushed away.

'I'm not a bloody cripple,' snapped John, then added ruefully, 'Sorry, Pat, it's meself I'm trying to kid. I know yer were only tryin' to 'elp but I've got to learn to manage on me own. The sooner I get back to normal . . .' His voice trailed away as he saw the expression on his friend's face. 'I can tell what yer thinkin'.' His mouth contorted. 'Yer wonder 'ow I'm gonna make a livin' like this. I've been thinkin' the same bloody thing: who'll want a cripple round their necks?' His bitterness touched Patrick deeply. Last time he had visited there had been grave pain, yes, but still a hint of the old humour. One would have imagined his improved health would have boosted that – but seemingly not.

'Come on, where's your spirit gone?' He nudged John.

'I can't be a barrel o' bloody laughs all the time!' snapped John. 'How the 'ell d'yer think I feel? I've a wife an' two kids relyin' on me an' 'ere I am neither use nor bloody ornament.' He calmed himself, propped the crutches by the side of the bed and lay down. 'I don't suppose yer've seen her by the way? T'wife I mean. She came to visit me day after t'fight, but I haven't seen her since. I were wonderin' if yer'd heard owt?'

Patrick moved his head slowly from side to side. 'Would ye like I should go round an' see what's going on?'

'No, it dunt matter,' replied John wearily, afraid of what Patrick would discover. 'I expect she'll be in to see me when she gets time.'

The Irishman handed over a bag. 'There's the oranges I promised ye – unsucked.'

John accepted the gift and laid it to one side without looking at it.

There was a lull, then Patrick asked, 'D'ye know how much longer it'll be before you're out?'

'Not long I 'ope. I can't wait to get me hands on that . . .'

'Oh, John, ye're not still on with that?' demanded Patrick, concerned at the way the conversation always found its way back to Fallon. 'Leave it I tell ye.'

'I won't leave it. I want to kill the bastard!' John's threat brought an orderly hurrying to his bedside, telling Patrick he would have to leave if he continued to upset the patients.

'I've not a very good bedside manner, have I?' Patrick stared down at his friend's wild face for some seconds, before slowly turning away, leaving John to drown in his self-pity.

Constant thoughts of Fallon gnawed at him on the way home. John would only succeed in getting himself killed if he tried to handle the tinker alone. On the other hand, if the tinker was out of the way when John came out of hospital . . .

Instead of going directly home, Patrick undertook a quick tour of the public houses which he usually frequented, not to drink but to seek assistance. If he was to face the tinkers again he would not be outnumbered this time.

There was little movement on the streets as Patrick and the six friends whose help he had enlisted set out on their mission. The bitterly cold weather had kept those with any sense behind either their own doors or that of the public houses. The snow gathered in damp, annoying clusters on their lashes, forced its way between chin and comforter to trickle icily inside their clothing and set teeth chattering. They came well armed. All walked awkwardly as if their limbs were made of wood, for inside trouser legs and coatsleeves were secreted long staves, cudgels and hammers.

Patrick held up his hand as they came to the shop on the corner of Paver Lane. ' 'Tis careful we'll have to be now,' he whispered. 'Not a sound. We need to take them by surprise.'

The men followed him into the lane, blinking rapidly to relieve their stinging eyes, feeling the excitement churn their stomachs as they edged further and further into tinker territory. The anticipation of a good battle was more thrilling than any woman.

Patrick halted again to issue orders. 'Right, we're nearly there. Another fifty yards or so an' 'tis every man for himself. Only leave the big fella to me.'

Ryan chuckled. 'I recall meself saying that once – have y'ever felt a clog-dance on your face?'

Patrick hushed him and proceeded stealthily to where the tinker camp should be. The others withdrew their cudgels in readiness, awaiting his command, creeping silently behind him. The snow continued to drive into their faces, hampering their sight.

Something was wrong. They had been crawling a lot further than fifty yards and still there was no smell of woodsmoke or the sound of gypsy recreation, though it could be that the weather had forced them all into their wagons.

Patrick suddenly disappeared from view as he stumbled over something in the blackness. Picking himself up he found that he was standing in the middle of a collection of small skeletons, tangled lumps of horsehair and waste paper; a rubbish pile. A groan of bitter disappointment turned to one of fury and he flung down the hammer that he carried with a violent curse. The lane, at this point usually flanked by brightly-coloured wagons, was empty – the tinkers had gone.

CHAPTER TWENTY-FOUR

SPRING BROUGHT A welcome change in the temperature and with the lighter mornings came the opportunity to make up for lost hours during the winter months. Light, fluffy clouds scudded across the sky as Patrick arrived at the building site and prepared to start work. It was good to be alive on such a morning as this, now that his ribs no longer pained him. The grass was still damp with dew and the streets almost deserted. He felt as if he had the world to himself.

Whistling a soft tune he crossed the site to the shed where the tools were kept. Someone had broken the lock; it rattled uselessly in the fresh breeze. To Patrick there was nothing untoward about this. People were always breaking in and stealing the tools. Still whistling, he flung open the door, flooding the interior with light.

'For God's sake can't a man 'ave any peace around 'ere?'

Patrick stepped back as the pile of rags in the corner suddenly came to life. 'John!' he cried in disbelief as the deformed face showed itself. 'What the hell are ye playing at? Ye nearly scared a litter o' pigs outta me.'

'I'm not playin' at owt,' yawned his friend. 'I was tryin' to get a bit o' sleep before this big Irish demick barges in. What're you doin' 'ere this early, any road?'

'Baxter wanted someone to put in a few extra hours to get this job finished. I thought I'd take the opportunity to boost the old coffers.'

'Isn't twelve hours a day enough for yer?' said John sourly. 'Workin' yerself to death, for what? When yer've half killed yerself to buy her all t'things she fancies she'll clear off, that's what. Take my word for it, mate, no woman's worth it.'

'Ye sound as though you're speaking from experience,' said Patrick carefully.

John lay back with his hands behind his head, his once curly brown hair hanging lank and unkempt with pieces of dried grass sticking out all over the place, his clothes covered in mud. 'Oh, I know all about it, pal.' His mouth twisted downwards in a bitter grimace. 'I gets 'ome from 'ospital an' what do I find? She's sloped off, takin' bairns with 'er. God knows where. She never left a note or owt. I opens door an' there's this family sittin' round table. "Who the hell are you?" I sez, an' t'fella gets up an' sez "I might ask you t'same question, what yer doin' in my bloody 'ouse?" Turns out he's been livin' there for t'past six weeks. So 'ere I am wi' only clothes yer see me in. That's what women do for yer, Pat.'

'They're not all the same,' said Patrick. 'Tommy doesn't ask me for anything. I do all this overtime of me own accord, so's I can buy her the things she'd really like but wouldn't dream of askin' of me.'

'Aye, an' once yer've worked yerself into ground, settin' her up in a big, fine 'ouse wi' cupboards full o' fancy clothes she'll not need yer any more, yer'll've outlived yer usefulness. They're all t'bloody same, you mark my words.'

Patrick made no attempt to argue the point further, knowing that John's opinion would not be altered; he had been badly disillusioned. Of course Patrick could have pointed out that John had not contributed very much to his marriage, that he had treated his wife like a chattel and subjected her to humiliation over his constant thieving, and therefore could not expect much loyalty from her; but instead he asked, 'Where've ye been living then?'

'Here an' there,' answered his friend, going outside to urinate against the shed. 'I been sleepin' 'ere Saturday and Sunday. I did spend a couple o' nights out in the open but I got so bloody nithered I couldn't sleep. I daren't sleep any road, 'cause it were that bloody cold that I might not've woken up again.' He shivered and went back into the shed.

'But why did ye not come to us?' asked Patrick incredulously. 'Ye know we'd've helped ye.'

'I didn't reckon that lass o' yours'd be too keen to 'ave me as a lodger. Specially as 'ow I got yer into trouble wi' gyppos.'

'Don't talk soft. Ye know she wouldn't turn ye away. I

wouldn't have let her anyhow, I'm still boss in me own home.'

'I thought I were,' replied John acidly. 'Women, yer can't trust 'em an inch.'

'Listen, get yourself round to my house right this minute,' ordered Patrick. 'Tell Tommy I sent ye an' she's to give ye something to eat. How've ye gone on for food?'

'Oh, no trouble,' replied John, limping towards a haversack in the corner. 'I 'ad me mates to 'elp me there.' He unbuckled the pack and delved into it, quickly withdrawing his hand with a sharp yell. 'You little swine!' He sucked his finger and swung the bag round violently. 'That'll shake the buggers up a bit. Come out, yer little varmints!' He put his hand swiftly inside and whipped out a squirming, somewhat dizzy creature with fur the colour of honey and thrust it at Patrick who stepped back quickly.

'Jazers, I don't want the bloody thing! What is it anyway?' He peered warily into the vicious, beady eyes.

'Ferret,' answered John, reaching into the bag again and pulling out another squirming animal. 'By, they've been worth their weight in gold 'ave these two little fellas. They're as good an investment as yer could ever make. Yer'll never go short o' meat if y'ave one o' these, Pat. Only trouble is,' he licked a bead of blood from his finger, 'they can be bad-tempered little devils when they want to be.'

'Be a good fella an' put 'em away, will ye?' begged Patrick. 'I don't like the way that one keeps eyein' me.'

John laughed and stuffed the ferrets back into the bag, slinging it over his shoulder. 'Right, Pat, I'll take y'up on that offer if yer sure yer wife won't chuck me out.'

'Sure t'will be all right I tell ye, Tommy'll make ye welcome. Now will ye get going an' leave me to get on with some work?'

Thomasin did not exactly welcome John with open arms. 'Gor, the bad penny turns up again,' she said, hands on hips, as she opened the door and found him there.

' 'Ello, Tommy,' he ventured, pulling a lock of his greasy hair.

'Don't you Tommy me, yer thievin' little devil, I've a bone

to pick wi' you. Gettin' my husband mixed up in your dirty goin's on . . .'

'I'm sorry.'

'. . . gettin' him a good hidin' off them tinkers . . .'

John became angry. 'Look, I've said I'm sorry, what d'yer want, blood? Oh, never mind, pardon me for breathin'. I'm off!'

'Oh, don't be so bloody stupid!' She grabbed hold of his arm as he turned to stalk off. 'Get inside an' get them clothes off.'

Two of her neighbours who had been gossiping nearby stopped to listen, loose-jawed, to her invitation.

'Oh, s'truth, what am I sayin'!' Thomasin put a hand to her face. 'They'll be talkin' about me for weeks now. What I meant to say was, yer not comin' to live with us till yer've got a bit o' that muck off yer.'

'Yer mean I can stay?' John followed her indoors, unslinging the bag from his shoulder and laying it on the floor.

'Well, I'm not goin' to all this trouble just to chuck y'out in street again,' she answered, dragging the tin bath in front of the fire. 'There we are, I'll soon 'ave some water heated. Ah, Erin!' She turned as the child came in from the yard. 'Go see to Dickie, will yer? He's screamin' his bum off up there.'

'Hello, Erin,' said John, trying to keep the right side of his face away from the child, but with little success.

'Oh, Uncle John!' she exclaimed. 'What've ye done to your face? 'Tis all funny. What ye got that black thing over your eye for, Uncle John?'

John looked uncomfortably at Thomasin. 'It's an eye-patch. I've lost me eye.'

Erin's mouth dropped open. 'Lost it? Where?'

'Erin, go see to Dickie, there's a good girl,' said Thomasin, but Erin retained her morbid curiosity.

'Will I go see if I can find it for ye, Uncle John?' She crept closer.

'Yer'll not find it, love,' sighed John, taking off his jacket in an effort to distract the child and asked, 'Where's this brother o' yours, then?'

'He's upstairs. What's under the eye-patch then, Uncle John?'

'A hole,' answered John bluntly.

'Can I just take a peek?'

'Erin, will you do as you're told!' shouted Thomasin, pushing the child towards the stairs. 'Sorry about that, John, yer know what kids are.'

'Aye,' said John, his own children springing to mind.

'Yer must miss 'em,' she said quietly.

He looked at her. 'The kids yes, the wife I reckon I'm better off without.'

'Oh, got a confirmed woman-hater on me hands 'ave I?' said Thomasin, tipping the hot water into the bath.

'Can yer blame me for feeling like that?'

She shrugged. 'S'none o' my affair. I always reckon there's two sides to everything. Anyhow, get them clothes off an' I'll give 'em a wash.'

He hesitated awkwardly.

'Oh, don't worry.' She waved aside his embarrassment. 'I'll be off in kitchen to feed bairn when Erin fetches 'im down.' She bellowed up the stairs, 'Erin, hurry up love, Uncle John wants to get a bath.'

When Erin brought Dickie downstairs Thomasin shooed them into the kitchen and spoke over her shoulder to John. 'There's a towel over t'chair an' some spare clothes o' Pat's.' Then added cheekily before closing the door, 'Don't worry, I'll not come an' peep. Yer've nowt of interest I want to look at.'

When Patrick returned from work that evening he was pleasantly surprised to see John still in one piece.

'I thought ye might not be too pleased,' he whispered to his wife as he washed his hands ready for tea.

'Yer good at understatement, aren't yer, Pat?' answered Thomasin. 'Ah well, I could hardly turf him out when you so kindly told him he should come here, after all he is your friend.'

'Ah, you're a fine lass.' Patrick wound his arms about her and nuzzled her neck. 'I knew ye'd make him welcome, but I wasn't so sure about the livestock.'

'Livestock?' Thomasin disengaged herself.

'Ah, he's not told ye?' Patrick ran a hand over the back of his neck.

'Told me what?' she asked sternly.

'Well, I don't know whether . . .'

'Told me what?' she repeated.

'He's er . . . he's brought some ferrets with him.'

'Ferrets! He never said anythin' to me about no ferrets.' She marched into the adjoining room. 'Oy!' She kicked John's feet off the fender and he came suddenly awake. 'What's all this about bloody ferrets?'

John closed his eyes again. 'Ah.'

'I'll give yer ah! Where are they?'

He pointed vaguely to his haversack under the table. 'In there.'

'What?' Thomasin nearly hit the roof. 'Yer mean to tell me them animals've been in 'ere all day?' She turned on Patrick. 'What are yer thinkin' about, lettin' 'im bring ferrets in 'ere? They could've killed that bairn.'

'Oh, no . . . they're safe enough . . .'

'Get 'em out!'

'But . . .'

'Get 'em out! I'll not 'ave them blasted things in my 'ouse.'

'Where shall I put 'em?' asked John picking up the bag.

'By, yer really tempting Providence, aren't yer?' answered Thomasin crossly. 'Get 'em out in t'yard.'

'But somebody might pinch 'em!'

'Yer think I care?'

'Yer won't say that when yer eatin' juicy rabbit pies,' said John. 'Tell yer what, I'll go up to Low Moor tonight and bag us a few.'

'Out!'

'All right, all right, they're goin'!' John put the bag of ferrets outside the door, then returned to sink back into the battered armchair and put his feet on the fireplace, with a wink at Patrick. 'Home Sweet Home.'

'An' don't be makin' yerself too settled there either,' ordered Thomasin. 'It's teatime, everybody up at table.'

'Is she always like this?' asked John, eyeing the food on the table hungrily.

'Always,' replied Patrick. 'Come on, sit yourself down, John, and get started.'

'Listen,' said John, looking from Patrick to Thomasin. 'I

213

know it must be a bit of a nuisance havin' me 'ere, an' I'd really like to thank yer for takin' me in. It's no fun living rough.'

'Don't mention it,' said Patrick, his mouth filled with bread.

'Oh, no, don't mention it,' echoed Thomasin sarcastically. 'We're filthy wi' money, we take in cadgers every day o' week.'

'There's no need for that,' said Patrick sharply.

'Well, how are we supposed to keep him?' asked his wife, still annoyed about the ferrets. She addressed John, 'I don't suppose yer've got a job to go to?'

'Have you seen any advertisements for a one-eyed, gammy-legged bricklayer?' replied John scraping a thin covering of butter onto his bread. Baxter had wasted no time in replacing him, having heard that John would be in hospital for some time. 'But don't worry yer head about where t'money's comin' from. I'm not that far gone I can't earn me livin'.'

'I do worry though, John,' Thomasin told him. 'Don't think I'm gonna act as a fence for your underhand dealings.'

'My, Tommy, yer do use strange terms,' laughed John. 'What's all this about a fence?'

'Yer know very well.' Thomasin wagged her knife at him. 'I don't want my 'ouse fillin' wi' stolen property.'

'I've finished wi' all that,' replied John gravely. 'I learnt me lesson.'

'I wonder.' Thomasin refilled the teacups. 'Erin, love, eat yer crusts up.'

'Look,' said Patrick, 'if the man says he's going straight why won't ye believe him? Leave the fella alone, will ye? Here, John, have another piece o' shortcake.'

'Oh aye, eat us out of 'ouse an' 'ome,' said Thomasin airily. 'Only mark my words, no shenanigans in this 'ouse, remember.'

'I don't even know the meaning of the word.' John finished eating and wiped his mouth on the back of his hand. 'Besides, I can't get mixed up in owt, I've got to save all me energy for that gyppo.'

'Sure you're not still on about that, are ye?' Patrick pushed his chair back and reached for a pipe from the mantelshelf.

'I told yer, that . . .' John remembered the child's presence, 'that so an' so's goin' to pay.'

'Ye know they've moved on?' Patrick lit a taper from the fire and touched it to his pipe.

'Aye,' nodded John. 'That was the first thing I did when I came out, went to check on 'em. But they'll be back.' He spoke with certainty.

'As long as yer don't get Pat mixed up wi' 'em this time,' said Thomasin, collecting the crockery to take to the kitchen. 'I'll not have him hurt again.'

Patrick gave her a cutting glare. 'Since when have you spoken for me?'

'I only meant . . .'

'I know what ye meant an' I'll thank ye to mind your own business. When the time comes that I have to hide behind a woman's skirts that's the time to order a coffin.'

'Aye well, I dare say your pal'll be able to provide that an' all.' She retired to the kitchen in a huff.

'Pat, don't be fallin' out on my account,' protested John. 'I can fight me own battles.'

'Oh, sure,' answered Patrick. 'Like ye did last time.' His friend lowered his face. 'Look, I'm sorry, John, but 'tis a fool y'are if ye think ye can take them on alone.'

'I wasn't reckoning to take 'em all on, just the big bloke.'

'An' him the size o' Goliath? Sure, he'd make a lace doily out o' ye in a matter o' seconds. No, you're goin' to need help an' when the time comes ye can rely on my support. Didn't the man give me a hiding too?'

'Yer a funny bloke, Pat.'

'What's so funny about wanting to help a friend?' asked Patrick.

'That's what I mean, yer still look on me as a friend, even after I got yer into that bother. Yer must've lost a good bit in wages over that. Anybody else'd've told me where to go.'

Patrick grinned. There was a great deal of truth in what John had said. A more unlikely partnership one would not find. While Patrick was a stickler for the truth and took pride in his integrity John was never as happy as when he had put one over on someone.

John sank lower into the chair. 'What I said before – about

women, I mean – well, it were a bit harsh. She's a good sort is your Tommy under all that bluster.'

'She is.' Patrick's eyes creased at the corners. 'She's the best. I wouldn't swap her for a brewery.' He examined his hands, probing at the many cuts which criss-crossed his knuckles. 'Ye know, John, ye were right in part about all this overtime I've been takin' on. I've been working like fifty Trojans an' getting nowhere. There's a limit to how many hours a man can work in one day. But,' he became intense, 'I want to buy her so many things . . .' A bout of thoughtful puffing on his pipe, then a smile. 'Still, I've a surprise lined up for the summer. Don't breathe a word but I'm taking them to the seaside. Tommy's always sayin' how she'd love to see the sea. I've almost enough saved for a good day out.'

'It dun't do to give 'em everything they want,' warned John. 'She'll start to take yer for granted.'

Patrick shook his head. 'Not my Tommy.' He looked up as Thomasin showed Father Kelly into the room. 'Well, hello Liam. What brings you here tonight, as if I need to ask.' Liam had been a constant visitor since Richard's birth, demanding to know when they were going to have the child baptised.

John stood up and struggled into his jacket – or rather Pat's jacket, as his own clothes were still drying on a rail over the fireplace. 'I think I'll just nip out for an hour or so, an' leave you two to talk in peace.' The last thing he wanted was to get into conversation with a priest.

'Don't be comin' 'ome sozzled,' threatened Thomasin, unrolling her sleeves having completed the washing-up. She passed a pile of rags to Erin and a pair of scissors. 'There y'are, yer can help me with this rug.' She sat down by the fireside and spread the half-finished rug over her knee.

'Ye've got yourselves a lodger then?' Liam sat opposite her.

'You're very adept at probing boils, Liam,' she answered.

'Sore point, is it? Well, so is the matter I'm about to raise.' Liam's green eyes were serious. ' 'Tis taking ye some time to decide about the child's baptism.'

Patrick looked at his wife, then back at Liam. 'We've finally come to a decision, Father, but ye may not like it.'

'Father, is it?' said Liam, the flames of the fire reflected in his brilliant eyes. 'Then I'm sure I'm not going to like it.'

'We've decided not to bother having the baby baptised,' Patrick told him.

'Not to bother? Now there's an odd choice o' phrase. Ye mean not into the Catholic faith?'

'Not into any faith, Liam.'

The priest digested Patrick's words, looking from one to the other. 'Ye cannot be serious?'

'Why not?' asked Thomasin casually. It had been her decision in the end; Patrick had not been able to make up his mind and had left it to her. 'What's the point of havin' him baptised when we don't believe ourselves? It's two-faced.'

'I find it hard to accept that ye don't believe in anything,' said Liam, who knew that Patrick, while insisting that he had finished with the church, might one day be persuaded to return. 'Is there nothing ye hold sacred?'

Thomasin shrugged and laid down the rug to rub at her stiff fingers. She took no enjoyment from what she was about to say. Liam administered help to those who needed it and he had been a good friend to Patrick. 'No, Liam, I don't believe in anything. There might be a God, but if there is I don't reckon He's all that good.'

Liam closed his eyes as if to shut out the pain. 'Hard as it is for me to stomach I can understand your feelings – but your children are a different matter. I beg you, don't deny young Dickie his right.'

'Liam, ye make it sound as though we're inflicting some sort o' torture,' said Patrick, though sorry for causing his friend so much hurt still unrepentant. ' 'Tis all decided. When he's old enough he can choose for himself but until then we'll continue as we are. I can't see the difference it'll make.' He attempted a diversion. 'Tommy, go fetch the Father a cup o' tea.'

Liam declined and rose wearily. 'Thank ye no, 'tis something stronger I'm in need of.'

Patrick began to rise too. 'Just the excuse I've been seeking.'

'An' did I say I wanted company?' demanded Liam sharply, then turned away.

'I'll show y'out, then,' offered Thomasin with a concerned look at her husband who had flopped back to his seat.

'Don't bother.' The priest waved her away. 'If I don't know me way now 'tis hard luck.' His hand paused on the knob and he stared down at it as he spoke. 'Ye'll be very welcome whenever ye bring Erin to church, Patrick Feeney. I've always been a friend, as Godless as y'are, but I have to tell ye,' he looked over his shoulder now, 'that I can no longer find the charity to visit a house that refuses to admit Our Lord. Until you choose to let Him in, any meeting we might have must be restricted to the church. It seems all you're intent on doing is flinging my friendship back in me face.' So saying, he closed the door gently behind him.

'Well, yer didn't expect him to stand on his hands an' sing hallelujah, did yer?' said Thomasin at Patrick's downcast face.

'There's no call to be facetious,' he answered glumly. 'Liam's been good to me over the years. I don't like to think of our friendship coming to such an end. Sure, I never thought he'd take it so hard. He didn't seem too concerned at me marrying a Protestant, and knowing how I felt about the church didn't stop him visiting my house before.'

'I think it was really me what upset the pittle-pot,' said Thomasin. 'But would he honestly have thought any better o' me if I'd said I'd 'ave Dickie baptised a Catholic, knowin' all the time I didn't believe a word o' what I were promisin'?'

Patrick did not know what to believe any more. He sighed and took Erin onto his lap, changing the subject by telling her a tale. At its climax he said, ' 'Tis time ye went to bed, girleen.'

'Aw, please let me stay up till Uncle John gets home,' pleaded his daughter.

Thomasin sided with Patrick. 'No, it's late enough. Uncle John might not be back until late. Off yer go, like a good lass.'

Erin lingered sulkily against her father's chest and rubbed his chin beseechingly. 'I don't have to, do I, Daddy?' Even after all this time she still resented Thomasin's orders.

'Now ye heard what your mammy said,' Patrick spoke unthinkingly.

The child lost her wheedling smile and jumped from his knee sharply, stalking up the stairs without a word of good-night.

'I wish yer wouldn't do that,' said Thomasin, listening to the bedroom door slam.

'Do what?'

'Refer to me as "mammy". Yer know she doesn't like it.'

Patrick rattled the poker around the coals. 'Look, it's been years since her mammy died. I'm getting a bit sick and tired of all these tantrums. 'Tis about time she buckled down to the idea that you're her mammy now.'

'I've told yer before, she'll accept me in her own good time,' replied Thomasin, folding up the rug and rubbing her aching shoulders. 'Anyway, I'm not bothered if she doesn't want to call me Mammy.'

'Don't try to cod me,' exclaimed Patrick. 'I'm your husband, remember?' I can see how it hurts ye. Sure, I thought things were getting better between the two o' ye.'

'They are,' answered his wife. 'An' they'll continue to get better if yer leave things to run their course instead of trying to speed them up. Now then, I've summat else I want to discuss. Where's this friend o' yours gonna sleep when he deigns to come home? An' he needn't think I'm waitin' up for him all night either.'

'Nobody's askin' yer to!' John clattered into the room, shaking the rain from his hair, and slung two rabbits on the table. 'There y'are, don't say I never bring y'owt.'

'We were just decidin' where you're going to sleep,' Thomasin told him. 'An' I 'ope you've left them blasted ferrets in t'yard?'

'I wouldn't dare do otherwise,' said John, rinsing the mud from his hands. 'Don't bother about me, I'll bed down anywhere.'

'I dare say yer will,' replied Thomasin. 'But I'm not havin' t'ouse cluttered up wi' bodies all over t'place. If yer gonna be part o' this family yer can get yerself out tomorra an' buy a bed. An' I mean buy, not steal. Wi' all your talents I dare say yer'll get the money somewhere.'

'Part o' family, eh?' grinned John, rubbing his hands in front of the fire. 'By, she's a good'n your missus, Pat. Is there any chance of owt to eat afore I go to bed, Tommy?'

'There's bread an' drippin', take it or leave it.'

'That'll do champion, thank yer,' said John.

'An' as soon as yer've eaten it,' ordered Thomasin, 'yer can brush off all that mud. I'm not washin' two sets o' clothes thank yer very much.'

John elbowed Patrick and made himself small. 'Yes, Mam.'

CHAPTER TWENTY-FIVE

JOHN'S PRESENCE PROVIDED Patrick with male support on the nights when they stayed too long at The Bay Horse. To the children he became a much-loved uncle, an ever-present playmate, which was strange because one look at his ravaged face could terrify most adults into speechlessness. Initially, Thomasin had treated John merely as a fulcrum for her discontent, her quick temper adopting an unsteady balance upon his shoulders. But his capacity for turning his hand to most tasks and the regular provision of rabbits which eked out the housekeeping money soon established him in her eyes as a valuable member of the family.

The balmy spring blended into a summer of sun and surprises. Such as the day when Patrick had suddenly announced that he was taking the family to the seaside. After many months of poring over advertisements in the newspapers, extolling the virtues of Scarborough, he had finally saved enough money for his dream to become reality.

What a marvellous day that had been, crammed with smells, tastes and sensations such as Thomasin had never before experienced. The captivating aroma of engine smoke which curled under their nostrils the moment they entered the busy station in Tanner Row. The gleaming engine with its lustrous, brass domes that had let off a sudden burst of steam making them all jump and squeal, then laugh at their own fright. The promenade with fine ladies sauntering along on the arms of prosperous gentlemen, with dresses of organdie, satin and crêpe de chine. The beach which sported a crowd of holidaymakers, ladies and children on horseback, flys, landaus, gigs, all manner of vehicles churning tracks in the sand. Weary donkeys bearing panniers of screaming infants, vendors lugging baskets overladen with cockles, periwinkles, crabs. The sand in the sandwiches, the bathing machines that lined the water's edge with their bevy of voluminously clad bathers.

And the sea. Oh, the sea! Stretching out before them, a great blue infinity sparkling in the early afternoon sun, as if someone had unrolled a vast length of deep blue silk and in its folds bobbed a flotilla of gleaming craft. The graceful sweep of its ebb tide rippled in white, foamy wavelets to meet the golden sands, like the scalloped lace on a lady's petticoats.

Then all too quickly it had been over. All that remained to them was to trudge reluctantly back to the station to fight their way through the immense crowds and onto the train, drunk with ozone, the tight, tingling feel of sunburnt skin, hair sticky with sea-salt, to be transported tired, but happy, homewards bound.

Such days were sadly infrequent for Patrick, who spent the majority of the sticky, summer months mixing mortar, digging ditches, demolishing houses. Not for him the leisurely country pursuits of John who whiled away the sultry hours scavenging the country lanes with only his ferrets and the birds for company, gathering wild strawberries and brambles for Thomasin to put in a pie. John watched his friend's struggles to provide his wife with a higher standard of living. He saw a change in the Irishman who often had little energy for anything other than sleep when he had eaten his evening meal, leaving John to go unaccompanied to the ale-house and Thomasin with no one to talk to. The man was taking on far too much.

Outside the city walls green turned to russet as the long hot summer finally burnt itself out. Cool breezes began systematically to strip the trees of their leaves and an occasional frost hung on the morning air. It was hard to visualise the passing of summer in their squalid microcosm. No trees lined their streets to give a gentle hint of the onset of winter and the cold weather sprang upon them without warning. Soon another Christmas loomed into view. For the Feeneys it would be a great deal more festive than the last. Patrick's overtime earnings and the money John had made from selling scrap, made valuable contributions to their home comforts.

St Stephen's Day arrived, the day of Dickie's first birthday. He was to have a party and the tiny dwelling was filled with merry laughter until Hannah's arrival rather dampened the proceedings. Hannah, to her disgust, had discovered that Thomasin had not been churched after Richard's birth and for some time the Fentons' home had been forbidden territory. As long as her father paid his weekly visits Thomasin cared not for her mother's pious debarment.

The Flahertys were not to attend this party – not because of superior beliefs but because they had not been told of its occurrence. Hannah had graciously repealed her judgement for the Yuletide period and with her mother present at the gathering Thomasin deemed it wise to keep mum to her Irish friends. Already Hannah's arrival had subdued things but her husband could be relied upon to relieve the gloom.

William tossed his grandson up in the air, laughing at his squeals. 'Happy Birthday, Dickie! Eh, look what I've got 'ere!' He held out his hand to Hannah who handed him a brown paper parcel. 'Ooh, what's this, eh? Come on, let's open it, shall us?' William sat the baby on his knee, struggling to open the package with his free hand. 'By, look at that! A whatjercallit!' He pulled forth a shiny, tin object which, when he had turned it the right way up, emerged as a soldier beating a drum.

William located the key on the soldier's back and wound it up. Immediately the soldier rat-tatted a tinny tune on the drum. 'Isn't that grand?'

'Oh, lovely,' said Thomasin without conviction. 'I'll enjoy listenin' to that racket all day.'

Dickie showed his appreciation by picking up the soldier and beating time on his grandfather's knee.

'Not like that, silly!' William took the toy from Dickie, then gave it back quickly as the baby howled a noisy protest.

Erin stood nearby, her eyes big and round, never leaving the clockwork soldier. William noticed her apprehension. 'Eh, Hannah, get the rest o' them whatsits out, will tha? Poor bairn here thinks she's not gerrin owt.'

Hannah distributed the rest of the presents, a blouse for Thomasin, some tobacco for Patrick, which had been William's idea not his wife's, and disappointingly for Erin, who eyed the tin soldier enviously, two flannel petticoats.

Thanking her parents for their gifts, Thomasin started to lay the table for tea, saying to Patrick, 'I wonder where John's got to. He's been out ages.'

'John?' enquired Hannah, at exactly the same time as the said person entered bearing a long, thin parcel.

'That's me name!' John pulled off his cap and grinned demoniacally. 'I thought me ears were burnin' when I was comin' down t'lane. Been talkin' about me, 'ave yer?'

Hannah was scarcely able to suppress a cry of alarm as John approached her, cap in hand, and Thomasin made hasty introductions.

'Mother, this is John, Pat's friend, yer might remember him from t'weddin'.'

Hannah grimaced. Would they ever let her forget that débâcle?

'Well, anyway,' added her daughter, 'he's lost his wife an' . . .'

Hannah's face softened. 'Oh, dear I am . . .'

John interrupted. 'No, love, Tommy doesn't mean lost as in dead, she means lost as in buggered off.'

'Oh!' Hannah put a hand to her throat at the familiarity of the man.

'Well, I could've phrased it a little better,' said Thomasin, 'but that's the long and short of it. John's wife's left him an' he's come to live with us.'

Hannah was struck dumb and unable to tear her eyes away from the terribly scarred face with its black eyepatch. The man looked an out and out rogue. What on earth was Thomasin thinking of? As if it was not humiliating enough to have one's daughter living among such people she had to start giving sanctuary to lame dogs and scoundrels.

John still held out his hand in friendship but now that Hannah had made it apparent that she found him unsavoury he transferred it to William.

'Hello, Billy, good to see yer again. When are we gonna 'ave another night like we had down at Spread Eagle? By God, didn't we sup some stuff.'

'Er hello, John,' replied William, anxiously eyeing Hannah.

'You seem to be well acquainted with this person,' hissed

Hannah suspiciously. 'And been drinking with him by the sound of it.'

'Aye, well he were 'ere last time I called yer see,' blustered William awkwardly. 'We mighta gone to t'thingummyjig, I can't really recall.'

Hannah buttoned her lips and glared at him while John retreated to the kitchen to wash his hands.

'Sorry about me mother,' said Thomasin.

'S'all right,' replied John indifferently. 'Yer get used to people lookin' at yer like that.'

'Do yer?' asked Thomasin seriously. 'Do yer really?'

He dried his hands and gave a caustic laugh. 'No, I'm lyin' again. I don't think I'll ever get used to lookin' like some sorta monster.'

'Aw, yer don't look like a monster, John.' Thomasin laid a sympathetic hand on his shoulder.

'Don't I? Would you fancy me?' asked John, then as she looked away uncomfortably. 'No. There's not a woman that would. That's what makes it so damned hard, Tommy.' He balled his fists and shook them angrily. 'They think that because I look like this I'm not human any more, that I don't have feelings like any normal man. Even the dollymops won't gimme time o' day. Eh, I shouldn't be talkin' to yer like this.' He picked up a comb and ran it through his brown curls. 'Better make meself presentable for t'party.'

'I don't mind, John,' she said kindly. 'If it helps to get it off yer chest yer can talk about it as much as yer like.'

'As long as it only is talk, eh?' he grinned.

'Eh, I should be very careful,' she laughed.

'Yer a queer'n, Tommy.' He tapped her lightly on the shoulder with the comb. 'Sometimes yer never off me back an' then others yer seem . . . Oh, I don't know . . . different anyway. I feel as though I could open me heart to yer when yer like this.'

'Aye, I'm nobbut queer,' admitted Thomasin, arranging tiny cakes on a stand. 'Now enough o' this maudlin talk o' yours. Grab a couple o' plates an' follow me.' Her great belly moved before her. She had fallen almost immediately after Dickie's birth. A pause as she poked the long package John had brought in with him. 'What's this yer've brought wi' yer?'

'Eh, don't be kickin' it about, that's my birthday present to Dickie!'

'Oh, beg pardon.'

When they returned to the living room Hannah was in the process of issuing Patrick with another piece of her mind. 'Just when are you going to pull yourself together?' she asked bitingly. 'I do grant that you have made some efforts to improve your standard of living; this carpet, for instance, would do credit to a much wealthier household.' Thomasin nudged John who was responsible for this luxury. 'But if you can afford to spend that on a carpet surely the money would be put to better use in saving for a larger house.'

Thomasin intervened before the angry flush on her husband's face manifested itself into a deadlier altercation. 'Ey, what's brought this on, Mother? Honestly, I can't leave the room for five minutes but yer on yer soap box again.'

'I was simply pointing out,' said Hannah, 'that there is more to life than two up and two down and the longer you stay here the harder it will be for you to pull yourselves from the quagmire.'

'Oh, I'm sorry,' replied her daughter casually, 'I was under the impression that you lived in a two up an' two down yerself.'

Hannah was not to be swayed. 'Quite correct – which is the reason I want more for my daughters. I realise what it is like to have a husband with no ambition. One has to have a certain push if one is to get anywhere in life. I do not want you to suffer the same dreary existence as myself.'

'Dun't it make thee feel good to know tha's appreciated?' said William lightly, dandling his grandson on his knee.

John, who had been listening with interest to the dialogue, finally unearthed the true reason for Patrick's compulsion to work. It was to prove this woman wrong, to show her that he could give her daughter as good a life as anyone could, to prove to her, and to himself, that he was a man.

Patrick finally spoke. 'Forgive me if I'm wrong, but I thought this was to be a birthday party. All I've heard so far is people tearing strips off each other. Hannah, I'll make a deal with ye. I promise not to offend ye with me uncouth manners if you promise not to say another word about me bettering meself. Now is it a deal?'

Hannah snorted. 'I'm sorry, I'm sure. I only intended my remarks to be helpful.'

'You can make yerself more helpful by fetchin' them cups an' saucers from kitchen,' commanded Thomasin. 'Now then, how many of us are there? One, two . . . wait a minute, where's Erin?'

Patrick fingered his new waistcoat. 'Ah, she was asking if she could invite Bridie to the party, so I told her it would be all right. Was I wrong?'

'No, that's fine,' replied his wife. 'As long as she doesn't bump into Molly. I think it'd be a bit of a squash with all her brood in here an' all. Oh s'truth, look at that!' She pointed to the present which John had brought and which Dickie had now opened. 'What yer gone an' brought him a sword for? He's bad enough without a weapon in his hands.'

'I thought it were rather good,' said John admiring his handiwork. 'He can't do much harm as it's only wood.' He drew in his breath as Dickie tested the sword on Uncle John's shins. 'Ah well, perhaps it was a mistake,' he decided, rubbing his bruised leg.

'I hope that child isn't long in fetching Bridie,' said Patrick. 'I'm ravenous.'

'We'll give her a couple o' minutes,' replied Thomasin. 'It's likely poor old Bridie that's holding her up.'

Erin skipped gaily into the alleyway that led to Britannia Yard, tripping a path through the rotting débris. She was about to tap at Bridie's door when someone crept up behind her, making her jump with his sneering question.

'What you doin' 'ere, Irish?'

She turned her nose up at Ned Raper's weasel-like face. 'None of your business, stinky Raper.'

He drew his jacket sleeve across his running nose, leaving a yellow film on the coarse material which made her feel sick. 'Yer gettin' too clever, Irish. Yer mates aren't 'ere to 'elp yer now.'

Erin's face paled at the rashness of her words and she looked nervously about for someone to help her. If she was quick she might just be able to grab hold of Bridie's door handle.

She made a sudden movement, but Ned anticipated her action and his arm went around her neck, squeezing the breath from her.

'Let go, I can't breathe,' she gasped, stars swimming before her eyes. But her pleas went unheeded. 'Not so cocky now, are yer?' Ned half dragged, half carried her towards the abattoir and leaned his back against the unbolted doors which swung obligingly open. 'I bet yer sorry yer called me names now, aren't yer?'

'Oh, I am, I am!' Erin had realised what he was going to do. 'Please, Ned, don't take me in there! I'll give ye anything ye want, here, I've got some sweeties in me pocket.' She fumbled in her pinafore pocket and pulled out a crumpled bag of sweets and waved them in the air.

Ned snatched the sweets, keeping one arm around her neck then threw them on the ground. 'Pah! I don't want nuthin' you've touched. Any road, yer wrong. I'm not takin' yer in there.' Erin let out a relieved sigh. ' 'Cause yer goin' in on yer own!' cackled Ned and giving her a mighty shove he slammed the doors shut behind her, making sure that she heard the bolt ram home.

There was the sound of his mischievous laughter for a moment, then all was quiet, save for Erin's panting breath. She pressed her terrified face against the wooden doors, trying to peer between the gaps in the planking but was unable to ascertain if Ned was still outside. Then panic gripped her.

'Let me out!' she screamed. Then quieter, 'Please, Ned, I'm sorry I said ye stink, ye don't really. Let me out, they're waiting for me at home.'

She waited for an answer, but none came and she turned her back to the doors peeping into the darkness through half-closed eyes. Even though the abattoir was not in use, the aura of past atrocities hung like an evil shroud all around her. Rows of steel hooks lined the gory walls, giant teeth bared in a maleficent snarl. Erin whimpered and tried to find another way out. Tiptoeing, shivering with fear, her back brushed against a dangling chain sending a noisy rattling around her prison. She began to cry; quiet sobs that seemed abnormally loud in the empty place. Someone would miss her, wouldn't they? They were all waiting for her, they would wonder where she was, wouldn't they? But what if they were too preoccupied with Dickie's party to notice she was not there?

In answer to her questions, she suddenly heard the bolt being unfastened. Light streamed in, highlighting the crimson smudges on the walls and silhouetted in the doorway was a figure, a man.

'Daddy?'

The door banged shut and the light was gone. She thought she was alone again, until the sound of stealthy footfalls advanced towards her. A funny, prickling sensation crept all over her body as she tried to see his face in the gloom. Backing away uncertainly, she suddenly found that she could go no further and her little hands felt the slimy coldness of the wall behind her as the man moved nearer.

The giddy relief made her legs buckle and she slid to the abattoir floor, for a chink of light had revealed his face. It was someone she knew, a friend.

'Have ye come to rescue me?' she asked, smiling uncertainly.

Without replying the man bent down and stroked her hair making her feel inexplicably afraid.

'Come on, shall we go out now?' She began to rise, but the man laid a restraining hand on her shoulder.

Slowly her smile dissolved. He was not going to let her go. A strange look had come to him; his eyes were all funny as he stood and towered over her. Then her feeling of terror returned tenfold as she watched his hand drop to his breeches and slowly begin to unfasten the buttons.

The guests sat drumming impatient fingers on the tablecloth.

'Where on earth has that bairn got to?' frowned Thomasin. 'She's been gone ages. Pat, will yer go see if yer can find her? All t'sandwiches'll start curlin' up at corners if we wait much longer.'

Excusing himself, Patrick slipped on his jacket and left the house. Trust Erin to hold up the festivities. She had probably done it on purpose just to spoil things for Thomasin. Well, she had done it once too often. She would have to have a damned good hiding to make her learn that her little displays of jealousy would be tolerated no longer.

He was still perusing these angry thoughts as he turned into Britannia Yard and immediately collided with a man who carried in his arms Patrick's limp, white-faced child. All the recriminations vanished and his skin crawled with shock and fear as he stared at the pitiful waif in the other fellow's arms.

'What in God's name are you doing with my daughter, Raper?' The words were delivered quietly but with great potency.

Raper's erubescence faded somewhat as he faced the trembling father.

'I were bringing her home, Feeney. There's been . . .' he faltered and swallowed before proceeding '. . . a bit o' trouble.'

Erin whimpered and reached out for her father who swiftly snatched her from the butcher and hugged her to his chest. No word had passed her lips, no greeting for her father. He feared the unspeakable.

The shade of his eyes altered with the pent-up rage that lay behind them. 'Now, Raper,' he fought to keep his voice steady, 'I'm going to take this child home to her mother, an' then I'm coming back to ask you what happened, an' if I don't get the right answers, if you've harmed her, Raper, if you've touched but one hair of her head . . .'

The butcher, mortally offended, broke in and lifted himself to his full height. 'Now, wait a minute, Feeney! What sorta man d'yer think I am? I might hate your guts, but I'd not touch a little bairn like that. I know kids're all frightened o' me, an' I might clip a few ear'oles now an' then, but I'd never touch her . . . that way.'

The effect of his last words travelled all the way through Patrick's body. 'What d'ye mean "that way"?'

Raper stared at the pathetic mite, averting his piggy eyes from the Irishman's face. 'Well, I don't know if I got there in time or . . .'

'Tell me, Raper!'

Patrick's fury jolted the butcher into relating the situation. Suspicious of his nephew's odd behaviour when he had returned from the yard, Raper had questioned the boy.

'I'll bet yer've been in that slaughterhouse again, haven't yer?'

Ned assumed a look of pure innocence. 'Who me, Uncle

Edwin? No, I been makin' meself useful like yer told me to do.'

Disbelieving the boy's protestations Raper had decided to take a look for himself. It would not do for them to start the killing and find that Ned had knotted all the chains together, or loosened the screws that held the hooks in place. On more than one occasion he had winched a carcase to the ceiling, only to have it miss his head by inches as the loosened hook gave under its weight and sent it crashing to the floor.

'Just as I thought,' he had nodded to himself on finding the doors unbarred. 'Better just 'ave a look inside an' see what that little get's been up to.'

A startled face had turned to meet him and the crouching figure raised himself.

'What the 'ell . . .?' started Raper, then his eyes had fallen on the weeping child, her skirt thrown carelessly over her face exposing slender, naked limbs. Jos Leach's erection had slowly wilted as the butcher advanced with fists upraised. 'Yer bastard! Yer filthy, rotten little pillock!'

Total lack of understanding held Leach rooted to the spot. Raper was angry, but why, what had he done? Hadn't he seen the butcher do the self same thing to Jos's mother? Tell her he loved her and done things to her, just like Jos loved Erin, loved her pretty face and the way she smiled at him. Why had she cried like that? He didn't want to hurt her. His mother hadn't cried. His blank expression turned to one of fear as Raper reached out for him and he cowered on the floor with his arms protecting his head, awaiting for the first blow. It never came.

'Christ,' spat Raper, placing his boot against the youth's shoulder and sending him sprawling. 'Yer don't even know what yer've done, do yer?' His fist dropped unused to his side and he let out a string of expletives to give vent to his anger. Then he turned to the girl, pulling down her skirts to cover her nakedness. Awkwardly he cradled her to him. Having little experience with children except to chastise them, he did not know how to comfort her. He dried her tears on his cuff. Fear and distrust looked out of the red-rimmed eyes and the child tried to pull away. 'I'm not gonna hurt thee, young'n,' he told her gruffly. 'I know yer don't like me but I'm not gonna hurt yer, honest. I'm gonna take yer 'ome that's all.'

Picking her up he had cast a venomous glare at Leach before stepping outside and into the alleyway, where he had almost collided with Patrick.

Rage and impotence fought for position in Patrick's mind. How could you punish a lunatic, who did not even know what he was being punished for? He glowered at the sky, cursing God, then brought his eyes down to Raper's face. Ashamed now of his erroneous judgment of the butcher he offered his apologies and thanked the man for his intervention, hoping that Raper had arrived in time.

'What'll have to be done about . . .?' He nodded towards the abattoir, unable to bring himself to foul his tongue with that despicable name.

Raper scratched his head. 'He'll 'ave to go to asylum I suppose, that's where t'bugger belongs. I'll see to that any road, he's my responsibility. You get that bairn 'ome, she needs her mam.'

'Come on, Erin,' Patrick whispered against the white cheek. 'Let's get ye home. Tommy'll know what to do.'

Thomasin had tired of waiting and the party was well under way with sounds of merry laughter escaping the house in Bay Horse Yard. But all sign of merriment fizzled out as Patrick violently kicked open the door and stood on the threshold bearing the molested child. Immediately he was enveloped in a press of concerned faces, all wanting to know what had befallen Erin.

'Has she fallen?' asked Thomasin, peering concernedly at Erin's knees. 'An' where's Bridie, isn't she comin'?'

'She never got to Bridie's,' replied Patrick levelly, then his voice cracked as Raper's story tumbled from his lips. 'Oh, Christ, Tommy,' he cried after relating the facts to the horrified listeners. 'Take her. Take her an' see what the filthy bastard has done to her.'

Disbelievingly, Thomasin gazed at Leach's victim in Patrick's outstretched arms, at the angry bruise on her forehead, her face streaked with cow dung. 'Oh, Pat, he's not . . .?'

'I don't know!' raged Patrick. 'The poor little darlin' can't tell us, she won't speak. She needs a woman! Please, Tommy, go take her somewhere an' have a look at her, I've got to know.'

'You hold her for a minute,' ordered Thomasin, going towards the kitchen.

'I'll help you,' shouted Hannah, but was restrained by William.

'Tha'll help most by keeping out of it,' he told her firmly. 'Bairn needs somebody who's close to her.'

Hannah examined his face to see if there were any recrimination in it, for she knew that her treatment of Erin in the past had been far from grandmotherly and, now that she looked at the crumpled little form in Patrick's arms, felt deeply ashamed and guilty. But William's face showed no reproval, only the warm understanding that stems from being married to someone for many years. 'You can make it up to her later' the look said.

When Thomasin returned she gently lifted Erin and carried her into the kitchen where a steaming bath awaited. Softly singing a lullaby to the child she began to peel off the dung-caked dress, as she did so, praying silently – Please, please don't let her be hurt. She then performed a discreet examination of the mud-streaked thighs, steeling herself for what she might find, but after a few seconds let out a great sigh of relief. There was no blood, no sign of violation. The butcher had got there in time. If Raper had been in the kitchen at that moment she would have thrown her arms around his neck and kissed him, such was her relief.

She placed Erin carefully in the bath, wringing out a rag and wiping away the filth of the abattoir. 'There, there, darlin'!' She held the black curls away from the bruised forehead and kissed it gently. 'You're safe now. The man won't hurt yer any more, I won't let him.'

Erin closed her dazed eyes and her little body shook with emotion as the tears rolled down her face, dripping from her chin into the bathwater. Thomasin suddenly found that she was crying, too. Noisy sobs of thankfulness broke from her lips as she felt two wet little arms grip her tightly around the neck, making her revise her opinion about the benevolence of the deity she had hitherto denied. There must after all be a God, or someone who watched over and protected them for here in her arms was the evidence as the child broke her silence.

'Mammy,' she wept. 'Oh, Mammy!'

PART THREE

CHAPTER TWENTY-SIX

'EASY AS SHELLIN' peas!' smiled Thomasin, looking down at the red, squawking bundle in her arms. The birth had been a relatively quick one, with the minimum of pain. Unlike last time, she had been able to potter about the house, involving herself with light tasks, until the second stage of labour was imminent. Then, no sooner, it seemed, than she had lain upon the bed, son number two made his swift arrival into the world.

Hannah, cheated over the birth of Thomasin's first child, had subjected them to daily visits as the birthdate had grown nearer. But Thomasin had insisted that Molly act as midwife, so Hannah had to content herself with a supervisory position, one in which she excelled.

'Well,' she beamed, as though the responsibility of producing the new infant had been solely hers. 'That wasn't too bad, was it?'

Molly rolled her eyes at Thomasin as she wrapped the placenta and membranes in the accouchement sheet and went downstairs to dispose of them.

Thomasin smiled and, tucking her hand into her nightgown, pulled out a breast and offered it to the baby. A spark of interest flickered in the wrinkled features as the warm skin touched his cheek.

'Away, lazy.' Thomasin stroked the downy skin, trying to coax him to accept the nipple.

Hannah watched them with satisfaction. 'Now, you cannot deny that this one takes after his mother. Just look at that hair.'

Thomasin had to agree. 'Aye, proper little carrot top, isn't he?'

The baby finally grasped what was expected of him and attached himself firmly to his mother.

'There's a good boy.' Thomasin looked up at Hannah. 'Yer'd best let 'em in now, Mother.'

Hannah appeared to be shocked. 'But surely not while you are feeding him?'

'Nay, don't be daft,' replied Thomasin amusedly. 'Go on, let 'em in, poor Pat's got a right to see his son, yer know.'

Hannah cleared her throat to register her disapproval and went to admit the rest of the family. Patrick's attempts to attend the birth of his second son had been sadly thwarted; Hannah had never heard anything quite so disgraceful as a man being present at a birth. The very idea.

'Now you can't stay long,' she informed Patrick and the children, shepherding them into the room. 'She's got to have her rest.'

Patrick stooped to kiss his wife and admire his new son. 'Jazers, look at that hair!' He laughed and fingered the baby's cheek. 'We'll have a right time with him when he gets a bit bigger. As if it's not bad enough having one hothead in the house.'

'Eh, you're not so calm an' collected yerself,' objected Thomasin, changing the baby to the other side. She craned her head past her husband. 'Where's that pal o' yours then?'

Hannah provided the answer. 'I told him to wait downstairs until the family had met the baby.'

Thomasin was exasperated. 'What a rotten thing to say! You might not consider it so but John is part of this family and he's every right to see t'bairn. What's up, did yer think his face'd curdle t'milk or summat?' She buttoned up her bodice, glaring at her mother. 'Anyway, I've finished now so yer can show him up.'

Hannah unwillingly complied and brought John to join the family gathering.

'But don't stay too long, mind.'

'Mother, he's only just got 'ere,' said Thomasin, indicating for John to sit on the bed alongside Patrick. 'It's safe to leave me with him, yer know. 'E'll not attack me.'

Her mother reddened. 'I did not for one moment suggest he would.' She gave John a half-smile which passed for an apology. 'Well, I think I shall go and help Mrs Flaherty to make the tea.' She disappeared.

Thomasin giggled. 'Poor Molly. Me mother's been drivin' her mad with her orderin' an' delegatin', makin' sure she washes her hands every five minutes. I'll bet Molly's hands've never seen so much soap in all their lives.'

John stroked the baby's cheek with a rough finger. 'Nah then, who've we got 'ere?'

'This,' said Thomasin proudly, to both John and her husband, 'Is John Patrick Feeney, named after his favourite uncle an' his father.' Neither she nor Patrick had decided on a name prior to the birth but as Thomasin had watched the two men sit side by side, one so handsome, the other cruelly mutilated, she knew there could be no other choice.

A shadow passed over John's face as he thought of his own children. Where might they be now? He had thought to find out where his wife had taken them but then dismissed the idea. What could he possibly have left to offer them? He stared down at the baby, reliving the moment when he had held his own son for the first time, how proud he had been. Normally unemotional, John was taken aback to find his throat constricted with sadness, making him unable to voice his thanks for the honour bestowed on him. Finally he took a deep breath and said, with a lightness he did not feel, 'To be hoped he doesn't take after his Uncle John, Tommy, or you an' me are gonna have some explainin' to do.' Then grinned at Patrick to make sure that his fiery-tempered friend knew it for a jest. 'But thanks for namin' him after me, it were a right kind thought.'

– Poor lad, thought Thomasin. Why should I have so much and he have nothing? She patted his hand. 'Nay, not kind, love, only fittin'. There weren't two finer blokes to name him after.'

The luxury of laying in bed began to pall. Thomasin was becoming increasingly impatient with her mother's fussing. Tears flowed frequently and unexplainedly. Eventually in a fit of pique she sprang from the bed and pulled on her clothes. Assuring her mother she would be fine she packed her off home and sank down in relief, enjoying the sudden emptiness of the house. Patrick had taken the children out for a walk and John was out Heaven knew where; there was only her and the baby at home.

She pushed herself from the chair, wincing, for she was still sore where the baby's quick exit had torn her. Looking around for jobs that needed tackling she could find none; her houseproud mother had swept away any trace of grime. The house was as clean as a new pin. A search of the cupboards revealed a surfeit of baking, so there was no option left but to return to her chair where she sat staring at the wall. Would they live like this always, she wondered, gazing at the rough bare plaster. Patrick's hard work had enabled them to furnish the house a lot more comfortably than most in their position, but it would be euphemistic to call it anything other than a hovel. Oh, to see some pretty flowered curtains at the windows instead of those dreary brown ones, or a couple of pictures on the walls to brighten them up. But, though essentially a materialistic person, Thomasin never regretted marrying Patrick and her protestations that he must not think he had to work all hours that God sent just to please her were sincere. The impoverished surroundings mattered not when she had three fine children and a good strong man to warm her bed.

Her thoughts were distracted by a knock on the door. Hoisting herself from the chair she opened it to find Father Kelly on the doorstep. 'Liam!' He was the last person she might have expected. 'Well, I never – come in.'

Liam scraped the mud from his boots and entered. 'I expect you're surprised to see me?'

'No, me hair allus stands on end like this. Sit down. Eh, Pat'll be sorry he missed yer. He's just taken t'bairns for a walk – never been known. Will yer 'ave a cup o' tea?'

'I will, an' very kind it is of ye to offer after the way I've treated ye.'

Thomasin raised her eyebrows. 'The way you've treated us? I would've thought it were t'other way round.'

'True,' replied Liam. 'But I reckon I was the guiltier of the two parties. 'Twas no way for a Christian to behave, walking out like a truculent child just 'cause I couldn't get me own way. An' truth to tell, in walking out I was admitting defeat, which is something a man in my profession should never do. He should stand by his friends an' help them overcome their prejudices. So, when I heard ye'd had a new addition . . .'

'Yer thought yer'd come an' have another try,' supplied Thomasin. 'Aye well,' she handed him a cup of tea and sat down opposite at the table, 'I shouldn't give up yet, Liam, yer might get yer own way in t'end.'

Her words whet Liam's interest and he leaned forward. 'Do I detect a hint of reason?'

Thomasin brought her grey eyes level with his and said honestly, 'I'm not sure yet, Liam.' She toyed with the handle of the cup.

'Something's happened since I saw ye last?' ventured the priest.

'Did yer 'ear about Erin's nasty episode?' Liam frowned. 'No, I don't expect anyone would've told yer.' She related the episode, at the end of which the priest's face crumpled.

'God . . . an' I wasn't here to comfort ye. What kind of a priest am I?'

'You weren't to know, Liam,' she absolved. 'Anyway, before that 'appened Erin was an evil little monkey, by she really was. I couldn't seem to do owt right for her. The way she looked at me sometimes . . . it were like she couldn't stand the sight o' me. An' I'm afraid I came close to feelin' the same way about her sometimes. Then, after this bad job it were like . . . oh, I can't describe the feelin' but we suddenly came together like that.' She locked her fingers to illustrate. 'Somethin' 'appened, Liam. Don't ask me what 'cause I couldn't tell yer. I were just so thankful an' happy that Jos Leach hadn't harmed her that I came to thinkin' there must be somebody up there after all, watchin' over us, yer know. It were such a lovely feelin'.' She gave a little laugh. 'Do I sound daft?'

Liam shook his head and said quietly, 'It sounds to me like ye've found God, Thomasin.'

'Ah well, I wouldn't know about that.' She sipped her tea. 'I just know that Erin's accepted me at last. Whoever's work that was I'm very grateful.'

'An' how is the wee girl now?' he asked concernedly.

Thomasin sighed. 'Physically she's fine, but mentally who can tell? She won't go to play in Britannia Yard any more, just stays 'ome wi' me or plays wi' little'ns in our own yard.'

'Ah well, I should try not to make too much of it,' advised

Liam. 'Scars like that take a long time healing. She liked and trusted somebody an' he let her down. She's bound to be a bit withdrawn at the moment. Give it a few months and she'll come round. She's a lot luckier than the young chap who set upon her. He's got to spend the rest of his life in that place, an' him little more than a child himself.'

'Surely yer didn't expect us to say nowt about it?' she asked amazedly. 'Just let him go his own sweet way molestin' little lasses whenever he felt like it?'

'No, no of course not,' answered Liam sadly. ' 'Tis just the thought of him mouldering away in that lunatic asylum, an' him not understanding why he's been locked up.'

'Well, I for one am glad he is locked up, Liam,' said Thomasin firmly. 'Where he can't do no more harm. It's Erin yer should be feelin' sorry for, not him.'

A meditative nod, then Liam returned to his former subject. 'So, ye think ye might've changed your mind about having the boys baptised?'

'We've discussed it, yes. Pat can't make up his mind.'

'Isn't that Patrick down to his boots? He'd sit on the fence an' watch the house fall down. D'ye feel I should have another go at him?'

'If yer like but I don't know that it'll work – oh but, Liam,' she smiled and touched his arm, 'he'll be that pleased to see yer in his 'ouse again, whatever the reason. He's missed yer company, yer know.'

'I've missed his too,' answered Liam. 'Tell him I'll call again when I get the chance – if you're sure I'll not get a bunch o' knuckles. I'm just off to visit Mrs Dougherty now. The poor thing is dying I fear.'

Thomasin fought down the urge to joke that she hoped the woman had hung on until Liam had finished jawing here; the priest might not appreciate her black humour. 'We'll look forward to seein' yer, Liam.'

Concern grew over Erin's dogged refusal to visit Britannia Yard. Thomasin had tried gentle coaxing: 'That nasty man isn't there, yer know, love,' but still Erin refused, preferring to stay at home in the company of her little brothers, her doll and her harp. Then, one drizzly morning, Erin had suddenly asked to be taken to visit Granny.

'Well, you certainly pick yer moments,' said a surprised Thomasin, up to her elbows in flour. 'Can't it wait till this aft?'

'No, I must go now,' replied the girl intensely, but when Thomasin enquired why the hurry she could not answer, for there was no tangible reason. 'Please, Mam,' she begged.

Thomasin smiled. It had taken some getting used to, hearing Erin calling her 'mam', and despite the inopportune moment she was glad that the child had made her own decision to go to Britannia Yard and had not had to be pushed into it. 'All right, I'll just finish this dough.' She pummelled away inside the large bowl. 'You go wrap Sonny up warm, then I'll be ready.' It had been necessary to give the new baby a nickname with two Johns in the house.

'I'll have to take my harp as well,' said Erin.

'Yer can't lug that great thing over there in this weather,' cried Thomasin, then sighed as a heavy rapping came at the door. 'All right, all right, I'm comin', don't break door down.'

'Oh, Mrs Feeney, sorry to bother yer.' Sarah Wilson hopped about on the doorstep, trying to avoid the rain. 'Can yer just spare me half a cup o' sugar? I've run short again.'

Thomasin admitted her. 'Aye, I suppose so – if you'll do me a favour in return. Can yer keep yer eye on these two bairns while I nip round to Brit Yard with Erin? I'll only be as long as it takes me to get drenched.'

Mrs Wilson put her hands on her knees, bending to speak to the youngest member of the family who rolled over and over on the mat in front of the fire. 'Eh, haven't you grown! By, it dun't seem like five minutes since he was born an' look at him.' She tickled Sonny's ribs, making him laugh. 'Eh, who could hurt 'em?'

'Y'oughta be 'ere when he's squawkin' his head off an' clarted up to t'eyeballs,' said Thomasin. 'Away, Erin, fetch yer harp. Shan't be long, Mrs Wilson.'

The rain drove into their faces, turning their hair into frizzy rats' tails. Erin glanced about her nervously as they entered Britannia Yard; even in the knowledge that Jos was incarcerated she was still afraid.

Her sudden entry to Bridie's kitchen startled the old woman from her nap in the rocking chair. 'Well, fancy coming out on a day like this,' she cried, rubbing her eyes. 'Oh, but 'tis glad I am to see ye an' no mistake.' She held out her hand to Erin who clasped it firmly and climbed onto the old woman's lap. Bridie screwed up her face in discomfort as the bony rump adjusted itself on her pained knees.

'I've missed ye,' she told the child. ' 'Tis like someone took a knife an' cut out a little piece o' me heart, what with you not payin' your normal visits lately. It must be ages since ye last called. I thought I'd seen the last o' ye. "Bridie," says I, "ye've taught the girl all ye know an' now she's forgotten all about ye." ' In the course of instructing Erin in the joys of the harp Bridie had realised that she had untapped genius. Often she had tried to fox Erin by giving her a difficult piece to play but had been invariably out-done. The girl was a natural. Soon she had been able to play the most exacting tunes without stumbling.

The sound of Erin's harp had seemed to revive and re-nourish her. Every time the girl played, Bridie was once more in the Emerald Isle, a girl again, long, long ago. How the boys had flocked about her then, bewitched by the strains of her harp, lured by a siren in a sea of green fields. In her memory it was always summer, always would be, with the laughing tanned faces of healthy young men wrestling for the privilege of walking her home. Ah, she could have had any man in County Mayo then, such was the power of her music, but the one she had finally chosen and with whom she had lived for forty years was gone now, and there had been no children. She was quite alone.

It was ironic, the way she had tried so hard to die when she had lost him to the Great Hunger, when all about her were falling like swatted flies. It must have been a will greater than her own which had kept her alive and brought her to this foreign land, where she had been surrounded by people, yet strangely alone – until she had met the child.

Erin was speaking. 'I'll never forget ye, Granny. I wanted to come but I was frighted.'

Bridie sighed and hugged the girl. 'Aye, I can understand that, my pet. 'Twas just that . . . well, an old lady gets to thinkin' strange thoughts. I got the feeling on me that I was never going to see ye again an' it made me sad, like.'

'Don't worry, Granny.' Erin checked for signs of tears on

the other's face. 'Look,' she pointed to the harp which was propped against the door jamb. 'I've come to play for ye.'

'Oh, that's grand.' Bridie helped the girl from her knee. 'An' did ye come on your own or did Thomasin bring ye?'

'Mammy brought me,' said Erin, surprising Bridie with the title bestowed on Thomasin. She dabbed the moisture from the curved frame and sat next to the old woman, wriggling her bottom between the arthritic knee and the chair arm.

' 'Tis good to have ye back,' whispered Bridie as the enchanting chords leapt from under the plucking fingers, producing a soporific melody which made her eyelids unaccountably heavy. Slowly they closed and at once she was far away in that green and luscious country, feeling the heather scratch her bare feet as she danced over its purple carpet. Her hair was no longer grey and wound into a restrictive bun, but flowed free and golden in the wind, streaking out behind her like a yellow banner. Her limbs were firm and supple carrying her over the dew-kissed grasses in a joyful, abandoned dance.

Erin finished playing and opened her eyes – Wouldn't you know it? Granny had fallen asleep. She tiptoed to the door, then turned to gaze at the wrinkled countenance with its peaceful expression and ran back to plant a soft kiss on Bridie's cheek. Opening the door quietly, so as not to disturb her friend, she slipped away to Molly's house where Thomasin was still sitting.

The woman looked up at the child's entrance. 'S'truth, 'ave I been here that long? I'd best get meself gone else Mrs Wilson'll think I've absconded. Have yer enjoyed yerself?'

Erin nodded. 'Except that Granny fell asleep halfway through my tune.'

Molly opened the door for them. 'Ah, 'tis her age, ye know – but I'll bet she enjoyed your visit. I'll go see her myself when this rain has eased up. Sure, the poor old divil gets mournful lonely.'

An hour after they had left and the rain had stopped, Molly picked her way through the muddy puddles in the yard and went to call on Bridie. Staring down at the strikingly beautiful face of the old woman Molly felt a brief ripple of shock and crossed herself. If she had needed further evidence of Bridie's departure the cold hand provided it and she shivered as she touched the icy fingers. Pulling a blanket from the bed in the corner she tucked it around the old woman, then berated herself for such a ridiculous act; as if Bridie was bothered about being warm now.

She took a final look at the body, just to make certain, then slipped outside, already making plans for the wake. They would have to give Bridie a proper send-off, her having no family to speak of. If everyone contributed they could have a high old time.

By the time she had reached her own front door the shock of death had turned to pleasure.

'Good to see y'again, Pat.' Liam shook the man's hand warmly. ''Tis only sorry I am it couldn't be a happier occasion. Ah, but you're looking fine, the pair o' ye.' He embraced Thomasin with his smile. 'And your handsome brood.' He put his face close to the child in her arms. 'Faith, what a bruiser. Ye'll be able to go ten rounds with your father before you're much older. Sure, wasn't he only a wee sprout of a thing the last time I saw him. An' young Dickie-me-lad, how are you? The ladies'll have to be sure an' watch out when you grow up. Ah, an' I see our beautiful young colleen will be treating us with her harp.' He straightened. 'My, it promises to be a fine wake.'

Thomasin glanced at the guest of honour in her plain wooden box, then at the table of food: oatcakes, scones, apples, bread, baskets of piping hot potatoes, the jugs of liquor and the pot of tobacco, the bowl of salt for those who were carrying the coffin to sprinkle in their pockets to ward off harmful spirits. Everyone was chattering and laughing and saying didn't the corpse look a picture of happiness. In fact it all appeared more like a party than a funeral.

'Sure, I can see our good lady's thinking we're crazy.' Liam was smiling when she looked at him. 'I'll wager ye've never been to a send-off like this, Tommy?'

'Last time I did, it was a weddin'.'

'Ah well, I guarantee it'll make your eyes widen as the day goes on,' predicted Liam.

It certainly did. As the wake progressed it became more of

a circus, the guests succumbing to the potent beverage with which Molly kept refilling their cups. Feats of strength began to be performed in the middle of the floor, along with wrestling, juggling, acrobatics and other games – some bordering on the obscene, which Father Kelly quickly vetoed. The latter, though, was a prime contributor to the stream of jokes and riddles that were bandied.

As Ghostie Connors was called upon to provide the music John announced loudly, 'Flamin' 'ell, it's the first time I've seen a corpse play at its own funeral!'

Ghostie, never appreciative of laughter directed at himself, threw his workmate a disdainful glare, shuffled to the centre of the floor where he proceeded to dish up the most inappropriate funeral music.

Thomasin was half-appalled, half-bewitched by this strange breed, one side of her wanting to join in the merriment, the other telling her it was disrespectful.

'Ah, I can understand your shock,' said Patrick, bouncing a child on his knee to the music. 'But don't y'agree this way is a lot better than standing round a big hole with long faces? After all, 'tis a better place Bridie's gone to.'

'I thought you didn't believe in that any more,' teased his wife.

Patrick shrugged, looked sheepish at being caught out. 'Nor do I – in the church anyways. But an afterlife? Well 'tis logical is it not? There must be somewhere better than this, otherwise what'd be the point of it all?'

'I think I'll bring Liam over to listen to this. I'd say he stood a pretty good chance of recapture right now.'

'Lord, don't do that. Sure, I was pleased enough to see him after so long but I couldn't do for him to go on an' on about having the boys baptised.'

'Why don't we 'ave it done an' that'd be an end to it?' coaxed Thomasin.

'Because I don't feel anything, that's why.'

'I think it's just 'cause yer don't want to back down.'

'Think what ye like – now will ye stop spoilin' me enjoyment an' come have a dance?'

A sigh. 'Whoever heard o' dancin' at a funeral?'

Molly came round just then with a pewter pot which she dashed against each of their cups. 'There, get that down yese

– oh no, wait. Wait, everybody! I'm forgetting meself. We've not yet drunk a toast to Bridie's health.' She burst out laughing, shocking Thomasin even further at this thoughtless display. 'Oh, have ye heard me? 'Tis a bit late for wishin' the poor old darlin' health. Anyway,' she raised her mug, 'here's to Bridie, may she have Eternal Peace.'

'Well, she's not likely to get that 'ere,' muttered Thomasin as everybody echoed 'To Bridie!'

'Ah, a drop o' pure gold,' gasped Molly. 'Takes the lining off your throat so it does. Come on, then, on with the wake.' And the festivities continued.

In time the potent liquor banished Thomasin's reserve and she consented to dance with her husband, asking her neighbour to take charge of Sonny. It had certainly been a long time since they had danced like this. The music – or was it the drink? created a mood of devilment in him and he pulled the pins from her hair, shaking it loose to stream around her shoulders.

'Ah, I love it like this.' He squashed his face into its red waves as he swung her round.

'Take that look out o' yer eye,' she warned him laughingly. 'I can't be doin' with another bairn just yet.' After Sonny's birth she had made it clear there would be no more additions to the family. Not for her a life such as Molly's with snot-nosed children dangling from every available appendage. Three was quite enough, thank you, considering the difficulty they had to feed and clothe them.

'Faith, ye wouldn't be that cruel,' he pleaded in her ear as they whirled around the room. 'Not tonight. We're havin' such a good time, 'twould be a pity to end such a day on a sour note.'

'If it's sweetness yer after I'll treat yer to an extra spoonful o' sugar in yer tea. Now dance.'

Hands clapped, feet drummed, urging the dancers on until they were ready to drop from exhaustion. It seemed as though Ghostie's fiddle was about to be sawn in half, so frantically was his elbow moving. Yet above the tortured instrument the grey face remained impassive, sepulchral. Finally the strain on his fiddle proved to be too much as one of the guts snapped with a noisy ping.

Thomasin sagged into a chair next to her husband. 'Phew!

I've only had one dance an' I'm worn out. I must be gettin' old.'

'Never,' smiled Patrick. 'You'll never grow old, Tommy.' He kissed her and looked over her shoulder at Erin. 'Erin darlin', if ye want to play your harp now's the time. 'Tis a captive audience ye'll have.'

Erin took her chance and pushed her way to the room centre, making no apologies for rapping some ankles with her harp on the way. They had had their bit of fun, now they must listen while she played something more respectful in honour of her friend. She then fingered out the saddest refrain in her repertoire, accompanying it with tragic words. The noisy drunken gabbling soon diminished to a deathly silence as everyone listened. She sang of the land after which she had been named, of its sons' and daughters' tragic exodus, its beauty, her sweet voice rising in pitiful lament. At the climax of her mournful song there was not an eye in the house that did not shine with tears and the applause was tumultuous.

'Oh, that was lovely, pet.' Molly blew her nose loudly and mopped the moisture from her deeply set eyes. 'Sure, I haven't enjoyed meself so much since me old mother died.'

And everybody laughed again.

Chapter Twenty-seven

How quickly the years flew past. True to Thomasin's declaration there had been no additions to their brood in the last four years, but the strain was beginning to tell. John became uncomfortably aware that all was not well in the Feeney household. It began with tight-lipped faces and the odd sarcastic remark then, as it gathered momentum, developed into something more violent with abusive tirades being volleyed back and forth across the breakfast table. Thinking that maybe he was no longer welcome, John questioned his friend after one such particular outburst.

Patrick waited until Thomasin was out of earshot before offering an explanation, then in a low voice said, ' 'Tis nothing to do with you, John boyo. 'Tis her an' me that's the problem. She's been keeping me at arms' length, I can't even . . . '

'Go on, tell him!' Thomasin had sneaked back into the room as their voices had lowered and glared at Patrick's guilty start. 'Tell him all about our private life, see if I care. There's a few things I could tell him about you an' all.' She stormed back into the kitchen, cursing as she tripped over a toy cart.

Patrick sighed his exasperation, then told John of Thomasin's reluctance to have any more children. 'I can't go on like this, John,' he ended dolefully. 'She's driving me to rape. No other man'd put up with it.'

John sympathised, understanding all too well how his friend was feeling. 'I should imagine that once she's made her mind up on summat there'd be no budgin' her.'

' 'Tis right you are,' replied his friend acidly. 'An' the frustrating thing is that it's not going to get any better while

I'm only bringing home thirteen bob a week. An' that's what it boils down to in the end, ye know.' He tapped his finger on the table as he spoke. 'Money. God, will I ever get out o' this place?'

'There's some would be quite happy wi' a place like this,' said John. 'I reckon you would if it weren't for Tommy's mother gettin' yer ridin' all the time.'

Patrick groaned. 'Ah, but she's right, John! I should be able to give Tommy more than this – an' it isn't just her, 'tis all of it. D'ye know, when I first came to England, about eleven years ago, I promised meself that as soon as I'd saved enough, I was going to buy meself a small piece o' land an' be me own master. Huh! What happened, I ask myself?' He swept his hand around the dreary room. 'Is this all that became o' my dream?' He pushed away his empty plate and sighed again.

'So, yer think a bit of extra cash'd solve yer problems?' asked John.

'It'd certainly help,' came the sour reply. 'What with there being no overtime lately I've had to dig into me savings.'

'There's only one solution then,' was John's simple answer. 'Yer'll 'ave to ask for a rise.'

'I can't do that,' argued Patrick. ' 'Tis the going rate.'

'Goin' rate be blowed. He could pay yer more if he wanted but he's not likely to unless yer kick up a fuss. Yer never get owt if yer don't ask.'

'Well,' answered Patrick dubiously. 'If ye think there's a chance it'll work I may as well ask him this morning.'

'You put me in an awkward position, Feeney,' was Baxter's reply to the Irishman's request.

'Well, the way I see it, Mr Baxter, ye've been getting my services pretty cheaply.' Patrick was determined to go out richer than he had come in. 'I was doing the work o' three men until recently.'

'I can't argue with that,' answered Baxter. 'But as you may have gathered there's not been much work put our way lately. Things haven't been too easy for me, financially speaking.'

'Oh, I can wait until things pick up a bit, Mr Baxter,' conceded Patrick. 'I didn't mean I wanted more money right this minute.'

'Either way you'd not get it, I'm afraid. It's a bit more difficult than that.' Baxter cleared his throat. 'As a matter of fact I was about to send for you to explain.'

One of Patrick's eyebrows formed a question mark. 'Explain?' he asked when Baxter was unforthcoming. 'Explain what?'

'Explain why I have to let you go,' said the other into his waistcoat.

'Let me go?'

Baxter sighed. 'I can't put it much plainer. There's no more work – you're finished. Last in, first out, that's how it goes, I'm afraid.'

'What're ye talking about "last in"?' cried Patrick. 'I've worked for you eleven years. What about Barley, or Watson? They've only been here a matter o' months.'

'I am aware of that,' replied his employer. 'An' they'll be going as well, only I haven't had time to tell them yet. I've got debts to meet, I can't be paying for men to sit idle. You know as well as I do there's hardly been enough work for two men lately, let alone half a dozen. No, I'm sorry, Feeney, there's no going back.'

Patrick was stunned. 'But doesn't loyalty count for anything with you? I've given ye eleven years of my life, doesn't that deserve more consideration? What's my wife going to say when I go home an' tell her I've lost me job? How am I supposed to feed me children?'

Baxter was unrepentant. 'Eleven years, you say? Well, when you've been at it as long as I have you'll come to learn there's no sentiment in business. There's many a time I've given men like you a chance in the past, only to be let down. Don't talk to me about loyalty, lad, loyalty won't pay my bills – an' I have children to feed too, you know. No, I'm sorry, I've tried to put it off as long as I could but you'll have to go.'

Patrick accepted his fate. What use was there in pursuing the argument?

'How long have I got then?'

'A week,' replied Baxter. 'And before you start upbraiding me again, I shouldn't, or I might decide to finish you right now. As far as I'm concerned I'm doing you a favour by allowing you to stay on till Saturday.'

Patrick curled his lip. 'Thank ye very much, Mr Baxter, sir. Remind me to do you a favour some time.'

All day Patrick rehearsed in his mind how to break the news to Thomasin. How would she take it? Now there was a silly question. He could end up like some bloodied object on one of Raper's hooks.

When he arrived home that night John asked eagerly if Patrick had had any luck. The latter glanced briefly at his wife, slung his haversack into a corner and sank into a chair, rubbing his dirty hands over his face.

'Well?' repeated John impatiently. 'How did yer get on?'

'I didn't,' muttered Patrick through his fingers. 'Tommy, where's me tea? Me belly thinks me mouth's been stitched up.'

Thomasin, in slightly better humour than the morning, placed his meal on the table. 'What's the matter wi' you? Yer look as if Liam's been castigating you again.'

' 'Tis worse than that, I'm afraid,' he responded. Her ears pricked. He raised his eyes to hers, then lowered them again. 'I've lost me job.'

'Stap me!' cried John and slapped the wall in anger. 'He's not gone an' finished yer just 'cause you asked for a rise? Blimey, I wish I'd never mentioned it.'

Thomasin, initially struck dumb with shock, now found her voice and used it on John. 'Oh, so it's you who's been puttin' silly ideas into his head, is it?'

'No, no,' Patrick intervened. ' 'Twas not John's fault. He only told me what to do for the best. The reason I got finished was that Baxter's having a difficult time of it financially.'

'Aw, poor old devil,' came the satirical rejoinder. 'My heart bleeds for him. It must be murder havin' to live in a ten roomed house with only pheasant to eat.'

' 'Tis no good you giving me all your clever talk,' replied Patrick. 'After next week I'll be out of a job an' nothing you can say will change it.'

'This is all your fault,' Thomasin accused John.

'No!' shouted Patrick. 'If anybody's to blame 'tis you.'

'Oh, it's all comin' out now!' jeered his wife. 'I knew it'd be my fault. Well, yer've cooked yer goose, Patrick Feeney, 'cause until yer get another job yer'll be sleepin' down 'ere with yer friend, then see how clever his ideas are.'

She stomped upstairs, closely followed by an incensed Patrick, where their argument continued vociferously for some time.

John sat at the table, leaning on his elbows and staring at Patrick's untouched meal as bangs and crashes erupted over his head. 'Oh well,' he decided, pulling the plate towards him, 'waste not, want not.'

He was halfway through the meal when he suddenly noticed that the noise had died to a rhythmic creaking. 'Stone the crows,' he muttered to himself, 'I wish I had Pat's powers of persuasion.'

'Ah, this weak flesh,' cursed Thomasin, retching in the privy some weeks later. She had never been quite sure whether the saying 'the luck of the Irish' actually meant the opposite; well, she was sure now. A deep depression settled upon her at the thought of another mouth to feed. Patrick's days at Baxter's were over and as yet he had been unable to find work elsewhere. They were now surviving on their savings and relying on John for income.

Their lodger, despite Patrick's denials, held himself responsible for their dilemma and racked his brains for a solution. Though they were at the moment existing on the money he made from selling scrap he knew that Patrick's pride would not allow him to rely on his friend for long. Perhaps they could set up some sort of business partnership. He decided to broach the subject with Patrick.

'What sort o' business partnership?' asked his friend.

'Well, brickyin' I suppose,' replied John. 'I'm not so crippled that I can't lay a few bricks any more, as long as you do all the humpin'.'

'An' just how d'ye suggest we go about this?' enquired Patrick. 'I mean it takes capital to start a business. I can barely afford to feed me family at the moment.'

'It all depends on how yer go about it,' answered John, lowering his voice, afraid that if Thomasin heard his good idea she would be sure to quash it out of hand. 'I've been weighin' the matter up very carefully. If we can get the materials cheap we'll be well away.'

'And how or where do we get cheap materials? Sure, ye know most o' the bricks used are reclaimed. Nobody uses new stuff, so are ye proposing to knock down a few houses to get them?'

'Aye, I thought we could start wi' Baxter's,' said John. 'Yer won't take me serious, will yer? Just leave it all to t'businessman.' He tapped his chest. 'I know where to lay me hands on t'stuff.'

'Ah, now where have I heard that before?' mused Patrick.

'Pat, if I've told yer once I've told yer a thousand times,' objected a wounded John. 'I've finished wi' all that lark. Just you leave everything to me an' don't worry, yer Uncle John's gonna make yer a rich man.'

A mere twenty-four hours later John stumbled into Bay Horse Yard, heaving under the weight of the handcart. He poked his head around the door, saying to Patrick, 'Away, I've got a surprise for yer.'

Surprise was not the word. Patrick could scarcely voice his incredulity at the piles of bricks, mortar, sand and horsehair that were crammed onto the handcart.

'Holy Souls,' he finally managed to whisper. 'How did ye get your hands on all this since yesterday?'

'I got it cheap off a man who's gone bankrupt,' replied John with his back to the Irishman, then pulled the tarpaulin back over the load.

Thomasin stood at her husband's shoulder, equally amazed, but not so easily misled. 'The truth,' she told John bluntly.

John turned around. 'Promise yer won't hit me?'

'Oh, God, it's stolen!' hissed Thomasin and pushed the two men into the house.

'John, ye promised;' accused Patrick. 'Now where did ye really get it?'

'Think of a name beginning wi' B,' answered John sheepishly.

'Oh, Jaze . . . an' ye brought it here? Christ, man, have ye no sense? I could end up in prison if someone should guess where it came from.'

John flapped a derisive hand. 'He doesn't know. I've had this up me sleeve for a while, been collectin' it bit by bit over t'past month or so an' stashin' it away.' Along with other things; John had these caches all over. 'He won't even notice it's gone.'

'Oh, John, John,' wailed Patrick. 'Why the hell d'ye think Baxter had to get rid o' me? Because he was in "financial difficulties", as he put it. There's no bloody wonder if some devil's been thievin' all his materials, is there?'

John was scornful. 'A tiny bit o' stuff's not gonna make much difference to him. Flamin' 'ell, he's had his whack out of us over t'years. I bet he couldn't survive on three bob a day like I used to before he gave me the boot – an' what about you? Eleven years yer gave him an' what has he given you except a kick up t'arse? No, I reckon we've only taken what's rightfully ours.'

'Well, I think John's right,' announced Thomasin, surprising both men. 'He deserves everything he gets after t'way he treated yer both. I don't hold wi' thievin' but I think yer a fool, Pat, if yer don't take advantage o' this.'

Patrick stared at his wife in her dowdy, ill-fitting dress, at the lines of worry that striped her forehead; had it been his failure to provide that had carved them there?

'All right,' he yielded, much to John's satisfaction. 'I'll go along with it for now. But,' he pointed a warning finger, 'the moment we start to make our fortunes this lot goes back. I'm having no one telling me my business was founded on dishonesty.'

John stared. 'Yer mad,' he breathed. 'Bloody mad. How will we get it back to Baxter? Trundle it onto t'site wi' t'handcart an' say "Sorry, Mr Baxter, we only borrowed it"?'

'Not "we", John,' replied Patrick. 'You – an' ye'd best get it out o' sight now before somebody starts askin' questions.' He flopped back into a chair and picked up yesterday's newspaper which had been passed on by William.

Thomasin left John to dispose of the handcart and joined Pat.

'Eh, I'm that relieved we're gonna 'ave some money coming in again.'

Patrick allowed himself a smile, though he questioned the efficacy of his brain. 'I don't expect it'll be much at first 'cause there's no point in running before we can walk. Best if we start by doing small jobs, nothin' too complicated, repairs an' alterations. Then when people get to know us maybe we can begin to be a little ambitious.'

She returned his smile. 'I don't feel too bad about the baby now, 'cause yer'll be earnin' a lot more than if you were workin' for Baxter.' She sat opposite him and gazed into the fire, dreaming of what Patrick's new venture might bring them.

Patrick turned over a page of the newspaper and let out a cry of delight, startling her. 'Listen to this: *On the tenth of September, eighteen hundred and fifty-eight, at the Festival Concert Rooms will be held a reading of "A Christmas Carol" by its celebrated author Mister Charles Dickens.'* He scanned the advertisement then let out a groan of disappointment. 'Oh, no, the cheapest tickets are a shilling; we can't afford it.'

Thomasin, realising how important this was to her husband, said, 'Yer in work again, remember? Or nearly. I daresay it won't break us?'

He was aching to go but, 'It seems so extravagant when we've hardly been able to find money for food lately.'

'There's a few bob left in tin. I dare say yer pal will keep supplyin' t'bunnies so we'll not starve.'

'An' you'll come with me?'

'Happen I will – we'll take Erin too. It'll make a nice evening out.'

Alas, when Patrick visited the music shop in Davygate to purchase the tickets there were none left. 'But perhaps,' the assistant told him, 'there may be a few on sale at the actual venue.'

'Aw, never mind, love,' Thomasin comforted his despondent admission. 'We'll still go. Even if we can't buy tickets yer might at least be able to see him arrive.'

Patrick cheered up. It would indeed be an honour just to see the man.

Chapter Twenty-eight

By the day of the Dickens reading Patrick was feeling pretty pleased with himself. John, with his silvery tongue, had convinced their clients that he and Pat were the best men for the job and the growing demand for their work gave them little time for leisure. Still, he would not miss the chance of seeing his favourite author if he could help it. Leaving the younger children in the care of their adoptive uncle he, Thomasin and Erin set out for the Festival Concert Rooms.

Thankfully the weather was mild as, to Patrick's deep chagrin, all the spare tickets had been snapped up. Thomasin said she and the child would wait with him for a glimpse of his hero. As the family settled on a bench close to the entrance, hordes of richly-trammelled gentlefolk began to arrive, mingling involuntarily with their poorer counterparts. Apparently Dickens had insisted on the tickets being reasonably priced so that the lower classes too would have a chance to hear his work.

Erin had brought along her harp which Patrick had seen as a good idea; if they were to have a long wait it would occupy fidgety hands. He noticed his wife shiver and pull her shawl more tightly round her. The weather had altered with a September contrariness; one moment gentle sunshine, the next a chilly breeze.

'Sure, ye can always go home,' he told her. 'I don't mind waiting on me own.'

'We've waited this long, we might as well stay a few minutes longer,' she answered. 'He can't be long now. Besides I'm rather curious to see a man whose books can still my husband's tongue for more than five minutes.'

Erin flexed her fingers and began to play as the queue outside the Rooms grew longer. Several heads turned to discover the source of the delightful sound, smiling in appreciation. One gentleman who had just alighted from a stately-looking carriage and whose conscience had obviously been pricked by the impoverished group held out a coin to Erin.

Patrick stopped Erin's hand from reaching out. 'Thank ye, but we're not beggars. My daughter is merely playin' for her own amusement. Anyone who cares to listen is welcome to do so with pleasure, but we seek no payment.'

The man raised his eyebrows admiringly. Such pride was rare amongst the peasant classes. He surveyed the man's ragged appearance, then looked back at the arrogant face. Although dressed in rags the man obviously regarded himself as an equal; the absence of the word 'sir' had not gone unregistered. He studied the child whose brilliant eyes brimmed with a wealth of knowledge – so young, he thought, yet the eyes could be those of an old woman. He then turned his attention to Thomasin, who stared back unabashed at his scrutiny. Now there was a tasty morsel: with a more flattering wardrobe she could keep pace with the best of the fillies.

He spoke at last. 'You have an extremely talented daughter,' he told Patrick thoughtfully. 'I am sure that her accomplishment deserves a wider audience. What are your thoughts on allowing her to play at the Hall one evening?'

'What hall would that be?' enquired Patrick suspiciously.

The man laughed, greatly amused that the other was ignorant of his identity. 'Why, Dunworthe Hall. The name is Herleigh by the way – and yours?' Patrick told him. 'I shall be giving a musical evening on Tuesday next and should be delighted to have your daughter entertain us.'

Patrick nodded slowly as he encountered Erin's eager face. 'If Erin wants to go I guess it'll be fine by me. Can ye tell us how to get there?'

The man appeared more amused than ever, then pointed. 'Ask my coachman, he will tell you. I look forward to hearing your daughter's talents on Tuesday eve.' So saying, he entered the building.

'Well, would yer credit that?' spluttered Thomasin. 'I suppose you know who that was?'

Patrick shook his head. 'Hurley or something or other.'

'It's only Lord Herleigh, yer big daft lummox. Yer weren't very polite to him, were yer?' She mimicked his statement: ' "My daughter is merely playing for her own amusement." By!'

Patrick defended his behaviour. 'Just 'cause he's a lord is that any reason I should kiss his arse?'

'Nobody asked yer to, did they? But yer never even called him sir.'

Patrick tutted. 'For God's sake, why did he have to pick on us? What're we gonna wear for this do?'

'Nay, don't ask me, I never got an invite.' Thomasin turned up her nose, faking offence.

Patrick put an arm round her. 'Ye know, 'twould be better for you to take Erin yourself. Ye'd enjoy it much more than I will.'

'I hope yer not expectin' me to feel sorry for yer?'

He laughed. 'Maybe you're right. It might be rather interestin' at that.'

So knocked sideways was he by the man's identity that Patrick, in his conversation with Thomasin, failed to notice the dark, bearded figure entering the building surrounded by chattering admirers. Only when the doors had closed did he realise that the man whom he had come to see had eluded him. Unable to catch a word of the reading through the door or even at a window, and seeing his pregnant wife stretch her aching back, Patrick decided to take them home. Although he had missed Dickens the evening had not been a complete waste of time, for despite his nonchalant acceptance of the invitation to Dunworthe Hall Patrick was quite looking forward to the musical evening – and who knew what might come of it?

He delved into his pocket for pipe and tobacco pouch; it was good to be able to afford a smoke again. He approached a tobacco store on whose doorpost was fixed a metal horse's head. Bending over it he touched his pipe to the gas jet that flared from its nostrils then put an arm round his wife and steered her home.

Thomasin awoke next morning regretting her outing. There was a dull ache in the small of her back due to all that hanging around, she told herself as she waved her husband and John off to work – I should take things a little easier. After all, there's none of us getting any younger. She smiled at the thought of Patrick with greying hair and stooped posture, then rubbed her back thoughtfully where the pain lingered in a persistent warning. Ignoring it she turned to the pile of crockery in the sink.

'Ah well, this won't buy the baby a new bonnet. Erin love, fetch rest o' them pots, will yer?' She went to the yard to fill a bucket with water.

In her daydreaming the bucket overflowed and splashed onto her boots. She jumped back then picked up the heavy container to carry it indoors. Erin heard her harsh cry of pain and came running out into the yard, eyes wide with bewilderment as she witnessed Thomasin's agony.

'Mammy, what's the matter?'

'Ooh, God, Erin!' The pain was excruciating and Thomasin clutched first at her back then at her belly. 'Go get somebody quick. It's the babby.'

'Take me arm, Mam,' ordered Erin and helped her stepmother into the house where Thomasin crumpled to the floor.

Sonny, who had followed them in from the yard started wailing. 'Mammy!'

Dickie stood nearby, staring at his stricken mother. 'Can I have something to eat, Mam?'

'Oh, shut up, Dickie!' stormed Erin. 'Can't ye see Mammy's poorly?' She bundled the two of them into a chair. 'Now sit there an' don't move. I'm off to Aunt Molly's, she'll know what to do.' She bent over Thomasin's convulsive form. 'I'll not be long, Mam,' then dashed off to Britannia Yard, forgetting the apprehension she usually experienced here, and assailed Molly with a garbled account of what had happened.

Molly listened calmly to the eleven year old's frightened pleas. 'Right, pet. I'll be over right away. Just let me find Norah to look after me little ones. Brendan!' she called to one of three tiny children who played on the floor, 'Stop doin' that to your brother.' She turned casually to Erin. 'Ah, 'tis a pity your mammy didn't see fit to have a bigger family. They're a joy are the little ones, a pure joy – Brendan, I'll not tell ye again, d'ye want a whoppin' when your daddy gets in?'

Erin tugged at her sleeve imploringly. 'Oh, please, Aunt Molly, come quickly! She's awful bad.'

'All right, all right, don't be gettin' all aereorated.' Molly followed her out of Britannia Yard and into Walmgate. 'Not so fast, pet, me poor old legs cannot keep up with ye.' She was certain that Erin was kicking up a fuss over nothing and that when they arrived Thomasin would likely have got over her twinge.

But the moment Molly set eyes on Thomasin she realised that things were not as they should be: the pain was so bad that she had lost consciousness. Further indication of the seriousness of Thomasin's condition was the red stain spreading slowly through the coarse material of her skirt. Molly threw a worried glance at Erin and began to roll up her sleeves.

'Go for the doctor, pet, your mammy's not well at all. I'll look after her while ye go. Hurry now, there's a good colleen.' Erin fled into the yard. 'An' see if ye can find your daddy when ye've been to the doctor's!' shouted Molly.

Patrick was enjoying one of John's jokes when Erin finally came upon him in Barleycorn Yard. His smile disappeared as his daughter came rushing breathlessly up to him and, clutching a hand over the stitch in her side, delivered her bad news. 'Oh, Daddy, Daddy, come home! 'Tis Mammy . . . the baby.'

Leaving Erin trailing far behind a distraught Patrick galloped towards his home. When he arrived Molly waylaid him before he could rush up the stairs.

'The doctor's with her, Pat, I should wait till he comes down.'

When the doctor eventually reappeared some good while later, looking tired and rumpled, Patrick, in his anxiety, took hold of him roughly. 'Well, man, how is she?'

The doctor, patiently unloosing Patrick's grip on his arm, told him the worst: Thomasin had lost the baby. No, there had been no fall or shock, the premature labour had been inexplicable and final. His wife had lost a fearful amount of blood and it had been touch and go but she would probably survive now.

'Final,' mouthed Patrick. 'You said final?'

'I am sorry,' the doctor informed him as kindly as possible.

'But I greatly doubt that your wife will ever conceive again; her internal organs have suffered badly from this ordeal.'

Patrick was aghast. My God, it was his fault. If he hadn't kept her hanging around waiting for Dickens last evening this would never have happened.

'Well, wherever the fault lies,' replied the doctor to Patrick's self-reproach, 'she is not to be moved. Any upheaval could restart the bleeding. Do you understand?' He spoke, as if to a child, into Patrick's ashen face. 'The slightest movement could be her death warrant.'

The last words brought Patrick from his stupor. 'She could die?'

'Have you not been listening to a word I have said?' reproved the doctor. 'Yes, die! So heed my words and under no circumstances is she to be allowed to leave her bed. She is to receive constant nursing and plenty of nourishment to build her up. I have instructed the nurse who accompanied me to take charge of your wife's welfare for the next few days. I shall call upon you again tomorrow.' He was in the motions of donning his coat when his eyes fell on Molly, on the scrawny neck seamed with grime, the dirt-laden finger-nails. Belonging to the new school of thought, he decided to utter a further word of caution. 'And if you value your wife's health, Mr Feeney, you would be wise to restrict visitors to the immediate family. Any infection brought into the sickroom, however unwittingly, would undoubtably kill her.'

As soon as he had left Patrick shot upstairs to invade the sickroom. The nurse looked up sharply and put a finger to her lips, then left the bedside and whispered to him, 'Your wife is sleeping at present. I shouldn't disturb her, she's very weak.'

He stared down at the pale face that blended with the white bed linen. Her brilliant hair was strewn over the pillow in damp wisps. Her lashes were dark against the deathly skin and, sensing his presence, fluttered open.

'I didn't mean to wake ye.' He moved closer to take hold of her limp hand. She did not speak, her half-closed lids tried to force themselves open but were too weak and sleep claimed her again.

'*Tommy?*' The panic rose as, for one terrifying moment he

thought that his nightmare with Mary was to be repeated. But no, he could still feel the slight rise and fall of her breast. He slumped over her, scooping her hands between his and clutching them to his chest. A thousand thoughts swirled within his despair: it was his fault, all of it. If he hadn't selfishly insisted on taking his marital rights she would not be lying here now. But oh, how could he stay away from her when he loved her so much? She was like a sickness within him, ever present, always demanding. If anything should happen to her . . . he could not go through it all again – Please, God, he suddenly found himself praying. please, I'll give You my sons, I'll do anything You ask an' I'll not deny You again but please, please, don't take this one, too.

He felt a hand on his arm and raised desolate eyes. 'You'd better go now,' instructed the nurse. 'She's very ill and needs rest. I'll be sure to call you when she awakes.' Patrick remained at the bedside, unwilling to leave her, afraid that if he left she would die.

Then he brushed his lips to the waxen cheek and went reluctantly downstairs where he found John talking to Molly and Erin trying to comfort the boys.

'How is she?' Both John and Molly asked simultaneously.

He dropped his chin to his chest and slumped into a chair. 'She looks terrible, terrible. I was afraid to leave her in case she . . . but the nurse says I'll be better off leavin' her to get some rest.'

'Huh, nurse,' sniffed Molly. 'Sure, I can't see why ye have to have a nurse when ye know there's one here who's willing to take care o' Tommy; payin' out all that good money just to have some old busybody pushing ye around. Will I go up an' tell her she's not wanted?'

'No, no, thank ye for your offer, Molly,' replied Patrick. 'But you have your own family to see to, an' ye heard what the doctor said. She has to have somebody with her all the time for the next day or two at least. I think 'tis best if the nurse stays – she seems very competent.'

'Ah, she might seem that way while you're here to keep an eye on her,' said Molly. 'But as soon as you're off to work it'll be out with the gin bottle an' not a thought for poor, darlin' Tommy. She needs someone who cares for her. D'ye want I should come an' keep an eye on her for ye?'

'Thanks, Molly,' he answered gratefully. 'But I shan't be needin' your surveillance for I'll not be going to work till Tommy gets well.' He looked at John. 'Sorry to impose like this but can ye manage for a while on your own?'

'Aye, 'course,' vouched John. 'But don't yer think yer'd be better off workin'? There's nowt yer can do 'ere but sit around an' mope all day an' that's gonna do yer no good, is it?'

'She's my wife, John. If anything's going to happen to her I want to be here.'

'Enough o' that sort o' talk,' exclaimed Molly. 'Tommy'll be as fit as a lop in no time. All she needs is a good rest an' a drop o' good broth to build her up. Now, are ye sure ye don't want me to get rid o' that nurse for ye? I still say you're wastin' your money.'

Patrick was kind but firm. 'You're a good friend, Molly, an' it would be taking advantage of ye to expect ye to look after Tommy with your own to see to. Don't worry about me wasting my money. Sure, I can afford it now.' He looked at Erin who sat next to Dickie and held Sonny on her lap. 'Erin'll help with the cookin', won't ye, darlin'?'

She nodded and formed a smile. 'Don't worry, Daddy, I'll take care of us all.'

'Ah well, if me services aren't required I'll be off home,' declared Molly. 'But I'll be back later with a big jug o' beef tea.' She patted Patrick's shoulder. ' 'Tis dreadful sorry I am about the baby. I know just how ye feel havin' lost so many meself.'

'Faith, 'tis not the baby I'm grievin' over, Molly,' replied Patrick quietly. ' 'Tis me wife. At least if she comes through this I'll know it won't happen again.'

'Do I take ye to mean she cannot have any more children?' To Molly, the mother of eleven live children and the Lord knew how many stillborn, this was the worst fate of all. 'Oh, the poor darlin', I didn't realise it was so bad.'

John broke in. 'Any road, I'll be off back to me work, Pat. If yer get sick of stayin' at 'ome yer know where to find me.'

'Oh, wait an' I'll walk with ye, son,' announced Molly and followed him outside, leaving Patrick with his head in his hands, watched by three frightened children.

CHAPTER TWENTY-NINE

THE NEXT DAY brought little change to Thomasin's condition. Her face was still deathly white and when she woke it was for but a minute at a time. Patrick, when allowed to by the nurse, sat by her bedside, gently wiping her face with a damp cloth, an action which immediately plunged him back into the past, to when he had sat by another bedside, urging another wife not to die. When banished from the bedroom he would pace the floor below like a wound-up tiger, snapping irritably at his children then feeling thoroughly ashamed for his abominable behaviour. How could he blame them? The two younger ones were not to know that he had gone through all this before. Only in Erin's face did he perhaps see a flicker of understanding, of apprehension.

Another day passed. He could neither eat nor sleep for fear of what might happen, and dark crescents materialised beneath his worried, weary eyes. As the week neared its end Patrick began to despair that his belated prayers had once again been flung back in his face; but when he tried to see Tommy the nurse softened at his haggard features. 'If you promise me that you'll go downstairs this minute and sample some of whatever your daughter has been cooking and also take a wash and smarten yourself up, then I think by that time I can safely promise you a just reward for your waiting.'

Patrick was suddenly alert; did she mean that Thomasin was going to be all right?

The nurse hesitated. 'Let us say that she is over the worst, but,' she held up her hand to ward off his attempts at re-entry, 'she is still very weak and is not going to be helped if she judges from your condition that you are unable to cope without her. What d'you think her first reaction will be if she sees you looking like that?'

Patrick guessed correctly. 'She'll insist on getting out o' bed to look after us.'

'Exactly – which is why you must make an effort to look presentable before you go in to see her. Now, will you do as I ask?'

Patrick spun round and bounded down the stairs, startling Erin who was carrying a pot to the table. He caught the look of fear in her eye. 'Oh, no, angel, 'tis all right, the nurse says Mammy's over the worst.' He seated himself at the table and ran his fingers through untidy hair. 'I'm going in to see her once I've been cleaned up. God, do I stink.' He pulled at his shirt in disgust.

Erin smiled for the first time in days. 'Ye'll be wanting something to eat then if she's better?' She placed the pot before him.

'Oh, Lord, Erin, I'm sorry . . .' began Patrick.

'Daddy, ye've not eaten a thing I've made for ye.' Her blue eyes filled with water. 'D'ye not like my cooking?'

Patrick stood and hugged her. 'Aw, 'tis nothing to do with your cooking, Erin, 'tis only that before I was too worried to eat an' now I'm too excited over Tommy getting better.' He sat down again. 'I promise after I've seen her I'll eat everything ye put in front o' me.'

Dickie scraped his plate clean. 'When is Mammy coming down? I don't like Erin's cookin'.'

'You ungrateful little wretch,' rebuked Patrick. 'Is that all ye can say with your mammy lyin' poorly up there?'

Dickie lowered his face and was silent for a while, then asked meekly, 'If Daddy doesn't want his, can I have it, Erin?'

She pursed her lips and scraped the remainder of the meal onto his plate. 'There, you greedy article an' I hope it chokes ye.'

Patrick pushed back the chair and set about making himself presentable, sharpening his razor on the doorstep and applying it to his whiskers over a layer of soapbubbles. Discovering there was no clean shirt he turned to Erin. 'Has your Uncle John had his dinner?'

'Aye, he went back to work as soon as he'd finished it.

Said he wanted to see a man about a dog. Are we getting a dog, Daddy?'

Patrick smiled. 'No, darlin', 'tis just an expression John uses when he's up to no . . .' His smile drooped slightly. 'Oh, God, I hope he's not getting mixed up in anything. I can well do without it at the moment. Ah.' He found what he had been seeking and pulled it over his head.

'That's Uncle John's shirt,' observed his daughter.

'Why d'ye think I asked where he was?' grinned her father. He combed his hair and stood up straight for his daughter's inspection. 'D'ye think I'll pass?'

Erin was about to answer when the nurse's voice rang out. 'Oh, there's your summons, Daddy.'

Patrick moved to the bottom of the staircase and looked up at the nurse who told him he could come up now. 'Come in, come in,' she beckoned as he paused at the bedroom door, and bustled about with towels and bowls of water.

He approached the bed cautiously and peered down at his wife, his heart sinking. She didn't look any better. Her eyes were closed, her face impassive – but no, he took a closer look. Her skin seemed to have lost that moribund hue and was now tinged with the faintest shade of pink. He bent closer, thinking that perhaps the pink sheen was merely the result of the sun shining through the red curtains, but as the nurse briskly drew them apart and allowed the light to stream in he almost collapsed with relief. The pink was definitely in her cheeks.

The nurse's bustle brought Thomasin's eyes slowly open and she blinked at the happy face which hovered over hers. 'Pat?'

He took hold of her hand and rubbed if affectionately. 'Oh, Tommy, Tommy, what a fright ye gave me.' He seemed not to know whether to laugh or cry and kept touching her face to reassure himself of her deliverance. 'I thought I'd lost ye.' The nurse made a diplomatic exit.

Thomasin gave a weak smile and said sleepily, 'Yer don't get rid o' me that easily.' She lifted a trembling finger to wipe away a tear that had trickled down his cheek, then after a short silence said, 'I've lost the baby.'

Patrick closed his eyes in affirmation.

Her hand fell to her side. 'I'm sorry, Pat.'

'Sorry? What have you got to be sorry about? Sure, I'm the one who should be saying sorry, bringing all this pain upon ye. If anything'd happened to ye because I couldn't take no for an answer . . .'

She placed a hand over his. 'No, no, love. It wasn't your fault, these things happen. Mind, I wouldn't like to go through it again.'

He hesitated. 'Did the doctor say anything?'

'Such as?' she asked, then when he did not answer immediately said, 'You mean I won't be able to 'ave any more, don't yer?' He nodded and she sighed. 'Oh well, wasn't that what I wanted in first place?' Then her act collapsed and her face crumpled in tears.

'Oh, Tommy, Tommy, don't.' He lifted her shoulders gently and held her close. 'Don't upset yourself.'

'Oh, I know it's stupid,' she sobbed. 'I know I said I didn't want any more – but that was when we couldn't afford it. When you decided to branch out in business I got used to the idea, was quite lookin' forward to another bairn. I know I shouldn't quibble, I've got three – but they're not babies any more, Pat. Erin's nearly a woman, Dickie only thinks I'm 'ere to cook his meals an' wash his clothes, I know our Sonny's fond of a cuddle but it's not the same, is it?' He shook his head, though not quite understanding her woman's reasoning. She sniffed and wiped her eyes on the sheet. 'I can't explain to you what it's like. You're a man, yer don't know what it feels like to have something growin' inside yer – even when it's not been there long, when it's really nowt more'n a tadpole, it's still a child. You picture what it'll look like when it's born, what sort o' person it'll grow into, then you lose it an' all those pictures vanish. You don't see anythin' any more, 'cept a bloodstained sheet an' a minute blob o' creation.'

'Ye saw it?' he whispered.

'Mmm – tiny little mite about this long.' She held her finger and thumb barely apart, then sighed. 'I think it was anyway, everything's so hazy, but it must've been 'cause the nurse covered it up ever so fast so's I wouldn't see it.' She wept again. 'I've let yer down, haven't I? I know you were so lookin' forward to another lad.'

'I was, yes,' he admitted truthfully. 'But, Tommy, if it

meant having to sacrifice you to get him, then my own life wouldn't be worth living.'

The nurse returned. 'Mr Feeney, I think that's long enough now, don't you?'

'Nurse, I've not had a chance to talk to me wife an' now you're raring to throw me out. Where's your heart?' He stifled a yawn.

'Tut, look at him, nurse,' said Thomasin. 'Bored to tears already. I bet you haven't slept all week, have yer? Look at the state o' yer.'

'An' here's me thinking I'd got meself all smartened up,' answered her husband, sounding hurt.

'Come along, Mr Feeney, there's a good boy.' The nurse took hold of his arm and piloted him to the door.

'Boy, is it?' laughed Patrick. 'Did ye hear her, Tommy? Will I show her what's what?'

'I don't advise that, Mr Feeney.' The nurse pushed him through the doorway as Thomasin issued a weak wave. 'Now go along and get some sleep, then I may allow you to see your wife later.' She closed the door in his face.

Far from showing anger at the nurse's officiousness, Patrick laughed aloud, so happy was he that Thomasin was on the mend. But once downstairs the happiness gave way to an acute weariness and he collapsed into a chair as Erin waited for his report.

'She's going to be all right, darlin',' he replied to her query. 'Another day or two an' she'll be helpin' me mix cement.'

'Thank the Lord,' breathed Erin, reminding him of his promise. 'An' now can I persuade ye to eat something, Daddy?'

Patrick wriggled his back into the chair and crossed his arms over his stomach. 'Ye can that. I could eat a Protestant between two stale cowpats.'

But when Erin returned ten minutes later bearing a plate laden with appetizing victuals, it was to find her father fast asleep.

Long after Mass had finished Liam emerged from the vestry buttoning his top coat. This was the time he loved most, the time when all the worshippers had departed and the tiny chapel was silent. He liked the echo of his footsteps around its emptiness, the smell of polish, of incense and candlewax. He paused to genuflect to the altar, locking his eyes with those of the man who hung in agonised splendour upon the brass rood.

Then his gaze was drawn involuntarily to the door at the opposite end of the short aisle which creaked and groaned as someone turned the handle.

The man pulled his cap from his dark head and stuffed it into his pocket, then walked slowly towards the figure by the altar, flanked on either side by a child – one dark and attractive, the other with flaming hair and solemn grey eyes. Liam watched silently as the trio approached, his green eyes warm and encouraging, smiling a little as the man stooped to right his youngest who had stumbled over his own feet. The three proceeded until they came to stand directly in front of Liam, the boys gazing in awe at their surroundings, the man returning the steady gaze of the green eyes.

He finally spoke. 'D'ye think ye could find room for three more, Father?'

Liam held out his hand and clasped the other's warmly. 'Of course I can,' he responded sincerely. 'Welcome home, Pat.'

CHAPTER THIRTY

THOMASIN ENDURED THE enforced bedrest ungraciously, feeling depressed about losing the baby and the thought of being unable to bear another. Her mother, who had been sent for after the nurse's departure and ignorant of the full extent of her daughter's suffering, made various comments designed to cheer but only succeeding in making Thomasin a thousand times worse.

'For God's sake, Mother, leave me alone,' snapped Thomasin from the rumpled bed, and turned her face abruptly to the wall. Patrick had not informed her mother until Thomasin was on the mend and the nurse no longer needed.

Mortally wounded by her daughter's ingratitude, Hannah slunk from the room and went to join the others downstairs.

'How's lass?' asked William at his wife's appearance. She sniffed into a handkerchief, trying to procure a tear of self-pity. 'Oh, bloody hell!' exclaimed her husband. 'What's wrong now? I 'ope th'asn't been upsettin' 'er.'

Hannah was offended. 'It is I who have been upset. I cannot seem to do anything right for her. One puts oneself out and is she grateful? No. She has just told me I'm not wanted.' She eventually succeeded in squeezing out a tear.

'I'm sure she didn't mean it.' Patrick pointed at the pot of tea to show there was a cup going. 'Ye have to make allowances for what she's been through. I expect a few more of us'll be feeling the edge of her tongue before she's on her feet again.'

A sudden diversion was created by Dickie who tripped and gashed his head on the corner of the table. Hannah, completely forgetting the contretemps with her daughter, flew about searching for a cloth with which to bathe the injured spot, clucking over him like a mother hen. Five year old Dickie made the most of this attention, sobbing theatrically.

'Now, now, big boys shouldn't cry,' his father told him, stemming the flow somewhat.

'Big boy?' cried William, picking up his grandson and sitting him on his lap. 'Nay, he's nobbut a goblin yet.'

'No, I'm not,' protested Dickie, measuring himself against his grandfather. 'I'm nearly as big as you.'

William laughed and patted the boy's glossy head. By, he were reet proud o' these lads.

'Of course,' Patrick was saying, 'all this means we can't possibly go to Dunworthe Hall on Tuesday.'

William could hardly believe his ears. 'Dunworthe Hall? Who's off to Dunworthe Hall?'

'Oh, me an' Erin,' replied Patrick casually and picked up the note that had arrived as confirmation of the summons. 'Lord Herleigh wants her to play at his musical evening. Sure, I thought I'd told ye, Billy?'

With these words Patrick claimed the honour of being the first person ever to make William speechless – or almost. His face turned a funny purplish colour. 'Bugger me,' he kept repeating. 'Bugger me.'

Patrick then dropped his faked indifference to tell them about the incident outside the Festival Concert Rooms. Their eyes grew wide in disbelief, and when he had finished Hannah's face wore a dreamy, abstracted look.

'Now, don't be gerrin' any ideas, lass,' warned William. 'It dun't mean we'll all be hobnobbin' wi' gentry. I can see by t'look on thy face tha's already married Erin off to Lord Herleigh's son.'

Hannah glared at him, then addressed herself to her son-in-law. 'You must go, of course. William and I will take care of the children and Thomasin.' Hopefully the venture would set Patrick an example for the future. She asked what he and Erin would be wearing, dreading that he was going to reply that it would be his present ensemble.

He wrinkled his brow. 'I suppose I'll have to buy meself a new outfit,' – then noticed her look of relief. 'Well, ye didn't think I was going in these old rags, did ye? Erin'll have to have something too – though I don't know how I'll cope without Tommy's help; I'm not very well-informed on ladies' fashions.'

'Leave everything to me,' said Hannah firmly, eyes guessing the child's measurements. 'I shall find something suitable.' She was not about to risk leaving such a vital undertaking to him. Adjusting her lace cap she sat, as a lady should, with rigid spine and hands clasped loosely on her lap. 'Such a pity that Thomasin is perforce a-bed,' she sighed. 'How she would have loved to go to the Hall. But, if she is ill I expect you must be the one to escort Erin – though I doubt that you will feel as comfortable there as Thomasin; she has had some experience of mixing with upper-class folk.'

Patrick ignored the jibe. 'Actually, Hannah, Tommy couldn't go even if she was well. Ye see,' he took great delight in informing her, 'she didn't get an invite.'

'Oh,' said Hannah.

Came Tuesday and the house was filled with Erin's excitement. She had told virtually everyone in the community where she was going, and each time she told the story she embroidered it just a little more to make them envious. Hannah and William arrived in the afternoon, bringing with them a brown package.

'Go try that on, my dear,' said Hannah, handing it to Erin who dashed up to her room.

A few moments later screams of delight were to be heard. Never had she owned anything like this. Hardly daring to touch the dress for fear of spoiling its immaculate prettiness she carefully took hold of the shoulders and held it against her. The dress escaped its folds, casting down its white flounces like a shower of snow, a sash of delicate blue at the waist.

Hurriedly slipping off her clothes she ran to the bowl and washed herself. Then, after patting herself dry, she gently lifted the dress over her head.

'Oh, a perfect fit,' cried Hannah, catching sight of the girl at the top of the stairs. 'Come, let me fasten those buttons and sash.'

Patrick gazed at the transformation. How like her mother she was, he thought, watching Hannah brush the raven hair, and what a difference from the child he had presented to

Thomasin six years ago. He leaned over to kiss her cheek but Hannah pushed him away.

'Patrick, have a care! I have taken great pains in choosing this dress and I am not going to allow you to crush it.' She tied a blue ribbon in the silky hair. 'There, dear.' She was more charitable towards Erin these days. 'Who would guess that you came from anything other than the best home?' The charity did not extend to Patrick, who parried with his own slice of irony.

'An' who knows, Hannah, she might get such a taste for the high life that she won't lower herself to talk to the likes o' you.'

'Tha'd best be off, Pat,' said William, forestalling another cutting remark from Hannah. 'It's a fair way to go. How's tha gonna get there, any road?'

'I thought we'd give the old shanks a little exercise.'

'You cannot possibly walk all that way,' exclaimed Hannah. 'What sort of condition will you be in when you arrive? If you haven't the money for transport I am sure that William . . .'

'Of course I've the money,' he cut in. 'Sure, I just didn't know how far it was, that's all.'

'Tha's sure?' asked William.

'I'm sure,' vouchsafed Patrick. 'Don't ye know I'm coming up in the world? I have me own business now, ye know.'

Hannah sniffed. 'Not a very reputable one if that partner of yours is anything to go by.' She was pleased that she had not been forced to suffer John's presence on this visit; he made her feel so uneasy.

'Nay, t'lad's all reet,' said William, before Patrick could spring to his friend's defence. 'He can't help lookin' like that.'

Dickie prevented any further character assassination by tripping over the edge of the rug and once more banging his head on the table.

'By gum, lad,' William scooped up his grandson, 'if tha keeps this up tha face'll look like an ordnance map by t'end o' week wi' all them bruises.'

'Well, I'll leave him to your care, Billy,' said Patrick, reaching for Erin's hand. 'We'd just better go say goodbye to Tommy.'

Thomasin met them with apathetic eyes. 'Have a good time,' she said unconvincingly.

Patrick was worried about his wife's low spirits. Nothing he said seemed to interest her – she just lay there staring at the ceiling. 'We could always stay at home.'

She was instantly guilty at having dampened Erin's obvious excitement. 'What, with Erin all dressed in her finery an' nobody to show her off to? Get away wi' yer. I'll be all right, honest.' She managed a smile as Erin kissed her. 'Yer look lovely, Erin, really lovely.'

But once they were through the door she sank back into her previous wretchedness.

Much later, Patrick and his daughter arrived at the gates of Dunworthe Hall. Luckily the weather had been kind as they had had to walk further than they had imagined, the transport they had chosen stopping far short of their destination. To Patrick the miles meant nothing, but he could tell that Erin was beginning to tire, for once or twice he had to stop her from stumbling over the cart ruts in the rough, country lane.

He hesitated briefly at the imposing appearance of the great house then, dragging Erin after him, marched up the long approach to the front entrance. The liveried footman nearly suffered an apoplexy when he opened the door and saw the pair. When he regained his equilibrium he jabbed a white-gloved thumb to the left and told them, 'Servants' entrance, round the back.'

'We're not servants,' frowned Patrick, but the door was already closed in his face. Although annoyed at the majestical command he obeyed the footman's instructions. On knocking at the servants' entrance he was admitted by a giggling maid; the news had apparently already reached the kitchen. 'Lord Herleigh asked us to call.' He flourished the invitation, bringing forth another gale of laughter.

'Oo, hark how the dogs do bark,' she chortled, then made a mocking curtsey. 'Pray come in, sir, how h'extremely honoured we h'are to have you here.'

Erin clung to her father's hand, bewildered and taken aback by their treatment, until the cook, a kindly soul, chased away the maid and bade them sit by the fire while someone went to enquire as to their orders.

The kitchen resumed its hectic air as the seven other maids completed preparations for the evening. How could anyone need so many servants? marvelled Patrick.

Five minutes later the same footman who had closed the door in their faces came down and announced that Erin was to accompany him upstairs.

'Not you.' He put a restraining hand on Patrick's arm, then quickly removed it on noting the spark in the Irishman's eye. 'His Lordship only wishes to see the girl,' he explained hastily.

Patrick gave a reassuring nod to Erin and held out her harp which he had carried for her. 'Go with the man, darlin'. I'll be here when ye get back.'

But when she returned to the kitchen Erin was not as excited as she had been on setting out. The people upstairs seemed not to consider her a person like themselves, only an object for their amusement. They had not even asked her name or how old she was like the friends of her parents would have done.

'They're not like us, Erin,' said Patrick to her question. 'They think we're not as good as them, just 'cause they've got money.' He nudged her. 'But we know better, don't we? We're as good, if not better than them. I'll wager none of those folk upstairs could play a harp as well as you, for all their fancy talk.'

He was right of course, thought Erin, but the adventure had gone flat. In a little while the cook put before them a delicious tea of buttered scones, crumpets, gingerbread and cake which all helped to soothe her bruised spirits. It was almost worth coming for the tea alone, said Patrick who up till then had been feeling most annoyed that his new outfit had been an unnecessary purchase; all that hard-earned cash for nothing. But the cook seemed to appreciate his smartness for she kept plying him with mountains of goodies until he begged her to stop or she would have to answer to his wife for his straining buttons.

After tea Erin offered to help Cook wash the pots as she did at home.

'Well, bless my soul,' cried the cook. 'What a good little thing you are. But, no, you sit there, we've got our own girl what does the washing up, and you don't want to spoil that pretty dress, do you?' She bellowed for the scullion to clear the table and ordered Patrick to sit down by the fire again where the two of them could have a nice chat while the underlings went off to change aprons. She settled into her chair and smiled at Patrick. What a lovely man – such a pity he was married.

The orchestra's discordant tones as its members tuned their instruments crept down to the kitchen where Patrick waited, more than a little put out. He had not expected to mix with the guests, but surely they could have allowed him upstairs, somewhere out of sight, to listen to his own daughter play. Erin had long since been marched away to receive instructions. Now, as the orchestra sprang into life, she sat nervously in the wings, awaiting her début. She was unfamiliar with the piece that was being played but soon found herself swaying to the rhythm and almost forgetting her apprehension for a while.

Then all at once the symphony came to an end and as the members of the orchestra sat back in their seats, Erin was given a hefty shove by someone unseen and came to land in front of the sparkling audience. The splendour of the ladies' gowns, coupled with the brilliance of the crystal chandelier that hung in glittering festoons over their heads, dazzled Erin into stupefaction. She stood there trembling, gripping her harp, forgetting why she was there, until the conductor leaned over and tapped her on the shoulder with his baton. She then sat down on the chair provided and began to play. Then, as always, she became lost in her music and all tension vanished as she immersed her soul in the melody.

Downstairs, Cook was listening with Patrick to the faint chords. 'Ah, it brings tears to your eyes. What a shame you couldn't be up there to hear her properly.' Then a sudden thought struck her and she nudged him. 'Listen, I've just thought: if you use that staircase, there,' she pointed, 'you'll be able to see her through the banisters; those stairs overlook the ballroom.'

'What'll I say if anyone catches me?' asked Patrick, rising eagerly to his feet.

'Nobody'll catch you. There's only the staff what uses that staircase an' they're all far too busy to notice you. Go on, off with you.'

Patrick gave her his flashing smile and, thanking her profusely, made his way slowly up the staircase. As Cook had said, he had a perfect view of his daughter through the banisters. The room below was a-dazzle, making him wish Tommy could be here to see it all, or better still that she could be part of it. The harp's dulcet tones meandered round the ballroom where the guests sat entranced. He settled down to watch and listen.

'My word, what have we here?' The softly uttered words startled him and he jumped up, nearly bowling the woman off her feet.

'Ah, may I assume from your expression of guilt that you should not be here; that I have caught you out?' As she spoke he had the strange impression of a honeypot being upturned over his head and the golden syrup dripping stickily over his shoulders.

'I was . . .' he faltered, silenced by the brazen eyes that roamed his body.

She stood with her weight on one foot, so that one of her hips jutted out provocatively, and wafted her face with an ornate fan. 'Do not be alarmed, my dear, I am not going to let your little secret out. I have simply come to join you as I was growing rather bored with the company below. It is far more interesting up here.'

Tired of the music, the woman had suddenly spied the handsome face that peeked between the banisters. Making her excuses to her companion she had slipped away to take a closer look. The view was even better from here, and although the man's apparel bespoke his humble lifestyle his good looks and strong body doubly compensated for any lack of breeding. It was so long since she had had such a pleasant diversion – and one had to take the opportunity when it arose. She took a step closer.

Patrick stepped back and felt the balustrade against his rear.

'Surely I do not frighten a big fellow like you?' purred the woman, raising a scented hand to his cheek. Her perfume tantalised his nostrils, filling his head with all kinds of thoughts. He cursed his boyish behaviour; women did not normally have this effect on him – but then this was no ordinary woman. Her beauty surpassed even Mary's. From her golden curls to her tiny, doll-like feet in their satin slippers she oozed femininity. Her voluptuous body pressed itself to his, spurred on by his obvious arousal. She lifted her face for his kiss and he tasted her sweetness. Taking his hand she led him further into the shadows.

'Come, let us seek somewhere more comfortable. I feel sure we can find a more enjoyable pastime than listening to this rubbish.'

Her words broke the spell that she had woven so expertly around him. Erin's harp chastised him – how could he? How could he have thought to make love to this woman while Thomasin lay sick and alone? The woman must be a witch to have driven every thought of his wife from his head. He broke free. 'I'm sorry.'

'Come now.' She pressed herself against him once more. 'You will get far more pleasure with me than from listening to that little slut.'

He felt the heat of her hand at his groin and sprang away as if fouled by her touch. 'That slut as you call her happens to be my daughter.'

'Oh, la!' She gave a tinkling laugh. 'Forgive my little *faux pas*; it was merely a jest. Come now, do not be angry with little Helly.' She pouted and inclined towards him, making him suddenly aware of the heavy stench of liquor and he wondered why he had not noticed it before; the woman was drunk.

God, she was like a bitch in heat, he thought, staring coldly at the exquisite face. Underneath all those fancy clothes she was nothing more than a high-class strumpet. He started to go but she blocked his way.

'Excuse me.'

'Oh no, darling, you are not to escape so lightly.' She hopped from side to side, evading his departure. 'Now that I have you cornered I am going to make full use of your attributes. Oh come, do not be so cruel. Can you not see that I ache for you?'

At this Patrick grabbed her by the upper arm and snarled into her face. 'Woman, I've never lain with a whore in me life an' I don't intend to start now.' With that he thrust her aside and dashed down the staircase.

The sound of Erin's harp followed him to the foot of the stairs, as did the woman's mocking laughter. But though she laughed her eyes were flint-like with the anger of rejection. How dare he? She swayed drunkenly. It appeared that Helena Cummings would have to find her pleasure elsewhere tonight.

The unlit country lanes made for a creepy journey home, doing nothing to lighten the anger which still smouldered beneath Patrick's apparently cheerful exterior. Erin also was not entirely happy with the evening. Though the ladies and gentlemen had applauded enthusiastically their admiration was patronising, as if it were a miracle that someone of her class could play at all. Still, she clutched three shiny coins in her fist. Hopefully they would cheer Thomasin.

At home, the boys had long been a-bed, albeit not asleep. They had passed a pleasant afternoon with their grandparents, even though Grandma was inclined to spoil things somewhat. Grandad, on the other hand had let them do as they pleased, within reason. He had not been cross when Sonny had leaned too far over a sheep pen at the cattle market and had fallen among the bleating creatures, emerging, as Grandad put it, smelling like a poke of devils. Grandma had been outraged and had plunged the child into a bath, complaining to Grandad that her resolution to see the boys become perfect gentlemen was being eroded by his total lack of breeding.

'D'ye mean like Uncle John breeds his ferrets?' asked Dickie as she put them to bed.

'Most certainly not!' Really, the things that man was filling their minds with. 'Now go to sleep at once and do not waken your mother with your chattering.'

Thomasin however was not asleep; she lay in the darkened room wondering what Pat and Erin were doing now. The depression crept in a black tide across her sleepless mind. It made her want to die.

But then her true spirit rebelled, refused to be submerged in the vortex of despair and came bobbing to the surface to clutch at straws of hope. She must count the good things in her life: the loving, steadfast husband who said that he lived only for her; the three fine children whom she must put before the one she had just lost. There and then she decided that this would be her last day in bed. She must find plenty of work to take her mind off events past. After all, what had she wanted with another child anyway? No, she must do her best for the ones she already had. She shook the cobwebs from her mind and violently plumped the pillow. Taking a hairbrush from the dressing table she pulled it through her tangled, lank hair, swearing at the lugs that fought against her. Then, straightening the sheets she awaited Patrick's homecoming.

'Nah then, didst 'ave a good time?' bawled William, shoving Erin before the fire to warm herself.

Patrick replied that they had. 'I danced with her ladyship an' a fine gentleman asked for Erin's hand in marriage.'

'Soft bugger, walk 'ome,' scoffed William. 'If tha dun't want to tell us . . .' he waved his hand in dismissal.

Patrick grinned. 'Oh, I don't mind telling ye, 'twasn't what we expected.' He related the events of the evening, carefully omitting the episode with the mysterious female.

'I'm sure Erin found it more to her taste,' said Hannah.

To which the girl replied, 'Well, the ladies' dresses an' jewels were very pretty, an' the Hall was enormous with great big glittery things like glass hanging from the ceiling. An' there was all this lovely food – mind, we never got none o' that although we did have a lovely tea. Then there was loads o' pictures around the walls, an' the furniture all had fancy gold bits on it. But,' she decided pensively, 'I think I'd rather live here; even though we haven't loads o' money we've plenty o' friends. Those ladies an' gentlemen didn't seem like real people somehow. 'Twas like being in a dream! Nobody seemed to notice you were there, they just carried on eatin' an' talkin' around ye like ye didn't exist. An' I'll tell ye something else: when it comes to looks none o' them could hold a candle to Mammy or Daddy.'

Patrick hugged the tired child with a surge of paternal pride. 'There y'are, Hannah, some folk realise the value of a happy home. We don't need your high-class baubles an' fancy talk.'

Hannah bristled. 'Happy home, you say? Hah! My daughter did not look too happy the last time I looked in upon her, in fact she looked positively melancholy. While you were out gallivanting she was lying there brooding over her circumstances.'

'But that's unfair,' protested Patrick. 'I was quite prepared to stay at home, 'twas you who urged us to go – an' so did Tommy, come to that.'

'Well, of course she would, wouldn't she? Thomasin is so unselfish, she must be to put up with all the hurt you have caused her.'

'Hurt? What're ye talking about, hurt?'

'I would have thought it patently obvious that it is the squalor in which you have condemned her to live which has resulted in her condition. She would never have lost the child had she been in a more sympathetic environment. I told her what would happen if she married a pauper, but would she listen?'

'Hannah!' barked William. 'That's enough.'

' 'Tis too late now, Billy,' said Patrick bitterly. 'What's said cannot be unsaid – an' 'tis nothing I didn't already know. You look down on me, Hannah, because I'm Irish an' because I'm poor. Ye cannot see through your own blind ambitions that Thomasin loves me for what I am – as I love her. But one day I'm going to make ye change your mind, not as ye might imagine by taking her to live in a mansion, but by proving to ye that two people can be happy without a potful o' money.' He turned to Erin. 'Erin darlin', I think ye should go tell your mammy what ye've just told us; it might make her feel happier. Pray God one of us should.'

Erin looked from her father's angry face to her grand-mother's unrepentant one, then slowly turned and crept up the stairs. Poor Daddy, why did Grandmother hate him so?

'Come in, lass,' said Thomasin as the child peeped into the bedroom. 'How did it go?' Erin told her all about the evening, repeating the statement she had made downstairs. 'Bless yer,' her stepmother raised a smile, 'but I don't reckon I could hold a candle to the ragman's horse just now.'

Erin replied that this was only because Thomasin had been ill, then held out her hand. 'I hoped this might make ye feel better.'

'What's this?' asked Thomasin, staring at the coins on her palm.

'That's me wages.' The pride on the young face radiated the dull room.

– The stingy devils, thought Thomasin. Still, Erin was obviously pleased with her gains. She smiled and folded the coins back into the girl's hand. 'That belongs to you, Erin, you earned it. Buy summat nice for yourself.'

Erin's face fell. 'But I want you to have it.'

Thomasin stared at the downcast face, then abruptly broke down. 'Oh, you are a good lass!' she sobbed, putting her arms round Erin who hugged her back. 'I'm sorry I've been so maungy these past couple o' days. I don't know what y'all must think o' me.'

'Oh, Mam,' soothed Erin. 'I explained to the boys and they understand that you're only sad 'cause the baby isn't coming any more. They've been quite good really.'

'By, you're growin' up,' breathed Thomasin, shaking her head. 'An' what about you, how've you been copin'?'

'Fine enough,' replied Erin, then bit her lip. 'I was a bit scared at first. When I saw all the blood I thought . . .'

'Yer thought I were gonna die?' said Thomasin gently.

The girl nodded, then burst into tears. 'You're not, are ye?' she wept into Thomasin's shoulder.

'Ee, lass, yer've been bottlin' all this up, haven't yer?' Thomasin wiped the child's eyes on the sheet. 'I bet yer never said a word to nobody.'

Erin gave a great sniff. 'I didn't like to say anything to Daddy, but I could tell he was thinkin' the same's me.'

'Aye well, yer needn't worry any more, I'll not be leavin' yer, love.' Thomasin patted her head. 'I take some gettin' rid of, yer know.'

Erin gave a sniffly laugh and hugged her again. 'Oh, Mam, I do love ye.'

CHAPTER THIRTY-ONE

PATRICK'S RETURN TO the church passed without comment from Thomasin, who had no need to ask his reasons for doing so. That he had enrolled her sons into the Catholic faith without consulting her instigated no wrath, on the contrary she was glad that he had at last come to terms with himself after so many years of inner struggle and though not committing herself in any way had dutifully accompanied him and their children to this evening's Mass.

Their return was marked by a torrential downpour which sent them scuttling – children laughing and shrieking, adults complaining – for the cover of the alleyway into Bay Horse Yard. When the rain had eased a little they made the last few yards' dash across the court and into the house.

'Merciful Mary, what a filthy night.' Patrick slammed the door on the heavens' distress. 'Let's have that fire stoked so's ye can get the kettle on, Tommy.'

His wife gave priority to relieving the children of their damp garments, rubbing each glistening head briskly with a towel, pulling off boots and stuffing them with newspaper, before placing the kettle over the renewed blaze. Fifteen minutes later each sat round the hearth clutching a cup of hot cocoa with burnished cheeks and glowing eyes.

Patrick balanced his cup on the fender and stood to reach for a pipe off the mantelshelf. In passing, his hand came to rest on the cocoa tin which held their savings and he rattled it appreciatively. 'Sounds nice, does it not?' He smiled at his wife.

She had to agree. Though the doctor and nurse's fees had

savaged their reserves somewhat, the quantity of sovereigns continued to grow steadily.

'Aye, I reckon it were best thing that ever 'appened to us, you gettin' finished from Baxter's. That tin's never been so heavy since it held cocoa.'

Patrick clamped his teeth round a pipe and applied a flame to it. 'If we go on like this we'll soon be able to think of moving to somewhere better. Have ye put your mind to where ye might like to live?'

Her eyes smiled over the cup. 'Anywhere you'd like to take me – Dunworthe Hall perhaps.'

'No, I'm serious.' He reseated himself to sprawl his long legs over the hearth rug. 'There's enough in there to take us somewhere really nice.' He nodded towards his elder son. 'An' we'll maybe think about sending Dickie to school.'

'I don't want to go to no school,' replied Dickie, wiping the ring of cocoa from his mouth.

' 'Course ye do,' said his father through volumes of smoke. 'I wish I'd had the chance to go to a proper school. I had to make do with what the parish priest could teach me an' though he was a clever man it didn't stretch the brain like a proper school would've.'

'I'll not like it,' repeated Dickie cussedly.

'Sure, how d'ye know if ye've never been? D'ye not want to learn to read an' write?'

The youngster shook his handsome head.

'An' how d'ye propose to get through life if ye cannot put your name to anything?' asked his father. 'There're people that'll always be ready to take advantage of a numskull.'

'Uncle John cannot read nor write very good,' countered his son, 'an' he don't let anybody take 'vantage of him. He's clever, is Uncle John.'

'Aye, too clever for his own good sometimes,' muttered Patrick. 'An' if you're thinking to follow in your Uncle John's footsteps then think again. You're going to school, whether ye like it or not!'

'Why do I have to go?' Dickie persisted. 'Why not one o' the others?'

'I'll go,' offered Erin eagerly.

'Ah, don't talk such nonsense, Erin,' said Patrick, careless of her feelings. 'You're a girl, what use would there be in your going to school? Why, in a few years' time ye'll be thinking o' marrying. A complete waste o' time it'd be.'

'Nay, don't be marryin' t'lass off just yet,' said Thomasin wiggling her numbed toes on the fender. 'It's no fun tending to four men on me own. An' any road, what's wrong with her wantin' to learn, might I ask? She might not want to get married, she mebbe wants to do more with her life.'

'Be one o' them blue stockings, ye mean?' Patrick's pipe fell from his open mouth and he brushed the hot ashes hurriedly from his lap. 'God forbid that any daughter o' mine should get mixed up with that sorta rubbish, she'd not set foot in the house again.' He replaced his pipe. 'Don't misunderstand; I'm not against her learning to read an' write, in fact I'm all for it, but she doesn't have to go to school to learn how to do that. I've seen to it that she knows enough to get her through life and anything else'd be, like I said, a waste o' time.'

'So now yer know,' pronounced Thomasin to a downcast Erin, who had great difficulty in hiding her bitter disappointment. Why on earth should he consider education a waste of time just because she was a girl?

Thomasin had already turned away and was speaking to her youngest. 'What about you, Sonny? How d'you feel about school?'

Sonny was all for it and had to be restrained from preparing himself immediately. 'Nay, yer a bit young yet, love.' Thomasin put her arm round him and kissed his coppery head. 'Next year, mebbe. I don't want to part wi' my baby yet a while.'

He pushed her off. 'I'm not a baby.'

'No, of course yer not. I'm sorry, it's just that if you all go off to school who'll I have left to sneak biscuits when me back's turned?' She rose suddenly. 'Anyway, come on now, it's time for bed.' There was a hail of objections.

'Aw, Mam, can we not stay up till Uncle John comes in?' begged Erin.

'Aye, we haven't had us story yet,' piped up Sonny.

'Your Daddy'll tell you a story,' answered Thomasin.

'But we like Uncle John's stories best,' complained Dickie, dragging at his mother's arm, hampering her journey to the stairs.

' 'Tis nice to know you're wanted,' grumbled Patrick lazily.

'Oh, we like yours, Daddy, but Uncle John's are, well . . .' Dickie sought for a word.

'Now let me hazard a guess,' replied his mother. 'More interestin'? Aye, there's a lot o' folks'd be interested in Uncle John's outpourings, specially them what wears blue helmets an' carry big sticks. Lord knows what he's teachin' 'em,' she added to Patrick.

She had all but dragged the children to the stairs when the door crashed open and the children cried in unison, 'Uncle John!' Though how they knew it was John was indeterminable, for the only recognisable thing about him was the one eye which gleamed from a mud-caked face.

'Come away!' shrieked Thomasin as they clustered round him. 'I've just got you lot dried. God in Heaven, John, whatever 'ave yer been up to now? Yer look as if yer've been pulled through a hedge backwards.'

'In a matter o' speakin' I 'ave,' replied John, flicking back his hair and spraying them all with rainwater. He unhooked his haversack and let it fall. 'Eh, come on, young 'uns.' He fought his way to the fireplace. 'Let's get me bum warm.' He pulled off his boots and was about to place them in the hearth when Thomasin objected.

'Not there, that's just been polished! Put 'em over near door, an' before yer settle yerself yer can get them filthy wet clothes off. I'm not 'avin' me new chairs clarted up. Look at that puddle yer've made already!'

John held out his hands beseechingly to Patrick. 'If she's like this now what's she gonna be like when yer get this fine 'ouse yer allus on about? Can't I just put a bit o' newspaper on chair, Tommy? Just while I say goodnight to these bairns an' get meself warm. I'm bloody saturated.'

Thomasin grudgingly conceded and the children thronged around him once more wanting to know if he had a tale to tell them.

'I'd be interested to hear it an' all,' said Thomasin, folding her arms. 'I think you were gonna tell us 'ow yer got so blathered up, weren't yer?' She fingered his jacket in disgust.

'I thought I just did,' said John with a wink at the children. 'I've been pulled through a hedge backwards.'

'Very funny,' threatened Thomasin.

'It's right! Well, a bramble bush to be precise, eh, an' d'yer know, you lads?' He poked Sonny and Dickie in the midriffs making them double over giggling. 'I've gone an' lost me ferrets. Would yer believe it? Damned good breeder one of 'em was an' all.'

'Enough of the biology lesson,' said Thomasin going to pick up his haversack where he had dropped it. 'An' if yer've lost yer ferrets what 'ave yer got in this bag? It feels awful plump.'

'Open it an' see.'

'Is it likely to leap out at me?' enquired Thomasin.

'Try yer luck,' grinned John wickedly. 'Yer never know what yer might find.'

Thomasin's caution was overthrown by her inquisitiveness and tentatively she unbuckled the strap, expecting some vicious creature to take a lump out of her at any minute. When nothing untoward happened she explored further, gingerly folding back the flap and pulling the bag open, then screamed as something brightly-coloured sprang out at her.

'Yer daft 'aporth,' snorted John, catching the bag as she flung it at him and impatiently delved into the haversack. 'Don't yer know what these are?'

'Pheasants!' squealed Thomasin, clapping her hands delightedly as he pulled forth his booty.

'Aye, yer soft devil. It were only tails that uncoiled an' made yer jump. I 'ad to fold 'em over so's nobody saw 'em. Well, yer said yer were gerrin' sick o' rabbits didn't yer?'

Patrick took his pipe from his mouth and pointed the stem at his friend. 'Ye've been poaching, John,' he said sternly.

'Me, poachin'? As if I would.' John's attempt at innocence was contradicted by his knavish appearance. 'It's right!' he said defensively, seeing their scepticism. 'Yer see, I went up to t'Moor as usual, undid me bag to get ferrets out, then I got taken short an' had to go behind t'hedge. Any road, I must've forgotten to fasten t'bag 'cause when I turned round little . . . demons were nowhere to be seen.' He rubbed his hand over his mutilated face and stared pensively at the dirt which came off on his palm. 'Anyhow, I thought, I daren't go 'ome emptyhanded 'cause Tommy'll kill us, so I 'ad a nosey round an' came up wi' them.' He nodded at the pheasants.

Thomasin leaned back against the table and said with a distrustful smirk born of familiarity, 'I suppose yer gonna tell us now that yer found 'em lyin' by t'roadside?'

'How did yer guess?' marvelled John. 'There they were, just waitin' for somebody to pick 'em up.'

'Enough of your lies!' cut in Patrick. 'Ye've poached them from Lord Herleigh's estate, haven't ye?'

'Now how could I do that when I never went out equipped for catchin' pheasants?' asked John. 'Yer don't just march up to 'em an' say "hop into this bag, mate"! It takes a lot o' snares an' bait, yer can't catch pheasant wi' ferrets.'

'So tell us.'

John's resolution was immovable. 'I've telled yer, I found 'em.'

'Then how did yer get in such a mess?' asked Thomasin calmly. 'Yer jacket ripped to shreds, yer face an' hands all scratched.'

'Ah, well, that was when t'real poacher came along an' caught me emptyin' all his snares,' John enlightened the gathering. 'By, he were really upset. If gamekeeper hadn't come along I wouldn't've been 'ere to tell t'tale.'

'Gamekeeper!' Patrick's noisy exclamation made the children jump visibly. 'God, how did ye manage to escape?'

'Ah, that's where t'bramble bush comes in. Y'see, I'd already got one pheasant outta snare an' was just about to knock off another when t'poacher arrives on t'scene an' starts on me. Any road, he were makin' that much row that gamekeeper hears 'im an' along he comes, God yer oughta've seen size of his gun. He doesn't see me 'cause poacher's given me a right bazzackin' an' I'm lyin' on t'floor. All he sees is t'other fella dancin' about like a looney an' takes a shot at 'im. I roll under t'bush while poacher takes off wi' gamekeeper after 'im. 'Course, I 'ad to pick a bramble bush, didn't I?' He tutted and examined his hands with their red crisscrosses. 'S'truth, I thought I were gonna be in there all night.'

'Well, I hope ye've learned your lesson,' said Patrick, puffing furiously and pacing about agitatedly.

'Oh, I have, Pat, I have. I learned not to waste me time when there's other soft devils ready to do yer work for yer. I'm off back tomorra night, see what else I can lay me 'ands on. See, when I were on me way 'ome I saw t'poacher lyin' in t'ditch, right mess he were, he'll not be goin' back for a few nights, so I thought I'd save 'im trouble an' go empty rest of 'is snares.'

Patrick slapped a hand to his forehead. 'The man's incorrigible. What about the poacher – was he badly hurt?'

John made an indifferent gesture. 'I didn't 'ang about to find out. That gamekeeper's a bit handy!'

'But he could be dying!' objected Patrick.

'Why should I worry about that? He were goin' to make meat paste outta me, yer couldn't expect me to 'elp 'im. Besides, he knew t'risks he were takin' when he decided on his trade.'

'I think it's time you children went to bed,' said Patrick, suddenly concerned at the effect John's attitude was having on them.

'Aw, Daddy!' Dickie wanted to ask how one killed a pheasant. Sonny was stroking the bird's resplendent plumage and Erin had her arm draped over John's houlder, all hoping their father would soften. But as Patrick's hands dropped to his belt buckle the three scrambled hurriedly for the stairs.

After their rapid disappearance Patrick addressed his friend. 'Sometimes, John, I despair of ye, I really do, going on like that in front o' the children.'

'Like what?' John was genuinely bewildered.

'It's no good tub-thumping at him,' said Thomasin, going to hang up the pheasants. 'He doesn't know what yer on about. Yer'll never change 'im. An' happen it'll all be forgotten tomorra when yer get yer teeth into these.' She turned to John. 'An' now yer've 'ad a warmin', my lad, yer can go get a blinkin' wash!' She caught hold of his collar and pushed him towards the back door.

'Wait on, Tommy, I want a word wi' Pat, it's business.'

'Not till yer clean,' said Thomasin, rifling the drawer for a change of clothing which she hung over the back of a chair. 'Now, outside an' get yer head under that water an' don't come back till yer white again, Mister Blackamoor.'

'Aren't yer even gonna heat water up for me, after I've brought yer two pheasants?' John's protests met with a pitiless rejoinder.

'An' have that mud all over me kitchen floor? Not likely – out!'

She watched, hawk-like, as he stripped off his upper clothes and stepped into the yard where he bent under the icy water's tortuous gush, groaning pathetically. When he had cleaned off all the mud, apart from that on his trousers, he was allowed back indoors to towel himself dry, change his clothes and sit shivering in front of the fire. Meekly grateful he accepted a mug of cocoa from Thomasin, swilling it down in one go and holding the mug out hopefully for a refill.

'If yer want another go get it yerself,' ordered Thomasin, sitting down to some darning.

'Y'ought to've been in t'army, Tommy, yer'd've made a good sergeant major.' Too lazy to refuel his mug John placed it on the hearth.

'What was the business ye wanted to talk about, John?' asked Patrick, tugging off his socks to trim his toenails.

'Oh, aye. I've been thinkin', we've been doin' quite well wi' this business of ours, haven't we?'

'We have.' Patrick glanced up from his delicate task and, seeing his wife's annoyed face began to gather up the nail clippings from the rug. 'I was just saying to Tommy here how much we've managed to save.'

'Well, instead o' savin' it, why don't we plough it back into t'business?' John hunched forward intently. 'Use it to buy more materials, take on some really worthwhile jobs. That's how all t'big boys get started, yer know, keep ploughin' their profits back into t'business.'

'We've just begun to save a little an' ye want me to give it back?'

'Not give it back, it'd still be your money. Listen, I thought when we started out we said we'd begin with little jobs an' when we got established we'd progress to summat a bit more ambitious. Well, I reckon we've established ourselves right enough now. People know we do a good job. I think it's about time we branched out a bit.'

'Don't ye think it's a bit soon?' said the other.

'We've got to start sometime,' answered John. 'Come on, Pat, what d'yer say?'

'We-ell, I'm not sure,' prevaricated the Irishman. ' 'T'won't be like the cash in hand jobs we're doing now. People'll expect to receive a bill, they won't be wanting to part with large amounts of money over the doorstep and that'll mean keepin' books. Who's going to have that responsibility, as if I didn't know?'

'Nah! We don't have to bother with no books,' scoffed John. 'Just scribble t'fee on a bit o' paper an' shove it through t'letterbox. I can't be doin' wi' all that legal stuff.'

'John, if a business is going to succeed it's got to be on a legal basis. I cannot get involved with anything less, I've a family to consider.'

'Oh, you are goin' to consider us then?' remarked Thomasin, whose eyes had been travelling from one face to the other. 'I was beginning to wonder.'

'Of course I am!' exclaimed Patrick. 'I wouldn't take such an important step without discussing it with you. 'What d'ye think?'

'I'll tell yer what I think,' answered his wife, resting her darning on her lap. 'I think you're bloody cracked. Listen, what business experience have either of you had? Eh? 'Cause yer can't call what yer doin' at the moment a real business.'

'Ye like the money it brings in well enough though, don't ye?' said Patrick, in a clipped tone.

'Of course I do, that's why I want to keep it, not go spendin' it on a pile of old bricks.'

'Look, me an' John are having a serious discussion about all our futures, if ye've nothing sensible to say keep your mouth shut.'

'If you ask me I'm the only sensible one here,' replied Thomasin. 'To listen to the two o' you it's almost like bein' in t'boardroom.'

'Will ye stop pouring scorn on our plans?' demanded her husband.

'I'm not, honestly I'm not,' pleaded Thomasin. 'I'm just tryin' to stop you running into summat before yer can walk. Yer've not been workin' for yerselves for five minutes an' here y'are talking like Tuke & Casson.'

'There you're at it again!' snapped Patrick. 'What's the matter with ye, woman? Sure, ye didn't imagine I was going to spend the rest o' me life doing repair jobs, did ye?'

'Of course not!' Thomasin was beginning to get ruffled. 'But I don't want yer gettin' yerself into anything yer not ready to handle. Oh!' She turned on John exasperatedly. 'What did you 'ave to go cramming his head with this rubbish for? You an' your clever ideas. We were just beginning to get on our feet, nice bit o' furniture, decent clothes . . .'

'I don't know what yer complainin' about,' John jumped in. 'All I've done is put forward an idea that'll get you that big, fine 'ouse.'

'This big, fine 'ouse keeps rising to the surface,' said Thomasin irritably. 'On whose suggestion, may I ask? Have I ever mentioned one? Have I?' She displayed her palms. 'It's me laddo here what keeps goin' on about that, not me. If this is all we can afford I'd be quite content to stay here. I don't want him puttin' a millstone round his neck on my account. I told you, didn't I?' she demanded of her husband. 'When we got married I said I had all I wanted, but do yer take any gorm? No! It's like talkin' to somebody wooden. When will yer stop this foolish thinkin' that yer somehow need to prove yerself?'

'When your mother stops tellin' him he isn't fit to kiss yer arse,' said John before he was able to stop himself.

Thomasin stared at the two men for a brief span before giving a moan of understanding. 'Aren't I bloody dense,' she said grimly. 'Here's me thinkin' that all this was proposed for my benefit when all along it's not me you've been tryin' to please, it's me blasted mother.' She nodded emphatically in her enlightenment. 'All this tripe about me deservin' better an' how you're gonna take us outta here, huh! I must've been blind not to have seen it afore.'

'It *was* for you, Tommy. *Is* for you.' Patrick took hold of her hands and pleaded into her vexed face. 'Everything I ever said, I meant. Ye do deserve better. Your mother is right in that.'

'But nobody takes any notice of what Mother says!' said Thomasin feelingly.

'I do!' he cried angrily. 'Because deep down I know it's true. When I came to this country I brought few things with me. I'd lost nearly everything I owned in the Hunger. But even in the worst times of my life, though I'd lost material things, I'd always held onto my pride. Your mother has tried her best to take that away from me, Tommy.' She laid her fingertips comfortingly on his arm and he lifted his own hand to her cheek. 'I see this as one last chance to redeem myself in her eyes, prove to her that everything she said about me was wrong.'

Thomasin moved her cheek against his palm. 'You're a daft 'aporth,' she uttered softly. 'By all means build your new life if that's what yer want. But never for one moment think that you have to prove yourself. However bad things might be, however little money we have, you'll always be a man, Patrick Feeney, an' don't let any silly, misguided woman tell you otherwise.' She put her arms round him and placed her head against his breast.

'Do I get one o' them?' asked John hopefully, receiving only a laughing cuff from Thomasin.

Patrick smiled as his friend flopped back into the chair. ' 'Tis all settled then. We have Tommy's seal of approval an' can start whenever we want.'

'Approval nothing,' said Thomasin, serious again. 'I still think you're mad, the pair of yer after t'little experience yer've had, but I know yer'll not listen to a word of advice from me.' She pointed a finger at her husband. 'I shall say it, yer know, if all this comes to nowt.'

'Say what?' enquired Patrick.

'I told yer so.'

CHAPTER THIRTY-TWO

THE LANDLORD OF The Square and Compass handed over two frothing tankards and scraped their coins off the bar. The friends sought a table and sat down.

'Ye know, John,' said Patrick wiping his mouth and lowering his tankard to the table, 'I've been giving some thought to what we were saying last night.'

John ran a finger over his froth-coated lip and flicked it at the floor. 'And?'

'There's one or two points I'd like to get clear. 'Tis comin' up to winter – what happens if it's a bad one an' we cannot work 'cause o' the frost? If we put all our money back into buying materials we're not gonna have any put by for emergencies.'

John seemed indifferent. 'What emergencies? We'll not starve. I can allus magic up a couple o' pheasants.'

'An' the rent, an' the children's clothes an' Christmas?'

'Christ, it's nobbut October an' he's worryin' about Christmas. Any road, we could allus have it written into contract that we get paid at halfway stage.'

'John,' Patrick tussled with his impatience. 'You're talking as if we already have a job lined up. That's the other thing I wanted to clarify: how do we go about finding these rich pickings? I know we've earned ourselves a good reputation lately but that's for small bait. Nobody who wants a large job doing would even consider us.'

John shrugged. 'Uncle John'll think o' summat.' Then he saw Ghostie at the bar and went to get his own tankard replenished. 'Now, Ghostie, yer not looking any better. How's work goin'?'

'As ever,' replied Ghostie mournfully.

'Plenty of it then?'

A shrug. 'Things're picking up a mite. Baxter's got plenty fixed up – well he will have if his tenders are approved.'

Something clicked in John's mind. 'Can I buy yer a jar, Ghostie, old lad?'

Never had it been known for Connors to refuse anything free. After the landlord had served them the two men went to sit with Patrick. 'Ghostie were just tellin' us, Pat,' John looked meaningfully at Patrick, 'things're much improved for our friend Baxter. Seems he's gotta lot o' work on.' He turned to Ghostie and asked nonchalantly, 'D'yer think he might have too much to cope with?' A shrug from Ghostie. 'See, me n' Pat are thinkin' o' going into partnership, aren't we, Pat? Thought you might be able to help.'

'I can't see how.'

'Is he er, is he payin' yer any better lately, Ghostie?'

Ghostie raised haunted eyes. 'Was that meant to be a joke?'

John glanced around him, then lowered his voice. 'How would yer like to earn yerself a few bob, then?'

Ghostie came as close to showing some form of life as he could muster. 'What would ye be wanting me to do?' John told him. 'Jesus Christ!' The cry was that of a banshee. 'I can't do it, John. Oh no, I can't do it.'

'Look, all y'ave to do is let us in t'office when Baxter's out o' road,' protested John. 'Me an' Pat'll do rest.'

'He means he will,' corrected Patrick.

After much bargaining it was agreed that Ghostie should carry out the service for the fee of one sovereign. 'Done! an' on the strength o' you two going to line me pockets I'll buy ye both a drink.'

'Good God yer'll 'ave us droppin' dead wi' shock next,' said John, and when Ghostie was out of range chuckled and raised his tankard. 'Here's to our funereal friend, may his embalming fluid never run dry.'

The following morning in the same alehouse Patrick handed over payment, thanking Ghostie for his help and offering him a drink.

'Next time, Pat. I can't stop, I've a funeral to attend.'

John looked alarmed. 'Not yer own, I trust?'

'D'ye want I should make it yours?' Ghostie could never see why they were amused by his looks.

'Sorry, mate,' John shouted after him. 'An' thank you kindly. If y'ever need a favour . . . don't come to me.' A grin at Pat.

By undercutting the tenders they had copied from Baxter's files they made sure that both were duly accepted. They decided to attack the bigger project first which, they surmised, would take a month to complete, depending on the cooperation of the joiner they contracted to assist. That would mean they could probably complete both jobs by Christmas, weather permitting.

Their first act was to use most of the contents of the cocoa tin to buy the required materials which did not please Thomasin. 'An' just how d'yer expect me to buy extra food an' presents for Christmas?' she asked sourly.

'Nay, Christmas is weeks off yet,' answered John cheerfully. 'That tin'll be twice as heavy by then.'

'Who pulled your strings?' snapped Thomasin. 'I was speakin' to Patrick.' She faced her husband squarely. 'Well? I'm waiting for an answer.'

'Ye've just had your answer,' replied Patrick curtly, indicating John with a nod. 'Now, will ye stop your nagging, you're beginning to sound like someone else I know.' Then his expression softened and he took hold of her shoulders. 'Tommy, stop worrying, everything's in our favour. Our luck is changing. Sure, we cannot fail.'

'Can't yer?' she asked bitterly. 'Why not? Since when has Fate ever been kind to us?'

'Sure, it brought us together, did it not?' he asked with a twinkle. 'Wasn't that a good thing?'

'Of course it was an' I want it to stay that way! That's why I'm beggin' yer not to go through wi' this. I've got this feeling that summat awful's gonna happen.'

'What can happen? The weather's mild, we've another job for when this one is finished. What could possibly go wrong?'

'I don't know,' she answered lamely. 'I've just got this feelin', that's all.' She pleaded with him. 'Please, Pat, we're just getting on us feet, don't go risking all yer've worked for, not yet.'

But as Patrick emptied the gold coins into a purse she knew that nothing would change his mind.

It transpired, however, that Thomasin's fears were groundless; the work completed towards the end of November was highly acclaimed by the gentleman for whom it had been carried out.

'Excellent!' cried Percival Dodd on inspecting the finished extension to his house. 'You are to be congratulated, gentlemen, on your diligence and craftsmanship. A most satisfying undertaking.'

'Thank you, sir.' John tugged his forelock. 'Er, would it be presumptuous o' me to ask, seein' as 'ow you're so pleased, like, if you're acquainted with h'anyone who needs work doin' to pass on our names?'

'Not presumptuous in the least,' replied Dodd. 'It will be a pleasure to bestow upon my friends the benefit of your skills. Indeed, I cannot express sufficient praise for your work.'

John grinned later as he watched Patrick make up Dodd's account. 'Let's 'ope he's as forthcomin' with the cash as he is wi' the flowery phrases.'

Patrick swore as his pen deposited a large blot on the paper. He screwed it into a ball and started again. 'What I want to know is what do we use for materials for our next job?' Dodd's extension had left them with only enough bricks to make crude beginnings on their next assignment. It might be weeks before Dodd settled up.

'We do what everybody else does,' answered John. 'Get the bricks first, pay later.'

'Will they let us do that?' asked Patrick, no businessman.

John laughed and slapped the other on the knee. 'Don't you know yer Uncle John by now?'

With a new supply of bricks they embarked on their second commitment. This too was accomplished within a matter of weeks and drew further commendation from the recipient. The two men began to envisage a great new career unfolding before them. Thomasin was not so impressed.

'Yer've not been paid for either of 'em yet. Christmas is only a few weeks away. When're we supposed to see some o' t'benefits?'

The arrival of a letter interrupted her reprimands. Patrick ripped it open and fluttered it between thumb and forefinger, beaming triumphantly. 'Look at that, Mrs Feeney.'

Thomasin scanned the letter which asked for a quotation on the building of a wall, then threw it on the table.

'What's wrong with ye, woman? Can ye not raise a smile? 'Tis more work we're being asked to do.'

'It's not money though, is it? Bits o' paper don't pay t'rent. D'yer know how much there is left in that tin? I'll tell yer: one sovereign, one bloody sovereign. That's hardly enough to last us a week never mind Christmas.'

As the day crept nearer Patrick began to share her concern. He had started to receive bills of his own, demanding payment for the building materials he and John had purchased, making them unable to secure any more until those were paid for. He had sent letter after letter to Dodd but as yet there had been nothing from that quarter. But with John's unquestionable talent for providing food and countless trips to the pawn shop they were able to keep their heads above the mire. Even so, a visit from his mother-in-law three days before Christmas did nothing to detract from Patrick's unease. Though Thomasin had done her best to arrange the furniture in order to hide the gaps, Hannah's sharp eye immediately noted the absence of two items.

'I seem to remember you had a what-not standing there, Thomasin,' she remarked, looking round for somewhere to lay her gloves. 'Have we been rearranging the furniture, dear?'

Thomasin lifted the kettle from the fire and filled the teapot. 'Aye, well it were gettin' a bit crowded in 'ere so I decided to shift it.'

Hannah smiled patronisingly. 'Come, come, dear, you cannot fool your mother. You have had to sell it, have you not? Short of money again, I presume. Hah. I might have known that all Patrick's fine talk about a business partnership was all nonsense, that all it would amount to would be to land you in Poverty Row once again. I can tell you now, dear, you will never succeed in escaping from here, but then I warned you before your marriage what would happen, did I not?'

Patrick caught the tail-end of her unbending criticism as he and John limped in after a hard day of tramping the streets enquiring after work.

'Good evening, Hannah,' he said with little cordiality.

Hannah balanced her cup and saucer elegantly. 'Ah, good evening, Patrick. Thomasin and I were in the process of discussing your business venture. It seems that it was short-lived.'

Patrick furrowed his brow. 'I can't think what leads ye to that impression, Hannah. In fact our business is proceeding in the manner that John and I foresaw it would.'

'I cannot imagine what inspired you to enter into such an undertaking if you anticipated its failure,' sneered Hannah, then sighed. 'I expect you will be wanting to spend Christmas with us. Of course you will be most welcome. I assume that you, Mr Thompson, will have made your own arrangements for the festive season . . .'

Patrick interrupted. ' 'Tis most gracious of ye to honour us this way, Hannah, but we were rather hoping that you an' Billy would care to spend your Christmas in our humble household, weren't we, Tommy?'

His wife looked at him blankly, then her lips parted in unconcealed surprise as Patrick began casually to build a pile of gold coins on the table. She had to bite back her exclamation and turn to Hannah who was much too taken aback to notice her daughter's surprise. 'Yes, we were discussing it last night, Mother, we thought it'd make a nice change for you.'

'But, your furniture,' said Hannah in a small voice. 'I assumed you had sold it to buy food.'

Thomasin appeared puzzled. 'I can't think what gave yer that idea. I told yer, I've shifted it, that's all. Now, can we expect yer for Christmas?'

'Oh, yes, dear, we will be happy to accept your kind invitation,' said Hannah deflatedly, unable to believe that she could have been so wrong about her son-in-law.

As soon as the door had closed behind Hannah, the three burst out laughing and Thomasin reached for the pile of sovereigns. 'Am I to assume that you've been paid at last?'

'Ye assume right,' said Patrick, then grasped her wrist. 'Not so fast, milady, 'tis bills we have to pay before I allow ye to get your lovely hands on it. But don't worry, there'll be plenty left to give us as fine a Christmas as we've ever had.

However, the bills must take priority else we'll not be able to get any more materials. An' it doesn't all belong to us, ye know, I do have another partner.'

John flung himself into a chair and eased the band on his eyepatch where it had made a red ridge on his forehead. 'Nay, what do I need money for? I get all me bodily needs 'ere – or nearly all.' He grinned devilishly at Thomasin who tucked her chin into her neck and narrowed her eyes. 'All I require is a couple o' bob to buy me ale an' I'll be happy.'

'And is this Dodd's payment?' asked Thomasin.

' 'Fraid not,' answered Patrick. 'Mr Dodd wasn't available when we called. This is for that second job we carried out. Still, once I've settled my own accounts we'll be ready to go again.' He separated a number of coins and put them into Thomasin's hand. 'That should be enough to organise a Christmas that'll impress even your mother.'

It was. That Christmas was the first that passed without one demeaning comment from Hannah, without Thomasin having to accumulate her fruit and vegetables by rooting under the market stalls at the close of business, and without any untoward incident involving John, Patrick or the children. Their table had never been so full; not one square of tablecloth showed between the plates of ham, beef, fowl, fruitcakes, plum pudding, pork pies, pickles, mincepies, oh . . . what a feast! The house overflowed with a happiness that one could almost reach out and touch. Even Hannah forsook her usually aloof posturings to wish Patrick all health in his newfound prosperity, an act that made his happiness complete.

CHAPTER THIRTY-THREE

AFTER THE CHRISTMAS period the demands for their work came flooding in, providing them with a healthy rota for at least the three months to follow. Apart from a brief delay due to heavy frosts, the weather had been their greatest ally.

The letters sent to Percival Dodd were still unanswered but this did not unduly worry the pair, for now that they had settled their own accounts they were able to obtain more credit. John suggested that they order sufficient bricks to complete the next three jobs – that way, by the time they were on to the last one, the first should have been paid for.

Their demand for such a large order was met with some reluctance. 'You're sure you're going to be able to pay for all this?' asked the merchant. 'You were a bit longwinded in coughing up for the last lot.'

John confidently assured the man that business was booming and that he would be paid forthwith. 'I hope so,' replied the merchant. 'I'll expect it to be paid before the last day of February.'

Their new supply was stacked under a tarpaulin in Bay Horse Yard.

The children were in bed, John had been sent – against his will – to replace the bricks borrowed from Baxter and Patrick was stooped over his ledger, squinting under the transient light of a candle, his pen making tortured scratchings over the parchment.

His wife bent over his shoulder, her auburn tresses dangling onto the page. 'My, we are comin' up in t'world,' she murmured and pointed to the figure at the foot of the column. 'Is that what we're worth?'

Patrick carefully lifted the strand of hair that obstructed his pen and curled it round his finger, pulling her face down to his. 'Sorry to disappoint ye, madam, but that's what we owe.'

She straightened in shock, as far as her captive hair would allow. 'You're pullin' me leg?'

'Chance'd be a fine thing.'

His joviality was not shared by his wife. 'Pat, it's no laughin' matter. Where are we goin' to find that much money?'

'From this column.' He unwound her hair and pointed to the column on the opposite page. 'Ye asked what we're worth, well, take away the other figure an' what ye have left is what we're worth.'

Thomasin could scarcely believe it and held the candle nearer to the page to make sure she had not misread the figures. Patrick smiled at her undisguised astonishment. 'It hasn't been paid o' course, but once we've completed these three jobs I think we'll be able to manage that new house out o' the profits. Are ye proud o' me?'

She linked her arms about his neck and settled her chin on his springy black hair. 'Pleased for yer, yes,' she answered quietly. 'But proud? Nay, I couldn't be more proud o' yer than I already was. It doesn't take a pocketful o' sovs to make me proud o' yer.' She swung herself round to sit on his lap. 'Eh, I must admit though it's nice not to have to worry where t'next penny's comin' from, to have plenty to eat an' drink, an' decent clothes.'

'D'ye know what I enjoy best, though?' asked Patrick, playing with the green ribbon at her throat. She looked at him expectantly. 'Not having the extra weight to carry – your mother, she's terrible heavy to have on me back all the time.'

Thomasin produced a bubbling laugh that came straight from the gut, just as John burst noisily through the door, his disfigured face twisted even further with fury.

'Yer'll not laugh when yer've heard what I've got to say,' he snapped harshly, bringing both of them anxiously from the chair.

'Whatever it is d'yer have to make so much row about it?' pleaded Thomasin. 'I don't relish havin' to sit readin' stories to Sonny at this time o' night.'

'Huh! I won't be the only one makin' a row when yer

know what I know.' He marched feverishly up and down.

'John, calm yourself,' implored Patrick. 'An' tell us what's wrong.'

'We're finished, that's what's wrong!'

They both guessed what he was about to say. 'Oh, Jazers,' breathed Patrick. 'Ye got caught putting those bricks back.'

Thomasin slumped into the chair and sighed noisily. 'I might've known you couldn't be trusted to do owt right.'

Showing a side of his character that neither had seen for some years John rounded on them. 'Well, clever buggers yer both wrong. I loaded t'bricks onto 'andcart, covered 'em, trundled 'em down to Baxters an' stacked 'em all nice an' neat without anybody sayin' as much as boo.'

'Then I can't understand why you're so angry,' said Patrick.

John slammed his palms onto the table and leaned on them, speaking into his shirt front. 'Because when I came back the yard was empty, that's why. Some thievin' swine's gone an' nabbed all our livelihood.'

'Taken all our stuff?' cried Patrick, then ran into the yard to stare at the ground where only a dusty patch marked their stockpile's previous existence. 'My God, I've been sitting here all night an' never heard a thing. How could they have stolen it from under our noses? The only sound I've heard all night is . . .' he groaned and leaned against the wall in despair. 'A cart.'

'Aye, that was the sound of our dream bein' carted away,' said John sourly, stamping back into the house. 'The thieving bastards. The idle, bloody wasters. Can't think of a way to earn a livin' except by pinchin' some bugger else's. Yer can't trust any bugger these days.'

Thomasin hastily hid her face beneath her hands, lending them to believe she was crying – Oh, I shouldn't, she rebuked herself. Here we are on the verge of disaster and what do I do – laugh. But the sight of John's indignance had been too much to remain straight-faced. He really believes what he's saying, she thought. She stirred as Patrick gripped her shoulder to offer comfort, and pretended to dry her eyes before looking up at him.

'It appears your mother was right,' he said bitterly. 'Once a pauper, always a pauper.'

Suddenly repentant for her private amusement she stood up and shook him gently. 'Oh, Pat, only you could possibly blame yourself for the dirty deed of another. It wasn't your fault the bricks were stolen. Anyway,' she turned to John, 'How can your career be finished? Pat's just been showin' me t'books: accordin' to what I've seen you could still afford another load.'

John glared savagely at Patrick who tried to explain the predicament to his wife. ' 'Tis not as simple as it sounds, Tommy. Those figures I showed ye were merely that – figures. Ye see, we haven't even enough available cash to pay for those bricks. John is right – without them we're finished.'

Patrick was roused the following morning by his younger son pounding up and down astride his chest.

'Look what I found growin' outside the window, Daddy. Daggers.'

Patrick bellowed as the icicles which Sonny brandished slipped from his little fingers and landed on his father's naked chest.

'Jazers, ye little varmint! I'll have the hide off ye, I will.'

Sonny leapt from the bed and retreated to the comparative safety of the doorway as Patrick flung back the bedclothes to retrieve the 'daggers'.

'Haven't I told ye 'tis dangerous to lean outta that window?' said Patrick grumpily as he stumbled from his bed and placed the icicles on the saucer which housed the bedtime candle.

Sonny chewed his lip and watched his father rummaging about in the semi-darkness for his trousers. 'Will my willie be as big as that when I grow up?' he asked with interest, a question he had asked many times, but repeated as he liked the reassurance of its answer. But today's response was different.

'Ye'll be lucky if ye grow up at all if ye go dropping icicles down me front of a morning,' warned Patrick. 'Think yourself lucky ye don't meet with the usual fate that greets harbingers of doom.' Sonny's news of the arrival of the true winter could only add to his problems.

'What d'ye mean, Daddy?'

'Never mind. Go tell your mother if me breakfast isn't on the table in ten seconds 'tis a widower I'll be.'

' 'Tis already on the table,' answered Sonny. 'That's what I came to tell ye.'

'Then why didn't ye?' Patrick wanted to know, tucking his son under his arm and marching downstairs.

'I gather you've looked outta the window,' said Thomasin seeing her husband's grumpy expression.

'I didn't need to,' replied Patrick plunging straight into his bacon and eggs, with every intention of enjoying it while he had the chance. 'Your son brought me the evidence.'

John, who slept downstairs, was always up before the rest of the household and was now poring over the ledger.

'Ye'll not magic that into money just by looking at it,' said Patrick, nipping a piece of gristle from his bacon. 'By my calculations we can raise about fifteen guineas without leaving ourselves destitute.'

'Don't yer think it's about time that Mr Dodd parted with his cash?' volunteered Thomasin. 'I know yer can't expect prompt payments but after all it's been three months since you did his extension. I reckon he's had enough time to scrape t'cash together now.'

'Well, I keep sending him reminders,' said Patrick, mopping his mouth. 'I've heard nothing.'

'Once he's paid,' said John thoughtfully, 'we could just about raise t'rest o' the money by doing odd jobs again.'

' "Once he's paid" being the catch-phrase,' said Patrick dismally. 'He hasn't taken much notice o' my reminders, has he?'

'Well, instead o' wondering,' suggested his wife, 'why don't you an' John pay him a visit an' demand yer money?' She looked out of the window at the glassy yard. 'Yer not gonna be able to do much else today.'

Later, when he was washed and shaved, Patrick caught John in the act of secreting a pickaxe handle up his sleeve. 'John, what in God's name are ye doing now?'

'Have yer thought what yer gonna do if he won't pay?' enquired his friend, hooking a finger under his eyepatch to scratch the sunken socket. Patrick replied that he had not. 'Well, I 'ave.' John tapped the piece of wood up his sleeve.

Patrick grabbed hold of the man's arm and extracted the shaft. 'John, ye cannot solve everything with violence. Anyways, I don't think there'll be any need for that. Mr Dodd seemed a respectable man, I'm certain he'll cough up when we explain the situation.'

Their journey to Heslington Road was hampered by cart tracks and people's footprints which had frozen into a corrugated skating rink. Once there, the men's spirits were not enlivened by the off-white curtains which blinded every window.

'Sure, they can't all be still in bed, can they?' wondered Patrick. ' 'Tis almost dinnertime.'

'Bed or not,' responded John, delivering three hearty raps on the brass door knocker, 'that'll soon get the buggers up.'

Several raps later there was still no reply and they decided to scout around the rear of the house for the servants' quarters. At the back entrance they tried again.

'It is futile to knock, young man,' came a quivering voice from the seclusion of a privet hedge.

Patrick and John exchanged glances, then approached the hedge and peered over it. Below them was a grey, stooped figure in a magenta cloak and the most bizarre headgear they had ever encountered, with ostrich plumes of scarlet and orange clashing superbly with the cloak.

'Beg pardon, ma'am,' Patrick addressed the woman. 'Could ye tell us where I might get in touch with Mr Dodd?'

The ageing dowager produced an eartrumpet from the confines of her cloak and, holding it to her ear, pointed it in the direction of Patrick's face.

'You will have to speak up, I am rather hard of hearing.'

Patrick took hold of the edges of the eartrumpet and shouted into it: 'We're looking for Mr Dodd. Can ye tell us where to find him please?'

'Are you friends of his?' asked the woman.

Patrick decided that this was going to be a long conversation if he went into details so replied that, yes, he and Mr Dodd were good friends.

'You will forgive me for asking,' replied the woman. 'But I thought it politic to keep an eye on Percival's property while he is away. There are so many unsavoury characters around these days.' She seemed not to include John in her generalisation as she smiled quite nicely at him.

'Away, ye said?' shouted Patrick. 'What time will he be back?'

'Oh, not until later in the year,' she answered. 'But then I thought you would have known that if you are acquainted with him. Percival always goes to the Continent during the winter, he suffers greatly from the cold. His rheumatics, you know. Indeed, my poor joints have not taken kindly to this icy spell they . . .'

Patrick cut her off in mid-sentence, saying worriedly, 'There's nobody in the house at all? A maid, anybody?'

'Yes, so do I!' responded the old lady and Patrick had to grip the trumpet impatiently to repeat the question.

When at last he had ascertained that the house was completely empty, that their last hope had been denied them, the two men returned home, deflated and angry.

'The inconsiderate, ould swine!' stormed Patrick to his wife. 'Would ye not think he'd've settled up before he went haring off to enjoy himself? What sorta trick is that to play on anyone?' He threw a cup violently at the wall.

'Well, raving like a madman isn't goin' to help,' said Thomasin, calmly picking up the pieces. 'If yer carry on like this we'll have nowt left to sell. 'Cause that's what it's gonna boil down to, yer know, sell as much as we can to raise t'money.'

The sale of the majority of their furniture raised nowhere near as much as they had hoped for, even by deviously spiriting away some of the children's larger toys they could not hope to meet the amount required. By the twenty-seventh of February they had only accrued a portion of the debt. Patrick's pride would not allow him to beg from either friends or family, yet every knock at the door sent him into a panic, only to breath easily again after each false alarm. There came the day, however, when the bad dreams were overtaken by the dreaded actuality; the arrival of the builders' merchant's demand.

'Well, here it is.' Patrick flattened the bill out on the only remaining table while John and Thomasin stared down worriedly at it. 'What're we to do?'

John offered to recoup the bricks he had restored to Baxter's site, drawing little applause from Patrick.

'Sure, 'tis bad enough being on the verge of seeing the inside o' the Debtors' Prison. I should hate to sample the felons' side as well.'

His words brought fresh horrors to Thomasin's mind. 'You don't really believe it'll come to that?'

'Prison? Why, of course. If I fail to meet that demand there's no other possible conclusion. Anyway,' he folded the demand into his pocket, 'I'll go offer him the money we've managed to raise an' hope he'll wait for the rest.'

Though the icy weather had abated, enabling them to take on odd jobs and repairs they could not hope to raise the rest of the cash by these methods. What little money they earned was spent, naturally enough, on food . . .

Dickie loped into the kitchen to explore the cupboards in search of something to eat, then turned indignantly to his mother. 'There's no cake in any o' these tins. Give us some money, Mam, an' I'll go buy a bag o' biscuits.'

In a trice Patrick was on his feet and had dealt the youngster a stinging blow round the ear. 'Your mother'll give ye nothing, my lad! D'ye think we're made o' the stuff? Ye've been taking too much for granted lately – all o' yese. There's Erin going on about wanting a new dress, Sonny pestering for books an' you!' he stabbed a finger at Dickie who had fallen under the blow and stared up at his father with a hurt expression, 'you're always thinking about your stomach. Ye never spare a thought for your mother an' me.'

'Patrick, don't take it out on t'lad.' Thomasin pulled Dickie to his feet and, rubbing his cheek in a motherly fashion sent him outside. 'They're only bairns, yer can't expect 'em to understand what we're up against.'

'They should be made to realise then!' shouted Patrick. ' 'Cause they'll realise soon enough when their father is sent to prison.'

Sonny poked his head experimentally into the room and said in a small voice, 'Rent man's in t'yard.'

Thomasin gave a groan of dismay, then whispered to her son, 'Go tell him I'm out an' I'll pay him next week.'

'Sure, what did ye go an' tell him that for?' demanded her husband when Sonny had gone to carry out his orders. 'Hiding behind a child.'

She whirled on him. 'Look, I'm sick of having to tell him I have nowt an' I'll be damned if I'm gonna humiliate myself another week.'

Unwittingly Sonny had bestowed a deeper humiliation upon his mother by telling Daniel Jones, as he was about to knock, 'Me mammy says she's out.'

Patrick and his wife were still involved in their argument as the rent collector ventured into the room. Both stopped in mid-sentence, Thomasin deeply embarrassed at having been caught out.

'Please, there's no need to apologise, Mrs Feeney,' he said in answer to her ashamed confession. 'I do understand, really I do.' His features became comparable to those of a spaniel dog rebuked by its master. 'It grieves me deeply to have to be the one to add to your troubles, but I feel forced to warn you that I can no longer hope to keep your arrears a secret. If it were up to me of course I should be all too willing . . .'

Thomasin sat down and bade him do likewise, which he declined, feeling uncomfortable. 'It's all right, Mr Jones, there's no reason for you to feel guilty. Of course you'll have to tell Mr Denton – an' thank you for giving us warning of what to expect.'

Spring came into bloom, a time of new life and bright hopes – for some. All it brought the Feeneys was a deep poverty. People began to hammer on the door demanding payment. There was nothing to give them. The money Patrick had given the builders' merchant had fended him off for a while but now he too was protesting. They cut food down to an absolute minimum in order to knock a few shillings off the debt. The crushing disgrace it brought was worse than any famine he had lived through.

One tender concession to his misery was that Hannah had not visited them since Christmas and was therefore unaware of the adversity into which they had been plunged. William – who would have been the first to offer assistance had he known of their plight – had suffered a severe bout of bronchial trouble for the last four weeks and so had not been there to see their furniture slowly disappearing.

Neither could John alleviate their plight by his normal methods, for Patrick had threatened that should he bring any more stolen goods into the house he would be immediately ejected, his previous fears about the felons' gaol still holding good.

As the days passed the Feeneys were forced to retreat deeper and deeper into the shadows of ruin.

Liam sat comfortably in his study, a glass of whiskey at his right hand, a book balanced in his left. He had just enjoyed an excellent lunch cooked by Mrs Ray, his housekeeper, and had decided to relax and perhaps snatch forty winks before his next pastoral commitment.

The book grew heavier and the level of the topaz liquid fell lower in the glass. His eyelids became increasingly heavy and, however hard he might fix his eyes to the page, they refused to digest another line. His head began to loll and his chin sank slowly to his chest. The hand which held the book was lowered inch by inch to the desk and pretty soon Liam was snoring peacefully.

His brief sojourn was abruptly fractured by a banging at his front door. Liam came suddenly conscious, almost knocking over the glass in his shock. He raised the hand that had stayed clamped automatically on the book while he slept and ran it around his chin, allowing the pages to flutter carelessly in the draught that came from the open window.

What had woken him so rudely? His stomach was quite churned up about it. He was about to reclose his eyes when the frantic knocking came again. Tipping the remainder of the whiskey down his gullet he eased himself from his chair and went to answer it. The knocking was repeated. Where was that infernal Mrs Ray?

He fumbled with the door knob in the darkened hallway, the stained glass sky-light above the door permitting the minimum of illumination. Mrs Ray must have gone out and, knowing he was asleep, had locked the door, fearing burglars. Damn and blast the woman. Where was his key?

'Will ye stop your knocking, I'm comin' as fast as I can!' He finally came across his key, secreted beneath the glossy leaves of an aspidistra. Flicking the soil from it he opened the door to see Thomasin standing forlornly on his doorstep, a bundle in her arms and three scared-looking children with tear-stained faces by her side.

'Oh, Liam, thank God you're in! I didn't know who else to come to.'

Liam voiced his concern as the woman and her brood stepped past him into the hall. 'Thomasin, ye look as though ye've had a death in the family. God help us ye've not, have ye?'

'Oh, Father, it's much worse than that!' she replied, gulping in an agitated breath. 'Much worse. Patrick's been arrested!'

CHAPTER THIRTY-FOUR

LIAM LISTENED ASSIDUOUSLY as Thomasin related her tale of woe. The deputation had arrived that morning with warrants for Patrick and John's arrest for non-payment of debts and to evict them from their home. Thomasin had had to undergo the acute indignity of being turfed out into the yard while the few remaining pieces of furniture were removed to go towards paying the debt and the house was boarded up. She had experienced a physical pain as each nail was hammered into the plank that spanned her doorway as if they were being driven into her heart. This was the house to which she had come as a bride, where her babies had been born. It was almost unbearable. The children had cried, the younger ones clinging to her skirts in bewilderment as the constable led their father away.

Liam interrupted. 'And what of your friend, John?'

'Hah! You may well ask,' she replied bitterly, cuddling Sonny on her lap. 'That . . . so-called friend hopped out o' the window an' was away like an oiled rabbit before ever the bailiff pulled the warrant from his pocket. Fine friend he turned out to be.'

'Ah sure maybe you're being a little hard on the man,' said Liam. 'I know he's a bit rough, but I can't imagine he's the sort o' fella who'd let ye down after ye've given him a home for all this time. 'Tis my prediction he'll be back. Ah, Tommy, Tommy, why did ye let things get this far without coming to me for help? Neither of ye said a word about it when ye last came to Mass.'

'Pat wouldn't let me ask anybody for financial help. He said it was beggin'.'

Liam watched the tears fill her eyes and damned the man

for a proud fool. 'An' does he think his friends are going to let him wilt away in that gaol? Does he think his pride is going to get him out o' there? Begging indeed. He's been on this earth for nearly forty years an' still the man doesn't know what friends are for.' He clapped his hands. 'Well, once we get you sorted out we'll make a start on raising that money.'

'I 'ope you 'ave more luck than me, then.' Thomasin buried her head in her hands and Erin chewed her nails. 'I don't want to sound ungrateful 'cause Molly's a good lass, but she's not much use when it comes to money or needing a place to stay. She'd need a shoehorn to fit another four bodies into her house.'

Liam stared ponderously at the whiskey bottle, wondering whether to offer any to Thomasin. He did not approve of women partaking of strong liquor, not from a moral stance, merely judging it a waste. However, Thomasin was in dire need of some stimulus to her jaded spirits and what better than a drop of Erin's brew? He measured out a small glass and handed it to her. 'Drink that down, ye'll feel better.' He waited for her to do so before proceeding. 'Ye say that ye didn't know where else to turn – what about your parents – do they know?'

Thomasin allowed a struggling Sonny to vacate her lap and lollop off to explore the bookshelves. 'Don't go touchin' owt, mind. No, Liam, they don't know. I daren't go for fear of what me mother'll say.'

'But surely your parents have a right to know their son-in-law's in prison? You're not going to tell me you're afraid of your own mother?'

'Not afraid of her,' corrected Thomasin. 'Afraid of what I'll do if she starts spoutin' the old story of Patrick the Pauper. I swear if she starts I'll kill her. Just one word, that's all it'll take and I'll . . .'

'Calm yourself, woman,' ordered Liam sternly. 'Ye must go to your parents right away an' tell them. They'll stand by ye, I'm sure of it – an' where else will ye lay your head now ye've no home? I can just hear the tongues wagging should I ask ye to lodge with me. Ah, I know your mother an' Pat have never seen eye to eye, but take my word for it, when she hears what he's suffered she'll not be too hard on him.'

Liam could not have been more wrong.

★

'Prison!' screeched Hannah. 'Oh, that it should come to this; my own daughter married to a convict.' She pressed fraught digits to her temples and continued to voice her horror. 'Oh, the shame of it. What am I to tell my neighbours when they enquire of your presence in my house – for enquire they will, oh yes, this is the opportunity they have been waiting for. How can I tell them that worthless man is in prison? Oh, Thomasin, how could you do this to me? Did I not tell you what would happen if you married that miserable wretch? But little in my constant warnings did I imagine he would drag you into such degradation.' She turned on her husband. 'I warned you! I warned you all but you would hear nothing against him and now all my fears have been realised. I was right from the beginning.'

'And aren't you bloody well pleased about it?' accused Thomasin with the ferocity of a cornered cat.

Hannah stared amazedly at her daughter. 'How can you suggest such a thing? I have never suffered such humiliation – and please do not speak to me in such a vulgar manner. This is the worst thing that has ever happened to me.'

'I wasn't aware of anything 'appening to *you*, Mother,' replied Thomasin angrily. 'It's *me* who's lost me house an' me husband.'

'But your misfortune reflects on me,' answered the other. 'And how you can possibly say I am pleased about it . . .'

'I'll tell yer why I can say it,' snapped Thomasin. 'Because it's right. Don't bother to deny it. I was watching your face before Christmas when yer thought Patrick's business 'ad failed an' when he pulled those sovereigns out of his pocket you were actually disappointed that you couldn't say what yer've been dying to say ever since we were wed, which is "I told yer so". I don't know how yer've managed to contain yerself all these years, Mother. Yer've been livin' for this moment, haven't yer? Well, come on, let's be 'earin' it. Spit it out: 'e's a pauper, a worthless good-for-nowt Irishman an' he'll never be anything else. Well, let me tell you a few facts, Mother!' There was no halting the flow of invective once it had begun. 'It's you who's responsible for 'is bein' in this mess. You who nagged and nagged 'im from the moment you set eyes on 'im, makin' 'im think he wasn't fit to kiss me feet, prodding him into aspirations he can't possibly achieve.

Well, I'll tell you summat else while I'm at it: I'd rather 'ave Patrick than all my sisters' 'usbands rolled into one.'

Hannah laughed uncomfortably. 'Thomasin, this episode has affected your rationality. You cannot really compare Patrick to Danvers or Roderick – or even Carlyle. They always show their mother-in-law the utmost respect. Why, the last time he called, Danvers . . .'

Here she was interrupted by her daughter. 'Yes, and when was that, Mother? I'd be interested to know. When was the last time that Danvers, or any of 'em for that matter, deigned to call?'

Hannah was about to give an affronted retort, then found that she could not remember the date of her other daughters' last visit.

'I'll bet it's a couple o' years ago at least,' said Thomasin. 'An' do you know why they don't come, except as a duty? Or what the little monetary gifts are for? They're to buy you off, Mother dear, so you won't embarrass 'em in front of mater an' pater. They're all bloody well ashamed to have you as a relation because for all your fantasies you're not, an' never will be, *in their class.*'

There was a short silence in which Thomasin remained poised for a counterblast. But she worried needlessly; Hannah was far too shocked to say anything.

'I think tha's said enough, daughter,' reproached William. 'What a blessin' them bairns're out in t'yard an' couldn't hear that. I'm ashamed o' thee, lass, upsettin' tha mother like that.'

Hannah, her face ashen but strangely for once undampened by tears, rose wordlessly and, trance-like, went upstairs.

'I've never seen her like that afore,' breathed William, commenting on the lack of histrionics. 'Tha's really knocked stuffin' out of her this time.'

'Well, it was all true!' snapped Thomasin, still fuming at her mother's inclemency. 'It was her who provoked me into sayin' it by speakin' about Pat like that.'

'Aye, it might well be,' replied William. 'But did thee have to deliver tha speech in such a callous manner? I know she says some bloody stupid things, Tommy – I should know better than anybody, an' I'll agree wi' thee she dun't gi' Pat much chance – but she is, after all, thy mother, lass. Tha'd no right to go speakin' like that to 'er.'

Thomasin was about to add to her defence then issued a long, drawn-out sigh and flopped into a chair like a rag doll. 'Oh, I know, I know. It were rotten o' me, Father – but when I think about the way she's treated Pat an' how she goes on about Danvers an' his crew as if sun shines out of 'em it makes me sick.' Her voice was in danger of rising again and she struggled to curb her temper. 'There's me poor 'usband locked away in a stinkin' prison an' all she thinks about is what people are goin' to say about her.'

'Well, that's Hannah all over,' voiced William, tugging up his breeches. 'Thee ought to 'ave learned by now to take what she says wi' a pinch o' salt.'

Thomasin nodded solemnly. 'Aye well, 'appen I'll go say I'm sorry when I've cooled down.'

'Nay, it's ower late for that,' said her father. 'No amount of apologisin' is gonna make up for what thee said. I'd be surprised if she'll even speak to thee, let alone forgive thee. Still,' he added, seeing her downcast face and considering she had enough to contend with already, ' 'appen things are better out in t'open. She couldn't go on wi' her head in t'sand thinkin' t'Baby Stork got fed up o' flying and dropped her here instead o' Windsor. Any road, I think she really knew it all along, about them being ashamed of her, I mean. That's why she's so 'ard on Pat – well, somebody had to be t'scape-goat, didn't they? What more likely candidate than him, most decent fella among 'em?' He chuckled. 'I reckon I've had me fair share of her yammerin' an' all over t'years, an' truth be known, if I'd realised what I were lettin' meself in for 'appen I'd've stayed single.'

'Perhaps if yer 'ad done I wouldn't be in this mess now,' moaned Thomasin. 'Oh, God, what am I goin' to do?'

'Tha's gonna stop thinkin' about thisself an' start plannin' a way to get lad out o' there. Why the hell tha didn't come to us before it got this far . . .' he tutted and shook his head.

'Yer right o' course,' she sighed. 'Oh, poor, poor Patrick, I wonder what all this has done to him?'

After the ordeal of being parted from his family, Patrick arrived at Silver Street police station where he was passed along the line with an assortment of life's unfortunate flotsam: thieves, murderers, debtors, all heaped together on the same dungpile, some to remain in the Debtors' Prison, some destined for longer journeys – Botany Bay or the 'Drop'.

His thoughts, though he tried to stop them, turned invariably to Thomasin and the children. She had seen this coming, had begged him not to be too ambitious before he was ready. But he had known better, had refused to listen to a woman's intuition – and this was where his superior judgment had taken him. How must she feel, married to a failure?

It was because of thoughts like this that when Thomasin made her first visit to the prison she found access to her husband denied her. 'But I've a right to see 'im,' she protested to the gaoler. 'I'm his wife.'

'None o' my doing if he doesn't want to see nobody,' replied the gaoler, jangling the keys at his belt, eyeing Thomasin with interest and questioning the sanity of one who did not want to see such a fine example of womanhood.

'Doesn't want to see anybody?' said Thomasin.

'That's what he sez.'

'But he wouldn't include his wife in that,' she argued, putting on her best wheedling voice for the gaoler. 'Come on, mister, you'd want to see your wife if you were locked up in 'ere, wouldn't yer?'

'No,' he answered lightly. 'Truth to tell, I'd be glad to be out of her way. But then my wife doesn't look anything like you, great fat lump o' pork she is.' He crooked a spindly finger. 'Away then, if yer want to see him.'

She hastily followed him through the cold stone corridors filled with obnoxious gases. The gaoler finally arrived outside a cell and ran his key over the grilled window on the inner wall. 'Hey, Feeney, yer've gorra visitor!'

There was a furtive rustling from a dim corner and an angry voice growled, 'I thought I told ye I didn't want any visitors?'

Thomasin thrust her face to the grill and peered into the dingy enclosure. 'Patrick, it's me.'

Her only welcome was a groan which embodied everything Patrick was feeling. 'Go away, Tommy, I'll not have ye see me like this. Gaoler, take pity on me.'

'It's pity yer need right enough if yer don't want to see a tasty dish like her,' muttered the gaoler. 'You must have a slate loose.'

'Please, Patrick,' she gripped the bars and tried to penetrate his hideaway. 'You must talk to me.'

There was no answer and she kept repeating her demand. 'For Christ's sake talk to her,' ordered one of his four cellmates, holding his head. 'It's bad enough in here without nattering women.'

Patrick ignored him, but nevertheless responded to her pleas. 'Why must I?' he asked dully. 'For you to tell me you were right an' I was wrong? Don't I have enough to bear without your recriminations?'

'D'yer think I care who was right, yer stubborn fool?' she cried. 'I only want to see yer 'cause yer my husband an' I miss yer.'

'Well, I don't want to see you. Take her away, gaoler, for God's sake.'

The man turned to Thomasin. 'Looks like your old man is off his head, me bonny – sometimes happens in here. How about you coming an' taking sup wi' me? If he doesn't want yer there's one here who's more than willin'.'

It was the best thing he could have said. In a split second Patrick scattered his bed of rushes, trampled his cellmates and was at the window with his arm reaching through the grille to grasp the gaoler round the neck. 'Have ye ever heard the sound a broken neck makes?' he snarled into the struggling man's ear.

'Patrick, oh, Pat,' cried Thomasin, disregarding the beleaguered gaoler to seize her husband's arm. 'Look at yer. What they been doing at yer? Oh, poor lad.'

'He'll be in a damned sight worse position if yer don't persuade him to let me go,' choked the gaoler, his face turning red from the pressure on his Adam's apple.

Thomasin coaxed her husband to let go.

'You think yerself lucky I'm a patient man,' the gaoler informed Patrick bad-temperedly. 'I could have you out of here an' danglin' on the end of a string for attempted murder of a prison official as quick as that!' He tried to snap his fingers but the sweat of fear had made them sticky and they slipped against each other without a sound. 'It's only because I take account o' the fact that you're not right in the head that I don't. Five minutes,' he warned Thomasin and retreated to the far end of the stone corridor.

Patrick tried to withdraw his arm from the grille but she gripped it tightly. 'Yer needn't think yer wrigglin' out o' seein' me now – an' what's all this about not wantin' visitors? I never heard owt so daft.'

'Is it daft I am not to want to be humbled further by my family an' friends seeing me in this position?' he asked with bitterness, then despair. 'Oh, Tommy, why did ye come? We both know there's no possibility of raising the money to get me out o' here, so ye might as well go home an' forget about me.'

'Like you seem to've done about me?' she enquired sternly. 'Buried yourself under a pile o' straw, turned yer back on everything an' everybody, thinkin' if you kid yerself into believing that yer've nobody relying on yer that we'll all go away? Well, here's one as won't.' She tapped her chest. 'An' no amount o' rejection on your part is gonna make me.'

He rammed both arms through the bars and pulled her clumsily to him, imagining he could feel her warm body against his instead of iron and stone. 'Oh, Tommy, Tommy, what are we going to do?' His anguished face had begun to lose its healthy tan. 'Is our marriage destined to be limited to a few snatched kisses through these damnable bars? 'Cause I couldn't bear it, seeing ye but not being able to love ye.'

'Better that than the way you tried to make it. Turning yer back on everything we ever had.'

He lifted a dirty hand to stroke her hair and hesitantly forced out a sentence that had taken so much courage to compose and that she knew he did not mean for one second. 'I wouldn't blame ye if ye wanted to forget about me. You're still a young woman, Tommy. What use to you is a husband that can offer ye nothing but his name? I'd understand if ye met someone else.'

'An' that was a sample o' your understanding, was it?' she asked dryly, with a sideways glance at the gaoler.

He found no humour in her implication. 'I mean it, Thomasin.'

She was suddenly angry. 'Patrick Feeney, I can't ever have meant much to you if yer ready to palm me off on somebody else the minute yer in difficulties. Let me make it perfectly plain: you are not going to be rid of me – ever. As for finding a new husband, well, Mr Feeney, I already have a husband, thank you very much, an' though he might not think he's worth the price of last week's newspaper I think differently. An' despite your predictions you *are* going to get out of this place because I am going to get you out – savvy? Whatever it takes, whether you like it or not. Now then, seeing as we've got that little matter out o' the way, yer can supply me with a list of your requirements. They can't be feedin' yer much in here by the look o' yer, an' I'll bring you 'em tomorra.' Her grey eyes never wavered in their determination, defying him to argue again.

'Tommy,' – there was a shadow of the old Patrick in his smile – 'how could I ever have thought you'd take this lying down?'

'There's only one thing I take lying down, Patrick Feeney,' she said, trying to coax laughter, 'an' when you get out of 'ere that'll be the first thing you get.'

Thomasin's pledge of freedom was rather easier to give than to accomplish. Though her parents had donated everything they could spare and friends had rallied round with minute, but nevertheless welcome, contributions, the effect on the debt was but a nibble. Father Kelly joined the campaign, choosing not to mention to Thomasin just how much soul-searching he had undergone to provide his donation. His leather-bound volumes of Shakespeare and Greek mythology were very precious to him, but he had parcelled up his beloved tomes and had set off to look for a buyer. Thomasin teased the lid from the cocoa tin – the one reminder of things past – and counted out the money. There must be a quicker way of raising the cash. She had toyed with the possibility of putting Erin into service but was reluctant to do this until she found a suitable household, and besides, a few shillings per week could not help much.

On her last visit to the prison Thomasin had recognised that Patrick's spirits would not stand much more of being cooped up like an animal, that to free him she would have to employ more drastic methods than she had already tried. Patrick, she knew, would rather die than have her do what she was about to, but the thought of this dreadful partition augmented her resolve – after all, Patrick need never know.

CHAPTER THIRTY-FIVE

'IF IT PLEASE m'Lud, would it be possible to call a short adjournment?' Roland Cummings addressed the judge. 'There has come to my notice further evidence which may prove crucial to my client's defence. I should be most grateful for the opportunity to converse with him.'

The judge readily agreed. His ageing joints had been troubling him unmercifully all morning and he was thankful for a chance to escape. It was nearly lunchtime anyway. He banged the gavel. 'Court adjourned until ten o'clock precisely tomorrow morning!' He was damned if he was sitting on this hard seat this afternoon.

'Court rise!'

Roland raised his eyes to study the ornate ceiling as the judge left the court, following the lines of the elaborate frieze encrusted with torch standards and festoons, rising to a circle of urns and honeysuckle. It was a fine room by any standards, the ribbed dome, at which he now stared, supported by eight unfluted columns, each decorated with gilded capitals, the walls lined with oak panelling. His gaze dropped abruptly as the judge disappeared and, gathering his brief, he reached over to exchange a few words with his client before the man was led away to the cells. Having told the man he would return to the prison this afternoon to discuss things in more detail he gave in to the pangs of hunger and, after removing his wig and robes, slipped out of the building to seek a tea shop.

Passing Clifford's Tower he felt the invariable shudder of unease. He could never explain this reaction, but somehow he always had the impression that something terrible had taken place at this spot. Perhaps it was only in his mind. Whatever, he was always relieved when it was out of sight, though even with the high outer wall of the castle between them the 'Mince Pie's' forbidding presence made itself felt. He had just emerged from the massive gatehouse into Tower Street, eager to be out of its grip, when someone tapped him on the shoulder.

'Fancy a good time, sir?'

The familiar voice made him spin round in surprise. 'Thomasin, my dear, how lovely to see you!' She grinned as, with obvious pleasure, he grasped her hand to kiss it. 'My, you look wonderful!' His eyes roved the green silk dress that had been brought out of storage for this occasion, recognising it immediately. 'Oh . . . such a delightful coincidence.'

She allowed him to keep her hand. 'Well, not exactly coincidence, Roly.'

Alertness and a shade more surprise. 'You were waiting for me?'

She nodded; then the vision of Patrick on the other side of this buttressed gritstone wall produced an expression of detachment.

His pleasure at seeing her after such a long absence caused him to misinterpret the situation. 'The Irishman . . . it's over?' His old prediction – that by marrying the Irishman she would add twenty years to her true age – had not been accurate. What lines she had accumulated made her all the more attractive in his eyes. Only the hand he clasped bore signs of the life she had chosen.

'Oh, no, no,' she said hurriedly, noting the flicker of disappointment that met her correction. 'He's in yon place.' She gestured at the prison wall.

'As a prisoner?'

'Well, no, he only went in to complain about the smell.'

He guessed now the reason she was here, resented it slightly even though it was lovely to see her. 'And you want me to get him out?'

She sensed his feelings. 'I know it's askin' a lot . . .'

He straightened and said smartly: 'Come, we cannot discuss your imbroglio here; we'll go somewhere private.' Tucking her hand under his arm he set off in the opposite direction to that which he had intended.

She might have guessed where the somewhere private might be. The house in Hull Road was just as she had left it. Roland unlocked the door and ushered her into the hallway. Had there been anyone since her, she wondered, then mocked herself for a fool. Of course there had, he was flesh and blood like her. On the way here, at Roland's request, they had stopped to purchase bread, butter and cooked ham. Throwing her shawl over the coatstand she took these into the kitchen and set out two plates whilst also making a pot of tea. It was all rather eerie, everything in the same place, as if time had travelled backwards.

Whilst they ate – Roland heartily, Thomasin barely at all – she told him everything; how she had raised a lot towards the debt but there was still a great deal outstanding.

The last of the bread disappeared into Roland's mouth. 'Has his case been tried?'

'He's been up before the beak but it's been adjourned.'

'And how many grounds of opposition can we expect?' He saw that she didn't understand and rephrased it. 'Creditors, how many?'

'Well . . . I'm not sure. He owes most of it to the builders' merchant . . . an' we couldn't pay the rent. 'Course, I don't suppose that matters now we've been chucked out.'

'God, the man wants horse-whipping!' He slammed the arm of his chair and rose to patrol the carpet. 'If you had listened to me there would have been none of this.'

But a look at her face calmed him. 'Oh well, I suppose I'll defend the blasted fool for your sake – but don't hold out too much hope. What date is the next hearing?'

'I don't know . . . but that doesn't matter. I didn't mean I wanted you to defend him, Roly. I was hopin' we could 'ave the matter settled before the case comes up – that could be months if there's another adjournment.'

He was only too aware of the workings of the legal system. 'So, what you are really asking, Tommy – correct me if I am wrong – is for me to pay off your husband's creditors so at the next hearing the case will most likely be dismissed.' His tone had again become rather peevish. At her affirmation he came to stand by her chair. 'And am I also right in thinking that you hoped this might just sway me?' His fingers picked at a frill on the green dress.

She could have choked herself for not handling this better; it must look so obvious to him now. 'I thought it might remind yer what good friends we used to be . . .'

'Used to be?'

'Still are, I 'ope. Look, Roly, I wouldn't ask yer for this if I weren't desperate.' She gave a sharp laugh. 'I did consider goin' on the streets first . . .'

'Until you thought of good old Roland. How charming to know where one stands in your affections, Thomasin.'

'I phrased that rather badly.' Panic was beginning to stir; Roland was her last hope of raising the money in one swoop. She reached up, entreating. 'What I meant was, I didn't want it to look like I was just usin' yer.'

'But you are.'

Her hand fell. 'Yes.'

He threw aside his childish pique then, to sit on the arm of her chair and clutch her to him, kissing her compassionately. 'Oh, Tommy, it's simply my jealousy speaking again. I do remember the good times we had – more frequently than you, I'd hazard. It makes me so angry to think what that fellow's put you through. I've missed you terribly, you know.' He tilted her chin with a long finger so that she was looking into his face. 'I thought for a moment when I saw you waiting for me . . . but it has just turned out to be another of your business propositions, hasn't it?'

An apologetic nod.

'Might it be too ambitious to hope that this could be conducted on a similar basis to our other ventures?'

The longing on his face had spoken long before his words; had been half expected. She wondered, then, why she should feel disappointed in him. 'I'm hardly in a position to barter, am I?'

He knew from the way she said it, from her play of feature what she was hoping for; knew that out of affection for their past sorties he should offer her the money she so desperately needed and not exact reward; but he couldn't; he wanted her.

Thomasin watched the opposing expressions flicker over Roland's unattractive features, where desire over-reached courtesy, and knew that her hopes of him were ill-founded. She could have said no, could have held her distance and drawn on the sympathy she knew was there, but fearing that

323

this might cost her Patrick's freedom, and telling herself it was only just exchange, she gave him what he sought.

There was no hesitation. Roland, being the weak-willed character he was, took her with the old familiar gusto. That she wanted only his money seemed no hindrance and he was actually surprised when his normal expertise failed to rouse her.

He paused and looked down into her troubled face. 'It's no use, is it?'

She found it strange that he even had to ask and said so. 'What we had was good fun, Roly, I'd be the first to say so, but that's all over now. I belong to someone else, someone who, if I don't get that money, is going to spend a long time in prison. Yer must understand that he's the only reason I'm doin' this; there's no "old time's sake" about it. I'm sorry to be so frank, but I must 'ave that cash.'

Far from sapping his potency the thought of taking something to which he had no entitlement excited him further and he plunged furiously into her again and again, while the unresponsive body beneath tried to detach her mind, feeling oh, so wretched.

It was over. Roland gave a last, satisfied shudder and was still. Seconds passed before he raised his face from the pillow and dared to look at her.

'Tommy, what a weak, selfish boor I am. Can you ever forgive me?'

'I seem to remember askin' the same thing o' you once,' she replied calmly. 'How could I refuse?'

'I don't know what came over me.' He rolled off her, then answered himself. 'Yes, I do. It's because I knew there'd never be another chance, because you're so dear to me I couldn't bear to pass up the opportunity . . . how disgusting I must seem to you.' She moved her head forgivingly. 'Oh, Tommy, how I envy that husband of yours.'

The mention of Patrick brought back the rush of guilt and she squeezed her eyes shut, trying to blot out the vision of his dejected figure in the prison cell, as if he could read her sin.

Rising suddenly from the bed she began to pull on her clothes as Roland watched her, sensing her shame. It was only now that he noticed the flawless body of yesterday had gone; tiny, silvery stretchmarks shone from the once sleek thighs and though her breasts were the same as he remembered them – full and firm – the nipples were darker; well-worn, he thought, from the mouths of the Irishman's children. He watched her brush out her long hair and wind it up on top. Taking the hairpins she had held between her teeth she stabbed them roughly into place as if trying to punish herself for this betrayal.

She was ready to go and waited expectantly. He got out of bed, exposing the naked, hairy body, and crossed the room to pick up his jacket. How did he give her the money without making her feel like a whore? He hesitated, feeling ridiculous in his nudity then, putting his jacket aside, he disappeared into another room where he rifled an escritoire for a pen. Returning to the bedroom he blew momentarily on the piece of paper in his hand before passing it to her.

'Take this to my bank,' he instructed. 'They will give you the money.'

There was a tinge of sadness in the smile she gave him. 'How am I goin' to repay you?'

'Thomasin, Tommy,' begged Roland. 'Please do not make me feel more ashamed than I do already. There is no question of repayment. It was worth ten times that amount just to be with you again. Treat the money, if you will, as penance for my weakness.'

She gave a sudden frown. 'What'll I tell Pat? He's sure to ask where the money came from so quick.'

Roland adjusted his clothing and inspected himself in the mirror. 'Didn't you say you were trying to find a post for your stepdaughter?'

'Aye, but I've had no luck.' Then she realised what he was suggesting. 'Oh no, I can't have her comin' to work for you! What'll yer wife say?'

'Doubtless she will wonder at my sudden interest in the hiring of servants,' he answered, 'but I do not think she will take it unkindly that I took it upon myself to add to her staff and thereby her status. She is forever telling me what a fifth-rate establishment my home is.' He turned away from the mirror. 'You can tell your husband that your step-daughter's kind-hearted employer heard of his plight and decided to pay her yearly earnings in advance.'

She was doubtful. 'Good wages you pay, Roly.'

'Naturally, my dear, I always pay well for services rendered.' He smiled an apology as she blushed crimson. 'I'm sorry, that was uncalled for. You have certainly suffered enough degradation without my mindless quips. Now, about the child's employment; shall we say the New Year? That would give you ample time to settle into a new life.'

'The New Year it is then . . . an' thank you, Roly.' She followed him downstairs.

'For what, Thomasin? For taking what you did not really want to give? I deserve not your thanks but your contempt. It would have been easy for me to give you that money without demanding your body in exchange, but alas I'm a weak wretch. Oh, your husband is a lucky man.'

'Lucky?' she laughed. 'Is it lucky to be stuck in a filthy prison cell an' to have yer wife beddin' with another man?'

'Not the former, I'll agree, but to have a woman care about one so much that she would consider undertaking an act which she obviously found so repulsive is a state to be envied.'

She bit her lip. 'Oh dear, Roly, I never meant it to sound as though I found yer repulsive. You're a good friend. I'm ever so grateful to yer for the money.'

'Enough said, my dear.' He pulled a watch from his waistcoat pocket. 'And now we really must part company, I have to get back to the castle . . .' It sounded, he knew, as though now he had had his money's worth he wanted to be rid of her, but the longer she stayed the harder it would be for him to say goodbye.

'Aye, of course,' said Thomasin hastily and opened the door. 'Goodbye, Roly – an' thanks again. I'll never forget it.'

– Nor I you, my dear, thought Roland as he watched her trip lightly down the garden path. Nor I you.

Evening came and with it a quiet tapping at the door. Weary after spending the afternoon dashing about the city in the course of securing Patrick's freedom, Thomasin looked imploringly at her parents.

'Thee sit where y'are, lass,' said William rising from his chair. 'I'll answer it.'

'Let me in,' hissed someone as he opened the door a crack and a figure brushed past him into the kitchen.

'Oh no, this really is the limit!' shrilled Hannah at the sight of their guest. 'William, close that door immediately before anyone should see him.'

'Well, the bad penny turns up again,' scoffed Thomasin, her weariness diffused in her eagerness to damn him for his perfidy. 'We thought we'd seen t'last o' you.'

John pretended to be hurt. 'If that's all t'welcome I get when I bring yer glad tidings I reckon I'll go.'

'Oh, aye,' said Thomasin sarcastically. 'An' what tidings might they be then?'

John delved into his pocket, brought out a purse and upturned it over the table to release a shower of glittering coins. 'There y'are,' he winked at William. 'Never let it be said that John Thompson deserts his friends.' He looked back at Thomasin, expectantly awaiting the kiss of gratitude.

Which made his surprise all the greater when, instead of throwing her arms about him, Thomasin broke down and wept.

CHAPTER THIRTY-SIX

THE BLINDING SUNLIGHT seared his deprived eyes and Patrick raised a protective hand over them as he took a step into freedom. He caught at the prison wall to steady himself, for the lack of proper exercise and the confined space had made his limbs weak and uncooperative; but then a few home-cooked meals would soon remedy that and chase the pallor from his cheeks.

The support of the wall became unnecessary as his brain became attuned to what was required of his legs and he set off again, this time with a jaunty spring to his step, racing to be free of that grim outer wall of the castle. Over and over, as he walked through the city streets, he relived in his mind that final court appearance; how the guard had ducked his head under the low lintel of the cell doorway to inform him that the debt had been paid and his Honour would likely decide that Patrick could be released if there was no further opposition. The hearing had been a formality. Patrick was now a free man.

His journey to his father-in-law's house was accompanied by a glowing current of gratitude for everyone who had been involved in his release. Thomasin had informed him on her last visit how kind everybody was being and how they had between them managed to raise nearly half the money towards cancelling the debt. He marvelled at how, in the space of one week, his wife had fulfilled her intent to gain his freedom; a remarkable feat, even for one so determined as Tommy. Thoughts of his wife produced an effusiveness that encompassed his whole being, making the streets endless in his longing to be home, to see her, hold her.

When at last he reached his destination he paused just long enough in the street to smooth down his hair and flatten his grimy collar before approaching the Fenton house. His knock brought a swift response and Patrick made ready his smile at the sound of the latch being lifted.

'Not today, thank you,' said a well-known voice whose owner made to shut the door in his face, but Patrick placed an adroit boot between door and threshold.

'John, you ould get!' he cried as his friend flung open the door, guffawing at his practical joke and slapping the Irishman on the back. 'Sure, I thought we'd seen the last o' you. Jazers, this is a surprise!'

'Nay, not you an' all,' replied John pushing him indoors. 'Yer as bad as that wife o' yours. I told her . . .' John rambled on, telling Patrick of his actions since their last encounter, but Patrick had eyes and ears only for his wife who stood motionless in the doorway, smiling, almost shyly.

They approached each other, yet neither dared to touch. John's volubility fizzled out as he became aware that his presence was superfluous. He cleared his throat.

'Aye, well, I'd best leave you two in peace. I'm sure yer must 'ave a lot to talk about. I'll be back in about an hour.'

'Make it two,' said Patrick, without taking his eyes from his wife.

John made a disrespectful sound and left.

'Hello,' murmured Thomasin softly, smiling up into his dear face.

For answer he lifted one of his great hands, cupping the dome of her skull like a ripe russet apple and lowered his mouth to hers. The fruits of freedom were sweet.

'God, I've missed ye, Tommy,' he breathed, dropping his hands to the small of her back and crushing her body to his. 'I thought I'd never get to hold ye like this again.'

Thomasin uttered a little laughing sob and wiped away a tear of happiness, then removed his hands gently from her body. 'You can hold me as much as you want,' she promised. 'But first, I hope yer won't mind if I ask yer to 'ave a bath? Yer stink like a bag o' ferrets.'

He gave a bellicose laugh; the old Patrick. 'That's what I love about you, wife, you're so romantic.'

Her eyes never leaving him she dragged the tin bath in

front of the fire and proceeded to fill it nearly to the brim with gallons of steaming water. She then began to help him off with his clothes, laughing at his protestations that somebody might come in.

'Mother an' Father've taken the children out for a walk. There'll be nobody to disturb us for a good few hours yet.'

He reclined in the luxury of it all, closing his eyes in ecstasy as she soaped and scrubbed him, kissed and petted his steam-dampened hair. He felt his body begin to respond to her ministrations, enjoying the hand that lingered below the water-line. Without opening his eyes he brought a dripping hand from the tub and placed it on her breast, leaving a sodden imprint on her dress. She held out a towel and he stood, the steaming water draining in rivulets over his thin body, until she wrapped the towel around him, gently patting him dry as she would a baby. His hair showered droplets onto her face as he bent to kiss her then, without further ado, they went upstairs.

Much, much later in the short time they found to talk, Thomasin told him how she had raised the money to pay the remainder of his debt. He was none too keen on taking Erin's wages in advance, or come to that of her entering into service at all. Things could happen to a girl in that position – and what if she were to hate it? She would have no choice but to remain there until she had exchanged her services for the advanced wage.

'I'm sorry,' said Thomasin, snug in his arms. 'I couldn't think of any other way out. All I could see was you spendin' the rest o' yer life in gaol – an' if you're really opposed we can repay the money before she's due to start in the New Year. The irony of it is that I wouldn't've had to place her in service at all if John had arrived earlier with his contribution.'
– If only you knew the full irony of it, she thought bitterly.

Patrick's face split into a wide grin. He had been so happy to discover that his friend had not deserted him. 'Aye, good old John. I feel so rotten about all the names I called him when I thought he'd left me to take the jug. An' you did the right thing, Tommy,' he squeezed her. 'If I had the choice to make meself between staying in gaol an' Erin going into service I know which I'd make. Besides,' he propped himself on an elbow and began kissing her again, ' 'tis a damned good wage she's getting. I think we'll let her keep the job. It sounds a fine house to work for – an' we'll need John's money to set up another home. I may just think about putting you into service an' all.'

Thomasin laughed, but inside her mind wept with the cruelty of John's ill-timed coup. Her sacrifice had been for nothing. She placed a deterring hand over his face. 'By, we'll have to have this 'ere beard off, fuzzy-phyz. It's wicked.'

He flopped onto his back, wriggling his body into the comfortable, if narrow, bed, basking in the freshly-starched linen. 'So, our friend's staying here, is he? I wonder that Hannah would allow him into the house – me too, come to that.'

Thomasin made a *moue*. 'Right on both counts, I'm afraid. But I think yer'll find she's not as hard on yer as yer might imagine.' Patrick looked at her questioningly. 'Well, yer might say we had a little thunderstorm which helped to clear the air. As for John, we've compromised. He's only stayin' for a couple o' nights till he can find lodgings.'

'I wonder where he got the money from,' mused Patrick. 'Not by honest means, I'll warrant.'

'Does it matter, when it was intended to set you free?' John had disclosed to Thomasin the source of the money, but she was too unsure of the reception this information would get from Patrick to pass it on to him. John's disappearance had taken him only as far as the city of Leeds. There was little sense in trying to raise the money he needed on his own doorstep. It had not been easy, for the streets that he walked were filled with similar people trying to earn a living from thievery and deception. The only difference being that, while they were old hands at the game, he – despite his exploits in the past – was in an entirely new field. Even so, his silver tongue had helped him to achieve his aim without trespassing on their patches too much.

That evening, in the time twixt tea and supper, the family, John included, discussed the need for Patrick and John to find employment.

'Well, I say we go ask Baxter for a job,' proposed John to the others' amazement.

'You're mad!' exploded Patrick, though half-amused. 'I don't know how ye've got the nerve to face him.'

'But it's not as if he knows I pinched his bricks,' argued John. 'An' after all I did put 'em back.' A fact which still stung.

'Granted,' said his friend. 'But he wasn't too sympathetic to ye after your spell in hospital. What makes ye think he'll be any more susceptible to your charm now?'

'Aye, well, 'appen it were a soft idea,' concluded John, folding his arms and looking decidedly sick. 'But I can't think what else to suggest other than cloggin' it round all t'sites – an' there'll not be much doing at this time o' year.'

Thomasin decided that a pot of tea might make the grey matter more responsive and went to fill the kettle.

'Aye, the answer to all our problems,' said William, drawing on his pipe. 'A nice cup o' tea.' He spoke to his wife. 'If these lads don't come up wi' summat tha might have to tap them wealthy relatives o' yourn for a loan.' Hannah merely nodded, untypically moderate since her daughter's outburst, yet still capable of summoning a riveting glare at Patrick's next remark.

'Well, if the worst comes to the worst,' he joked, 'we can always send Tommy out on the streets.'

A cup crashed to the floor.

'Steady on, lass,' cried William. 'Tha's eatin' us out of house an' home, don't be smashin' all t'crockery an' all.'

Thomasin affected a weak smile and stooped to pick up the shattered pieces. She threw a sidelong glance to see if anyone had noticed her discomfiture and was relieved to observe that the conversation had steered back to its original topic.

'Ye know,' said Patrick ruminatively, 'I think ye were right about Baxter, John. Maybe we should pay him a visit. He's not such a bad old stick.' Here, Thomasin reminded him of past vilification. 'Well, I know I've called him a few choice names,' granted Patrick, 'but sure, he might consent to help us. Anyway, we can but try.'

'I'll say this for you, Thompson,' said Baxter to John's request for a letter of recommendation. 'You weren't at back o' t'queue when it came to handing out cheek. You set up in business against me an' now you're asking for references. What happened to that partnership I heard about – didn't last long, did it?'

John dared not look at his friend for fear that Patrick was going to tell Baxter the truth. But even Patrick wasn't that big a fool, answering simply, 'We decided we weren't cut out to be businessmen, Mr Baxter.'

The man nodded and reached for a sheet of paper, speaking as he wrote. 'Well, you've both done good work for me in the past. I'll not hold it against you that you set up as rivals.' He folded the sheet and handed it to John. 'I do hear they want a few men at Wilson & Franks – only temporary, mind. This should swing some weight for you.'

The men thanked him and left, doffing caps, John hardly able to withold his laughter. 'If only he knew,' he cackled. 'If only he knew about them bricks.' He kissed the letter and waved it in the air, then gave Patrick a playful, but hefty, nudge, sending him hurtling into the road. Jeering, his ravaged face twisted in demoniacal amusement, he ran off hurling insults at his pal who leapt up and sprang at him, wrestling him to the ground.

'Mind the bloody letter!' shouted John as they rolled around in the dirt like a couple of schoolboys.

Patrick laughed and struggled to stand, pulling John after him. It was odd that in his regained freedom he seemed to experience everything so much more acutely, as though in his happiness he wanted to laugh and shout and generally play the fool, as though acting the child somehow helped to take his mind off his sense of shame. Panting from his exertion he dusted himself down and asked, 'Shall we go for a jar to celebrate?'

But his query received no answer. John's hand, which had been in the motion of sweeping back his untidy hair, stopped. Patrick followed his friend's stare to see what had gained his interest and saw, halfway along Paver Lane, the brightly-coloured wagons, the grey spiral rising from the campfire.

They were back.

CHAPTER THIRTY-SEVEN

THE FACT THAT Patrick and John were good workers during their temporary employment paid dividends. On the recommendation of Wilson and Franks they found regular employment at another firm. As the festive season arrived Thomasin was able to tell her mother that, because of this, they hoped soon to be moving to accommodation of their own.

'I expect you'll be glad to see t'back of us,' she said.

Hannah could hardly disagree; two women in one kitchen was not conducive to good relations, especially when one of them was her impetuous daughter.

Thomasin's hands paused in the task of preparing vegetables for the next day's Christmas dinner. 'Mother?' she began awkwardly.

Hannah glanced up absently from the mixing bowl which cradled the aroma of crushed sage and onion, added zest for the forcemeat stuffing. 'Yes, dear?'

'While we're alone I'd like to say something about what I said when I first came here . . . when Pat was in prison.'

Hannah's face lost its abstractedness and took on a hard expression at the memory of it. 'I hardly think your statement needs enlargement, Thomasin. It was quite plain to see you hold me responsible for all your troubles.'

Thomasin expanded her ribcage, then bit back the retort. 'Well, anyway, I just wanted to say I'm sorry if I was cruel.'

'Indeed you were!' replied her mother, drawing forth her lace handkerchief. 'Oh, the pain you caused by your wicked words. I could perhaps have understood if what you said was true, but to accuse me of such falsehoods when all I wanted was your well-being . . . oh!' She sobbed heartrendingly into the handkerchief, nary a tear in sight.

Despite her mother's apparent grief Thomasin was able to smile, thankful for the return of the old Hannah; so much easier to cope with than the muted aggrievement they had had to endure since Thomasin's admonishments.

'Away, Mam, I'll put kettle on.'

Cold air swept under her skirts and she shivered. 'Put wood in t'oil,' she commanded Patrick whose dirty smiling face appeared round the door.

He threw down his dusty rucksack and pulled off his boots while Thomasin brought his meal from the oven. ' 'Tis quiet we are tonight,' he said as he washed his hands. 'Where is everyone?'

'In bed,' replied Thomasin happily.

'At this time? Why, 'tis only just dark.'

'That is because it's Christmas,' provided Hannah, undergoing a prodigious transformation for one so previously consumed by grief.

'Ah, they're afraid Father Christmas'll pass them over if they're not abed when he calls,' deduced Patrick. 'An' where's Billy gone? To the boozer?'

'William,' said Hannah correctively, 'has gone to conduct business.'

'An' that's what I'll be doing after I've had me tea,' said Patrick, winking at his wife.

Thomasin poured out three cups of tea. 'I'll finish doin' those veg later, 'cause it looks like this is all I'm goin' to see of me husband tonight.'

Some time later, feeling refreshed after his catnap, Patrick went upstairs and returned looking spruce in his best outfit.

'Oh, aye,' scoffed his wife. 'Rat's leavin' t'sinkin' ship. Leavin' t'women to do all t'work while you go off suppin'.'

'Sure, you're welcome to come,' replied Patrick airily. 'If ye don't mind sharing me with all me other lady friends.'

'I'll give yer lady friends,' warned Thomasin. 'Get on if yer goin', an' don't be comin' back 'ere in a newtlike state.'

He peeped back round the edge of the door. 'Er, Merry Christmas, love.' He ducked as a sprout flew past his head. Thomasin grinned at her mother's baffled expression.

★

The Ham and Firkin was a-swill with patrons as Patrick stepped into its merry embrace. In this lively anchorage he found his friend, John who was living now in a room at Mistress Armstrong's boarding house in Church Lane, along with Ghostie, Jimmy and Molly, Riley, Ryan and many more of his old friends. Ah, 'twas going to be a good night! He could feel it in his water. 'God bless all here!'

'Pat, me poor, wee boy, let me look at ye!' Molly swayed up to him, her narrow eyes peering from a florid, befuddled face. 'Aw, God love ye, 'tis good to see ye a free man an' lookin' so bonny. Ah, sure, 'twas my money what helped to free ye, ye know. I sez to Tommy, Tommy, I sez, here's a shillin' to help free that man o' yours. 'Tis the only money I have in the world but if it helps to get me dear Patrick outta that there prison 'tis worth every drop o' gin it woulda bought me.' She looked at him coyly.

'Ah, 'tis a lucky man I am to have friends such as you, Molly.' Patrick put his arm around her and gave her a big kiss, which made her bridle and preen in front of her long-suffering husband. 'An' seein' as how I should hate to be responsible for you dyin' o' thirst, I'm here to pay ye back every penny. Landlord, set them up. Come on, Jimmy, Ghostie, get your glasses filled. Tonight we're going to sup this place dry.'

A great cheer arose and empty tankards began to clatter onto the counter, impatient for refills. For the next hour the liquor flowed as liberally as water, with John keeping the company in yuletide spirits with an unwilting supply of jokes and tales. Inevitably – for Patrick's gesture was founded upon generosity of nature, rather than funds – the ale supply began to dry up and, reduced to purchasing their own drinks, his circle of friends grew gradually smaller. Patrick emptied out the entire contents of his pocket.

'Mm, just enough to buy me another jar before I go home.' He banged on the bar top shouting, 'Let's have another glass o' froth and a pound out o' the till.'

'I've only one pair of hands,' answered the landlord from the other end of the bar. 'Wait your turn while I'm finished with this fella.'

Patrick gave a good-natured riposte and was about to turn away when a second glance at the man who was being served brought a tingle of anticipation, the harsh rasping voice of its owner jarring a distant memory. He opened his mouth and whirled to inform John, but the expression on his friend's face told him it was unnecessary. The one eye sparkled with bitterness and the old lust for revenge. 'You're seeing the same as me?' asked Patrick. John merely nodded grimly. 'Hey, boyos,' the Irishman hissed to the six remaining men. 'How d'ye fancy a nice bit o' sport to round the night off?'

They enquired suspiciously what the sport was and Patrick quietly explained the situation.

'Oh, sure I remember now,' exclaimed Riley. 'He's the one that gave ye the pasting. Aye, o' course we'll help ye sort him out, there's nothing I like better than a good scrap.'

' 'Tis a few shillelaghs we could do with,' stated Flaherty with a loud belch. 'Have y'ever seen the size o' that one?'

'Sure, there's only the two o' them,' encouraged Patrick. 'An' eight of us. As long as we don't let them get to their camp an' raise help we're away. 'Tis time that bastard was copped.'

'Do we get him in here, then?' enquired Ryan.

' 'Tis no good wastin' good drinking time,' replied Patrick. 'We'll wait till he leaves.'

'Will ye look at the size o' them things on the end of his arms,' breathed Riley, watching Fallon lift his tankard. 'Sure, eight of us or no he could flatten a few. What d'you say, John?'

– They think it's a game, thought John, listening to their laughter. He made no reply to Riley's question, merely leaned on the bar and fixed his eye upon Fallon, waiting for him to make his exit.

At that moment the tinker looked in their direction and his swarthy complexion drained to a wary pallor at the seven and a half pairs of eyes that seemed to be fused to his. Though he could not remember meeting any one of them before it did not take his mother's crystal ball to tell him what was on their minds. For a moment his senses were clouded by edginess. He nearly rushed out of the place there and then. But while there were eight of them he and his companion stood no chance at all. Better to sit here awhile and think matters out over a drink. It was doubtful they would make their attack in here.

Only when his eyes fell on John a second time did he begin

to get an inkling of the seriousness of his predicament. This was where the real danger lay.

Thirty minutes later the tinker and his companion left. Fallon knew that their only hope lay in making a run for the camp. Once there they would find support.

Patrick slammed down his tankard and straightened his jacket. 'Right, we're off.' He faltered as he saw John lean over the bar and extract two empty bottles while the landlord's back was turned. 'John, ye'll not go losing your head over this?' he asked worriedly as the man shoved the bottles into his pockets.

'Don't worry, Pat,' replied John, his voice lacking its usual humour. 'I know exactly what I'm doing.'

The men jostled their way out of The Ham and Firkin, adjusting their eyes to the darkened streets. Fallon was nowhere to be seen.

'That way!' John's keen ears had picked up the distant clatter of boots. He set off in pursuit with the others close behind. 'Come on, the bastards are gettin' away.'

They did not catch up with the tinkers until the latter had reached their caravans, but luckily their reinforcements only consisted of two men and a couple of old women. Patrick hastily searched the roadside for a weapon as the tinkers produced knives. He found a thick, fallen branch and held it before him.

In a second the tinkers had struck, giving John only sufficient time to take out one of the bottles and tap it against the wheel of a caravan, hurling the other to Flaherty who caught it deftly and did likewise. The antagonists circled one another like dogs, searching for a weak spot. Then suddenly Fallon lunged for the nearest man's skull with an iron bar. Patrick held up his branch to parry the blow, using it like a pikestaff to force his opponent backwards. John crouched like a cat ready to spring, the moon catching the bottle's jagged edges. He lurched violently at one of the tinkers, but the man side-stepped and dealt a heavy blow to John's neck with his fist, knocking him to the ground. John rolled over to avoid the tinker's boot and sprang to his feet. Blood had begun to seep from a cut on Riley's forehead but he and Flaherty had succeeded in disabling two of the tinkers while Ghostie and Ryan, despite strenuous harassment, were trying to keep the screaming women from laying brooms across the others' backs.

John fought desperately to subdue his own combatant. He must get to Fallon. His friend suddenly cried out in agony as Fallon's iron bar made painful contact with the hand that had been grasping the staff. He fell back, involuntarily dropping the branch and clutching injured fingers. At that same instant the only other remaining tinker reeled screaming and covering his face where John's weapon had finally reached its target. The blood ran through his fingers, down his arms as he sank to the ground, writhing. His screams stabbed through Patrick's own agony; it wasn't supposed to be like this.

John hovered over his victim an instant, the bottle still poised, then looked around for his main quarry. 'Fallon!' His animal cry halted the tinker as he stood astride Patrick's frame, the iron bar raised above his head.

Fallon looked about him for his comrades. The only ones left standing were the screeching women who hurled incessant abuse at the assailants. He remained like a statue, the iron bar clasped in upstretched hands, his eyes wild and staring. Then, unexpectedly, before anyone could stop him, he flung down the weapon, missing Patrick's head by inches and was gone.

In a flash John too had disappeared into the murk in his single-minded pursuit. Ghostie and Ryan hurried across to where Patrick was being hauled up by the others, arms aloft as protection against the women's brooms.

'Where's John?' grimaced Patrick, staring at the carnage, and when told his friend had gone after Fallon groaned again. 'Oh, Jazers, he's going to get himself kilt if we don't stop him. He's no match for that madman. Come on!'

Fallon's breath came in shallow gasps. He pressed his back to the cold wall, straining his ears for the sounds of following footfalls, trying frantically to think what to do. If they split up he could handle them, even two at a time; God's mercy they would.

His hearing, made sharper by the flow of adrenalin that lashed through his veins, picked up a soft movement and he tensed in readiness. The group *had* split up and from the minimum of sound he guessed it was only one person. All the hair on his body stood on end. He felt an urgent need to scratch at his crotch and under his arms where the fear lingered in prickling annoyance.

The noise came again, closer this time. He made himself ready, holding his breath as the sound came once more. Very close. With a sudden bound he leapt from his hiding place to face his aggressor, his only weapons – his hands – positioned for the first blow . . . and startled the foraging cat which leapt onto a wall with a wail of dismay.

Patrick lifted his head at the sound. 'It came from over there. Sounded like someone was hurt.'

'No, 'twas only a cat, I'm sure of it.' Ryan shook his head and lifted the rag he had tied around his hand to examine the gash.

The men lifted their heads at another cry. 'Fallon!' John's voice resounded through the maze. 'Fallon, I know you're in there! I'm comin' after yer.'

'Well, that was no bloody mowler,' said Patrick. 'C'mon, spread out an' we'll try an' corner him.'

Dividing into groups of two with Patrick going it alone, they took off in different directions into the twisting skeins of alleyways.

But Fallon, after his stupid mistake, had already slipped the net and was now out of the maze and running down Long Close Lane towards Fishergate and the river, the fear lending speed and strength to his aching legs. Long-forgotten memories returned in his dash towards the Foss. As the blood pumped through his body so his mind was jarred into a confusion of events and happenings, people and places. Like a magic lantern show he had once seen at a fairground, the pictures slipped in and out of his memory like slides into the machine. The faces of his sons and baby daughter smiled out from his brain and lingered a second before being replaced by that of his wife, her tanned features wrinkling into the sly grin that so endeared her to him.

He was on Castle Mills Bridge now. The frosty atmosphere tore at his lungs with a thousand knives. Below lay the Foss, wind rippling its inky waters. Fallon clambered down the rough stone steps and paused at the bottom, undecided on which way to go. There were two enormous barges moored there. He waited for the moon to go behind a cloud, thankful for the chance to regain his breath.

*

Patrick proceeded carefully along the alley, peering cautiously into every dark corner, his heart thumping in his chest. Up until now the search had proved fruitless. Fallon could be miles away by now. He heard a church clock strike the half hour, and wondered half past what? Tommy would be wondering where he was. He'd likely get a caning when he got home. He suddenly damned Fallon for his untimely appearance. If the tinker had not favoured The Ham and Firkin as a watering hole they would all be home in bed right now. Well, it was obvious that they were not going to find him in here – one more alley, thought Patrick, and I'll be out of this tangle of streets. With the end of the maze in sight he relaxed his guard, shoved his hands into his trouser pockets and began to whistle softly, anticipating the reception of his late homecoming.

All at once his whole body was encompassed by an excruciating agony which sent him staggering to the ground. Immediately the man was astride him, hands locked round Patrick's throat. His eye glinted insanely as he tried to throttle the life out of Patrick – His eye! thought the Irishman, his eye. John, John, 'tis me! he wanted to shout, but the grip on his throat permitted no sound to escape. He writhed and bucked beneath the weight of his friend but although John was the lighter the added strength of his temporary madness made it impossible for Patrick to break free. The Irishman's hands clawed at the other's face, his injured fingers trying to seek a hold on anything which might remove the encumbrance.

Then suddenly the weight was gone and the sweet night air came rushing back into his bursting lungs. 'John, ye mad bugger, is it tryin' to kill your best friend y'are?' Ryan and Ghostie hauled the Englishman to his feet and shook him savagely.

John wiped a hand over his brow and stared down at Patrick who rubbed his throat with one hand, his groin with the other, breathing heavily. 'Christ, Pat, what did yer want to go an' do a soft thing like that for?' he asked, pulling his friend up. 'I thought you were Fallon.'

'Well, God help him for he'd have no balls left.' Patrick still squirmed from John's initial attack. 'Look, d'ye not think we've had enough? I've been half-strangled, beaten, had me plums crushed an' probably got a busted finger into the bargain. I can't take much more.'

The others agreed. 'Sure, we've had our bit o' fun,' said Riley. 'Can we not go home? I like a fight as much as the next man but faith that was a bit real.'

'You buggers can do what yer like,' answered John. 'But I'm not givin' up now.' He pleaded with Patrick. 'Come on, Pat, we've nearly got him. Let's just check down by t'river. If he isn't there we'll call it a day.'

Patrick held up his hands to the others as John turned on his heel. 'What can ye do with the man? Are you as puddled as I am?' After much grumbling the others finally agreed.

'But only as far as the river, mind,' warned Flaherty. 'Me feet're like frozen turds.'

Fallon watched from the safety of the shadows as the moon outlined their figures on the bridge, willing the benign countenance to slip behind a cloud, which she obligingly did. Above him Patrick narrowed his blue eyes and tried to infiltrate the darkness.

' 'Tis out o' luck y'are, John, there's no sign o' the bugger down there.' He was about to turn towards home and then looked back sharply. 'Hold on, I thought I saw something down there. C'mon, let's go take a look.' His feet trod the same steps as the tinker's and Fallon held his breath as the man seemed about to pierce his hideaway. There was nothing else for it. He must make a run for it now; now, while the moon was hidden and make for one of the barges. Once on board he could cut through the mooring line and drift down river.

But at the moment he chose to make his bid for the barge the moon broke her own cover, fixing him in her silvery spotlight as he ran. At what point Fallon realised he was not going to make it he could not tell. Whether it was when the gathering current forced the barge to shift in its ill-tied moorings, or when his heel encountered the patch of oil on the quayside as he made his leap. A look of horror and understanding coloured the tinker's face as his legs skidded from under him and his body hurtled headlong into the space twixt wharf and hull, hands clawing frantically at the barge as he plunged with a great splash into the icy water.

Patrick jumped down the remaining steps and hurried to the quayside as Fallon threshed about in the freezing river, his mouth agape with the shock of its coldness.

John rushed up to stand beside him and found it difficult to believe what his eyes were seeing when Patrick lay on the wharf and reached a rescuing arm towards the water. 'What yer doin', man?' he gaped.

'What's it look like?' grunted the Irishman. 'Enough is enough, John.' He succeeded in clasping Fallon's slippery hand and began to haul him up when he felt a pressure on his arm and looked up awkwardly. 'John, will ye take your boot off me arm an' gimme a hand?'

John glowered at him. 'I'm not wastin' all this bloody time just to let him go. He's stayin' where he is.' He squatted at Patrick's shoulder and spoke persuasively. 'What's up wi' yer, man? He nearly killed us once, remember?'

'I remember.' With the removal of John's boot Patrick started to heave on Fallon's arm again. 'But ye'll not ask me to stand by an' watch a man drown, 'tis not in me. That would only make us as bad as he is.' His face was suffused with blood from the effort of the struggle. 'Now, for God's sake, John, help me get him up.'

But John made no attempt at assistance.

Fallon gripped the proffered hand with all his might and effectively gained a foothold on the slimy wall, using Patrick's shirt to pull himself out of the water. During a brief pause in the climb he looked up breathlessly into John's face and knew that the one-eyed man shared none of his rescuer's sentiments. Somehow he must create a diversion if he were to come out of this alive, and the only way to do that was to turn the tables on the man who was hauling him out of the water. It mattered not that Patrick had just saved his life when the one-eyed man had no intention of allowing him to live.

He was nearly out now and had brought his right knee up over the edge of the wharf. As he did so he grabbed a handful of Patrick's shirt and tugged.

'Easy,' grunted Patrick, almost losing his balance. 'Ye'll have us both in.'

But the tinker ignored his plea and began to shunt Patrick lower and lower over the side. Too late Patrick realised the man's purpose, his boots scrabbling over the damp ground as he was pulled further towards the water. 'John, for pity's sake!'

'I wondered just how long it'd be before yer realised,' said his friend, who had been watching the struggle with a twisted smile and now stepped forward in an attempt to extricate the tinker's iron grip from Patrick's shirt. 'See what thanks yer get for all yer fine efforts?'

Patrick barely heard the mocking words; he was straining every muscle to keep his grip on dry land. The other men came rushing up to watch the battle just as a terrible scream split the night. Unable to remove Fallon by the strength of his hands, John had sunk vengeful teeth deep into the tinker's fingers, relishing the taste of his enemy's blood. He accomplished his aim. Patrick fell back as the tinker abruptly released his hold and began to slip towards the water, hands flailing for anything that might save him.

John turned his face to his friends with a satisfied grin, which was to prove fatal. With his blind side towards the tinker he did not see the falling man's last desperate grab for life. The pressure on his ankle took him completely by surprise, pulling his feet from under him and with a resounding splash both men plummeted into the river.

Patrick and his companions peered anxiously into the black space between wharf and barge where the waters of the Foss threshed and foamed as each tried to push the other under its deadly coverlet. Once more Patrick stretched himself out on the cold stone and reached down a liberating arm, this time to his friend. Riley and Ryan hung onto his legs as he inched himself further, making frantic grabs for John's collar but each time grasping only air. His shirt had freed itself from his trousers, bearing his midriff to the chafing stone. The veins in his neck bulged with the effort as he continued to call for his friend to take his hand.

John, however, saw nothing save the man with whom he grappled, recounting the hardships that this tinker had heaped upon him: the loss of his eye, his job, his family.

'Jesus, Mary an' Joseph,' breathed Flaherty, grasping Connors' arm. 'Will ye look? For Christ's sake pull him up now.' The force of the current against the hull had teased the laxly tied mooring free. Egged on by the waves that the violent combat had produced one end of the barge began to drift towards the wharf.

'Jazers, 'tis going to crush the lot o' them if we don't get him up!' screamed Riley. 'Give us a hand, you lot.' He and Ghostie tucked a hand into Patrick's belt and began to pull him up.

Patrick bellowed in annoyance as he felt himself being dragged away from his goal. 'Get off, I've nearly got him!'

'Pat, the barge is movin'!' shouted Flaherty. 'We'll have to pull y'out else you're going to go the same way as them two.' He spoke to the man next to him. 'Grab his left foot, I'll take his right. C'mon, boyos, haul away.'

'No!' Patrick tried to reach up with his arm to beat them off. 'We can't let John drown. We've got to save him.'

' 'Tis no use, Pat, we can't save the lot o' yese!'

With three men on either side they began to heave the struggling Irishman upwards.

'No!' Patrick's anguished cry rang out again, but to no avail.

The swaying vessel continued its stealthy movement, sending icy ripples over the struggling figures below. Hands sought futilely to shove it away. To the observer a boat on water appears lightweight, but this was oh, so heavy. Behind the tons of wood and metal lay the greater strength of water. It would not be deterred.

It was a sight Patrick would never forget. One moment his friend's face glittered in triumph, his hands clawing Fallon's head beneath the water, laughing at the flurry of air bubbles that peppered the surface. Then his mouth came open in surprise, his face held an expression of incomprehension as the breath was squeezed noisily from his broken body, and his one eye shone out of the darkness, etching itself indelibly on Patrick's memory.

At last the barge became bored with its game, relinquished its deadly embrace. Its bow nosed itself into the main current, straining at the remaining tether. Gentle waves lapped in its wake, all that remained of the previous turmoil.

Released, Patrick knelt at the edge of the quay and gazed spellbound into the watery void, sure that his friend would miraculously reappear, that in a moment his grinning, ugly face would burst through the murky backwash crying, 'Fooled yer!'

'Pat?' Riley's sharp enquiring tone brought little response. Hands in pockets, shoulders hunched against the cold that bit through his thin shirt, he walked briskly away from them. From the river.

'Pat, where ye goin'?' repeated Riley, running after him, followed by the others.

'Home,' came the quiet reply. 'Just home.'

The warmth that hit him on opening the kitchen door came as a restorative after the horrors of the evening, but his comfort was shortlived. Thomasin looked up as he entered, the smile of welcome dying on her lips when she caught sight of his filthy shirt and bruised face.

'Oh, is it Christmas again?' she asked sarcastically, flinging down her darning to point at the signs of violence on him. 'I can't let you out for five minutes, can I? Every Christmas it's t'same, yer get a few drinks down yer an' yer seem to go completely barmy. An' what, if I may ask, has 'appened to your best jacket? My God!' She paced up and down in front of him, snatching tugs at his sleeves as she passed. 'Look at the muck on that shirt. It's oil, yer know, it won't come out. I suppose fella me lad's got yer into another of his scrapes, has he? Don't suppose we'll be seein' his face for t'next couple o' weeks. Huh!' She frowned at Patrick's reticence. 'Well, out with it! Aren't yer gonna make excuses for 'im like yer usually do?'

He shuffled to a chair and collapsed into it, ignoring her questions to ask one of his own. 'Is everyone in bed?'

' 'Course they are,' she snapped. 'Have yer any idea o' what time it is? There's only soft Lizzie here waitin' up like a wiltin' daisy to see yer get 'ome safe. By God, I'll give that little so an' so what for when I see 'im.'

'Ye'll have a job,' replied Patrick wearily. 'Unless ye've powers that I don't know about.'

'What the hell are you talkin' about?' she demanded, hands on hips.

'He's dead, that's what I'm talking about,' replied her husband sharply. 'Now are ye bloody satisfied?' He glared at her stunned face momentarily, then lowered his face abruptly.

346

'Dead?' she repeated disbelievingly. She stared at her husband's hunched frame, watching his shoulders heave. A minute had passed before she realised he was weeping. 'Oh, Pat!' She flung herself upon him, cradling his wet face in her arms, lamenting the hurtful outburst. She edged herself onto the chair alongside him, gripping him fiercely, rocking him to and fro like she did with the children when they came home hurt. She pulled out a handkerchief and lifting his face, mopped at his cheeks gently. 'Do you want to talk about it?' Her grey eyes held everything he needed at this moment; warmth, security, comfort.

He took a deep breath and shook his head. 'Later, perhaps.'

'It'll be better if yer get rid,' she prodded, laying her head on his shoulder. 'Come on, love, let's go to bed – or would yer like a nice cup o' tea?' She laughed as Patrick chorused the last four words.

'Ah, Tommy, you always make everything seem better. You and your cups o' tea.'

She stood up and held out her hand. 'I think I can manage summat better than a cup o' tea, if yer up to it. We'll leave talkin' till you're feelin' better. There's nowt like a bit o' mother's love to buck yer spirits up. An' when yer ready to tell me, I'll be here.'

PART FOUR

CHAPTER THIRTY-EIGHT

THE NEW YEAR opened up before them, a bright, clean page awaiting the indelible words that they might choose to write upon it. Patrick fought hard to put the events of the previous year behind him, though with each evening came the recurring nightmare of his friend's death. He would thrash and whimper in his sleep, tossing his head from side to side, until his wife shook him gently and he would awake, drenched in sweat.

The worst part had been when a man's body was reported to have been discovered wedged against the lock gates in the Foss. From the description Patrick knew that it could not be John and so the agonising wait continued.

By this time, the Feeneys had found a house of their own to rent. The small, terraced property was, as their other homes had been, situated off Walmgate, for Patrick wished to remain among his Irish friends. This one, though, was a vast improvement on their previous abodes, having its own supply of running water and, joy of joys, their very own closet in the back yard.

However, such luxury required a steep price and Patrick could not afford the high rent out of his wage. But Thomasin, who had fallen in love with the house the moment she stepped over the threshold, said she would go out to work for the extra money. She could not bear to think of someone else living in 'her' house.

Though she had been overjoyed when he accepted her plan the ease of his capitulation worried her. She had expected to have to fight very hard over this issue. Perhaps, she thought, the added years had made him more pliable, but she knew that the truth was more likely to be that his imprisonment had scaled away a little of his arrogance; had given him time to reflect on his assumed self-importance. Maybe that was not such a bad thing. Pride in a man was to be admired but Patrick could be very pig-headed at times.

She had flung her arms round his neck voicing her thanks. 'An' I promise the job will only be part-time, yer'll not have to get your own meals.'

'I should hope not,' he replied sternly. 'I shall expect my meal on the table, working wife or no.'

'An' here's me thinkin' yer mellowin' in yer old age.' She pulled away smiling, then put a thoughtful finger to her chin. 'I'm just wonderin' how we're gonna be able to furnish this new place.'

Patrick reminded her that there was still some of John's money left. Thomasin, hoping to patch his battered ego, suggested that he might perhaps like to use that money to start up in business again, in a small way of course.

He gave a brittle laugh. 'Sure, there'll be no more business gambles for me. I know when I'm beaten.'

'You're sure you are Pat Feeney?' she teased. 'The Patrick I know wouldn't give in so easily. Where's the old fightin' spirit?'

'I left that behind at the Debtors' Prison,' he replied glumly. 'Along with a lot of other things. Ye've got to face it, Tommy, as I have, I'll never be anything other than what ye see before ye; a labourin' man. It was never meant to be that I should be one o' the masters.'

'Well I don't know how yer've come to that conclusion,' she answered. 'You hardly had a chance to find out – an' yer will keep talkin' as if it were your fault that yer failed. It was because yer fell foul of a bunch o' thievin' scoundrels.'

Patrick was not to be heartened. 'Ah, well, whatever, 'tis in the past an' as far as I'm concerned there'll be no danger of a repetition. It was John who was the businessman, not me. Before I came here I knew little else but farming. No, I think I'll just stick with what I've got. I doubt Hannah will be able to find fault with the house we've chosen an' with poor John's money we oughta be able to furnish it nicely.'

'She still creeps in, doesn't she?' Thomasin smiled but her eyes were sorrowful. 'And don't pretend yer don't know who I'm meaning.'

'Ye know what they say about old habits,' he replied with a wry expression. 'But, make no mistake, Tommy. This is for you, for all I've put ye through. All right, I would prefer it if your mother could produce just one complimentary remark about me, but if she can't find it in her then 'tis not as important as it once might've been. I'm through trying to prove myself to her – to anyone, most of all to myself. All I've proved so far is that I'm not the man I thought I was. No, the important thing is to make ye happy. I'm sorry I cannot do any better for ye, 'tis eternally grateful I'll be for the way ye've stuck by me. Ye've not a lot to thank me for, I know.'

Thomasin frowned. This was not like Patrick at all. 'Pat, yer talkin' as if I'm some stranger. I'm yer wife, lad! When we were wed I made a promise to stick beside yer for better for worse, yer surely didn't expect me to leave yer when we came to the first hurdle, did yer? I do wish yer'd stop all this defeatist talk. Much more an' yer'll be havin' me believe it.' She tapped his cheek playfully.

On their return to financial stability they had decided to re-examine the question of the boys' education. Dickie, who had enjoyed a short reprieve due to his father's business collapse, did not take kindly to finding himself once again destined for school. Sonny, on the other hand, was delighted. Why, he had wanted to know, could Dickie start two weeks earlier than himself? Because, Thomasin had replied, Dickie was the elder and also they had insufficient means to equip both boys for school at the same time. If Sonny had guessed the true reason he would have been further infuriated. It was such a big step, Thomasin had told her husband, she could not possibly part with both her sons at once, especially her little, carrot-haired baby, the wrench would be too severe. Just wait till she had acquired a little job then she would have something to assuage the soreness of parting . . .

The Feeneys' arrival at their new home excited great curiosity from Nelly Peabody who was unmarried, fiftyish and extremely nosey. The moment their cart pulled up she rushed outside to offer assistance.

'It's very kind of yer, Mrs Peabody,' smiled Thomasin and pointed at the menfolk who were unloading the furniture, 'but I think we've enough hands for t'job. Some o' these things are very heavy, I'd hate yer to hurt yerself.' She turned as Erin and the boys came trundling a handcart down the street, laden with crates and curtains, pots and pans.

'I shan't break anything,' promised Nelly.

'Oh, I wasn't suggestin' . . .' Thomasin sighed and indicated the handcart. 'Well, if yer'd like to help you could carry one of those smaller boxes, thank yer very much.' She left the chair on the pavement and took hold of the other end of a table which Patrick had dragged from the cart.

Nelly, when the children arrived, pushed them aside and, struggling with a box, followed the others into the house. She waited until Patrick and Thomasin had positioned the table and had gone back to fetch another item of furniture before she placed the box on the floor and started to lift out the objects inside which had been packed with newspaper. The children, who had trailed in with burdens of their own, made disapproving faces behind her back. By the time Patrick and his wife returned Nelly was up to her elbows in discarded newspaper.

'Er, Mrs Peabody, I think 'tis best we get the big stuff in before ye start unpacking the crockery,' suggested Patrick, making her jump.

'Oh, ahem! I was just admiring your wife's taste,' said Nelly, holding a teacup up to the light. 'Very pretty. Bone china too.' She placed the cup on the floor and delved again into the box. The way she sat on her heels and rubbed her hands together gleefully reminded Patrick of the red squirrel he had seen on Lord Herleigh's estate. The brown eyes bright with curiosity, the little paws rifling the horde of goodies.

'I was just saying,' Patrick looked unamusedly at Nelly who was unwrapping yet another of their belongings. 'I think we should . . .'

'Oh, very nice.' Nelly seemed intent on examining the entire contents of the box. 'Oh, Mrs Connel's got one of these.' She beamed and held up a cheese dish decorated with pink and yellow roses. 'She got hers from Leak & Thorp's sale.'

Thomasin sagged at the opposing end of the iron bedstead which she and Patrick were trying to manipulate up the stairs. 'Mrs Peabody . . .'

'Miss!'

– Is there any wonder thought Thomasin? 'Miss Peabody, can yer just nip upstairs and open t'bedroom door for us so's we can see where we're goin'?'

Nelly was only too pleased to grasp the opportunity of investigating the contents of the bedrooms and was on the landing before one could draw breath.

'Sure, what did ye send her up there for?' grumbled Patrick, walking backwards up the stairs. 'She'll be telling everyone what we've got.'

'Well, she's already seen half o' t'stuff, she might as well see t'rest,' gasped his wife, easing the bed onto the landing and pausing for breath. 'Any road, I'm not bothered if she does tell everybody. My new furniture can stand comparison wi' anyone's in this street.'

'I still don't like all and sundry knowing my business,' hissed Patrick and glowered at Nelly who was busy opening and shutting the drawers of a tallboy. 'Will ye look at the ould biddy? Has she nothing better to do?'

'Probably not,' replied Thomasin lifting the bed once more.

'Shall I unpack that?' Nelly was pointing to a battered, leather trunk.

'That'll not be necessary,' said Patrick brusquely, swinging the bed into position and drawing a spanner from his pocket.

'Oh, it's no trouble.' Nelly began to unsnap the locks on the trunk. 'Your clothes will be all creased if you leave them in there all day.'

'Mrs . . .!' began Patrick crossly, then fought down his temper. 'I don't want . . .'

'We don't want to put you to any trouble,' finished Thomasin rapidly, not wanting to alienate her neighbour at this early stage. 'But, if yer'd really like to help?'

'Oh, yes, of course.' Nelly clasped her hands eagerly.

'Then would yer be so kind as to make us all a nice cuppa tea?'

Patrick chuckled to himself at the popular phrase as Nelly, not bothering to hide her disappointment, went downstairs to put the kettle on, then finding no fire in the grate took Thomasin's teapot with a quota of tea into her own house to brew it.

'There,' said Thomasin, some time later, dusting her hands.

'We've just t'beddin' to put on and t'curtains to 'ang then we're about done up here.'

Together they inspected the bedrooms. There was a double bed in each, one for them, one for the boys and a mattress for Erin until she was summoned to her new employment, which would be any time now.

'I wonder how that lot are faring downstairs?' Thomasin hoisted her skirts and hurried below, followed by Patrick who went outside to pay the carter for his services. This done, he joined his wife to find Nelly having words with their elder son. The children, it seemed, had not appreciated her instructions on where to place the furniture and a heated exchange had developed.

'What a disagreeable child,' said Nelly, arranging the cups on the table. 'Most unmannerly.'

'Sure, I only said 'tis rude to poke about in things that don't belong to ye,' provided Dickie when asked. Hadn't his mother told him so?

Thomasin took hold of his collar and sent him outside with a stern warning, then sat down. 'By, this is a welcome cuppa tea, Miss Peabody. Just what we need to warm us up till we get fire lit.'

'Yes, everyone says I make the finest cup of tea in York,' boasted Nelly. 'And though I say it myself I have to agree. Though of course this is not up to my usual standard. I would normally use a better quality tea.' She sat next to Sonny and tweaked his ear lobe. 'And what have you to say, young man?'

'S'all right, I suppose,' granted Sonny, jerking his ear from her torment. 'S'not as good as me Mam makes though.' He hoped Nelly's visit would not be a regular occurrence. 'Won't yer dad be worried if yer out too long?' he enquired hopefully.

'He means yer husband,' enlightened Thomasin. 'Miss Peabody isn't married, Sonny.'

'But yer old,' replied Sonny unflatteringly. 'All old people are married.'

'Not all, my good fellow,' corrected Nelly firmly.

'Why aren't you married then?' pressed Sonny.

'Because I choose not to be,' said Nelly looking somewhat uncomfortable.

'Oh.' Sonny seemed surprised at this and pondered upon

it a while before adding, 'Haven't ye even got any children, then?' causing his father to clear his throat noisily.

Nelly blushed and attempted a coy laugh, taking great pains to avoid an answer, sipping her tea prissily.

'Well, have ye?'

'Er, Sonny, will you go outside and check that we've got all the stuff off t'cart?' asked Thomasin with a crafty kick of Patrick's ankle who was smiling into his teacup.

Sonny's mouth turned down and he placed his cup heavily on the table.

The woman turned her attention on Erin who, as usual, had been merging quietly with the background. 'What long hair, dear, you must ask your mother to tie it up in a more suitable style or it will sap your strength.'

'I like it like this,' replied Erin coolly. This woman would make a worthy companion for grandmother.

'It is very nice, of course,' agreed Nelly. 'But most unhealthy, especially in the hot weather. It can produce an extreme attack of the vapours if one does not take care.'

'Well, I like it like this,' repeated Erin stubbornly. She put down her cup and went to join her brothers outside.

Nelly, unmoved by the hostility she had engendered, finished the tea and rose to continue with her inventory. 'This has a chip out of it.' She held up a pottery figurine before placing it on the mantelshelf. 'Did you know?'

'Yes, I am aware of it, Miss Peabody.' Thomasin glanced at her husband who was in danger of setting fire to himself in trying to constrain his temper.

'How much did you pay for this?'

That was too much. Patrick gave a strangled gasp, clashed his cup and saucer together and marched outside. Thomasin decided that enough was enough and began to side the teacups.

'Well, thank you for all your help, Miss Peabody,' she smiled, hoping that Nelly could take the hint.

'Oh, it's my pleasure.' This was obviously true. Nelly, never one to take a cue, failed to grasp Thomasin's attempt at subtlety and started to arrange various articles on the mantelshelf until the effect was to her satisfaction.

'There! Now, I think we could just do to move this chair over to that corner.' She hauled the chair to the required spot.

'Look, I don't want to seem as though I'm throwing you out,' said Thomasin slowly. 'But I'll have to get our meal ready in a minute.'

'Pray proceed, Mrs Feeney,' cried Nelly. 'I can cope quite well alone.'

'I'm quite sure that's true, Mrs Peabody . . .' Here Thomasin was again corrected on Nelly's status. 'I'm sorry, Miss Peabody,' she laid great emphasis on the Miss, 'but I wouldn't dream of allowing yer to undertake any more o' my duties. I'm certain you 'ave enough to do at home.' She stifled Nelly's objections and escorted her down the passage.

Outside the children, coatless but with an added comforter to keep the cold at bay, had made a slide on the pavement. They careered noisily up and down, eyes alight, joined by an equally ecstatic father.

'What a foolhardy caper!' exclaimed Nelly, wringing her hands. 'Oh, dear. What if I should walk upon that and break a limb, or even worse?'

'That was the general idea,' muttered Patrick in a sly aside to the children who giggled, then laughed even louder when their father slithered abruptly onto his bottom.

Nelly disappeared for a few moments then returned bearing a shovelful of ashes which, despite the childrens' vociferous protests, she sprinkled over the onyx-like strip on the footway.

'Upon my soul, we cannot have you being responsible for someone hurting themselves, can we?' she said, mainly for the benefit of Patrick who, she reasoned, should know better.

The children, robbed of their game, trooped back indoors as Nelly retreated to her own domicile, brushing her skirt which held a trace of ash. She turned, before closing the door, shouting to Patrick as if nothing had happened, and to his further annoyance, 'I hope you enjoy your kippers.'

'Tell the whole street, why don't ye?' fumed Patrick scathingly when Nelly's door had closed. 'Jazers, have ye ever known the like of her?'

But Thomasin was still meditating on Nelly's parting words. 'How on earth did she know?' she breathed amazedly. 'I haven't even taken 'em outta t'paper yet.'

'Thomasin, there's nothing in our house she doesn't know

about,' answered Patrick resentfully. 'She probably inspected the privy just to see what colour the . . .'

'All right, we don't want to know!' Thomasin interrupted.

'Well, honestly,' said her husband, gripping the handles of the cart. 'The woman's a menace. Had I known what we were letting ourself in for I'd never've taken the place. There's no need to ask why the last occupants moved, is there?' He prepared to wheel the handcart away.

'Where d'yer think yer off to now?' enquired Thomasin. 'I'm just gonna put them kippers on.'

'I'll not be long,' he answered over his shoulder. 'There's things I want to buy.'

'What things?'

'Praties!' The conversation grew louder as the distance between them widened.

Thomasin curled her lip. 'Why d'yer need handcart for a few taties?'

'Who said anything about a few?' shouted Patrick. 'Sure, I'm not humping ten stone o' praties home on me back when I can wheel 'em in comfort.'

'What the devil d'yer want ten stone for? We don't need that many.'

'What's all this "we" business? They'll be my praties, for me own personal use. An' before y'ask,' he added, tapping his nose, 'never you mind.'

'Right, that's your rations cut off for a week,' shouted his wife and slammed the door.

CHAPTER THIRTY-NINE

'WILL YOU GET up? This bed stinks like a rats' nest! Thomasin's bellow ricocheted off the walls, threatening to bring the house down. Taking hold of her elder son's ankle she hauled him from his bed.

'S'truth, child, yer worse than yer father. Come on now, Sonny's been up for hours. Yer'll be late for school.'

She threw open the window and peered into the street which rang with the sound of men's boots, their breath coming in silvery balloons as they laughed and joked their way to work. In the neighbouring house Nelly Peabody, up since first light lest anything of import should occur, sat at her usual position behind the lace curtain, noting the coming and going of the male population, making sure that everyone came out of the right house and keeping a particular eye on the door directly opposite hers, the home of Ruby Sinnington, the street's scarlet woman.

Thomasin pulled her shawl tighter and leaned over the windowsill to shout a merry salute to another of her neighbours and told herself what a good choice they had made in coming to live here. Little more than a fortnight had passed since their arrival but she felt as if she had lived here all her life, so friendly and embracing was the house's atmosphere. They never really talked about it but she knew the others felt as she did. At night, while the wind rattled bad-temperedly at the door knocker and whined through the gaps in the windows, the family would sit cosy and warm around a blazing log fire; Thomasin and Erin darning, the boys playing dominoes and Patrick puffing dreamily at his pipe, his long legs stretched over the hearth, a book propped upon his stomach, occasionally each catching another's eye to smile contentedly. Yes, this certainly felt like home. She broke off her dreaming to reissue the warning.

'Come on, Dickie, let's be havin' yer, else I shall be up wi' a pail o' water!' She went downstairs.

Dickie yawned and rubbed his head which had made smarting connection with the floorboards, the thin, bedside rug offering no protection. Monday again. How he hated Mondays. Monday meant school, an end to the fun of the break. School meant an end to everything. The twice-weekly trips to the cattle market with Grandad, the good times he and Sonny had spent with Uncle John on Low Moor, when he had taught them the tricks of his trade and would often reward them with a couple of rabbit skins to be exchanged for a halfpenny at the rag and bone merchant's, which in turn was exchanged for a bag of confectionery at the corner shop. He wondered fleetingly when Uncle John would come back. Daddy said he had gone away but did not say where and for how long.

Now there was only Saturday and Sunday in which to have fun, and half of that was taken up by church. What was the point of it all? he asked himself. School was such a bloody waste of time.

With wearisome effort and half-open eyes he pulled his trousers on over the shirt which he had worn for bed. No such luxuries as nightshirts for the Feeneys. Although there was a time, he ruminated, when even the bedside rug would have been classed as a luxury, now it was accepted as normal. He had often wondered where their newfound wealth had sprung from. It seemed to happen after his father had been away, when they had had to live with Grandma. Perhaps he had been earning his fortune then, though when Richard had asked where his father was during those months his mother had always changed the subject; the question had seemed to make her unhappy, he did not know why. Grandma and Grandad stayed tight-lipped about it too.

He rubbed briskly at the gooseflesh on his upper arms, longing for the summer, then went down to the kitchen.

At the breakfast table, with cheeks that glowed red like the unruly hair that had been plastered down with water, sat Sonny, his small hands wrapped around a mug.

'Oh, yer've decided to honour us wi' yer presence at last.' Thomasin, sweat gleaming on her brow from the heat of the oven, put the bowls of dough that she had mixed onto the range to rise. 'I suppose yer'll be wantin' some breakfast?' She pushed the bowl of dripping at Dickie who had flopped lethargically at his brother's side. 'There y'are, help yersel'.'

'He's had bacon.' Dickie scowled and pointed with a knife to his brother's empty plate.

'An' I had a dip o' me Dad's egg,' Sonny informed him gloatingly, bringing upon himself a bombardment of nips and digs.

'Do we have to have this every morning?' sighed their mother. 'An I'll tell yer why he's had bacon, me laddo,' she directed a rigid finger at Dickie, 'because he's been up since crack o' dawn fillin' t'coal bucket an' layin' t'fire, while you were lozzockin' in t'pit. I've told yer before, if yer can't be bothered to get yer bum up in a morning yer'll have to make do wi' what's left. Lazy article. Yer didn't think yer were gonna get breakfast in bed, did yer? Why should I put meself out when yer never do owt for me?' She turned her back on Dickie's downcast face, knowing it was only put on for her benefit and he was not really impressed by her chastisement.

'Go fetch us the salt, Son.' Dickie began to spread the dripping over the crust.

'What's the matter, have you run out of legs?' said Thomasin, then: 'Stay where you are!' she ordered as Sonny was about to comply. 'If he wants salt he can get it himself. He wants a blinkin' servant does that one.'

Dickie shrugged and ate the bread and dripping without salt.

Thomasin puffed crossly at a stray hair that had floated down to tickle her nose, then wound it back into the bun at the nape of her neck. How different they were, she sighed to herself, giving Sonny the benefit of her sparkling smile as he brought his plate to the sink. Looking at her youngest was like looking into a mirror. There was the auburn hair, the grey eyes, and if the generous mouth was perhaps just a little less ready to turn up at the corners it was still her mouth that she saw.

He was just like a little robin this morning, all chirpy and bright-eyed at the prospect of learning to read and write. Such an eager face. She hoped he was not going to be disillusioned.

Dickie pushed the last of his crust into his mouth and came alongside her, putting his arms round her thighs, his head against her hip, sneaking a beseeching gaze with one of his brilliant blue eyes. This fine chap was solely his father's son, with not a drop of Fenton blood in him. A beautiful child. The crisp black hair, the eyes that danced and twinkled when he smiled; in years to come this one was going to be a great attraction for the ladies – just like his father – but unlike Patrick, who had never taken seriously his magnetizing effect on the opposite sex, even at this early age she could tell by the tactics he employed on his mother that Dickie would break many a heart. How could anyone resist such charm, such beauty?

Her eyes softened and she placed a forgiving hand on his head. 'Come on, cupboard love, we don't want Sonny being late on his first day.'

She reached for the bowl of dripping and hurriedly prepared two slices while the boys put on their jackets, then wrapping each slice, she put one into Dickie's pocket, the other into Sonny's. 'There y'are, special treat for playtime.' Poor little mite, he looked so innocent standing there. A sudden tear stung her eye and she bent to hug him.

Dickie pulled on his boots and laced them up. 'Away then, our lad, 'tis a hidin' we'll get if we're late.'

Thomasin smiled to herself. That was one thing they shared at least – the curious accent, a conflicting mixture of Irish and Yorkshire, at times musical, at others blunt, basic.

Sonny wriggled out of his mother's embrace, wiping the spot where her lips had moistened his cheek and peered under the peak of his cap. 'I'm off then, Mam. Are yer sure ye'll be all right on yer own?'

His concern touched her. 'Aye, love, I've got a busy day ahead o' me. I've got to go with Erin to her new job an' then I'm goin' after one o' me own.' Last evening she had spied, in the Situations Vacant column of the local newspaper, a post which would suit her requirements admirably. A part-time assistant at a grocery store down Goodramgate. 'So, it looks as though we're all venturing into new territory. Oh, I will miss yer though!' She was about to kiss him again but Sonny, seeing his brother open the door, dashed after him, shouting an apology. 'I'll have to go, Mam! Look after yersel'.'

'I will,' laughed Thomasin. 'An' think on, no fightin'. An' mind the road!'

Outside the younger boy danced and skipped excitedly beside his brother. 'Will I be in your class?'

'Dunno.' Dickie was still trying to prop his eyes open.

'What's yer teacher like? Is he nice? Will I like him?' Sonny tugged at the older boy's sleeve, firing questions like peas from a reed.

'For God's sake, our lad, will ye shut your gob?' Dickie shook him off. 'Sure, I don't know what yer getting so excited about. Ye'll be sick of it by the end o' the week. Sure, I can think of a million better things to do wi' me time than sit in a stuffy ol' classroom.'

Sonny would not be deterred by his brother's usual bout of 'morning moroseness' as Thomasin had dubbed it, knowing that by dinnertime Dickie would have found his good humour again. It took him all morning to wake up.

'Will I have a desk? What will I be doin' today? Sums?'

Dickie grabbed a handful of his jacket and growled into his face, 'I don't know about sums but ye'll be doin' bloody somersaults if ye don't shurrup.'

'Awmmm! I'm gonna tell me Mam ye been swearin',' cried Sonny, though the threat was empty for he knew that should he do so he would probably get a good hiding for telling tales.

Dickie knew this too and gave his brother a sardonic sneer as they arrived at the school, whose open gates revealed a hotch-potch of juvenile humanity. Boys of diverse sizes, differing standards of dress ran amok, their collective noise having all the attributes of a pack of young hounds.

Dickie, hands in pockets, strolled up to a small group who squatted in a circle, firing pebbles at something on the ground. His brother, gazing wide-eyed at the turmoil around him, stayed close to his elbow.

'What ye doin'?' Dickie placed his hands on a boy's shoulders and leaned over to peer into the centre of the circle.

The skinny, freckle-faced boy glanced up then resumed his cannonade. 'We're havin' a race,' he answered, flicking yet another stone at the unfortunate cockroaches. 'Mine's winning.'

' 'Tis not!' cried another boy. 'Look, 'tis going the wrong way.'

The freckle-faced boy plucked the cockroach from its intended escape route and placed it in the right direction. 'Go on, yer bugger! Go on!'

Amid much cheering and jeering, howling and cursing the cockroaches finally staggered up to the piece of string that was the winning line, the freckle-faced boy's coming first as he had predicted.

He scooped up the insect with a whoop. 'I won! I won!' For the first time he noticed the younger boy at Dickie's side and thrust the cockroach under Sonny's nose. 'Look at that. What d'ye think? Is it not a beauty?'

Sonny did not flinch as the insect wriggled inches away from his face. 'Ye cheated,' he accused.

The other boy's exultant smile vanished. 'What d'ye mean by that?'

'When ye picked it up and straighted it ye put it down a few inches nearer the winning post.'

The freckle-faced boy stared at Dickie who shrugged. He certainly was not going to get involved in the argument.

'What's yer name?' asked the boy suddenly.

'What's yours?' replied Sonny defiantly.

The boy frowned. 'I asked you first, an' don't cheek your elders.'

'You're not older than me.' Sonny's jaw protruded obstinately.

'Look, son,' the boy adopted a haughty posture, trying to increase his height, 'I'm nearly eight, so ye'd best watch out for yerself.'

Sonny was scornful. 'You're never eight! You're only as big as me an' I'm six.'

'Thump him,' urged someone in the crowd that had gathered.

'Show him who's master,' goaded another.

The freckle-faced boy glared and took a step towards Sonny who raised both his fists like a prize-fighter.

At this point Dickie stepped in and took hold of his brother's ear. 'Off to a good start, are ye not? Didn't Mam say for ye not to get into any trouble?'

The freckle-faced boy addressed Dickie. 'Does he belong to you, then?'

'Aye, he belongs to me,' said Dickie. 'More's the pity. Look,' he said to Sonny, 'what did ye want to go accusing my friend o' cheating for?'

' 'Cause he was, I saw him!'

'Well, if he's a cheater,' Dickie informed him, 'then you're a liar, 'cause ye said you were six an' y'aren't.'

'I nearly am!'

'Will ye stop arguin'! 'Tis nothing to do with you anyway, I don't know why ye had to interfere. Now make friends an' tell the boy your name.'

Sonny glowered under golden lashes and clamped his lips together. He was not going to back down. 'He's got to tell me his first.'

'I'll clatter ye, now tell him!' Dickie proceeded to shake him until his teeth rattled.

But Sonny merely glared in stubborn defiance until suddenly a bell clanged its noisy invitation, sparing him further man-handling and the playground's confusion formed into six, untidy lines.

Sonny kept a firm hold on his brother as they edged their way into the classroom through the tumult of wriggling, streaming bodies.

'Ah, and who might we have here?' A pair of kind-looking brown eyes smiled into Sonny's grey ones as the two boys emerged from the press to stand gazing up at the master's tall desk.

'This is our Sonny, Brother Francis – I mean John!' Dickie shoved his brother forward. 'He's come to start school.'

The master raised his eyebrows. 'You do not mean to tell me that this fiery-haired little chap is your brother? Why, you are as different as chalk and cheese.'

'I didn't know where to take him, Brother Francis,' said Dickie.

'Well, perhaps he had better sit next to you for the time being,' answered the master, 'so that you can take care of him. I am sure he must be feeling apprehensive on his first day.

'I don't need no taking care of,' supplied Sonny. 'An' I don't want to sit next to him.' He was still angry about the incident in the playground.

Brother Francis laughed. His young face, rather like that of a plaster saint, shone with goodness. 'Ah, you must be the little fellow whom Father Kelly warned me about. He said I might find you . . .' he paused 'well to use Father Kelly's own words, a "proper little Tartar" he said you were an' no mistake.'

Sonny did not know whether a Tartar was good or bad so said nothing.

Brother Francis became serious. 'But you would do well to curb that tendency to speak your mind, my good chap. There are many in this school who are not so lenient as I. Now, I think it best that you seat yourself beside your brother as I am about to begin registration.'

When all the boys had been accounted for Brother Francis laid down his pen and addressed the class. 'Now, pay attention my fine fellows! After Mass most of you will be going to take your lesson from Brother Simon Peter.'

'Oh, God,' muttered Dickie under his breath. 'I hope that doesn't mean us.'

'Did you speak, Richard Feeney?' Brother Francis enquired sternly.

'No, Brother Francis.' Dickie hung his head.

'Very well, then might I continue with what I was saying?' He waited for any other interruption then proceeded. 'I require a deputation to transport certain monies to the Post Office. Now, who can I trust, I wonder, to undertake this important task?'

Every boy, with the exception of Sonny who did not understand the implication of the master's request, shot up his hand, waving it in the air frantically. 'Me, Brother!' It came as one voice. 'Please, me, Brother!' The chance of being spared the agony of Brother Simon Peter's class was not to be passed over lightly. Brother Francis toured the pleading faces, feeling like a hanging judge. Which boy would earn the stay of execution? Dickie Feeney came under his indecisive eye, his arm flapping wildly, straining at the socket, desperate to be chosen. The boy's good-looking charm was infallible.

'Very well, Richard Feeney and . . . you and you.' He pointed at two other boys who grinned their relief while the others grimaced jealously.

'Please, Brother Francis, can I take me brother with us?' asked Dickie.

The master's answer was drowned by Sonny's objection. 'I don't want to go! This is my first day at school, I want to learn things.'

'Young man,' said Brother Francis. 'The first thing that you must learn is not to speak unless spoken to. This is the second such time I have to warn you. Now, I shall ignore your outburst this time, attributing it to the insecurity you are so obviously encountering on your first day and your unfamiliarity with school etiquette. But I warn you for the last time, another such interruption will not be tolerated.' He turned to Dickie. 'Master Feeney, I suggest you acquaint your brother with the manner in which a scholar should conduct himself before he finds himself in deep water.' He addressed the whole class. 'And now, my friends, to Mass.'

Noisily, the boys shuffled their way into the draughty corridor and joined the other classes then, all assembled, they trooped back outside and crossed the playground to the church.

CHAPTER FORTY

AFTER THE BOYS had gone to school Erin came in from the back yard, making Thomasin exclaim, 'Eh, I thought you were gonna sit there all day.'

'I've got the runs.' The pale-looking girl rubbed her abdomen and made a face. A letter had arrived the other day summoning her to her new employment, since when she had been in this state.

' 'Sonly nerves, love.' Thomasin patted her kindly. The child was bound to be feeling anxious with such a big step ahead of her. 'You'll be all right when yer get settled in.'

'I hope so,' replied Erin. 'All of a sudden I'm feelin' really frightened. 'Tis the first time I've been away from all o' yese.'

'Oh, there's sure to be somebody there who'll take care o' yer,' Thomasin reassured her.

Erin chewed her fingernail. 'What if they don't like me? What if I should smash the best pots or something silly like that?'

Thomasin was concerned that she was responsible for putting Erin in this position. 'You won't.' She hesitated, then added: 'Erin . . . can you keep a secret?' At the girl's nod she went on, 'You know you're supposed to've received yer wages in advance for this job?' Another nod. 'Well . . . that was a lie in a way. Yer see, yer father is a very proud man an' he'd be ever so mad if he knew where it really came from . . . I borrowed it from someone, he's got pots o' money an' he says he doesn't mind when I pay it back, but I had to concoct this tale for yer dad. I know it's wrong, but it was better than him being in prison, weren't it?' Erin agreed. 'I could've paid this person back with the money John brought, but then we wouldn't've

369

been able to furnish this house . . . anyway, what I'm tryin' to say is you'll be receiving wages as well.'

'But why?' Erin wanted to know.

'Eh, lass, it's far too complicated to explain. Just believe it's all for the good of yer father – an' yer must never tell him or he'll blow his top. Take the wages they give yer an' slip 'em to me in secret an' just act as if it's a normal job to the other servants. We don't want them noseyin', all right?'

Erin smiled, ' 'Tis our secret,' making Thomasin cringe.

Feeling treacherous, the woman took her stepdaughter to Monkgate. The door of the grand house was opened by Alice Benson who directed them into the balmy kitchen, telling them they were expected. Thomasin bent to kiss Erin, then prepared to leave.

'You'll be welcome to stay for a cup of tea, Mrs Feeney,' offered Rose Leng, the cook. 'After all, it'll be a fair while before you see your daughter again.' The staff was granted one day off per month and one free evening a week.

Thomasin thanked her and sat down, eyeing the spotless kitchen. It was quite clearly a very well-run household. She examined the large, rectangular room as Alice filled the teapot. The length of one side of it was covered by a huge dresser which displayed an assortment of jugs, tureens, plates and dishes on its top shelves. Stacked beneath were numerous pans of different sizes. In the centre of the room was the table at which she now sat and where the food was prepared. This was also where the servants took their meals. On another wall stood the kitchen range, flanked on one side by a hot closet and on the other by an alcove, in which hung copper pans and a pair of bellows. Light was provided by one tiny window beside the outside door and in the evenings by gasflame, the pipes of which hung down from walls and ceiling in ungainly intrusion, lacking the ornamental glass globes which graced those of the upstairs rooms.

Against another of the distempered walls was a small table with two wooden stools and on the remaining wall was hung a variety of cooking implements, a sampler with 'Bless This House' embroidered on it by the daughter of that house and a mincing machine. The red-tiled floor was naked save for a fireside rug, on either side of which was a chair, the property of Rose and Johnson the manservant. Finally a doorway led to two whitewashed larders, the store cupboard and the laundry room.

Thomasin accepted the cup of tea, grateful for the opportunity to ask the cook about the mistress. She knew, naturally, that Roland's was a marriage in name only and that his wife had rejected her daughter at birth, but little about the way in which she treated her staff. Rose, a devout gossip, was only too pleased to fill in the missing details.

'By, she's a proper brazen little thing,' she nudged Thomasin confidentially. 'D'you know, I've lost count of the number of men that's been here this week. Man mad, she is, man mad. Pretends she's giving dinner parties, but we all know what goes on afterwards. I swear, it's like living in a brothel.'

Alice Benson snorted and gave Thomasin a crafty wink. 'How d'you know that, Mrs Leng?' she asked innocently. 'Have you lived in one?'

'Alice Benson!' shouted the cook. 'Stop your nebbin' and make yourself useful. There's plenty I can find for you to do down here if you've done upstairs.'

The maid flounced off sulkily and Rose turned back to Thomasin. 'Cheeky young madam.' She bristled with indignation. 'She's more idea of what one o' them places looks like than I do. Real flighty piece, you know.' She looked at Erin. 'I hope you won't catch any of her bad habits?'

Erin shook her head, though not fully understanding the cook's meaning.

'I can't think how she's kept her position,' Cook went on. 'I've been expecting her to come in any day and announce she's . . . you know . . . with child.' She mouthed the last two words behind a plump hand. 'The mistress, two-faced hussy that she is, doesn't allow us to have followers – how d'you like that?' Thomasin made sympathetic noises. 'But Alice, she manages somehow.'

Thomasin smiled as Rose took her empty cup away, her wide beam wobbling like a jelly, the dimpled flesh of her upper arms trembling at her every breath.

'But don't you go worrying about your little girl, Mrs Feeney.' Rose returned to her seat. 'I'll see she doesn't come to no harm. Look after her like my own child, I will.'

'Does Mr Leng work here too?' enquired Thomasin.

'Oh no, dear, I'm not married.' Only the cook's status in the household afforded her the marital title.

'Are there just the two o' you, then? Apart from Erin, I mean.'

Rose shook her head and her whole body shivered like a blancmange. 'No, there's Mr Johnson – valet, he calls himself, more like a general dogsbody if you ask me. Proper snobby, he is an' all, thinks he's a cut above. By, he's a strange cove. There's something not quite right about that one. Nothing I can put my finger on, mind, but it's just the way he . . . well, I do declare the price of coal nowadays!' She hurriedly changed the subject as a pair of highly-polished boots appeared on the stair, followed by a pair of rather bandy legs, a stocky body and finally a face with a Grecian nose, dark chips of eyes and a mouth which might have been fashioned from granite.

Thomasin, puzzled at Rose's sudden change of subject, turned as the manservant came into the kitchen then, seeing the faint traces of annoyance on Johnson's face, hurriedly gathered her shawl about her and rose. 'Well, I'd better be on my way. Thank you for the tea, Mrs Leng.' She touched Erin's cheek. ' 'Bye, love, I expect we'll see you on your evenin' off.'

Johnson made a barbed comment, suggesting that if Erin ever got an evening off it would be more than he ever had.

Thomasin decided that she did not like him. Most men were pleasant and attentive in her company; this one was eyeing her as though she was something the cat had chewed up. 'I sincerely hope she *will* get an evening off,' she told him, coolly polite. 'She has had strict instructions from her father to attend Mass on one evening per week and on Sundays.'

'Well, I can tell you now,' replied Johnson with a smirk, 'she'll not be allowed to go to any Catholic church; if she goes anywhere it'll be to Chapel on Sunday morning with the rest of us servants.'

Thomasin was about to lay about him verbally when she caught Erin's eye. The girl seemed to be imploring her not to make trouble. 'Well, we'll see,' she uttered eventually, then bent to kiss Erin and whispered in her ear, 'Try to go if yer can, love, but don't worry if they force yer to go with them. Nobody's goin' to hold it against yer if yer can't get to your own church.'

'What about Daddy?' asked Erin softly.

'What he doesn't know can't harm him,' responded Thomasin. 'Anyway, it might not come to owt, just wait an' see how yer get on.' She gave Johnson one more glare, then took her leave.

Out on the street she shivered and paused to look back at the handsome residence, her admiring eyes meeting another pair that held her gaze levelly – So that is Roland's wife, she thought, staring up at the beautiful but cold face at the bedroom window. How could Roland ever have taken a second glance at me when he has a wife who looks like that? She's lovely.

– What on earth is that common woman staring at? thought Helena. And more to the point what business has brought her to my house? There was something very familiar about the red-haired woman. Where had Helena seen her before and why should such a plain-looking creature inspire such curiosity?

Her hair was scarlet against the white of the pavement as she stared unwaveringly at the window, refusing to be intimidated by Helena's imperious sneer. Helena frowned as she tried to recall the occasion of their meeting – though it was doubtful that Helena had ever debased herself to talk with such a jade; she was more suited to Roland's . . . my God, that was it! Helena stepped back sharply as the memory smote her, the indignity of witnessing this creature on her own husband's arm.

Why, the audacity of the man! The outrage. How dared he bring his mistress into her house? The anger fluttered inside the exquisite breast as Helena stood on tiptoe, in order to see into the street without reapproaching the window, but the woman had gone – Well, gone or not, fumed Helena, I shall get to the bottom of this, and if I discover that that woman has spent the night under my roof then heads are going to roll.

As the door of the big house closed behind Thomasin so Erin's introduction to working life began. Rose instructed Alice to get the girl kitted out in her uniform, which was several sizes too large and had to be hitched up and tucked in.

'At least you don't have to pay for it,' said Alice at Erin's complaint. 'That'd be a nice slice out o' yer wage before yer begin.' She moved off. 'Away, I'll show you round the house. We might as well start at the top an' work our way down to the kitchen.' She led Erin up four flights of stairs, pausing on each landing for the breathless child to catch up with her.

'Don't worry, yer'll soon get accustomed to running up an' down these a dozen times an hour.' At the top of the house Alice turned a knob and flung open the door of the small attic room. 'This is my room – or should I say ours now.'

She pushed Erin into the room which was little more than a cupboard and must have required a lot of ingenuity to fit in the articles of furniture it contained, which were: a bed of cast iron, a chest of drawers, a washstand complete with jug and bowl in plain white enamel. There were no cupboards or wardrobes, merely a rail fixed to the wall on which hung Alice's two dresses and spare uniform. Neither was there any gaslight here, the only decoration on the wall being a picture of an angel surrounded by cherubs, and the only source of artificial light a stub of candle on a saucer.

Alice wriggled to adjust her stays. 'Down we go.'

On the storey below she tapped on a door and placed her ear to it before entering. 'This is her ladyship's boudoir, where it all happens.' She rolled her eyes at Erin's blank expression. 'Never mind, innocent, yer'll learn. Go an' have a look on her dressing table, there's some right pretty things.'

Erin crept into the room, afraid that her boots would mark the carpet. Alice sailed across the room and threw open the wardrobe doors. 'What about that lot then?'

Erin gasped at the splendid range of gowns that shimmered and dazzled from within, and thought of Thomasin's pitiful collection.

'No wonder she can never make up her mind,' sniffed Alice, roughly stuffing the escaping gowns back inside the wardrobe, then closing the door.

Next she took Erin on a fleeting inspection of the master's room, and then on to his daughter's.

'Oh, sorry, Miss Caroline,' she apologised. 'I thought yer'd be in the schoolroom, otherwise I woulda knocked.'

'It is perfectly all right, Alice,' smiled the child rising from the window seat and shaking out her lacy skirts. 'Miss Elwood is not feeling too well so we did not have lessons today.' She looked at Erin who curtsied.

'This is the new maid, Miss Caroline,' provided Alice. 'Her name's Erin.'

'How do you do, Erin? Will you not stay and talk to me

for a little while? I would be so glad of the company. It can be terribly lonely up here.'

Alice looked peeved. 'Well, I don't know about that, Miss. She's supposed to be here to help me. Can't have her natterin' to you all day.'

'Oh, please, Alice,' coaxed Caroline. 'Do be a sport. It's simply awful up here with no one to talk to.'

'You'd find it a lot worse down in the kitchen,' reprimanded Alice. 'Still, seein' as how she didn't choose to arrive 'till all t'mucky work was over I suppose I can grant her half an hour. Soon be dinnertime any road.' She flicked a hand at Erin. 'You certainly know how to time your entrances.' She left Erin in Caroline's care and bustled towards the stairs, then turned and added a chafing rejoinder. 'Best get your bit o' pleasure while yer can, 'cause tomorra yer won't know whether yer on yer arm or yer elbow.'

When Alice had left, Caroline smiled and returned to the window seat, patting the cushion for Erin to join her. 'Now, you must tell me all about yourself.'

Erin asked what she wanted to know.

'Well, you can begin by telling me your age,' replied Caroline.

'Twelve, Miss,' said Erin, much to Caroline's surprise.

'Oh, are you really? I assumed you were much older, my age at least. You are very tall, aren't you?'

Erin nodded. 'I expect I get that from my Daddy. How old are you then?' she asked familiarly, then, remembering to whom she was speaking, added a hasty 'Miss'.

'Fourteen,' answered Caroline.

Now it was Erin's turn to be astonished. 'Jazers, ye don't look it!' she cried, making Caroline laugh at her funny accent.

'Why do you speak like that?' asked the other girl, who never ventured outside the house except to Chapel on a Sunday so had only come into contact with the Yorkshire voices of the servants and the accentless English of her parents.

' 'Cause I'm Irish,' replied Erin. Sure the girl must be a bit of an eejit if she didn't know that.

'You will have to forgive my ignorance,' said Caroline, 'but I have never had the pleasure of speaking with an Irish person until now.' She grabbed a cushion from behind her back and hugged it to her chest, clearly delighted at having someone of her own age to talk with. 'Tell me more. Have you any sisters?'

'No.' Erin made a face. 'I've got two brothers. Right little devils they are an' all.'

'I wish I had a sister,' sighed Caroline. 'Or even a brother would do, as long as it was someone to talk to.'

'Ye wouldn't like having brothers.' Erin shook her head. 'They're a real arse-ache.' She clapped a hand to her mouth. 'Sorry, Miss, I shouldn't've said that.'

'Oh, that's all right,' replied Caroline casually. 'It is one of Alice's words. Perhaps you might tell me what it means? Alice will never tell me.'

Erin seemed reluctant to enlighten the young lady.

'Come, I won't tell,' pleaded Caroline. 'Alice is always saying naughty words when she thinks I'm not listening. I made a note of them all.' She then came out with such a stream of oaths as Erin had ever heard, even from her stepmother's lips.

'Ye oughtn't to say things like that,' she gasped. ' 'Tisn't nice for a lady.'

'I don't want to be a lady,' sulked Caroline. 'I want to be like you, it is more fun. Now, tell me what they mean.'

Erin interpreted those words which she knew the meaning of. 'But don't ye go telling anyone I told ye.'

Caroline promised, then asked: 'If you are only twelve then why are you not at school? Have you left?'

'I haven't never been to school,' replied Erin flatly. 'I wished I could. Me brothers go, both of 'em, but nobody seemed to think it was important for me to go.'

'And would you really have liked to?' prompted Caroline.

'Oh, yes! I'd love to learn to read an' write proper. Me Daddy taught me a little bit but I'd really love to learn things about other countries an' that.'

Caroline was thoughtful for a moment then went on to ask about Erin's parents. Erin, after informing the girl that her father built houses and her mother was going after a job in a grocery enquired about Caroline's parents.

'I hardly ever see mine,' Caroline told her sadly.

'But how can ye not see them when ye live in the same house?' Erin wanted to know. 'Sure, ye must meet at dinner-time.'

'Mama does not allow me to dine with her and Papa. I eat

in the kitchen and, apart from the time in the schoolroom, all my days are spent up here.'

Erin was astounded. 'Don't ye ever see your mother at all?'

Caroline shook her head and her face clouded over. 'Only by accident. I do not think she likes me because I'm not pretty like her.'

'But y'are pretty,' Erin cut in.

Caroline smiled weakly. 'It is very decent of you, Erin, to try and cheer me up but you must be wrong. Mama has always made it perfectly clear to me why she finds my presence so hard to bear. It is because I am so ugly.'

Erin stared back at the girl pityingly. Not by even the most hypercritical standards could Caroline be judged ugly. Her hair, like skeins of molten gold, bunched in ringlets over the immature shoulders, framed a heart-shaped face set with eyes the colour of the sky on a June day.

'Have ye never looked in the mirror?' she asked.

'Oh, yes, it became quite a regular habit some years ago. Each night after Mama had been to see me I would stare into the glass for hours, praying that in the morning some miracle would have occurred.'

'But I thought ye just said she didn't come to see ye.' Erin was confused.

Caroline explained. 'I am referring to when I was a little girl. She used to come and see me quite often then, I remember quite clearly although I cannot have been more than three years old. I would be lying in bed, all quiet, and the door would creak. I used to be able to tell that it was Mama who lingered outside by the scent of her perfume, it would float into my room before she entered. Sometimes she would pause outside the door for an age without speaking or making any sound and often the smell of perfume would fade, then I knew that she was not coming, she had changed her mind. Other times she would creep to the side of my bed and stare down at me and ask if I loved her. Then I would reply that I did and ask if she could love me, just a little, and she would say, "But you are so ugly. How could anyone love you?" and then she would go and I would cry.'

Erin covered her newfound friend's hand comfortingly.

'Then,' continued Caroline with misted eyes, 'one night her visits stopped completely. I missed her so.'

Erin was amazed. 'But don't you hate her?'

'Hate her?' said Caroline, perplexed. 'I love her, she is my mother.'

'But she told you those cruel lies. Ye aren't ugly at all, but very pretty.'

Caroline could not be convinced. 'Then why would she say it, if it were untrue?'

'Sure, I don't know that,' replied Erin. 'Perhaps she's just jealous of ye.'

Here Caroline had to laugh. 'Oh, Erin, you have obviously not encountered Mama yet or you would know why that statement is so ridiculous. Mama is the most beautiful, adorable creature on earth. She is without comparison.'

Beautiful she might be, thought Erin, but no one who said such things to a little child could be called adorable. However, she decided to shift the conversation to Caroline's father. 'What about your Daddy, do ye see him?'

Caroline's face brightened. 'Oh, yes, Papa loves me, he always comes up to kiss me goodnight. Well, mostly,' she added in retrospect. Her father often disappeared without trace for days on end; still, when he was at home he always made a point of spending a little time with his daughter.

All at once Erin felt a rush of gratitude for her own parents' love which she had so often taken for granted. How she pitied this poor girl, for all her wealth and comforts. Delving into her apron pocket she produced a bag of sweets. 'Here, would ye like a barley sugar?'

Caroline extricated one of the sticky sweets from the bag and tested it on her tongue.

'Me Mam bought me 'em on the way here,' said Erin, then wished she had not for Caroline's face had the forlorn look about it again. She shoved the bag towards the other girl. 'Go on, have another. Me Mam said I had to share 'em with me friends.'

Caroline looked at the other earnestly. 'And are you my friend, Erin?'

'If ye want me to be, then I am.' Erin grinned and popped another sweet in her mouth, little guessing that if anyone was in need of a friend in this household it would be her.

CHAPTER FORTY-ONE

AFTER MASS, DURING which the freckle-faced boy had paraded his victorious cockroach along the rim of the pew in front to alleviate the tedium and to draw envy from his tiny, ginger-haired opponent, the boys returned to the classroom.

Before setting off on his errand for Brother Francis, Dickie offered his brother a few words of advice.

'Try and behave yourself while I'm away,' he warned. 'Just watch yourself with old Codgob.'

Sonny knotted his brow. 'Who?'

'Codgob – Brother Simon Peter,' replied the other. 'A right villain he is. If ye start spouting off like ye've done to Brother Francis he'll tear the ears from your head.'

Dickie did not have time to elaborate further as Brother Francis summoned his delegates and sent the remainder of the class in the direction of Brother Simon Peter's classroom.

The moment Sonny encountered the man who was to take the next lesson his brother's choice of nickname was clarified. Indeed, never had a pseudonym been so descriptive; the master looked just like the specimens he had seen on the fishmonger's slab. His dark eyes were cold and unfriendly, staring lifelessly at the little boys who ambled silently past him. The eyebrows met in a permanent-vee above the nose from which sprang ugly black hairs. But it was the lips that gave rise to the alias; thick and wide, most definitely cod-like, ballooning out in blubbery disapproval of his unfortunate pupils.

He spoke and Sonny, his eyes glued to the extraordinary face, felt a desperate urge to laugh. The words seemed to cascade all lopsidedly from the distorted mouth.

'You find something amusing, boy?'

Startled, Sonny gulped and smiled into the muddy eyes. 'No, Brother.'

'Then why, may I be permitted to ask, do you wear that stupid grin?' There was no outward indication that the man was angry; the words were delivered softly.

'Me Mammy says "Life'll treat ye better if ye always wear a smile".' Though Sonny doubted the validity of Thomasin's anecdote as he looked at the sullen face of the master.

'I see,' replied the Brother thoughtfully. 'I had always assumed that it was only lunatics who went around with a permanent grin on their faces. Have we then, I ask myself, a lunatic in our midst?'

Nobody laughed.

'What is your name boy?'

'Sonny Feeney.'

'Hah! A lunatic indeed.' The mouth laughed, its thick lips quivering. 'Who but a lunatic would sport a name such as that? Have you no proper name, boy?'

Sonny was beginning to lose his temper. 'My real name is John,' he said firmly. 'But my friends call me Sonny.'

'Well, Feeney,' replied the master, 'when you have been here longer you will realise that to number me among those to whom you refer as friends would be ill-advised. I am not here to be your friend but to knock some education into that stupid brain of yours – if you have one. This,' he took a thick leather strap from a hook on the wall, 'is my only friend. It commands respect. I would ask you to remember that in future when you are in my classroom, you will behave with decorum and mind your manners. My friend does not allow smirkers in this room, and it would be most unwise of you to anger him.' He toyed with the wicked-looking strap for a few moments, stroking its fringed end over the palm of his white hand.

'Mr Kearney knows all too well what happens when my friend becomes angry, do you not, Kearney?' He addressed the freckle-faced boy whom Sonny had been dismayed to find sitting next to him.

But the boy was not as bold as his companion had been. 'Yes, Brother.' It came out as a whisper.

'Yes, Kearney has very good reason to remember my

friend's anger,' said Brother Simon Peter, tapping the strap gently against his hand. 'Which makes his behaviour during Mass this morning all the more unaccountable.'

The boy cringed visibly as the master went on, 'Perhaps you will tell me, Kearney, indeed, tell all of us the reason you have just attended Mass?'

'To pray to our Lord, Brother.' The answer was delivered into his collar.

'I cannot hear you, Kearney. Speak up.'

'To pray, Brother.'

'To pray, Kearney! That is correct. To pray to our Maker for all the good things of life. To pray for His forgiveness for all the vile deeds we commit.' He flung his arm wide as he spoke, encompassing the whole class, then turned back abruptly and leaning towards the freckle-faced boy spat: 'Then did my eyes deceive me when I observed in the church, in Our Lord's house, a contemptible, dirty-nosed little cretin sporting a cockroach on the pew? Did they, Kearney?'

'No, Brother.' The boy shrank further into his seat as the master hovered over him.

'No! You admit that in the house of God you chose not to pray, to beg forgiveness for the revolting little creature you are, but to give your attention to a form of life even lower than yourself?' He straightened sharply. 'Do you still have this inspiring being in your possession?'

'Yes, Brother.'

'Then pray fetch it out. Let us all have the benefit of this wonderful piece of creation, so wonderful that it can lead one away from the path of righteousness.'

The boy inserted trembling fingers into his pocket and, feeling the insect's tickling limbs, brought it out and made to place it on the desk. Before he could withdraw his hand there was a flash of movement and the painful taste of leather over his wrist. He cried out and held his smarting hand to his chest, leaving an upturned cockroach wriggling helplessly on the desk.

Sonny stared pop-eyed as the master made a brief visit to his own desk and fumbled among a tin of miscellany, then returned to Kearney's place. Taking the object he had selected from the tin, a pin, he brought his hand down in a stabbing movement and skewered the writhing cockroach to the desk.

'There! Now he may entertain us all for the rest of the lesson.'

Replacing the strap on its hook he returned to his desk, allowing everyone to breathe a little easier.

Sonny stole a glance at his neighbour who could not tear his eyes from his struggling pet and was still rubbing his pained wrist tearfully. Though they had not set out on the best of terms Sonny felt that he must offer some morsel of comfort, so defeated did the child appear.

'He's a rotten old pig, isn't he?'

The master looked up sharply, his opaque stare touring the rows of shifty-eyed boys. 'Did someone dare to speak? I was not aware that I had invited comment.'

'It was me,' piped up Sonny, drawing the master's impatient glare.

'Ah, the lunatic once again.' Brother Simon Peter drummed his fingers on the desk. 'Perhaps it is rash of me to ask, for what pearl of wisdom could a lunatic have to offer? But pray repeat your statement as I failed to hear it the first time.' He waited; his bulbous lips held a sardonic warp.

Sonny was not to be intimidated as the other boy had been, but decided to moderate his former opinion. 'I said: I think you're rotten.'

There was a collective intake of breath and those seated in front spun round involuntarily to gaze at the new boy.

'Eyes front!' snapped the master and the boys quickly averted their admiring eyes.

'So, you find my punishment of Kearney not to your liking, Feeney?' said the master calmly. 'That is truly most distressing, and there was I thinking that Kearney had been let off rather lightly. Tut, tut.' He suddenly slammed his palm down onto his desk, dislodging a container of pens which clattered noisily to the floor. 'Feeney, you tempt my patience to the point of violence. I do not like your face, Feeney, neither does my friend. Be very, very careful.'

How dearly Sonny would have loved to answer: 'I don't like yours much either', but that would be seeking an introduction to Codgob's 'friend'.

'Very well, we will, if Mr Feeney will allow us, proceed with our lesson which today is rather special. Instead of us employing the usual charcoal for our drawings, Brother Francis has instructed that we use these paints which he has provided – though why he should want to waste his own, personal property on scrofulous louts such as you is questionable – nevertheless, if that is his wish who am I to disobey? Shaughnessy and Connel, do the honours, if you please, while Mr Feeney provides us with a subject.'

Sonny inspected the room, pretending to think of a subject, knowing as he did what his reply would be.

'Well, Feeney, have you sufficient intelligence to understand my request?'

Sonny nodded. 'I have.'

'Then what is it to be? Do not keep us all in suspense.'

'I can only think of one thing I'd like to paint,' said Sonny. ' 'Tis yourself.'

Brother Simon Peter raised the vee above his nose in mild surprise. 'Why, boy, I am beginning to revert my opinion of you. Perhaps you do display a modicum of intelligence after all.' He turned to the rest of the boys who were spellbound by the repartee. 'Let us hope that the end result of Master Feeney's suggested subject will do credit to its owner.'

Sonny examined the large sheet of paper in front of him and felt the quality of the brush with his thumb. Though he had never painted before, the moment he picked up that brush something magical happened. Almost warily he dipped it into the paint and applied it to the paper. Then he withdrew the brush and studied the result: one black blob. A surge of excitement. One black blob in the middle of all that virgin sheet. All that white just waiting to be filled in.

After the first, few testing strokes he became more confident. The colours began to flow, taking shape of their own accord, as if it were not he who wielded the brush but some mysterious force outside him. It was at that moment Sonny decided that this was what he was here for. This was to be his life.

The man sat perfectly still. Each time Sonny looked up to study the model he met with cold, fathomless eyes, as if the master knew what was in his mind, as if there were only the two of them in the room. The large mahogany-framed clock ticked portentously, its brass pendulum beating away the seconds to the moment of judgment. Sonny, his original intention dissolved in the rush of creative discovery, painted on, dipping his brush from paint to paper, paper to water, water to paint.

When it was finished, Sonny laid down his brush and stepped back to inspect his masterpiece, and realised, even in his self-congratulation, that he had made a terrible mistake. But it was too late to alter it now for the subject had risen from his chair and, ignoring all the others, came straight to him.

The room was still, save for the ticking of the clock. All eyes were upon them, sensing that something was about to happen. Brother Simon Peter lurked behind Sonny and stared at the painting; at the enormous lips, red and bloated, the protruding eyes beneath the angry black vee. Though hardly audible his voice held patent menace.

'This is your idea of a jest, Feeney?' Something stirred in the opaque eyes, but what, the boy could not measure as he looked up, attempting innocence.

'Why no, Brother.' He returned his eyes to the painting which, viewed by any unbiased observer would have drawn immediate acclaim for the accuracy of its brilliant caricature.

The other boys exchanged glances and fidgeted uneasily. Someone ought to have told the new boy one did not play jokes on old Codgob. For one precious minute they thought that the man was going to laugh as his mouth twitched precariously at the corners. They should have known better.

Brother Simon Peter snatched up the paper and in a mad frenzy ripped and twisted Sonny's beautiful painting until it resembled fine snow and was scattered to all corners of the room. Worse was to come. Grabbing the amazed boy by the collar he hauled him roughly to the front of the class where he glowered and slobbered over him, grinding his teeth, clenching and unclenching his hands.

'Imbecile or not you have gone too far this time.' The nostrils flared white with anger. 'You are about to learn that your attempts at humour can bring you nothing but pain. Take down your breeches.'

Sonny's jaw dropped. He had been prepared for a punishment but not the humiliation that the Brother intended to mete out. He hesitated then said, with a resolute jut of his chin: 'I'll not.'

An air of apprehension from the gathered onlookers wavered under his nose. He could smell the fear from their grimy little bodies as the master, calmer but no less menacing, reached out and lifted the strap from the wall.

'My friend is waiting,' Brother Simon Peter said evilly. 'The longer he has to wait, the angrier he becomes.'

Sonny was frightened now. His face grew pale, making his hair appear more vivid than ever. Still he did not move.

'Feeney, my friend is growing most impatient.' The master began to tap the leather strap agitatedly. 'Do you wish me to enroll the services of two of your peers who will divest you of your breeches and hold you down while I administer punishment? Are you a coward, Feeney, that you dare not take your comeuppance like a man?'

'I'm no coward!' cried Sonny, fumbling with his trousers and at the same time trying to unravel the sickening knot in his stomach.

He allowed his loosened garment to drop to his ankles, his face not white any more but red, trying to cover his nakedness with his hands.

'Hands by your sides, boy.' The thick lips trembled gloatingly and then with no further warning, the master grabbed his jacket, thrust him roughly over a bench and began to administer a harsh punishment to the little white rear, appearing to enjoy every lash.

Sonny squeezed his eyes and mouth tightly shut, trying to blot out the pain, counting each stroke. Five! Six! Seven! The sadistic teacher was totally absorbed in his task, almost drooling over the pink marks that began to multiply on the clenched buttocks. 'Have you had enough, boy? Do I see you cry? Are you not sorry for the ungracious manner in which you treated your master?' Saliva flew in all directions as he delivered his breathless demands, still beating enthusiastically.

But Sonny refused to give in, would never cry. He tasted the salty blood that swelled from his bitten lips. Eleven! Twelve!

– Cry, boy, cry! willed the master.

But Sonny remained silent. Thirteen! Fourteen!

A quiet murmuring arose from the watching boys. Nobody had ever lasted this long before. Why did he not cry? Did he not understand that the blows would continue until he begged for mercy?

Brother Simon Peter's arm rose again and again, his energy unflagging, beating himself into a trance, seeing not the boy

Feeney but himself, cowering under the hand of his tyrannical father: 'You will cry, boy! You will!' Bells began to ring inside his head, joined by a steady buzzing noise. Not until his arm had risen and fallen many more times did he realise that the clanging was not in his head but in the corridor outside, signalling the mid-morning break. The buzz of consternation from the boys percolated his madness and he stopped, panting for breath, allowing Sonny to rise from the bench.

Painfully, but still dry-eyed, the boy pulled up his trousers and limped back to his place to help with the tidying of the paints. This done he followed the others to the corridor, and though he did not spare a glance for the master, Brother Simon Peter could not fail to detect the triumphant light in the boy's eye.

The classroom was silent again. He was alone. Alone save for a pinioned, wriggling insect at which he now stared, his gleaming face alight with animosity. Leaning over, he detached the pin from the wood holding the skewered cockroach speculatively, turning the pin in his fingers so that the creature revolved.

'He thinks he can beat me,' murmured the Brother vaguely, studying the insect whose struggles were becoming weaker. 'But we shall see.' Very gently he placed his thumb and forefinger against the pin, pushing the insect towards the point, thereby releasing it. It fell to the desk, amazingly on its feet, and attempted to crawl away. The master placed a finger in its path, making it confused. It attempted to detour the obstruction but on turning found its way blocked yet again. Futilely the cockroach sought for an escape while the master looked on half-interestedly. 'Yes, we shall see,' he said again, and promptly brought his thumb down upon the insect, putting an end to its misery. Sonny was not to receive such mercy.

CHAPTER FORTY-TWO

SOMEONE LINGERED AT Sonny's elbow. He pretended not to notice and proceeded in his proud-shouldered gait.

'You were daft you know.'

Only now Sonny fixed his grey eyes on his unwelcome companion. 'Who asked you?'

The boy repeated his statement, undaunted by the glare of hostility. 'You were daft. He'll be after you every lesson now. Why did you not cry? He would've stopped hitting you then.'

'I never cry,' scowled Sonny jerking a thumb at his chest. 'Anyways, it never hurt. Well, not much any road.'

He walked on, the freckle-faced boy still at his shoulder.

'Sorry about your painting,' the boy sympathised. 'I thought it was real good, just like him.'

Sonny grinned. 'Aye, it was, wasn't it?'

The other grabbed his arm, drawing him to a halt. 'Look, I've decided to forget about the way you insulted me this morning, seeing as how you stuck up for me with old Codgob.'

' 'Tis very kind of ye,' answered Sonny, but his attempt at sarcasm was lost on the other.

'Aye well, we lads have to stick together, don't we? 'Tis the least I can do, to make up for the beating you took.'

'I've had worse,' lied Sonny.

The boy held out his hand which still bore an angry red weal. 'Are we friends, then?'

'If ye tell me your name,' challenged Sonny. It was back to the argument of this morning.

The boy hesitated before answering, then decided that it would not be losing face to back down to a hero. 'My name is George,' he said, then gave a grin that was minus two front teeth.

Sonny, his own face creasing into a smile, took the hand that George offered. 'Mine's Sonny.'

'I know that,' laughed George, making Sonny remember that he had had to deliver his name to Brother Simon Peter.

He gave a sheepish grin. 'Oh, aye.'

They walked on. George stepped aside as they came to the outer door, allowing Sonny to enter the playground first. Seeing them, Dickie, his stockings sagging tiredly around his ankles, ran over to meet them. He and his helpers had been hiding round the corner until they were certain that Brother Simon Peter's lesson was over, but news had already reached him of his brother's exploits.

'I can't leave ye for five minutes, can I?' he sighed, apeing their mother. 'Did I not warn ye what he was like? Did I not say he'd give ye a hiding if ye crossed him?'

'He was real brave,' cut in George. 'He never cried.'

'Our Son never cries,' replied Dickie contemptuously. 'Has he done much damage then?' he asked, tugging at the waist-band of his brother's trousers. 'Let's be having a look at your bum.'

'Will ye get your hands off!' yelled Sonny indignantly, knocking his brother's hand away, then relented. 'Oh, all right, then. Away.'

A long crocodile of eager spectators followed their course to the privy and fought for a good ringside seat.

'Eh, look at that,' breathed Dickie as Sonny gingerly prised away his trousers, which had begun to stick to the broken, weeping skin. 'Stand back everybody. Go on, back!' he yelled herding the interested party out of viewing distance. 'If ye want to see it ye'll have to pay. Farthing a time. C'mon, those with no money can sling their hook.'

Amid a lot of grumbling George turned away. 'I ain't got no money.'

'Nay, ye cannot charge him,' Sonny told his brother. 'He's a pal.'

'Look,' replied Dickie who was busy holding back the crush of boys. 'If we let him in for nowt they'll all expect to get in free. Have ye no head for business?'

' 'Tis *my* bottom they've come to see,' objected Sonny. 'I say who comes in an' who doesn't.'

'Suit yerself,' replied Dickie releasing the pressure on the spectators; allowing them all to crowd in. 'A rich man ye'll never be.'

Sonny gave an exclamation. ' 'Twas your pockets ye were thinking to line. Now, c'mon, stop arguing and let 'em look if they want to.'

He moved this way and that so that everyone was able to get a good look at his injured bottom, basking in victorious recognition. It was only his first day at school and already he was a hero.

Dickie winced in sympathy. 'Oh, our Son, how are ye gonna hide that from me Mam? She's bound to see it some-time.'

'Don't you go saying anything,' warned Sonny swivelling his bottom as those around him 'oohed' and 'aahed' in admir-ation. 'Else I'll likely get another hiding off her. Then she'll probably tell Dad and he'll come down and give old Codgob a bazzacking, and then he'll take it out on us, and me bum'll be like mincemeat.' He groped in his pocket for the bread and dripping which was by now somewhat the worse for wear and looked most unappetising. Nevertheless he bit into it with relish. 'No, we men have got to keep these things to ourselves,' he mumbled sagely. ' 'Tis nothing to bother the womenfolk with.'

Dickie laughed uproariously. 'Get away, me Mam's the only one you're scared of.'

Sonny stuck his bread between his teeth and hauled up his trousers threateningly. 'I'm not scared of anybody! I'm gonna have ye for that.'

But once again the sound of the bell intervened and the crowd rapidly dispersed, leaving Sonny to button his trousers and hurriedly bolt down the remainder of his snack.

In school he perched painfully on the edge of the bench and took the slate that someone handed to him, awaiting instructions. Brother Francis noticed the tiny, ginger-haired boy wince and gave a sigh of regret. It was inevitable, of course. Brother Simon Peter would brook no spirited behaviour nor tolerate any backtalk from cheeky little boys. He had never yet known a new boy to return from one of

Brother Simon Peter's classes without the customary stripes on his rear. He hoped the young chap had not suffered too badly; he had taken a great liking to Sonny, despite his readiness with a bold answer, and his colleague could be very severe. But no, he watched Sonny chattering happily to his neighbour – it would take more than a beating to break this young fellow's spirit.

Brother Francis leaned over his desk and said in an authoritative voice: 'Very well, boys, let us proceed with our arithmetic, shall we?'

The unanimous groan that met this suggestion relayed the fact that the boys did not hold him in the same awe as his grim-faced counterpart. They knew quite well that, beneath the stern exterior, the man was smiling.

At dinnertime Sonny managed to stop himself wincing with discomfort, even when his mother delivered a playful slap to his bottom.

'How did yer like school, then?' she asked, putting a bowl of potatoes on the table.

' 'Tis all right,' said Sonny noncommittally, tucking hungrily into his meal.

'By, that's a change from this morning,' replied Thomasin in surprise. 'Yer don't sound too sure about it. Is it not what yer expected?'

'Oh, aye, 'tis all right,' repeated her son, his eyes never leaving his plate.

'Ye've not been fighting again, have ye?' asked his father suspiciously. There was not a day went by without his younger son getting into one scrape or another. 'Your mother's right, ye don't sound very enthusiastic.'

'No!' cried Sonny indignantly, then with a sideways glance at his brother pushed his empty plate towards Thomasin. 'Can I have some more, Mam?'

'There's a bit of pork left – that's if yer dad doesn't want it?'

Patrick waved his knife indicating the negative.

'Is it pig pork?' asked Sonny, making them all laugh.

'Is there any other?' replied Thomasin, sharing the remnants of the Sunday joint between Sonny and his brother. 'An' can yer not sit still? Yer fidgetin' around as though you were sat on an ants' nest.'

Sonny threw another glance at his brother and tried to keep still, but it was hard; he could feel his trousers beginning to stick to his skin again – they would be the very devil to get off at bedtime.

After dinner he and Dickie returned to school, where George and his gang were waiting at the gate, bearing gifts to shower upon the conquering hero. Thomas Shaughnessy had brought two badges, Joseph Hagan, a small ball of twine which had miraculously fallen into his pocket in the haberdashery store when he had been sent to purchase a packet of pins for his mother, and George himself handed over four blue and white marbles, much cherished possessions.

The afternoon session was a quiet contrast to that of the morning. Sonny really enjoyed himself, learning how to write his name on a piece of slate. The only trouble was, when he had to rub it out in order to do something else he could never remember how to write it again. But Brother Francis was a man of infinite patience, never turning the little robin away whenever he appeared at his shoulder to ask for assistance.

Throughout the afternoon Sonny listened attentively to all that he was told, soaking up knowledge like Jimmy Flaherty soaked up ale. His fingers lovingly stroked the pages of the books that Brother Francis had allowed him to look at, enjoying the shape of the words, although he could not yet decipher them. At the end of the school day he, as did the others, handed in his slate. But unlike the rest Sonny lingered at the master's desk while his brother gestured impatiently from the doorway.

'You seem reluctant to go, Sonny.' Brother Francis's saint-like face peered down at him. 'Have you enjoyed your first day at school?'

'Oh, yes, Brother Francis,' Sonny replied eagerly, but seemed loath to move.

'Was there something else?' enquired the master, lacing his fingers, still smiling.

Sonny faltered, then, with a quick glance at his gesticulating brother, broke out, 'Please, Brother Francis, could I have one o' them books to take home? Just to borrow, like,' he added hastily.

Brother Francis seemed surprised; he had never had such a request before. He looked down into the expectant little face, hesitating. Would he be making a mistake? Would he ever see the book again if he complied with the boy's request? He stared into the honest grey eyes before smiling and answering, 'I do not see any reason why I should not loan you a book, my son. Have you any particular preference?' He indicated the bookcase.

Sonny's face burst with eagerness. 'Oh, yes! I know exactly which one.' He leapt towards the bookcase and, curbing his exuberance, reverently lifted out the book of his choice.

'May I see?' Brother Francis held out his slim fingers and Sonny placed the volume into his hand.

The master seemed pleased with his choice. His pious face reflected the splendour of the colourplates in the book. 'You have chosen well, Sonny,' he murmured.

'Yes, Brother,' replied the boy, not giving his real reason for choosing that particular book, that it was the vivid colours and not the religious content that transfixed his eye. If only he could paint pictures like that. His heart sank as he wondered how he could get some paints of his own; if he saved up all his pocket money perhaps one day . . .

He smiled again as Brother Francis handed over the book. 'Take very good care of it, my boy.'

'I will, Brother,' shouted Sonny and, shoving it down the inside of his jacket, ran to join his brother.

'What the devil have ye been gassing about?' enquired Dickie crossly. 'I'm famished.'

'I asked Brother Francis to lend me a book an' he did,' said Sonny, still delighted at the teacher's generosity. He tugged it from his jacket to show to his brother. 'Just look at those pictures,' he breathed. 'Aren't they just grand?'

Dickie sniffed and reached for the book which Sonny pulled out of his grasp.

'Take your dirty hands off it! Sure, I'll get the blame if there's mucky fingerprints all over it.'

'All right, keep your shirt on,' replied Dickie airily. 'I'm not interested anyway. Only I wouldn't leave it lying around if I were you. Izzy Smith'll pay me a good few shillings for that.'

'Ye wouldn't?' barked Sonny, having visions of Brother Francis discovering his book in the pawnshop window.

'Would I not?' grinned Dickie. 'Well, leave it lying around and see what happens to it.'

Sonny had just stuffed it back inside his jacket when he felt a cruel hand grasp a fistful of his hair, and was pulled up sharply.

Brother Simon Peter focused baleful eyes on his victim, twisting his hand into Sonny's hair. 'Well, well . . . the lunatic is also a thief.'

'I'm not!' cried Sonny, looking to his brother for support. But Dickie sidled into the shadows.

'Then what, may I ask, is this?' The master reached into Sonny's jacket and withdrew the book, waving it under the boy's nose.

'I didn't steal it,' protested Sonny, wriggling like a hooked fish. 'Brother Francis lent it to me.'

'A likely tale,' scoffed Brother Simon Peter. 'As if a master would allow a wretched little maggot such as you even to finger such a priceless edition.'

'But he did.' Sonny screwed his eyes shut in discomfort as the man tightened his grip. 'Ask my brother, he knows.'

'Even if your brother were here,' answered the Brother, indicating the empty corridor, 'I should give as much credit to his explanation as I do to yours. He is a liar too. All boys are liars.'

To Sonny's dismay the master began to drag him back into the dimmed corridor. He struggled against the superior strength.

The cruel eyes narrowed and the master hissed into his captive's ear, 'You thought to beat me this morning, did you not? Well, you are about to find out that nobody beats me, boy. Nobody.'

'What seems to be the trouble, Brother?' The angry teacher started as Brother Francis appeared at his classroom door, his hands clasped calmly in front of him.

'Trouble?' spat Brother Simon Peter. 'I shall tell you what the trouble is, Brother.' His hand twisted Sonny's hair once again, turning the boy to face the other master. 'This boy, this thief – yes, I say thief!' He brandished the book under Brother Francis' nose. 'For what other explanation can one offer when one finds such a book in his possession?'

'I can give you a quite feasible explanation, Brother,' interceded the other quietly. 'If you had cared to enquire I would have told you that I have given Sonny the loan of this book.'

Brother Simon Peter appeared not to believe this. 'Loaned?' he whispered. 'You loaned one of the school's priceless books to this, this . . .'

'That is what I said,' confirmed Brother Francis. 'Now, will you kindly release the boy? I am sure you must be hurting him.'

Brother Simon Peter quivered. 'Hurting him? But boys are meant to be hurt, Brother. How else will they learn?'

Sonny continued to wriggle.

Brother Francis sighed, then looked deep into the other's face. His usually kind eyes were hard. 'Brother, have I not just informed you that I am responsible for the boy having possession of the book? What, pray, is there for him to learn? If you were to see me walking out of the school with a book under my arm would you then treat me in such a fashion?'

Brother Simon Peter grimaced sarcastically. 'Naturally I would not, but that is a different matter entirely. These boys were plotting to sell the book they had stolen.'

'Brother, I have already stated the book was not stolen. Do I really have to keep repeating myself?'

The thick lips pursed out argumentatively. 'Whether it was stolen or not they were still conspiring to sell it, I heard it for myself.'

'I am sure you must have been mistaken, Brother,' replied Brother Francis. 'If that is so then where is his accomplice?'

'Are you suggesting that I am lying?' hurled Brother Simon Peter.

'My dear Brother, I would not dream of such a thing. I am merely pointing out that we should perhaps ask the boy to offer an explanation.'

'Is not my word sufficient for you?' snapped the other.

Brother Francis sighed again. 'Of course I believe what you think you overheard, but that does not necessarily mean that you understood their intentions. Perhaps the boy would be good enough to give his version?'

Sonny was quick to leap to his own defence, and his brother's, even though Dickie had deserted him. 'We didn't mean any harm, Brother. 'Twas just Dickie's way of a joke.'

'I accept your explanation, Sonny,' replied Brother Francis. 'I am quite certain that you would not misuse the book in any way.'

'Oh, no, Brother.' Sonny was adamant.

'Then we can forget all about the matter,' decided the master.

'Forget?' spluttered Brother Simon Peter, still holding on to Sonny.

'Brother, you heard the boy's story, you have his choice of book in your hand, would you believe that a boy who makes such a choice could find it in his heart to lie?'

Brother Simon Peter felt his case begin to collapse. He glared into his opponent's stern face then thrust the book roughly at Brother Francis and stormed off. Brother Francis held the book towards Sonny. 'Off you go, boy,' he said kindly.

In the schoolyard George waited patiently for his hero and was relieved to see him still in one piece. His freckled face relaxed into a happy smile as Sonny, along with Dickie who had emerged from his hiding place, bounced towards him.

'I thought you'd had it when I saw old Codgob grab a hold on you,' he said, skipping along beside them.

'Huh! I'm not scared of him.' Sonny straightened his jacket huffily.

'Just 'cause ye got the better of him today doesn't mean to say ye'll do it every time,' said his brother. 'Ye'll not be so cocky when it's time for another of his lessons. He takes us for P.T. as well, ye know.'

'What's P.T.?' enquired Sonny, squinting under his cap, then disappearing momentarily as he slipped on a patch of ice.

Dickie laughed and hauled him to his feet. 'Physical torture. Well, training really, but with Codgob it's torture.'

Sonny brushed the ice from his breeches and frowned. If an art lesson could produce such violent treatment from the master, what on earth would be the outcome of all this P.T. stuff?

'Can I come to your house to play?' enquired George, lifting their minds from the dreaded subject.

'If ye like,' replied Sonny nonchalantly, playing the big man when all the time he was as pleased as punch that a boy of eight wanted to be his friend.

When they arrived home he asked his mother if George could stay to tea.

'I'll clip your ear'ole,' she scolded, when she had dragged him into the scullery. 'There's hardly enough for you two, let alone three. I've told you before about inviting people to tea. I can hardly turn him away when you've asked me in front of him, can I?'

'I don't mind sharing me tea with him,' replied Sonny. 'He's my pal, he gave me these.' He pulled the spoils of war from his pocket and held them up proudly as they returned to the other room.

'By, you must be popular,' exclaimed his mother. 'I can't think why. Here you are, then, make yourself useful, carry this plate o' bread an' butter an' I'll fetch yer a cup o' tea.'

Black with the grime of the schoolyard, the boys began to reach for the bread with sooty fingers.

'Oy, hands washed first!' bellowed Thomasin, then noticed the bulge in Sonny's jacket. 'What the blazes have you got down there?'

Sonny pulled out the book and told her about Brother Francis's kindness.

'Well, fancy that! Best put it somewhere it won't get mucky or torn.' She turned over the pages, her eyebrows becoming a little higher each time. 'By, your teacher must be a trusting soul! It's a right fancy book is this.'

'He likes me,' explained her son, following the others to wash his hands.

When they returned Thomasin handed the plate of bread and butter to George and said, 'Take some, George, there's plenty for all,' and gave a crafty glance at her younger son as George took three slices – That'll teach you, said her eyes when Dickie had taken his and there was only one slice left. But Sonny did not seem to mind, he was too busy nudging his marbles around the table – until he received a sharp slap on the hand.

'It was kind o' yer to give our Sonny those, George,' said

Thomasin. 'It's nice for him to make friends on his first day.'

'Oh, everybody likes Sonny, Mrs Feeney,' enthused George. 'He's a real hero. Why, d'you know what he did today?'

'I'm all ears,' replied Thomasin with interest.

'Er, is there any more bread, Mam?' Sonny tried to veer the conversation away from the dangerous course it was taking.

'Now yer know very well what I told you before.' His mother glared at him, then turned back to the other boy. 'What were you sayin', George?'

'Well, your Sonny . . .'

Sonny sank lower and lower into his chair, trying to reach his erstwhile friend's ankle under the table, attempting to convey the silent message with murderous eyes.

'We were in Codgob's class – that's Brother Simon Peter, well . . .'

'Look out, 'tis the man with the stick!' Patrick's noisy arrival brought his sons leaping from the table in a relieved greeting at this fortuitous intervention.

'Why, 'tis popular I am today an' no mistake,' laughed their father as his sons clambered over him. 'Do I detect trouble in the air?'

'Excuse me, George,' said Thomasin. 'I'll listen to your story in a minute, I just have to get their dad's tea.' She pushed her sons back to the table and followed her husband through to the scullery.

Their parents gone, the boys descended on the hapless George. 'Big gob! Are ye trying' to get us a hiding?'

Poor George was mortified. 'I just thought . . .'

'Aye, an' ye know what Thought did? Followed a muck cart an' thought it were a weddin',' growled Dickie. 'Did ye not hear us say this mornin' that me mam'd kill us if she found out?'

'Is it daft y'are?' hissed Sonny. 'I thought ye wanted to be my friend?'

'I do,' pleaded George.

'Then sit down an' shut yer gob,' ordered the smaller boy.

'Now, George,' said Thomasin, reappearing with her husband's meal and pulling up a chair for Patrick to sit down. 'What were you tryin' to tell me before?'

The boy looked helplessly at the glowering faces across the table and decided that diplomacy was required if he were to escape unscathed. 'Sorry, Mrs Feeney,' he crammed the last of his bread into his mouth and quickly washed it down with the tea. 'I'll have to tell you some other time. Me Mam'll wonder where I am.'

Thomasin frowned as the boy bade them all a hasty goodbye and left, reappearing seconds later to say, 'Thank you for having me.'

'Well, that's nice, isn't it?' she sniffed. 'He eats all our tea then buggers off. What's up, doesn't his mother feed him?'

'Thomasin, will ye mind your foul tongue in front of the children?' said Patrick, wolfing down his meal.

'Please may I leave the table?' asked Dickie of his father, who nodded.

Sonny made to follow him but a tap on the hand from Patrick's knife held him in his seat. 'Please may I leave the table?'

'That's better,' said his father, mopping his plate with a piece of bread. 'Now, off ye go, an' try to stay outta trouble until bedtime.'

'Neither of yer are going anywhere till yer get wrapped up,' said their mother, threading a scarf around each neck and reaching for two pairs of 'gloves', the cuffs sawn off two old jumpers and stitched up at the ends to make mittens.

'I'm sure there's something gone off there,' she mused, when they had gone.

'Where?'

'At school. Yer know what our Sonny's like. I 'ope he hasn't been in trouble already.'

'Ah, well, boys will be boys.' Patrick stretched his long body, then rose from the table to fetch his pipe.

'I'll wager we won't hear yer sayin' that in ten years time when they've got some poor maid into trouble!'

The January wind grew teeth which nibbled and gnawed at their noses, but the boys seemed unconcerned at its assault as they danced like dervishes on the pavement outside their home. Sonny showed his brother how he could write his name, but unfortunately the wall which he chose to autograph belonged to Miss Peabody. She chastised them most strenuously and demanded that they clean it off, but when she reappeared with pail and scrubbing brush they had vanished. However, when they trooped back into the house some time later it was to find that Miss Peabody had lodged a complaint. Their mother stood prepared holding a big wooden spoon; the boys knew what for; many's the time they had felt its convex edge against their rumps.

'Well, what have yer got to say for yerselves?' demanded Thomasin sternly.

'I was only writing me name to show our Dickie,' explained Sonny.

'Aye, and all the rest,' declared Thomasin. 'Miss Peabody was very upset, said you'd been cheeky to her.'

'Oh, come on, Tommy,' coaxed her husband. 'Sure, you're not going to give them a beating for so mild an offence? You know as well as I that the woman is a blasted killjoy. They were only having a bit o' fun.'

Dickie edged up to his mother and leaned his head against her, gazing up pleadingly with those big, blue eyes. 'You're not going to clout us, Mam, are ye?'

'By, I must be goin' soft.' Thomasin hung up the spoon and gave each boy a shove towards the back yard. 'Off yer go to t'closet then we'll decide if yer goin' to get any supper.'

After they had been outside, had polished their boots and placed them on the fender for morning, Patrick took one on each knee where they sat complacently until Thomasin hauled them off for a wash. When her rough ministrations were completed, once again they leaned their faces against their father's broad chest, cups in hand, a ring of greasy cocoa around each mouth, while Patrick related another of the Irish folk tales from his childhood.

'Sure, ye got off very lightly with your mother,' whispered Patrick, when his tale was over. ' 'Tis a hanging offence in your grandmother's opinion, ye know, upsetting the neighbours.'

Sonny threw up his eyes. 'Women!' he expostulated. 'They should be attacked more often.'

'I heard that,' came Thomasin's voice. 'Bed!'

Upstairs the boys took off their trousers, Sonny very carefully, then stood silently for a moment, listening for any movement on the stairs.

'Right, get the pot,' commanded Dickie when the coast was clear.

Sonny complained that he always had to fetch it, to which his brother replied that this was as it should be because Sonny was the youngest, so Sonny reached under the bed and pulled out a large, white champerpot.

'Put it over near the wall,' ordered Dickie, lifting his shirt in readiness.

'You'll never hit it from there,' hissed Sonny.

'How much do ye bet?' said Dickie, taking aim.

'And what if ye miss and it goes through the floorboards onto me Dad's head?' protested Sonny, making his brother giggle and causing him to misfire. The stream of urine sprayed over the bedroom floor in a damp, irregular pattern. 'See, I told ye ye couldn't hit it.'

A giggling fight ensued.

'Stop, I'm wetting meself,' chuckled Sonny as his brother tickled him. 'Let me have my go.' He then sent an undeviating fountain tinkling into the chamberpot.

'Look out, me Mam's coming!' exclaimed Dickie, foiling Sonny's accuracy and sparking off another bout of pummelling.

'Have you boys said your prayers?' Patrick's voice floated up to their room, putting a stop to their horseplay.

'Yes, Dad,' lied Dickie.

'May God have mercy on ye, Richard Feeney,' replied his father. 'All I've heard so far is a lot of shenanigans. I'll be having a word with the priest about that lying tongue o' yours.'

Dickie grinned and knelt down, putting his hands together. 'God bless Mam, our Sonny, Grandma and Grandad, Aunty Molly, Uncle Jim an' all me friends,' he chanted loud enough for his father to hear. 'And please, God, could Ye send me a new daddy? 'Cause the one I have is awful cruel to us. Thank Ye very much, amen.'

Patrick chuckled and closed the downstairs door.

'Ye can forget about the last bit, God, I was only joking,' said Dickie to the ceiling.

'Ye shouldn't say things like that,' reproached Sonny. 'Ye'll go to Hell.'

He knelt and offered his own prayer. 'God bless Mam,

Dad, Dickie, all the people that our lad said an' would You possibly be able to make old Codgob very poorly in time for the next P.T. lesson? Thank You, amen.'

On the wall beside their bed was a wooden crucifix and, under this, a small container of holy water which they applied to their foreheads and breasts in the sign of the cross. Then, snuggling under the blankets and clinging to each other for extra warmth, they soon drifted into the land of dreams.

Much later, as Thomasin lay beside her husband in the aftermath of passion, she had an idea.

'Pat?' She elbowed him.

'Sure, have ye not had enough that ye can find the strength to talk as well?'

'I've been thinking. Now that there's a bit more brass coming in, how about us havin' a housewarmin' party?'

'Well, so long as ye don't go inviting the ould faggot from next door,' he mumbled. 'She'd put a damper on the whole affair.'

'Aw, she's not that bad,' said his wife charitably. 'She can't help it if she's nowt better to do than to live other people's lives for 'em. And she does have her uses, does Nelly. She'll always tell yer whose prices are lowest or if there's owt going off that we need to know about. Now then, about this party,' she droned on, unaware that her husband had fallen asleep. 'I think it's best if we wait until the summer. I don't want people trailing slushy boots into my new house. We'll have to arrange it so it falls on Erin's day off. 'Appen she'll need a bit o' relaxation after all that hard work she's got in store for her . . .'

CHAPTER FORTY-THREE

POOR ERIN, ACCUSTOMED to rising at seven-thirty or eight o'clock, was startled into wakefulness by Alice's rough shaking.

'Come on, it's half past five! You'll have to get that fire lit.'

Erin leapt out of bed, splashed some water on her face from the bowl on the dresser, hastily pulled on her clothes and followed Alice down to the kitchen.

'Right', said Alice, taking a bucket which contained some brushes and rags from a cupboard. 'Here's your cleaning things, go an' do t'range while I go and spread some tea leaves on t'upstairs carpets.'

Erin looked blankly from the range to Alice, who snapped testily, 'S'truth, I thought I was in for a rest now you're here. Come on, useless, I'll help you. But just this morning, mind.'

She knelt upon a piece of sacking and showed Erin how to clean out the grate, brush off the bars and hob, then how to mix a lump of blacklead with water and apply it with a round-headed brush, taking care to get into all the nooks and crannies.

'It's best if you can clean the grate out on a night, then there isn't so much to do on a mornin'. Still, that means you stayin' up till her ladyship's guests have gone, so you can't win either way really. Now then, got the idea? When it's dried you polish it with that brush there.'

Erin nodded. 'Where do I put the ashes?'

Alice put her hands on her hips. 'Out in that bin in the yard o' course. I hope you're not gonna be wantin' to know the far end of a fart all day. You'll have to use your noddle a bit, you know. I've got me own work to do, I can't be playin' nursemaid to you.'

Erin went to dispose of the ashes.

'And hurry up, you haven't got all day!'

Rose came into the kitchen. 'What, no kettle on, Alice?'

'S'not my fault,' replied Alice haughtily, collecting the used tea leaves. 'Erin hasn't cleaned the range yet.'

'Oh, God gimme strength, girl!' hollered the cook. 'You'll have to do better than that if you're to work in my kitchen. Come on, put some elbow grease into it.'

Erin pushed back her hair and wiped a black smudge onto her nose from her grimy hands, rubbing energetically at the range.

'And where is your cap?' asked Rose. 'The mistress'll go spare if she sees all that hair loose.'

'Wouldn't put it past her to cut it off,' said Alice. 'She's like that. Spiteful.'

'I'm sorry, I left it upstairs,' Erin apologised.

'No good up there, dear, it wants to be on your head.' Rose plonked herself onto her chair.

'Shall I go and fetch it, then?' Erin ventured.

'Lord, no!' cried Rose. 'You get that done first, we want our cup of tea.'

'For goodness sake it's like Bedlam in here.' Johnson, his collar awry and a dark stubble on his chin, slouched into the kitchen and looked around him. 'Pour me a cup of tea, girl.' This to Erin, who looked back at him helplessly.

'It may have escaped your notice, Mr Johnson,' said Cook, rising to lumber about the kitchen agitatedly, 'but there is no *fire*, and therefore no tea.'

'No fire!' roared Johnson, grabbing a ladle and whirling on Erin. 'How will I manage to shave without my hot water? I have my duties to perform.'

'Now, Mr Johnson, don't go getting yourself all het up,' pleaded Rose, pushing the manservant into a chair. 'It won't do no good shouting at the girl, she's in enough of a dither without you adding to it. Erin!' she snapped. 'Don't stand there gawping, get that fire seen to, else your life won't be worth living.'

Finally the task was completed and Rose came to inspect it. 'Well, not bad I suppose, but you'll have to get into those corners. Look at that.' She wiped a podgy finger along the edge of the range and showed Erin the stale grease. 'Can't have that in my kitchen, dear. Next thing you know we'll be infested with beetles and rats.'

Erin cleaned the parts that she had missed and Alice, having swept the upstairs carpets and laid the table for breakfast, put the kettle on as soon as the fire was going, saying, 'Thank God, I'm gaspin'.'

'Sure, I'm ready for one an' all,' breathed Erin, edging up to the table and planting herself on a chair.

'Nay, you haven't time for that yet,' cried Cook. 'Go get a bucket from the scullery and scrub the floor and the steps. You've loads to do before you can even think of sitting down.'

Erin chewed her lip and went to fetch the bucket. On the previous day she had decided that she would be able to cope with the work apportioned to her, little guessing that her workload had been reduced on her first day, out of Rose's kindness. There was scant trace of that kindness now.

'You'll have to buck your ideas up,' the cook was saying sternly, scratching at her bottom which hung over the sides of the chair. 'You can't be washing the floor with cold water every day. First thing you do when you've cleaned the range is to get that fire started to heat the water, that's top of the list every morning. No, no!' she waved her hands at the girl's enquiring glance. 'You haven't time for it to heat up now. Just get on with it.'

Erin kneeled down and began to scrub the floor, shivering as she dipped her hand into the freezing water. Soon it became numb and she no longer felt the pain when her knuckles accidentally scraped the floor. Was it going to be like this every day? she wondered, changing the brush to her other hand. If she were at home now she would still be in bed, snuggled down under the warm covers. She tried to straighten her aching back and examined her hands; they were sore and blistered from the knocks she had unwittingly received from the wainscoting whilst getting into the corners.

'Stop daydreaming, girl!' Rose's sharp reprimand made her start her hasty scrubbing again.

Johnson pushed back his chair, drinking the last of his tea as he rose. 'Right, I'll have some of that hot water from the kettle for my ablutions!'

Erin, not realising that the man was addressing her, continued her back-breaking chore. Johnson expelled a noisy breath and snatched up the kettle from the range, sprinkling boiling water over Erin's bare arm as he swung it round.

She screamed and leapt up. 'Ye burnt my arm!'

'Did you hear that, Cook?' bayed Johnson. 'I burnt her arm, says she. You will be most fortunate if you escape with no more than a scalded arm the way you transport yourself, for I cannot see the mistress enduring your incompetence. If you had attended to your duties properly and had the fire lit I wouldn't have to be getting my own water.'

'Well, 'tis not my fault if no one told me what was expected,' replied Erin, snatching a reproving look at Alice.

'Eh, don't be shiftin' t'blame onto me,' snapped Alice. 'If you can't do the job right then you shouldn't be here.'

'Well, I wish I wasn't,' said Erin stubbornly.

'Hey, we'll have less of that cheek, girl!' ordered Cook. 'You'll speak in a civil manner when addressing your betters. Now, will you kindly finish scrubbing that floor, else none of us is going to get any work done at all.'

Scowling, Erin sank to her knees and resumed her chore, her temper lending elbow grease to her arm, until the floor and steps were sparkling. This time Mrs Leng could have no cause for complaint. She rose, grimacing at her semi-paralysed knees and emptied the dirty water in the yard, then waited for Cook's approval.

'Right, that deserves a cup of tea,' nodded Cook, reaching over the table for a cup. 'If you'd just got on without antagonising Johnson we'd all be a lot happier. There you are.' She held out the cup. 'You have done the sitting room fire, by the way?'

Erin shook her head and reached to take the cup of tea. 'Not yet.'

'Oh, heavens above, child, what are you thinking of?' Rose retrieved the cup from the child's grasp. 'You'd better hope and pray that her ladyship's having a sleep-in this morning or we'll all be for it. Go on, off you go – and mind you put on your cap first!' she shouted after the fleeing child.

Erin shot up the stairs to her room carrying with her the bucket of cleaning implements. Once there, she pulled on her cap, tucking the black locks under it as she hastily descended the stairs.

Peeping around the sitting room door she was relieved to find the room empty and hurriedly raked the ashes through the grate. That done, she polished the hearth and set the fire. It would not light. Try as she might, every time she put light to the wood it would crackle optimistically, then promptly die.

'Oh, please, please light,' she begged it, seeking assistance from a pair of bellows, giving the unwilling fire a hefty blast. 'I don't want to get into any more trouble today.'

It took pity on her and suddenly sprang to life, the yellow flames licking hungrily around their black food. Relieved, Erin sat back on her heels and looked around the room for the first time, soaking up the luxury that surrounded her.

In the centre of the room were two armchairs and a sofa, upholstered in a rich, chocolate-coloured velvet. To one side of these, stood a small cottage piano on which were arranged numerous ornaments and photographs, a clever trap for the inexperienced duster. On the opposing wall, looking strangely out of place in the oppressive room with its dark red walls and tasselled drapes, was a writing bureau, its delicate marquetry providing a welcome relief from the rest of the heavily-carved mahogany furniture.

On the walls hung giant pictures of the Royal family in varying poses and ensembles. Erin thought it rather amusing to see the Queen frowning through the forest of potted palms and aspidistras that obscured her majestical gaze. Above the mantelpiece of the ornately-carved fireplace was a very large mirror in gilded frame, and on the mantelpiece itself, between two clownish pot dogs, were more photographs.

Erin rose and, wiping her hands down her apron, selected one of the pictures that had caught her eye. The beautiful woman stared back at her coldly from the silver frame. This must be the mistress, Caroline had told Erin how lovely she was and she had been right. What lovely hair she had, and look at the necklace she wore, she was like a princess.

'If you are thinking to steal that I would advise against it.'

Erin spun round. The photograph slipped from her grasp and its glass shattered on the hearth.

Helena Cummings swept into the room in an aura of perfumed loveliness, the skirt of her hooped, plum-coloured gown swaying from side to side. She was in the foulest of moods. This morning she had received from her current lover, Walter, a touching epistle which had assured her of his undying love but told her that unfortunately he was to be given a posting in India and therefore they would be unable to spend any more turbulent afternoons together. In point of fact he was extremely grateful for the posting; it had given him the excuse he had needed to put an end to her cloying affections without incurring her wrath.

Helena was none too pleased; it meant a period of boring frustration until she found a replacement.

'I wasn't thinking to steal it, ma'am, honest.' Erin's blue eyes dilated as the woman advanced upon her. 'I was only looking at it 'cause I thought you were so pretty.'

The flattery cut no ice with Helena; she took it for granted that people found her beautiful. 'Who gave you permission to touch my possessions?'

'No one, ma'am,' whispered Erin, then explained, 'I'm the new maid. I came in to light the fire, I didn't think anyone'd mind.'

'Oh, you did not?' said Helena loftily. 'Then you were mistaken. As to the fire, why was this task not completed at the correct hour?'

'I'm ever so sorry, ma'am. What with me being new I didn't know . . .'

The repetition of Erin's excuse sharpened Helena's suspicion. Could this child's appearance be somehow connected with that woman's visit yesterday?

'What is your name?'

'Erin Feeney, ma'am.' Erin stooped to pick up the pieces of broken glass from the frame. 'An' I'm really sorry about breaking this.'

Helena ignored the apology. 'Well, in future, Feeney, I shall expect this fire to be well-established when I come down to breakfast. Also you will refrain from touching any object in this room other than when it requires dusting. Do I make myself clear?'

'Yes, ma'am.'

'Very well. Before you depart maybe this will serve to emphasise my words.' Quite without warning her hand shot out and caught Erin sharply on the cheek, making her drop the photograph with a little cry.

Shocked, for no one had ever laid a finger on her before, Erin raised a hand to her face which was now an angry red, and stared at her mistress with tears of bewilderment in her eyes.

'Now you may clear up that mess and get out,' crackled Helena.

Erin put the photograph on the mantelpiece and, placing the broken glass in her bucket, rushed from the room, almost bumping into the master on her way.

'Steady child,' chuckled Roland, stepping aside for her to pass.

'What possessed you to employ a useless dolt like that?' Helena enquired as he came into the room.

'I?' answered Roland. 'The servants are your responsibility, my dear, not mine.'

'I am quite aware of that,' came the curt reply. 'But do I not recall you telling me some weeks ago that you had attended the Martinmas Hirings and had secured another maid.'

'Ah,' Roland remembered. – That must be Tommy's step-daughter. Poor little thing, rubbing Helena up the wrong way on her first day. 'I humbly beg your pardon, my dear, you are quite correct. I did hire her. It is to be regretted that my choice does not rise to your standards – but pray, give the child a chance. She has barely had time to learn.'

'Do I detect a little more than an employer's interest in that girl?'

'I cannot imagine what you mean, Helena,' he replied coolly. 'I am merely asking you not to be too harsh on the child out of consideration for yourself. Servants are very hard to come by; if you frighten them away you may have to soil your own lily-white hands.'

'I remember thinking it odd at the time, you concerning yourself with the running of the household.' She narrowed her eyes. 'If you have brought one of your by-blows into this house . . .'

'Helena!' He appeared outraged. 'The very suggestion.'

She ignored the ragging tone. 'I do not suppose you would care to enlighten me as to your whereabouts since yesterday morning?'

'I do not think you would wish to hear my explanation, Helena,' smiled her husband.

'Perhaps it is of such an unsavoury nature that you cannot divulge it to your wife?' retorted Helena, then sauntered casually to the mantelpiece to make a play of examining the broken picture. 'No matter, I have little interest in your whereabouts, but I think it a great shame that you were not present to witness a rather interesting incident.' She paused to wait for his response, then continued, 'After I had breakfasted I returned to my bed-room to prepare for my morning commitments. There, I chanced to look from the window and saw a red-haired woman leaving my house. She caught my gaze and returned it very boldly, as if she were an equal. I do not suppose her visit has any connection with your employment of the brat?'

Roland shook his head, assuming a flummoxed stance, his eyes almost disappearing under the furry eyebrows. 'I really cannot say, my dear. Before the Hirings I had never laid eyes on the girl.'

'And the woman?'

'How can I say if I have ever met the woman if, as you yourself said, I was not present to witness her visit? Even if I had been at home I doubt whether I would have seen her as I am not privy to your bedchamber. The window of my room overlooks the garden, not the street.'

She curled her lip at this adroit side-stepping. 'Then you have no idea of her interests in this house?'

'None at all.' He moved towards the door and opened it. 'Shall we go to breakfast?'

She swept past him into the breakfast room where Johnson served them then was dismissed; Helena had no wish to converse about such a matter in the hearing of servants. Although she often treated them as though they were not there, she was intelligent enough to realise that they did have ears and, given the opportunity, would repeat what they had heard to servants of other households.

'So, you deny ever having met the woman?' she continued.

'Deny?' cried Roland. 'My dear, what a very odd choice of word. You make it sound like some sort of accusation.'

'Oh, enough of this taradiddle,' she spat, reaching for a honeycomb. 'I am neither blind nor deaf. I know what goes on under my own nose.'

'Do you indeed? Then I would be very pleased if you would enlighten me as I have not the faintest idea to what you are referring.'

'I am referring to your mistresses.' There, it was out in the open, after all those years of pretence. 'And in particular to that red-headed woman whom I spoke of earlier. Do not bother to lie, I have an exceedingly good memory, I well remember the humiliation of seeing her in your company at the Theatre Royal, flaunting yourselves for all to see.'

Roland rested his fork on his plate and threaded his fingers thoughtfully. 'Forgive me, Helena, my memory is not as acute as your own. If you recall the occasion so clearly perhaps you can remember who accompanied you?' She fumed silently as he went on, 'I seem to think he was rather a youngish fellow, much too young to be your dear papa.'

The mention of her father brought a vindictive spark to her eye. 'You would not be so bold if it had been Papa. Had he been there to perceive your faithlessness you would not be sitting there so smugly.'

'If you are so beset by my misdemeanours why did you not tell him, my dear? Shall I tell you? Because you know as well as I that there is more than one miscreant in this woeful tale and I suspect, Helena, that however many mistresses I may have had their total would look sadly inadequate when compared to your string of lovers.'

'How dare you! My father would break you if he knew the way you treated me.'

'I dare because it is quite true,' said Roland. 'And if it is in your mind to raise the question of divorce, might I remind you that, however badly off you consider yourself to be at this moment, being the wife of a "poor" lawyer, this house and everything in it is mine. In the case of a divorce you would receive nothing.'

She smiled grimly. 'Are you not forgetting my father's promise, Roland?'

'I have not forgotten, my dear, I am quite certain your dear papa would delight in ruining my career if there was any scandal. But if my memory serves me correctly, he said that you would be cut off without a penny should you ever contemplate divorce. Which means that without support from either party, you would be in a very sorry state of affairs.' He grinned at her barely suppressed rage. 'We are both adults, Helena. Surely it is far better to continue our charade while we engage in our separate pursuits?' Roland recommenced his breakfast and his mind switched to thoughts of Tommy.

Helena observed him sourly. He seemed to have quite forgotten about their difference of opinion, and one would almost think he had forgotten her presence too, judging by the way he smiled straight through her. She dipped a delicate fork into her scrambled eggs. 'You look very pleased with yourself,' she said bitterly.

'I am enjoying my breakfast, Helena,' he replied cheerfully.

'I really cannot imagine anything on this table which would compel you to wear such an inane grin.'

He threw her an ambiguous look under beetle brows. 'You would be most surprised what sparks my appetite, my dear.' With an even wider smile he plunged his fork into his devilled kidneys.

CHAPTER FORTY-FOUR

'WHERE THE HELL'S that child?' raged Alice, storming about the kitchen and getting under Cook's feet.

'Alice, will you get out of my way!' ordered Rose, wobbling back and forth between oven and table. 'How should I know? Go have a look in the sitting room.'

'Surely she can't still be there?' shouted Alice as she ran up the stairs.

There was no sign of the girl. Perhaps she was in her room – though God knew why. She pelted breathlessly to the attic and found Erin spreadeagled on her bed, sobbing her heart out.

'Christ, what you doin'?' yelled Alice. 'You haven't got time to blubber up here all day. Get down to that kitchen, there's a pile o' pots wants doin'.' Then in a somewhat kinder tone she asked, 'What's the matter? Has the old baggage been telling you off?'

'She hit me,' wept Erin into the bedclothes.

'Well, I dare say it won't be the last time,' said Alice. 'I've had a few clouts off her meself. Come on, it's not the end o' the worl', gerrup. Oh, look! You've gone an' got soot all over the bedspread.' Erin started to cry again. 'Oh, away,' coaxed Alice, shaking her gently. 'I'll help you to do beds else we'll be running late all day.'

Wiping her eyes Erin shadowed Alice down to the bedrooms and collected the chamberpots which were emptied and scoured out – a most distasteful duty and one which Erin had to do unaided; Alice had placed herself above such tasks now. Instead, she consigned herself to picking up the clothes which Helena had flung willy-nilly over the carpet and hung them in their rightful place.

While they were making the beds Alice spied a piece of paper secreted none too expertly between the pages of a book on the bedside table, and pounced upon it hungrily. 'Cor, it's another of Her Highness's love letters, I'll bet. Let's see what it says.' She pored over it eagerly, having learnt to read at Sunday School – though doubtless the girl's teacher had not foreseen her talents put to this use.

Erin paused to wipe the sweat from her brow. 'Are ye supposed to do that?'

' 'Course not, stupid,' returned Alice scathingly. 'We're not supposed to do anything around here. Look, now yer've made me lose me place.' She ran a finger down the page, the nail of which was ragged and dirty. 'Eh, there's no wonder she's seen her backside this mornin',' she exclaimed, finding the place where she had left off. 'Gone an' given her the order of the boot, he has. S'truth, I'll bet we're in for a right time of it now.'

Erin, having little interest in Helena's affairs, had resumed the bed-making. Her fingers were tucking the sheets neatly under the mattress when they came into contact with a hard object. Lifting the corner of the mattress she inserted her hand and withdrew the object, which turned out to be a sovereign.

She held it up to Alice who was still poring over the letter. 'Look what I've found.'

'Mmm?' Alice looked up absently, then opened her eyes wide. 'Good grief, are yer trying to get us all the push?' She snatched the coin from Erin and quickly pushed it back under the mattress. 'Crikey, have you gorra lot to learn.' She folded up the letter and replaced it in the book.

'But won't the mistress be looking for it?' asked Erin. 'I would if I'd lost all that money.'

'She hasn't lost it, yer dumbcluck,' sighed Alice. 'She's hidden it there on purpose to test us. See if we're honest. She's got hordes of 'em hidden all over t'house. So if you see another one, think on, leave it where it is. Away, let's get this bathwater shifted.'

They struggled down the many flights of stairs with the hip bath, the water slopping noisily between them. After emptying it they returned to do Cook's bidding.

'Oh, you finally found her, did you?' asked Rose, up to her armpits in flour. 'And, if I might make so bold as to ask, what happened to her?'

'She hit her,' replied Alice matter-of-factly.

'Aw, poor lamb,' said Rose, taking the impatience from her voice, a total reversal of her earlier attitude. 'Here, sit you down and have some breakfast.' She pulled a chair away from the table and Erin sat down gratefully.

'Mr Johnson's just brought the breakfast things down, there might be a bit of something left for you.' She lifted the lids of the silver tureens. 'Eh, the cat, look what she's done!' Rose pointed to the disgusting mess, her layers of lard quivering in indignation. Helena, in a childish burst of vindictiveness, had poured tea dregs into the scrambled egg and speared the concoction with broken honeycombs.

'One'd think she was still in the nursery the way she performs,' said Cook. 'She's only done it so we can't eat it, spiteful little madam. If her father knew what she puts us and Miss Caroline through he'd take a horse whip to her. He's proper gentry; he knows how to treat his staff.'

Alice told Cook about the letter.

'Oh, well, you might know,' answered Rose, then turned to Erin. 'You'd best just snatch a few biscuits, child. I haven't got time to do you owt decent what with us being all behind this morning.'

Erin took two biscuits from the barrel, then sneaked four into her pocket when Cook was not looking.

'You'll soon get used to it, love.' Rose patted her hand then went to continue with her baking. 'She's a hard piece is that one, but don't think it's only you that bears the brunt of her ill-humour. She takes it out on all of us. You'll be all right when you've learned to keep out of her way.'

Erin crunched thoughtfully on the biscuits, making them last, until Rose said, 'When you've eaten your biscuits you'd best make a start on those pots.' She made a floury gesture at an enormous pile of dirty crockery and pans coated with dried-on scrambled egg.

It was incredible how two people could get through such an array of crockery, thought Erin.

'Then when you've done that,' Cook was saying, 'you can give Alice a hand upstairs.'

Erin brushed the crumbs from the table and went to fetch a receptacle in which to do the washing up. It was barely nine o'clock and already she felt like going back to bed. She poured some hot water from the big kettle into the bowl and yelped as it stung her sore knuckles. It was not fair. There was Alice sauntering about, making herself look busy and leaving the hardest of the work to Erin.

She waded through the washing up, wondering what her new friend, Caroline, was doing now; certainly not this. She was probably in the schoolroom taking her lessons. Lucky Caroline, how she longed to change places with her. Finally the pile diminished, leaving only a bowlful of grey, scummy water to be disposed of.

'Right, grab a duster and follow me,' ordered Alice, and Erin trudged wearily after her. 'Change your apron first,' said the maid. 'You can't go upstairs looking like summat that's been stuck up t'chimney.'

Erin looked askance.

'In here!' said an exasperated Alice, opening a drawer and pulling out a clean apron. She thrust it towards Erin then made for the stairs.

After a busy hour in the drawing room the girls trooped up another flight of stairs to attend to the cleaning of the landing. As she trailed half-heartedly after Alice, Erin caught sight of Caroline through the open door of the schoolroom and dawdles outside to catch her friend's eye, which she succeeded in doing, until Alice pulled her away with a sharp rebuke.

'Don't you be gettin' fancy ideas just 'cause she asked you to stay and talk to her yesterday,' she said acidly. 'Your place is with us in the kitchen.'

Miss Elwood, the governess, looked up from her book to see what had distracted Caroline's attention, and was just in time to see Erin disappear down the corridor.

'To whom were you waving, Caroline?' she asked.

'Oh!' Caroline started. 'Please excuse my manners, Miss Elwood, but I was so pleased to see my new friend, Erin, she is the new maid. I do hope you will forgive my inattention?'

'Of course,' smiled Louisa Elwood, then pretended to look stern. 'But I am not sure that your parents would approve of such a friendship. After all, you are a young lady and must choose your friends accordingly.'

'And where do you propose I should meet these friends, Miss Elwood?' asked Caroline petulantly. 'I am never allowed out of the house. The only people to whom I may converse are servants. Besides which,' she added stubbornly, 'I happen to like Erin and cannot imagine a more "suitable" friend in any sphere. She has such a sympathetic ear and is so pretty. And I suspect that she is fond of me, too.'

'How long has she been here?' enquired the governess. 'I do not recall having seen her before today.'

'She only started her employment yesterday,' divulged Caroline. 'But already she is such a good friend that I feel that I have known her for years.'

Miss Elwood's mouth flickered good-humouredly at the girl's impetuosity. Caroline saw the reserved half-smile and reared up defensively. 'You think I cannot possibly attain such a friendship in the course of one day, but I can! It is so unfair. I have never had anyone of my own age to talk to. In fact, no one seems to want to talk to me at all.'

'You wound me, Caroline,' cried the governess, drawing an instant apology from her pupil.

'Pray forgive me, you know that I did not mean it to sound as it did. I look forward immensely to the times we spend together. But,' Caroline sighed, 'I really do like Erin.'

Louisa looked at her charge's wistful face and decided that, maidservant or no, Erin was much needed here. She herself had endured the same loneliness as a child, though perhaps not quite so harshly as Caroline for her own parents had been very loving, and Louisa felt it was her duty to attend to all aspects of Caroline's happiness, not just her education.

'I agree,' she said at last, 'that it will be nice for you to have someone of your own age in the house. Perhaps we could arrange for the two of you to spend a little time together.'

Caroline decided that this was the right time to make her request. 'Do you think it might be possible for Erin to join my lessons sometimes? She desperately wants to learn. It seems unfair that her brothers are allowed to go to school but she isn't.'

'I see no reason why not,' replied Louisa kindly. 'I shall speak to your papa about the matter. Provided,' she added sternly, 'that you now cease your daydreaming and let us continue with our lesson.'

'Yes, Miss Elwood,' smiled Caroline, and happily buried her nose once more in the book.

*

'You'd better go down now,' said Alice, rising from the chair where she had been idly watching Erin do all the work. 'Cook'll give you the shopping list. I've got to clean the silver, though I don't see why I should. It's old Johnson's job truth be known, but he's gone over to the mews to collect a carriage for Titifollol.'

Erin gave a final flourish of her feather duster then returned to the kitchen.

'Ah, there you are,' said Rose, picking up a piece of paper and handing it to Erin along with a basket. 'You know where Goodramgate is, don't you?' Erin nodded. 'Well, halfway along you'll find a grocer's shop, you can't miss it. You'll get everything on that list from there. Then,' she gave the girl another list, 'drop this in at the butcher's, that's two doors along from the grocer's. You won't have to wait for that, he delivers.'

Erin wrapped her shawl tightly around her and picked up the large basket.

'Poor little soul,' said Rose to Alice, who came in carrying a tray of silver. 'I'll have to have a word with the master about giving her one of Miss Caroline's old coats. It's a crying shame to see a pretty little thing dressed like that. And you, madam, can stop throwing your weight about so much!' She pounded away at her dough. 'Just because you've been promoted doesn't mean to say you can make her life a misery. Don't think I haven't noticed you pushing her around.'

'Me?' said Alice incredulously. 'What have I done?'

'Nothing,' replied the cook. 'That's just my point. I know she's the scullery maid and by rights she gets all the dirty jobs to do, but it's only her first day, you oughtn't to push her around so. If she gets sick of it and leaves then you'll have it all to do again.'

'I like that!' cried Alice indignantly. 'You've been shoving her around as much as I have.'

'I'm entitled,' replied Rose airily. 'You're not. Now get on with whatever you're supposed to be doing.' She plaited the bread and put it into the oven.

A bell jingled from a rail on the wall, craving attention in the drawing room.

'Oh, damn that blasted thing,' sighed Alice flinging down

her cleaning rag. 'I wonder what Lady Arsey wants now?'
Erin shivered and felt the goose-pimples begin to form. She
walked briskly to increase her sluggish circulation. In spite of
the cold it was nice to escape from that hostile atmosphere
for a while. Crossing the road she tramped up Goodramgate
until she found the grocery. After carefully purchasing every
item on the list Erin left in search of the butcher's shop.

Pausing outside, she stared at the bloody carcases that hung
at its open frontage, at the smiling, lifeless faces of the pigs
suspended by their hind legs, their narrow eyes screwed shut.
Never would she be able to enter a butcher's shop without her
mind conjuring up terrible memories. Her fingers trembled
unconsciously as she felt once again the walls still tacky with
blood, heard the ghoulish rattling of chains. She stared,
horrified, at the ghastly array on the let-down shelf, the
piles of slippery liver, sinewy chitterlings, and sheep's heads
grinning back at her in a terrifying rictus, beasts' hearts
pulsating before her very eyes.

'Well, are yer comin' in or aren't yer?'

Startled, she spun round to find a tall, grinning boy at her
shoulder, his blond hair spiking from under his butcher's cap.
Fresh-complexioned he was, with white even teeth and a
cheeky smile, pleasant blue eyes that glittered with youthful
merriment at the sight of this pretty girl. He was the sort of
boy for whom many a maid would have mooned into her
pillow.

But Erin could see none of these things. Her eyes saw only
the blood on his clothes, the tiny pieces of flesh under his
fingernails and the slavering, pimply face of Jos Leach.

The boy leapt back in alarm as Erin gave a piercing scream
and ran wildly down the street. She did not know where she
was going but simply ran, black hair streaming, boots ringing
and skidding on the frosty pavement, the shawl slipping from
her terrified shoulders as her arms worked furiously to aid
her escape.

'I thought I told you to keep your hands to yourself, Samuel
Teale?' The butcher emerged from his shop to see what all
the commotion was about.

Sam blushed, still taken aback by his reception. People
were staring at him, pointing accusingly. 'I didn't touch her,
Mr Simons, honest,' he protested. 'She must be a loony. All

I said was "Are yer coming in?" and she gave a big scream. Scared the livin' daylights outta me, she did.'

'Are you sure you didn't touch her, you randy little devil?' His employer lowered his eyebrows.

'Cut me throat an' hope to die,' swore Sam, quite upset about the whole business.

'All right, son, you'd better go and deliver those orders then.'

Sam followed the butcher back into the shop, still trying to work out what the girl had found so frightening about him, and was unable to chase her pretty, terrified face from his thoughts for the rest of the day.

CHAPTER FORTY-FIVE

ERIN KEPT ON running until the big house was in sight, then almost fell down the steps to the basement. Safely round the back of the house she leaned against the wall and shut her eyes, gasping and puffing with the exertion of her flight. When she had collected her senses she picked up the basket of groceries and opened the kitchen door.

'Did you get everything?' asked Rose, who was preparing a menu for the evening meal.

'Yes, Cook,' replied Erin, putting the basket on the table for Rose's inspection.

'And did you leave the list at the butcher's?'

The question hit her like a wet fish in the face. The list! In her panic she had forgotten all about it. She touched a tremulous hand to her face.

'Oh, don't tell me you forgot?' Rose slammed down the pencil on the table, breaking the lead. 'We'll have no meat for supper, the mistress'll go mad. Oh, you are useless, girl.'

Erin hung her head and crossed her fingers behind her back, praying that the cook would not send her back to the shop.

'Well, you haven't got time to go back now,' said Rose crossly, much to Erin's relief. 'I want some help in the kitchen and you obviously aren't to be trusted to run errands. Alice!' she bellowed to the maid who had just appeared on the staircase. 'Alice, Erin's forgotten to go to the butcher's, be a love and go, will you? We've got to have a joint for tonight.'

For once Alice made no complaint. On the contrary, she was only too happy to comply. She enjoyed her trips to the butcher's, revelled in the saucy company there, and she could have a good old stroll around the shops while she was at it.

'Right, Erin,' snapped Rose. 'You put those groceries away sharp, and get that cap back on. The mistress usually comes down to inspect the kitchen about this time.'

Feverishly Erin tucked her hair under her cap and straightened her apron, and none too soon, for Helena's tiny feet tripped lightly down the stairs under a rustle of silk.

'Good morning, Cook.' She swayed about the room like a handsome, deadly cobra, sharp eyes darting about the kitchen, waiting to strike.

'Good morning, madam,' replied Rose. 'Would you care to study the menu?'

'No, I will leave it to your discretion, Cook,' replied Helena silkily. 'I am sure that whatever you prepare will be quite adequate.'

– Adequate indeed, sniffed Rose, that's about her limit. Never a word of praise for all the hard work you put in. You could slave all day, preparing a banquet fit for a king and what would you get? 'Oh, that is quite adequate, Cook.' Bitch.

Helena was trailing a manicured digit along the range. 'This really is quite disgraceful, Cook!' She held up her finger distastefully and wiped away the grease on a cloth which Rose swiftly handed to her. 'Who was responsible for cleaning it this morning?'

Rose hesitated then looked pointedly at Erin, who had been trying to make herself look small.

'I might have known!' expostulated Helena. 'It seems that my little rebuke this morning was not severe enough.' She gestured for Erin to come closer, which the girl did fearfully. 'Now, listen very carefully. I understand that the house in which you live is probably crawling with all manner of vermin, but I expect my house to be kept spotlessly clean at all times.' She tried to remember Erin's name but it escaped her and she had to ask once more.

'Feeney, ma'am,' whispered Erin, expecting another blow at any minute.

'Oh, yes, the Irish girl,' nodded Helena. 'I might have expected it. The Irish have such filthy habits. I really cannot think what possessed the master to employ one. Or can I? I wonder, does your mother have red hair by any chance?'

Erin nodded, alert for any movement from Helena's hands.

The woman turned her back on Erin and marched slowly along the length of the kitchen, her face darkening. So, her assumption had been correct. Well, her dear husband would live to regret his rash decision to bring his bastard to work in this house. And so would the child.

She turned and sauntered back to stand before Erin once more. 'Yes,' she said thoughtfully, staring right through Erin as she spoke. 'I thought that might be your mother, a true slut if ever I saw one.' Her voice lost its abstractedness and she added sharply, 'Let me inform you, Feeney, that any "understanding" your mother may have reached with the master is irrelevant to me. What is, is that you are here to work and work you will. By that I do not mean to your mother's standards but to mine. I hope I will not have to clarify the matter again?' She did not wait for an answer. 'Very well. You will now clean the range again and when you have finished I shall wish to inspect it. If it is still not to my satisfaction you will earn yourself a beating.' Laying her palms against her whispering skirts she glided up the staircase and was gone.

'Well!' Rose was astounded. 'She's certainly taken a dislike to you, hasn't she? I wonder why?' Her inquisitive mind ticked over. From what the mistress had said, or rather not said, Erin could be one of the master's illegitimates; Lord knew there would probably be a few about. But then he would hardly set her to work in his own kitchens if that was the case. You'd think he would take a bit more care of her than that.

'Is your mam a friend of the master's then?' she asked casually.

'What?' Erin was still hearing Helena's words and was most upset by them. Fancy saying those awful things about her mam. She felt the tears sting her eyes and turned her face away from Cook before they brimmed over.

Rose repeated her question.

'No, I don't think so,' replied Erin, though rather uncertainly, wondering now if Helena's words were entirely without foundation. Thomasin had been very vague about her relationship with Mr Cummings. Whatever the case she was not going to add fuel to the flame that Helena had obviously sparked in Rose's inquisitive mind. She knew what a gossip Rose was.

'What shall I do after I've put the groceries away?' she asked, diverting the conversation.

Rose saw that she was not going to get anything out of Erin so decided to let it rest for now. But she was too curious to forget about it completely and would bring it out for an airing at a later date.

'You can peel some potatoes for our dinner,' she answered. 'I've got some nice steak and kidney in the oven, should be ready soon. You'll like that, everybody likes my steak and kidney pie.'

Erin set about peeling the potatoes, but just as she applied the knife to the first one Johnson descended the stairs looking decidedly out of humour.

'Girl, get a pail of water and go clean the front step instantly!'

'But . . .'

'I have no time for any of your backchat!' snapped the manservant. 'I said instantly. A dog has fouled the front step and the mistress wishes to go for her morning ride. She cannot do so until the step has been cleaned. Go now.'

Erin filled a bucket, threw in a scrubbing brush and, holding a shovel in her free hand, went out of the back door to clean the offending mess. Johnson, having made a suitable change of clothing, rushed after her to where the carriage stood outside the front door and tipped the boy who had been holding the reins.

'Hurry, girl, the mistress will be down at any moment!'

Erin offered up a silent prayer for the cold weather which had made the dog excreta quite easy to remove and sloshed her scrubbing brush onto the step to scrub away the evidence. The noise of her scrubbing covered the sound of the front door opening and she was unaware of Helena's arrival until two dainty feet appeared under her nose.

She was about to apologise for her presence, was just going to return her brush to the bucket when, without so much as an excuse me, Helena raised one of her prettily-shod feet and trod heavily on Erin's fingers, purposely screwing her foot round to increase the pain.

Erin stood clutching her bleeding fingers, the tears streaming down her cold face as Helena climbed into the carriage and it pulled away. *Why?* she asked herself over and over again. *Why?*

★

At lunchtime Caroline came down to the kitchen to take her meal. Miss Elwood, as usual, took hers on a tray in her room.

'Sit down, Miss Caroline.' Rose placed a steaming plate of meat pie and vegetables in front of her. 'And try to cheer that girl up, will you?' She pointed at Erin. 'She looks like a bit o' wet lettuce.'

Caroline smiled at her neighbour. 'Are you not happy in your new post?'

Erin made a face behind Rose's back and the other girl's smile widened.

'I expect you are finding it pretty hard?' Caroline, who had never lifted a finger in her life, had no inkling of just how hard.

She looked at Erin's hand which Cook had kindly bandaged after Erin had returned weeping. 'Have you had an accident?'

' 'Twas no accident,' said Erin sullenly. 'The mistress stood on my hand.'

Caroline lost her smile. 'I think you must be mistaken, Erin. Mama would never do a thing like that except by accident.'

Erin gave an embittered chuckle. ' 'Twas no accident I tell ye. She hates the sight o' me. I got a clout this morning just for nothing.'

'Really, Erin.' Caroline was no longer the sweet-natured girl of yesterday. 'I do think you are rather over-dramatising the situation. If you truly knew Mama you would realise that she is far too beautiful a person ever to contemplate such an act as you are suggesting. I think you are being most unjust in your accusations when she is not here to answer them.'

Erin was just going to argue with Caroline when she caught Alice's wary glance. The meal progressed in silence, apart from the scraping of knives and forks upon plates. Erin wondered at Caroline's inability to see the mistress for what she was. Erin noticed that none of the other servants spoke about Helena in front of her daughter, at least not in the derogatory manner in which they did when Caroline was not present. It was quite obvious why. Caroline would hear no wrong said about her mother and was apt to become extremely distressed at the least little criticism.

Erin decided that in future it was better to remain silent

about Helena's persecution rather than alienate the only friend she had there.

Though Caroline's over-sensitivity was quick to rise in defence of her mother, she was not one to sulk and before the meal was over she was chatting amiably once again to her neighbour.

'I am most sorry that you have had such a dreary morning,' she told Erin. 'But no matter, I have some news which should cheer you. You remember how you told me that you wished you could go to school? Well,' here she pressed her lips together secretively, before blurting out: 'I have asked Miss Elwood about the possibility of you joining my lessons and she has agreed to ask Papa if it can be arranged. What do you think of that?'

Erin could hardly believe her ears. She looked agog at Rose who said, 'That's all well and good, Miss Caroline, but who's going to do her work down here?'

'This bloody mug,' provided Alice bitterly.

'Alice! Mind your language in front of Miss Caroline,' shouted Cook.

'I am sure it will not interfere with her work,' said Caroline. 'It will only be for one hour after lunch. Surely one hour will not make any difference? Oh, please, Cookie, do say yes.'

'Well, it isn't up to me, is it?' replied Cook. 'If the master says yes, well, we'll all have to grin and bear it.' She looked at Erin's pleading face and softened. 'Oh, I suppose it'll be all right! Just for one hour and provided you make up for lost time.'

Caroline squealed in delight and threw her arms around Erin, who blushed at this impulsive behaviour. 'Marvellous! I shall inform Papa that you do not mind, Cookie.'

'Don't you go letting him think it's my idea,' cautioned Cook.

'I must say, it all sounds very irregular to me.'

All faces turned to Johnson.

'What harm will it do?' argued Alice, who had changed her tune on realising that Erin's absence would not affect her. 'Long as she catches up with her work and don't expect anybody else to do it.'

'Servants should know their place,' Johnson insisted quietly, 'and should not be getting ideas above their station.'

'Oh, and I suppose that means me!' Alice flung down her knife and fork with a clatter.

'If the cap fits . . .' replied Johnson tauntingly. His softly superior manner had a habit of being more infuriating than his words.

'Just 'cause you're after getting yerself in my bed . . .'

'Alice!' commanded Rose. 'That is quite enough.'

'Well, he's always on at me,' sulked the maid, prodding viciously at the leftovers on her plate with a fork. 'And it's only 'cause he's jealous.'

Johnson did not rise to this charge, simply smiled his dark, secretive smile, giving nothing away.

After lunch Caroline returned to the schoolroom, taking Erin with her.

'Ah, Caroline,' said Miss Elwood. 'I have approached your papa who was most affable to my proposals.'

Erin expelled the breath she had been holding and grinned happily at the other girl. This would make up for all the indignities and insults. At last she was going to school. She was shown to a desk and provided with a stack of exercise books, and for the next hour neither thought of nor heard anything other than the governess' voice.

But the time sped all too quickly and pretty soon she found herself once more faced with a pile of dirty crockery and the promise of a hard afternoon to come.

Many hours later, she collapsed into bed beside Alice. It felt as though she had been there for a week – a month even – not one single day. However, she was not to be allowed any rest for Alice wanted to talk. Now, snuggling under the blankets with the older girl Erin received a true insight of what life was really like in the big house.

'Such goings on,' whispered Alice, putting her cold feet against Erin's legs. 'The mistress has a string o' fellas – 'cause they don't bother with one another, her an' the master. An' he's a rum'n an' all, always winking at me. I shall have to be very careful o' my virtue. I often expect him to come creepin' into bed of a night after his oats. I hear he's very fond of his oats, is the master.'

Erin was thoroughly confused now. Why should the master want to eat oats in bed? Was it not a little messy?

Alice laughed gleefully. 'Hasn't yer mother told you anything?' She reached up to snuff the candle and in the privacy of darkness introduced Erin to the intricacies of human nature.

Erin was disgusted, revolted. 'I'm not going to do that when I grow up.'

'You just wait,' chuckled Alice. 'How d'you think you came about then? Certainly not from under a gooseberry bush.'

Erin was silent. She knew where babies came from, but never for one moment did she believe that her parents had indulged in such actions – and certainly not for enjoyment as Alice so obviously implied.

'Put yer arms round me, I'm cold,' commanded Alice. This Erin did. Alice shoved her bottom against Erin's warm belly and, pulling the child's hands up to her breast, tried to sleep.

In the bedroom directly below theirs Helena stared into the darkness from her pretty, canopied bed, wondering what her husband was up to. He had not returned home yet, but that was not unusual. Often he did not arrive until well after she was asleep, if at all. He would likely be bouncing on some willing trollop. The thought made her annoyed even though she no longer cared for him. It was merely the thought of him enjoying himself while she lay here alone that was irksome. Grumpily she turned over and squeezed her eyes shut, attempting to blank out the erotic pictures.

Rose lay in her bed thinking of tomorrow's menu, then yawned and, accompanied by a groan of complaint from the sagging mattress, turned over and fell instantly alseep.

Below, in a small room off the kitchen, Johnson had been asleep for some time.

Only Erin remained awake, too exhausted for sleep. Alice grunted and moaned in her dreams, and pulled Erin's hand closer to her breasts. Erin felt the hard nipple thrust against her palm and, deriving a primeval comfort, she leaned her head against Alice's shoulder and finally achieved unconsciousness.

CHAPTER FORTY-SIX

THE FOLLOWING MONTHS brought no lightening of Erin's workload – quite the reverse in fact. Her days seemed to be filled with an endless mountain of dirty crockery, unmade beds, slop buckets. She cleaned the kitchen range over and over in her sleep, only to find it once again thick with grease in the morning. She ploughed mechanically through her work with heavy eyelids and stiff arms like an automaton, until the time came when she could throw herself into bed and catch a few, blessed hours' respite.

She gained no benefit from her spare time, for when her evening off came around it was spent hurrying between Mass – due to Helena's disinclination to allow her to go on Sundays – and making brief visits to her home.

Patrick and Thomasin had been horrified at her appearance on the first visit. Her face, though naturally pale, looked more like that of a middle-aged woman than a young girl. Her father had immediately forbidden her to go back – they would sell something and pay back the advanced wages – but with an inherited stubbornness she had stated that, like himself, she would not have her integrity questioned; she had taken her money in advance and therefore must see the year out. The secret smile she gave Thomasin when saying this cut to the quick.

However hard, one gets used to anything after a time and slowly Erin became acquainted with the routine. Alice had found an admirer and though it was very awkward sneaking out to meet him it made life all the more exhilarating, thereby putting her in a better frame of mind.

Rose was quite happy with Erin's performance now that

she had a good grasp of the work rota, and even let her help with the baking sometimes – allowing her membership to the cook's book of secrets, which contained such items as using best butter to increase the amount of dripping from the roast which she then sold at the door for a nice profit.

Even Johnson's attitude showed a slight improvement, though Erin could not say that he liked her or that she liked him but as long as she did her work he remained quite civil.

There was, however, one person in the house who would never soften to Erin's presence. Helena, still convinced that Erin was Roland's child, continued her single-minded persecution. At their every encounter she would find some excuse, however shallow, to scold the child, choosing a time when Roland was present so that he should witness the folly of his loose-living. Poor Erin's arms were black and blue from all the nips she had received from her mistress and, despite the other servants' reaffirmation that Helena treated them all as badly, the little Irish girl knew that for some reason of her own the mistress hated her.

The one ray of sunshine in this life of drudgery was the hourly lesson she received each afternoon. No longer did she have to listen enviously on her home visits when her younger brothers would boast of their attainments at school. Now she was able to match their abilities and with each week surpass them. Unchained, her intellect devoured the books with which she was provided, gobbling up each grain of knowledge and proving to be more than a match for Caroline.

Roland had said nothing to his wife about the lessons. For himself he could not see the harm in them, but knew that Helena would object most strongly. At this moment of the day he was thinking of Tommy. Oh, he had found a new playmate as she had forecast – a handful of them in fact – but none was quite so exciting after her. He wasn't sure he could even be bothered to meet his current mistress tonight, which was why Helena found herself accompanied at the dinner table, much to her surprise.

'To what do I owe this pleasure?' she asked, raising her wine glass to delicate rose-petal lips.

'Pleasure, my dear?' Roland feigned astonishment.

'I speak figuratively of course,' she replied blandly.

'Of course, of course,' nodded Roland, selecting a cluster

of grapes from the fruit bowl. 'Well, my dear, it is simply that I am feeling rather too tired to venture out tonight and thought perhaps I might retire early. I have been working too hard of late. The rest will do me good.' He dabbed at his mouth with a napkin to conceal a smile.

She watched him select a cigar and sink into an armchair with his brandy. 'You say you will retire early; will you be expecting anyone to join you?'

'Do my ears deceive me? Are you inviting yourself into my bed?'

'I most certainly am not.' Helena did not appreciate his joke.

'Then to whom do you refer, my dear?' Roland curled the cigar smoke around his tongue.

She ignored this to tell him, 'You may goad me all you wish, dearest,' – the endearment sounded as if she were wiping dung-caked boots on him – 'but I should like you to bear in mind that my ability to overlook your decadent habits when they occur outside this house does not extend to those few occasions when you are under this roof. I will tolerate no lewd behaviour in my home. You know how the servants gossip and I would not have my daughter submitted to . . .'

'Your daughter?' Roland's surprise was real. 'Since when have you been concerned with Caroline's welfare? You have persistently ignored her since the day she was born. She is now fourteen years of age and you suddenly decide that you want to be a mother.'

'I admit that I may not have shown as much interest as I might have done,' allowed Helena. 'But that was purely because I believed her to be happier with a nurse – you know how awkward I am with young children.' She waved a small hand. 'But pray, do not let us digress from the pertinent subject. What we have been speaking of is all in the past and I intend to remedy any unintended hurt our daughter may have suffered quite shortly.'

'In what way?'

'As you say, our daughter is now fourteen, an impression-able age, one at which she must be advised and schooled in various matters. She will soon be a young lady with thoughts of marriage. A mother must be there to mould and steer her in the right direction. After considerable soul-searching I have decided that I must put aside my admittedly selfish pursuits and dedicate my attention to her well-being.'

There had been a great deal of consideration on Helena's part. She had thought about the matter very carefully indeed and had come to the conclusion that Caroline, with her virginal beauty, could become her mother's passport to higher circles. For however often Helena may have told her daughter that she was ugly, it was merely a cruel lie designed to wound. Even Helena was not so self-deceiving that she could not see that the girl would be a great draw for the gentlemen. The first steps towards shaping Caroline's future would involve sending her away to a suitable school. The young governess was very efficient but was hardly qualified to teach Helena's daughter how to conduct herself when mixing with lords and ladies.

Roland started as Helena voiced her intentions to dispense with the governess. 'And what if Caroline does not wish for all this?' he asked when she had outlined her arrangements. 'She may be quite happy to marry a lawyer as you did.'

Helena was astounded at this preposterous conjecture. 'Don't be so ridiculous. She will leap at the chance to improve her status. Apart from which she has very little choice in the matter. I, as her mother, have already designated what is best for her.'

'Aren't you forgetting something?' queried Roland. 'Am I not to be consulted? I am her father.'

'Are you?' There was an insinuating twinkle in Helena's eye.

But Roland waved aside the innuendo. 'You know very well I am. You would not have married me otherwise. Do I not have a say in her upbringing? You have always left it to me in the past.'

Knowing that Roland would put a stop to her plans if he discovered her true motives, Helena injected a fawning tone to her voice. 'Surely your last statement proves my point? You have had to bear the responsibility alone for fourteen years, is it not time I began to act like a mother?'

'I have long ago given up hoping for that, Helena.'

'Please, Roland, give me a chance to prove to you that I am thinking only of our daughter's happiness – as you should be. She must come first, I realise that now. We must do all we can to ensure that, unlike ourselves, Caroline makes a suitable marriage.'

'Our ideas on marriage may differ somewhat.'

'I think you will support my idea when I tell you my choice.' She then told him of her plan to invite the Snaith-Buxbridges to dinner one evening. 'It is time Caroline was given an airing, to show people what a beautiful daughter we have.'

'I have always subscribed to that idea,' said Roland. 'But Caroline is young yet. It is a little premature to be seeking a marriage partner for her.'

'What nonsense! It is never too early to introduce one's daughter to respectable society. Come, Roland, don't spoil it for her.'

He swallowed his brandy and, placing the glass on a silver tray, rose abruptly. Did Helena think she fooled him with her fake concern? He had known her too long to believe she had anything other than her own interests at heart. 'I regret I cannot give your propositions my undivided attention to-night, Helena. I am quite worn out. However, I will leave the arrangements for Caroline's future to your discretion on the understanding that the question of marriage is postponed until she is much older.'

'But I can invite the Snaith-Buxbridges?'

A tired nod. 'And now goodnight.'

PART FIVE

CHAPTER FORTY-SEVEN

SUMMER . . . WHEN THE children of more budget-conscious mothers cast off their boots and ran barefoot. When front doors were wedged open from dawn to dusk and curtains hung in their stead. When the butter spread a little easier and grandmothers hauled their chairs on to the pavement, to sit and watch the world at play while the sun comforted their brittle bones.

Yet in the schoolyard where the boys assembled for their physical training ordeal, Brother Simon Peter's cold, codfish gaze made it seem more like the depths of winter. His icy scorn, as his eyes ran up and down the lines of unwilling participants, made them shiver, and suddenly the sun, as though intimidated, retired behind a cloud to leave the yard in shadow.

The blubbery lips quivered as Brother Simon Peter's eyes came to rest on Sonny. This damnable boy. Even after several months of savage beatings, the severity of which increased with each misdemeanour, the boy was as wilful and obstinate as ever. Not one tear had he cried. Though his lips were often beaded with blood from the extreme punishments, his eyes remained dry and defiant. Brother Simon Peter squinted threateningly into those seemingly innocent grey eyes which returned his inspection levelly. Sonny was wondering what delight the master had up his sleeve today.

The teacher finally spoke. 'Pay attention, you odious collection of offal. Today's lesson is designed to test your stamina. It is what might be termed a cross-country run, but as I am reluctant to unleash such savages on the unsuspecting yokels your journey will take the following route. You will run, I repeat *run*, down Walmgate, go under the Bar, turn right . . .' he broke off and addressed Sonny out of habit. 'I assume,

Feeney, that you do know which is your right? Pray hold up your right hand.'

Sonny, unsure, slowly raised his left hand.

'Well, that is no more than I expected,' replied the master tiredly. 'Can anyone tell this imbecile which is his right hand?'

The few boys who did know were nervous of putting up their hands for fear of being thought goody-goodies.

The master sighed heavily. 'I wish someone would tell me how I am supposed to educate a class of morons who do not even know their right from their left. When you have gone under the Bar you will turn this way.' He swung out his right hand, catching the child who was unfortunate enough to be standing next to him a vicious clout on the ear. 'Do you understand?'

'Yes, Brother.'

'From there you will follow the line of the Walls until you reach Fishergate Postern, and from there you will return to school.' He spoke pointedly at Sonny. 'I will brook no short cuts under Fishergate Bar, nor any shirking. Any boy who is not back within three minutes of the leader will be punished. Shaughnessy, lead on.'

The boys jogged out of the playground, accompanied by the faint sound of girlish singing from the female side of the school and the slightly off-key piano playing of Sister Mary. They spilled into Walmgate, a motley selection of ruffians. Forty pale, scab-encrusted faces bobbed up and down, the ragged edges of their trousers dangling above darned socks. The dust eddied around their plodding feet and soon even those who were not wearing boots looked as though they were. The hot sun bore down upon them, turning their faces from white to pink to red. Their hair became plastered in cowlicks to glistening foreheads; but they ran on.

Before they had reached Walmgate Bar, Dickie began to flounder and gradually fell further to the back of the heaving serpent of bodies.

Sonny looked over his shoulder. 'Come on, Dick, they'll be leavin' us behind.'

'Bugger 'em,' puffed Dickie and slowed to a casual gait. 'I've had enough o' this lark. 'Tis too hot. I say we take a short cut.'

Sonny and George who had also stopped, stared at Dickie then back at the line of bobbing heads which trickled into the distance. 'I don't think we should,' was Sonny's opinion. 'Ye heard what he said about short cuts.'

'Ah, sure ye know he'll give ye a hiding anyway,' retorted Dickie. 'He don't need no excuses. Can yc tell me of any lesson where ye've not had one?'

Sonny could not, but said reprovingly, ' 'Tis fine for you to talk, you're not the one who gets the beatings. If he should catch us . . .'

'He'll not catch us,' scoffed Dickie. 'The man can't be hiding around every corner can he? We're bound to be able to get back into school one road without he sees us – but if you're scared.' He pretended to run on, fully aware that it would rile his brother.

'I didn't say I wouldn't do it, did I?' replied Sonny hotly. 'I just meant what if we're back too soon? He'll know.'

'We won't be,' promised Dickie. 'We'll hang around for a while, go an' see what old Bacon Neck's up to.' This was the name with which they had dubbed Edwin Raper, his skin being the very colour of boiled bacon.

His two compatriots finally agreed and, making sure that they were unobserved, they slipped down the narrow passage-way to Britannia Yard.

'Eh, look,' whispered Sonny, delving into one of the bins that stood outside the abattoir and holding up his prize. 'Hens' heads.'

'Well, if there's no more ye'll have to share 'em with me,' ordered his brother, rummaging in the bin, then crowed noisily as he found something more interesting. 'Ey, we'll have a bit o' fun wi' these! We can shove 'em down t'lasses' necks.' He thrust his hand into the bin again. 'Let's see how many there is, we can sell 'em for a ha'penny each.' He pulled out another brace of hens' claws and waved them in George's face.

George retreated slightly, then bent to peep through the cracks in the abattoir doors. Inside, the murky shadow that was Edwin Raper had just administered the coup de grace to a steer which was suspended from a hook in the roof. The boy watched quiveringly as the animal was skinned and disembowelled.

'Ugh, look at that.' George was unable to contain his disgust as the butcher's knife drew a deep incision along the lifeless belly, sending miles of tangled intestines slithering to the dirty floor. Grey, blue, red, brown, green, almost every colour under the sun lay upon that floor. George thought he was going to be sick but couldn't tear himself away.

'Come out, ye've had your turn.' Dickie elbowed him out of the way and squinted through the crack.

'S'not your turn, 'tis mine,' argued Sonny and a ferocious jostling for position began, until the doors swung open knocking them all onto the filthy yard.

'What the hell are you up to?' bawled Raper, brandishing a red-tipped knife. 'No good, I'll be bound.' He advanced on them.

The terrified boys, without daring to take their eyes from the knife, tripped and stumbled into the alleyway and out into the street, pursued by the maniacal butcher. He shook the knife at them and bellowed like one of his victims. 'I'll cut your bloody throats if ever I catch yer round 'ere again!'

They ran like the devil himself was on their heels, until they were sure that he was no longer following. 'Phew! I wonder what time it is?' panted Dickie, making certain that his pocket still contained the hens' feet. 'D'ye think we'd best be goin' back?'

There was half-hearted agreement and together they cut through a lane that led to the school, hoping to rejoin the group of runners on their return.

But their plan was foiled. As they were about to run towards the school, the appearance of an all-too-familiar figure had them hastily springing back around a corner.

'Blinkin' 'ell, what we gonna do now?' asked George, goggling at Brother Simon Peter in alarm. 'Look, there's the rest o' the lads.' He pointed in the direction of George Street where the first of the breathless competitors had appeared. However fast they might sprint across the road to join them Brother Simon Peter would most certainly see them.

'I told ye 'twas a silly idea,' bewailed Sonny.

The line of boys was halfway past the truants now, who could already feel the strap across their rumps. It would take witchery to get them out of this one.

And then appeared a person whom they had always accused of possessing that power, but for which they had never dreamt they would ever have cause to be grateful. 'Coo-ee, Brother Simon!' whinnied Nelly Peabody and bounded across the road to greet the master, omitting to use his full name as she always did; it was such a mouthful.

The master tried to ignore her presence and concentrate on counting the runners as they streamed past, but Nelly tugged at his sleeve demanding his attention and so confusing his addition.

'Oh, Brother Simon,' said Nelly. 'I was beginning to think that you were avoiding me.'

'Whatever gave you that impression, Miss Peabody?' The smile lacked conviction. 'Twenty-one, twenty-two.'

'Well, that last time I saw you, you did say that you might take tea with me one afternoon. That was some time ago.' Nelly had successfully entertained just about everyone who was of any importance in the district. The schoolmaster had so far managed to evade her.

'I'm very sorry, Miss Peabody, but as you know a schoolmaster has numerous duties to perform – twenty-seven, twenty-eight – I do trust that you are enjoying more reasonable health since our last meeting?'

'Oh, my dear Brother Simon, you cannot begin to imagine the pain I have to endure . . .' Nelly ranted on and on and on, while the master tried futilely to keep his attention on the runners.

Here was their chance. As the last boy padded towards them the three leapt into the queue, passing the stragglers and positioning themselves behind the thirtieth runner; a place where they might be expected to be. At that moment Brother Simon Peter returned his calculating eyes to the boys, craning his neck over Nelly's shoulder as she moaned continuously over her rheumatism. Forty boys staggered past him, thirty-seven of their number in red-faced exhaustion, the other three eyeing him nervously.

With a modicum of diplomacy the master finally disengaged himself from Nelly and followed the boys into the yard where he scrutinised each face closely.

'Very well,' he said at last. 'You may return to the classroom.'

The three recalcitrants made to follow the rest, sneaking congratulatory smiles at each other.

'One moment, those three boys.' They stopped dead as he came up to them. 'Running appears to be your forte, does it not?' They stole apprehensive glances at one another, unfamiliar with his phrase. 'What I mean by that, Feeney,' said the master as he bent towards Sonny, speaking in his quiet, minatory way, 'is that whilst the rest of the class are obviously worn out from their exercise, you and your companions seem not to have sustained any ill-effects whatsoever. On the contrary, you are positively bounding with fitness.'

'It was quite easy really, Brother.' Sonny could have bitten off his tongue, but the words could not be reclaimed.

'Good, good,' smiled the master reflectively. 'Then, as you apparently enjoyed it you will be pleased to learn that I have decided to allow you to complete the course again. One cannot have too much of a good thing, can one, Feeney? But this time, instead of coming into school after completing the first circuit you will go round once more, which should add to your enjoyment even further.'

Sonny could feel his brother's accusing glare.

'Very well, off you go – oh, and Feeney?' Both Dickie and Sonny turned back as he warned them: 'Just so you will not take it into your heads to cut your journey short, I am going to position a boy on all entrances to Margaret Street and George Street.'

There was no way out this time. The three set off, Sonny and George berating Dickie for his bright idea of a short cut. By the time they reached the Bar their legs were beginning to ache, weighed down by the heavy boots. There was no dodging the hot sun which bounced from the pavements and settled upon their heaving shoulders. Towards the Cattle Market they staggered, panting dry-tongued past Fishergate Bar where one of Codgob's spies lounged in bored antagonism, onto Fishergate Postern, clomping up Lead Mill Lane and back to the school.

'Keep those knees up!' shouted the master as they ran past the gates. 'I shall allow you another eight minutes to go round again.'

'D'ye think we can do it?' panted George hopefully.

'Doesn't matter if we do or not,' replied Sonny dully. 'We're still for it.'

Their windpipes started to feel as though they had been scoured with sandpaper. Ballooning lungs, tortured limbs – Holy Mary, Mother o' God, pray for us sinners! Left, right, left, right! Eyes stinging, heads throbbing. Sweet Jesus, the landmarks seemed to be getting further apart. Slogging, plodding onwards.

'I can't go any further,' wheezed Dickie painfully. 'I'll have to have a rest.'

Sonny and George, though exhausted themselves, heaved him to his feet and dragged him between them.

'Come on, our lad,' gasped Sonny, wiping a hand around his dripping face. ' 'Tis not far now. There'll be trouble if we're not back in time, or worse trouble I should say.'

Each step became agonising. The pain clutched at their calves and, gaining a hold, crept higher into their thighs, their hips. Everywhere.

Suddenly Dickie fell. A long, ragged gash appeared on his shin. He began to cry. Sonny helped him up and pulled a grimy rag from his pocket, dabbing at his brother's eyes; a diminutive patriarch. The blood oozed from the cut in a scarlet trickle towards his boot, soaking into the stocking that hung around his ankle.

Sonny straightened the handkerchief and tied it around his brother's leg. 'Can ye tie a double knot?' He looked at George who came to his aid.

Then once more they continued the tortuous trek, feeling no benefit from their brief rest. Eventually, after what seemed like hours, they reached the school gates where Brother Simon Peter still lurked, a black-hearted vulture.

'A fine effort,' he praised as they limped after him into the classroom, his lips twisting into what was supposed to be a smile. 'Unfortunately you failed to arrive back within the allotted time.'

' 'Tis not fair,' Sonny objected. 'My brother fell an' cut his leg, that's why we didn't get back in time.'

The vee above the master's nose seemed as though it were ready to take flight. 'So, you stayed to look after him? An admirable trait is compassion, Feeney. Highly commendable.' He reached for the strap on the wall. 'And, as you so rightly shared his pain then, you will have no objection to sharing it now. That is only "fair", as you put it. Come here, boy.'

Sonny advanced and, without having to be instructed, unbuttoned his trousers and bent over the bench.

'Now, how many shall we give him today, boys?' The master tapped the strap across his palm, prolonging the agony. 'For his failure to complete the course in the given time might I suggest six would be suitable?' Sonny knew that he would not get away so lightly. 'Then six for taking a short cut in the first instance . . .'

'We didn't!' Sonny interjected.

'. . . and a further six for his insolence towards his master.'

Sonny took his punishment with the invariable silence, gritting his teeth as the thick leather strap bit into him. The Brother, recognising that he would kill this boy before subduing him, wisely kept his temper, administering the blows in cool, calculating accuracy.

'Next!'

George stepped forth and duly received twelve welts, finding no difficulty in producing the required tears.

Then it was Dickie's turn.

'Now, Feeney,' said Brother Simon Peter, almost gaily. 'How many do you think you deserve?'

The boy studied his boots and remained silent, knowing that any answer he might give would be the wrong one.

'Have you no tongue, boy?' hissed the master, wetting his lips as he watched Dickie unbutton his trousers and produce his white rump for retribution.

'Let me see. Feeney Minor received eighteen, did he not? And I believe you were the person who hindered the others by your careless action. Therefore I think it only fair that you receive an extra six, making a total of twenty-four.'

Dickie looked at his brother, then closed his eyes as the punishment commenced. By the sixth stroke the tears were beginning to form. By the twelfth he was crying profusely, sobbing noisily into his clenched fists.

Sonny watched his brother's anguish in angry silence, guessing that anything he might say would only procure sterner retaliation for Dickie. The wily master had finally found his opponent's Achilles heel: his brother's pain could reach Sonny in a way no flogging could.

The strokes, instead of decreasing in strength as they neared the fifteenth, became heavier. Each time the man's hand fell he looked towards Sonny, urging him to cry, to put a stop to his brother's pain. Dickie yelled heartrendingly, begging the master to stop. But only Sonny could do that, and Sonny would not cry.

Everyone's eyes were upon him. Seventeen! Eighteen! Dickie was almost screaming now. Sonny bit his lip. Why? Why was everyone looking at him? He had taken his punishment like a man, why could not his brother do the same? He knew that he could put a stop to all this, but why should he? Why? It was always he who had to be the strong one, even though he was the youngest; sticking up for his brother, fighting his battles. Angrily he listened to Dickie's screams and knew that he could not stand by and do nothing. He would have to do it. At that moment he hated his brother. This time it was not punches that were required, but tears. It took a different kind of courage.

Slowly a drop of moisture welled up in the corner of his eye. It hung on his lower lashes for an age, then trickled down the side of his nose, pursued by another, and another. The master's eyes lit up with a triumphant gleam. He slapped the twentieth stroke over the red and broken skin, then dropped the strap to his side.

'I think we can dispense with the other four, Feeney,' he said magnanimously. Dragging Dickie to his feet he gloated as the boy painfully fastened his breeches and limped back to his seat.

The room was silent. All gazes were cast to the floor, sharing in Sonny's humiliation as the tears coursed down his face. He had been their hero – their one spark of light in this golgotha – now he was just the same as all the others.

Sonny looked around at his friends who now presented their backs and refused to meet his eyes.

Later, in the playground, though Sonny tried to avoid them, George and his comrades edged up to him, jackal-like, scuffing their boots on the gravel, prompting each other into speech. Eventually it was left to George to state their claim.

'We want our things back,' he said bluntly.

Two sharp lines appeared between the sandy eyebrows. 'They're not yours now, ye gave 'em to me.'

'That was before.' The rest of the boys grew braver and circled around him. 'You've got to give 'em back, else we'll tell.'

Furiously, Sonny rammed his hand into his pocket and drawing out the marbles, badges and string flung them into their turncoat faces. Then, swivelling on his heel, he marched briskly away. If that was their idea of friendship, then he wanted none of it.

And as usual, when there was trouble, his brother was nowhere to be seen.

That evening Erin came, armed with a basket of groceries which Cook had sneaked from the larder.

'Will ye look at her, Tommy!' cried Patrick, kissing his daughter delightedly. 'Has she not grown into a little lady?'

Thomasin put down her darning and came to welcome her stepdaughter. 'She is that. And look at all these lovely things she's brought with her.' She lifted the napkin from the basket. 'By Jove, I shan't know what to do with all this.' She turned to address her sons, holding up a brown, speckled egg. 'How would yer like a chucky egg for your supper, then?'

'Eggs for supper!' exclaimed Patrick in mock horror. 'Sure, ye'd think she was laying 'em herself.'

'Well, yer've got to do summat to cheer 'em up,' answered his wife. 'I've never seen such long faces in all me life. They've been sat like two book ends since they came in from school.'

The boys eyed her noncommittally from their separate chairs.

'They've been fightin',' whispered Thomasin to Erin, who took the groceries through to the scullery where she slipped her wages into Thomasin's pocket.

'How's the mistress treatin' yer these days?' asked Thomasin sitting down again.

'About the same,' replied Erin quietly. 'I'm beginning to think she's got something personal against me.'

Thomasin flinched. 'Nay, she's no reason to, has she?'

'I thought perhaps you might be able to tell me,' ventured her stepdaughter. 'She's been saying . . .' she paused.

'Saying what?' asked Patrick interestedly, sucking on his pipe and filling the room with clouds of familiar perfume.

'Ah, 'tis nice to be home with all the old smells,' breathed Erin as the smoke swirled around her head.

'By, yer make it sound as though we stink,' sallied Thomasin, glad that Erin had changed the subject.

Erin laughed softly. 'Now ye know what I meant – Dad's tobacco and the like.'

Patrick smiled too but was not to be distracted. 'Ye were saying that the mistress says things. What about?'

'Oh just . . . awful things,' answered Erin. 'None of it has

444

any substance, she just says things to hurt people.' She looked at Thomasin who was obviously suffering some discomfort from this dialogue, then changed the subject again. 'There's one thing anyway,' she said brightly. 'The mistress seems to have taken a liking to Caroline all of a sudden. We never see her in the servants' hall now, she always takes her meals upstairs.'

'As it should be,' said Patrick firmly. 'Whoever heard of a lady making her daughter eat with the servants? Though I don't expect the girl is very keen about taking her meals with the miserable ould witch after the fun she's had with you.'

'Ye'd not think so,' agreed Erin. 'But Caroline doesn't see the mistress in the same light as we do. She'll not hear a wrong word said about her. I miss her though.'

'Well, perhaps 'tis for the best,' Patrick puffed thoughtfully. 'It doesn't do to get too attached to someone of her class.'

'Why ever not?' asked Erin. 'Just because she's rich doesn't mean to say we can't be friends.'

'That's quite true in theory,' admitted Patrick. 'But such friendships usually end in one o' the parties being hurt, an' there'll be no prizes for guessing which one.'

'Ye don't understand, Dad,' sighed his daughter. 'Caroline isn't like that at all. Well, she can be a bit high an' mighty at times, but that's only her upbringing, she's a good friend really. Think of all the things she's done for me. These nice clothes I'm wearing, they belonged to her – and the school lessons.'

'They're to continue then?' asked Patrick, fighting to keep the bitterness from his voice. It needled that Caroline, with a wave of her hand, could give his daughter what he could not.

'Of course,' said Erin. 'Why wouldn't they?'

'Does the mistress know about them yet?' asked Thomasin. She had been greatly surprised when Erin had informed her about the lessons.

'D'ye think I'd still be taking them if she knew?' grinned Erin, then went on to tell them the rest of the news, about the dinner parties Helena had given and the new gowns she had bought, describing them down to the last button.

'I wish ye wouldn't talk about all this grand stuff in front of your mother,' reproved Patrick, though only in fun this time. 'She'll be expecting me to buy them for her next.'

'Now yer know what I've always told yer,' retorted Thomasin. 'I have everything I want right 'ere.'

Pale creases fanned out from the outer edges of Patrick's blue eyes, where they had been screwed up against the glare of the sun. It looked as if someone had taken a paintbrush and applied white, feathery strokes to his tanned skin. 'I know what ye say,' he teased. 'But if it was handed to ye on a plate I'll wager ye'd not turn it down. Come on now, be truthful.'

Thomasin shook her head wearily. 'No matter how many times I tell yer it's like talkin' to a stuffed donkey.' She turned her attention back to Erin. 'Your talk of dinner parties brings me to our bit o' news. Well, not so much dinner parties as housewarming . . .'

'Oh, you're having it at last!' squealed Erin, springing to her feet.

Thomasin laughed with her husband. 'Aye, we've finally got round to it. We've set it for next Saturday.'

Erin's face crumpled and she sat down deflatedly. 'Oh, but I'll miss it. My afternoon off is on the Sunday.'

'Eh, I'm sorry, lass, but it's all arranged now, we can hardly tell t'guests we've changed our minds, can we, Dad?' said Thomasin, then her face relaxed into a motherly smile and she leaned forward to chuck Erin under the chin. 'Yer daft 'aporth. I'm havin' yer on a bit o' string. Yer don't think we'd have a party without you, do yer?'

Erin laughed in relief and blinked away the tears that had been stinging her eyes. 'Oh, you are a one, Mam.' She sprang up excitedly and caught up her basket. 'Ooh, I must go an' tell Caroline me news. By, I'm that lookin' forward to it.'

'To be hoped your brothers have altered their faces by then,' commented Thomasin. 'They'll scare all the guests away.' She poked at Sonny with her toe and he huffily shifted his position. 'Come on, maungy, crack yer face.'

'I think Erin's enthusiasm'll make up for any miserable mugs,' observed Patrick as his daughter kissed him and prepared to leave. 'Ye'd think we were having a banquet the way she's performing.'

Erin squeezed his hand then dashed to the door. 'Oh, ye don't know how much I'm looking forward to it,' she cried happily. 'I can't wait for Sunday!'

CHAPTER FORTY-EIGHT

SUNDAY DAWNED UNINSPIRINGLY through a thick blanket of grey cloud, and it was not until mid-morning that a valiant sun fought free of its prison to remind the inhabitants of the big house that it was summer.

But Erin was too busy and far too excited about the party ever to notice the weather. She sailed through the morning chores at twice the speed, as if working faster would make the time go quicker, too.

As there would be no lesson today, which meant that Erin would not see her friend, she decided to spend her short morning break chatting to Caroline and at eleven o'clock placed two cups of tea on a tray and slipped up to the other girl's room.

Caroline had just returned from chapel and was in the act of replacing her prayer book and gloves in the drawer when Erin marched in.

'Oh, Erin, you are a darling, I'm absolutely parched.' She snatched one of the cups and sank gratefully into a chair, kicking off her shoes and propping white-stockinged feet on the dressing table. 'Chapel was infinitely dreary, as usual. I thought it would never end. How lucky you are not to have to go.'

Erin, clutching her own cup, pushed away a hairbrush and comb then perched on the edge of the dressing table. 'Ye've got a hole in your stocking,' she observed.

'Have I, where?' Caroline twisted her foot around. 'Oh, yes, so I have. Oh, well, I dare say you will not mind darning it for me this afternoon.'

'Not this afternoon, I'll not,' replied Erin. ' 'Tis my free period. I'm goin' to our housewarming party.'

Caroline wriggled her toes. 'Oh, yes, I remember now. That should be fun, but no more than you deserve. You work much too hard, Erin.' She handed over her empty cup. 'Put that on the tray, would you?'

'Shall I go down for another?'

Caroline wrinkled her nose. 'No, stay and tell me about the party. What will you be having to eat? Mama says that at her next dinner party I am to be present, just think of that! I am to be treated like a grown up, and I shall have wine to drink.'

'Well, I don't suppose there'll be anything of that sort at our party,' said Erin. 'But nevertheless it should be a grand do. There's all our old friends coming.'

'What are you to wear?' asked Caroline.

'I thought perhaps I'd wear the brown dress which you kindly gave me,' said Erin.

'Oh, but you cannot possibly wear that drab old thing, it's positively ancient!' cried Caroline. 'And besides, you need something pretty and bright for a party.'

'Well, maybe I could wear one o' the others ye gimme,' replied Erin slowly, and when Caroline told her that they were all far too shabby for a party, said, 'They'll have to do 'cause I've nothing else.'

'Nothing else?' answered Caroline disbelievingly. 'Oh, come – you are not going to tell me you have only the old things I gave you.'

'We can't all be rich like you,' snapped Erin springing from her perch and grabbing the tray.

'Oh, don't be such a ninny, Erin.' Caroline jumped up and caught hold of Erin's arm. 'I did not mean to be insulting. I was genuinely surprised. Here!' She ran to the wardrobe and flung open the door. 'You may choose any one of these.'

Erin stood motionless with the tray, still a little angry. 'Don't talk soft, I can't take one o' those. The mistress'd go loony if she saw me in one o' your dresses.'

'I don't mean to keep,' said Caroline. 'Just to borrow. I am sure Mama will not mind. Come, you cannot go to a party in such an old rag. I know how much you have been looking forward to it, please, take one.'

Erin put down the tray and wiped her hands involuntarily

down her apron, then went to select a dress from the rail. After much suggestion and criticism from Caroline, she finally chose a lavender gown with a simple lace collar and cuffs which, when donned, changed the colour of her eyes from blue to amethyst.

'Oh, Caroline, it's lovely!' Erin twirled before the glass. 'Wait till Daddy sees me in this.'

'I wish that I was going with you,' said Caroline. 'But I have to stay in my room till tea and do nothing more strenuous than read a book. I abhor Sundays.'

Erin, with profuse thanks, took the dress to her room then returned to the kitchen to resume her work.

'You're looking bright today,' said Cook, as Erin began to peel the vegetables for lunch.

' 'Tis my party this afternoon,' replied the girl gaily.

'How could you forget, Cook?' said Alice who was also helping with the preparation of lunch. 'She never talks of anything else.'

Erin told them of Caroline's contribution to her party apparel.

'Then we'd best see what we can do, hadn't we, Alice?' Cook waddled to the larder and returned with a basketful of newly-baked pies, eggs, butter, cheese and a jar of beetroot.

'Oh, Cook, you're ever so generous!' exclaimed Erin. 'Mam won't half be pleased.'

'Aye, she's good at being generous with other people's stuff is Cook,' joked Alice, and beat violently at the Yorkshire Pudding mixture. 'I'm surprised she hasn't put a bottle o' the master's best sherry in an' all. Eh, Mr Johnson!' she shouted, as the manservant appeared with a great selection of silver that required polishing. 'You don't fancy makin' a donation to Erin's party, do you? How about leavin' t'cellar keys on table by accident?'

Johnson, dourfaced as usual, rolled up his sleeves and began to clean the silver.

'Keep that polish away from my cooking,' warned Rose. 'We don't want to poison her ladyship.'

'You speak for yourself,' muttered Alice, adding cheekily, 'Any road, a bit o' polish in the gravy might brighten her up a bit.'

'Oh, Alice, you are a caution,' laughed Rose, taking the

joint from the oven to baste it. 'I don't know where you get it from.'

'Why, I get it from you, Cook,' replied Alice. 'Don't think I didn't notice you letting them ashes fall into that roasting tin.'

Cook spun round indignantly, then saw the gleam of mischief in Alice's eye. 'Well,' she chortled, 'it adds to the flavour, that's what I always say.'

Despite Erin's fears that the afternoon would never come, the little hand eventually crept up to the two and she dashed off to wash and change. Within ten minutes her face was clean and pink, devoid of the sooty smudges from the flue, her hair hung down in loose waves, gleaming like an ebony cape over the lavender dress. Before returning to the kitchen she dashed to Caroline's room to say a last goodbye.

'You look simply lovely, Erin,' praised Caroline. 'That gown suits you much better than it ever did me. And to put your mind at rest, I have told Mama about lending it to you and she did not mind one bit.'

'She didn't?' said Erin doubtfully.

'Of course not, I told you she wouldn't. You really do paint her in a bad light, Erin. She is not as you imagine her to be at all.'

'If ye say so.'

'I do. She's been most terribly kind to me of late. She has apologised for all my years of loneliness and has explained that our separation was not of her making. She is to make it all up to me, she says, and I must confess that I have never been so happy in all my life.'

Erin smiled. 'I'm glad for ye, Caroline. I'm glad you're happy. Though I do miss not seeing so much of ye.'

'And I miss you too, Erin.' Caroline hugged her tightly. 'But we still have our lessons together, do we not?'

'Yes, we do, but I wonder for how long?' said Erin into the other girl's shoulder. The lessons could not remain undiscovered forever.

'Why, for as long as we continue to be friends of course,' said Caroline. 'And that is for always. For if ever I should lose your friendship, Erin, I am certain I would die.'

'Oh, Caroline, you're so intense.'

'No, I am serious,' cried the other. 'You are the best friend

I shall ever have. I could not possibly bear the thought of us parting.' She sniffed and wiped her eyes. 'Oh, there, I've gone and put teardrops on your dress.'

'Doesn't matter,' replied Erin happily. 'They'll soon dry. Anyway, I must go if I'm not to miss the party.' She kissed Caroline and with a hasty look at herself in the mirror went down to the kitchen to collect her gifts for Thomasin.

'Oh, Alice, come and take a look at Erin,' cried Cook. 'She's a real picture.'

Alice, though feeling slightly envious of Erin's beautiful appearance, considered it childish not to agree. 'Aye, she looks more like a lady than Miss Caroline,' she said kindly. 'Don't she, Mr Johnson?'

'Very nice,' said the manservant with a cursory glance from his newspaper. 'Don't be too late back, girl, else the door will be locked.'

'That's as near a compliment as you'll get from him,' whispered Alice, then said loudly, 'Have a nice time and don't drink too much of the master's sherry.'

'What's that, Alice?' barked Johnson.

'I'm only jokin',' said Alice and distorted her mouth at Erin. 'Go on, lass, off yer go.'

'Bye, Alice. Bye, Cook,' shouted Erin swinging the basket onto the crook of her arm. 'Bye, Mr Johnson.'

'And may one ask where you are going, girl?'

Everyone turned to the staircase, the jovial atmosphere fizzling out. No one had heard her come down.

Erin blinked nervously at Helena who waited impatiently for an answer.

" 'Tis my afternoon off, ma'am.'

'On whose instructions?' challenged Helena.

'Why, it was just taken for granted that it was my Sunday afternoon, ma'am.'

'It seems to me that rather too much is taken for granted around here,' replied the mistress imperiously. 'For instance, the dress which you are wearing; I believe that it belongs to my daughter.'

'Caroline said I could borrow it,' objected Erin, but Helena cut off her words.

'When referring to my daughter, Feeney, you will use the correct term of address, which is Miss Caroline or Miss

Cummings.' She lowered her gaze to Erin's arm. 'And what of the basket of groceries? Do you also take the food in my larder for granted?'

'That was my fault, madam,' Rose owned up. 'It was only a few bits and pieces for her to take to the party. Only a few leftovers.'

Helena stalked up to Erin and lifted the cover on the basket. 'You call those "bits and pieces", Cook? I would call it thievery!'

'Madam!'

'Can you think of another word for it?' demanded Helena. 'No. Sheer and blatant thievery. If I were a vindictive woman, Cook, then you would find yourself in the most serious trouble. I sometimes think that you overestimate my leniency.'

'Oh, no, madam,' said Cook. 'I'd never do that.'

'Be quiet! Feeney, replace those items in the larder and be quick about it.'

Erin shot past the mistress to the larder while Helena turned her wrath on Johnson. 'Johnson, I had assumed you to be a responsible person yet you allow this sort of behaviour. Why?'

'I knew nothing about it, madam,' answered Johnson.

'Then you should make it your business to know,' snapped Helena. 'You incompetent fool. Very well,' she turned back to Cook, 'I will overlook your dishonesty this one time, but any similar occurrence will earn you a place in one of Her Majesty's prisons. Feeney, you will go at once to my daughter and return the dress which you took without permission, and then you will return to the kitchen to carry out your duties. By your actions you have forfeited your right to time off.'

'But they're expecting me at the party,' protested Erin.

'Are you questioning my authority?' snarled Helena. 'I said you are to return to your duties. And your insolence has just cost you dearly. From today you will receive one month's notice, is that understood? A month should give me sufficient time to replace you.' With that she was gone.

'Oh, the cruel bitch,' spat Alice going over to put her arm round Erin. But Erin slipped from her grasp and with a strangled sob ran up the stairs to her own room.

*

The guests began to arrive in dribs and drabs; Jimmy and Molly with their horde of children, two of Patrick's workmates and their spouses, old neighbours, new ones (though not Miss Peabody) and the indispensable fiddler who was closely followed by Father Kelly. The latter proffered his bestowal to Patrick as his fellow Irishman showed him in.

'Ye'll not be holding Communion this week then, Father?' said Patrick, taking the bottle from him.

'We'll have less o' the blasphemous talk, Pat Feeney,' replied Liam. 'That happens to be a first class Madeira if ye don't mind, given to me by one o' my admirers.'

Patrick laughed. 'Sure, there cannot be many o' those about.' He steered Liam into the party, where the other guests were being handed glasses by Thomasin.

Liam thanked her as she handed one to him, then looked inside it. 'But sure, 'tis no good empty!'

'If you hold yer tongue you might get it filled,' she told him. 'Your glass, I mean, not your tongue. Right, hold out yer glasses, everyone, we might as well make a start on Father Kelly's communion wine.'

'Now don't you start,' spluttered Liam. 'I've had enough o' that irreverent chat from your husband.'

A knock came at the door, interrupting the filling of glasses.

'I'll get it,' said Patrick. 'It'll be your Mam an' Dad.'

He put down his glass and went to open the door. 'Hello, Billy, Hannah, sure ye didn't have to knock.'

'Some of us have to have manners, Patrick,' answered Hannah and slipped past him.

'See tha's got spies out,' observed William, inclining his head towards the neighbouring window where the lace curtains moved ever so gently.

'Aye, there's not much goes on without Mrs P. knowing about it,' Patrick told him, then shoved William indoors. 'You watch, I'll give her five minutes an' she'll be round with some excuse.'

'Ah, yer here at last, are yer?' said their daughter. 'Pat, fetch me Mam an' Dad a glass.'

Hannah apologised for being the last to arrive. 'It's your father,' she explained. 'He always insists on leaving it until the last few minutes to get ready.' She eyed the Flaherty family warily. 'I see that terrible woman is here. Let us hope we will not have a repetition of your wedding reception.'

'By, God yer've got a long memory, Mother,' said her daughter. 'I'm quite sure yer can all get along if yer put yer minds to it.'

Patrick took William's arm and drew him aside. 'Here, have a taste o' that, Billy.' He offered his father-in-law a glassful of colourless liquid which he had poured from the earthenware jug.

'What the 'ell's this yer givin' me, bloody water?' William examined the drink dubiously.

'Water is it? I'll bet ye cannot knock that back in one go,' wagered Patrick.

William raised the glass and tipped the liquid down his throat.

'Hell's teeth!' he gasped, and wafted his mouth furiously to quash the fire within.

'Keep yer language down,' commanded Thomasin from the other side of the room. 'There're ladies present.'

'Drop o' good stuff, eh, Billy?' laughed Patrick.

'S'truth, it nigh on blows top of yer 'ead off,' returned William. 'What the 'ell is it?'

Patrick winked. 'Come, I'll show ye.' He led William towards the scullery.

'Don't be slopin' off,' called Thomasin. 'I'm dependin' on you to keep people's glasses filled.'

'I will be but a second, oh light of my life,' replied her husband, guiding William through the kitchen, where he flung open a cupboard door.

'There, what d'ye think o' that?'

'I'm still no wiser,' said William, staring at the container full of frothy water with tubes leading out of it into earthenware casks.

'Why, ye just said it, man – *still*.' A grin. 'I cannot think why I never had the gumption to make one before. All these years I've been pouring my money into the publicans' pockets an' it never crossed me mind.' He poured himself a cupful from one of the casks. 'Ah, 'tis a wee drop o' heaven, Billy, d'ye not think?'

William had to agree and asked Patrick how it was made.

'Praties,' replied the Irishman succinctly. 'An' a little bit o' knowhow.'

'Mmm, could do wi' one o' them at 'ome,' mused William sipping at his refilled glass, very carefully this time. 'By, tha wouldn't need much o' that to get thee feelin' frisky, would tha'?'

'Yoo hoo, anybody in?'

'There y'are!' exclaimed Patrick. 'What did I tell ye? Did I not say she'd be round?' He knocked back his drink. 'I'll be right with ye Mrs P.!'

William followed him back to the front room as Nelly came in. She checked as if in surprise. 'I'm most awfully sorry to incommode you, I didn't realise you had visitors. I just came to let you know what has happened to Mrs Fry.'

'Come in, Miss Peabody,' answered Thomasin pulling Nelly into the throng. 'I was going to come round and invite yer anyway. Yer might as well stop now that yer here.'

'Well, I should hate to intrude,' replied Nelly.

'Nonsense, yer'll be very welcome, won't she, Pat?'

Patrick nudged his father-in-law. 'Aye, about as welcome as a dose o' pox in a brothel,' he muttered from the side of his mouth. He stood and walked over to Nelly. 'Ah, truly you're welcome, Mrs P., and may I say you're lookin' very handsome today? Anyone would think ye were dressed for a party.' He winked at William, then taking Nelly's arm he asked courteously, 'Would ye like to wet your whistle now you're here, Mrs P.?'

'Well, I'm not really a drinking woman, Mr Feeney,' simpered Nelly.

'Ah, go on, a drop o' this won't harm ye.' He poured out a glass of poteen. 'Look, 'tis like water really.'

'Patrick,' warned Thomasin in a threatening manner. 'Perhaps our guest would rather 'ave a glass o' this wine?'

'No, I'd better not,' said Nelly. 'I'm not used to strong liquor. A small glass of the other stuff will be fine, just to drink your health you know.'

'A discerning woman.' Patrick smiled sweetly and handed her the glass. 'Good health to ye, Mrs P.'

She sipped at it daintily. 'It's a bit strong.'

'Here, let me put a drop o' water in it for ye.' Patrick poured some liquid from another jug into her glass, filling it to the brim. 'There, tell me how that tastes.'

'Ah, yes, much better,' agreed Nelly, unaware that the

455

liquid that he had added was not water but more poteen.

Patrick sat back next to William and waited smugly for the drink to take its effect, grinning at his wife who scolded him with her eyes.

After checking that everyone was enjoying themselves Thomasin went to sit with her husband. 'I can't think where that lass has got to,' she puzzled. 'She oughtta have been 'ere by now.'

'Knowing the old witch that she works for,' said Patrick sipping respectfully at his poteen, 'she's probably found a lot of extra work to do. I expect she'll be along shortly.'

Caroline almost dropped her book as Erin burst in and stood panting in the doorway. 'Erin, whatever has happened? I thought you would be at the party by now.'

'There isn't to be no party!' yelled Erin. 'Leastwise, not for me. You said she didn't mind about the dress. Well she does, an' she's stopped me going to the party. I hate her!'

'Do you mean Mama?' asked Caroline perplexedly. 'But it was true what I said, she did not seem to mind. Oh, Erin, I'm sure you must have got mixed up somewhere. She would not do a wicked thing like that.'

'Mixed up am I?' shouted Erin tearing off the dress and flinging it at Caroline. 'I'll tell ye how mixed up I am. In another month ye won't be seeing any more o' me 'cause I'm leaving, that's how mixed up I am.'

'Oh, surely not because of this?' Caroline came towards her pacifyingly.

'Because I've got the push,' howled Erin, standing indignantly in only her underwear.

Caroline was alarmed. 'But you can't go, you're my friend!'

'Your mama doesn't like us being friends,' sniffed Erin, hoisting up her petticoat to wipe her face.

Caroline was nonplussed. 'I cannot believe all this. It is most unlike Mama to do a cruel thing like keeping you from your party.'

'Well, 'tis right.'

'Then it is most unfair of her,' decided Caroline. 'In fact I would go so far as to say she is a . . . a gastropod.'

'That won't do me no good,' sulked Erin.

'Yes it will, because I have decided that since Mama is

being so beastly she is not to be obeyed on this matter. You are going to the party, Erin,' said Caroline boldly, 'and I am to go with you.'

Erin's lips parted. 'But you cannot go!'

'And why not, might one ask?' said Caroline. 'Anyway, you are wrong. A lady may go wherever she pleases, and has Mama not told me that I am a lady? Very nearly anyway. Oh, come on, Erin.' She threw the lavender dress back at her friend. 'Put that back on quickly while I change.'

'But what if the mistress should find out?' said Erin, struggling back into the dress while Caroline rifled her wardrobe. 'An' how do we get out without being seen?'

'What if she does find out?' Caroline donned a jade-coloured dress and jacket to match, dainty satin slippers and a bonnet covered in silk roses. 'I shall tell her that she has no right to treat my friend in such a manner and that I shall speak to Papa about your reinstatement.'

'I'm not sure I want to stay here,' replied Erin, fastening Caroline's sash and brushing out her blonde hair.

'Don't ever say such a thing!' Caroline swirled on Erin and gripped her arms. 'Don't ever say you'll leave me. I could not bear it without you.'

'I thought ye were a lady,' said Erin dryly. 'Ladies don't have scullery maids as friends.'

'Why do you always have to make everything so difficult?' She kissed Erin fondly. 'Now come, we will be late for our party.'

Once their outfits were completed the two girls crept downstairs to the kitchen to tell Cook so that she would not worry over Erin's disappearance. But worry Cook did.

'Lor, what am I going to tell the mistress if she asks, Miss Caroline?' she protested. 'I daresn't lie for you else she'll finish me for sure.'

'Then tell the truth,' said Caroline calmly. 'That as I disagree totally with the manner in which she has handled the situation I am countermanding her orders. Erin and I are going to a party.'

CHAPTER FORTY-NINE

' 'TIS A SHAME but there y'are,' Patrick was saying to his wife, 'we can't hold up the festivities for her. Ghostie!' he shouted. 'Let's be hearing a tune from your fiddle, or has he lost his voice?'

Ghostie took a swig from his glass and smacking his lips tucked the fiddle under his sagging chin and struck up a jig.

'Oh dear,' said Hannah faintly. 'That music sounds very familiar, I hope it is not going to be like the last time we heard it.'

'Oh, don't be such a grump, Mother.' Thomasin clapped her hands to the music. 'C'mon, there isn't much room for dancin' but I want to see everyone enjoying themselves. All of yer, get them boots tappin', hands clappin'. Away, Molly, have yer gone to sleep over there?' she shouted.

'Indeed I have not,' slurred Molly, her eyes bright slits above the sculptured cheekbones; she looked amazingly clean for once. 'I was just admiring all your nice paraphernalia. Sure, ye've come a long way since Britannia Yard. Ye've certainly got taste.'

'Whatever would she know about that?' breathed Hannah.

Thomasin ignored her mother and spoke to Molly. 'Never mind pokin' about in my cupboards, get your bottom up and give us a demonstration of yer dancin' prowess.'

Without needing to be asked twice Molly cackled, sprang up and seized Patrick's hands, pulling him from his seat.

'Molly, will ye have a heart? I was just resting me poor ould feet,' he moaned.

'Ould be damned,' replied his would-be partner. 'I'm not dancin' unless 'tis with me favourite fella. Now will ye pump some life into those feet or do I have to roll up me sleeves to ye?'

Patrick hastily grabbed her around the waist and set off at a gallop. They careered between the clapping, stamping guests, eyes a-gleam from the poteen, cheeks red from the dancing, the oddest couple you ever did see, with Patrick's tall frame towering over Molly's wizened five feet two, laughing and teasing, swinging each other round in wild frivolity. The noise was deafening with the shrill cackle of the inebriated Molly accompanying the frenzied sawing of Ghostie's fiddle. They staggered and collided with the onlookers, righted themselves and set off again, their dance interspersed with howls from Patrick as Molly stamped upon his toes.

All of a sudden Molly faltered and leaned against Patrick, opening and closing her eyes and breathing heavily. 'Begob, Pat, I'll have to sit down, that drink's gone right to me head. Sure, I'm startin' to see things that should never be there.'

' 'Tis not like you to be unable to hold your drink,' laughed Patrick.

'I know, I know, but I'm seeing things I tell ye. Will ye look over in the doorway? I'll swear I saw an angel standing there.'

'Oh? Then ye'd best have the baby clothes at the ready, Molly,' chuckled Patrick, but turned around to investigate. He stopped laughing.

Everyone else looked round interestedly.

There, in the doorway, stood Caroline. Molly was right, she did look like an angel, with the light from the open front door behind her casting a golden halo around her ringleted head.

Erin stepped into the circle of astonished guests and led Caroline with her. 'Hello, everybody, sorry I'm late. Oh, this is Caroline by the way,' she added matter-of-factly.

Everyone stared at the lovely child who stood clutching her bonnet and looking around the room, then saying to the person nearest to her who happened to be Father Kelly, 'How do you do?'

The magic was broken by Sonny who sat among the knot of Flaherty children with his brother, clutching a bottle of ginger ale. 'What did ye bring her for?' he asked, eyeing Caroline from head to foot.

'John, have you no manners?' Hannah came out of her trance and bustled forward to take Caroline under her wing. 'How do you do, my dear? I am Mrs Fenton, Erin's grandmother, and this is my husband, and these are Erin's parents.'

Thomasin and Patrick edged forward and shook hands with the girl, muttering polite greetings.

'I do hope that you will forgive the impropriety of inviting myself to your party,' said Caroline, slipping off her jacket and handing it to Erin who took it away for safe-keeping. 'But we had a slight problem at home. Mama did not want Erin to come.'

Patrick looked expectantly at his daughter. 'Then how . . .?'

'Oh, it is all my doing, Mr Feeney,' provided Caroline, looking confidently at one of the female guests who gave up her seat to Caroline's superior presence. 'Erin has told me so much about you that I decided I would like to come and see for myself. I must say it is very . . .' she examined the poor furnishings, the almost bare room, bare except for the human decoration which eyed her distrustfully '. . . it is very nice, very homely.'

'Thank you, Caroline,' said Thomasin, at last regaining her normal poise. 'But what will your mother say when she finds you're gone? Won't she be annoyed?'

'At first perhaps,' admitted Caroline. 'But I think she will understand when I explain.'

'Let's hope so,' said Patrick. 'I should hate my daughter to get the blame for your folly.'

Hannah gasped; had the man no idea of how to talk to civilised people?

'Mr Feeney!' Caroline's eyebrows arched haughtily. 'You are not suggesting that I would allow my friend to take the blame, are you?' She rose stiffly. 'If my presence is an imposition I can just as quickly go home. Come, Erin!'

'I'm sorry!' Patrick leapt in front of her and gestured for her to reseat herself; though still feeling uncomfortable in the girl's presence he would not have Erin miss the party. 'Pray, sit down, we were just about to eat when you arrived.'

Hannah seated herself between Caroline and her neighbour, squeezing her ample rear onto the row of chairs. 'Would you care for a pastry, my dear? They are freshly-made.'

Caroline thanked her and placed one of the pastries onto a plate, accepting a cup of tea which Thomasin put into her other hand.

'I must apologise in advance,' whispered Hannah solicitously, 'if you find my daughter's guests a little, how shall we say? . . . *base*.' She touched refined lips to her teacup, then lowered it. 'Especially Mrs Flaherty over there, such a terrible woman. But what can one expect from someone of her class?'

Caroline leaned towards Erin who had returned to sit at her friend's side, saying in a stage whisper, 'Isn't she a frightful snob?'

Erin winced as her grandmother, with a disquieted cough, retreated to the kitchen to shed her tears. 'She doesn't mean any harm,' she explained.

'I must say,' piped up Caroline, 'everyone seems to have gone terribly quiet. I do hope your reticence is not the result of my arrival?'

The guests looked at each other over their cups, not knowing what to say. They were unaccustomed to taking tea with the gentry.

'I daresay we'll all be a bit more talkative after we've finished eating,' said Thomasin.

William, the only one who remained unencumbered by Caroline's invasion, trotted over with a plate of assorted cakes and, never one to stand on ceremony, said, ' 'Ere, grab yerself a whatsit, lass, before all them greedy buggers eat 'em.'

Thomasin shrank visibly but to her amazement Caroline burst out laughing. 'Oh, I can see that I am going to have such an enjoyable time.'

Caroline's amusement at William's blunt comment made things start to perk up a little. Tea over, Thomasin organised a singsong, which went quite well until some of the male guests started to put their own words to the songs.

Father Kelly clapped his hands. 'Enough of this bawdiness. Are ye not forgetting ye have a lady in your midst? If ye cannot consider the morals of your own children I beg you to think of hers.' Though Liam imagined that Caroline was enjoying the singing as much as everyone else, her face was fiery and her blue eyes fevered from the small glass of sherry that Erin had filched from the table.

'Ladies and gentlemen,' proceeded Liam. 'It seems a pity,

now that we have young Erin amongst us, not to take advantage of her musical skills. How about it, Erin? Will ye give us a taste of your harp?'

A roar of approval went up from the guests.

Erin asked where it was.

'I'll go fetch it,' said her father, and bounded up the stairs to his bedroom.

The harp had stood in silence for many months now. Dust had collected in the carved recesses of its forepillar. Patrick traced his hand lightly over its magnificence and thought of his beloved father, left behind in Ireland and surely long-dead by now. Lifting the precious instrument carefully, he went downstairs and set it down in front of his daughter.

'Erin, what an absolutely wonderful instrument!' Caroline leapt from her seat and ran slim fingers over the harp. 'You did not tell me that you could play.'

'It never seemed to crop up in our talks,' said Erin simply, then bade her friend be seated and carried the harp to the centre of the floor where she sat on a stool and prepared to play.

Molly, who was seated next to Nelly, swayed against her neighbour. 'Have ye never heard our Erin play, Missus P.?'

Nelly shook her head and refilled her glass with 'water', her hand trembling under the weight of the jug, her vision becoming blurred.

'Ah,' said Molly. ' 'Tis like being with the angels. There'll be enough tears to do the washing-up before her song is halfway through.'

' 'Tis right y'are, Molly,' agreed Patrick. 'Look at the child, 'tis like a little sprig of lavender she is in her new dress, and twice as bonny.'

'Pat Feeney,' said Thomasin, 'if talk were brass we'd all be very rich indeed. Now, will yer let the lass get on wi' it?'

Erin, her tuning completed, held the harp to her shoulder and closed her eyes. The guests became silent as the first chords escaped her fingers to caress their ears, trickling like an Irish mountain stream to wash away the poverty in which they lived. They listened intently, but with a dreamy look in each eye, these Irish souls thinking fondly of their homeland. Only Nelly remained unmoved, too far gone to hear the playing, tipping the jug yet again towards her glass.

The music neared its climax, soaring dramatically into a wonderful crescendo, then fading to nothingness. It took a few seconds for the listeners to return to reality, then a burst of hearty applause shook the room. Erin opened her eyes, which were smiling, and put the harp from her. She always felt drained after each playing, as though the harp were drawing out all her vitality through her fingertips.

'Erin,' cried Caroline through the applause, 'I did not know that you were so talented. When we return home you must bring your harp with you so that Miss Elwood may sample the delights which I have heard tonight.'

The evening wore on with the guests reminiscing about the old days, how things used to be, the liquor chasing away any trace of discomfort at Caroline's presence. Father Kelly watched Nelly sway precariously on her chair and hurried over to offer assistance.

'Pat,' he remarked, ' 'tis a treacherous man y'are to let her get in such a state. Have ye no common decency? The woman is almost pickled.'

Patrick shrugged and winked at his sons who were enjoying the spectacle immensely.

Liam prised the jug from Nelly's hand and waved his fingers in front of her face. 'You're looking dangerous pale, Miss Peabody, would ye like to lie down?'

Nelly tried to focus on the blurred image before her. Squinting her eyes she leaned forward drunkenly, sniffed, and with no consideration for his priestly garb slurred, 'Have you trumped?'

'Oh, cover his ears somebody,' cried Thomasin, rushing over to save Father Kelly from further embarrassment through peals of laughter.

The children, who often bore the brunt of Miss Peabody's annoyance, fell about in near hysterics.

Liam coughed blusteringly, though not really upset. 'It's been a grand party, Thomasin, but I fear I may have outstayed my welcome. I'll be moving on.'

'Aye, I think we'd all better call it a day before Nelly really upsets somebody,' agreed Thomasin. 'Pat, you and me father can take Miss Peabody home, seein' as how you're responsible for her condition.'

Still guffawing Patrick said his farewells as the other guests surged noisily into the street, then he and William propped Nelly between them and guided her to her own house. After much banter about who was going to take off her clothes and put her to bed, the men laid her on the sofa and covered her with a crocheted blanket then left, still chuckling.

Caroline was shaking hands with Thomasin as Patrick and his father-in-law returned. 'Goodnight, Mrs Feeney, and thank you for a lovely party. I have had a marvellous time, it was so entertaining.'

– I'll bet it was, thought Thomasin, then smiled. 'I'm glad you enjoyed it, love. Patrick, you'd best accompany these two young ladies home, it's gettin' quite dark.'

'Right y'are.' Patrick tugged at his forelock and took the harp which his daughter was holding. 'Give that to me, 'tis too heavy for you to carry all that way. Come now, we'd best be off before it gets any darker.'

When they reached Walmgate Caroline faltered and peered down the road which, in the dim light and with its dingy buildings, had begun to look quite sinister. 'Do you think we might take a cab, Mr Feeney?' she asked nervously. 'It is getting rather dark.'

'I'm afraid my wages don't run to cabs, Caroline,' answered Patrick firmly. 'Don't worry, ye'll be quite safe with me.'

The girls chatted quietly on their way through the city. Patrick listened thoughtfully, the smoke from his pipe flowing over his shoulder as he walked briskly beside them. At times one would think the two girls were equals the way they addressed each other, but sometimes he detected a slightly superior note come creeping into Caroline's voice, and feared for his daughter's emotions.

When they finally arrived Erin was about to descend the steps to the basement when Caroline stopped her. 'No, we shall not go that way.'

'But we came out this way,' answered Erin.

'No,' replied Caroline. 'I shall not go sneaking in by the servants' entrance like a whipped dog. I shall go through the front door like everyone else and you as my friend shall come with me.'

'Caroline, do ye think that's wise?' asked Patrick, seeing the uneasiness cloud his daughter's face.

'I am sure I know what is wise in my own house, Mr

Feeney.' The superior tone came to the fore again.

Patrick was unimpressed. 'I wasn't thinking of you, I was thinking of what might happen to my daughter if she's caught disobeying the rules. The mistress seems to be very strict on these matters.'

'Oh, pooh.' Caroline marched up to the front door dragging Erin with her. Erin shrank, hoping Caroline would not mention the dismissal. He would have to be told of course, but not yet. 'Everyone seems to think Mama is some sort of ogre. I promise no harm will come to Erin. Once Mama understands that Erin is my friend then everything will be fine. Anyway,' she added with her hand on the knob, 'if we go in quietly perhaps she will not even hear us.'

Patrick followed, bearing the harp under his arm, and stepped into the spacious hall.

Caroline turned and proffered her hand. 'Thank you very much for escorting us, Mr Feeney. I hope it has not been too much of an imposition.'

'Why no, 'tis my pleasure, Miss Caroline.' Patrick laughed at himself. All evening he had been referring to her as plain Caroline. It must be the grandness of the house that had caused him, unconsciously, to add the deference. He compared this hall with its mahogany panelling, marble-tiled floor, valuable antiquities and chandelier to his own dim little front passage with its peeling wallpaper and crude lighting arrangements. What must have gone through Caroline's mind as she had entered his home? He pushed all thoughts from his head and bending low over her hand touched his lips to her knuckles, making her squirm girlishly.

'Goodnight to the pair of ye.' He turned and was about to leave when there came a human sound.

'Psst!'

They all looked in the direction of the servants' quarters and there stood Cook waving her hands about in a frantic semaphore, jabbing a finger at the drawing room door in an attempt to warn them.

'What is the matter?' hissed Caroline, trying to decode the cook's message.

The drawing room door was suddenly flung open and out stalked Helena exuding violent waves of perfume, the only sweetness about her.

'So!' she spat. 'You have decided to return. How thoughtful of you. Stay where you are, Cook!' she commanded without turning as Rose was about to disappear. 'I have matters to discuss with you also.'

And then words failed her as she beheld the man who accompanied her daughter and the maid. Oh, la! She raised a delicate hand to her cheek. It was all she could do to refrain from laughing. Here she was bullying the child to take revenge on Roland's mistress and all the time she had been extracting penance from another enemy without even being aware of it.

How could she have thought that Roland could ever have sired such a handsome creature? It was quite obvious who the child's father was, and there he stood with the harp as further evidence of that night at Dunworthe Hall. Helena wondered why she had never noticed the resemblance, but then she had taken little notice of the daughter on that night, only the man, the man who had insulted her.

She was also confused about the red-haired woman who seemed to be the link between these two men, and could only surmise that her first suspicion had been half-correct, that the woman had been Roland's mistress but was now this Irishman's wife. Oh, what fun she was going to have! But not yet, she had been taken too much by surprise to be able to glean maximum enjoyment from this incident. She must first deal with her disobedient daughter.

'Caroline, please go to your room.'

'But, Mama.' Caroline stepped forward and touched Helena's arm. 'Please allow me to explain. It was all my fault. I made Erin take me to the party.'

Helena chose to ignore the imploring hand on her arm. 'Caroline, you will do as you are ordered. I shall speak to you later. Please do not disobey me again.'

With an entreating look at Erin, Caroline fled up the stairs.

'As for you,' Helena addressed Erin. 'Was it not enough for you to countermand my strict instructions without filling my house with vagrants?' She eyed Patrick distastefully from head to foot.

'But this is my father,' cried Erin. 'He escorted us back.'

Patrick remained uncharacteristically silent. He had recognised her also, remembered how she had set fire to him with her hands, how he had pushed her away and fled. Each knew that the other had not forgotten, but not one word of recognition passed between them.

'So,' said Helena officiously. 'You are Feeney.'

Patrick nodded curtly.

'May one ask what you are doing in my reception hall?'

'Your daughter invited us in,' he submitted, reflecting her contempt. 'I believe she assumed that, as she had been welcomed into our home, we in turn would be welcomed into yours. She insisted that we accompany her through the front entrance.'

'So, it is my daughter with whom I have to remonstrate?' said Helena.

'Caroline didn't mean no harm,' blurted Erin.

'Do you not mean Miss Caroline, Feeney?' enquired Helena.

'Yes, ma'am,' answered Erin quietly, then added recklessly, 'But please don't be too hard on her. I shouldn't've let her persuade me to take her.'

'You should not indeed,' stated Helena. 'Which you will discover to your detriment.'

'Now wait a minute,' cut in Patrick, taking a step forward.

'I have nothing further to say to you, Feeney,' replied Helena. 'Other than to warn you that should I find you in my private quarters again I shall send for the police. You may go.'

'If you touch my daughter . . .' began Patrick.

'Cook,' ordered Helena briskly. 'Go and inform Johnson to fetch a constable.'

'Don't bother, I'm going,' snarled Patrick. 'But I'm warning ye, if ye touch that girl ye'll be sorry.'

'You may go,' repeated Helena forcefully, and Patrick, after kissing his daughter, stormed from the house leaving the door wide open.

'Kindly close and lock the door, Cook,' instructed Helena. 'Then I wish to speak to you.'

Rose waddled undignifiedly to the door and closed it, shooting the bolts into place.

'Now.' Helena folded her hands over her skirts. 'I wish to inspect the kitchen.'

'At this time, madam?' asked Rose incredulously.

'Are you deaf, Cook, or simply insolent?'

Cook lumbered to the servants' entrance and led the way down to the kitchen with Erin, clutching her harp, at the rear.

Helena sauntered over to the range and traced a finger over its warm surface. 'This is intolerable.'

She turned her Medusa stare on Erin and her eyes took in the thick, black mane that streamed over the girl's shoulders. 'It is quite obvious that this girl has been neglecting her duties to attend to more vain pursuits.'

'But I cleaned it this morning,' objected Erin.

Rose supported her. 'Yes, she did, madam. I saw her do it myself.'

'Then your eyesight is failing, Cook,' said Helena. 'Perhaps I should replace you also?'

Rose said no more.

'Very well, girl, since you use the time which should have been spent working in the pursuit of personal fripperies, I suggest that you now attend to your proper duties and clean the range.'

'But, ma'am – the fire's not gone out yet,' argued Erin. 'I cannot clean it till it cools off.'

'Then you must wait until it does,' answered the mistress disdainfully.

'But that'll be hours,' blurted Cook.

Helena gave her a withering glare. 'I trust you are not arguing with me again, Cook?'

Rose looked at her feet. The little minx would not hesitate to throw her out, discounting all those years of loyal service as cook and before that housemaid at Helena's father's house.

'I am most gratified to hear it,' said Helena at Rose's negative reply. She walked to the staircase. 'Oh, and Cook?' she said in the casual voice that the servants knew was a precursor to some vile order. 'Tomorrow you will instruct Benson to cut that girl's hair. I cannot possibly tolerate such appearance in my kitchen. Imagine the embarrassment if one of my guests should find a hair in his meal.'

Erin parted her lips in alarm and was about to complain, but Rose gave her a warning nudge as they watched Helena's dainty slippers disappear up the staircase.

'The cat!' expostulated Rose noisily. 'The absolute cat.' She examined Erin's crestfallen face and put a podgy hand on the girl's shoulder. 'We'll have to do it, love, otherwise there'll be hell to pay.'

'But she can't,' voiced Erin faintly. 'She can't.'

'You've been here long enough to know that she can do exactly as she likes,' said Rose. 'If we don't do it she'll get rid o' the lot of us, and then where will we be?' She walked away from Erin and began to punch at the cushions in her chair. 'All of this is Miss Caroline's fault! She's got very headstrong since the mistress allowed her to take her meals upstairs.'

Erin's eyes filled with tears. She was thinking of what her father would say when he found out.

'Who's got her back up then?' Alice stampled down the stairs rattling a trayful of used glasses. 'She nigh on pushed me down the blasted stairs just now.'

Rose told her.

'Oh, blimey!' cried Alice turning to Erin. 'What did I tell you? Didn't I tell her, Cook? "If you don't cover that hair up," I said, "she'll have it off".' She rinsed the glasses out, broke one in the sink, swore, then said she would leave it until morning to clear up. 'I suppose I'll get that job an' all?' she snapped, pointing at Erin's head. 'Aye, I thought so. God, as if there isn't enough to do.'

'Don't bother about the glass, Alice,' said Erin wearily. 'I've got to stay up to do the range so I might as well do that an' all.'

'Oh, good lass,' replied Alice drying her hands. 'Right then, I'll get meself off to bobies. 'Night everyone.'

Rose bade Alice goodnight then spoke to Erin. 'I'm afraid you'll have to wait up on your own. I hope you don't mind, but I'm like a bear with a sore head if I don't get my sleep. You can sit in my chair if you like.'

Erin thanked her and sank into the cushions. She stared into the still glowing fire, making pictures from the embers, wishing she were at home in her lumpy, little bed, arguing with her brothers, laughing with her father. She was so tired, so very, very tired.

Patrick ran all the way home, trying to expel the surfeit of anger by punishing his body. The spiteful harridan. Now he understood why she had treated Erin in such a manner – she remembered the child from that night at Dunworthe Hall. God, he would like to break her neck. But he must calm himself before he reached home. What explanation would he give Tommy? How could he say: 'Mrs Cummings is taking it out of Erin because of me'? She would want to know all the details. She would see it in his eyes that, had Erin's music not broken the spell, he would have made love to this evil woman.

If Thomasin noticed his subdued attitude after the high spirits of the evening then she did not comment upon it.

'Did they get home safely?' she asked, helping him off with his jacket.

'Aye.'

'It was a grand party, wasn't it?' She hung the jacket on a peg.

'It was.'

'Poor Nelly, you oughtn't to have done that to her, yer know. She'll have a right headache tomorra.'

'Aye, well . . .'

'Are yer comin' to bed then?'

Jerked from his anger, he put his arms around her and squeezed. 'I love ye, ye know.'

'Eh, what 'ave I done to deserve all this?' She laughed, as he kissed her.

'Did I hear ye mention something about bed?' he asked, the former twinkle back in his eye.

'Aye, I could do wi' some sleep after such a hard day,' she yawned, then laughing softly, hitched a tow on his belt and followed him upstairs.

CHAPTER FIFTY

ERIN AWOKE WITH a start and rubbed her eyes. Where was she? She opened her eyes wider, then closed them as her senses began to operate. That was it, she had been supposed to wait for the fire to go out and clean the range. Sure, it was well and truly out now. She must have slept for a long time because when she touched the grate it was cool under her fingers. The gas jet still cast its yellow flicker around the walls; she had forgotten to turn it out.

Rising from Cook's chair she pressed a hand to the small of her back and leaned on it, then pulled at the skirts of the lavender dress which were creased and crumpled. Looking towards the clock on the mantelpiece she saw that it was a quarter to four – Oh well, she yawned, there was no sense in going to bed now, in a few hours the house would be alive with turbulent activity. Might as well have a nice blaze going for when Cook came down.

She put on an apron and went to fetch the brushes and polish. With great diligence she raked out the ashes and cleaned into all the corners, making sure that Helena would have nothing to complain about today. Perhaps if Erin were super-efficient the mistress would forget about the haircut. She set the fire which, with a little help from the bellows, soon sprang into yellow flower. Filling the big kettle with water she put it on to boil and went to pick the pieces of glass from the sink.

The door opened and a tousled Johnson slouched in. 'I thought my watch was wrong when I heard all the movement,' he grumbled. 'What are you doing up so early?'

He took one of the glasses from the draining board and filled it with water while Erin related the events of the previous evening, including Helena's orders that Erin's hair must be cut.

He swilled the water around his mouth then spat it into the sink as if making a comment upon Helena's treatment. 'That is a great pity,' he sympathised and replaced the glass on the draining board. 'You have lovely hair.' He took one of her ruffled curls between his fingers and rubbed at it.

Erin stared at him in surprise for he had never spoken to her so before. One could hardly manage to draw two civil words from him. He gazed at the hair, his granite face suddenly transformed into that of a kind, caring man. And then it was gone. He dropped the hair abruptly.

'I shall take a little of this water for my shaving,' he said, lifting the kettle and tipping it towards the shaving mug which he had brought from his room. Then he was gone, leaving Erin to shake her head and carry the teapot to the range.

It was still early as she reached into the bread bin and, cutting herself two slices from a loaf, pressed one of them onto a toasting fork and held it to the fire. The flames almost hypnotised her into sleep again and she had to keep forcing her eyes open. A light, golden brown began to cover the surface of the bread and she turned it over to toast the other side.

Some twenty minutes later, when Erin sat at the table munching toast and sipping tea, Rose came down, followed directly by Alice.

'Wonders'll never cease,' scoffed Alice flopping down beside Erin. 'You're up early. Whose bed've you been sleepin' in?'

'Alice, that's enough of that kind of talk, thank you,' threatened Rose. 'She isn't like you, our Erin, she's a good girl.'

'Shall I pour ye a cup?' Erin asked them both.

'That would be very nice, dear,' replied Rose plonking herself into her own chair. 'This is a real treat to come down to.' She held her hands to the now well-established fire and rubbed them together.

Erin confessed that she had fallen asleep in the chair.

'Oh, you'll pay for it, my dear! Come dinnertime and you'll feel as though you could sleep for a week. I know, I've done it many a time myself.'

After her early breakfast Erin went to change into her

working clothes and attend to the drawing room fire, pleased that she had ample time so as not to encounter Helena. That done, she returned to the kitchen and assisted Rose in the preparation of breakfast for upstairs, after first, of course, scrubbing the floor.

'Well, Caroline. Have you anything to say to your Mama?' Helena unfolded her napkin and draped it over her mustard-coloured skirts.

Caroline looked up guiltily from her plate to which her eyes had been cast since she had seated herself.

'I am sorry, Mama,' she said humbly.

'I am most pleased to hear it, Caroline,' answered her mother. 'You cannot know the hurt I have suffered over your intransigence.' After dealing with Erin the previous night Helena had gone on to confront her daughter.

There had been a terrible scene with Caroline nearing hysterics at one point, and Helena had thought it better to let matters cool off a little.

'May one enquire to what intransigence you refer?' asked Roland through a mouthful of bacon.

Helena found it impossible to conceal her disgust. 'Really, my dear, what hope is there for the child if you persist in this uncouth habit of yours? I find it hard to comprehend what you are saying with your mouth full of food.'

'I humbly crave your pardon, Helena,' said Roland, dabbing his mouth. 'It was my eagerness to join in the family discussion which led me to forget my manners.'

'If you had been here to assume your fatherly duties last night,' said Helena, 'you would have no need to ask. Your daughter took it upon her shoulders to absent herself without my permission and I had to exercise the discipline which should have been administered by you.'

'And to where did you absent yourself, Caroline?' asked Roland lightly.

Caroline looked at her mother who answered for her. 'She went to the home of one of the servants.'

'To be precise I went to Erin's party,' provided Caroline. 'Mama had been beastly to Erin and would not allow her to go home on her afternoon off. So I said she could go, as long as she took me with her.'

'And did you have a pleasant time?' asked her father.

'Roland!' Helena banged upon the table in a most unladylike fashion. 'Will you please desist from this facetious attitude? How can I possibly hope to discipline our daughter when you seem to have such a low regard for our status.'

'Quite right, my dear.' Roland was repentant and turned to his daughter. 'Caroline, you should not have done such a thing. I am certain that your mother must have been desperate with worry at your disappearance.'

'Not to mention what could have happened to you in that den of thieves,' put forward Helena.

'I am truly, truly sorry for the hurt I have caused,' wailed Caroline, then leapt up to grip her father's shoulders beseechingly. 'I know it was wrong but please, Papa, do not allow Mama to vent her anger on Erin. She was not to blame for any of it. I lent her the dress and Mama thought that she had taken it without permission, though I did inform Mama of my intention,' she added reprovingly. 'And now Mama has dismissed her.'

Roland's face lost its mild expression as he looked sharply at his wife.

'I expressly forbid you to dismiss that child!'

'I am afraid it is already done,' replied Helena carelessly.

'Then it must be undone,' said Roland. 'For I will not have an innocent child made to suffer for one of your whims.' He leaned forward, his heavy brow balanced on the hook of his nose. 'Do not think that I am unaware of your reasons for this persecution, Helena. But you are wrong, so very wrong.'

'I think not,' smiled Helena smugly. 'But no matter. If you are determined that the girl should stay, then however incompetent or insolent she might be, I must bow to your superiority.'

'Oh, Mama, thank you!' Caroline rushed around the table to kiss her mother and Helena manufactured an indulgent smile.

'Really, Caroline, you must try to curb this impetuosity, it is not fitting in a lady. One trusts that you will conduct yourself with a little more dignity this evening.'

Roland and his daughter looked at Helena inquiringly.

'Following our discussion I have invited some friends to dine with us. As they are most anxious to meet our daughter I have decided that she shall be present.'

Caroline's face underwent a series of expressions, from

disbelief to rapture. 'Oh, Mama!' She was about to leap up again, then recalled Helena's admonishment and remained fixed to her seat.

'I trust you will not require my presence also,' said Roland. The thought of being cooped up for an entire evening with Helena's lickspittle friends left him cold.

'But naturally,' replied his wife. 'Are you not interested in your daughter's future?'

'If I understand your meaning correctly,' answered Roland, 'I had assumed that we were to leave that certain business until a later date.'

'But surely it is more sensible to take the opportunity as soon as it arrives? Believe me, Roland, you will not find a more suitable match anywhere.'

'I shall be the judge of that,' replied Roland.

'Of course,' said his wife. 'That is why you must be present tonight. I realise that you shrug most of your responsibilities on to me, but surely you could find the time to meet your prospective son-in-law.'

Caroline stared from one to the other unable to understand their words, but too excited at the thought of her first dinner party to worry.

'As you wish,' sighed Roland, and prepared to leave for work. 'I only hope it will be worth the inconvenience.'

For some time after he had gone Caroline was all of a twitter about what she should wear and how one should behave, until finally Helena, tiring of the girlish enthusiasm, dismissed her to the schoolroom until later in the morning when they would go out to buy a new outfit for her.

Directly Helena and Caroline had returned from their morning's outing Rose was summoned to the drawing room to discuss the menu for the evening. She handed over her idea for Helena's approval.

'Read it out to me, Cook,' sighed the mistress, rubbing her temples. 'I have such a headache with listening to my daughter's incessant chatter.'

'I'm very sorry to hear that, madam,' said Rose insincerely, and proceeded to reel off the menu. 'I thought for the first course, Mock Turtle Soup, Fried Fillets of Sole, Saddle of Mutton – or I thought I might do Beef à la Jardiniere (she had some difficulty getting her tongue around this) and for afters . . .'

'Yes, yes,' sighed Helena impatiently. 'Very well, Cook, I shall leave it entirely to you. That will be all.'

As Rose turned to leave her mistress suddenly remembered. 'Oh, and inform the Feeney chit that I have decided to overlook yesterday's digression and she may stay in my employ, provided she smartens herself up – I trust she has had her hair attended to?'

Although glad of the first part of Helena's sentence Rose's heart went out to Erin; she had hoped that the mistress had forgotten. 'Not yet, madam, Alice is going to do it when she's finished her work.'

'Very well, then I shall wish to inspect it before you begin preparations for tonight's meal.'

Rose returned to her domain and told Erin the bad news. Later Alice brought out a pair of scissors and trimmed three inches from the long, glossy waves. 'D'yer think that'll satisfy her ladyship?' She brushed the snippets of hair from Erin's shoulders.

'I swear I don't know what will satisfy her,' sighed Rose. 'But we'll have to find out. Come on, Erin, let's face the Inquisition.'

They left Alice to sweep up the discarded locks and went upstairs.

Helena reclined in the armchair, rubbing pensively at the brown velvet upholstery. She was deciding which was the best course of action to take in the pursuance of the eligible Charles Snaith-Buxbridge.

Someone opened the door and she looked up annoyed at the diversion in her plotting. 'Ah, Cook! Let us see if the work has been carried out to my instructions. Turn around, girl.'

She frowned at Erin's back and turned to Rose. 'But this is hardly any better,' she exclaimed angrily. 'It seems that I must teach you the way in which it should be done. Fetch the scissors.'

Rose hurried downstairs while Helena tapped her foot impatiently. Erin stood trembling, feeling the waves of hate from Helena's eyes. When Rose returned, her mistress snatched the scissors and began to slice viciously at Erin's hair, not just snipping but wielding the scissors as though she were clipping a privet hedge. Rose looked on in horror as the shears flashed over the girl's head, hacking and slashing at the hair, which fell profusely to the carpet. Soon the Persian weaving was hidden beneath the pool of savaged black waves.

'There, that is much better.' Helena thrust the scissors back at Rose, while Erin stared in dismay at the pile of hair on the floor. 'And kindly clear up that mess,' ordered their mistress, then stalked out of the room.

Rose put a hand to her mouth and gaped at the ragged, uneven mess that Helena had inflicted on the girl. There was hardly any hair left at all, just a pitiful, fluffy cap. She put her arm around Erin. 'Come on, love,' she said quietly. 'You come and help your Aunt Rose; take your mind off things.'

All through the day the kitchen bubbled and boiled with alacrity. Erin was plunged headfirst into the maelstrom, with hardly a moment to dwell on her shorn locks, so busy did Rose keep her, fetching and carrying, dicing vegetables, washing up. It was not until tea-time, when the workers gratefully sat down, that her hand crept under the mob cap to explore the damage.

She sucked in her breath as her fingers encountered the place where Helena's scissors had slashed too close to the skin. On purpose? Who could tell what went on in that woman's mind! The relief that Erin had felt on being told that she was to stay in the Cummings' employ was fast disappearing.

'What're you going to do on your evening off?' asked Alice, licking some icing from her fingers. 'About yer hair, I mean.'

'Alice, sometimes I despair of you,' said Cook impatiently. 'Here I am trying to keep the child's mind off it by giving her plenty to do and then you go and shove your big oar in.'

'Well, it's got to be faced,' replied Alice. 'I mean, her parents aren't goin' to be very pleased, are they?'

'Perhaps I won't go,' said Erin, nibbling a piece of fruit-bread.

'Well, if you're waiting for it to grow yer'll have a long wait,' voiced Alice.

Rose sighed at Alice's bluntness, then said, 'She's right, you know – you can't stay hidden forever. Maybe if you put one o' Miss Caroline's bonnets on they won't notice.'

Alice sniggered. 'No, I'm sure I wouldn't notice if my daughter had three foot of hair one day an' none the next.'

Coinciding with Cook's exclamation Erin said, 'Ye don't think I'd dare borrow anything else from Miss Caroline!'

'Oh, no . . .' Cook put a finger to her chin. 'Eh, Alice . . .'

'Oh, I know what you're off to say, Cook – well don't.'

'Go on, it'll do no harm,' begged Cook. 'The poor little lass.'

'Well . . . I don't see why I should,' sulked the maid. 'But all right, she can borrow mine – only don't let owt happen to it, you hear? With your luck it'll come back in tatters.'

'Thank you, Alice,' said Erin. 'I'll take good care of it.'

Johnson finished his tea and rose. 'Come along, Alice, we have no time for shillyshallying, there's work to be done upstairs.'

'God, I've just sat down,' protested Alice, then shoved back her chair and trailed after the manservant.

'Don't you take no notice what Alice says,' Rose told Erin, patting her hand. 'If you push all those untidy bits inside the bonnet I'm sure your parents won't notice.' She gathered the tea things. 'Well, we'd better not sit here gossiping all day, there's still plenty to do for this here dinner party.' She went to check on the pans that simmered on the range, leaving Erin faced with another giant pile of dirty crockery.

The evening was as hectic as the afternoon. Alice rushed down to the kitchen, fighting her way through clouds of steam and stacks of red-hot tureens. 'S'truth, it's like Hades down here. Listen, they want some more plates up there, Mr Johnson's going mad.' She dropped a pile of plates into Erin's arms. 'Here, put these on the lift quick, else it'll be more than yer hair getting cut.'

'Alice, do you have to say things like that?' said Cook crossly, shaking and quivering like a jelly as she whipped a bowl of cream.

Alice ignored the reprimand. 'Ooh, Cook, you oughtta see the young gentleman what's partnering Miss Caroline, he's a real beau. His hair all falls about in waves, like that.' She demonstrated upon her own head, undulating her hands down from her parting, then gave an exclamation. 'Oh God, I'm not supposed to talk about hair falling down, am I?'

'Alice, get back up them stairs before you feel my foot round your backside,' ordered Rose.

And Erin plunged herself back into the washing up, still trying to think of what she was going to tell them at home.

CHAPTER FIFTY-ONE

'EH, I HOPE you've got eyes in the back of your head this mornin',' Alice warned Erin as they collected their cleaning implements. 'She's in a Bramah of a mood.'

Erin, still suffering the after-effects of the dinner party and too preoccupied with her mutilated hair to take much notice merely nodded.

'Morning, Cook,' shouted Alice as Rose came down. 'I'm just saying to Erin she'll have to keep clear of Lady Cowclap. I don't know what went off after that party but it obviously wasn't to her liking. She took lumps out o' me last night when I was taking her hair down.'

'Her little arrangement must've gone awry,' said Cook, planting herself by the fire. It was common knowledge in the kitchen what Helena was up to.

'Shame 'cause that young Mr Charles what was invited for Miss Caroline was a bonny fella.'

'Eh, I don't know,' sighed Rose. 'One minute she can't stand the sight of the child and the next she's trying to marry her off.'

'Miss Caroline's getting married?' asked Erin.

'Oh, awake now, are we?' skitted Alice. 'Well, yes, I reckon she will be soon as she's old enough and the mistress can get hold of a rich enough fella for her. S'obvious this one's slipped the net.'

'Now don't stand there gossiping, Alice.' Johnson had entered. 'Attend to your duties.'

'God, the minute he comes in he starts. All right, I'm off. Erin, you can go do the mistress' bedroom, I'm keepin' out of her road.'

But Erin went instead to the schoolroom where she peeped around the door to find Caroline awaiting Miss Elwood.

The girl leapt at her. 'Oh, Erin, I've so much to tell you! I had the most wonderful time last night. The meal was a dream and I met the most interesting people.'

'Yes, so Alice's been saying,' responded Erin, feeling if her cap was on straight so that no one could see her hair. 'I hear your gentleman was very handsome.'

'Erin, don't be such a silly,' laughed the other. 'He wasn't my gentleman, he was just one of Mama and Papa's friends – anyway, I found him the least charming of the company.'

'Then 'tis not true you're going to marry him?' ventured Erin.

Caroline laughed even louder. 'Marry him? Why, I am barely fifteen. Why should I even think of marriage to any-one?'

'Oh, 'twas just what Alice said . . .'

'Pooh, to what Alice says,' retorted Caroline. 'I shall not marry until I am at least twenty-one, and when I do it will certainly not be to anyone as boring as Charles. Though I must say he was very handsome.' She poked at Erin's temple. 'What have you been doing to your face? It's all scratched. Why, it goes all the way under your . . . oh, Erin!' Caroline gasped as she lifted the edge of the cap and saw the mess which Helena had caused. She pulled the headwear completely off. 'Erin, whatever happened?'

Erin grabbed the cap back and pulled it almost over her eyes. 'Ye wouldn't believe me if I told ye,' she said crossly. 'But if ye must know it was your dear mama.'

'Erin, now you are being an ass,' scoffed Caroline. 'Mama would never do that.'

'If there's an ass in this room 'tis you!' yelled Erin. 'You're too stupid to know the truth when ye see it, an' what's more it was done all because o' you, because ye made me take ye to the party.'

'I'll thank you to have a little more respect when speaking to your betters,' snapped Caroline, suddenly reminding Erin of a younger version of the mistress.

The Irish girl's spirit flared up again. 'Oh, now we're really getting to the truth! Ye don't look upon me as a friend at all. I was just somebody who came along at the right time when ye were feeling lonely. Now that your precious mama is taking an interest in ye, ye think ye don't need me any more.'

'Now you are being downright stupid,' replied Caroline. 'Think of all the fun we've had together, all the secrets I have shared with you. Of course I look upon you as my friend.'

'Real friends don't treat each other like you treat me,' responded Erin, and mimicked Caroline: ' "I'll thank you to have a little more respect when speaking to your betters." '

'Erin, don't be silly. You know I did not mean anything!'

'Did ye not? Then why did ye say it? I'll tell ye, because ye don't look upon me as a friend, Caroline, someone who's an equal! All ye see when ye look at me is a scullery maid who ye can boss about.'

'Well, aren't you?' demanded Caroline haughtily. 'Isn't that what you are, a scullery maid?'

The pause which followed was pregnant with disgust which emanated solely from Erin. 'I may only be a scullery maid but I do know well enough to have a bit of respect for people's affections.'

'Girls, girls!' Louisa bustled into the schoolroom and took hold of each girl's arm. 'One can hear you at the other side of the house. Whatever your differences I am certain they do not need to be aired so vociferously.'

'I'm sorry, Miss Elwood,' said Erin softly. 'I'm going back to the kitchen now. Thank ye for all the time ye've spent with me; a shame it's been wasted.'

'And why should it be wasted?' asked Louisa.

'Because I'm not coming to lessons any more,' replied Erin, and made to leave.

Caroline bounced forward and grabbed Erin around the waist. 'Erin, don't be such a goose. You cannot possibly sacrifice your education just because of a silly little tiff.'

' 'Twas rather more than that, Miss Caroline.'

'Will you please stop calling me Miss? Look, I apologise for what I said. It was very wrong of me – I'm such a pig.'

'Caroline, your language,' reprimanded Miss Elwood.

Caroline was not listening. 'Please, Erin, forgive me. You know I'll die if ever you desert me.'

Erin viewed her steadily but made no reply.

'Please, Erin,' begged the other. 'If not for my sake then

for your own. If you give up your lessons now I shall hold myself responsible.'

– As well you might, thought Erin, then forced an unconvincing smile. 'All right, I'll be here this afternoon. Now I'll have to go.'

Caroline had beamed at this apparent forgiveness and now asked, 'Erin, before you leave would you please, please give Miss Elwood a sample of your musical talents. I've told her all about your harp and I'm certain she would be delighted to hear it.'

Erin gave way. 'But only for a short while, mind,' and went to fetch the harp.

'What an exquisite piece of craftsmanship,' Louisa exclaimed when Erin returned with the instrument. 'My word, you must take very good care of this and keep it in a safe place.' She wondered how the little maid had come to possess such a valuable article.

'Oh, I do,' confirmed Erin. ' 'Tis like a part o' me. If I lost it, well, I dread to imagine what it would do to me.' She began to play, leaving Caroline wishing rather wistfully that she were the recipient of Erin's love and not the harp.

Helena's temper over the previous night's fruitless episode had still not waned. Of all the audacity, to accept her lavish hospitality and make it look as if they had accepted the bait and then have the gall to announce Charles's intended engagement to someone else. All those weeks of preparation wasted. Now she would have to start looking all over again.

She rose from her chair, grasped the bellpull for Alice to clear away then, with the intention of going for a mid-morning ride, she went upstairs to change.

As she passed the schoolroom, however, she heard sounds of girlish laughter, a sound so strange to this house as to warrant investigation. Behind the closed door Erin was playing while Caroline performed a clumsy dance in accompaniment, exemplifying the jig which Molly and Patrick had done at the party. When the door opened the three faces turned towards it guiltily.

'So, this is what you teach my daughter, Miss Elwood!' Helena scowled resentfully at the traces of happiness that were fast disappearing. 'Foolish behaviour and lack of discipline.'

She marched into the room. 'And what is that servant doing here?'

The governess's smile dissolved. 'Your husband gave his approval for Erin to take lessons with Caroline, Mrs Cummings. We thought that the companionship might be good for your daughter.'

'I cannot imagine why you should hold that fraternisation with the servants might be good for her – quite the reverse I suspect.'

'But I've always taken my meals with the servants until lately, Mama,' offered Caroline. 'We did not think you would mind.'

'You did not think I would mind?' repeated Helena. 'Really, Caroline, after our conversation of the other evening I had thought you would have been conversant with my wishes. I do mind! I mind very much that no one saw fit to consult me in this matter. I am sure that Miss Elwood was quite aware that I would never give my permission for this child to intrude upon your education and lower your standards, that is why she did not ask.'

'That is unfair,' cried Louisa. 'Erin is a most intelligent girl. Do you suppose that I would have allowed Caroline's education to suffer?'

Helena stared back at the governess. 'Whatever I suppose is of little consequence now, Miss Elwood, as Caroline will no longer be requiring your services, poor as they are. Feeney, go to the kitchen where you belong.'

As Erin tried to duck past her Helena caught her arm and twisted it viciously. 'If ever I should find you in here again you will pay dearly – and kindly dispose of that.' She indicated the harp. 'Or I shall dispose of it for you.' She thrust the child from the room.

'Mrs Cummings, what did you mean about Caroline?' enquired Louisa.

Helena turned back to the governess. 'I mean that Caroline will be going to an establishment for young ladies quite soon, and apparently not before time.'

'No, I don't want to go!' Caroline was filled with panic at the thought of leaving her friend. She had been cooped up for so long in this house that to be pushed into the outside world held nothing but terror.

'Do not want? Of course you will go,' replied Helena flatly. 'It is plain to see that you are not going to learn the refinements of a lady under Miss Elwood's tutorage.' She took a step towards her daughter and stroked her cheek, though there was no affection in the gesture. 'Caroline, my dear, I know that the thought of leaving your parents must be quite heart-rending for you, but it will not be for long. Why, in a few years you will be ready for marriage . . .'

'I won't, I won't!' Caroline was horrified. 'I do not want to marry. I refuse to leave and go to a horrid school, I am perfectly happy with Miss Elwood. Mama, do not make me.'

'Stop that at once!' commanded Helena. 'You will do as you are told. What I have suggested is for your own good. As for you,' she addressed Louisa, 'your services will be dispensed with as from today. From the display I have just witnessed you are setting a bad example to my daughter.'

'But you cannot do that!' objected Louisa.

'I beg your pardon?' replied the other stiffly. 'Pray tell me why not?'

'I shall appeal to Mr Cummings!'

A curt laugh. 'Miss Elwood, if you imagine that a plain little creature like yourself could possibly appeal to my husband then you are certainly with insufficient wits to be teaching my daughter.' She consulted the fob watch that was pinned to her dress. 'You have precisely thirty minutes to pack and get out of my house.'

CHAPTER FIFTY-TWO

THE EPISODE OF his subjugation had been almost forgotten, by all but Sonny. Brother Simon Peter could hardly believe that this was the same boy, had it not been for the ginger thatch that bespoke his identity. No longer did Sonny answer back, except with a polite reply, much to the disgust and disappointment of his peers. The lessons progressed with few interruptions, apart from the occasional beating of an unlucky child.

Although the master had emerged as victor in their private battle, he was, nevertheless, annoyed that there was no other worthy adversary to tangle with. Several times he had tried to bait Feeney, but since that day the boy had simply hung his head, refusing to be drawn.

Sonny felt the master's expressionless eyes upon him, but kept his own glued to the book in his hands. He guessed that the others had dubbed him a coward, but did not care; they were no better than he. He had been the first one to stand up to Codgob and now, because he had defended his brother in the only possible way, they despised him.

When school finished Sonny and his brother made their way home, ignoring the elbows that dug into their ribs as they passed into the corridor and out into the yard. Someone pushed Sonny hard in the back, almost lifting him off his feet, but when he turned in defiance the perpetrator had merged into the crowd; though they called him Cowardy Custard behind his back, none of them had the courage to face him fairly. Even the older boys were rightly cautious of baiting young Feeney.

Shoulders hunched and hands in pockets, the brothers veered out of the schoolyard.

'Have ye still got them hens' heads, Son?' asked Dickie, in

an attempt at peace-making. Sonny had refused to talk to him for a long time after the incident of the cross-country run.

Sonny felt in his pocket and pulled out the hens' heads. 'Aye.' He smelt them. 'Phew, they're a bit ripe though.' He thrust them under his brother's nose.

'Ye'd best sling 'em.' Dickie knocked his brother's hand away. ' 'Tis a wonder me mam hasn't played war about t'smell. Here, ye can have one o' these instead.' He handed a yellowed claw to Sonny, feeling that he had to make amends for his brother's unpopularity at school.

Sonny brightened, and pulled the tendons in the foot, setting the claws grasping at air. 'Eh, isn't that our Erin down there?' He pointed with the claw to a figure farther down the street. 'Look at her, all dressed up like a dog's knob. C'mon, let's have her on.'

They started to run until they came within five yards of their sister, then crept up stealthily behind her. Erin felt something touch her cheek and absently put up a hand to brush it away. Her fingers felt something sharp and horny, making her scream and spin round.

'Ye little devil!' she cried, slapping wildly at Sonny who danced around her with a terrible grimace on his face and the hen's claw stuck up his jacket cuff like a hand.

'Argh, I'm a monster what's gonna eat this grand lady,' he yelled, stabbing at her smart clothes.

'Wait till me dad finds out, he'll tan your arse for being so cheeky!' Erin stormed off.

'It can't be a lady, Son,' shouted Dickie, pursuing his sister. 'That's not how ladies talk. I'm thinking it must be our Erin dressed up in ladies' clothes. Let's see.'

Before Erin could stop him he had reached up and snatched the flowered bonnet from her head.

'Bloody hell!' Both boys stopped dancing round her to stare at the untidy, cropped hair.

'Give me that here!' Angrily she snatched the bonnet from Dickie and, ramming it on her head, proceeded towards home, her skirts boiling round her calves and tears of frustration in her eyes.

Shaking off their surprise the boys chased and overtook her, barging into the house shouting, 'Look what's happened to our Erin!'

'Less noise,' ordered their father, then, 'Hello, me darlin', come in, come in!' He kissed his daughter and held her by the shoulders to examine her. 'Why, I do believe 'tis another new bonnet you're wearing.'

Erin mumbled that, no, it was just on loan.

'Yer look lovely,' said Thomasin, and offered to take Erin's bonnet and shawl.

The girl refused hastily. 'I'll not stop long, I have to go to Mass before it gets dark.'

The two boys giggled and rolled about like young puppies.

'What's up with you two eejits?' demanded Patrick.

'She daren't take her hat off,' chortled Sonny behind a grubby hand. 'She's frightened you'll see her hair.'

'Ye mean not see her hair, don't ye?' joked his brother, and the pair fell about laughing again.

'Don't take any notice,' said Erin nervously. 'They're just being daft.'

Patrick stared from his chuckling sons to his apprehensive daughter. Then, ignoring Erin's please, he carefully untied the bonnet and lifted it from her shorn head.

Thomasin let out a gasp of horror. 'Godfrey Norris, what the hell's 'appened to your 'air?'

Erin raised swimming eyes from the carpet to steal a blurred glance at her father, who was too shocked to speak for the moment.

'I wasn't going to tell ye,' she sobbed. 'I knew ye'd be angry. After me dad left the other night I got a right roastin', an' the mistress said I had to have me hair cut 'cause it was too long, an' Alice cut it but it weren't short enough, so the mistress took the scissors to it an' she . . . she cut it all off!' Once she had released the scrambled sentence she broke down.

'I'll kill her,' swore Patrick softly. Then louder: 'I'll bloody kill her!'

Pushing Erin aside he marched to the cocoa tin and emptied its contents into his pocket. Then without a word to anybody, he flew from the house, not stopping to slam the door.

'Pat! Patrick, don't!' yelled Thomasin after him, but her shout went unheeded. He was already on his way.

She turned to her sons who had stopped laughing, alarmed by the suddenness of their father's anger. 'You two, up to bed, now.'

'But, Mam! We haven't had our tea.'

Thomasin's hand groped for the big wooden spoon. 'Bed! Yer've had yer little laugh at our Erin's expense, now see how yer like my little joke.'

Without daring to argue they scampered up the stairs, falling over each other in their rush to escape the dreaded spoon, and flung themselves onto the bed, bewildered and rather afraid.

Helena reclined in the armchair and closed her eyes, recapping the events of the last few days. Roland had been very displeased over the dismissal of the governess. Well let him – see if she cared. Suddenly she was almost thrown from her chair with the impact of Patrick's violent entry.

'You bitch!' He marched up to stand directly in front of her, his hands clenching and unclenching at his sides, his face suffused with anger.

'I'm sorry I couldn't stop him, ma'am,' bleated Alice, hopping about in the doorway holding a freshly-laundered pile of linen.

Helena, though frightened by the raging Irishman who towered over her, felt a surge of excitement. 'It does not matter, Benson,' she said, fighting to keep her voice level. 'I have a few words which I would like to say to our visitor.'

Alice closed the door, then bent immediately to the keyhole.

'Now, to what do I owe the honour, Feeney?' said Helena, urging her breath not to come so rapidly. She began to rise.

'Sit down!' Patrick gave her a rough shove and she made an ungainly return to her chair.

'Well, really!' she gasped, then cringed as he placed his arm on either side of the chair and leaned towards her. 'Before ye have your few words with me, Mrs Cummings,' his voice was less harsh, but no less threatening, 'I have a few words of me own. I'd like to know why ye deemed it necessary to cut my daughter's hair?'

'Now, look here!' Helena was becoming more and more nervous. 'I do not have to answer to you for my actions.'

'Yes, ye do,' he said gravely. 'And your answer had best be convincing.'

'Very well,' she snapped. 'Not that it is any of your concern.

I expect my servants to be clean and tidy. I will not have them dropping long hairs into my food.'

'Clean an' tidy, is it?' snarled Patrick. 'What would you know about clean, woman? You're filth. Like a turd in the gutter. Don't think I don't realise why you've done this to her. 'Twas to get back at me, wasn't it?' He pushed his menacing face closer to hers.

'Don't touch me!' Helena cowered in the chair, really afraid now.

'Touch ye? Hah! I wouldn't touch ye with a ten foot pole.'

'You are insulting. Get out! Get out!'

'Don't worry. Now that I've told ye what I think of someone who treats a child in that manner I'm going.'

Much to her relief he straightened. Then her fear returned as he delved into his pockets.

'What are you doing?' she almost screamed.

'Don't fret,' he sneered, ''tis not a knife.' He flung the sovereigns which he had taken from the cocoa tin at her and she shrieked.

'I do not understand!' She stared at the gold coins which spangled her gown.

'D'ye not recall my daughter received her wages in advance?' asked Patrick. 'Well, as she's not worked the full year ye can have the balance, for I want nothing from you. Ye'll find six pounds there.'

'Six pounds?' roared Helena, forgetting her fear. 'But she would only receive five pounds for the whole year.' She paused as she saw the flicker of doubt in Patrick's eyes; used it to her advantage. 'You say she was paid in advance?'

'I did. Have ye so much money that ye could forget about fourteen pounds?'

'Why, there has certainly been some skulduggery here,' spat Helena. 'What of the wage she receives every month?'

'You're talking nonsense,' said Patrick. 'She's received no wages.'

'I have personally delivered that chit's wage into her hand. Do you propose further slander?' Her face altered then. 'May I presume it was my husband who gave you the child's earnings in advance?'

'He paid them to my wife actually,' replied Patrick with a growing unease. Erin had definitely brought no money home.

'Ah yes, your wife.' Helena had by now lost all sign of nervousness and actually smiled. 'That would account for it. My husband can be over-indulgent with his favours at times.'

'An' why would a rich man like your husband possibly want to favour my wife?' he asked brashly . . . and then his eyes fell on the portrait.

Helena did not reply – she did not have to . . . the suggestive, pouting mouth told volumes without ever parting in speech.

For one moment she saw murder in his eyes and the terror returned, but she need not have been afraid; she was not to be the recipient of his wrath. As quickly as he had entered he was gone, barging into Alice on his way out and knocking the pile of linen from her arms.

Helena gave a long sigh and followed him from the room to make certain he had left the house. 'Get out of my way!' She kicked at Alice with an impatient foot. 'And what is that linen doing on the floor?'

Alice mumbled that the Irishman had made her drop it.

'Ah, and I suppose you were at the door eavesdropping,' guessed Helena. Deliberately she placed her foot on the sparkling linen, ground it into the carpet, then gave it a disparaging toss with her toe. 'That linen is positively filthy, Benson,' she said lightly. 'It will all have to be washed again.'

A sly smile took over her face as she went upstairs. What fun and games there would be in the Feeney household when the oaf got home.

Patrick strode purposefully towards home, disregarding the complaints as he elbowed aside all who crossed his path. How could he have been such a fool not to see it? He had believed her, trusted her, how could she have lied so coolly when she said she loved him, when all the time she had a lover stashed away? – Just hold on a minute there, Pat, he told himself, are ye not jumping to conclusions? Would you go believing that woman's insinuations before your own wife has a chance to speak? Give her a chance to defend herself. Don't go thinking the worst all the time. There could be a perfectly reasonable explanation for her taking money from that man . . . but what of the money Erin was supposed to have brought home every month? There was still that to answer.

Outside his front door he paused, wanting to know the truth yet scared of hearing it.

Thomasin looked up as the door slammed. 'Well?' she said eagerly.

'Erin, go upstairs.' He leaned against the wall, breathing heavily.

Wordlessly, Erin obeyed.

'My God,' breathed Thomasin. 'Yer've not gone an' done for her?'

'An' tell me, why would I want to do that, Thomasin?' he asked stiffly. 'When the woman's been so helpful, so enlightening.'

'Patrick, yer talkin' in riddles. Will yer please tell me what yer've done?'

' 'Tis not what *I've* done,' he answered darkly. ' 'Tis what *you've* done that we're about to discuss.'

Her heart sank; he knew. 'Pat . . .'

He held up his hand. 'No, just bide a second. I've a question to put to ye, Thomasin. I'll only put it the once, so I expect ye to give me the right answer an' none o' your hedging.' So quietly were his words delivered that they could have been a caress: 'Where did you get the money to buy my release?'

She gave a nervous laugh. 'I told yer, it's Erin's wages in . . .'

'Sure, I know what ye told me, Thomasin,' he replied coldly. 'An' now I know ye for the liar ye are, because ye see Mrs Cummings has just kindly informed me that her servants get nowhere near the amount that you purport to have received – beside the fact that she gets the impression she's been paying the girl every month. So, ye've got me to wondering, like, why Mr Cummings would want to be so generous as to pay Erin so much more than the going rate? Aye, he must be a very benevolent man this Mr Cummings.'

'Look, I'm sorry,' she said shamefacedly. 'I should've told yer the whole truth – but I knew what a proud old thing you were, yer wouldn't've liked it if I'd told yer I got the money from an old friend o' mine.'

'Especially if it were a male friend, isn't that what you're sayin', Thomasin?'

She wanted to go to him, to hug him and explain why she had had to do it, but Patrick's eyes held no welcome. 'All right, so I knew yer'd be jealous,' she shrugged. 'Now yer know the truth, what're yer gonna do?'

'Ah, but I don't know the whole truth, do I, Thomasin? I mean, ye say he's an old friend an' who am I to argue with ye? A very close friend, was he?' He laid great emphasis on the word close.

She begged him not to go on.

'Why ever not? Sure, I'd like to meet this close friend o' yours. In fact why don't ye take me an' introduce the pair of us right now?' He grabbed her arm.

'Stop it, Patrick! Please, stop.' She struggled and he looked at her in amazement.

'Why, I do believe you're reluctant for me to meet this friend o' yours. Sure, I cannot think why. D'ye think he's too good to meet me?'

'Of course not, don't be silly.' She rubbed her arm and turned her face away but he caught hold of her chin and wrenched it around so that she was facing him again.

'Then I can think of no possible explanation for your unwillingness, Thomasin,' he said softly, 'other than this: you don't want me to meet this man because he's not just your friend, Thomasin – he's your lover.'

'No, you're wrong!' she cried but dared not look into his eyes.

'Am I? Am I?' he shouted, fingers tightening on her chin, making her wriggle in discomfort. 'And was his wife wrong when she saw the pair o' yese together?' It was a lie but he had to know.

'That was years ago!' she objected shrilly, finally freeing her chin from his cruel fingers.

'Years ago it might be!' he raged. 'But can ye deny that 'tis still going on?'

'Of course I deny it! It's not true.'

'You're a liar!' He picked her up and shook her like a rag doll, throwing her this way and that. 'My God, ye must both have had a bloody good laugh about me. When I think of all the hours I've slaved to buy ye the things ye wanted, the months I spent in prison . . .'

'Don't, oh please, don't,' she sobbed, and tried to support herself against his chest but he shoved her away. 'I never wanted all those things. It was you who insisted on buyin' 'em for me. I told yer not to work too hard, I told yer I was happy just as we were.'

'Oh, ye were happy all right!' he laughed sarcastically. 'Who wouldn't be with a lover who can buy her anything she wants an' a husband who's willing to sweat his balls off 'cause the eejit thinks she loves him? It must've taken a great deal of energy to keep the both of us happy, Thomasin.'

'Please! Please, let me explain,' she begged. 'I saw in Roland a way to get you out of prison. I knew you wouldn't like it, but what else could I do? Leave you to rot in there forever?'

'Isn't the truth more likely that, with me in prison, ye got to feeling kinda itchy? That ye couldn't wait until the cell door was locked before your tongue was hanging out for it?'

There was the briefest of pauses, then her hand clapped resoundingly upon his cheek. 'All right, you've had your say! Now I'll have mine. Yes! I did sleep with him, and in return he gave me the money to get you out. And no, before you ask, I didn't enjoy it, not one bit, it was degrading, horrible. I hope to God I never have to feel that way again. My only thoughts were for you, locked up in there like an animal. It was the only way I could get the money, Patrick. Do you think I would've descended to that before I'd tried everything else?'

'There's just one thing wrong with your explanation, Thomasin,' he answered. 'While I was at the Cummings' house I couldn't help but notice a very large portrait on the wall. 'Twas of a man, a very ugly fella he was, with a face I'd hardly be likely to forget. 'Tis the man who ye were living with before ye met me, isn't it?'

She nodded. 'But I swear, Patrick, I'm tellin' yer the truth. I've never set eyes on him since that day until . . .'

'Until ye rutted with him in exchange for fourteen pieces of gold,' he cut in viciously. 'Funny, I always thought the price of betrayal was thirty pieces o' silver.'

'You want to watch your own tarnished halo, mate!' she cried. 'I've done things that no woman should ever have to do an' this is all the thanks I get for it.'

'Thanks?' Patrick burst out laughing, but the sound was far from happy. 'Next, I suppose, ye'll be asking me to thank the man for making my wife into a whore.'

She lashed out again but this time he caught her hand and

twisted it behind her back. 'Not this time, ye filthy bitch. Ye've contaminated me for the last time.' He pushed her towards the doorway. 'There's only one place for dirt like you an' that's in the gutter.'

'Patrick, can't yer see that I did it because I love you?' she pleaded.

'What a way ye have of showing it.' They struggled together as he tried to push her through the doorway. 'Besmirching my daughter with your fornications, getting her to lie to her father . . .'

She had never seen him so angry. He was almost insane. The curses ripped from his lips but in his anger he had reverted to his native tongue and she could not understand them. *'Striapach! Tréatúir!'* He was a crazy, maddened foreigner, a stranger, not Patrick. Every time he succeeded in opening the door she lashed out with her feet and kicked it shut, for she knew that once outside she would never get back in.

'God, I wish I'd never set eyes on ye!' he gasped and wrenched at the door while still trying to pinion her arms to her body with one of his, but she struggled and fought him. He finally managed to open the door and wedged his foot in the space he had created then began to edge her over the threshold. 'To think that I've worked every hour that God sent just to please a whore like you! Well, ye can take your filthy, lying tongue and get out o' my house, and don't come back!'

With another curse he thrust her out onto the pavement where she fell upon her face, grazing the dome of her cheek and pushing one of her teeth through her lip. He filled the doorway, glaring down at the pile of skirts that heaved and cried and turned her face towards him pleadingly. He struggled with the automatic response to run to her, pick her up and hold her, to beg her forgiveness.

Thomasin shook the fuzziness from her head and staggered at the door. 'Pat, think of the children.'

Her persistence seemed to jerk him from the horror of what he had done to her. With a brief grimace of distaste he slammed the door in her face.

'You have no children,' came the muffled, brutal reply.

But she had. The commotion had brought them to the top of the stairs where they had watched in horror as their mother was cast from the house. Sonny tripped and stumbled down the stairs, flew at his father and punched at him wildly as Thomasin pounded at the door. 'Stop it! Let Mam in!' he screamed, trying to wrest the key from Patrick, while the tear-stained faces of his siblings spied down on them, wedged in the banisters unable to move.

Patrick flung aside his son as if he was not there. 'Forget her,' he mumbled. 'Ye have no mother now – never did have.'

With these cruel words he charged into the back yard and locked himself in the closet, where he punched the walls in frustration. He felt betrayed and sickened – Tommy, how could ye? He sank to the privy seat, buried his head in his hands and wept.

Inside, Sonny laid his palms and face against the front door, sobbing, trying to feel his mother through the unyielding wood. While on the other side, Thomasin still hammered and thumped until the blood began to trickle down her arms.

CHAPTER FIFTY-THREE

HE PROLONGED HIS cramped exile for two hours, head in hands and deep in thought. Try as he might, he could not push away those pictures of his wife lying naked with another man. An ugly ape of a man, pawing at her, slobbering over her . . . Holy Mother, he wanted to scream as he visualised those great, obscene hands touching her there, and there. And all because the bastard was rich, filthy, stinking rich. I love you, she had said. How many times? He snatched a piece of newspaper from the wad that hung on the wall and tried to drown himself in the words. But there were only half-stories, nothing which might hold his attention, and the visions of Thomasin with her lover were too buoyant. However he screamed at his eyes to cling to the newsprint, the naked couple appeared, stretched out between the lines, using the words as their bed, writhing, copulating. He clamped his fingers around the newspaper and reduced it to a tiny, black walnut.

'I did it for you,' she had said. Did she not know him well enough to understand that he would rather die in prison that be indebted to another man for buying his wife's favours?

A tap came at the door. The pictures faded, but did not die.

'Daddy?' Sonny tried to peep through the hole where the latch was fixed to the wood. 'Dad, are ye in there?'

'Go away.'

'I want to pee, Dad, I'm bustin'.'

Patrick growled and tried to cover his ears. 'Go in the yard.'

'I can't, Dad, our Erin's in t'yard.' This was mere pretence to lure his father out. Sonny squinted through the crack. For a good two minutes there was no answer. Sonny continued to tap and whine through the crack. Then there came a snort of impatience and the sound of the sneck being lifted, and his father stood there, morose and pathetic. The three children stepped back and stared at him accusingly.

'What did ye hurt me Mam for?' demanded Sonny, an angry robin.

Patrick looked down with puffy, bloodshot eyes at the image of his wife, then pushed the boy aside. 'I thought ye wanted to go to the privy?'

The children watched him slouch back into the house.

'What we going to do?' asked Dickie worriedly. 'There's nobody to get our supper.'

Erin and Sonny glared at him. Was that all he could think about? Dickie hung his head, then followed the others inside where once more they silently observed their father.

'If ye've nothing better to do than stand an' watch me then ye can go to bed,' muttered Patrick, leaning on his elbow.

'I want to know why ye chucked me Mam out,' persisted Sonny.

Patrick opened his mouth to shout: 'Because she was a harlot!' but instead he answered evenly, ' 'Tis none o' your business, Sonny. Now, will ye please go to bed?'

'When's me Mam coming back?' asked the tiny boy.

Patrick could not look at his son. His mind went back to the time when, after Mary died, he could not stand the sight of Erin. It was the same sensation he was experiencing now. God, the boy was so like her.

'Your mother isn't coming back,' he said to all of them, then rose abruptly and went to the scullery, returning with a jug of poteen. 'Well, did ye hear what I said?' he barked at their shocked expressions. 'She's not coming back so ye might as well get used to it.'

His younger son stared at him, the grey eyes disbelieving, the mouth forming a startled O. Then, 'I hate you!' he cried and fled up the stairs, closely followed by his brother.

Patrick groaned and took a drink straight from the earthenware jug. The liquor splashed onto his shirt but he didn't appear to notice.

'Will it be all right if I go now?' asked Erin tremulously.

'To bed? Aye,' he replied disinterestedly.

'No, I meant back to the big house.'

He slammed the jug onto his knee and the liquid slopped noisily inside it. 'You'll not set foot in that house again,' he issued dramatically.

Erin was shocked. 'But, Daddy, my harp is still there – an' there's Miss Caroline to consider.'

'Don't you argue with me, girl!' She had only once seen her father in such a foul temper and that had been long ago. 'Miss Caroline, Miss Caroline! I'm sick o' hearing about her. Ye'll have nothing further to do with any member of that family – an' what about this money you and that woman've been hiding away? I thought better of you than to scheme against your father.'

'I didn't, I didn't! Mam . . .'

'Ah, I know . . . it wouldn't be your fault, she made ye do it . . . I'm not mad at you . . . as for the harp, well, ye'll just have to leave it where it is. We all have to make sacrifices, Erin. All have to make . . .' his voice disappeared into the jug as he took another drink.

'But ye know what it means to me!' She jumped back as he leapt from his seat.

'Can a man get no peace in his own house?' he roared. 'Dammit, I'm going to the ale-house. At least there I can get drunk without anyone wittering in my ear about bloody stupid harps!' The choice of one of his wife's words – wittering – made her spring back like a Fury into his mind's eye. Damn her! 'You can get the boys their supper when I've gone. And if that woman should show her face,' he warned, 'don't you dare let her in. There's no place for her in this house any more.' He marched down the passage and out of the house.

Erin watched the boys pick at their supper, unable to eat anything herself. Poor Mam – and poor Dad.

'I suppose we'll have to put up with your cookin' if me Mam doesn't come back,' complained Dickie, receiving a cuff for his insensitivity.

'Just get that supper down ye and shut up,' ordered Erin, donning Alice's bonnet and wrapping a shawl around her shoulders. 'And don't let me catch ye still up when I come in.'

'Where y'off to?' enquired Sonny, gnawing at his crust.

'I'm off to the big house to get me harp,' replied his sister. 'I don't care what Dad says, I'm going. With a bit o' luck he'll be too drunk when he comes back to notice I'm missing. Now, are ye sure ye'll be all right on your own? I'll not be long.'

' 'Course we will,' answered Sonny. 'We're not daft, ye know.'

'Well remember, no messing,' she cautioned. 'An' lock the door behind me. We don't want any bogeymen creepin' in an' eating y'up.' She said this purposefully in the knowledge that Dickie, at least, would now not dare to poke his nose out into the street.

Roland was very drunk. It was not his usual practice to imbibe so heavily, he was just so damned depressed. His current mistress had cleared off with a young subaltern – not that this had made him broken-hearted. She couldn't hold his interest like Tommy had done; none that had ever followed her would bear comparison. He fished out a watch and tried to decipher the time, then put it away again. What difference did it make? No one would miss him if he were late, in fact no one would miss him if he never came home again. Nobody cared. The clink of bottle against glass seemed to amplify and fill his eardrums. He decided he'd better go. After settling the bill he accomplished the walk to the exit without stumbling, placing each foot firmly in front of the other in the way of inebriates. He saw not the wink between two dandies as he weaved his way to the door, supposed it to be an accident when they fell against him in the street outside, and accepted their apologies gracefully, unaware that his gold watch and a number of sovereigns had found themselves a new home.

It was very dark. People passed him, laughing, singing, forming a chain with their partners. He watched them as they wound a detour around him as he swayed on the spot. Their action made him dizzy.

'Well, if it isn't Johnathon!' The heavily-painted face materialised from a darkened doorway, its owner linking arms with his. 'How about a spot of fun, Johnny?'

He tried to recall her name. Johnathon was the pseudonym he gave to the street girls if they should bother to ask. She had obviously encountered his custom before.

He put a massive hand up to her breast, which was almost hanging out of the gawdy dress, and squeezed. 'Not tonight, my dear, thank you. As you see I am a little indisposed. It would be rather like trying to raise Lazarus.'

' 'Ere, you've changed your tune, yer randy old devil!' she shrilled. 'I wouldn't've let yer get away wi' that if I thought yer weren't gonna buy. Yer wouldn't go into a shop an' squeeze the bleedin' tomatoes then walk out without payin', would yer?'

Roland grimaced and fumbled in his pockets. 'How odd,' he mumbled, patting each pocket in turn. 'I could have sworn . . .'

'Oh, Christ,' muttered the woman. 'How many bleedin' times 'ave I heard that one? Yer cheeky swine, if yer ain't got no money yer can go jig yerself.'

'Ah.' Roland eventually found a coin that had escaped the pickpockets. He held it to his eyes to find out its value, but the woman quickly snatched the sovereign and thrust it down her cleavage.

'Cor, thanks, Johnny.' She patted his cheek. 'You can feel 'em any time!'

Roland raised his hat and stumbled on. The streets seemed to be lined with women who had made his acquaintance, calling, 'Now then, Johno, give us a kiss!' Or 'Come up an' show us yer testimonials.'

He smiled politely, remembering none of their names. How ironic to know so many women yet there was not one among them whom he could call a friend.

The bridge arched its back at his shuffling feet. He stopped and leaned over the abrasive stone, stared down into the blackness. He ran his teeth over his furred tongue. The taste was appalling. What was he doing getting drunk? He never got drunk. It was all that silly girl's fault that he felt like this. Well, he would show her! He would show her exactly what she had done to him. What would her feelings be when she read about it in the newspaper? 'Today, the body of a man was found floating down the Ouse' . . . no, that was not right. How long did bodies stay down for? Was it three days? Never mind, she would know when she read those words that it was Roland, and it would serve her right, throwing him over for a soldier.

He peered slyly to his left. There was only a young couple, and so engrossed were they in themselves that he doubted they had even noticed his presence. What a pity – perhaps he should wait till he got an audience, for he wanted it to make a big splash in the newspaper. Oh, very droll! he chuckled. Big splash, what?

He turned to his right. Further along the bridge a solitary woman leaned in the same stance as himself, as if she too were contemplating suicide. Maybe they could do it together, he thought stupidly. A lovers' pact. He screwed up his eyes. There was something familiar in the way she held her head, cupping her hands to conceal her face.

At that moment, sensing his gaze, she turned her face to him and his heart leapt. 'Tommy!' he cried joyfully and began to lumber towards her.

She stood upright, thinking, hoping, that it was Patrick. Her optimistic smile faded as he staggered up to her. 'Oh, hello, Roly. Yer look as if yer've had a drop too much.' She leant over the bridge again.

'More than a drop, I fear,' he stuttered, and touched her arm, not believing it was really Thomasin. 'Goodness gracious.' He brushed aside her hair. 'What has happened to your face?'

She turned down her mouth and the cut on her lip cracked open. 'Patrick found out about you an' me,' she said simply. 'He's thrown me out.'

'Oh, heavens!' he exploded, forgetting all about the girl. 'Who told him?'

'Your dear wife,' she answered wryly.

'But . . . but how did this come about?' asked Roland. 'I mean, she did not know for sure that you were . . . and how did she match the two of you together? How did she come to meet your husband?' the questions poured out.

Thomasin told him how his wife had cut off Erin's hair, and how Patrick had gone storming up to the Cummings' house to seek retribution. 'How could you 'ave let her do it to that poor lass, Roly?' she said reproachfully.

'I had no idea that it was so bad,' breathed Roland. 'I realised of course that Helena had taken a dislike to the child, but the extent of her torment escaped me. I am rarely at home, you see.' It seemed a lame excuse. 'I would never have allowed it had I known.' The poor little scrap. To have suffered such indignities at the hands of his wife. 'Why, I could kill her!'

Thomasin disregarded the startled looks from passers-by. 'That'll not do any good.'

He calmed down a little. 'Do you know, it is odd but not five minutes ago I was contemplating killing myself.'

'Ditto.'

'Not you?' He took hold of her hand and gently squeezed her fingers. 'You are not the type to go and do a silly thing like that.'

'Why not?' She stared down at the long, artistic fingers that intertwined with hers. 'I've nowt to lose now. No husband. No children.'

'But surely,' he said, 'surely you explained to him your reasons for doing what you did?'

'Oh, aye. But he didn't see it the way it was meant. Patrick thinks I've been cuckolding him ever since we were married. He won't believe that it was only the once, as if it mattered,' she sighed. 'I'm all mixed up, I can't think straight. All I can think of are them bairns. I'll never see 'em again, God help me.' There were no tears, just a resigned gesture of despair.

'Thomasin, it was all my fault,' said Roland. 'If I had given you the money without . . . you know. But I could not help it. I love you, Tommy. Oh, to have ruined your life is too much for me to bear.' The alcohol still mingled with his blood, making his thinking totally irrational. With an astonishingly agile movement for one so drunk, he leapt onto the parapet and prepared to jump.

'Roly, stop!' Thomasin tried to grab hold of him. 'Don't be a fool. Yer drunk. Yer wouldn't even be dreamin' o' doing this if yer weren't.'

'Oh, now you have made me feel worse,' he wailed, swaying dangerously. 'I must go, it is the best for everyone.'

Seeing that she was making no impression, Thomasin altered the tone of her voice. 'Roland, come down 'ere at once! You know very well that you 'ave no intentions of jumpin'.'

With a hangdog look he sat on the parapet and lowered himself back to firm ground. Putting his arms around her he begged her to forgive him.

' 'Course I forgive yer, yer soft old devil,' she said dispassionately, 'but yer've got to promise me that yer won't do owt stupid like that again.'

'But you were going to,' he protested.

'Nah.' She screwed up her nose. 'Like you said, I'm not the type. Though Lord knows what I'm gonna do now.' She fell against him and cushioned her head on his broad chest.

And this was how Patrick saw them as he scoured the town for her that night. During the time it had taken him to reach the city centre, he had come to the conclusion that, while she had wronged him terribly, life without her would not be worth living. He had decided to forgive her, even though he would never be able to forget her betrayal. He loved her, needed her . . . that is, until he saw them there, holding each other. How could he guess that she was in Roland's arms only for comfort? All he could see was a man and a woman locked in a loving embrace; that everything she had screamed at him in her defence had been lies. After all her protestations of love she had finally gone slinking back to her lover. He backed into the shadows, unable to tear his eyes away as the man rested his chin on Thomasin's scarlet head. Patrick wanted to kill him.

'Where will you go?' Roland was asking her.

She shrugged. 'To my parents, I've nowhere else.'

There was a tiny hesitation, then Roland said, 'If you like we could perhaps . . .'

She looked up sharply. 'Oh, no, Roly! I'm sorry, I just couldn't.' Lord, the man would never alter.

He nodded sadly, then kissed her. 'I understand – but if ever you should need me . . .' How foolish; they both knew that she would never need him.

Patrick did not see them break apart and go their separate ways. Broken of heart and spirit, he had already gone home.

CHAPTER FIFTY-FOUR

THE CITY AT night was full of noisy people, jeering and laughing, pushing and fighting. Erin remained close to the wall and walked as fast as her legs would carry her to the other side of town, stifling a scream as filthy fingers clutched at her from a doorway and pulled the bonnet from her head. She ran on, before whoever it was could kill her to steal her clothes as well.

It was with great relief that she reached the Cummings' house and slipped noiselessly through the kitchen door.

'Blinkin' 'ell – where you been?' hissed Alice. 'There's been a right to-do over you – an' where's my hat? Oh God! I told yer what'd happen, Cook.'

'I'm ever so sorry, Alice,' replied Erin soulfully. 'Someone attacked me.'

'Aye, there'll likely be another one will, too! Oh, you are careless – that was a good hat that was. What's happening then?'

'I'm not to come here any more,' Erin told her. 'I've only come for me harp.'

'Oh, no!' wailed Alice. 'Don't tell me I've got it all to do on me own again. Can't you even help wi' them pots before yer go?'

Erin shook her head, disregarding her ugly haircut; there were other things on her mind. 'I daren't. Me dad'll kill me. I'm not meant to be here at all.'

Alice smirked at Cook. 'Aye, he's a bit of a lad by all accounts is your dad, isn't he?'

'I don't know what you're talking about,' said Erin, and attempted to push past Alice.

'Oh, come on. I was there. I saw him an' the mistress going at it, hammer an' tongs. I thought he were goin' to give her a right good brayin'. Callin' her all sorts o' pretty names he was.'

'I tell ye, I know nothing,' said Erin. 'And if he was then 'tis only what she's had coming to her. Now, would ye mind moving outta me way so's I can get me harp?'

'Well, I don't know about that,' prevaricated Alice. 'What do you think, Cook? I say we don't let her go till she lets on.'

'Oh, please, Alice, just leave me alone.' Erin suddenly burst into tears.

'Now look what you've done!' Cook hurried over to comfort Erin. 'The poor little girl's got enough to contend with. Leave her be.'

Alice rolled her eyes. 'Oh, s'truth, I didn't mean owt, honest. Eh, come on, Erin.' She tugged at the edge of Erin's shawl. 'I'll come with yer to fetch your harp. An' I think you'd best have a word wi' Miss Caroline while we're there. She's been going frantic 'cause her ma's gone an' told her you're not comin' back.'

As Alice led her away Cook mouthed the words. 'Try and find out what's gone off.'

Together Alice and Erin climbed up to the attic and re-trieved the harp. Then the Irish girl went to say goodbye to Caroline. She paused briefly outside the schoolroom, running her eyes over the bookshelves, feeling a great ache that she would not be coming here any more.

'Oh, Erin! I knew you would come back!' Caroline leapt from her bed where she had been crying into her pillow. 'Mama has been saying such horrid things about you. She told me you are not to live here any more, but it isn't true, is it? You will not leave me?'

Erin did not know how to break the news gently so gave it to Caroline straight. 'I'm sorry, but it is true. I just came back to fetch this.' She touched her harp.

'But why? *Why*?' sobbed her friend. 'You promised that you would never leave me. You are the only friend I have. Except for Alice of course,' she added politely to the other girl, who stole nervous glances down the stairs.

'I know what I said, an' I'm sorry,' replied Erin. 'But I

cannot go against my father. Anyway, I can't bear to stay in this house any longer.'

'It's all the mistress' fault,' volunteered Alice boldly. 'It was her who caused all this trouble, cutting Erin's hair an' upsetting her dad.'

This time Caroline did not bristle at the condemnation of her mother.

'Yes, I can understand that your father would be upset when he saw your hair,' she granted. 'But surely after things have cooled down . . .'

' 'Twasn't just the hair,' said Erin. 'He came storming up to your house to see the mistress and they had a big row. Alice heard it, didn't ye?' She looked at Alice who nodded eagerly.

'What was it about?' asked Caroline.

Erin glanced uneasily at Alice and said cagily, 'Well, I don't really know. But whatever she said it must've been something awful 'cause . . .' she faltered.

'Oh, don't stop now,' begged Alice.

'Well, not that it's any of your business,' said Erin. 'But . . . he's gone and thrown me Mam out.'

'He hasn't,' breathed Alice. Wait till she told Cook. What a to-do!

'Anyhow, now ye know why I have to leave,' said Erin, moving to the landing.

Caroline followed her, crying and begging for her friend not to leave.

'I have to,' insisted Erin, tucking the harp firmly under her arm. 'I'll be sorry to leave ye, Caroline, I'll miss ye something terrible. But I have to go.' It was true, she would miss Caroline. But oh, she would miss the lessons a great deal more. Caroline was a nice girl when she wanted to be, but Erin had come to understand the wisdom of her father's warning. Rich and poor, the two did not mix.

The noise of Caroline's distress finally brought Helena from the drawing room and she positioned herself at the foot of the stairs.

'What is the meaning of all this noise?' she demanded. 'And what is that girl doing up there?'

It was Caroline who answered. 'Oh, please, Mama, do not let Erin go away. I love her.'

'Love?' spat Helena. 'Are you out of your mind? How can one possibly love a despicable creature such as she? A common guttersnipe who has caused nothing but trouble from the moment she entered this house.'

'What a terrible thing to say!' Caroline's face was mottled and tear-stained, her blonde curls tangled from rolling about on the pillow. 'Erin is my friend. I will not allow you to speak about her like that.'

'Caroline, have you completely lost all sense of reason?' answered Helena. 'And please will you kindly desist from shouting and come down this instant.'

'I won't!' said Caroline obstinately.

'Come down this minute!' snapped Helena, then: 'Benson, do not stand there gaping like a fish. Bring my daughter to me.'

But as Alice tried to take Caroline's arm, the girl leapt nearer to Erin and clung to her, crying and shouting.

'Caroline, if I have to come up then it will be the worse for you!' Helena set her mouth and watched as Alice coaxed Caroline to release the Irish girl.

'Very well,' she said at last. 'I shall illustrate just what happens to people who disobey me. You are to receive a whipping, my girl!'

'Please let go,' whispered Erin urgently as Helena advanced up the stairs.

'No, I won't let go!' shrieked Caroline, her eyes wild. 'Stay away, Mama. Erin was right all along and I was too blind to see it. You are a horrid, horrid woman. I hate you!'

Helena had by now reached the top of the staircase. 'Caroline, you are becoming hysterical. You do not know what you are saying.' She paused uncertainly, not knowing the best way to handle this highly-strung girl. Caroline could spoil all her plans if she chose. Helena fought down the impulse to smack that stupid face, and attempted a motherly gesture. 'Come, we will forget about the whipping, you are not yourself and do not know what you are saying. Please, Caroline, allow the girl to leave. I am sure that you will find many more suitable friends when you go to Miss Dearly's Academy for . . .'

But the mention of school exacerbated the matter. 'I won't go! I won't!' screamed Caroline. 'I want to be taught by Miss Elwood.'

'You are being unrealistic, Caroline,' said Helena. 'Do you not remember that Miss Elwood has left us?'

'Yes, I do remember! You sent her away. You send everyone away whom I love. I hate you!'

Helena could control herself no longer. 'I suppose it is you who has taught my daughter to behave in this disgusting manner?' she accused Erin, who was trying to calm Caroline. 'Well, you shall see how I deal with people who disrupt my life. Benson, take Caroline to her room and lock the door. She will remain there until she can behave in a more respectable fashion.'

'No!' screeched the girl as poor Alice tried once more to detach her from Erin.

Annoyed at Alice's feeble attempts to separate the girls, Helena joined the struggle. She tried to wrestle Caroline free but Erin's harp, to which the Irish girl clung protectively, got in the way.

She grabbed the harp from the startled girl and dashed it against the balustrade, trying to smash it to pieces in her anger. Splinters of polished wood flew from the instrument. The strings shrieked in a tortured cacophany as she raised it again and again, chipping the beautiful marquetry, attempting to break its back. But the harp refused to die.

Erin freed herself from Caroline and made to stop Helena, but only succeeded in receiving a blow from the harp, and fell back holding a hand to her cut head.

'You fiend!' Brimming with hysteria, witnessing her friend's hurt was the last straw. With a sudden dash, Caroline placed her hands against Helena's back and pushed.

The banging stopped. All that was to be heard was Helena's scream as she toppled over the balustrade and soared towards the tiled floor below. At that same moment Roland opened the front door and sucked in his breath, staring into his wife's terrified maw as she flew towards him, her skirts rippling and billowing above the lace-trimmed drawers, and landed with a ghastly thud at his feet.

So quiet; quiet as death. Roland looked up at the tableau on the landing, where Alice peered over the broken balcony, her hands clasped to her cheeks, and Caroline's eyes shone blue and round in the white, white face. Then his gaze slowly fell to his wife.

Erin, the first to regain her senses, stepped tentatively down the staircase and regarded Helena's prostrate form. Then, stooping, she gripped the harp which had fallen with its attacker and tugged it free of the body. She moved her eyes from Helena to examine its battered frame. Though terribly scarred and sporting half a dozen broken strings, the harp still lived. Erin folded her arms around it and held it defensively to her breast.

Alice prodded herself from her immobility and, leading a benumbed Caroline after her, came slowly down the stairs as Roland searched for Helena's pulse, but found none.

'I did it,' whispered Caroline disbelievingly.

Roland looked sharply at Alice, who answered: 'Miss Caroline doesn't know what she's sayin', sir. She's a bit shocked-like. It was an accident. The mistress leaned too far over the banisters and toppled over. Me an' Erin saw it, didn't we?'

Erin looked at Caroline, who seemed to be in some sort of trance, then supported Alice's claim. 'Yes, sir, it was an accident.'

Roland stared at the maids' divided faces and hoped that an inquest jury would find them more convincing than he did. He looked down at his wife again, and felt, apart from the shock, a wonderful sense of release.

Caroline stood as if paralysed, gazing down at the beautiful corpse. The coroner would understand if Roland suggested that his daughter be spared the ordeal. The maids' evidence should be sufficient.

'Thank you, Alice,' he said quietly.

'What for, sir?' she asked innocently. 'Like I said, it was an accident. Now, you come along wi' me, Miss Caroline, let's get yer tucked into bed wi' a nice cup o' chocolate an' you'll feel lots better.' She took the girl's arm and gently but firmly steered her towards the staircase.

Roland turned his attention to Erin who was watching Caroline ascend the stairs. He laid a heavy arm across her shoulders. 'I regret that your time in this house has not been a happy one. I hold myself to blame for that, and for the unhappiness of your family.' He felt Erin's big blue eyes on his face but could not look into them. 'If you should see your mama, tell her . . .' – Tell her what? That he was sorry he had ruined her life? He suddenly fished in his pocket then, not finding any money, disappeared into the drawing room and came back with three sovereigns. 'Would you allow me to give you these?'

Erin made no move to take the coins. 'I don't think my father will accept them, sir.'

'They are not for your father,' he told her. 'They are for you, to repair your harp. It is such a beautiful instrument and deserves better than to be scarred for life.'

'Then I accept, thank you, sir.' She folded the coins into her pinafore and twisted it into a knot. 'And now I must go, for me Dad will be angry if I'm missing when he gets back.'

Roland opened the door and shouted to a passing youth to go fetch a cab, rewarding him with a sixpence on his return. He helped Erin to board the cab and passed a coin to the driver.

'Take this young lady wherever she wishes to go.' ·

The cabbie doffed his hat and flicked the reins. As the cab drove away, Erin heard Roland address the youth again.

'Go to Doctor Haines' residence, will you, boy? Tell him there has been an accident at the Cummings' house.'

Patrick rattled the doorknob, then attacked the door itself. 'Erin, open up!'

Dickie grappled with the key and opened the door.

'Where's your sister?' Patrick staggered in, kicked the door shut and, flopping into a chair, reached for the jug of poteen.

The boys dared say nothing, but were saved from further interrogation by the sound of Erin's arrival in the hansom. It was a sound that was out of place in their street, and Nelly Peabody's curtains moved slightly as Erin alighted and paused on the pavement as the horse clattered off towards the city centre. What a field day Nelly had had. There had been enough ammunition today to arm her tittle-tattle for the rest of the year.

At Erin's entry the boys vanished up the stairs. Patrick lowered the jug and observed the harp with an apathetic, bloodshot eye.

'I thought I'd made me views clear?' he slurred.

Erin held her chin high. 'What are ye going to do about it? Hit me like ye hit Mam?'

'Why, you impertinent . . .' He thrust aside the jug of poteen, spilling the remains over the carpet and came upon her, arm upraised.

Erin flung up her arm to stave off the attack and cried the first words that came into her mouth. 'She's dead!'

He paled. She couldn't be! Had he not just seen her half an hour ago? He grabbed his daughter roughly by the arms. 'What d'ye mean, dead? How? When?' He started to shake her. 'For pity's sake, tell me, child!'

She stuttered out her story, and watched the colour return to his cheeks as he realised that she had been referring to Helena.

'Good riddance,' he snarled callously, and slouched to the scullery for another jug of liquor. 'May the devil rot her evil carcase.'

'Oh, Dad,' reproved Erin. 'Ye shouldn't oughta speak so of the dead.'

He waved his hand deprecatingly. 'Ah, away off to bed with ye an' leave me in peace.'

Erin crept up to her bedroom. After she had undressed, she knelt before the wooden crucifix which had been her mother's, prayed for her father's forgiveness, her mother's return, and Helena's soul.

CHAPTER FIFTY-FIVE

THE SUMMER DIED. Swallows congregating on the telegraph wires for their winter migration draped the countryside in twittering necklaces. In the hedgerows and forests hedgehogs rooted for a warm hollow in which to spend their winter sleep. Even the house itself seemed to have entered into a state of hibernation, as if waiting for Thomasin's return.

Though Erin had done her best to rekindle the feeling of home, rising early to bake the bread and provide a welcoming blaze for the boys to come down to, neither the mouth-watering smell of baking nor the wholesome meals that awaited them could mask the sour smell of their father's unwashed body which greeted them on a morning. The place stank like a tap-room. Each day they rose to face the obstacle of his drunken form slumped across the furniture, one finger still hooked unconsciously around the jug handle, clinging to the one friend he had left.

For the first two weeks after Thomasin's departure it was a hard enough task to get through to him, let alone persuade him to go to work. The chair had become his world; he would not move from its womb except to stagger into the yard to relieve himself. A permanent feature of this world was the jug of poteen which was replenished at waking intervals. Once, Erin had tipped the whole stock of liquor down the drain, but she had succeeded only in driving him from the house and into the taverns where the last of his money was swallowed away, leaving her only Roland's sovereigns to fall back on for food. It seemed that the harp was destined to remain silent.

It was dreadful, trying to do the housework with him

sitting by the hearth all day. She would bang and clatter the dustpan round the tiles, knock his ankles with her brush, hoping for something more than the usual unresponsive grunt; but there was nothing. He was so insensible that when she rose on a morning she would even find mice droppings scattered on his chest, where the creatures had picnicked on the crumbs which stuck to his clothes.

If anyone had tried to ask Patrick to voice his feelings he would have told them: 'I was once lost in a fog, back home ye know. Thick and dense it was, almost like a stirabout that ye'd eat for breakfast. Ye couldn't see five yards in front of ye, and held your hands up to feel your way like a blind man, using them to cut through the mist, hoping ye wouldn't fall into any bogs. I didn't know where I was going, couldn't hear one friendly sound. The mist crept into my ears and plugged them up. Then all of a sudden, I came upon this little man. I was a bit wary at first, 'cause I took him for one o' the little people. 'Twas only when I got right up to him that I found he was made of stone; a lump of granite that had dropped off the mountain.

'He had moss-green clothes and a perky, lichen hat with a sprig of broom growing out like a feather, and he sat there looking at me out of his chiselled, weathered face with the stirabout lapping all around him.

'Twelve times I came upon that little fella, as I laboured through the mist. He seemed to be following me wherever I went, laughing at me, like. It got to be very unnerving. 'Twas only when the mist lifted that I realised that 'twas not him who had been moving, but me who'd been going in circles. I was only twenty yards from where I'd started, but the mist had set a worm in my brain so that I could not move any way but round.

' 'Tis like that now. I'm in a fog, coming across the same landmark again and again. Only this time 'tis no little green man I'm seeing, but Thomasin. The harder I try to fight my way through that mist, the more I find myself coming back to her.'

Eventually Patrick was able to claw his way to the edge of the mist, not quite escaping, yet coming far enough out to save himself from falling into the bottomless abyss that lay beneath the fog. He had been that way before, and had no wish to return.

Erin's fervent prayers to the Holy Mother were rewarded by Patrick's return to work. Not to his old job, for that had been filled by someone more reliable, but nevertheless a job, which meant that Erin need no longer worry about the elasticity of her sovereigns.

But still she had worries of another kind. Though Dickie, now that he had sampled Erin's new-style cooking, was not too unhappy, Sonny was taking his mother's absence very badly. He and his father would have terrible fights over Thomasin, well, not so much fights as Sonny taking the part of a worrisome mosquito and Patrick the enraged horse, which always ended with Sonny in tears and Patrick disappearing to the ale-house.

On one such evening, when Patrick had flown into a rage, Erin went upstairs to find Sonny tying up his belongings in a large 'kerchief.

'I'm running away,' he told Erin sulkily when she asked. 'I'm off to find me Mam.'

'She'll not take much finding,' answered Erin calmly. 'She's at Grandma's.'

'How d'ye know?' he asked eagerly, dropping his bundle. 'Have ye seen her?'

'No, but where else would she be? Look,' she took the 'kerchief and laid his possessions on top of a chest of drawers, 'even if she is, what good will it do if ye go up there? Me Dad'll only fetch ye back.'

'I'll fight him,' boasted Sonny.

'A lot o' good that'll do,' replied his sister. 'Jeez, ye're like a couple o' fightin' cocks, the pair o' ye. I don't know how I keep sane. D'ye think he's going to stand there an' let ye clout him? No, he'll drag ye off home and then we'll be back where we started.'

'Then I'll keep running away till he gets tired of it,' replied Sonny, beginning to pack his things again.

'Look, will ye put that lot away an' come down?' said Erin forcefully. 'There's things I want to say to you an' Dickie. Important things, like how we can get me Mam to come back.'

Later the three of them sat with mugs of tea and slices of toast round the fire, discussing the best way of dealing with their troublesome parents.

'What we need,' said Erin, 'is a plan of attack. Any suggestions?'

Dickie raised his hand and the others turned to him expectantly. 'Can I have the last piece of toast?'

Erin cuffed him. 'We're trying to discuss something of the greatest import an' all you can think about is your guts. Are ye not bothered about seeing your Mammy again?'

' 'Course I am,' he protested. 'But sure, I cannot think on an empty stomach. Me Mam'd let me have it if she was here.'

'Well, she's not, greedy swine,' said Sonny angrily.

'Sonny, such language!' chided his sister. 'Come on now, be serious. We'll have to think of something that'll get Mam an' Dad back together. I can't stand much more o' Dad's goings-on.'

'Nor can I,' said Dickie, watching the piece of toast. 'He stinks.'

'So do you!' argued Sonny.

'Sonny, please!'

'Well, somebody has to stick up for me Dad,' replied Sonny.

'I like that,' said Erin. ' 'Tis you who've been calling him the worst names.'

'All right, shurrup.' Sonny calmed down. 'I'm trying to think.' He wrinkled his brow and twitched his nose from side to side. 'What about if one of us goes to me Mam an' says me Dad's had an accident?'

'Won't work,' replied Erin, playing with the tufts of her hair. 'I shouldn't think me Mam'd give a mouldy sprout about himself after what he's done to her. Still, you're on the right lines. Now, if we were to go to her and say one of us had had an accident, then go to me Dad and say the same thing, then I'll bet both of them would come running. Once they were together and saw the joke they might decide to patch things up. What d'ye say?'

Sonny leaned forward. 'Which one of us is going to have the accident? I reckon it should be me, 'cause I'm Mam's favourite.'

The others laughed scornfully at his arrogance, then Erin said: 'Perhaps you're right, but let's make a proper plan. Sonny, you're supposed to have been knocked over and nearly dying. I'll go to the place where me Mam works and tell her, while Dickie goes to me Dad's site and tells him. Now, we've got to get the timing right so's they both arrive together.'

Sonny giggled. 'By, won't they laugh when they find out I'm really all right.'

'Well, let's hope they're not disappointed,' retorted Erin. 'Right, let's go through it once more before me Dad gets home.'

After leaving Roland, Thomasin had gone straight to her parents' home, where she had fallen into a deep state of shock. For the next couple of days she had been tucked up in bed, shivering violently between two hot water bottles, forced to listen to her mother's prattling about Patrick's cruel treatment, about the Irish being a race of drunken ruffians and, 'Oh, what is to become of those children with that brute?'

William, naturally, had been more understanding, even though he was extremely annoyed at Patrick's treatment of his daughter.

'Come on, Tommy,' he had said. 'Everything'll work out, you'll see. Why, in t'mornin' Pat'll forget all about whatever it is that's upset 'im an' he'll be round here first thing to tek thee 'ome.'

But he didn't. Thomasin now lying peacefully in her bed knew that he would never forgive her. The tears came. She let them take their course, then angrily she wiped her eyes and dressed. What was the point of lying in bed thinking about it? She would have to earn a living if the worst came to the worst and she had to live here permanently. So she had better make a start now. But oh, the children . . .

Mr Penny, the grocer, was shocked at Thomasin's appearance as she bade him a solemn good morning and apologised for her absence.

'Eh, you shouldn't have come here in a state like that.'

'Thank you, that's made me feel a whole lot better.' She took off her shawl and turned the Closed sign to Open.

'Nay, I didn't mean, I meant . . . Oh, hell, sit down and tell me what happened.' He pulled up a crate and planted himself firmly on it.

'Nowt much to tell.' She began to refill the shelves which had been sadly neglected in her absence.

'Come on,' he coaxed. 'It must've been summat serious judging by that face. Away, put t'kettle on an' tell me all about it over a cup o' coffee.'

Between sips, Thomasin told him the whole story. It seemed easier to unburden her mind on someone who was not a member of her family.

'Well, I can't say as I blame him,' said Arnold Penny, when she had done. 'I daresay I'd have done the same if you were my wife.' He looked at his coffee cup. 'By, Thomasin, you've really shocked me, you have. I'd never have thought you the type to do unseemly things like that.' He shook his head and sighed.

'Yer don't have to tell me I've been a fool,' she said sadly. 'But I were that desperate I didn't know how to raise t'money.'

'Eh, lass,' he covered her small hand with his gnarled one, 'what are we going to do with you? I'll tell you what we're going to do, we're going to forget all about it, that's what. Happen I've done some worse things in my time, who am I to condemn you for trying to save your husband? All things considered, that husband o' yours ought to think himself lucky that he's got someone to care for him like you.'

She was grateful for the wafer of comfort, but doubted that Patrick would think so.

A customer entered the store and Thomasin went to serve her. Reading the items from the list the woman said, 'Half a pound of dried peas, a pound of butter, a pound of Cheshire cheese . . .' As each item was reeled off, Thomasin placed it on the counter. 'A box of matches, five candles, half a pound of . . . no, I said five candles, there's only four,' snapped the woman, then returned to her list as Thomasin mumbled apologies. 'A box of shortbread, half a pound of tea and some of that soap, there. That'll do, I think.' She folded her list and replaced it in her basket. 'One moment, you haven't given me the matches.'

'What's that, a coffin?' enquired Thomasin, stabbing at the box of matches.

'I beg your pardon?' bristled the woman. 'You need to learn a few manners I think.'

'Silly bugger,' muttered Thomasin under her breath as she turned away.

'What did you say?' The woman narrowed her eyes.

Thomasin turned back. 'I said, have you got your sugar?'

Mr Penny rushed forward to intervene. 'Nice morning, madam!'

'Hmm! You wouldn't think so to look at her,' replied the customer. 'I should be careful, she'll be losing all your customers for you if you don't watch her.'

The grocer hastily wrapped two rashers of bacon and placed them in her basket. 'A special offer just for today,' he told her. 'For our first customer of the morning. I do trust you will call again?'

'I do not think so for one moment,' replied the woman, though tucking the bacon out of sight so that he could not grab it back. She left, muttering about one never seeming to get good service nowadays.

'She's right, you know,' he said to Thomasin. 'You've got a face like last week's rice pudding. Don't you know that the customer is always right? Even if you can't stand the sight of 'em you've got to be civil, lass, else I'll not have any customers left. I think I'd best see to 'em this morning and you fill t'shelves while you get in better humour.'

She said that she was sorry. It was not fair of her to take it out of the customers.

Arnold Penny bade her sit down and take a breather. He thought an awful lot of his assistant. From that first week when she had saved him from certain ruin by uncovering a scheme between the previous assistant and the carters who delivered the goods, he knew his decision to employ Thomasin had been a sound one. It appeared that the pair of embezzlers were inserting extra items on one copy of the invoice and not the other, and then splitting the pilfered goods between them while Mr Penny stood the charge. He had not noticed anything odd, for he had always allowed Joanna to attend to the bookwork.

'She always seemed so efficient,' he had said.

'Oh, she was that all right,' replied Thomasin. 'So efficient that she's now probably running a chain of shops on the proceeds.'

Thomasin had offered to go through the books for him to

help sort them out. Mr Penny's claim that she might not be able to understand Joanna's methods of book-keeping became swiftly apparent as Thomasin tried to unravel the reams of unintelligible figures. Not only were the books cooked, she had quipped, they were well and truly burnt to a frazzle. Mr Penny had been tremendously impressed by her integrity and her keen eye and since that time had praised her every good deed with 'I'll remember you in my will!'

'I'd rather keep busy,' she told her employer.

'Well,' he slapped her lightly, 'then you'd best get some bloody work done.'

She laughed, then the door burst open and an agitated child danced about in front of the counter.

'Erin!' Thomasin's face lit up, but Erin did not give her time to say further.

'Oh, Mam! 'Tis our Sonny, he's had an accident!' She waved her hands excitedly.

'What? Where?' stammered Thomasin.

'Come on, I'll take ye,' cried Erin.

'Here, get your shawl on, lass,' said Mr Penny and helped her on with the garment. 'Go on, off you go and see to your boy. And I hope he's not too badly hurt!' he yelled as she raced after Erin.

Sonny and Dickie had set off for school as usual, but only Sonny would be going in, for Dickie must be free to drag his father to the scene of the 'accident'. At the end of the street they paused to press their noses against Mrs Swale's shop window.

'I wonder if she's got any bottles round the back?' said Dickie, his idea being to steal a couple of empty bottles and hand them over the counter to claim the deposit. 'C'mon.'

Sonny watched his brother cram the bottles in every spare pocket and himself picked one up thoughtfully. He grinned as a marvellous idea formed itself. Reuniting his parents was not the only fun he was going to have today. He pocketed the bottle and said goodbye to his brother, joining up with a crowd of schoolmates as they chattered and sallied down the street.

Brother Simon Peter watched the boys drift unenthusiastically into his classroom. Today was another art lesson. He half hoped that Feeney would take it into his head to do something silly, so providing the excuse to give him a hiding.

But Sonny was wise to his taunts by now and behaved impeccably. Then Brother Simon Peter spotted the ginger beer bottle which protruded from the boy's pocket and seized upon this chance for some sport.

'A moment, Feeney.' He reached out as Sonny passed and withdrew the bottle, sitting it on his desk to read the lettering upon it. 'Well, well, a present for his master. My word, the boy is learning at last.' He waited for Sonny to put his objections, but none came – confound the boy, he raged. Was there no way to provoke him? 'Where is your brother, Feeney?' he asked as Sonny made his way to the bench.

'He's ill, Brother,' replied the boy, then sat down.

'Oh, nothing serious I trust?' said the master. 'Black Death? Cholera?'

But still not a glimmer of defiance from the pupil.

At the end of the lesson, before the boys returned to their own class, Sonny approached Brother Simon Peter's desk and asked if he might have his property returned.

'Return it, Feeney?' blubbered the master. 'But I took it to be a gift. Are you then the kind of person who gives with one hand and takes away with the other?'

'No, Brother,' answered Sonny and looked at his boots, running the toe of one of them over the other, an act which would have brought stern measures from his mother had she seen it.

'Then the beer is mine,' said the master.

'No, 'tis mine,' replied Sonny. 'An' ye'll be sorry if ye drink it.'

– Ah, at last! sighed the master to himself. At last, at last. He stood imperiously and grasped the bottle of ginger beer. The other boys halted their exodus to stand and watch amazedly. Feeney had risen again!

'So,' commented Brother Simon Peter. 'I shall be sorry, shall I? Well, boy, I think not, for I am extremely partial to ginger beer. In fact I think I shall consume it here and now and when I have thoroughly enjoyed it I can tell you that you are the one who will be sorry.'

He removed the cork which Sonny had picked from the gutter that morning and gloatingly lifted the earthenware cask to his lips. His head went back, his thick lips smothered the neck of the bottle, his eyes closed in anticipated pleasure – then suddenly flew open as the taste of lukewarm urine hit the back of his throat. He spluttered and choked, gagged and retched as the boys burst into spontaneous laughter, hanging onto each other in undisguised mockery. The room became filled with their howls and the spitting and coughing of their enemy.

Sonny's victorious grin quickly disappeared as the master, still gagging, grappled for the boy's collar. Oh no, the man was not going to beat him again. Let him take it out on that load of gibbering jackasses, they deserved it anyway. Quick as a flash he fled to the corridor and into the yard, pursued by the manic schoolmaster. Laughing and whooping and well out of range of Codgob he turned as he ran to thumb his nose at his persecutor, then darted out into the street and across the road towards the safety of home.

He never knew what hit him. One moment he was giggling delightedly, the next . . . nothing. The man driving the hackney carriage bellowed a warning and tried to rein in his horse, but it was too late. The creature lost the rhythm of its high-stepping gait, reared with a frightened whinny and Sonny's white face disappeared under the tangle of horseflesh.

Brother Simon Peter shunted to a halt and supported himself in horror on the school gate, the tanginess of urine still on his tongue, then slumped to the low wall as a muttering crowd grew around him.

CHAPTER FIFTY-SIX

THE ROOM WAS dark; the curtains had been pulled across the window so that the light would not hurt his eyes when he awoke. When.

Thomasin, Patrick, their other two children and the priest, a host of outlines, grouped around the bed on which lay the inert form of their son, their brother.

He had been unconscious for two days now. The doctor had said that there was nothing he could do to speed the wakening, that it was the body's way of healing itself and the boy would wake in his own good time. But, he had added cautiously, there was always the possibility that their son could just slip quietly away, and they must steel themselves for such an eventuality. He had known cases, he said, where the child had lain in such a coma for many weeks then suddenly woken as if merely from a good night's sleep. They must pray for such an outcome, for Sonny's life depended on one more powerful than he.

And they had prayed. Prayed and prayed. Liam had dashed over right away when Molly had explained the reason for the Feeneys' non-appearance at Mass, and now stood at the foot of the bed fingering his rosary, his murmured supplications emulated by the boy's family.

The white face was minus a blemish, save the faint scattering of gold-dust over the bridge of his nose. Long, curled fringes of reddish-gold rested upon the mauvish hollows beneath his eyes. Thomasin from time to time leaned over to smooth an imaginary slick of hair from his forehead, laid her cool fingers upon the clammy skin. She could feel Patrick's eyes boring into her as she stroked her son's face – He's blaming me, she thought painfully, but no more than I blame myself. Oh, Sonny, my baby!

They had been together, if one could call it together, for forty-eight hours and in that time had exchanged few words, the bulk of their communication restricted to looks; accusing looks, hurt looks, needing looks. And how badly they needed each other at this time, with their son's life dangling on a slender thread. But neither would make the first move.

Patrick sat with his elbows resting on his patched knees, his fingers scratching worriedly at the black stubble on his chin. He was sober, yet with a jumble of thoughts that harrowed his brain – *Oh, Tommy, Tommy, why did ye have to come back? Just when I was getting used to being without ye, without your sweet honey lips breathing hot fire into me, drowning me, without your body drawing me further and further inside of ye, sinking, warm, suffocating, joyous. Please, Sonny, don't die, you're all I have left of her now. Stay with me, love me. Mary would never have done this to me. Sweet, gentle Mary who never did a wrong thing or uttered an unkind word in all her short life, who personified the Ireland that I long for so badly now, who . . . who never had one ounce of passion in her young girl's body. Ah, Tommy, Tommy!*

Erin, a waxen-faced urchin with her half-hair, like a fledgling sparrow, part-naked, part-dressed in a wispy covering of down over the vulnerable flesh, watched Thomasin's eyelids droop. Her stepmother had not slept since the night before Sonny's accident. Neither had her father. Though he had gone to his lonely bed, taking Dickie with him, Erin knew that it was only done so that he would not have to be alone with his wife. She wept inside for them both, and for Sonny. Poor, dear Sonny lying like a limp doll in that big bed, barely a swell in the patchwork quilt – *Dear, Holy Mother, please don't take him. It was all my fault. I let him be the one to pretend to have the accident, it should be me who is lying there now, not Sonny, whom everyone loves, not the baby.*

Dickie squatted on a footstool, hugging his grubby, knobbly knees which were dotted with scabs, relics of the playground. He applied his thumbnail to a crust, prising around the edges, lifting, exploring, trying to lever it off all in one piece.

'Stop picking,' said his father, without a glance in his direction.

Dickie let his hand drop to his bootlaces and began to poke the loose ends into the laceholes. Anything to keep his mind from screaming out with boredom. Why did he have to sit here all day waiting for Sonny to wake up? Why couldn't he go out to search for horse chestnuts or collect beechnuts? Still, Sonny had earned him a few days off school, he supposed he should be grateful for that. If only he weren't so bored, and his parents weren't so grumpy. They only seemed to notice he was here when he did something wrong – Come on, Son, hurry up and wake, then we can go to Heso and get conkers.

Erin touched Thomasin's arm. 'Why don't ye try to catch up on some sleep, Mam? Sure, ye're nearly dropping off that chair.'

Thomasin jolted, shuffled to bring her spine flush with the chair-back, then shook her head wearily. She would not move from Sonny's side until he woke. Or didn't wake – No, don't think that way! she censured. He is going to get better, he is. But what then? He might as well be dead to Thomasin, for once the danger was over she knew that Patrick would tell her to leave. Oh, Patrick, please touch me. Hurt me, anything, so that I don't feel so alone.

'Shall I make a cup of tea then, Mam?' persisted Erin.

'I can't speak for anyone else, but I'm absolutely bogged down with tea. I can feel it slopping around when I as much as blink. Still,' she added half-heartedly, 'I suppose you've got to do summat to keep yer from goin' mad, haven't yer? Aye, go on, lass, put water on. Liam, will you have one?'

Liam's green eyes lacked the usual spark of vitality. He grieved deeply for them all, they were as his family – Have they not suffered enough, Lord, without You taking their baby too?

'Thank ye, no,' he answered dully, winding the rosary in and out of his fingers. ' 'Twill be time for Mass shortly, I must leave ye.'

'Is it that hour?' replied Thomasin half-surprised. 'I seem to 'ave lost track of what day it is, never mind about time. Will we see yer later, Liam?'

'If I'll not be intruding,' he answered, pocketing his beads.

She raised a brief smile. 'Yer'll not be intruding, Father.'

'Then I'll come later this evening.'

'Thank you, I'd like that,' she said sincerely, then her eyes were slowly drawn back to her son's face.

'I'll be off then. Keep your spirits up, ye hear? See ye later, Patrick.'

'What?' Patrick jumped. His mind had been taken over by that sickly, tumbling motion that precedes sleep. 'Sorry, Father, I didn't catch what ye said.'

Liam returned to the bedside and gripped Patrick's shoulder. 'Ye'll not give up on Him this time, Pat?'

Patrick glanced up at him, then gave a slight shake of his head. 'No, I'll not give up, Father, that's my son lying there. I'll keep on praying 'til he comes back to me.'

Liam patted his shoulder. 'I'm thinking ye should try one or two prayers for yourself while you're at it.' He looked at Thomasin, gave a strengthening smile then moved to the door again. 'Take care, God be with ye both.'

Erin escorted the priest to the front door, leaving only Dickie to intrude on their silent grief.

'Shall I fetch me soldier?'

'Sorry, son – what did ye say?' asked Patrick guiltily.

'Shall I fetch me soldier for when our Sonny wakes up?' repeated Dickie, his fingers straying back to his scabby knee. 'He likes it.'

'You're a good lad.' The rigidity of Thomasin's face relaxed somewhat. 'I'm sure he'd love that.'

' 'Tis only to lend, not to keep,' explained Dickie hastily, then went to dig the soldier from a drawer, winding it up on his return and placing it on the bed.

The door creaked and Erin admitted Brother Francis to the bedroom.

'My dear people, do remain seated,' he whispered as they were about to rise. 'I would have come sooner but knowing how ill your son is I felt that it would not be appropriate.'

'Why does everybody think they're intruding?' sighed Thomasin, sitting on the bed and offering her chair to the schoolmaster. 'Yer get the feeling that nobody cares when they all stay away.'

There had been two very noticeable absences, those of William and Hannah. On the evening of Sonny's accident Thomasin had, without thinking, asked Erin to slip over to her grandparents' house to break the bad news. They would be sure to be worried about their daughter's failure to come home, and would have to be told about Sonny. Patrick had immediately lost his temper.

'Is it not enough that I have to suffer your presence,' he demanded, 'without having your mother's dictatorial prattling?'

'Is my presence then so loathsome?' she had answered quietly, watching that beloved face contort into a hateful, grief-consumed mask.

He had swung away from her then and had started to open and shut drawers, lift ornaments and look underneath them as if searching for something so that he might not have to answer: 'Yes, you *are* loathsome! But I want you, woman. Oh, how I want you.'

'But they've a right to come!' she had cried then. 'They love Sonny, he's their grandson.'

'He's my son!' Patrick had rounded on her.

'And he's my son too! I have the right to say who sees him.'

'Ye have no rights, woman! No rights whatsoever. This is my house and I say who comes into it. I will not have that woman here.' – Because she'll blame me, he thought, I know she'll blame me. 'Do ye hear me?'

'But they'll be terribly worried, Patrick,' she had implored. 'At least let my father in to see Sonny, yer know how he dotes on him, please, Pat.'

He took a step towards her but did not touch her. He knew what would happen if he touched her. 'Listen to me, woman. You are in this house because ye are the boy's mother, though I pity him in having one such as you for a mother. But do not look upon my charity as a sign of weakness, or get any fool notions that by allowing ye in here I want ye back, because I don't. And don't think that your staying here gives ye any rights, because it doesn't. As soon as that boy is well, ye'll be through that door in a flash. Sure I don't know what possessed me to ask ye in the first place, you're doing no good here at all. Not to anybody.'

It was not so much his words that hurt as the way he kept calling her 'woman', as though the very utterance of her name caused him pain. Which it did.

In the end he had given Erin permission to tell William and

Hannah about their grandson, but with strict orders that they were not to try and visit him. He would perhaps allow the boy to visit them when he recovered – This will kill me Dad, thought Thomasin grimly. He thinks the world of those lads. It'll kill him.

The schoolmaster was speaking. 'I am sure that everyone is as worried as you are, Mrs Feeney. It is simply, I suspect, that they do not wish to impose upon your grief or hurt you by their probing references.'

'Oh, don't listen to me,' sighed Thomasin. 'I know they care really, an' I know they don't come because they don't know what to say. It's just that you get this awful, empty loneliness when nobody asks how he is.'

The schoolmaster nodded in agreement, then began to un-wrap the package he had brought. 'It may seem a rather foolish thing to offer when your son is . . . Well, I thought perhaps when he wakes he might like to look at this again.' He pulled the paper from the book which Sonny had borrowed on his first day at school. 'I recall how much he enjoyed the pictures. It may help a little towards his recovery.' He laid the book gently on the chest of drawers as Thomasin struggled with her tears. He might never be able to read that book again . . .

'Thank ye, Brother Francis,' said Patrick, for both of them. 'I don't know when we'll be able to return it.'

When Brother Francis smiled it was as if someone had held a candle to his face. The eyes generated warmth and encouragement. 'Tell Sonny he may keep the book as long as he wishes. He will no doubt be able to bring it with him on his return to school.'

'You think he will return?' asked Thomasin, doubtful, hoping.

The man took her hand comfortingly. 'I am sure of it. Your son is a very determined character, Mrs Feeney. He has had to face adversity before and has sailed through it.'

'I'm sorry?' Thomasin was confused.

'No, it is I who am sorry, I ramble so,' said the schoolmaster, not wishing by his inference to implicate Brother Simon Peter as the cause of Sonny's accident. That little matter was about to be dealt with personally. He had stood by for too long and allowed his colleague's cruelty to go unchecked. Now he must act before someone was seriously hurt, or had that happened already? No, he would not allow himself to consider the possibility that Sonny might not wake. 'I was referring to your son's tenacity in the playground, Mrs Feeney. He will not, I think, be bullied?'

Here even Patrick effected a smile. 'I'm afraid my son is a bit of a fighter, Brother. I trust he hasn't caused too much upset?'

'On the contrary, Mr Feeney,' said Brother Francis. 'You can thank Heaven for that fighting spirit, for it is that which will bring him through. I am sure of it.'

'What a grand man,' murmured Thomasin when the schoolmaster had gone.

Patrick nodded but did not look at her. Could not look at her – Oh, Tommy, Tommy, please don't speak. The sound of your voice kills me . . .

When Erin returned with a tray of tea she was accompanied by another visitor. Molly crept into the darkened room, apologising as she tripped over Patrick's chair-leg.

'I've brought the rest o' the family. I hope ye don't mind?' she said in a loud whisper. 'I'd hate to wake the little fella up.'

'Yer don't have to whisper, Molly,' said Thomasin listlessly, shuffling up her chair to make room around the bed. 'We'd be glad if yer can wake him up. Bring 'em all in, then, don't have 'em littering staircase.'

The Flaherty tribe crowded into the small room, the larger ones taking their places behind Thomasin and Patrick, the babies crawling on the bed wearing only short shifts, the soles of their feet and their naked bottoms bearing the familiar imprints of Britannia Yard.

Molly held out a grubby paper bag. 'I brung the wee fella a bit o' somethin' for when he wakes up. 'Tis toffee, I made it meself.'

'It's very good of yer, Molly,' answered Thomasin, wondering what recipe Molly had used. A pound of sugar, butter, half a pound of muck from Molly's fingernails . . . She screwed the bag into her hand. 'We were just sayin' as how nobody's been an' the next minute we're inundated wi' visitors.'

'Ah, 'twas only that we didn't like to poke our noses in before, like,' answered Molly. 'I was all for coming round straight away when I met up with Miss Peabody in the butcher's, but Jimmy said ye wouldn't be wanting us round at a time like this.'

'Well, I'm glad yer decided to come, Molly,' replied Thomasin. 'A little chat helps to take yer mind off things. Yer tend to go inside of yerself when yer've nobody to talk to.' Her eyes fluttered over Patrick who, after an abbreviated greeting to the Flahertys, had reverted to his dejected silence.

'Ah, Himself is takin' it hard, is he?'

Patrick prickled at the woman's muted lilt. They were talking about him as if he was not there.

Thomasin nodded. 'I suppose Miss Peabody also told yer about . . .?'

'She did,' replied Molly. 'An' not just me. 'Tis all over Walmgate about you an' Pat. Sure, I'd never've thought it, well who would, him bein' so well-favoured like. How could ye bring yourself to look at another fella?'

Thomasin stiffened. 'You know nothing, Molly, nothing. It's not the way you're thinkin' at all.'

'Ah, sure, what's the fuss?' returned Molly. 'It looks like ye've patched up your differences now.' She frowned at Thomasin's negative gesture, the furrows on her brow made more pronounced by the dirt that had collected in them. 'Well, you're back aren't ye?'

'I'm only here 'cause of Sonny,' muttered Thomasin. 'He's made it very clear that once the lad's better I'm to go.'

'Ah, but 'tis wicked he is,' cried Molly, and dug Patrick hard in the ribs. 'Hey, 'tis you I'm talkin' about, ye dizzy poltroon. Can ye not see ye were made for each other? An' you behaving like a dog with hydrophobia. Ye oughta be shot.'

'Molly, if ye've come to see Sonny then you're very welcome,' he answered. 'But if it's to interfere in my affairs then I'll thank ye to mind your own. There's enough busybodies around here with Missus P.'

'Well, 'tis sorry I am,' said Molly, smarting at the rebuff. 'But if a friend can't be concerned that you're making a fool of yourself then who can?'

'A fool is it?' Patrick raised his voice. 'Sure, you'd know all about that.'

Thomasin sighed. 'Will you both please stop it? I won't have you arguin' while Sonny is like that.'

'Ah, I'm sorry, pet.' Molly bent over the bed to examine Sonny. 'Sure, he looks as good as gold, don't he, Jimmy? Ye'd never think he was such a little varmint to look at him there. Jimmy, d'ye mind when we took the children to see Connor Killeen? Did he not look just like Sonny does now, like a little angel?'

'Molly,' said Thomasin sharply. 'Connor Killeen was dead! Sonny's still alive, he's just asleep that's all.'

'Ah, I know, I know,' cried Molly, baring long, burnt umber teeth. 'I meant nothing by it. 'Twas just the look about him. Peaceful like. I often think when I look at me little ones asleep, how angelic they look. 'Tis almost a shame when they have to wake up.'

A soft mewing caused everyone to look at Erin, whose face was interred in a huge, red handkerchief.

Molly threw up her pruney-skinned hands. 'Ah, God will ye look what I've done now! Erin, colleen, I wasn't meaning that Sonny was going to die. I was just trying to think of something nice to say about the wee fella, to cheer your Mammy up.'

Erin sobbed piteously and no one could stem her tears.

'Jazers, woman,' breathed Jimmy Flaherty. 'Can a man not take ye anywhere? D'ye always have to go upsetting folk? Can ye not see that they're all worried outta their minds?'

'And so am I,' objected his wife. ' 'Tis not my fault that everyone takes my words the wrong way. Don't ye know I love Sonny like me own? Won't I cry enough tears to fill the Ouse if he should die?' Her lower lip quivered. 'Why, 'twas me who brought him into this world . . .'

'We know yer didn't mean anything, Molly,' sighed Thomasin, trying to comfort Erin.

'Come on now, Molly.' Jimmy swung a baby under his arm and took another by the hand, dragging it from the bed. 'We'd best leave Pat an' Tommy in peace. We'll call again tomorrow maybe.'

'Aye, maybe the lad'll've woken by then,' said Molly encouragingly. Then spoilt it by adding: 'But if the Lord decides to take him I've got a lovely little nightgown that'll . . .'

'Molly!' It was not very often that Jimmy raised his voice to her, but when he did it meant he must be obeyed.

Molly said a hasty farewell and, with accompanying slaps and prods, herded her family down the stairs and through the front door.

Erin still wept. 'He isn't really going to die, is he, Mam? He can't die, not our Sonny.'

Thomasin drew the girl to her and kissed the tufty-sprigged head. 'Why don't yer fetch yer harp and play us a little tune? Something to cheer us.'

'Oh, ye don't know.' Erin sucked in her breath, that horrific night rushing back to her. 'My harp, 'tis broken.' She laid quick fingers on Thomasin's lips. 'Please, don't ask how. I couldn't bear the telling of it again, not just yet. Maybe later, when Sonny . . .' she changed her mind. 'I think we ought to say another prayer, don't you?' She dipped her fingers into the puddle of holy water beneath the crude statuette of the Virgin Mary and knelt down, resting her forehead against the coverlet.

Patrick clasped his work-abused hands against his brow, nipping the bridge of his nose between his thumbs, then slowly dropped to his knees. Dickie too knelt and prayed, and some minutes later Thomasin also sank to the bedside rug and pleaded for her son's life.

A tan-coloured skin had formed upon the untouched cups of tea. Outside could be heard the sound of children, other people's children, scurrying and laughing as Miss Peabody chased them away from her front. A lone dog's bark echoed in the lane. A starling perched on the guttering and went through his repertoire of impersonations. The prayers seemed to dry up.

Thomasin pushed herself from the rug and sank back into her chair. Dickie dragged himself to his feet, clasping a handful of his mother's dark blue skirts and looked into her face. She was so sad. He wished that he could say something to make her better. He knew they all played war about his selfishness, but he loved his Mam really. He hated to see her looking so old and ugly.

' 'Twas only supposed to be a trick ye know,' he explained solemnly. 'We just wanted ye to come home. We were only pretending that Sonny had had an accident. It was his idea. He said what a good laugh it would give ye when ye found out he was all right. We didn't know he was going to have a real accident.'

531

It was too much for Thomasin. She bowed her head and wept quietly into her chest. Yes, that was just the sort of mad thing her Sonny would do. And it was all her fault. Her mind was crammed with pictures of her son as a baby, a little carrot-topped head wobbling against her shoulder, the greedy pulling at her breast, all the funny things he had ever said came back to haunt her. Snug on her knee around the winter blaze, cuddled in a blanket to hear the bedtime story, patting her chest indignantly – 'Mammy, your humps are getting in my way' – his goodnight kiss, the lips that tasted of caramel – *dear God, don't let him die!*

The sound of her pitiful weeping filled Patrick's ears, filled his brain, his whole body, enraging him, making him want to hit her, silence her.

'Stop it!' he demanded loudly. 'Stop it! For God's sake stop!'

But her sobbing only increased. He could stand no more. Leaping from his seat he lurched to the side of the bed where she crouched. 'See what ye've done?' he shouted, sinking iron fingers into the tender flesh of her upper arms. He took hold of the wet face that stared at him dumbly and screwed it around to face the boy on the bed. 'Look at him. I said look at him! He's lying there because of you. Because he wanted ye to come home. God damn you!' His tanned face was hewn with such despair that it added ten years to his shoulders. To Thomasin he suddenly looked so old, so lost.

The once-merry eyes were sunken and dispirited, the mouth an agonised incision as he shouted and raved at her. 'Was it not enough for ye to destroy me? Will ye not be bloody satisfied until ye've killed the lot of us?' His fingers bit deep into the marshmallow flesh but she felt no pain, only that of his accusing eyes. 'What sort of a mother are ye? Eh? Tell me, what sort of a woman? Damn ye, I'm asking ye, answer me. Answer me! Oh, Thomasin!' And she suddenly found herself in his arms, being scolded and hugged and sworn at and kissed all at the same time with the full length of his body pressed tightly against her, crushing her as she quivered and sobbed. 'Why did ye do it, Tommy! Why? Ye knew that ye were my life, *are* my life, look at the state of me without ye.' He jabbed at his anguished face. 'Look at them!' He stabbed at the children who cried with them. 'Do we look like we're alive? Ah, God, Tommy, I worship ye, why did ye do it to me? I could kill ye.'

'I'm sorry, I'm sorry!' She wept the words into his hard chest, the tears and mucus intermingling, sniffing, pleading, loving. 'Oh, I'm so sorry!' Breathing in the comforting man smell, drowning in his hardness, finding solace even in his anger. 'But it was for you. Only for you. Forgive me.'

'Ah, God no, 'tis me who should be forgiven,' shivered Patrick, nuzzling her herb-scented hair, sinking deep into it, behind her ears where the scent blossomed warm and familiar, aching for her. 'Come back. Come back to me, Tommy. I love ye. I don't care about him. Yes, I do, I could kill him! I could kill you. But I need ye. We all need ye.'

They clung together fiercely, kissing tears, tasting sorrow, infecting their children who wept copiously, but this time with the happiness of having their mother delivered safely back to them. And then they were all kissing each other and crying, hugging and stroking and the house began to come alive again.

'What day is it? Ow, my head hurts.'

The four ceased their noisy reunion to stare disbelievingly at the bed as Sonny repeated his sleepy question.

Patrick and Thomasin came simultaneously to his side, eyes still misty, expectant, not daring to hope . . .

Patrick gave a throaty laugh, then wiped the moisture from his face. 'Jeez, son, ye've kinda caught me out there for I don't rightly know what day it is.' He hugged his wife to him, the old Patrick smile there again. 'I think maybe 'tis Thursday, no Friday . . .'

'Oh Jazers,' groaned Sonny. 'Bloody physical torture again . . .' He squinted at the dim figures that ringed his bedside. 'Sure, what are ye all doing in my bedroom in the middle of the night?' And then he noticed Thomasin and his mouth turned up into that cheeky grin which they had dreaded they might never see again. 'Good trick eh, Mam? Knew ye'd come back. Told them lot that I'm your favourite. Knew ye'd come. Got a headache. Could I miss school today? 'Tis Codgob, I don't like him . . .' Then he yawned, laid his russet head to one side and promptly sank into a peaceful, healing sleep.

EPILOGUE

IT TOOK MANY months, but with forgiveness and remorse from both sides they picked up the shards of their marriage and began to piece them together. The form that partnership took was a different one: how could anything possibly be as it was after all the pain, bitter words and loss of trust? But despite this, maybe because of it, theirs became a deeper relationship, one which would last, forged by the tribulations they had endured together, bonded by the love of their children.

Thomasin laid the heel of her hand firmly against the window, in an effort to dislodge the snow that obscured her view. 'Looks like yer going to be laid off again,' she told her husband. 'Yer might know it'd do this just when it's coming up to Christmas an' we need the extra brass.'

She went to the cupboard and lifted out Patrick's best suit, then as an afterthought picked up his boots and parcelled both up separately. 'Take these down to Izzie's will yer, lad?' she told Dickie. 'We'll have to have a few bob an' it don't look like yer Dad's goin' to need his suit for Church, unless he's got a dog sledge tucked away. I shan't be shiftin' far in this lot either.'

'I like the way you're sending *my* things to the pawnshop,' accused Patrick. 'What if I should have an important meeting or something?'

'D'yer mean down at The Spread Eagle?' smirked his wife. 'Aye, well 'appen I'm gettin' you in trainin' for Christmas. Yer needn't think you're goin' to be pumping gallons of bilge-water down your throat this year. I intend it to be a nice, quiet family do.'

'If it's a quiet Christmas then it'll be the first one ever,' grinned her husband, then reached under the sofa for a newspaper to read.

Dickie seemed loath to move from his fireside seat. 'Aw, Mam – why can't our Sonny go to t'pawnship?'

' 'Cause I told you to go, that's why,' shouted Thomasin. 'Now shift!'

Dickie's sulky departure was forestalled by the arrival of his grandfather who burst through the door in a flurry of snow.

'Nah then, young fella me lad!' bellowed William, ridding his boots of the surplus snow, his face and ears bright red above the checked comforter. 'Where're thee off to? Tha'll get buried alive in this bloody lot.' He slammed the door, leaving the knocker reverberating in irritation. 'An' how's young Nobbut?' He bobbed down in front of the fire beside Sonny who smiled and held up the picture which he had just completed. 'By, that's grand! What's it supposed to be? Oh, I see, Father Christmas.' He caught the child's nose gently between his knuckles. 'By, he's a good drawer is our Sonny.' The hurt he had felt at Patrick's snub when Sonny was ill had now worn off.

'I'm going to be an artist when I grow up,' Sonny informed him.

'Nay,' scoffed his grandfather, unwinding the comforter from his neck and unbuttoning his coat to let the fire reach his body. 'That's no job for a man. Tha wants to be an engine driver or summat clever like that. Artist? I've never heard owt so daft.'

Sonny grinned and made a start on another picture. Whatever his grandfather might think, an artist he was going to be.

'Why aren't yer at school, any road?' asked William.

'School's closed for Christmas,' answered Sonny.

'I'll bet yer pleased about that, aren't yer?'

Sonny smiled and shrugged. 'Our lad is, but I wanted to go. I like school.' He recalled the relief he had felt when Dickie had returned one afternoon to tell him the good news; Codgob was gone. No one seemed to know the circumstances of his departure, but it was hinted that Brother Francis had been instrumental in the man's dismissal. It was a strange thing, said Dickie, but on the day that Codgob left he had been sporting a black eye. Some said that Brother Francis had been seen leaving Codgob's classroom looking very pleased with himself. But it was hardly likely that one so charitable had delivered the blow. Was it? Whoever the culprit, he had the eternal thanks of every boy in the school.

'What you doin' 'ere at this time of a mornin' any road?' asked Thomasin.

'That's a nice welcome, I'm sure,' sniffed her father. 'After I've trudged through frozen wastes, up to me ears in snow, talk about brass monkeys, fetchin' yer this letter an' . . .'

'What letter?' Thomasin wiped her hands on her apron and reached for the envelope that William fluttered tauntingly.

'Nay, it's not for thee,' he said airily. 'It's for t'master.' He handed it to Patrick. 'I thought mebbe someone was sendin' me some money, 'till I saw yon fella's name on it. Tha mother said it might be summat important an' I had to bring it round right away.'

'Ye didn't have to put yourself out on such a disgruntled day, Billy,' answered Patrick. ' 'T'won't be nothing important with my moniker on it.' He frowned at the envelope on which was scrawled a mass of redirections. Apparently it had gone first to Bay Horse Yard, then to William's address, and by the condition of the envelope had been through many hands before reaching Patrick's.

He ripped it open carelessly – and gasped as a collection of banknotes fluttered to the carpet. He stared down at them, making no move to pick them up, far too astonished to move at all.

William's mouth dropped open. 'Well, I'll be damned!'

Patrick slowly spread out the letter while his wife, who was also too amazed to speak, gathered up the large white notes and began to tally them. She then watched his face as he read and re-read the letter to make sure he had understood it correctly.

To Messrs. Feeney & Thompson
Dear Sirs,
 It is with my deepest apologies that I send this remittance for work carried out by yourselves on my property. A member of my staff had inadvertently

placed your bill in a drawer, where it lay unopened for some time before
being discovered. I do trust that my delay in settling the account has not
caused too great an inconvenience. I thank you once again for your excellent
workmanship,

Yours respectfully
P. Dodd Esq.

'When yer've finished reading it are yer gonna tell us what it says?' asked Thomasin impatiently, as Patrick mouthed the words to himself.

He looked up, his mouth beginning to twitch at the corners. 'See for yourself.'

She quickly scanned the words. 'P. Dodd. Where have I heard that name before? Dodd. Dodd. Oh no, it's not that fella that skipped off to t'Continent while you spent your holidays in t'Castle? Well!' She seethed with the effrontery of it and testily repeated the words of the letter. ' "I trust it has not caused too great an inconvenience." Oh no, just a stay in gaol, and a nearly-broken marriage, that's all, nothing to get steamed up about. Why, of all the bloody cheek!'

And then a splutter of mirth exploded from her lips as the hilarity of it all caught up with her, and she saw that Patrick too was trying very hard not to laugh. Both collapsed into uproarious laughter, holding their sides in exquisite agony, hooting, braying, the tears coming in torrents. Oh, the irony! The months of needless suffering, of deprivation, of heart-break – but it was so, so funny.

'Give us that suit back,' giggled Thomasin, grabbing the parcel from Dickie who, along with his brother, sister and grandfather, stood nonplussed, astonished at their antics. 'Old Skinny Brassballs can stick his measly handouts. What do we want his piddlin' few bob for when we've got all this?' She squealed, then threw the banknotes into the air and began to dance around the room again.

William stared as if his daughter had gone mad. 'Well, do I get to share in this good joke?' he demanded, hands on hips.

Thomasin, still in stitches, could not speak. She crossed her legs and doubled over, jumping up and down on the spot, then gathered the money up and waved it, fan-like, in front of William's face.

'Come on, silly bugger!' roared William, unable to contain

his curiosity any longer. 'Else I'm off to fetch tha mother. What does it say?'

'Oh, Dad,' choked Thomasin, the tears streaming down her face, and hanging on to her husband for support. 'It says: this is goin' to be your merriest Christmas ever.'

Patrick nodded and laughed until he was fit to burst, then echoed her words. 'Aye, Merry Christmas, Billy boy. Merry bloody Christmas!'

BESTSELLING FICTION FROM ARROW

All these books are available from your bookshop or news-agent or you can order them direct. Just tick the titles you want and complete the form below.

☐	THE COMPANY OF SAINTS	Evelyn Anthony	£1.95
☐	HESTER DARK	Emma Blair	£1.95
☐	1985	Anthony Burgess	£1.75
☐	2001: A SPACE ODYSSEY	Arthur C. Clarke	£1.75
☐	NILE	Laurie Devine	£2.75
☐	THE BILLION DOLLAR KILLING	Paul Erdman	£1.75
☐	THE YEAR OF THE FRENCH	Thomas Flanagan	£2.50
☐	LISA LOGAN	Marie Joseph	£1.95
☐	SCORPION	Andrew Kaplan	£2.50
☐	SUCCESS TO THE BRAVE	Alexander Kent	£1.95
☐	STRUMPET CITY	James Plunkett	£2.95
☐	FAMILY CHORUS	Claire Rayner	£2.50
☐	BADGE OF GLORY	Douglas Reeman	£1.95
☐	THE KILLING DOLL	Ruth Rendell	£1.95
☐	SCENT OF FEAR	Margaret Yorke	£1.75

Postage _____

Total _____

ARROW BOOKS, BOOKSERVICE BY POST, PO BOX 29, DOUGLAS, ISLE OF MAN, BRITISH ISLES

Please enclose a cheque or postal order made out to Arrow Books Limited for the amount due including 15p per book for postage and packing both for orders within the UK and for overseas orders.

Please print clearly

NAME..

ADDRESS...

....

Whilst every effort is made to keep prices down and to keep popular books in print, Arrow Books cannot guarantee that prices will be the same as those advertised here or that the books will be available.